Essays and Sketches of
MARK TWAIN

Essays and Sketches of MARK TWAIN

Selected and with an Introduction by

Stuart Miller

BARNES & NOBLE
BOOKS
NEW YORK

This edition published by Barnes & Noble, Inc.

1995 Barnes & Noble Books

ISBN 1-56619-879-8

Text design by Nicola Ferguson

Printed and bound in the United States of America

2 4 6 8 10 M 9 7 5 3 1

Contents

Twain and Nature

Twain and Human Nature

Twain and the Learning Process

Twain and Literature

Twain the Traveler

Twain Looks Back

Introduction

Twain's Concerns

That human beings are perfectable is a relatively modern idea. One of its corollaries might be that human beings are, at heart, pretty much the same. This is what makes human perfectability plausible—that our fears and desires are similar, however our habits and histories may differ.

It would seem necessary to a comic vision of the world that it include at least this notion of people as, in a benign sense, interchangeable. Comedy, after all, depends upon an ability to empathize, to be able to say "That's so true. I've seen that happen a million times," the recognition of folly as a universal human trait. Satire, by contrast, underscores the distance between author and target, laying claim to superior virtue or, at least, understanding. If you laugh along with a Swift or a Mencken, you laugh on the side of the angels.

How contrary is it, then, to claim that Mark Twain, a genuinely comic rather than satiric writer, rejected the idea of human perfectability, and that his assessment of the human family was that it was a family divided? To be sure, when we read Twain we find the aforementioned identification of reader with both author and subject; we laugh at the portrait of humanity Twain paints, willingly finding glimmers of ourselves about the eyes and mouth. This is partly due to Twain's similar willingness to etch some of his own features into these collective portraits. Twain does not exempt himself from the frenzies and furies, the bumblings and bafflements of human existence.

Yet Twain was never disposed to see his fellow creatures as all sharing the same needs and yearnings. Differences, as much as similarities, are at the core of Twain's vision of the human race. The sense that people are nature's flaw, if not God's botch, is worked out in many of Twain's nonfiction writings, both long and short. When Twain takes it upon himself to step away from the comic rostrum, and up to a more serious one, this sense can lead to some surprisingly uncharacteristic views. Uncharacteristic, that is, if we insist on seeing Twain as a cigar-smoking man-in-a-white-suit, a good democrat (small *d*) full of wisecracking candor about foreigners and bluff observations of his American brethren, each blow delivered in plain-spoken, right-between-the-eyes prose. For as much as Twain colluded in this image of himself, his essays and sketches touch on a wider range of concerns, and a more variegated and stratified depiction of the human species, than such an image allows. *Dark* is a word that might well come to mind. However, with one or two exceptions, "dark" is not the appropriate adjective to describe the tone of the pieces presented here. Such a word, sometimes used in relation to Twain's very last works, does not do justice to his active, irascible, mistrustful disenchantment with people as individuals and in groups.

Disenchantment implies expectation, and while Twain saw through a large number of chimerical human poses, he did hold folks large and small, himself included, to some basic common-sense standards: courtesy without obsequiousness, dignity without pretense, compassion without sentimentality, modesty and discretion without incivility. He was never a nihilist, even in the darkest of his final days of loneliness. On the other hand, he was not a simple "wit" or small-town humorist either. In order to better understand the particular bent of Twain's mind, it might be instructive to look at one very short sketch, written near the beginning of his career and placed first in one of his earliest collections.

"My Watch" seems, at first reading, not to have very much to say about the world in general. Yet Twain subtitles the piece "An Instructive Little Tale" and we would do well to take him at his word. This is not the place to retell the whole story—the sketch runs only a few pages and is included in this volume—but the gist of it will reveal a good deal of what Twain was all about. Twain's watch tells more than time. It tells us something about the timeless difficulties of the human being thrown among his fellows.

The mechanism performs beautifully on its own, but due to Twain's momentary negligence—he forgets to wind it—stops being reliable. In fact, it stops altogether. Succumbing to the advice of those around him, Twain subjects his prize watch, against his better judgment, to adjustments. The problem is that no amount of adjustment can return the watch to its original reliability. The watch had been his familiar. Now, unfamiliar quirks appear. The watch runs so fast that Twain skips hours, then days, then months. Soon, he's paying his bills way ahead of schedule. Readjustment to correct this costly flaw only makes the watch run slow, so that Twain misses appointments, commitments, and even stands in danger of being left behind by history. In the end the watch can never be made right—never, that is, be returned to its old, serviceable ways. It might as well be scrapped . . . along with the thousands of inept, nameless mechanics whose infernal tinkering (with something comfortable, or something loved, or something "good enough") has spoiled everything.

The reader can see fairly clearly where this is heading. Twain is often concerned with origins, with looking at what things were like before the human deluge. He asks what a thing might have been in its essence: what did God or Nature intend a thing to be, and what has Man made of it? A sensible man gets full value out of something by leaving it, insofar as he can, alone. But there are very few sensible men in Twain's universe. And Twain's universe casts its net very wide indeed.

Ultimately, what Twain is really wondering about, however, is not the ruined state of things, but the ruined state of man. What must this creature be like to have so blighted the earth he was meant to inherit? While not seeing the earth in paradisiacal terms (even in Eden before the Fall there were some fairly familiar problems—see "Extracts from Adam's Diary" and "Eve's Diary," included in this volume), Twain has a healthy reverence for unspoiled nature. This feeling is implicit, for instance, in his scathingly funny sketch of the resort town of Niagara, New York—as bogus an experience of natural wonder as ever existed. But Nature didn't tell the lie. It is meddling humanity that is the inevitable spoiler.

Human intervention is rarely for the good in Twain. It usually causes diminishment, and it is human nature, vain and self-deluding, that causes those interventions. Notice that in "My Watch" Twain is partly at fault. Not so much because he forgets to wind his watch—that's hardly a character flaw—but because he finally consents to allow the "experts" to take over. His gut feeling is that the watch only needs to be reset properly, but his sense of decency and forbearance demand that Twain at least listen to these people of good intention. He deludes himself into believing what his instincts warn him against, and quickly finds himself at the mercy of people with a much bigger flaw: the firm belief that they are possessed of superior knowledge. Armed with this knowledge they "fix" things, rushing in with mallet and wrench where angels fear to tread. They are not malicious people, they are . . . simply people. And, Twain cautions, when people are allowed to lead armies, head governments, cut your hair, make your bed, fix your watch, or try to teach you their language, they can make life a living hell. Only occasionally, and in Twain's work usually only if those people are female (as in the case of Eve with Adam, and Twain's own wife and daughters—see Twain's heartbreaking tribute to his younger daughter "The Death of Jean") can they make it a heaven.

Something precipitously American is going on here, and going wrong. The idea of a workable natural order, free of the larger encroachments of entrenched human self-interest and assumed privelege, provides the essential prerequisite for what Twain imagines to be a reasonable earthly life. But the figures in the landscape are poised to upset it. Unlike Emerson, Twain will not conceive of a society in which the first principles of nature, divined and adhered to by the individual, might lead to a well-balanced human community. Not that it's too late for that—for Twain it was always too late—but because it is written into our very souls that human beings must be clever to survive, and cleverness so easily turns to cunning and deceit: as though our humanity itself were our original sin, predating even the Fall. There is no grace period of human innocence. As evidence, Twain confesses in "My First Lie, and How I Got Out of It" that his own career as a liar began before the age of nine—*days*!

Twain's attitude, therefore, can never become nostalgic; this is the way of the world. The reader would be well advised to pay attention to the religious undertones of such a worldview. The Old Testament is perhaps given more weight in this view than the New. Salvation eludes us. The covenant has been broken, and we are wandering through our various deserts. Twain's is a very conservative attitude (again, small *c*). Over and over again in these essays and sketches the reader will find the sense that things fall apart, especially when human beings handle them. If these things are man-made, so much the worse—they are destined to crumble at a glance.

How to preserve the modicum of grace and gentility that makes living endurable? It's a large question for Twain (though the white-suited cigar smoker mentioned earlier wouldn't care a fig . . . but remember, that isn't Twain). The answer partly lies in savoring the small pleasures of life. This is a very important aspect of Twain's work, more important in the long run than his skewering of the pompous and his savaging of the gullible. Twain celebrates the pleasures of a good cigar (or even a bad one, provided it's one's chosen brand), the conquest of gravity in learning to ride a bicycle, the joy of inventing a remarkable way of teaching one's children the boring details of history. Though Twain plunges up to his elbows in the circus-tent mendacities of civic life, the reader will quickly sense that the finest and most attentive of Twain's short prose works deal with the more private areas of social life. Many of the public turmoils of Twain's time have changed their terms considerably in ours—though essays such as "Lionizing Murderers" and "A New Crime" seem frighteningly contemporary. But the terms of our relations with our books, our toys, our loved ones, and even our pocket-watches—if we remember to care for them *and not to fuss*—remain constant. It is frequently in the life lived locally and personally that Twain finds satisfaction. But the reader of these essays and sketches is challenged to find one false tear, one crocodile smile, one pathetic whine among them. When it comes to using prose to dissect the human condition, Twain's sense of balance, unlike his work atop a two-wheeler, is nearly faultless.

One reason is humor. Humor can put almost all man-made disasters into perspective. (The reader is reminded by Twain that his literary debut was occasioned by a shipwreck at sea.) When people are the victims of unmotivated, faceless cruelty, however, Twain never sneers or revels in their sufferings. Another way Twain gains perspective is to separate the human species into types. It may be a commonplace to say that comic laughter—again, unlike satire—is based on types, not personalities. When you begin to know another human being, see him close up, learn how he ticks, you're more likely to fall in love with him or murder him than to laugh at him. Intense interest in individual character is more likely to produce tragedy or melodrama than comedy. So be it. There is nothing inherently sinister in discussing men and women in aggregate, provided that the conclusions drawn are understood as having only provisional force. It's the stereo(fixed/firm/unshakable)type to beware of. Twain clearly falls on the righteous side of this line. (One complicated exception will be noted below.) He appeals as much to our sense that people are different in being alike as to our sense that they are alike in being different.

Twain's interest in human types is easily discovered in these short works. Travel had a good deal to do with this. It may surprise some readers to realize that Twain, in addition to living and working in the American Northwest, Southwest, Midwest, and East, spent large amounts of time in Europe, especially after the deaths of his wife, son, and one of his daughters, rendered him isolated and restless at his home in Hartford. Germany was a favored nation in Twain's itinerary. Twain admired many things about the Germans that we, with the hindsight of the late twentieth century, have come to dislike: their respect for rank and order, their fascination with ritual, their sharp political practicality, their somewhat stick-to-it literalness. But Germany was still largely a collection of cities and principalities in the 1880s, not an omnivorous nation-state, and to Twain these qualities spoke to that heritage of civility and grace he most approved. To his credit, Twain was able to spot in Richard Wagner and his idolators models of noxious grandiosity and self-importance. However, Twain was not a cultural thinker of the first water, and could not see, as Nietzsche finally did, the malign forces early at work in such Germanic self-constructions. (The reader is encouraged to turn to "At the Shrine of St. Wagner" for an example of Twain's beautiful sense of comic balance: attacking the institution known as Richard Wagner, while managing to say something eloquent and respectful about German culture, and even about some of Wagner's music.) England too was a grand source of amusement and bewilderment to Twain, a chance to look close-up at near family members and say, "There's what we Americans, for better *and* worse, might have become." France was, of course, Twain's *bête noire.* No humorist, Twain seems to have felt, has any ground to stand on in the case of France, for no humorist can top the inherent ridiculousness of the French and their stylized, attentuated, lascivious culture.

The point to remember here is that travel stimulated Twain's natural curiosity about human types. He was not so enlightened a man that this attraction to types circumvented the realms of nation, religion, or race. He was, in his understanding of social life, a man of his time and in no way prescient. Perhaps here, a more truly satirical, less reductive view of human nature would have greater appeal to us, but what we'd have to give up—Twain's life-size replica of human weakness and folly—might not be worth it. Still, one of the most troubling aspects of Twain's work for the modern reader is the relative ease with which Twain holds to typologies along these lines, even—and this should be emphasized in what follows—when his intention is to defend and honor a national, religious, or racial group.

In regard to this last point one could set in evidence Twain's essay "Concerning the Jews." Twain's purpose in this essay is a wholehearted defense of the Jew's common humanity and his specific virtues. It is meant to be a refutation of the unreasoned anti-Semitism of Twain's time. Yet it is difficult to argue with the fact that Twain's depiction of the normal Jewish citizen comes fraught with many of the worst stereotypes of the period. So what, runs one of Twain's arguments, if the Jew is a preternaturally successful businessman? This shrewdness is a virtue, really, and Gentiles would do well to admit it and try to acquire the same skills. Despite giving some historical explanations for the Jewish predominance in the business world (a predominance never questioned, by the way), Twain upholds the clannish, clever, slightly rank portrait of the Jew prevalent in his time. He does redraw the lines between vice and virtue in the Jew's favor, but he continues to think in terms of types, of races, of predetermined patterns of behavior based on groups. Twain's attempt to bring the Jew into the bosom of the human family is somewhat nullified by the terms, antiquated in enlightened circles even at the time, under which he conducts that admirable effort.

But it is Twain's fecundity as a humorist which should remain the focal point of any reasonable likeness. About this almost everything has been said, and one is tempted only to reiterate that among Twain's works can be found almost every comic device, situation, and gimmick in the arsenal of American humor. There are gestures in Twain's writing that are the verbal equivalents of slipping on a banana peel or banging heads together. There are coarse, ungainly dialect stories. There's Twain's persona of *faux-naïf*, presenting himself to his readers as the guileless man of good will and good sense, left to the mercy of those who would take him in—all the better to flush them into the open, so that the savvy author-narrator may expose them for the sly creatures they are. (This backfires beautifully in "A Mysterious Visit," where Twain the author seems just as eager to lampoon himself as a character in the farce.) There is some extravagant absurdist wordplay—most saliently in the famous essay on the German language—and, even more interestingly, situational punning, where the very narrative is a kind of reverberating joke, echoing other stories that surround it or are implied. Finally, at the upper end of the spectrum, there's that most sophisticated and subtle sort of humor, where the complex edifice of human pretense and self-delusion is completely demolished—and yet the defenseless human creature inside remains standing, supported by the author's larger human sympathies.

There is one feature of Twain's humor which the reader will find in great abundance among these short works. Although Twain, like any author, concocted many imaginary situations and documents in the course of his writing life (inventing diaries for characters as far back as Adam and Eve, for instance), a great deal of Twain's humor is a result of merely quoting. Twain's ability to sit back and let the defendant, or even a witness, hang himself is a hallmark of his style. Readers will find that Twain interpolates letters from widows, chapters from scholarly works, newspaper headlines, grammar exercises, obituaries, death threats, income tax questionnaires, actuarial statistics, stories overheard in train stations, and pseudo-scientific medical treatises into his essays. This is not done to pad the work, but to provide the essential human testimony that proves the point under consideration more convincingly than any argument. You only have to hear it from their own mouths to believe it.

It is very likely this notion of verisimilitude, born of Twain's years of knockabout journalism, that is also at the heart of his complaint against the author of *The Leatherstocking Tales*. In his famous blast "Fenimore Cooper's Literary Offenses," Twain lays out his concept of an American realist art. This art is based on getting the details right. Imagination is a poor excuse for having Indians, supremely skilled hunters and trappers, fail in their attempts to leap about two feet onto a boat sixteen feet wide and one hundred and forty feet long—a boat, by the way, moving at the exalted speed of one mile per hour! This famous attack on a narrative moment in Cooper's *The Deerslayer* is sometimes turned against Twain himself to point up the crudity of his literary criticism—mere griping, according to some. But the point he's making here is really about larger aesthetic issues. Out of what will our American art be made? Does the writer have an obligation to know something about what he records? Is the imaginative faculty the ability to construct a plausible world, or a merely fanciful one? Don't readers have the right to expect the same honesty and integrity from their authors as they do from their hotel porters? (See Twain's admiring essay on the European practitioners of that profession, included.) Or will our art be made of half-truths and fancies . . . like the French!

Twain's stand on the "Shakespeare question" will serve nicely to conclude the case for his aesthetic concerns, as well as his views on the natural limits of human attainment. It has been said that where a writer begins to discuss Shakespeare, he winds up largely talking about himself. That is, in all the guesswork concerning Shakespeare's possible life and talents, there is plenty of room to construct a genius in our own image—either we see ourselves as the hero of the drama, or else we positon ourselves within Shakespeare's story as we do in the world. A good deal can be discerned by considering what Twain made of Shakespeare in his lengthy meditation "Is Shakespeare Dead?"

The possibility that a world-class writer might have been made out of such a young man as we know William Shakespeare to have been—a humbly educated son of a small-town notable; a teenager apprenticed in a local trade, so that he might make his way in an entirely provincial world; a young man who bolted from this stultifying situation to find a more adventurous life, traveling (possibly as an actor) until he reached the big city—all this might seem stuff tailor-made for Twain's enthusiastic assent. It is similar enough in outline to his own story. Yet Twain flatly rejected the idea. Like Cooper's Indians, the son of the Stratford glover seems to miss the boat entirely. The wide technical knowledge of worldly things, especially the law, combined with the sheer proficiency of dramatic craft evinced by the plays themselves, excludes Shakespeare from being their author in Twain's estimation. The author of these works, he insists, had to be a man of larger public experience and more education than Shakespeare could possibly have been. Imagination? Twain once again minimizes the influence of sheer power of imagination on the abilty to create a complex art. Skills, learned through years of patient attentiveness (as young Twain attended to both a master printer and a riverboat pilot) are at the core of this great body of work. A lawyer and diplomat, Twain argues, constructed these works. No amount of imagining—even by a gifted presumer—could replace firsthand experience. Boys were even less likely in Elizabethan times than in Twain's youth to rise by virtue of natural gifts. Sir Francis Bacon (or someone very like, if one could be found) gets Twain's vote for authorship.

Here, the intention is not to refute the original point about the writer's projecting himself into the role of Shakespeare. Instead, we might be able to find in Twain's support of Bacon an alternative view of Twain himself. Not a brash, clever upstart, as some of Twain's lovable writings about his own youth propose. Nor a young man of unbounded though unfledged natural gifts and irrepressible enthusiasms. But a citizen of the world who had traveled great distances, learning through experience many crafts and skills, supreme among them the art of literary composition. He had earned, he felt, the right to his podium. The humor in these essays, and in all of Twain's work, should be seen in the light of his deeper, more serious concerns.

—*Stuart Miller*
1995

YOUNG MARK TWAIN

My First Lie, and How I Got Out of It

As I understand it, what you desire is information about "my first lie, and how I got out of it." I was born in 1835; I am well along, and my memory is not as good as it was. If you had asked about my first truth it would have been easier for me and kinder of you, for I remember that fairly well; I remember it as if it were last week. The family think it was week before, but that is flattery and probably has a selfish project back of it. When a person has become seasoned by experience and has reached the age of sixty-four, which is the age of discretion, he likes a family compliment as well as ever, but he does not lose his head over it as in the old innocent days.

I do not remember my first lie, it is too far back; but I remember my second one very well. I was nine days old at the time, and had noticed that if a pin was sticking in me and I advertised it in the usual fashion, I was lovingly petted and coddled and pitied in a most agreeable way and got a ration between meals besides. It was human nature to want to get these riches, and I fell. I lied about the pin—advertising one when there wasn't any. You would have done it; George Washington did it; anybody would have done it. During the first half of my life I never knew a child that was able to rise above that temptation and keep from telling that lie. Up to 1867 all the civilized children that were ever born into the world were liars—including George. Then the safety-pin came in and blocked the game. But is that reform worth anything? No; for it is reform by force and has no virtue in it; it merely stops that form of lying; it doesn't impair the disposition to lie, by a shade. It is the cradle application of conversion by fire and sword, or of the temperance principle through prohibition.

To return to that early lie. They found no pin, and they realized that another liar had been added to the world's supply. For by grace of a rare inspiration, a quite commonplace but seldom noticed fact was borne in upon their understandings—that almost all lies are acts, and speech has no part in them. Then, if they examined a little further they recognized that all people are liars from the cradle onward, without exception, and that they begin to lie as soon as they wake in the morning, and keep it up, without rest or refreshment, until they go to sleep at night. If they arrived at that truth it probably grieved them—did, if they had been heedlessly and ignorantly educated by their books and teachers; for why should a person grieve over a thing which by the eternal law of his make he cannot help? He didn't invent the law; it is merely his business to obey it and keep still; join the universal conspiracy and keep so still that he shall deceive his fellow-conspirators into imagining that he doesn't know that the law exists. It is what we all do—we that know. I am speaking of the lie of silent assertion; we can tell it without saying a word, and we all do it—we that know. In the magnitude of its territorial spread it is one of the most majestic lies that the civilizations make it their sacred and anxious care to guard and watch and propagate.

For instance: It would not be possible for a humane and intelligent person to invent a rational excuse for slavery; yet you will remember that in the early days of the emancipation agitation in the North, the agitators got but small help or countenance from any one. Argue and plead and pray as they might, they could not break the universal stillness that reigned, from pulpit and press all the way down to the bottom of society—the clammy stillness created and maintained by the lie of silent assertion—the silent assertion that there wasn't anything going on in which humane and intelligent people were interested.

From the beginning of the Dreyfus case to the end of it, all France, except a couple of dozen moral paladins, lay under the smother of the silent-assertion lie that no wrong was being done to a persecuted and unoffending man. The like smother was over England lately, a good half of the population silently letting on that they were not aware that Mr. Chamberlain was trying to manufacture a war in South Africa and was willing to pay fancy prices for the materials.

Now there we have instances of three prominent ostensible civilizations working the silent-assertion lie. Could one find other instances in the three countries? I think so. Not so very many, perhaps, but say a billion—just so as to keep within bounds. Are those countries working that kind of lie, day in and day out, in thousands and thousands of varieties, without ever resting? Yes, we know that to be true. The universal conspiracy of the silent-assertion lie is hard at work always and everywhere, and always in the interest of a stupidity or a sham, never in the interest of a thing fine or respectable. Is it the most timid and shabby of all lies? It seems to have the look of it. For ages and ages it has mutely labored in the interest of despotisms and aristocracies and chattel slaveries, and military slaveries, and religious slaveries, and has kept them alive; keeps them alive yet, here and there and yonder, all about the globe; and will go on keeping them alive until the silent-assertion lie retires from business—the silent assertion that nothing is going on which fair and intelligent men are aware of and are engaged by their duty to try to stop.

What I am arriving at is this: When whole races and peoples conspire to propagate gigantic mute lies in the interest of tyrannies and shams, why should we care anything about the trifling lies told by individuals? Why should we try to make it appear that abstention from lying is a virtue? Why should we want to beguile ourselves in that way? Why should we without shame help the nation lie, and then be ashamed to do a little lying on our own account? Why shouldn't we be honest and honorable, and lie every time we get a chance? That is to say, why shouldn't we be consistent, and either lie all the time or not at all? Why should we help the nation lie the whole day long and then object to telling one little individual private lie in our own interest to go to bed on? Just for the refreshment of it, I mean, and to take the rancid taste out of our mouth.

Here in England they have the oddest ways. They won't tell a spoken lie—nothing can persuade them. Except in a large moral interest, like politics or religion, I mean. To tell a spoken lie to get even the poorest little personal advantage out of it is a thing which is impossible to them. They make me ashamed of myself sometimes, they are so bigoted. They will not even tell a lie for the fun of it; they will not tell it when it hasn't even a suggestion of damage or advantage in it for any one. This has a restraining influence upon me in spite of reason, and I am always getting out of practice.

Of course, they tell all sorts of little unspoken lies, just like anybody; but they don't notice it until their attention is called to it. They have got me so that sometimes I never tell a verbal lie now except in a modified form; and even in the modified form they don't approve of it. Still, that is as far as I can go in the interest of the growing friendly relations between the two countries; I must keep some of my self-respect—and my health. I can live on a low diet, but I can't get along on no sustenance at all.

Of course, there are times when these people have to come out with a spoken lie, for that is a thing which happens to everybody once in a while, and would happen to the angels if they came down here much. Particularly to the angels, in fact, for the lies I speak of are self-sacrificing ones told for a generous object, not a mean one; but even when these people tell a lie of that sort it seems to scare them and unsettle their minds. It is a wonderful thing to see, and shows that they are all insane. In fact, it is a country full of the most interesting superstitions.

I have an English friend of twenty-five years' standing, and yesterday when we were coming down-town on top of the bus I happened to tell him a lie—a modified one, of course; a half-breed, a mulatto: I can't seem to tell any other kind now, the market is so flat. I was explaining to him how I got out of an embarrassment in Austria last year. I do not know what might have become of me if I hadn't happened to remember to tell the police that I belonged to the same family as the Prince of Wales. That made everything pleasant, and they let me go; and apologized, too, and were ever so kind and obliging and polite, and couldn't do too much for me, and explained how the mistake came to be made, and promised to hang the officer that did it, and hoped I would let bygones be bygones and not say anything about it; and I said they could depend on me. My friend said, austerely:

"You call it a modified lie? Where is the modification?"

I explained that it lay in the form of my statement to the police.

"I didn't say I belonged to the royal family: I only said I belonged to the same family as the Prince—meaning the human family, of course; and if those people had had any penetration they would have known it. I can't go around furnishing brains to the police; it is not to be expected."

"How did you feel after that performance?"

"Well, of course I was distressed to find that the police had misunderstood me, but as long as I had not told any lie I knew there was no occasion to sit up nights and worry about it."

My friend struggled with the case several minutes, turning it over and examining it in his mind; then he said that so far as he could see the modification was itself a lie, being a misleading reservation of an explanatory fact; so I had told two lies instead of one.

"I wouldn't have done it," said he: "I have never told a lie, and I should be very sorry to do such a thing."

Just then he lifted his hat and smiled a basketful of surprised and delighted smiles down at a gentleman who was passing in a hansom.

"Who was that, G——?"

"I don't know."

"Then why did you do that?"

"Because I saw he thought he knew me and was expecting it of me. If I hadn't done it he would have been hurt. I didn't want to embarrass him before the whole street."

"Well, your heart was right, G——, and your act was right. What you did was kindly and courteous and beautiful; I would have done it myself: but it was a lie."

"A lie? I didn't say a word. How do you make it out?"

"I know you didn't speak, still you said to him very plainly and enthusiastically in dumb show, 'Hello! you in town? Awful glad to see you, old fellow; when did you get back?' Concealed in your actions was what you have called 'a misleading reservation of an explanatory fact'—the fact that you had never seen him before. You expressed joy in encountering him—a lie; and you made that reservation—another lie. It was my pair over again. But don't be troubled—we all do it."

Two hours later, at dinner, when quite other matters were being discussed, he told how he happened along once just in the nick of time to do a great service for a family who were old friends of his. The head of it had suddenly died in circumstances and surroundings of a ruinously disgraceful character. If known, the facts would break the hearts of the innocent family and put upon them a load of unendurable shame. There was no help but in a giant lie, and he girded up his loins and told it.

"The family never found out, G——?"

"Never. In all these years they have never suspected. They were proud of him, and always had reason to be; they are proud of him yet, and to them his memory is sacred and stainless and beautiful."

"They had a narrow escape, G——."

"Indeed they had."

"For the very next man that came along might have been one of these heartless and shameless truth-mongers. You have told the truth a million times in your life, G——, but that one golden lie atones for it all. Persevere."

Some may think me not strict enough in my morals, but that position is hardly tenable. There are many kinds of lying which I do not approve. I do not like an injurious lie, except when it injures somebody else; and I do not like the lie of bravado, nor the lie of virtuous ecstasy: the latter was affected by Bryant, the former by Carlyle.

Mr. Bryant said, "Truth crushed to earth will rise again."

I have taken medals at thirteen world's fairs, and may claim to be not without capacity, but I never told as big a one as that which Mr. Bryant was playing to the gallery; we all do it. Carlyle said, in substance, this—I do not remember the exact words: "This gospel is eternal—that a lie shall not live."

I have a reverent affection for Carlyle's books, and have read his *Revolution* eight times; and so I prefer to think he was not entirely at himself when he told that one. To me it is plain that he said it in a moment of excitement, when chasing Americans out of his back yard with brickbats. They used to go there and worship. At bottom he was probably fond of them, but he was always able to conceal it. He kept bricks for them, but he was not a good shot, and it is matter of history that when he fired they dodged, and carried off the brick; for as a nation we like relics, and so long as we get them we do not much care what the reliquary thinks about it. I am quite sure that when he told that large one about a lie not being able to live, he had just missed an American and was over-excited. He told it above thirty years ago, but it is alive yet; alive, and very healthy and hearty, and likely to outlive any fact in history. Carlyle was truthful when calm, but give him Americans enough and bricks enough and he could have taken medals himself.

As regards that time that George Washington told the truth, a word must be said, of course. It is the principal jewel in the crown of America, and it is but natural that we should work for all it is worth, as Milton says in his "Lay of the Last Minstrel." It was a timely and judicious truth, and I should have told it myself in the circumstances. But I should have stopped there. It was a stately truth, a lofty truth—a Tower; and I think it was a mistake to go on and distract attention from its sublimity by building another Tower alongside of it fourteen times as high. I refer to his remark that he "could not lie." I should have fed that to the marines: or left it to Carlyle; it is just in his style. It would have taken a medal at any European fair, and would have got an Honorable Mention even at Chicago if it had been saved up. But let it pass: the Father of his Country was excited. I have been in those circumstances, and I recollect.

With the truth he told I have no objection to offer, as already indicated. I think it was not premeditated, but an inspiration. With his fine military mind, he had probably arranged to let his brother Edward in for the cherry-tree results, but by an inspiration he saw his opportunity in time and took advantage of it. By telling the truth he could astonish his father; his father would tell the neighbors; the neighbors would spread it; it would travel to all firesides; in the end it would make him President, and not only that, but First President. He was a far-seeing boy and would be likely to think of these things. Therefore, to my mind, he stands justified for what he did. But not for the other Tower: it was a mistake. Still, I don't know about that; upon reflection I think perhaps it wasn't. For indeed it is that Tower that makes the other one live. If he hadn't said "I cannot tell a lie," there would have been no convulsion. That was the earthquake that rocked the planet. That is the kind of statement that lives forever, and a fact barnacled to it has a good chance to share its immortality.

To sum up, on the whole I am satisfied with things the way they are. There is a prejudice against the spoken lie, but none against any other, and by examination and mathematical computation I find that the proportion of the spoken lie to the other varieties is as 1 to 22,894. Therefore the spoken lie is of no consequence, and it is not worth while to go around fussing about it and trying to make believe that it is an important matter. The silent colossal National Lie that is the support and confederate of all the tyrannies and shams and inequalities and unfairnesses that afflict the peoples—that is the one to throw bricks and sermons at. But let us be judicious and let somebody else begin.

And then— But I have wandered from my text. How did I get out of my second lie? I think I got out with honor, but I cannot be sure, for it was a long time ago and some of the details have faded out of my memory. I recollect that I was reversed and stretched across some one's knee, and that something happened, but I cannot now remember what it was. I think there was music; but it is all dim now and blurred by the lapse of time, and this may be only a senile fancy.

The Turning-Point of My Life

I

If I understand the idea, the *Bazar* invites several of us to write upon the above text. It means the change in my life's course which introduced what must be regarded by me as the most *important* condition of my career. But it also implies—without intention, perhaps—that that turning-point *itself* was the creator of the new condition. This gives it too much distinction, too much prominence, too much credit. It is only the *last* link in a very long chain of turning-points commissioned to produce the cardinal result; it is not any more important than the humblest of its ten thousand predecessors. Each of the ten thousand did its appointed share, on its appointed date, in forwarding the scheme, and they were all necessary; to have left out any one of them would have defeated the scheme and brought about *some other* result. I know we have a fashion of saying "such and such an event was the turning-point in my life," but we shouldn't say it. We should merely grant that its place as *last* link in the chain makes it the most *conspicuous* link; in real importance it has no advantage over any one of its predecessors.

Perhaps the most celebrated turning-point recorded in history was the crossing of the Rubicon. Suetonius says:

> Coming up with his troops on the banks of the Rubicon, he halted for a while, and, revolving in his mind the importance of the step he was on the point of taking, he turned to those about him and said, "We may still retreat; but if we pass this little bridge, nothing is left for us but to fight it out in arms."

This was a stupendously important moment. And all the incidents, big and little, of Cæsar's previous life had been leading up to it, stage by stage, link by link. This was the *last* link—merely the last one, and no bigger than the others; but as we gaze back at it through the inflating mists of our imagination, it looks as big as the orbit of Neptune.

You, the reader, have a *personal* interest in that link, and so have I; so has the rest of the human race. It was one of the links in your life-chain, and it was one of the links in mine. We may wait, now, with bated breath, while Cæsar reflects. Your fate and mine are involved in his decision.

While he was thus hesitating, the following incident occurred. A person remarked for his noble mien and graceful aspect appeared close at hand, sitting and playing upon a pipe. When not only the shepherds, but a number of soldiers also, flocked to listen to him, and some trumpeters among them, he snatched a trumpet from one of them, ran to the river with it, and, sounding the advance with a piercing blast, crossed to the other side. Upon this, Cæsar exclaimed: "Let us go whither the omens of the gods and the iniquity of our enemies call us. *The die is cast.*"

So he crossed—and changed the future of the whole human race, for all time. But that stranger was a link in Cæsar's life-chain, too; and a necessary one. We don't know his name, we never hear of him again; he was very casual; he acts like an accident; but he was no accident, he was there by compulsion of *his* life-chain, to blow the electrifying blast that was to make up Cæsar's mind for him, and thence go piping down the aisles of history forever.

If the stranger hadn't been there! But he *was*. And Cæsar crossed. With such results! Such vast events—each a link in the *human race's* life-chain; each event producing the next one, and that one the next one, and so on: the destruction of the republic; the founding of the empire; the breaking up of the empire; the rise of Christianity upon its ruins; the spread of the religion to other lands—and so on: link by link took its appointed place at its appointed time, the discovery of America being one of them; our Revolution another; the inflow of English and other immigrants another;

their drift westward (my ancestors among them) another; the settlement of certain of them in Missouri, which resulted in *me.* For I was one of the unavoidable results of the crossing of the Rubicon. If the stranger, with his trumpet blast, had stayed away (which he *couldn't,* for he was an appointed link) Cæsar would not have crossed. What would have happened, in that case, we can never guess. We only know that the things that did happen would not have happened. They might have been replaced by equally prodigious things, of course, but their nature and results are beyond our guessing. But the matter that interests me personally is that I would not be *here* now, but somewhere else; and probably black—there is no telling. Very well, I am glad he crossed. And very really and thankfully glad, too, though I never cared anything about it before.

II

To me, the most important feature of my life is its literary feature. I have been professionally literary something more than forty years. There have been many turning-points in my life, but the one that was the last link in the chain appointed to conduct me to the literary guild is the most *conspicuous* link in that chain. *Because* it was the last one. It was not any more important than its predecessors. All the other links have an inconspicuous look, except the crossing of the Rubicon; but as factors in making me literary they are all of the one size, the crossing of the Rubicon included.

I know how I came to be literary, and I will tell the steps that led up to it and brought it about.

The crossing of the Rubicon was not the first one, it was hardly even a recent one; I should have to go back ages before Cæsar's day to find the first one. To save space I will go back only a couple of generations and start with an incident of my boyhood. When I was twelve and a half years old, my father died. It was in the spring. The summer came, and brought with it an epidemic of measles. For a time, a child died almost every day. The village was paralyzed with fright, distress, despair. Children that were not smitten with the disease were imprisoned in their homes to save them from the infection. In the homes there were no cheerful faces, there was no music, there was no singing but of solemn hymns, no voice but of prayer, no romping was allowed, no noise, no laughter, the family moved spectrally about on tiptoe, in a ghostly hush. I was a prisoner. My soul was steeped in this awful dreariness—and in fear. At some time or other every day and every night a sudden shiver shook me to the marrow, and I said to myself, "There, I've got it! and I shall die." Life on these miserable terms was not worth living, and at last I made up my mind to get the disease and have it over, one way or the other. I escaped from the house and went to the house of a neighbor where a playmate of mine was very ill with the malady. When the chance offered I crept into his room and got into bed with him. I was discovered by his mother and sent back into captivity. But I had the disease; they could not take that from me. I came near to dying. The whole village was interested, and anxious, and sent for news of me every day; and not only once a day, but several times. Everybody believed I would die; but on the fourteenth day a change came for the worse and they were disappointed.

This was a turning-point of my life. (Link number one.) For when I got well my mother closed my school career and apprenticed me to a printer. She was tired of trying to keep me out of mischief, and the adventure of the measles decided her to put me into more masterful hands than hers.

I became a printer, and began to add one link after another to the chain which was to lead me into the literary profession. A long road, but I could not know that; and as I did not know what its goal was, or even that it had one, I was indifferent. Also contented.

A young printer wanders around a good deal, seeking and finding work; and seeking again, when necessity commands. *N.B.*—Necessity is a *Circumstance;* Circumstance is man's master—and when Circumstance commands, he must obey; he may argue the matter—that is his privilege, just as it is the honorable privilege of a falling body to argue with the attraction of gravitation—but it won't do any good, he must *obey.* I wandered for ten years, under the guidance and dictatorship of Circumstance, and finally arrived in a city of Iowa, where I worked several months. Among the books that interested me in those days was one about the Amazon. The traveler told an alluring tale of his long voyage up the great river from Para to the sources of the Madeira, through the heart of an enchanted land, a land wastefully rich in tropical wonders, a romantic land where all the birds and flowers and animals were of the museum varieties, and where the alligator and the crocodile and the monkey seemed as much at home as if they were in the Zoo. Also, he told an astonishing tale about *coca,* a vegetable product of miraculous powers, asserting that it was so nourishing and so strength-giving that the native of the mountains of the Madeira region would tramp up hill and down all day on a pinch of powdered coca and require no other sustenance.

I was fired with a longing to ascend the Amazon. Also with a longing to open up a trade in coca with all the world. During months I dreamed that dream, and tried to contrive ways to get to Para and spring that splendid enterprise upon an unsuspecting planet. But all in vain. A person may *plan* as much as he wants to, but nothing of consequence is likely to come of it until the magician *Circumstance* steps in and takes the matter off his hands. At last Circumstance came to my help. It was in this way. Circumstance, to help or hurt another man, made him lose a fifty-dollar bill in the street; and to help or hurt me, made me find it. I advertised the find, and left for the Amazon the same day. This was another turning-point, another link.

Could Circumstance have ordered another dweller in that town to go to the Amazon and open up a world-trade in coca on a fifty-dollar basis and been obeyed? No, I was the only one. There were other fools there—shoals and shoals of them—but they were not of my kind. I was the only one of my kind.

Circumstance is powerful, but it cannot work alone; it has to have a partner. Its partner is man's *temperament*—his natural disposition. His temperament is not his invention, it is *born* in him, and he has no authority over it, neither is he responsible for its acts. He cannot change it, nothing can change it, nothing can modify it—except temporarily. But it won't stay modified. It is permanent, like the color of the man's eyes and the shape of his ears. Blue eyes are gray in certain unusual lights; but they resume their natural color when that stress is removed.

A Circumstance that will coerce one man will have no effect upon a man of a different temperament. If Circumstance had thrown the bank-note in Cæsar's way, his temperament would not have made him start for the Amazon. His temperament would have compelled him to do something with the money, but not that. It might have made him advertise the note—and *wait*. We can't tell. Also, it might have made him go to New York and buy into the Government, with results that would leave Tweed nothing to learn when it came his turn.

Very well, Circumstance furnished the capital, and my temperament told me what to do with it. Sometimes a temperament is an ass. When that is the case the owner of it is an ass, too, and is going to remain one. Training, experience, association, can temporarily so polish him, improve him, exalt him that people will think he is a mule, but they will be mistaken. Artificially he *is* a mule, for the time being, but at bottom he is an ass yet, and will remain one.

By temperament I was the kind of person that *does* things. Does them, and reflects afterward. So I started for the Amazon without reflecting and without asking any questions. That was more than fifty years ago. In all that time my temperament has not changed, by even a shade. I have been punished many and many a time, and bitterly, for doing things and reflecting afterward, but these tortures have been of no value to me: I still do the thing commanded by Circumstance and Temperament, and reflect afterward. Always violently. When I am reflecting, on those occasions, even deaf persons can hear me think.

I went by the way of Cincinnati, and down the Ohio and Mississippi. My idea was to take ship, at New Orleans, for Para. In New Orleans I inquired, and found there was no ship leaving for Para. Also, that there never had *been* one leaving for Para. I reflected. A policeman came and asked me what I was doing, and I told him. He made me move on, and said if he caught me reflecting in the public street again he would run me in.

After a few days I was out of money. Then Circumstance arrived, with another turning-point of my life—a new link. On my way down, I had made the acquaintance of a pilot. I begged him to teach me the river, and he consented. I became a pilot.

By and by Circumstance came again—introducing the Civil War, this time, in order to push me ahead another stage or two toward the literary profession. The boats stopped running, my livelihood was gone.

Circumstance came to the rescue with a new turning-point and a fresh link. My brother was appointed secretary to the new Territory of Nevada, and he invited me to go with him and help him in his office. I accepted.

In Nevada, Circumstance furnished me the silver fever and I went into the mines to make a fortune, as I supposed; but that was not the idea. The idea was to advance me another step toward literature. For amusement I scribbled things for the Virginia City *Enterprise.* One isn't a printer ten years without setting up acres of good and bad literature, and learning—unconsciously at first, consciously later—to discriminate between the two, within his mental limitations; and meantime he is unconsciously acquiring what is called a "style." One of my efforts attracted attention, and the *Enterprise* sent for me and put me on its staff.

And so I became a journalist—another link. By and by Circumstance and the Sacramento *Union* sent me to the Sandwich Islands for five or six months, to write up sugar. I did it; and threw in a good deal of extraneous matter that hadn't anything to do with sugar. But it was this extraneous matter that helped me to another link.

It made me notorious, and San Francisco invited me to lecture. Which I did. And profitably. I had long had a desire to travel and see the world, and now Circumstance had most kindly and unexpectedly hurled me upon the platform and furnished me the means. So I joined the "Quaker City Excursion."

When I returned to America, Circumstance was waiting on the pier—with the *last* link—the conspicuous, the consummating, the victorious link: I was asked to *write a book,* and I did it, and called it *The Innocents Abroad.* Thus I became at last a member of the literary guild. That was forty-two years ago, and I have been a member ever since. Leaving the Rubicon incident away back where it belongs, I can say with truth that the reason I am in the literary profession is because I had the measles when I was twelve years old.

III

Now what interests me, as regards these details, is not the details themselves, but the fact that none of them was foreseen by me, none of them was planned by me, I was the author of none of them. Circumstance, working in harness with my temperament, created them all and compelled them all. I often offered help, and with the best intentions, but it was rejected—as a rule, uncourteously. I could never plan a thing and get it to come out the way I planned it. It came out some other way—some way I had not counted upon.

And so I do not admire the human being—as an intellectual marvel—as much as I did when I was young, and got him out of books, and did not know him personally. When I used to read that such and such a general did a certain brilliant thing, I believed it. Whereas it was not so. Circumstance did it by help of his temperament. The circumstance would have failed of effect with a general of another temperament: he might see the chance, but lose the advantage by being by nature too slow or too quick or too doubtful. Once General Grant was asked a question about a matter which had been much debated by the public and the newspapers; he answered the question without any hesitancy. "General, who planned the march through Georgia?" "The enemy!" He added that the enemy usually makes your plans for you. He meant that the enemy by neglect or through force of circumstances leaves an opening for you, and you see your chance and take advantage of it.

Circumstances do the planning for us all, no doubt, by help of our temperaments. I see no great difference between a man and a watch, except that the man is conscious and the watch isn't, and the man *tries* to plan things and the watch doesn't. The watch doesn't wind itself and doesn't regulate itself—these things are done exteriorly. Outside influences, outside circumstances, wind the *man* and regulate him. Left to himself, he wouldn't get regulated at all, and the sort of time he would keep would not be valuable. Some rare men are wonderful watches, with gold case, compensation balance, and all those things, and some men are only simple and sweet and humble Waterburys. I am a Waterbury. A Waterbury of that kind, some say.

A nation is only an individual multiplied. It makes plans and Circumstance comes and upsets them—or enlarges them. Some patriots throw the tea overboard; some other patriots destroy a Bastille. The *plans* stop there; then Circumstance comes in, quite unexpectedly, and turns these modest riots into a revolution.

And there was poor Columbus. He elaborated a deep plan to find a new route to an old country. Circumstance revised his plan for him, and he found a new *world.* And *he* gets the credit of it to this day. He hadn't anything to do with it.

Necessarily the scene of the real turning-point of my life (and of yours) was the Garden of Eden. It was there that the first link was forged of the chain that was ultimately to lead to the emptying of me into the literary guild. Adam's *temperament* was the first command the Deity ever issued to a human being on this planet. And it was the only command Adam would *never* be able to disobey. It said, "Be weak, be water, be characterless, be cheaply persuadable." The later command, to let the fruit alone, was certain to be disobeyed. Not by Adam himself, but by his *temperament*—which he did not create and had no authority over. For the *temperament* is the man; the thing tricked out with clothes and named Man is merely its Shadow, nothing more. The law of the tiger's temperament is, Thou shalt kill; the law of the sheep's temperament is, Thou shalt not kill. To issue later commands requiring the tiger to let the fat stranger alone, and requiring the sheep to imbue its hands in the blood of the lion is not worth while, for those commands *can't* be obeyed. They would invite to violations of the law of *temperament,* which is supreme, and takes precedence of all other authorities. I cannot help feeling disappointed in Adam and Eve. That is, in their temperaments. Not in *them,* poor helpless young creatures—afflicted with temperaments made out of butter; which butter was commanded to get into contact with fire and *be melted.* What I cannot help wishing is, that Adam and Eve had been postponed, and Martin

Luther and Joan of Arc put in their place—that splendid pair equipped with temperaments not made of butter, but of asbestos. By neither sugary persuasions nor by hell fire could Satan have beguiled *them* to eat the apple.

There would have been results! Indeed, yes. The apple would be intact to-day; there would be no human race; there would be no *you;* there would be no *me.* And the old, old creation-dawn scheme of ultimately launching me into the literary guild would have been defeated.

My First Literary Venture

I was a very smart child at the age of thirteen—an unusually smart child, I thought at the time. It was then that I did my first newspaper scribbling, and most unexpectedly to me it stirred up a fine sensation in the community. It did, indeed, and I was very proud of it, too. I was a printer's "devil," and a progressive and aspiring one. My uncle had me on his paper (the *Weekly Hannibal Journal,* two dollars a year in advance—five hundred subscribers, and they paid in cordwood, cabbages, and unmarketable turnips), and on a lucky summer's day he left town to be gone a week, and asked me if I thought I could edit one issue of the paper judiciously. Ah! didn't I want to try! Higgins was the editor on the rival paper. He had lately been jilted, and one night a friend found an open note on the poor fellow's bed, in which he stated that he could not longer endure life and had drowned himself in Bear Creek. The friend ran down there and discovered Higgins wading back to shore. He had concluded he wouldn't. The village was full of it for several days, but Higgins did not suspect it. I thought this was a fine opportunity. I wrote an elaborately wretched account of the whole matter, and then illustrated it with villainous cuts engraved on the bottoms of wooden type with a jackknife—one of them a picture of Higgins wading out into the creek in his shirt, with a lantern, sounding the depth of the water with a walking-stick. I thought it was desperately funny, and was densely unconscious that there was any moral obliquity about such a publication. Being satisfied with this effort I looked around for other worlds to conquer, and it struck me that it would make good, interesting matter to charge the editor of a neighboring country paper with a piece of gratuitous rascality and "see him squirm."

I did it, putting the article into the form of a parody on the "Burial of Sir John Moore"—and a pretty crude parody it was, too.

Then I lampooned two prominent citizens outrageously—not because they had done anything to deserve, but merely because I thought it was my duty to make the paper lively.

Next I gently touched up the newest stranger—the lion of the day, the gorgeous journeyman tailor from Quincy. He was a simpering coxcomb of the first water, and the "loudest" dressed man in the state. He was an inveterate woman-killer. Every week he wrote lushy "poetry" for the *Journal*, about his newest conquest. His rhymes for my week were headed, "To Mary in H——l," meaning to Mary in Hannibal, of course. But while setting up the piece I was suddenly riven from head to heel by what I regarded as a perfect thunderbolt of humor, and I compressed it into a snappy footnote at the bottom—thus: "We will let this thing pass, just this once; but we wish Mr. J. Gordon Runnels to understand distinctly that we have a character to sustain, and from this time forth when he wants to commune with his friends in h—l, he must select some other medium than the columns of this journal!"

The paper came out, and I never knew any little thing attract so much attention as those playful trifles of mine.

For once the *Hannibal Journal* was in demand—a novelty it had not experienced before. The whole town was stirred. Higgins dropped in with a double-barreled shotgun early in the forenoon. When he found that it was an infant (as he called me) that had done him the damage, he simply pulled my ears and went away; but he threw up his situation that night and left town for good. The tailor came with his goose and a pair of shears; but he despised me, too, and departed for the South that night. The two lampooned citizens came with threats of libel, and went away incensed at my insignificance. The country editor pranced in with a war-whoop next day, suffering for blood to drink; but he ended by forgiving me cordially and inviting me down to the drug store to wash away all animosity in a friendly bumper of "Fahnestock's Vermifuge." It was his little joke. My uncle was very angry when he got back—unreasonably so, I thought, considering what an impetus I had given the paper, and considering also that gratitude for his preservation ought to have been uppermost in his mind, inasmuch as by his delay he had so wonderfully escaped dissection, tomahawking, libel, and getting his head shot off. But he softened when he looked at the accounts and saw that I had actually booked the unparalleled number of thirty-three new subscribers, and had the vegetables to show for it, cordwood, cabbage, beans, and unsalable turnips enough to run the family for two years!

My Début as a Literary Person

In those early days I had already published one little thing ("The Jumping Frog") in an Eastern paper, but I did not consider that that counted. In my view, a person who published things in a mere newspaper could not properly claim recognition as a Literary Person: he must rise away above that; he must appear in a magazine. He would then be a Literary Person; also, he would be famous—right away. These two ambitions were strong upon me. This was in 1866. I prepared my contribution, and then looked around for the best magazine to go up to glory in. I selected the most important one in New York. The contribution was accepted. I signed it "MARK TWAIN"; for that name had some currency on the Pacific coast, and it was my idea to spread it all over the world, now, at this one jump. The article appeared in the December number, and I sat up a month waiting for the January number; for that one would contain the year's list of contributors, my name would be in it, and I should be famous and could give the banquet I was meditating.

I did not give the banquet. I had not written the "MARK TWAIN" distinctly; it was a fresh name to Eastern printers, and they put it "Mike Swain" or "MacSwain," I do not remember which. At any rate, I was not celebrated, and I did not give the banquet. I was a Literary Person, but that was all—a buried one; buried alive.

My article was about the burning of the clipper-ship *Hornet* on the line, May 3, 1866. There were thirty-one men on board at the time, and I was in Honolulu when the fifteen lean and ghostly survivors arrived there after a voyage of forty-three days in an open boat, through the blazing tropics, on *ten days' rations* of food. A very remarkable trip; but it was conducted by a captain who was a remarkable man, otherwise there would have been no survivors. He was a New-Englander of the best sea-going stock of the old capable times—Captain Josiah Mitchell.

I was in the islands to write letters for the weekly edition of the Sacramento *Union,* a rich and influential daily journal which hadn't any use for them, but could afford to spend twenty dollars a week for nothing. The proprietors were lovable and well-beloved men: long ago dead, no doubt, but in me there is at least one person who still holds them in grateful remembrance; for I dearly wanted to see the islands, and they listened to me and gave me the opportunity when there was but slender likelihood that it could profit them in any way.

I had been in the islands several months when the survivors arrived. I was laid up in my room at the time, and unable to walk. Here was a great occasion to serve my journal, and I not able to take advantage of it. Necessarily I was in deep trouble. But by good luck his Excellency Anson Burlingame was there at the time, on his way to take up his post in China, where he did such good work for the United States. He came and put me on a stretcher and had me carried to the hospital where the shipwrecked men were, and I never needed to ask a question. He attended to all of that himself, and I had nothing to do but make the notes. It was like him to take that trouble. He was a great man and a great American, and it was in his fine nature to come down from his high office and do a friendly turn whenever he could.

We got through with this work at six in the evening. I took no dinner, for there was no time to spare if I would beat the other correspondents. I spent four hours arranging the notes in their proper order, then wrote all night and beyond it; with this result: that I had a very long and detailed account of the *Hornet* episode ready at nine in the morning, while the correspondents of the San Francisco journals had nothing but a brief outline report—for they didn't sit up. The now-and-then schooner was to sail for San Francisco about nine; when I reached the dock she was free forward and was just casting off her stern-line. My fat envelope was thrown by a strong hand, and fell on board all right, and my victory was a safe thing. All in due time the ship reached San Francisco, but it was my complete report which made the stir and was telegraphed to the New York papers, by Mr. Cash; he was in charge of the Pacific bureau of the New York *Herald* at the time.

When I returned to California by and by, I went up to Sacramento and presented a bill for general correspondence at twenty dollars a week. It was paid. Then I presented a bill for "special" service on the *Hornet* matter of three columns of solid nonpareil at *a hundred dollars a column*. The cashier didn't faint, but he came rather near it. He sent for the proprietors, and they came and never uttered a protest. They only laughed in their jolly fashion, and said it was robbery, but no matter; it was a grand "scoop" (the bill or my *Hornet* report, I didn't know which); "pay it. It's all right." The best men that ever owned a newspaper.

The *Hornet* survivors reached the Sandwich Islands the 15th of June. They were mere skinny skeletons; their clothes hung limp about them and fitted them no better than a flag fits the flagstaff in a calm. But they were well nursed in the hospital; the people of Honolulu kept them supplied with all the dainties they could need; they gathered strength fast, and were presently nearly as good as new. Within a fortnight the most of them took ship for San Francisco; that is, if my dates have not gone astray in my memory. I went in the same ship, a sailing-vessel. Captain Mitchell of the *Hornet* was along; also the only passengers the *Hornet* had carried. These were two young gentlemen from Stamford, Connecticut—brothers: Samuel Ferguson, aged twenty-eight, a graduate of Trinity College, Hartford, and Henry Ferguson, aged eighteen, a student of the same college. The elder brother had had some trouble with his lungs, which induced his physician to prescribe a long sea-voyage. This terrible disaster, however, developed the disease which later ended fatally. The younger brother is still living, and is fifty years old this year (1898). The *Hornet* was a clipper of the first class and a fast sailer; the young men's quarters were roomy and comfortable, and were well stocked with books, and also with canned meats and fruits to help out the ship-fare with; and when the ship cleared from New York harbor in the first week of January, there was promise that she would make quick and pleasant work of the fourteen or fifteen thousand miles in front of her. As soon as the cold latitudes were left behind and the vessel entered summer weather, the voyage became a holiday picnic. The ship flew southward under a cloud of sail which needed no attention, no modifying or change of any kind, for days together. The young men read, strolled the ample deck, rested and drowsed in the shade of the canvas, took their meals with the captain, and when the day was done they played dummy whist with him till bedtime. After the snow and ice and tempests of the Horn, the ship bowled northward into summer weather again, and the trip was a picnic once more.

Until the early morning of the 3d of May. Computed position of the ship 112° 10′ west longitude; latitude 2° above the equator; no wind, no sea—dead calm; temperature of the atmosphere, tropical, blistering, unimaginable by one who has not been roasted in it. There was a cry of fire. An unfaithful sailor had disobeyed the rules and gone into the booby-hatch with an open light to draw some varnish from a cask. The proper result followed, and the vessel's hours were numbered.

There was not much time to spare, but the captain made the most of it. The three boats were launched—long-boat and two quarter-boats. That the time was very short and the hurry and excitement considerable is indicated by the fact that in launching the boats a hole was stove in the side of one of them by some sort of collision, and an oar driven through the side of another. The captain's first care was to have four sick sailors brought up and placed on deck out of harm's way—among them a "Portyghee." This man had not done a day's work on the voyage, but had lain in his hammock four months nursing an abscess. When we were taking notes in the Honolulu hospital and a sailor told this to Mr. Burlingame, the third mate, who was lying near, raised his head with an effort, and in a weak voice made this correction—with solemnity and feeling:

"*Raising* abscesses! He had a family of them. He done it to keep from standing his watch."

Any provisions that lay handy were gathered up by the men and the two passengers and brought and dumped on the deck where the "Portyghee" lay; then they ran for more. The sailor who was telling this to Mr. Burlingame added:

"We pulled together thirty-two days' rations for the thirty-one men that way."

The third mate lifted his head again and made another correction—with bitterness:

"The Portyghee et twenty-two of them while he was soldiering there and nobody noticing. A damned hound."

The fire spread with great rapidity. The smoke and flame drove the men back, and they had to stop their incomplete work of fetching provisions, and take to the boats with only ten days' rations secured.

Each boat had a compass, a quadrant, a copy of Bowditch's *Navigator,* and a nautical almanac, and the captain's and chief mate's boats had chronometers. There were thirty-one men all told. The captain took an account of stock, with the following result: four hams, nearly thirty pounds of salt pork, half-box of raisins, one hundred pounds of bread, twelve two-pound cans of oysters, clams, and assorted meats, a keg containing four pounds of butter, twelve gallons of water in a forty-gallon "scuttle-butt," four one-gallon demijohns full of water, three bottles of brandy (the property of passengers), some pipes, matches, and a hundred pounds of tobacco. No medicines. Of course the whole party had to go on short rations at once.

The captain and the two passengers kept diaries. On our voyage to San Francisco we ran into a calm in the middle of the Pacific, and did not move a rod during fourteen days; this gave me a chance to copy the diaries. Samuel Ferguson's is the fullest; I will draw upon it now. When the following paragraph was written the ship was about one hundred and twenty days out from port, and all hands were putting in the lazy time about as usual, as no one was forecasting disaster.

> MAY 2. Latitude 1° 28′ N., longitude 111° 38′ W. Another hot and sluggish day; at one time, however, the clouds promised wind, and there came a slight breeze—just enough to keep us going. The only thing to chronicle to-day is the quantities of fish about; nine bonitos were caught this forenoon, and some large albacores seen. After dinner the first mate hooked a fellow which he could not hold, so he let the line go to the captain, who was on the bow. He, holding on, brought the fish to with a jerk, and snap went the line, hook and all. We also saw astern, swimming lazily after us, an enormous shark, which must have been nine or ten feet long. We tried him with all sorts of lines and a piece of pork, but he declined to take hold. I suppose he had appeased his appetite on the heads and other remains of the bonitos we had thrown overboard.

Next day's entry records the disaster. The three boats got away, retired to a short distance, and stopped. The two injured ones were leaking badly; some of the men were kept busy bailing, others patched the holes as well as they could. The captain, the two passengers, and eleven men were in the long-boat, with a share of the provisions and water, and with no room to spare, for the boat was only twenty-one feet long, six wide, and three deep. The chief mate and eight men were in one of the small boats, the second mate and seven men in the other. The passengers had saved no clothing but what they had on, excepting their overcoats. The ship, clothed in flame and sending up a vast column of black smoke into the sky, made a grand picture in the solitudes of the sea, and hour after hour the outcasts sat and watched it. Meantime the captain ciphered on the immensity of the distance that stretched between him and the nearest available land, and then scaled the rations down to meet the emergency: half a biscuit for breakfast; one biscuit and some canned meat for dinner; half a biscuit for tea; a few swallows of water for each meal. And so hunger began to gnaw while the ship was still burning.

> MAY 4. The ship burned all night very brightly, and hopes are that some ship has seen the light and is bearing down upon us. None seen, however, this forenoon, so we have determined to go together north and a little west to some islands in 18° or 19° north latitude and 114° to 115° west longitude, hoping in the mean time to be picked up by some ship. The ship sank suddenly at about 5 A.M. We find the sun very hot and scorching, but all try to keep out of it as much as we can.

They did a quite natural thing now: waited several hours for that possible ship that might have seen the light to work her slow way to them through the nearly dead calm. Then they gave it up and set about their plans. If you will look at the map you will say that their course could be easily decided. Albemarle Island (Galapagos group) lies straight eastward nearly a thousand miles; the islands referred to in the diary indefinitely as "some islands" (Revillagigedo Islands) lie, as they think, in some widely uncertain region northward about one thousand miles and westward one hundred or one hundred and fifty miles. Acapulco, on the Mexican coast, lies about northeast something short of one thousand miles. You will say random rocks in the ocean are not what is wanted; let them strike for Acapulco and the solid continent. That does look like the rational course, but one presently guesses from the diaries that the thing would have been wholly irrational—indeed, suicidal. If the boats struck for Albemarle they would be in the doldrums all the way; and that means a watery perdition, with winds which are wholly crazy, and blow from all points of the compass at once and also perpendicularly. If the boats tried for Acapulco they would get out of the doldrums when half-way there—in case they ever got half-way—and then they would be in a lamentable case, for there they would meet the northeast trades coming down in their teeth, and these boats were so rigged that they could not sail within eight points of the wind. So they wisely started northward, with a slight slant to the west. They had but ten days' short allowance of food; the long-boat was towing the others; they could not depend on making any sort of definite progress in the doldrums, and they had four or five hundred miles of doldrums in front of them yet. *They* are the real equator, a tossing, roaring, rainy belt, ten or twelve hundred miles broad, which girdles the globe.

It rained hard the first night, and all got drenched, but they filled up their water-butt. The brothers were in the stern with the captain, who steered. The quarters were cramped; no one got much sleep. "Kept on our course till squalls headed us off."

Stormy and squally the next morning, with drenching rains. A heavy and dangerous "cobbling" sea. One marvels how such boats could live in it. It is called a feat of desperate daring when one man and a dog cross the Atlantic in a boat the size of a long-boat, and indeed it is; but this long-boat was overloaded with men and other plunder, and was only three feet deep. "We naturally thought often of all at home, and were glad to remember that it was Sacrament Sunday, and that prayers would go up from our friends for us, although they know not our peril."

The captain got not even a cat-nap during the first three days and nights, but he got a few winks of sleep the fourth night. "The worst sea yet." About ten at night the captain changed his course and headed east-northeast, hoping to make Clipperton Rock. If he failed, no matter; he would be in a better position to make those other islands. I will mention here that he did not find that rock.

On the 8th of May no wind all day; sun blistering hot; they take to the oars. Plenty of dolphins, but they couldn't catch any. "I think we are all beginning to realize more and more the awful situation we are in." "It often takes a ship a week to get through the doldrums; how much longer, then, such a craft as ours." "We are so crowded that we cannot stretch ourselves out for a good sleep, but have to take it any way we can get it."

Of course this feature will grow more and more trying, but it will be human nature to cease to set it down; there will be five weeks of it yet—we must try to remember that for the diarist; it will make our beds the softer.

The 9th of May the sun gives him a warning: "Looking with both eyes, the horizon crossed thus +." "Henry keeps well, but broods over our troubles more than I wish he did." They caught two dolphins; they tasted well. "The captain believed the compass out of the way, but the long-invisible north star came out—a welcome sight—and indorsed the compass."

May 10, "latitude 7° 0′ 3″ N., longitude 111° 32′ W." So they have made about three hundred miles of northing in the six days since they left the region of the lost ship. "Drifting in calms all day." And baking hot, of course; I have been down there, and I remember that detail. "Even as the captain says, all romance has long since vanished, and I think the most of us are beginning to look the fact of our awful situation full in the face."

"We are making but little headway on our course." Bad news from the rearmost boat: the men are improvident; "they have eaten up all of the canned meats brought from the ship, and are now growing discontented." Not so with the chief mate's people—they are evidently under the eye of a *man.*

Under date of May 11: "Standing still! or worse; we lost more last night than we made yesterday." In fact, they have lost three miles of the three hundred of northing they had so laboriously made." "The cock that was rescued and pitched into the boat while the ship was on fire still lives, and crows with the breaking of dawn, cheering us a good deal." What has he been living on for a week? Did the starving men feed him from their dire poverty? "The second mate's boat out of water again, showing that they overdrink their allowance. The captain spoke pretty sharply to them." It is true: I have the remark in my old notebook; I got it of the third mate in the hospital at Honolulu. But there is not room for it here, and it is too combustible, anyway. Besides, the third mate admired it, and what he admired he was likely to enhance.

They were still watching hopefully for ships. The captain was a thoughtful man, and probably did not disclose to them that that was substantially a waste of time. "In this latitude the horizon is filled with little upright clouds that look very much like ships." Mr. Ferguson saved three bottles of brandy from his private stores when he left the ship, and the liquor came good in these days. "The captain serves out two tablespoonfuls of brandy and water—half and half—to our crew." He means the watch that is on duty; they stood regular watches—four hours on and four off. The chief mate was an excellent officer—a self-possessed, resolute, fine, all-round man. The diarist makes the following note—there is character in it: "I offered one bottle of brandy to the chief mate, but he declined, saying he could keep the after-boat quiet, and we had not enough for all."

HENRY FERGUSON'S DIARY TO DATE, GIVEN IN FULL

MAY 4, 5, 6, doldrums. May 7, 8, 9, doldrums. May 10, 11, 12, doldrums. Tells it all. Never saw, never felt, never heard, never experienced such heat, such darkness, such lightning and thunder, and wind and rain, in my life before.

That boy's diary is of the economical sort that a person might properly be expected to keep in such circumstances—and be forgiven for the economy, too. His brother, perishing of consumption, hunger, thirst, blazing heat, drowning rains, loss of sleep, lack of exercise, was persistently faithful and circumstantial with his diary from the first day to the last—an instance of noteworthy fidelity and resolution. In spite of the tossing and plunging boat he wrote it close and fine, in a hand as easy to read as print. They can't seem to get north of 7° N.; they are still there the next day:

> MAY 12. A good rain last night, and we caught a good deal, though not enough to fill up our tank, pails, etc. Our object is to get out of these doldrums, but it seems as if we cannot do it. To-day we have had it very variable, and hope we are on the northern edge, though we are not much above 7°. This morning we all thought we had made out a sail; but it was one of those deceiving clouds. Rained a good deal to-day, making all hands wet and uncomfortable; we filled up pretty nearly all our water-pots, however. I hope we may have a fine night, for the captain certainly wants rest, and while there is any danger of squalls, or danger of any kind, he is always on hand. I never would have believed that open boats such as ours, with their loads, could live in some of the seas we have had.

During the night, 12th–13th, "the cry of *A ship!* brought us to our feet." It seemed to be the glimmer of a vessel's signal-lantern rising out of the curve of the sea. There was a season of breathless hope while they stood watching, with their hands shading their eyes, and their hearts in their throats; then the promise failed: the light was a rising star. It is a long time ago—thirty-two years—and it doesn't matter now, yet one is sorry for their disappointment. "Thought often of those at home to-day, and of the disappointment they will feel next Sunday at not hearing from us by telegraph from San Francisco." It will be many weeks yet before the telegram is received, and it will come as a thunder-clap of joy then, and with the seeming of a miracle, for it will raise from the grave men mourned as dead. "To-day our rations were reduced to a quarter of a biscuit a meal, with about half a pint of water." This is on the 13th of May, with more than a month of voyaging in front of them yet! However, as they do not know that, "we are all feeling pretty cheerful."

In the afternoon of the 14th there was a thunder-storm, "which toward night seemed to close in around us on every side, making it very dark and squally." "Our situation is becoming more and more desperate," for they were making very little northing, "and every day diminishes our small stock of provisions." They realize that the boats must soon separate, and each fight for its own life. Towing the quarter-boats is a hindering business.

That night and next day, light and baffling winds and but little progress. Hard to bear, that persistent standing still, and the food wasting away. "Everything in a perfect sop; and all so cramped, and no change of clothes." Soon the sun comes out and roasts them. "Joe caught another dolphin to-day; in his maw we found a flying-fish and two skip-jacks." There is an event, now, which rouses an enthusiasm of hope: a land-bird arrives! It rests on the yard for a while, and they can look at it all they like, and envy it, and thank it for its message. As a subject of talk it is beyond price—a fresh, new topic for tongues tired to death of talking upon a single theme: Shall we ever see the land again; and when? Is the bird from Clipperton Rock? They hope so; and they take heart of grace to believe so. As it turned out, the bird had no message; it merely came to mock.

May 16, "the cock still lives, and daily carols forth His praise." It will be a rainy night, "but I do not care if we can fill up our water-butts."

On the 17th one of those majestic specters of the deep, a water-spout, stalked by them, and they trembled for their lives. Young Henry set it down in his scanty journal with the judicious comment that "it might have been a fine sight from a ship."

From Captain Mitchell's log for this day: *"Only half a bushel of bread-crumbs left."* (And a month to wander the seas yet.)

It rained all night and all day; everybody uncomfortable. Now came a swordfish chasing a bonito; and the poor thing, seeking help and friends, took refuge under the rudder. The big swordfish kept hovering around, scaring everybody badly. The men's mouths watered for him, for he would have made a whole banquet; but no one dared to touch him, of course, for he would sink a boat promptly if molested. Providence protected the poor bonito from the cruel swordfish. This was just and right. Providence next befriended the shipwrecked sailors: they got the bonito. This was also just and right. But in the distribution of mercies the swordfish himself got overlooked. He now went away; to muse over these subtleties, probably. "The men in all the boats seem pretty well; the feeblest of the sick ones (not able for a long time to stand his watch on board the ship) is wonderfully recovered." This is the third mate's detested "Portyghee" that raised the family of abscesses.

> Passed a most awful night. Rained hard nearly all the time, and blew in squalls, accompanied by terrific thunder and lightning, from all points of the compass.—*Henry's Log.*
>
> Most awful night I ever witnessed.—*Captain's Log.*

Latitude, May 18, 11° 11′. So they have averaged but forty miles of northing a day during the fortnight. Further talk of separating. "Too bad, but it must be done for the safety of the whole." "At first I never dreamed, but now hardly shut my eyes for a cat-nap without conjuring up something or other—to be accounted for by weakness, I suppose." But for their disaster they think they would be arriving in San Francisco about this time. "I should have liked to send B—— the telegram for her birthday." This was a young sister.

On the 19th the captain called up the quarter-boats and said one would have to go off on its own hook. The long-boat could no longer tow both of them. The second mate refused to go, but the chief mate was ready; in fact, he was always ready when there was a man's work to the fore. He took the second mate's boat; six of its crew elected to remain, and two of his own crew came with him (nine in the boat, now, including himself). He sailed away, and toward sunset passed out of sight. The diarist was sorry to see him go. It was natural; one could have better spared the "Portyghee." After thirty-two years I find my prejudice against this "Portyghee" reviving. His very looks have long passed out of my memory; but no matter, I am coming to hate him as religiously as ever. "Water will now be a scarce article, for as we get out of the doldrums we shall get showers only now and then in the trades. This life is telling severely on my strength. Henry holds out first rate." Henry did not start well, but under hardships he improved straight along.

Latitude, Sunday, May 20, 12° 0′ 9″. They ought to be well out of the doldrums now, but they are not. No breeze—the longed-for trades still missing. They are still anxiously watching for a sail, but they have only "visions of ships that come to naught—the shadow without the substance." The second mate catches a booby this afternoon, a bird which consists mainly of feathers; "but as they have no other meat, it will go well."

May 21, they strike the trades at last! The second mate catches three more boobies, and gives the long-boat one. Dinner "half a can of mince-meat divided up and served around, which strengthened us somewhat." They have to keep a man bailing all the time; the hole knocked in the boat when she was launched from the burning ship was never efficiently mended. "Heading about northwest now." They hope they have easting enough to make some of those indefinite isles. Failing that, they think they will be in a better position to be picked up. It was an infinitely slender chance, but the captain probably refrained from mentioning that.

The next day is to be an eventful one.

> MAY 22. Last night wind headed us off, so that part of the time we had to steer east-southeast and then west-northwest, and so on. This morning we were all startled by a cry of *"Sail ho!"* Sure enough we could see it! And for a time we cut adrift from the second mate's boat, and steered so as to attract its attention. This was about half-past five A.M. After sailing in a state of high excitement for almost twenty minutes we made it out to be the chief mate's boat. Of course we were glad to see them and have them report all well; but still it was a bitter disappointment to us all. Now that we are in the trades it seems impossible to make northing enough to strike the isles. We have determined to do the best we can, and get in the route of vessels. Such being the determination, it became necessary to cast off the other boat, which, after a good deal of unpleasantness, was done, we again dividing water and stores, and taking Cox into our boat. This makes our number fifteen. The second mate's crew wanted to all get in with us and cast the other boat adrift. It was a very painful separation.

So those isles that they have struggled for so long and so hopefully have to be given up. What with lying birds that come to mock, and isles that are but a dream, and "visions of ships that come to naught," it is a pathetic time they are having, with much heartbreak in it. It was odd that the vanished boat, three days lost to sight in that vast solitude, should appear again. But it brought Cox—we can't be certain why. But if it hadn't, the diarist would never have seen the land again.

> Our chances as we go west increase in regard to being picked up, but each day our scanty fare is so much reduced. Without the fish, turtle, and birds sent us, I do not know how we should have got along. The other day I offered to read prayers morning and evening for the captain, and last night commenced. The men, although of various nationalities and religions, are very attentive, and always uncovered. May God grant my weak endeavor its issue.

Latitude, May 24, 14° 18′ N. Five oysters apiece for dinner and three spoonfuls of juice, a gill of water, and a piece of biscuit the size of a silver dollar. "We are plainly getting weaker—God have mercy upon us all!" That night heavy seas break over the weather side and make everybody wet and uncomfortable, besides requiring constant bailing. Next day, "nothing particular happened." Perhaps some of us would have regarded it differently. "Passed a spar, but not near enough to see what it was." They saw some whales blow; there were flying-fish skimming the seas, but none came aboard. Misty weather, with fine rain, very penetrating.

Latitude, May 26, 15° 50′. They caught a flying-fish and a booby, but had to eat them raw. "The men grow weaker, and I think, despondent; they say very little, though." And so, to all the other imaginable and unimaginable horrors, silence is added—the muteness and brooding of coming despair. "It seems our best chance to get in the track of ships, with the hope that some one will run near enough to our speck to see it." He hopes the other boats stood west and have been picked up. (They will never be heard of again in this world.)

> SUNDAY, MAY 27. Latitude 16° 0′ 5″; longitude, by chronometer, 117° 22′. Our fourth Sunday! When we left the ship we reckoned on having about ten days' supplies, and now we hope to be able, by rigid economy, to make them last another week if possible.[1] Last night the sea was comparatively quiet, but the wind headed us off to about west-northwest, which has been about our course all day to-day. Another flying-fish came aboard last night, and one more to-day—both small ones. No birds. A booby is a great catch, and a good large one makes a small dinner for the fifteen of us—that is, of course, as dinners go in the *Hornet*'s long-boat. Tried this morning to read the full service to myself, with the communion, but found it too much; am too weak, and get sleepy, and cannot give strict attention; so I put off half till this afternoon. I trust God will hear the prayers gone up for us at home to-day, and graciously answer them by sending us succor and help in this our season of deep distress.

The next day was "a good day for seeing a ship." But none was seen. The diarist "still feels pretty well," though very weak; his brother Henry "bears up and keeps his strength the best of any on board." "I do not feel despondent at all, for I fully trust that the Almighty will hear our and the home prayers, and He who suffers not a sparrow to fall sees and cares for us, His creatures."

Considering the situation and circumstances, the record for next day, May 29, is one which has a surprise in it for those dull people who think that nothing but medicines and doctors can cure the sick. A little starvation can really do more for the average sick man than can the best medicines and the best doctors. I do not mean a restricted diet; I mean *total abstention from food for one or two days.* I speak from experience; starvation has been my cold and fever doctor for fifteen years, and has accomplished a cure in all instances. The third mate told me in Honolulu that the

1. There are nineteen days of voyaging ahead yet.—M.T.

"Portyghee" had lain in his hammock for months, raising his family of abscesses and feeding like a cannibal. We have seen that in spite of dreadful weather, deprivation of sleep, scorching, drenching, and all manner of miseries, thirteen days of starvation "wonderfully recovered" him. There were four sailors down sick when the ship was burned. Twenty-five days of pitiless starvation have followed, and now we have this curious record: *"All the men are hearty and strong; even the ones that were down sick are well,* except poor Peter." When I wrote an article some months ago urging temporary abstention from food as a remedy for an inactive appetite and for disease, I was accused of jesting, but I was in earnest. *"We are all wonderfully well and strong, comparatively speaking."* On this day the starvation regimen drew its belt a couple of buckle-holes tighter: the bread ration was reduced from the usual piece of cracker the size of a silver dollar *to the half of that, and one meal was abolished from the daily three.* This will weaken the men physically, but if there are any diseases of an ordinary sort left in them they will disappear.

> Two quarts bread-crumbs left, one-third of a ham, three small cans of oysters, and twenty gallons of water.—*Captain's Log.*

The hopeful tone of the diaries is persistent. It is remarkable. Look at the map and see where the boat is: latitude 16° 44′, longitude 119° 20′. It is more than two hundred miles west of the Revillagigedo Islands, so they are quite out of the question against the trades, rigged as this boat is. The nearest land available for such a boat is the American group, *six hundred and fifty miles away,* westward; still, there is no note of surrender, none even of discouragement! Yet, May 30, "we have now left: *one can of oysters; three pounds of raisins; one can of soup; one-third of a ham; three pints of biscuit-crumbs."* And fifteen starved men to live on it while they creep and crawl six hundred and fifty miles. "Somehow I feel much encouraged by this change of course (west by north) which we have made to-day." Six hundred and fifty miles on a hatful of provisions! Let us be thankful, even after thirty-two years, that they are mercifully ignorant of the fact that it isn't six hundred and fifty that they must creep on the hatful, but *twenty-two hundred!* Isn't the situation romantic enough just as it stands? No. Providence added a startling detail: pulling an oar in that boat, for common seaman's wages, was a *banished duke*—Danish. We hear no more of him; just that mention, that is all, with the simple remark that "he is one of our best men"—a high enough compliment for a duke or any other man in those manhood-testing circumstances. With that little glimpse of him at his oar, and that fine word of praise, he vanishes out of our knowledge for all time. For all time, unless he should chance upon this note and reveal himself.

The last day of May is come. And now there is a disaster to report: think of it, reflect upon it, and try to understand how much it means, when you sit down with your family and pass your eye over your breakfast-table. Yesterday there were three pints of bread-crumbs; this morning the little bag is found open and *some of the crumbs missing.* "We dislike to suspect any one of such a rascally act, but there is no question that this grave crime has been committed. Two days will certainly finish the remaining morsels. God grant us strength to reach the American group!" The third mate told me in Honolulu that in these days the men remembered with bitterness that the "Portyghee" had devoured twenty-two days' rations while he lay waiting to be transferred from the burning ship, and that now they cursed him and swore an oath that if it came to cannibalism he should be the first to suffer for the rest.

> The captain has lost his glasses, and therefore he cannot read our pocket prayer-books as much as I think he would like, though he is not familiar with them.

Further of the captain: "He is a good man, and has been most kind to us —almost fatherly. He says that if he had been offered the command of the ship sooner he should have brought his two daughters with him." It makes one shudder yet to think how narrow an escape it was.

> The two meals (rations) a day are as follows: fourteen raisins and a piece of cracker the size of a cent, for tea; a gill of water, and a piece of ham and a piece of bread, each the size of a cent, for breakfast.—*Captain's Log.*

He means a cent in *thickness* as well as in circumference. Samuel Ferguson's diary says the ham was shaved "about as thin as it could be cut."

> JUNE 1. Last night and to-day sea very high and cobbling, breaking over and making us all wet and cold. Weather squally, and there is no doubt that only careful management—with God's protecting care—preserved us through both the night and the day; and really it is most marvelous how every morsel that passes our lips is blessed to us. It makes me think daily of the miracle of the loaves and fishes. Henry keeps up wonderfully, which is a great consolation to me. I somehow have great confidence, and hope that our afflictions

will soon be ended, though we are running rapidly across the track of both outward and inward bound vessels, and away from them; our chief hope is a whaler, man-of-war, or some Australian ship. The isles we are steering for are put down in Bowditch, but on my map are said to be doubtful. God grant they may be there!

Hardest day yet.—*Captain's Log.*

Doubtful! It was worse than that. A week later *they sailed straight over them.*

JUNE 2. Latitude 18° 9′. Squally, cloudy, a heavy sea. . . . I cannot help thinking of the cheerful and comfortable time we had aboard the *Hornet.*

Two days' scanty supplies left—ten rations of water apiece and a little morsel of bread. *But the sun shines, and God is merciful.—Captain's Log.*

SUNDAY, JUNE 3. Latitude 17° 54′. Heavy sea all night, and from 4 A.M. very wet, the sea breaking over us in frequent sluices, and soaking everything aft, particularly. All day the sea has been very high, and it is a wonder that we are not swamped. Heaven grant that it may go down this evening! Our suspense and condition are getting terrible. I managed this morning to crawl, more than step, to the forward end of the boat, and was surprised to find that I was so weak, especially in the legs and knees. The sun has been out again, and I have dried some things, and hope for a better night.

JUNE 4. Latitude 17° 6′, longitude 131° 30′. Shipped hardly any sea last night, and to-day the sea has gone down somewhat, although it is still too high for comfort, as we have an occasional reminder that water is wet. The sun has been out all day, and so we have had a good drying. I have been trying for the last ten or twelve days to get a pair of drawers dry enough to put on, and at last succeeded. I mention this to show the state in which we have lived. If our chronometer is anywhere near right, we ought to see the American Isles to-morrow or next day. If they are not there, we have only the chance for a few days, of a stray ship, for we cannot eke out the provisions more than five or six days longer, and our strength is failing very fast. I was much surprised to-day to note how my legs have wasted away above my knees: they are hardly thicker than my upper arm used to be. Still, I trust in God's infinite mercy, and feel sure he will do what is best for us. To survive, as we have done, thirty-two days in an open boat, with only about ten days' fair provisions for thirty-one men in the first place, and these divided twice subsequently, is more than mere unassisted *human* art and strength could have accomplished and endured.

Bread and raisins all gone.—*Captain's Log.*

Men growing dreadfully discontented, and awful grumbling and unpleasant talk is arising. God save us from all strife of men; and if we must die now, take us himself, and not embitter our bitter death still more.—*Henry's Log.*

JUNE 5. Quiet night and pretty comfortable day, though our sail and block show signs of failing, and need taking down—which latter is something of a job, as it requires the climbing of the mast. We also had news from forward, there being discontent and some threatening complaints of unfair allowances, etc., all as unreasonable as foolish; still, these things bid us be on our guard. I am getting miserably weak, but try to keep up the best I can. If we cannot find those isles we can only try to make northwest and get in the track of Sandwich Island bound vessels, living as best we can in the mean time. To-day we changed to one meal, and that at about noon, with a small ration of water at 8 or 9 A.M., another at 12 M., and a third at 5 or 6 P.M.

Nothing left but a little piece of ham and a gill of water, all around.—*Captain's Log.*

They are down to *one* meal a day now—such as it is—and *fifteen hundred miles to crawl yet!* And now the horrors deepen, and though they escape actual mutiny, the attitude of the men became alarming. Now we seem to see why that curious accident happened, so long ago: I mean Cox's return, after he had been far away and out of sight several days in the chief mate's boat. If he had not come back the captain and the two young passengers would have been slain by these sailors, who were becoming crazed through their sufferings.

NOTE SECRETLY PASSED BY HENRY TO HIS BROTHER

Cox told me last night that there is getting to be a good deal of ugly talk among the men against the captain and us aft. They say that the captain is the cause of all; that he did not try to save the ship at all, nor to get provisions, and even would not let the men put in some they had; and that partiality is shown us in apportioning our rations aft. —— asked Cox the other day if he would starve first or eat human flesh. Cox answered he would starve. —— then told him he would be only killing himself. If we do not find these islands we would do well to prepare for anything. —— is the loudest of all.

REPLY

We can depend on —— I think, and ——, and Cox, can we not?

SECOND NOTE

I guess so, and very likely on ——; but there is no telling. —— and Cox are certain. There is nothing definite said or hinted as yet, as I understand Cox;

but starving men are the same as maniacs. It would be well to keep a watch on your pistol, so as to have it and the cartridges safe from theft.

Henry's Log, JUNE 5. Dreadful forebodings. God spare us from all such horrors! Some of the men getting to talk a good deal. Nothing to write down. Heart very sad.

Henry's Log, JUNE 6. Passed some seaweed, and something that looked like the trunk of an old tree, but no birds; beginning to be afraid islands not there. To-day it was said to the captain, in the hearing of all, that some of the men would not shrink, when a man was dead, from using the flesh, though they would not kill. Horrible! God give us all full use of our reason, and spare us from such things! "From plague, pestilence, and famine, from battle and murder, and from sudden death, good Lord, deliver us!"

JUNE 6. Latitude 16° 30′, longitude (chron.) 134°. Dry night and wind steady enough to require no change in sail; but this A.M. an attempt to lower it proved abortive. First the third mate tried and got up to the block, and fastened a temporary arrangement to reeve the halyards through, but had to come down, weak and almost fainting, before finishing; then Joe tried, and after twice ascending, fixed it and brought down the block; but it was very exhausting work, and afterward he was good for nothing all day. The clue-iron which we are trying to make serve for the broken block works, however, very indifferently, and will, I am afraid, soon cut the rope. It is very necessary to get everything connected with the sail in good, easy running order before we get too weak to do anything with it.

Only three meals left.—*Captain's Log.*

JUNE 7. Latitude 16° 35′ N., longitude 136° 30′ W. Night wet and uncomfortable. To-day shows us pretty conclusively that the American Isles are not there, though we have had some signs that looked like them. At noon we decided to abandon looking any farther for them, and to-night haul a little more northerly, so as to get in the way of Sandwich Island vessels, which fortunately come down pretty well this way—say to latitude 19° to 20°—to get the benefit of the trade-winds. Of course all the westing we have made is gain, and I hope the chronometer is wrong in our favor, for I do not see how any such delicate instrument can keep good time with the constant jarring and thumping we get from the sea. With the strong trade we have, I hope that a week from Sunday will put us in sight of the Sandwich Islands, if we are not safe by that time by being picked up.

It is twelve hundred miles to the Sandwich Islands; the provisions are virtually exhausted, but not the perishing diarist's pluck.

JUNE 8. My cough troubled me a good deal last night, and therefore I got hardly any sleep at all. Still, I make out pretty well, and should not complain.

Yesterday the third mate mended the block, and this P.M. the sail, after some difficulty, was got down, and Harry got to the top of the mast and rove the halyards through after some hardship, so that it now works easy and well. This getting up the mast is no easy matter at any time with the sea we have, and is very exhausting in our present state. We could only reward Harry by an extra ration of water. We have made good time and course to-day. Heading her up, however, makes the boat ship seas and keeps us all wet; however, it cannot be helped. Writing is a rather precarious thing these times. Our meal to-day for the fifteen consists of half a can of "soup and boullie"; the other half is reserved for to-morrow. Henry still keeps up grandly, and is a great favorite. God grant he may be spared!

A better feeling prevails among the men.—*Captain's Log.*

JUNE 9. Latitude 17° 53′. Finished to-day, I may say, our whole stock of provisions.[1] We have only left a lower end of a ham-bone, with some of the outer rind and skin on. In regard to the water, however, I think we have got ten days' supply at our present rate of allowance. This, with what nourishment we can get from boot-legs and such chewable matter, we hope will enable us to weather it out till we get to the Sandwich Islands, or, sailing in the mean time in the track of vessels thither bound, be picked up. My hope is in the latter, for in all human probability I cannot stand the other. Still we have been marvelously protected, and God, I hope, will preserve us all in his own good time and way. The men are getting weaker, but are still quiet and orderly.

SUNDAY, JUNE 10. Latitude 18° 40′, longitude 142° 34′. A pretty good night last night, with some wettings, and again another beautiful Sunday. I cannot but think how we should all enjoy it at home, and what a contrast is here! How terrible their suspense must begin to be! God grant that it may be relieved before very long, and he certainly seems to be with us in everything we do, and has preserved this boat miraculously; for since we left the ship we have sailed considerably over three thousand miles, which, taking into consideration our meager stock of provisions, is almost unprecedented. As yet I do not feel the stint of food so much as I do that of water. Even Henry, who is naturally a good water-drinker, can save half of his allowance from time to time, when I cannot. My diseased throat may have something to do with that, however.

Nothing is now left which by any flattery can be called food. But they must manage somehow for five days more, for at noon they have still eight hundred miles to go. It is a race for life now.

This is no time for comments or other interruptions from me—every

1. Six days to sail yet, nevertheless.—M.T.

moment is valuable. I will take up the boy brother's diary at this point, and clear the seas before it and let it fly.

HENRY FERGUSON'S LOG

SUNDAY, JUNE 10. Our ham-bone has given us a taste of food to-day, and we have got left a little meat and the remainder of the bone for to-morrow. Certainly never was there such a sweet knuckle-bone, or one that was so thoroughly appreciated. . . . I do not know that I feel any worse than I did last Sunday, notwithstanding the reduction of diet; and I trust that we may all have strength given us to sustain the sufferings and hardships of the coming week. We estimate that we are within seven hundred miles of the Sandwich Islands, and that our average, daily, is somewhat over a hundred miles, so that our hopes have some foundation in reason. Heaven send we may all live to see land!

JUNE 11. Ate the meat and rind of our ham-bone, and have the bone and the greasy cloth from around the ham left to eat to-morrow. God sent us birds or fish, and let us not perish of hunger, or be brought to the dreadful alternative of feeding on human flesh! As I feel now, I do not think anything could persuade me; but you cannot tell what you will do when you are reduced by hunger and your mind wandering. I hope and pray we can make out to reach the islands before we get to this strait; but we have one or two desperate men aboard, though they are quiet enough now. *It is my firm trust and belief that we are going to be saved.*

All food gone.—*Captain's Log.*[1]

JUNE 12. Stiff breeze, and we are fairly flying—dead ahead of it—and toward the islands. Good hope, but the prospects of hunger are awful. Ate ham-bone to-day. It is the captain's birthday; he is fifty-four years old.

JUNE 13. The ham-rags are not quite all gone yet, and the boot-legs, we find, are very palatable after we get the salt out of them. A little smoke, I think, does some little good; but I don't know.

JUNE 14. Hunger does not pain us much, but we are dreadfully weak. Our water is getting frightfully low. God grant we may see land soon! *Nothing to eat,* but feel better than I did yesterday. Toward evening saw a magnificent rainbow—*the first we had seen.* Captain said, "Cheer up, boys; it's a prophecy—*it's the bow of promise!*"

JUNE 15. God be forever praised for his infinite mercy! LAND IN SIGHT! Rapidly neared it and soon were *sure* of it. . . . Two noble Kanakas swam out and took the boat ashore. We were joyfully received by two white men—

1. It was at this time discovered that the crazed sailors had gotten the delusion that the captain had *a million dollars* in gold concealed aft, and they were conspiring to kill him and the two passengers and seize it.—M.T.

Mr. Jones and his steward Charley—and a crowd of native men, women, and children. They treated us splendidly—aided us, and carried us up the bank, and brought us water, poi, bananas, and green cocoanuts; but the white men took care of us and prevented those who would have eaten too much from doing so. Everybody overjoyed to see us, and all sympathy expressed in faces, deeds, and words. We were then helped up to the house; and help we needed. Mr. Jones and Charley are the only white men here. Treated us splendidly. Gave us first about a teaspoonful of spirits in water, and then to each a cup of warm tea, with a little bread. Takes *every* care of us. Gave us later another cup of tea, and bread the same, and then let us go to rest. *It is the happiest day of my life.* . . . God in his mercy has heard our prayer. . . . Everybody is so kind. Words cannot tell.

JUNE 16. Mr. Jones gave us a delightful bed, and we surely had a good night's rest; but not sleep—we were too happy to sleep; would keep the reality and not let it turn to a delusion—dreaded that we might wake up and find ourselves in the boat again.

It is an amazing adventure. There is nothing of its sort in history that surpasses it in impossibilities made possible. In one extraordinary detail—the survival of *every person* in the boat—it probably stands alone in the history of adventures of its kind. Usually merely a part of a boat's company survive—officers, mainly, and other educated and tenderly reared men, unused to hardship and heavy labor; the untrained, roughly reared hard workers succumb. But in this case even the rudest and roughest stood the privations and miseries of the voyage almost as well as did the college-bred young brothers and the captain. I mean, physically. The minds of most of the sailors broke down in the fourth week and went to temporary ruin, but physically the endurance exhibited was astonishing. Those men did not survive by any merit of their own, of course, but by merit of the character and intelligence of the captain; they lived by the mastery of his spirit. Without him they would have been children without a nurse; they would have exhausted their provisions in a week, and their pluck would not have lasted even as long as the provisions.

The boat came near to being wrecked at the last. As it approached the shore the sail was let go, and came down with a run; then the captain saw that he was drifting swiftly toward an ugly reef, and an effort was made to hoist the sail again: but it could not be done; the men's strength was wholly exhausted; they could not even pull an oar. They were helpless, and death imminent. It was then that they were discovered by the two Kanakas who achieved the rescue. They swam out and manned the boat and piloted her through a narrow and hardly noticeable break in the reef—the only break in it in a stretch of thirty-five miles! The spot where the landing was made was the only one in that stretch where footing could have been found on the shore; everywhere else precipices came sheer down into forty fathoms of water. Also, in all that stretch this was the only spot where anybody lived.

Within ten days after the landing all the men but one were up and creeping about. Properly, they ought to have killed themselves with the "food" of the last few days—some of them, at any rate—men who had freighted their stomachs with strips of leather from old boots and with chips from the butter-cask; a freightage which they did not get rid of by digestion, but by other means. The captain and the two passengers did not eat strips and chips, as the sailors did, but *scraped* the boot-leather and the wood, and made a pulp of the scrapings by moistening them with water. The third mate told me that the boots were old and full of holes; then added thoughtfully, "but the holes digested the best." Speaking of digestion, here is a remarkable thing, and worth noting: during this strange voyage, and for a while afterward on shore, the bowels of some of the men virtually ceased from their functions; in some cases there was no action for twenty and thirty days, and in one case for forty-four! Sleeping also came to be rare. Yet the men did very well without it. During many days the captain did not sleep at all—twenty-one, I think, on one stretch.

When the landing was made, all the men were successfully protected from overeating except the "Portyghee"; he escaped the watch and ate an incredible number of bananas: a hundred and fifty-two, the third mate said, but this was undoubtedly an exaggeration; I think it was a hundred and fifty-one. He was already nearly full of leather; it was hanging out of his ears. (I do not state this on the third mate's authority, for we have seen what sort of person he was; I state it on my own.) The "Portyghee" ought to have died, of course, and even now it seems a pity that he didn't; but he got well, and as early as any of them; and all full of leather, too, the way he was, and butter-timber and handkerchiefs and bananas. Some of the men did eat handkerchiefs in those last days, also socks; and he was one of them.

It is to the credit of the men that they did not kill the rooster that crowed so gallantly mornings. He lived eighteen days, and then stood up and stretched his neck and made a brave, weak effort to do his duty once more, and died in the act. It is a picturesque detail; and so is that rainbow, too—the only one seen in the forty-three days—raising its triumphal arch in the skies for the sturdy fighters to sail under to victory and rescue.

With ten days' provisions Captain Josiah Mitchell performed this memorable voyage of forty-three days and eight hours in an open boat, sailing four thousand miles in reality and thirty-three hundred and sixty by direct courses, and brought every man safe to land. A bright, simple-hearted, unassuming, plucky, and most companionable man. I walked the deck with him twenty-eight days—when I was not copying diaries—and I remember him with reverent honor. If he is alive he is eighty-six years old now.

If I remember rightly, Samuel Ferguson died soon after we reached San Francisco. I do not think he lived to see his home again; his disease had been seriously aggravated by his hardships.

For a time it was hoped that the two quarter-boats would presently be heard of, but this hope suffered disappointment. They went down with all on board, no doubt, not even sparing that knightly chief mate.

The authors of the diaries allowed me to copy them exactly as they were written, and the extracts that I have given are without any smoothing over or revision. These diaries are finely modest and unaffected, and with unconscious and unintentional art they rise toward the climax with graduated and gathering force and swing and dramatic intensity; they sweep you along with a cumulative rush, and when the cry rings out at last, "Land in sight!" your heart is in your mouth, and for a moment you think it is you that have been saved. The last two paragraphs are not improvable by anybody's art; they are literary gold; and their very pauses and uncompleted sentences have in them an eloquence not reachable by any words.

The interest of this story is unquenchable; it is of the sort that time cannot decay. I have not looked at the diaries for thirty-two years, but I find that they have lost nothing in that time. Lost? They have gained; for by some subtle law all tragic human experiences gain in pathos by the perspective of time. We realize this when in Naples we stand musing over the poor Pompeian mother, lost in the historic storm of volcanic ashes eighteen centuries ago, who lies with her child gripped close to her breast, trying to save it, and whose despair and grief have been preserved for us by the fiery envelope which took her life but eternalized her form and features. She moves us, she haunts us, she stays in our thoughts for many days, we do not know why, for she is nothing to us, she has been nothing to any one for eighteen centuries; whereas of the like case to-day we should say, "Poor thing! it is pitiful," and forget it in an hour.

TWAIN
and the
AMERICAN SCENE

Niagara

Niagara Falls is a most enjoyable place of resort. The hotels are excellent, and the prices not at all exorbitant. The opportunities for fishing are not surpassed in the country; in fact, they are not even equaled elsewhere. Because, in other localities, certain places in the streams are much better than others; but at Niagara one place is just as good as another, for the reason that the fish do not bite anywhere, and so there is no use in your walking five miles to fish, when you can depend on being just as unsuccessful nearer home. The advantages of this state of things have never heretofore been properly placed before the public.

The weather is cool in summer, and the walks and drives are all pleasant and none of them fatiguing. When you start out to "do" the Falls you first drive down about a mile, and pay a small sum for the privilege of looking down from a precipice into the narrowest part of the Niagara River. A railway "cut" through a hill would be as comely if it had the angry river tumbling and foaming through its bottom. You can descend a staircase here a hundred and fifty feet down, and stand at the edge of the water. After you have done it, you will wonder why you did it; but you will then be too late.

The guide will explain to you, in his blood-curdling way, how he saw the little steamer, *Maid of the Mist,* descend the fearful rapids—how first one paddle-box was out of sight behind the raging billows and then the other, and at what point it was that her smoke-stack toppled overboard, and where her planking began to break and part asunder—and how she did finally live through the trip, after accomplishing the incredible feat of traveling seventeen miles in six minutes, or six miles in seventeen minutes, I have really forgotten which. But it was very extraordinary, anyhow. It is worth the price of admission to hear the guide tell the story nine times in succession to different parties, and never miss a word or alter a sentence or a gesture.

Then you drive over to Suspension Bridge, and divide your misery between the chances of smashing down two hundred feet into the river below, and the chances of having the railway-train overhead smashing down onto you. Either possibility is discomforting taken by itself, but, mixed together, they amount in the aggregate to positive unhappiness.

On the Canada side you drive along the chasm between long ranks of photographers standing guard behind their cameras, ready to make an ostentatious frontispiece of you and your decaying ambulance, and your solemn crate with a hide on it, which you are expected to regard in the light of a horse, and a diminished and unimportant background of sublime Niagara; and a great many people *have* the incredible effrontery or the native depravity to aid and abet this sort of crime.

Any day, in the hands of these photographers, you may see stately pictures of papa and mamma, Johnny and Bub and Sis. or a couple of country cousins, all smiling vacantly, and all disposed in studied and uncomfortable attitudes in their carriage, and all looming up in their awe-inspiring imbecility before the snubbed and diminished presentment of that majestic presence whose ministering spirits are the rainbows, whose voice is the thunder, whose awful front is veiled in clouds, who was monarch here dead and forgotten ages before this hackful of small reptiles was deemed temporarily necessary to fill a crack in the world's unnoted myriads, and will still be monarch here ages and decades of ages after they shall have gathered themselves to their blood-relations, the other worms, and been mingled with the unremembering dust.

There is no actual harm in making Niagara a background whereon to display one's marvelous insignificance in a good strong light, but it requires a sort of superhuman self-complacency to enable one to do it.

When you have examined the stupendous Horseshoe Fall till you are satisfied you cannot improve on it, you return to America by the new Suspension Bridge, and follow up the bank to where they exhibit the Cave of the Winds.

Here I followed instructions, and divested myself of all my clothing, and put on a waterproof jacket and overalls. This costume is picturesque, but not beautiful. A guide, similarly dressed, led the way down a flight of winding stairs, which wound and wound, and still kept on winding long after the thing ceased to be a novelty, and then terminated long before it had begun to be a pleasure. We were then well down under the precipice, but still considerably above the level of the river.

We now began to creep along flimsy bridges of a single plank, our persons shielded from destruction by a crazy wooden railing, to which I clung with both hands—not because I was afraid, but because I wanted to. Presently the descent became steeper, and the bridge flimsier, and sprays from the American Fall began to rain down on us in fast increasing sheets that soon became blinding, and after that our progress was mostly in the nature of groping. Now a furious wind began to rush out from behind the waterfall, which seemed determined to sweep us from the bridge, and scatter us on the rocks and among the torrents below. I remarked that I wanted to go home; but it was too late. We were almost under the monstrous wall of water thundering down from above, and speech was in vain in the midst of such a pitiless crash of sound.

In another moment the guide disappeared behind the deluge, and, bewildered by the thunder, driven helplessly by the wind, and smitten by the arrowy tempest of rain, I followed. All was darkness. Such a mad storming, roaring, and bellowing of warring wind and water never crazed my ears before. I bent my head, and seemed to receive the Atlantic on my back. The world seemed going to destruction. I could not see anything, the flood poured down so savagely. I raised my head, with open mouth, and the most of the American cataract went down my throat. If I had sprung a leak now I had been lost. And at this moment I discovered that the bridge had ceased, and we must trust for a foothold to the slippery and precipitous rocks. I never was so scared before and survived it. But we got through at last, and emerged into the open day, where we could stand in front of the laced and frothy and seething world of descending water, and look at it. When I saw how much of it there was, and how fearfully in earnest it was, I was sorry I had gone behind it.

The noble Red Man has always been a friend and darling of mine. I love to read about him in tales and legends and romances. I love to read of his inspired sagacity, and his love of the wild free life of mountain and forest, and his general nobility of character, and his stately metaphorical manner of speech, and his chivalrous love for the dusky maiden, and the picturesque pomp of his dress and accoutrements. Especially the picturesque pomp of his dress and accoutrements. When I found the shops at Niagara Falls full of dainty Indian beadwork, and stunning moccasins, and equally stunning toy figures representing human beings who carried their weapons in holes bored through their arms and bodies, and had feet shaped like a pie, I was filled with emotion. I knew that now, at last, I was going to come face to face with the noble Red Man.

A lady clerk in a shop told me, indeed, that all her grand array of curiosities were made by the Indians, and that they were plenty about the Falls, and that they were friendly, and it would not be dangerous to speak to them. And sure enough, as I approached the bridge leading over to Luna Island, I came upon a noble Son of the Forest sitting under a tree, diligently at work on a bead reticule. He wore a slouch hat and brogans, and had a short black pipe in his mouth. Thus does the baneful contact with our effeminate civilization dilute the picturesque pomp which is so natural to the Indian when far removed from us in his native haunts. I addressed the relic as follows:

"Is the Wawhoo-Wang-Wang of the Whack-a-Whack happy? Does the great Speckled Thunder sigh for the war-path, or is his heart contented with dreaming of the dusky maiden, the Pride of the Forest? Does the mighty Sachem yearn to drink the blood of his enemies, or is he satisfied to make bead reticules for the pappooses of the paleface? Speak, sublime relic of bygone grandeur—venerable ruin, speak!"

The relic said:

"An' is it mesilf, Dennis Hooligan, that ye'd be takin' for a dirty Injin, ye drawlin', lantern-jawed, spider-legged divil! By the piper that played before Moses, I'll ate ye!"

I went away from there.

By and by, in the neighborhood of the Terrapin Tower, I came upon a gentle daughter of the aborigines in fringed and beaded buckskin moccasins and leggins, seated on a bench with her pretty wares about her. She had just carved out a wooden chief that had a strong family resemblance to a clothespin, and was now boring a hole through his abdomen to put his bow through. I hesitated a moment, and then addressed her:

"Is the heart of the forest maiden heavy? Is the Laughing Tadpole lonely? Does she mourn over the extinguished council-fires of her race, and the vanished glory of her ancestors? Or does her sad spirit wander afar toward the hunting-grounds whither her brave Gobbler-of-the-Lightnings is gone? Why is my daughter silent? Has she aught against the paleface stranger?"

The maiden said:

"Faix, an' is it Biddy Malone ye dare to be callin' names? Lave this, or I'll shy your lean carcass over the cataract, ye sniveling blaggard!"

I adjourned from there also.

"Confound these Indians!" I said. "They told me they were tame; but, if appearances go for anything, I should say they were all on the war-path."

I made one more attempt to fraternize with them, and only one. I came upon a camp of them gathered in the shade of a great tree, making wampum and moccasins, and addressed them in the language of friendship:

"Noble Red Men, Braves, Grand Sachems, War Chiefs, Squaws, and High Muck-a-Mucks, the paleface from the land of the setting sun greets you! You, Beneficent Polecat—you, Devourer of Mountains—you, Roaring Thundergust—you, Bully Boy with a Glass Eye—the paleface from beyond the great waters greets you all! War and pestilence have thinned your ranks and destroyed your once proud nation. Poker and seven-up, and a vain modern expense for soap, unknown to your glorious ancestors, have depleted your purses. Appropriating, in your simplicity, the property of others has gotten you into trouble. Misrepresenting facts, in your simple innocence, has damaged your reputation with the soulless usurper. Trading for forty-rod whisky, to enable you to get drunk and happy and tomahawk your families, has played the everlasting mischief with the picturesque pomp of your dress, and here you are, in the broad light of the nineteenth century, gotten up like the ragtag and bobtail of the purlieus of New York. For shame! Remember your ancestors! Recall their mighty deeds! Remember Uncas!—and Red Jacket!—and Hole in the Day!—and Whoopdedoodledo! Emulate their achievements! Unfurl yourselves under my banner, noble savages, illustrious gutter-snipes—"

"Down wid him!" "Scoop the blaggard!" "Burn him!" "Hang him!" "Dhround him!"

It was the quickest operation that ever was. I simply saw a sudden flash in the air of clubs, brickbats, fists, bead-baskets, and moccasins—a single flash, and they all appeared to hit me at once, and no two of them in the same place. In the next instant the entire tribe was upon me. They tore half the clothes off me; they broke my arms and legs; they gave me a thump that dented the top of my head till it would hold coffee like a saucer; and, to crown their disgraceful proceedings and add insult to injury, they threw me over the Niagara Falls, and I got wet.

About ninety or a hundred feet from the top, the remains of my vest caught on a projecting rock, and I was almost drowned before I could get loose. I finally fell, and brought up in a world of white foam at the foot of the Fall, whose celled and bubbly masses towered up several inches above my head. Of course I got into the eddy. I sailed round and round in it forty-four times—chasing a chip and gaining on it—each round trip a half-mile—reaching for the same bush on the bank forty-four times, and just exactly missing it by a hair's-breadth every time.

At last a man walked down and sat down close to that bush, and put a pipe in his mouth, and lit a match, and followed me with one eye and kept the other on the match, while he sheltered it in his hands from the wind. Presently a puff of wind blew it out. The next time I swept around he said:

"Got a match?"

"Yes; in my other vest. Help me out, please."

"Not for Joe."

When I came round again, I said:

"Excuse the seemingly impertinent curiosity of a drowning man, but will you explain this singular conduct of yours?"

"With pleasure. I am the coroner. Don't hurry on my account. I can wait for you. But I wish I had a match."

I said: "Take my place, and I'll go and get you one."

He declined. This lack of confidence on his part created a coldness between us, and from that time forward I avoided him. It was my idea, in case anything happened to me, to so time the occurrence as to throw my custom into the hands of the opposition coroner on the American side.

At last a policeman came along, and arrested me for disturbing the peace by yelling at people on shore for help. The judge fined me, but I had the advantage of him. My money was with my pantaloons, and my pantaloons were with the Indians.

Thus I escaped. I am now lying in a very critical condition. At least I am lying anyway—critical or not critical. I am hurt all over, but I cannot tell the full extent yet, because the doctor is not done taking inventory. He will make out my manifest this evening. However, thus far he thinks only sixteen of my wounds are fatal. I don't mind the others.

Upon regaining my right mind, I said:

"It is an awful savage tribe of Indians that do the beadwork and moccasins for Niagara Falls, doctor. Where are they from?"

"Limerick, my son."

Science *vs.* Luck

At that time, in Kentucky (said the Hon. Mr. K——), the law was very strict against what is termed "games of chance." About a dozen of the boys were detected playing seven-up or old sledge for money, and the grand jury found a true bill against them. Jim Sturgis was retained to defend them when the case came up, of course. The more he studied over the matter, and looked into the evidence, the plainer it was that he must lose a case at last—there was no getting around that painful fact. Those boys had certainly been betting money on a game of chance. Even public sympathy was roused in behalf of Sturgis. People said it was a pity to see him mar his successful career with a big prominent case like this, which must go against him.

But after several restless nights an inspired idea flashed upon Sturgis, and he sprang out of bed delighted. He thought he saw his way through. The next day he whispered around a little among his clients and a few friends, and then when the case came up in court he acknowledged the seven-up and the betting, and, as his sole defense, had the astounding effrontery to put in the plea that old sledge was not a game of chance! There was the broadest sort of a smile all over the faces of that sophisticated audience. The judge smiled with the rest. But Sturgis maintained a countenance whose earnestness was even severe. The opposite counsel tried to ridicule him out of his position, and did not succeed. The judge jested in a ponderous judicial way about the thing, but did not move him. The matter was becoming grave. The judge lost a little of his patience, and said the joke had gone far enough. Jim Sturgis said he knew of no joke in the matter—his clients could not be punished for indulging in what some people chose to consider a game of chance until it was *proven* that it was a game of chance. Judge and counsel said that would be an easy matter, and forthwith called Deacons Job, Peters, Burke, and Johnson, and Dominies Wirt and Miggles, to testify; and they unanimously and with strong feeling put down the legal quibble of Sturgis by pronouncing that old sledge *was* a game of chance.

"What do you call it *now?*" said the judge.

"I call it a game of science!" retorted Sturgis; "and I'll prove it, too!"

They saw his little game.

He brought in a cloud of witnesses, and produced an overwhelming mass of testimony, to show that old sledge was not a game of chance but a game of science.

Instead of being the simplest case in the world, it had somehow turned out to be an excessively knotty one. The judge scratched his head over it awhile, and said there was no way of coming to a determination, because just as many men could be brought into court who would testify on one side as could be found to testify on the other. But he said he was willing to do the fair thing by all parties, and would act upon any suggestion Mr. Sturgis would make for the solution of the difficulty.

Mr. Sturgis was on his feet in a second.

"Impanel a jury of six of each, Luck *versus* Science. Give them candles and a couple of decks of cards. Send them into the jury-room, and just abide by the result!"

There was no disputing the fairness of the proposition. The four deacons and the two dominies were sworn in as the "chance" jurymen, and six inveterate old seven-up professors were chosen to represent the "science" side of the issue. They retired to the jury-room.

In about two hours Deacon Peters sent into court to borrow three dollars from a friend. [Sensation.] In about two hours more Dominie Miggles sent into court to borrow a "stake" from a friend. [Sensation.] During the next three or four hours the other dominie and the other deacons sent into court for small loans. And still the packed audience waited, for it was a prodigious occasion in Bull's Corners, and one in which every father of a family was necessarily interested.

The rest of the story can be told briefly. About daylight the jury came in, and Deacon Job, the foreman, read the following:

VERDICT

We, the jury in the case of the Commonwealth of Kentucky *vs.* John Wheeler *et al.*, have carefully considered the points of the case, and tested the merits of the several theories advanced, and do hereby unanimously decide that the game commonly known as old sledge or seven-up is eminently a game of science and not of chance. In demonstration whereof it is hereby and herein stated, iterated, reiterated, set forth, and made manifest that, during the entire night, the "chance" men never won a game or turned a jack, although both feats were common and frequent to the opposition; and furthermore, in support of this our verdict, we call attention to the significant fact that the "chance" men are all busted, and the "science" men have got the money. It is the deliberate opinion of this jury, that the "chance" theory concerning seven-up is a pernicious doctrine, and calculated to inflict untold suffering and pecuniary loss upon any community that takes stock in it.

"That is the way that seven-up came to be set apart and particularized in the statute-books of Kentucky as being a game not of chance but of science, and therefore not punishable under the law," said Mr. K——. "That verdict is of record, and holds good to this day."

The Late Benjamin Franklin

Never put off till to-morrow what you can do day after to-morrow just as well.

—B.F.

This party was one of those persons whom they call Philosophers. He was twins, being born simultaneously in two different houses in the city of Boston. These houses remain unto this day, and have signs upon them worded in accordance with the facts. The signs are considered well enough to have, though not necessary, because the inhabitants point out the two birthplaces to the stranger anyhow, and sometimes as often as several times in the same day. The subject of this memoir was of a vicious disposition, and early prostituted his talents to the invention of maxims and aphorisms calculated to inflict suffering upon the rising generation of all subsequent ages. His simplest acts, also, were contrived with a view to their being held up for the emulation of boys forever—boys who might otherwise have been happy. It was in this spirit that he became the son of a soap-boiler, and probably for no other reason than that the efforts of all future boys who tried to be anything might be looked upon with suspicion unless they were the sons of soap-boilers. With a malevolence which is without parallel in history, he would work all day, and then sit up nights, and let on to be studying algebra by the light of a smoldering fire, so that all other boys might have to do that also, or else have Benjamin Franklin thrown up to them. Not satisfied with these proceedings, he had a fashion of living wholly on bread and water, and studying astronomy at meal-time—a thing which has brought affliction to millions of boys since, whose fathers had read Franklin's pernicious biography.

His maxims were full of animosity toward boys. Nowadays a boy cannot follow out a single natural instinct without tumbling over some of those everlasting aphorisms and hearing from Franklin on the spot. If he buys two cents' worth of peanuts, his father says, "Remember what Franklin has said, my son—'A groat a day's a penny a year' "; and the comfort is all gone out of those peanuts. If he wants to spin his top when he has done work, his father quotes, "Procrastination is the thief of time." If he does a virtuous action, he never gets anything for it, because "Virtue is its own reward." And that boy is hounded to death and robbed of his natural rest, because Franklin said once, in one of his inspired flights of malignity:

> Early to bed and early to rise
> Makes a man healthy and wealthy and wise.

As if it were any object to a boy to be healthy and wealthy and wise on such terms. The sorrow that that maxim has cost me, through my parents, experimenting on me with it, tongue cannot tell. The legitimate result is my present state of general debility, indigence, and mental aberration. My parents used to have me up before nine o'clock in the morning sometimes when I was a boy. If they had let me take my natural rest where would I have been now? Keeping store, no doubt, and respected by all.

And what an adroit old adventurer the subject of this memoir was! In order to get a chance to fly his kite on Sunday he used to hang a key on the string and let on to be fishing for lightning. And a guileless public would go home chirping about the "wisdom" and the "genius" of the hoary Sabbath-breaker. If anybody caught him playing mumble-peg by himself, after the age of sixty, he would immediately appear to be ciphering out how the grass grew—as if it was any of his business. My grandfather knew him well, and he says Franklin was always fixed—always ready. If a body, during his old age, happened on him unexpectedly when he was catching flies, or making mud-pies, or sliding on a cellar door, he would immediately look wise, and rip out a maxim, and walk off with his nose in the air and his cap turned wrong side before, trying to appear absent-minded and eccentric. He was a hard lot.

He invented a stove that would smoke your head off in four hours by the clock. One can see the almost devilish satisfaction he took in it by his giving it his name.

He was always proud of telling how he entered Philadelphia for the first time, with nothing in the world but two shillings in his pocket and four rolls of bread under his arm. But really, when you come to examine it critically, it was nothing. Anybody could have done it.

To the subject of this memoir belongs the honor of recommending the army to go back to bows and arrows in place of bayonets and muskets. He observed, with his customary force, that the bayonet was very well under some circumstances, but that he doubted whether it could be used with accuracy at a long range.

Benjamin Franklin did a great many notable things for his country, and made her young name to be honored in many lands as the mother of such a son. It is not the idea of this memoir to ignore that or cover it up. No; the simple idea of it is to snub those pretentious maxims of his, which he worked up with a great show of originality out of truisms that had become wearisome platitudes as early as the dispersion from Babel; and also to snub his stove, and his military inspirations, his unseemly endeavor to make himself conspicuous when he entered Philadelphia, and his flying his kite and fooling away his time in all sorts of such ways when he ought to have been foraging for soap-fat, or constructing candles. I merely desired to do away with somewhat of the prevalent calamitous idea among heads of families that Franklin *acquired* his great genius by working for nothing, studying by moonlight, and getting up in the night instead of waiting till morning like a Christian; and that this program, rigidly inflicted, will make a Franklin of every father's fool. It is time these gentlemen were finding out that these execrable eccentricities of instinct and conduct are only the *evidences* of genius, not the *creators* of it. I wish I had been the father of my parents long enough to make them comprehend this truth, and thus prepare them to let their son have an easier time of it. When I was a child I had to boil soap, notwithstanding my father was wealthy, and I had to get up early and study geometry at breakfast, and peddle my own poetry, and do everything just as Franklin did, in the solemn hope that I would be a Franklin some day. And here I am.

The Petrified Man

Now, to show how really hard it is to foist a moral or a truth upon an unsuspecting public through a burlesque without entirely and absurdly missing one's mark, I will here set down two experiences of my own in this thing. In the fall of 1862, in Nevada and California, the people got to running wild about extraordinary petrifactions and other natural marvels. One could scarcely pick up a paper without finding in it one or two glorified discoveries of this kind. The mania was becoming a little ridiculous. I was a brand-new local editor in Virginia City, and I felt called upon to destroy this growing evil; we all have our benignant, fatherly moods at one time or another, I suppose. I chose to kill the petrifaction mania with a delicate, a very delicate satire. But maybe it was altogether too delicate, for nobody ever perceived the satire part of it at all. I put my scheme in the shape of the discovery of a remarkably petrified man.

I had had a temporary falling out with Mr. ——, the new coroner and justice of the peace of Humboldt, and thought I might as well touch him up a little at the same time and make him ridiculous, and thus combine pleasure with business. So I told, in patient, belief-compelling detail, all about the finding of a petrified man at Gravelly Ford (exactly a hundred and twenty miles, over a breakneck mountain trail from where —— lived);

how all the savants of the immediate neighborhood had been to examine it (it was notorious that there was not a living creature within fifty miles of there, except a few starving Indians, some crippled grasshoppers, and four or five buzzards out of meat and too feeble to get away); how those savants all pronounced the petrified man to have been in a state of complete petrifaction for over ten generations; and then, with a seriousness that I ought to have been ashamed to assume, I stated that as soon as Mr. —— heard the news he summoned a jury, mounted his mule, and posted off, with noble reverence for official duty, on that awful five days' journey, through alkali, sage-brush, peril of body, and imminent starvation, to *hold an inquest* on this man that had been dead and turned to everlasting stone for more than three hundred years! And then, my hand being "in," so to speak, I went on, with the same unflinching gravity, to state that the jury returned a verdict that deceased came to his death from *protracted exposure.* This only moved me to higher flights of imagination, and I said that the jury, with that charity so characteristic of pioneers, then dug a grave, and were about to give the petrified man Christian burial, when they found that for ages a limestone sediment had been trickling down the face of the stone against which he was sitting, and this stuff had run under him and cemented him fast to the "bed-rock"; that the jury (they were all silver-miners) canvassed the difficulty a moment, and then got out their powder and fuse, and proceeded to drill a hole under him, in order to *blast him from his position,* when Mr. ——, "with that delicacy so characteristic of him, forbade them, observing that it would be little less than sacrilege to do such a thing."

From beginning to end the "Petrified Man" squib was a string of roaring absurdities, albeit they were told with an unfair pretense of truth that even imposed upon me to some extent, and I was in some danger of believing in my own fraud. But I really had no desire to deceive anybody, and no expectation of doing it. I depended on the way the petrified man was *sitting* to explain to the public that he was a swindle. Yet I purposely mixed that up with other things, hoping to make it obscure—and I did. I would describe the position of one foot, and then say his right thumb was against the side of his nose; then talk about his other foot, and presently come back and say the fingers of his right hand were spread apart; then talk about the back of his head a little, and return and say the left thumb was hooked into the right little finger; then ramble off about something else, and by and by drift back again and remark that the fingers of the left hand were spread like those of the right. But I was too ingenious. I mixed it up rather too much; and so all that description of the attitude, as a key to the humbuggery of the article, was entirely lost, for nobody but me ever discovered and comprehended the peculiar and suggestive position of the petrified man's hands.

As a *satire* on the petrifaction mania, or anything else, my Petrified Man was a disheartening failure; for everybody received him in innocent good faith, and I was stunned to see the creature I had begotten to pull down the wonder-business with, and bring derision upon it, calmly exalted to the grand chief place in the list of the genuine marvels our Nevada had produced. I was so disappointed at the curious miscarriage of my scheme, that at first I was angry, and did not like to think about it; but by and by, when the exchanges began to come in with the Petrified Man copied and guilelessly glorified, I began to feel a soothing secret satisfaction; and as my gentleman's field of travels broadened, and by the exchanges I saw that he steadily and implacably penetrated territory after territory, state after state, and land after land, till he swept the great globe and culminated in sublime and unimpeached legitimacy in the august London *Lancet,* my cup was full, and I said I was glad I had done it. I think that for about eleven months, as nearly as I can remember, Mr. ——'s daily mail-bag continued to be swollen by the addition of half a bushel of newspapers hailing from many climes with the Petrified Man in them, marked around with a prominent belt of ink. I sent them to him. I did it for spite, not for fun. He used to shovel them into his back yard and curse. And every day during all those months the miners, his constituents (for miners never quit joking a person when they get started), would call on him and ask if he could tell them where they could get hold of a paper with the Petrified Man in it. He could have accommodated a continent with them. I hated —— in those days, and these things pacified me and pleased me. I could not have gotten more real comfort out of him without killing him.

General Washington's Negro Body-Servant

A Biographical Sketch

The stirring part of this celebrated colored man's life properly began with his death—that is to say, the notable features of his biography begin with the first time he died. He had been little heard of up to that time, but since then we have never ceased to hear of him; we have never ceased to hear of him at stated, unfailing intervals. His was a most remarkable career, and I have thought that its history would make a valuable addition to our biographical literature. Therefore, I have carefully collated the materials for such a work, from authentic sources, and here present them to the public. I have rigidly excluded from these pages everything of a doubtful character, with the object in view of introducing my work into the schools for the instruction of the youth of my country.

The name of the famous body-servant of General Washington was George. After serving his illustrious master faithfully for half a century, and enjoying throughout this long term his high regard and confidence, it became his sorrowful duty at last to lay that beloved master to rest in his peaceful grave by the Potomac. Ten years afterward—in 1809—full of years and honors, he died himself, mourned by all who knew him. The Boston *Gazette* of that date thus refers to the event:

> George, the favorite body-servant of the lamented Washington, died in Richmond, Va., last Tuesday, at the ripe age of 95 years. His intellect was unimpaired, and his memory tenacious, up to within a few minutes of his decease. He was present at the second installation of Washington as President, and also at his funeral, and distinctly remembered all the prominent incidents connected with those noted events.

From this period we hear no more of the favorite body-servant of General Washington until May, 1825, at which time he died again. A Philadelphia paper thus speaks of the sad occurrence:

> At Macon, Ga., last week, a colored man named George, who was the favorite body-servant of General Washington, died at the advanced age of 95 years. Up to within a few hours of his dissolution he was in full possession of all his faculties, and could distinctly recollect the second installation of Washington, his death and burial, the surrender of Cornwallis, the battle of Trenton, the griefs and hardships of Valley Forge, etc. Deceased was followed to the grave by the entire population of Macon.

On the Fourth of July, 1830, and also of 1834 and 1836, the subject of this sketch was exhibited in great state upon the rostrum of the orator of the day, and in November of 1840 he died again. The St. Louis *Republican* of the 25th of that month spoke as follows:

> ANOTHER RELIC OF THE REVOLUTION GONE
>
> George, once the favorite body-servant of General Washington, died yesterday at the house of Mr. John Leavenworth in this city, at the venerable age of 95 years. He was in the full possession of his faculties up to the hour of his death, and distinctly recollected the first and second installations and death of President Washington, the surrender of Cornwallis, the battles of Trenton and Monmouth, the sufferings of the patriot army at Valley Forge, the proclamation of the Declaration of Independence, the speech of Patrick Henry in the Virginia House of Delegates, and many other old-time reminiscences of stirring interest. Few white men die lamented as was this aged negro. The funeral was very largely attended.

During the next ten or eleven years the subject of this sketch appeared at intervals at Fourth-of-July celebrations in various parts of the country, and was exhibited upon the rostrum with flattering success. But in the fall of 1855 he died again. The California papers thus speak of the event:

ANOTHER OLD HERO GONE

Died, at Dutch Flat, on the 7th of March, George (once the confidential body-servant of General Washington), at the great age of 95 years. His memory, which did not fail him till the last, was a wonderful storehouse of interesting reminiscences. He could distinctly recollect the first and second installations and death of President Washington, the surrender of Cornwallis, the battles of Trenton and Monmouth, and Bunker Hill, the proclamation of the Declaration of Independence, and Braddock's defeat. George was greatly respected in Dutch Flat, and it is estimated that there were 10,000 people present at his funeral.

The last time the subject of this sketch died was in June, 1864; and until we learn the contrary, it is just to presume that he died permanently this time. The Michigan papers thus refer to the sorrowful event:

ANOTHER CHERISHED REMNANT OF THE REVOLUTION GONE

George, a colored man, and once the favorite body-servant of General Washington, died in Detroit last week, at the patriarchal age of 95 years. To the moment of his death his intellect was unclouded, and he could distinctly remember the first and second installations and death of Washington, the surrender of Cornwallis, the battles of Trenton and Monmouth, and Bunker Hill, the proclamation of the Declaration of Independence, Braddock's defeat, the throwing over of the tea in Boston harbor, and the landing of the Pilgrims. He died greatly respected, and was followed to the grave by a vast concourse of people.

The faithful old servant is gone! We shall never see him more until he turns up again. He has closed his long and splendid career of dissolution, for the present, and sleeps peacefully, as only they sleep who have earned their rest. He was in all respects a remarkable man. He held his age better than any celebrity that has figured in history; and the longer he lived the stronger and longer his memory grew. If he lives to die again, he will distinctly recollect the discovery of America.

The above résumé of his biography I believe to be substantially correct, although it is possible that he may have died once or twice in obscure places where the event failed of newspaper notoriety. One fault I find in all notices of his death which I have quoted, and this ought to be correct. In them he uniformly and impartially died at the age of 95. This could not have been. He might have done that once, or maybe twice, but he could not have continued it indefinitely. Allowing that when he first died, he died at the age of 95, he was 151 years old when he died last, in 1864. But his age did not keep pace with his recollections. When he died the last time, he distinctly remembered the landing of the Pilgrims, which took place in 1620. He must have been about twenty years old when he witnessed that event, wherefore it is safe to assert that the body-servant of General Washington was in the neighborhood of two hundred and sixty or seventy years old when he departed this life finally.

Having waited a proper length of time, to see if the subject of this sketch had gone from us reliably and irrevocably, I now publish his biography with confidence, and respectfully offer it to a mourning nation.

P.S.—I see by the papers that this infamous old fraud has just died again, in Arkansas. This makes six times that he is known to have died, and always in a new place. The death of Washington's body-servant has ceased to be a novelty; its charm is gone; the people are tired of it; let it cease. This well-meaning but misguided negro has now put six different communities to the expense of burying him in state, and has swindled tens of thousands of people into following him to the grave under the delusion that a select and peculiar distinction was being conferred upon them. Let him stay buried for good now; and let that newspaper suffer the severest censure that shall ever, in all future time, publish to the world that General Washington's favorite colored body-servant has died again.

Lionizing Murderers

I had heard so much about the celebrated fortune-teller Madame ——, that I went to see her yesterday. She has a dark complexion naturally, and this effect is heightened by artificial aids which cost her nothing. She wears curls—very black ones, and I had an impression that she gave their native attractiveness a lift with rancid butter. She wears a reddish check handkerchief, cast loosely around her neck, and it was plain that her other one is slow getting back from the wash. I presume she takes snuff. At any rate, something resembling it had lodged among the hairs sprouting from her upper lip. I know she likes garlic—I knew that as soon as she sighed. She looked at me searchingly for nearly a minute, with her black eyes, and then said:

"It is enough. Come!"

She started down a very dark and dismal corridor—I stepping close after her. Presently she stopped, and said that, as the way was so crooked and dark, perhaps she had better get a light. But it seemed ungallant to allow a woman to put herself to so much trouble for me, and so I said:

"It is not worth while, madam. If you will heave another sigh, I think I can follow it."

So we got along all right. Arrived at her official and mysterious den, she asked me to tell her the date of my birth, the exact hour of that occurrence, and the color of my grandmother's hair. I answered as accurately as I could. Then she said:

"Young man, summon your fortitude—do not tremble. I am about to reveal the past."

"Information concerning the *future* would be, in a general way, more—"

"Silence! You have had much trouble, some joy, some good fortune, some bad. Your great grandfather was hanged."

"That is a l—"

"Silence! Hanged sir. But it was not his fault. He could not help it."

"I am glad you do him justice."

"Ah—grieve, rather, that the jury did. He was hanged. His star crosses yours in the fourth division, fifth sphere. Consequently you will be hanged also."

"In view of this cheerful—"

"I *must* have silence. Yours was not, in the beginning, a criminal nature, but circumstances changed it. At the age of nine you stole sugar. At the age of fifteen you stole money. At twenty you stole horses. At twenty-five you committed arson. At thirty, hardened in crime, you became an editor. You are now a public lecturer. Worse things are in store for you. You will be sent to Congress. Next, to the penitentiary. Finally, happiness will come again—all will be well—you will be hanged."

I was now in tears. It seemed hard enough to go to Congress; but to be hanged—this was too sad, too dreadful. The woman seemed surprised at my grief. I told her the thoughts that were in my mind. Then she comforted me.

"Why, man,"[1] she said, "hold up your head—*you* have nothing to grieve

1. In this paragraph the fortune-teller details the exact history of the Pike-Brown assassination case in New Hampshire, from the succoring and saving of the stranger Pike by the Browns, to the subsequent hanging and coffining of that treacherous miscreant. She adds nothing, invents nothing, exaggerates nothing (see any New England paper for November, 1869). This Pike-Brown case is selected merely as a type, to illustrate a custom that prevails, not in New Hampshire alone, but in every state in the Union—I mean the sentimental custom of visiting, petting, glorifying, and snuffling over murderers like this Pike, from the day they enter the jail under sentence of death until they swing from the gallows. The following extract from the *Temple Bar* (1866) reveals the fact that this custom is not confined to the United States:—"On December 31, 1841, a man named John Johnes, a shoemaker, murdered his sweetheart, Mary Hallam, the daughter of a respectable laborer, at Mansfield, in the county of Nottingham. He was

about. Listen. You will live in New Hampshire. In your sharp need and distress the Brown family will succor you—such of them as Pike the assassin left alive. They will be benefactors to you. When you shall have grown fat upon their bounty, and are grateful and happy, you will desire to make some modest return for these things, and so you will go to the house some night and brain the whole family with an ax. You will rob the dead bodies of your benefactors, and disburse your gains in riotous living among the rowdies and courtesans of Boston. Then you will be arrested, tried, condemned to be hanged, thrown into prison. Now is your happy day. You will be converted—you will be converted just as soon as every effort to compass pardon, commutation, or reprieve has failed—and then! Why, then, every morning and every afternoon, the best and purest young ladies of the village will assemble in your cell and sing hymns. This will show that assassination is respectable. Then you will write a touching letter, in which you will forgive all those recent Browns. This will excite the public admiration. No public can withstand magnanimity. Next, they will take you to the scaffold, with great *éclat,* at the head of an imposing procession composed of clergymen, officials, citizens generally, and young ladies walking pensively two and two, and bearing bouquets and immortelles. You will mount the scaffold, and while the great concourse stand uncovered in your presence, you will read your sappy little speech which the minister has written for you. And then, in the midst of a grand and impressive silence, they will swing you into per—Paradise, my son. There will not be a dry eye on the ground. You will be a hero! Not a rough there but will envy you. Not a rough there but will resolve to emulate you. And next, a

executed on March 23, 1842. He was a man of unsteady habits, and gave way to violent fits of passion. The girl declined his addresses, and he said if he did not have her no one else should. After he had inflicted the first wound, which was not immediately fatal, she begged for her life, but seeing him resolved, asked for time to pray. He said that he would pray for both, and completed the crime. The wounds were inflicted by a shoemaker's knife, and her throat was cut barbarously. After this he dropped on his knees some time, and prayed God to have mercy on two unfortunate lovers. He made no attempt to escape, and confessed the crime. After his imprisonment he behaved in a most decorous manner; he won upon the good opinion of the jail chaplain, and he was visited by the Bishop of Lincoln. It does not appear that he expressed any contrition for the crime, but seemed to pass away with triumphant certainty that he was going to rejoin his victim in heaven. *He was visited by some pious and benevolent ladies of Nottingham, some of whom declared he was a child of God, if ever there was one. One of the ladies sent him a white camellia to wear at his execution.*"—M.T.

great procession will follow you to the tomb—will weep over your remains—the young ladies will sing again the hymns made dear by sweet associations connected with the jail, and, as a last tribute of affection, respect, and appreciation of your many sterling qualities, they will walk two and two around your bier, and strew wreaths of flowers on it. And lo! you are canonized. Think of it, son—ingrate, assassin, robber of the dead, drunken brawler among thieves and harlots in the slums of Boston one month, and the pet of the pure and innocent daughters of the land the next! A bloody and hateful devil—a bewept, bewailed, and sainted martyr—all in a month! Fool!—so noble a fortune, and yet you sit here grieving!"

"No, madam," I said, "you do me wrong, you do, indeed. I am perfectly satisfied. I did not know before that my great-grandfather was hanged, but it is of no consequence. He has probably ceased to bother about it by this time—and I have not commenced yet. I confess, madam, that I do something in the way of editing and lecturing, but the other crimes you mention have escaped my memory. Yet I must have committed them—you would not deceive a stranger. But let the past be as it was, and let the future be as it may—these are nothing. I have only cared for one thing. I have always felt that I should be hanged some day, and somehow the thought has annoyed me considerably; but if you can only assure me that I shall be hanged in New Hampshire—"

"Not a shadow of a doubt!"

"Bless you, my benefactress!—excuse this embrace—you have removed a great load from my breast. To be hanged in New Hampshire is happiness—it leaves an honored name behind a man, and introduces him at once into the best New Hampshire society in the other world."

I then took leave of the fortune-teller. But, seriously, is it well to glorify a murderous villain on the scaffold, as Pike was glorified in New Hampshire? Is it well to turn the penalty for a bloody crime into a reward? Is it just to do it? Is it safe?

A New Crime

Legislation Needed

This country, during the last thirty or forty years, has produced some of the most remarkable cases of insanity of which there is any mention in history. For instance, there was the Baldwin case, in Ohio, twenty-two years ago. Baldwin, from his boyhood up, had been of a vindictive, malignant, quarrelsome nature. He put a boy's eye out once, and never was heard upon any occasion to utter a regret for it. He did many such things. But at last he did something that was serious. He called at a house just after dark one evening, knocked, and when the occupant came to the door, shot him dead, and then tried to escape, but was captured. Two days before, he had wantonly insulted a helpless cripple, and the man he afterward took swift vengeance upon with an assassin bullet had knocked him down. Such was the Baldwin case. The trial was long and exciting; the community was fearfully wrought up. Men said this spiteful, bad-hearted villain had caused grief enough in his time, and now he should satisfy the law. But they were mistaken; Baldwin was *insane* when he did the deed—they had not thought of that. By the argument of counsel it was shown that at half past ten in the morning on the day of the murder, Baldwin became insane, and remained so for eleven hours and a half exactly. This just covered the case comfortably, and he was acquitted. Thus, if an unthinking and excited community had been listened to instead of the arguments of counsel, a poor crazy creature would have been held to a fearful responsibility for a mere freak of madness. Baldwin went clear, and although his relatives and friends were naturally incensed against the community for their injurious suspicions and remarks, they said let it go for this time, and did not prosecute. The Baldwins were very wealthy. This same Baldwin had momentary fits of insanity twice afterward, and on both occasions killed people he had grudges against. And on both these occasions the circumstances of the killing were so aggravated, and the murders so seemingly heartless and treacherous, that if Baldwin had not been insane he would have been hanged without the shadow of a doubt. As it was, it required all his political and family influence to get him clear in one of the cases, and cost him not less than ten thousand dollars to get clear in the other. One of these men he had notoriously been threatening to kill for twelve years. The poor creature happened, by the merest piece of ill fortune, to come along a dark alley at the very moment that Baldwin's insanity came upon him, and so he was shot in the back with a gun loaded with slugs.

Take the case of Lynch Hackett, of Pennsylvania. Twice, in public, he attacked a German butcher by the name of Bemis Feldner, with a cane, and both times Feldner whipped him with his fists. Hackett was a vain, wealthy, violent gentleman, who held his blood and family in high esteem, and believed that a reverent respect was due to his great riches. He brooded over the shame of his chastisement for two weeks, and then, in a momentary fit of insanity, armed himself to the teeth, rode into town, waited a couple of hours until he saw Feldner coming down the street with his wife on his arm, and then, as the couple passed the doorway in which he had partially concealed himself, he drove a knife into Feldner's neck, killing him instantly. The widow caught the limp form and eased it to the earth. Both were drenched with blood. Hackett jocosely remarked to her that as a professional butcher's recent wife she could appreciate the artistic neatness of the job that left her in condition to marry again, in case she wanted to. This remark, and another which he made to a friend, that his position in society made the killing of an obscure citizen simply an "eccentricity" instead of a crime, were shown to be evidences of insanity, and so Hackett escaped punishment. The jury were hardly inclined to accept these as proofs at first, inasmuch as the prisoner had never been insane before the murder, and under the tranquilizing effect of the butchering had immediately regained his right mind; but when the defense came to show that a third cousin of Hackett's wife's stepfather was insane, and not only insane, but had a nose the very counterpart of Hackett's, it was plain that insanity was hereditary in the family, and Hackett had come by it by legitimate inheritance. Of course the jury then acquitted him. But it was a merciful providence that Mrs. H.'s people had been afflicted as shown, else Hackett would certainly have been hanged.

However, it is not possible to recount all the marvelous cases of insanity that have come under the public notice in the last thirty or forty years. There was the Durgin case in New Jersey three years ago. The servant girl, Bridget Durgin, at dead of night, invaded her mistress's bedroom and carved the lady literally to pieces with a knife. Then she dragged the body to the middle of the floor, and beat and banged it with chairs and such things. Next she opened the feather beds, and strewed the contents around, saturated everything with kerosene, and set fire to the general wreck. She now took up the young child of the murdered woman in her blood-smeared hands and walked off, through the snow, with no shoes on, to a neighbor's house a quarter of a mile off, and told a string of wild, incoherent stories about some men coming and setting fire to the house; and then she cried piteously, and without seeming to think there was anything suggestive about the blood upon her hands, her clothing, and the baby, volunteered the remark that she was afraid those men had murdered her mistress! Afterward, by her own confession and other testimony, it was proved that the mistress had always been kind to the girl, consequently there was no revenge in the murder; and it was also shown that the girl took nothing away from the burning house, not even her own shoes, and consequently robbery was not the motive. Now, the reader says, "Here comes that same old plea of insanity again." But the reader has deceived himself this time. No such plea was offered in her defense. The judge sentenced her, nobody persecuted the governor with petitions for her pardon, and she was promptly hanged.

There was that youth in Pennsylvania, whose curious confession was published some years ago. It was simply a conglomeration of incoherent drivel from beginning to end, and so was his lengthy speech on the scaffold afterward. For a whole year he was haunted with a desire to disfigure a certain young woman, so that no one would marry her. He did not love her himself, and did not want to marry her, but he did not want anybody else to do it. He would not go anywhere with her, and yet was opposed to anybody else's escorting her. Upon one occasion he declined to go to a wedding with her, and when she got other company, lay in wait for the couple by the road, intending to make them go back or kill the escort. After spending sleepless nights over his ruling desire for a full year, he at last attempted its execution—that is, attempted to disfigure the young woman. It was a success. It was permanent. In trying to shoot her cheek (as she sat at the supper-table with her parents and brothers and sisters) in such a manner as to mar its comeliness, one of his bullets wandered a little out of the course, and she dropped dead. To the very last moment of his life he bewailed the ill luck that made her move her face just at the critical moment. And so he died, apparently about half persuaded that somehow it was chiefly her own fault that she got killed. This idiot was hanged. The plea of insanity was not offered.

Insanity certainly is on the increase in the world, and crime is dying out. There are no longer any murders—none worth mentioning, at any rate. Formerly, if you killed a man, it was possible that you were insane—but now, if you, having friends and money, kill a man, it is *evidence* that you are a lunatic. In these days, too, if a person of good family and high social standing steals anything, they call it *kleptomania,* and send him to the lunatic asylum. If a person of high standing squanders his fortune in dissipation, and closes his career with strychnine or a bullet, "Temporary Aberration" is what was the trouble with *him.*

Is not this insanity plea becoming rather common? Is it not so common that the reader confidently expects to see it offered in every criminal case that comes before the courts? And is it not so cheap, and so common, and often so trivial, that the reader smiles in derision when the newspaper mentions it? And is it not curious to note how very often it wins acquittal for the prisoner? Of late years it does not seem possible for a man to so conduct himself, before killing another man, as not to be manifestly insane. If he talks about the stars, he is insane. If he appears nervous and uneasy an hour before the killing, he is insane. If he weeps over a great grief, his friends shake their heads, and fear that he is "not right." If, an hour after the murder, he seems ill at ease, preoccupied, and excited, he is unquestionably insane.

Really, what we want now, is not laws against crime, but a law against *insanity.* There is where the true evil lies.

About Barbers

All things change except barbers, the ways of barbers, and the surroundings of barbers. These never change. What one experiences in a barber's shop the first time he enters one is what he always experiences in barbers' shops afterward till the end of his days. I got shaved this morning as usual. A man approached the door from Jones Street as I approached it from Main—a thing that always happens. I hurried up, but it was of no use; he entered the door one little step ahead of me, and I followed in on his heels and saw him take the only vacant chair, the one presided over by the best barber. It always happens so. I sat down, hoping that I might fall heir to the chair belonging to the better of the remaining two barbers, for he had already begun combing his man's hair, while his comrade was not yet quite done rubbing up and oiling his customer's locks. I watched the probabilities with strong interest. When I saw that No. 2 was gaining on No. 1 my interest grew to solicitude. When No. 1 stopped a moment to make change on a bath ticket for a new-comer, and lost ground in the race, my solicitude rose to anxiety. When No. 1 caught up again, and both he and his comrade were pulling the towels away and brushing the powder from their customers' cheeks, and it was about an even thing which one would say "Next!" first, my very breath stood still with the suspense. But when at the culminating moment No. 1 stopped to pass a comb a couple of times through his customer's eyebrows, I saw that he had lost the race by a single instant, and I rose indignant and quitted the shop, to keep from falling into the hands of No. 2; for I have none of that enviable firmness that enables a man to look calmly into the eyes of a waiting barber and tell him he will wait for his fellow-barber's chair.

I stayed out fifteen minutes, and then went back, hoping for better luck. Of course all the chairs were occupied now, and four men sat waiting, silent, unsociable, distraught, and looking bored, as men always do who are waiting their turn in a barber's shop. I sat down in one of the iron-armed compartments of an old sofa, and put in the time for a while reading the framed advertisements of all sorts of quack nostrums for dyeing and coloring the hair. Then I read the greasy names on the private bay-rum bottles; read the names and noted the numbers on the private shaving-cups in the pigeonholes; studied the stained and damaged cheap prints on the walls, of battles, early Presidents, and voluptuous recumbent sultanas, and the tiresome and everlasting young girl putting her grandfather's spectacles on; execrated in my heart the cheerful canary and the distracting parrot that few barbers' shops are without. Finally, I searched out the least dilapidated of last year's illustrated papers that littered the foul center-table, and conned their unjustifiable misrepresentations of old forgotten events.

At last my turn came. A voice said "Next!" and I surrendered to—No. 2, of course. It always happens so. I said meekly that I was in a hurry, and it affected him as strongly as if he had never heard it. He shoved up my head, and put a napkin under it. He plowed his fingers into my collar and fixed a towel there. He explored my hair with his claws and suggested that it needed trimming. I said I did not want it trimmed. He explored again and said it was pretty long for the present style—better have a little taken off; it needed it behind especially. I said I had had it cut only a week before. He yearned over it reflectively a moment, and then asked with a disparaging manner, who cut it? I came back at him promptly with a "You did!" I had him there. Then he fell to stirring up his lather and regarding himself in the glass, stopping now and then to get close and examine his chin critically or inspect a pimple. Then he lathered one side of my face thoroughly, and was about to lather the other, when a dog-fight attracted his attention, and he ran to the window and stayed and saw it out, losing two shillings on the result in bets with the other barbers, a thing which gave me great satisfaction. He finished lathering, and then began to rub in the suds with his hand.

He now began to sharpen his razor, on an old suspender, and was delayed a good deal on account of a controversy about a cheap masquerade ball he had figured at the night before, in red cambric and bogus ermine, as some kind of a king. He was so gratified with being chaffed about some damsel whom he had smitten with his charms that he used every means to continue the controversy by pretending to be annoyed at the chaffings of his fellows. This matter begot more surveyings of himself in the glass, and he put down his razor and brushed his hair with elaborate care, plastering an inverted arch of it down on his forehead, accomplishing an accurate "part" behind, and brushing the two wings forward over his ears with nice exactness. In the mean time the lather was drying on my face, and apparently eating into my vitals.

Now he began to shave, digging his fingers into my countenance to stretch the skin and bundling and tumbling my head this way and that as convenience in shaving demanded. As long as he was on the tough sides of my face I did not suffer; but when he began to rake, and rip, and tug at my chin, the tears came. He now made a handle of my nose, to assist him shaving the corners of my upper lip, and it was by this bit of circumstantial evidence that I discovered that a part of his duties in the shop was to clean the kerosene-lamps. I had often wondered in an indolent way whether the barbers did that, or whether it was the boss.

About this time I was amusing myself trying to guess where he would be most likely to cut me this time, but he got ahead of me, and sliced me on the end of the chin before I had got my mind made up. He immediately sharpened his razor—he might have done it before. I do not like a close shave, and would not let him go over me a second time. I tried to get him to put up his razor, dreading that he would make for the side of my chin, my pet tender spot, a place which a razor cannot touch twice without making trouble; but he said he only wanted to just smooth off one little roughness, and in the same moment he slipped his razor along the forbidden ground, and the dreaded pimple-signs of a close shave rose up smarting and answered to the call. Now he soaked his towel in bay rum, and slapped it all over my face nastily; slapped it over as if a human being ever yet washed his face in that way. Then he dried it by slapping with the dry part of the towel, as if a human being ever dried his face in such a fashion; but a barber seldom rubs you like a Christian. Next he poked bay rum into the cut place with his towel, then choked the wound with powdered starch, then soaked it with bay rum again, and would have gone on soaking and powdering it forevermore, no doubt, if I had not rebelled and begged off. He powdered my whole face now, straightened me up, and began to plow my hair thoughtfully with his hands. Then he suggested a shampoo, and said my hair needed it badly, very badly. I observed that I shampooed it myself very thoroughly in the bath yesterday. I "had him" again. He next recommended some of "Smith's Hair Glorifier," and offered to sell me a bottle. I declined. He praised the new perfume, "Jones's Delight of the Toilet," and proposed to sell me some of that. I declined again. He tendered me a tooth-wash atrocity of his own invention, and when I declined offered to trade knives with me.

He returned to business after the miscarriage of this last enterprise, sprinkled me all over, legs and all, greased my hair in defiance of my protest against it, rubbed and scrubbed a good deal of it out by the roots, and combed and brushed the rest, parting it behind, and plastering the eternal inverted arch of hair down on my forehead, and then, while combing my scant eyebrows and defiling them with pomade, strung out an account of the achievements of a six-ounce black-and-tan terrier of his till I heard the whistles blow for noon, and knew I was five minutes too late for the train. Then he snatched away the towel, brushed it lightly about my face, passed his comb through my eyebrows once more, and gaily sang out "Next!"

This barber fell down and died of apoplexy two hours later. I am waiting over a day for my revenge—I am going to attend his funeral.

Running for Governor

A few months ago I was nominated for Governor of the great state of New York, to run against Mr. John T. Smith and Mr. Blank J. Blank on an independent ticket. I somehow felt that I had one prominent advantage over these gentlemen, and that was—good character. It was easy to see by the newspapers that if ever they had known what it was to bear a good name, that time had gone by. It was plain that in these latter years they had become familiar with all manner of shameful crimes. But at the very moment that I was exalting my advantage and joying in it in secret, there was a muddy undercurrent of discomfort "riling" the deeps of my happiness, and that was—the having to hear my name bandied about in familiar connection with those of such people. I grew more and more disturbed. Finally I wrote my grandmother about it. Her answer came quick and sharp. She said:

> You have never done one single thing in all your life to be ashamed of—not one. Look at the newspapers—look at them and comprehend what sort of characters Messrs. Smith and Blank are, and then see if you are willing to lower yourself to their level and enter a public canvass with them.

It was my very thought! I did not sleep a single moment that night. But, after all, I could not recede. I was fully committed, and must go on with the fight. As I was looking listlessly over the papers at breakfast I came across this paragraph, and I may truly say I never was so confounded before.

> PERJURY.—Perhaps, now that Mr. Mark Twain is before the people as a candidate for Governor, he will condescend to explain how he came to be convicted of perjury by thirty-four witnesses in Wakawak, Cochin China, in 1863, the intent of which perjury being to rob a poor native widow and her helpless family of a meager plantain-patch, their only stay and support in their bereavement and desolation. Mr. Twain owes it to himself, as well as to the great people whose suffrages he asks, to clear this matter up. Will he do it?

I thought I should burst with amazement! Such a cruel, heartless charge! I never had *seen* Cochin China! I never had *heard* of Wakawak! I didn't know a plantain-patch from a kangaroo! I did not know what to do. I was crazed and helpless. I let the day slip away without doing anything at all. The next morning the same paper had this—nothing more:

> SIGNIFICANT.—Mr. Twain, it will be observed, is suggestively silent about the Cochin China perjury.

[*Mem.*—During the rest of the campaign this paper never referred to me in any other way than as "the infamous perjurer Twain."]

Next came the *Gazette,* with this:

> WANTED TO KNOW.—Will the new candidate for Governor deign to explain to certain of his fellow-citizens (who are suffering to vote for him!) the little circumstance of his cabin-mates in Montana losing small valuables from time to time, until at last, these things having been invariably found on Mr. Twain's person or in his "trunk" (newspaper he rolled his traps in), they felt compelled to give him a friendly admonition for his own good, and so tarred and feathered him, and rode him on a rail, and then advised him to leave a permanent vacuum in the place he usually occupied in the camp. Will he do this?

Could anything be more deliberately malicious than that? For I never was in Montana in my life.

[After this, this journal customarily spoke of me as "Twain, the Montana Thief."]

I got to picking up papers apprehensively—much as one would lift a desired blanket which he had some idea might have a rattlesnake under it. One day this met my eye:

> THE LIE NAILED.—By the sworn affidavits of Michael O'Flanagan, Esq., of the Five Points, and Mr. Snub Rafferty and Mr. Catty Mulligan, of Water Street, it is established that Mr. Mark Twain's vile statement that the lamented grandfather of our noble standard-bearer, Blank J. Blank, was hanged for highway robbery, is a brutal and gratuitous LIE, without a shadow of foundation in fact. It is disheartening to virtuous men to see such shameful means resorted to to achieve political success as the attacking of the dead in their graves, and defiling their honored names with slander. When we think of the anguish this miserable falsehood must cause the innocent relatives and friends of the deceased, we are almost driven to incite an outraged and insulted public to summary and unlawful vengeance upon the traducer. But no! let us leave him to the agony of a lacerated conscience (though if passion should get the better of the public, and in its blind fury they should do the traducer bodily injury, it is but too obvious that no jury could convict and no court punish the perpetrators of the deed).

The ingenious closing sentence had the effect of moving me out of bed with despatch that night, and out at the back door also, while the "outraged and insulted public" surged in the front way, breaking furniture and windows in their righteous indignation as they came, and taking off such property as they could carry when they went. And yet I can lay my hand upon the Book and say that I never slandered Mr. Blank's grandfather. More: I had never even heard of him or mentioned him up to that day and date.

[I will state, in passing, that the journal above quoted from always referred to me afterward as "Twain, the Body-Snatcher."]

The next newspaper article that attracted my attention was the following:

> A SWEET CANDIDATE.—Mr. Mark Twain, who was to make such a blighting speech at the mass-meeting of the Independents last night, didn't come to time! A telegram from his physician stated that he had been knocked down by a runaway team, and his leg broken in two places—sufferer lying in great agony, and so forth, and so forth, and a lot more bosh of the same sort.

And the Independents tried hard to swallow the wretched subterfuge, and pretend that they did not know what was the *real* reason of the absence of the abandoned creature whom they denominate their standard-bearer. *A certain man was seen to reel into Mr. Twain's hotel last night in a state of beastly intoxication.* It is the imperative duty of the Independents to prove that this besotted brute was not Mark Twain himself. We have them at last! This is a case that admits of no shirking. The voice of the people demands in thunder tones, "WHO WAS THAT MAN?"

It was incredible, absolutely incredible, for a moment, that it was really my name that was coupled with this disgraceful suspicion. Three long years had passed over my head since I had tasted ale, beer, wine, or liquor of any kind.

[It shows what effect the times were having on me when I say that I saw myself confidently dubbed "Mr. Delirium Tremens Twain" in the next issue of that journal without a pang—notwithstanding I knew that with monotonous fidelity the paper would go on calling me so to the very end.]

By this time anonymous letters were getting to be an important part of my mail matter. This form was common:

How about that old woman you kiked of your premises which was beging.

POL. PRY.

And this:

There is things which you have done which is unbeknowens to anybody but me. You better trot out a few dols, to yours truly, or you'll hear through the papers from

HANDY ANDY.

This is about the idea. I could continue them till the reader was surfeited, if desirable.

Shortly the principal Republican journal "convicted" me of wholesale bribery, and the leading Democratic paper "nailed" an aggravated case of blackmailing to me.

[In this way I acquired two additional names: "Twain the Filthy Corruptionist" and "Twain the Loathsome Embracer."]

By this time there had grown to be such a clamor for an "answer" to all the dreadful charges that were laid to me that the editors and leaders of my party said it would be political ruin for me to remain silent any longer. As if to make their appeal the more imperative, the following appeared in one of the papers the very next day:

> BEHOLD THE MAN!—The independent candidate still maintains silence. Because he dare not speak. Every accusation against him has been amply proved, and they have been indorsed and reindorsed by his own eloquent silence, till at this day he stands forever convicted. Look upon your candidate, Independents! Look upon the Infamous Perjurer! the Montana Thief! the Body-Snatcher! Contemplate your incarnate Delirium Tremens! your Filthy Corruptionist! your Loathsome Embracer! Gaze upon him—ponder him well—and then say if you can give your honest votes to a creature who has earned this dismal array of titles by his hideous crimes, and dares not open his mouth in denial of any one of them!

There was no possible way of getting out of it, and so, in deep humiliation, I set about preparing to "answer" a mass of baseless charges and mean and wicked falsehoods. But I never finished the task, for the very next morning a paper came out with a new horror, a fresh malignity, and seriously charged me with burning a lunatic asylum with all its inmates, because it obstructed the view from my house. This threw me into a sort of panic. Then came the charge of poisoning my uncle to get his property, with an imperative demand that the grave should be opened. This drove me to the verge of distraction. On top of this I was accused of employing toothless and incompetent old relatives to prepare the food for the foundling hospital when I was warden. I was wavering—wavering. And at last, as a due and fitting climax to the shameless persecution that party rancor had inflicted upon me, nine little toddling children, of all shades of color and degrees of raggedness, were taught to rush onto the platform at a public meeting, and clasp me around the legs and call me PA!

I gave it up. I hauled down my colors and surrendered. I was not equal to the requirements of a Gubernatorial campaign in the state of New York, and so I sent in my withdrawal from the candidacy, and in bitterness of spirit signed it, "Truly yours, *once* a decent man, but now

MARK TWAIN, I.P., M.T., B.S., D.T., F.C., and L.E."

A Mysterious Visit

The first notice that was taken of me when I "settled down" recently was by a gentleman who said he was an assessor, and connected with the U.S. Internal Revenue Department. I said I had never heard of his branch of business before, but I was very glad to see him all the same. Would he sit down? He sat down. I did not know anything particular to say, and yet I felt that people who have arrived at the dignity of keeping house must be conversational, must be easy and sociable in company. So, in default of anything else to say, I asked him if he was opening his shop in our neighborhood.

He said he was. [I did not wish to appear ignorant, but I *had* hoped he would mention what he had for sale.]

I ventured to ask him "How was trade?" And he said "So-so."

I then said we would drop in, and if we liked his house as well as any other, we would give him our custom.

He said he thought we would like his establishment well enough to confine ourselves to it—said he never saw anybody who would go off and hunt up another man in his line after trading with him once.

That sounded pretty complacent, but barring that natural expression of villainy which we all have, the man looked honest enough.

I do not know how it came about exactly, but gradually we appeared to melt down and run together, conversationally speaking, and then everything went along as comfortably as clockwork.

We talked, and talked, and talked—at least I did; and we laughed, and laughed, and laughed—at least he did. But all the time I had my presence of mind about me—I had my native shrewdness turned on "full head," as the engineers say. I was determined to find out all about his business in spite of his obscure answers—and I was determined I would have it out of him without his suspecting what I was at. I meant to trap him with a deep, deep ruse. I would tell him all about my own business, and he would naturally so warm to me during this seductive burst of confidence that he would forget himself, and tell me all about *his* affairs before he suspected what I was about. I thought to myself, My son, you little know what an old fox you are dealing with. I said:

"Now you never would guess what I made lecturing this winter and last spring?"

"No—don't believe I could, to save me. Let me see—let me see. About two thousand dollars, maybe? But no; no, sir, I know you couldn't have made that much. Say seventeen hundred, maybe?"

"Ha! ha! I knew you couldn't. My lecturing receipts for last spring and this winter were fourteen thousand seven hundred and fifty dollars. What do you think of that?"

"Why, it is amazing—perfectly amazing. I will make a note of it. And you say even this wasn't all?"

"All! Why bless you, there was my income from the *Daily Warwhoop* for four months—about—about—well, what should you say to about eight thousand dollars, for instance?"

"Say! Why, I should say I should like to see myself rolling in just such another ocean of affluence. Eight thousand! I'll make a note of it. Why man!—and on top of all this am I to understand that you had still more income?"

"Ha! ha! ha! Why, you're only in the suburbs of it, so to speak. There's my book, *The Innocents Abroad*—price $3.50 to $5, according to the binding. Listen to me. Look me in the eye. During the last four months and a half, saying nothing of sales before that, but just simply during the four months and a half, we've sold ninety-five thousand copies of that book. Ninety-five thousand! Think of it. Average four dollars a copy, say. It's nearly four hundred thousand dollars, my son. I get half."

"The suffering Moses! I'll set *that* down. Fourteen-seven-fifty—eight—

two hundred. Total, say—well, upon my word, the grand total is about two hundred and thirteen or fourteen thousand dollars! *Is* that possible?"

"Possible! If there's any mistake it's the other way. Two hundred and fourteen thousand, cash, is my income for this year if *I* know how to cipher."

Then the gentleman got up to go. It came over me most uncomfortably that maybe I had made my revelations for nothing, besides being flattered into stretching them considerably by the stranger's astonished exclamations. But no; at the last moment the gentleman handed me a large envelope, and said it contained his advertisement; and that I would find out all about his business in it; and that he would be happy to have my custom—would, in fact, be *proud* to have the custom of a man of such prodigious income; and that he used to think there were several wealthy men in the city, but when they came to trade with him he discovered that they barely had enough to live on; and that, in truth, it had been such a weary, weary age since he had seen a rich man face to face, and talked to him, and touched him with his hands, that he could hardly refrain from embracing me—in fact, would esteem it a great favor if I would *let* him embrace me.

This so pleased me that I did not try to resist, but allowed this simple-hearted stranger to throw his arms about me and weep a few tranquilizing tears down the back of my neck. Then he went his way.

As soon as he was gone I opened his advertisement. I studied it attentively for four minutes. I then called up the cook, and said:

"Hold me while I faint! Let Marie turn the griddle-cakes."

By and by, when I came to, I sent down to the rum-mill on the corner and hired an artist by the week to sit up nights and curse that stranger, and give me a lift occasionally in the daytime when I came to a hard place.

Ah, what a miscreant he was! His "advertisement" was nothing in the world but a wicked tax-return—a string of impertinent questions about my private affairs, occupying the best part of four fools-cap pages of fine print—questions, I may remark, gotten up with such marvelous ingenuity that the oldest man in the world couldn't understand what the most of them were driving at—questions, too, that were calculated to make a man report about four times his actual income to keep from swearing to a falsehood. I looked for a loophole, but there did not appear to be any. Inquiry No. 1 covered my case as generously and as amply as an umbrella could cover an ant-hill:

What were your profits, during the past year, from any trade, business, or vocation, wherever carried on?

And that inquiry was backed up by thirteen others of an equally searching nature, the most modest of which required information as to whether I had committed any burglary or highway robbery, or by any arson or other secret source of emolument had acquired property which was not enumerated in my statement of income as set opposite to inquiry No. 1.

It was plain that that stranger had enabled me to make a goose of myself. It was very, very plain; and so I went out and hired another artist. By working on my vanity, the stranger had seduced me into declaring an income of two hundred and fourteen thousand dollars. By law, one thousand dollars of this was exempt from income tax—the only relief I could see, and it was only a drop in the ocean. At the legal five per cent., I must pay to the government the sum of ten thousand six hundred and fifty dollars, income tax!

[I may remark, in this place, that I did not do it.]

I am acquainted with a very opulent man, whose house is a palace, whose table is regal, whose outlays are enormous, yet a man who has no income, as I have often noticed by the revenue returns; and to him I went for advice in my distress. He took my dreadful exhibition of receipts, he put on his glasses, he took his pen, and presto!—I was a pauper! It was the neatest thing that ever was. He did it simply by deftly manipulating the bill of "DEDUCTIONS." He set down my "State, national, and municipal taxes" at so much; my "losses by shipwreck, fire, etc.," at so much; my "losses on sales of real estate"—on "live stock sold"—on "payments for rent of homestead"—on "repairs, improvements, interest"—on "previously taxed salary as an officer of the United States army, navy, revenue service," and other things. He got astonishing "deductions" out of each and every one of these matters—each and every one of them. And when he was done he handed me the paper, and I saw at a glance that during the year my income, in the way of profits, had been *one thousand two hundred and fifty dollars and forty cents.*

"Now," said he, "the thousand dollars is exempt by law. What you want to do is to go and swear this document in and pay tax on the two hundred and fifty dollars."

[While he was making this speech his little boy Willie lifted a two-dollar greenback out of his vest pocket and vanished with it, and I would wager anything that if my stranger were to call on that little boy to-morrow he would make a false return of his income.]

"Do you," said I, "do you always work up the 'deductions' after this fashion in your own case, sir?"

"Well, I should say so! If it weren't for those eleven saving clauses under the head of 'Deductions' I should be beggared every year to support this hateful and wicked, this extortionate and tyrannical government."

This gentleman stands away up among the very best of the solid men of the city—the men of moral weight, of commercial integrity, of unimpeachable social spotlessness—and so I bowed to his example. I went down to the revenue office, and under the accusing eyes of my old visitor I stood up and swore to lie after lie, fraud after fraud, villainy after villainy, till my soul was coated inches and inches thick with perjury, and my self-respect gone for ever and ever.

But what of it? It is nothing more than thousands of the richest and proudest, and most respected, honored, and courted men in America do every year. And so I don't care. I am not ashamed. I shall simply, for the present, talk little and eschew fire-proof gloves, lest I fall into certain dreadful habits irrevocably.

TWAIN *and* NATURE

Curing a Cold

It is a good thing, perhaps, to write for the amusement of the public, but it is a far higher and nobler thing to write for their instruction, their profit, their actual and tangible benefit. The latter is the sole object of this article. If it prove the means of restoring to health one solitary sufferer among my race, of lighting up once more the fire of hope and joy in his faded eyes, or bringing back to his dead heart again the quick, generous impulses of other days, I shall be amply rewarded for my labor; my soul will be permeated with the sacred delight a Christian feels when he has done a good, unselfish deed.

Having led a pure and blameless life, I am justified in believing that no man who knows me will reject the suggestions I am about to make, out of fear that I am trying to deceive him. Let the public do itself the honor to read my experience in doctoring a cold, as herein set forth, and then follow in my footsteps.

When the White House was burned in Virginia City, I lost my home, my happiness, my constitution, and my trunk. The loss of the two first-named articles was a matter of no great consequence, since a home without a mother, or a sister, or a distant young female relative in it, to remind you, by putting your soiled linen out of sight and taking your boots down off the mantelpiece, that there are those who think about you and care for you, is easily obtained. And I cared nothing for the loss of my happiness, because, not being a poet, it could not be possible that melancholy would abide with me long. But to lose a good constitution and a better trunk were serious misfortunes. On the day of the fire my constitution succumbed to a severe cold, caused by undue exertion in getting ready to do something. I suffered to no purpose, too, because the plan I was figuring at for the extinguishing of the fire was so elaborate that I never got it completed until the middle of the following week.

The first time I began to sneeze, a friend told me to go and bathe my feet in hot water and go to bed. I did so. Shortly afterward, another friend advised me to get up and take a cold shower-bath. I did that also. Within the hour, another friend assured me that it was policy to "feed a cold and starve a fever." I had both. So I thought it best to fill myself up for the cold, and then keep dark and let the fever starve awhile.

In a case of this kind, I seldom do things by halves; I ate pretty heartily; I conferred my custom upon a stranger who had just opened his restaurant that morning; he waited near me in respectful silence until I had finished feeding my cold, when he inquired if the people about Virginia City were much afflicted with colds? I told him I thought they were. He then went out and took in his sign.

I started down toward the office, and on the way encountered another bosom friend, who told me that a quart of salt-water, taken warm, would come as near curing a cold as anything in the world. I hardly thought I had room for it, but I tried it anyhow. The result was surprising. I believed I had thrown up my immortal soul.

Now, as I am giving my experience only for the benefit of those who are troubled with the distemper I am writing about, I feel that they will see the propriety of my cautioning them against following such portions of it as proved inefficient with me, and acting upon this conviction, I warn them against warm salt-water. It may be a good enough remedy, but I think it is too severe. If I had another cold in the head, and there were no course left me but to take either an earthquake or a quart of warm salt-water, I would take my chances on the earthquake.

After the storm which had been raging in my stomach had subsided, and no more good Samaritans happening along, I went on borrowing handkerchiefs again and blowing them to atoms, as had been my custom in the early stages of my cold, until I came across a lady who had just arrived from over the plains, and who said she had lived in a part of the country where doctors were scarce, and had from necessity acquired considerable skill in the treatment of simple "family complaints." I knew she must have had much experience, for she appeared to be a hundred and fifty years old.

She mixed a decoction composed of molasses, aquafortis, turpentine, and various other drugs, and instructed me to take a wine-glass full of it every fifteen minutes. I never took but one dose; that was enough; it robbed me of all moral principle, and awoke every unworthy impulse of my nature. Under its malign influence my brain conceived miracles of meanness, but my hands were too feeble to execute them; at that time, had it not been that my strength had surrendered to a succession of assaults from infallible remedies for my cold, I am satisfied that I would have tried to rob the graveyard. Like most other people, I often feel mean, and act accordingly; but until I took that medicine I had never reveled in such supernatural depravity, and felt proud of it. At the end of two days I was ready to go to doctoring again. I took a few more unfailing remedies, and finally drove my cold from my head to my lungs.

I got to coughing incessantly, and my voice fell below zero; I conversed in a thundering bass, two octaves below my natural tone; I could only compass my regular nightly repose by coughing myself down to a state of utter exhaustion, and then the moment I began to talk in my sleep, my discordant voice woke me up again.

My case grew more and more serious every day. Plain gin was recommended; I took it. Then gin and molasses; I took that also. Then gin and onions; I added the onions, and took all three. I detected no particular result, however, except that I had acquired a breath like a buzzard's.

I found I had to travel for my health. I went to Lake Bigler with my reportorial comrade, Wilson. It is gratifying to me to reflect that we traveled in considerable style; we went in the Pioneer coach, and my friend took all his baggage with him, consisting of two excellent silk handkerchiefs and a daguerreotype of his grandmother. We sailed and hunted and fished and danced all day, and I doctored my cough all night. By managing in this way, I made out to improve every hour in the twenty-four. But my disease continued to grow worse.

A sheet-bath was recommended. I had never refused a remedy yet, and it seemed poor policy to commence then; therefore I determined to take a sheet-bath, notwithstanding I had no idea what sort of arrangement it was. It was administered at midnight, and the weather was very frosty. My breast and back were bared, and a sheet (there appeared to be a thousand yards of it) soaked in ice-water, was wound around me until I resembled a swab for a Columbiad.

It is a cruel expedient. When the chilly rag touches one's warm flesh, it makes him start with sudden violence, and gasp for breath just as men do in the death-agony. It froze the marrow in my bones and stopped the beating of my heart. I thought my time had come.

Young Wilson said the circumstance reminded him of an anecdote about a negro who was being baptized, and who slipped from the parson's grasp, and came near being drowned. He floundered around, though, and finally rose up out of the water considerably strangled and furiously angry, and started ashore at once, spouting water like a whale, and remarking, with great asperity, that "one o' dese days some gen'l'man's nigger gwyne to get killed wid jis' such damn foolishness as dis!"

Never take a sheet-bath—never. Next to meeting a lady acquaintance who, for reasons best known to herself, don't see you when she looks at you, and don't know you when she does see you, it is the most uncomfortable thing in the world.

But, as I was saying, when the sheet-bath failed to cure my cough, a lady friend recommended the application of a mustard plaster to my breast. I believe that would have cured me effectually, if it had not been for young Wilson. When I went to bed, I put my mustard plaster—which was a very gorgeous one, eighteen inches square—where I could reach it when I was ready for it. But young Wilson got hungry in the night, and—here is food for the imagination.

After sojourning a week at Lake Bigler, I went to Steamboat Springs, and, besides the steam-baths, I took a lot of the vilest medicines that were ever concocted. They would have cured me, but I had to go back to Virginia City, where, notwithstanding the variety of new remedies I absorbed every day, I managed to aggravate my disease by carelessness and undue exposure.

I finally concluded to visit San Francisco, and the first day I got there a lady at the hotel told me to drink a quart of whisky every twenty-four hours, and a friend up-town recommended precisely the same course. Each advised me to take a quart; that made half a gallon. I did it, and still live.

Now, with the kindest motives in the world, I offer for the consideration of consumptive patients the variegated course of treatment I have lately gone through. Let them try it; if it don't cure, it can't more than kill them.

The Bee

It was Maeterlinck who introduced me to the bee. I mean, in the psychical and in the poetical way. I had had a business introduction earlier. It was when I was a boy. It is strange that I should remember a formality like that so long; it must be nearly sixty years.

Bee scientists always speak of the bee as she. It is because all the important bees are of that sex. In the hive there is one married bee, called the queen; she has fifty thousand children; of these, about one hundred are sons; the rest are daughters. Some of the daughters are young maids, some are old maids, and all are virgins and remain so.

Every spring the queen comes out of the hive and flies away with one of her sons and marries him. The honeymoon lasts only an hour or two; then the queen divorces her husband and returns home competent to lay two million eggs. This will be enough to last the year, but not more than enough, because hundreds of bees get drowned every day, and other hundreds are eaten by birds, and it is the queen's business to keep the population up to standard—say, fifty thousand. She must always have that many children on hand and efficient during the busy season, which is summer, or winter would catch the community short of food. She lays from two thousand to three thousand eggs a day, according to the demand;

and she must exercise judgment, and not lay more than are needed in a slim flower-harvest, nor fewer than are required in a prodigal one, or the board of directors will dethrone her and elect a queen that has more sense.

There are always a few royal heirs in stock and ready to take her place—ready and more than anxious to do it, although she is their own mother. These girls are kept by themselves, and are regally fed and tended from birth. No other bees get such fine food as they get, or live such a high and luxurious life. By consequence they are larger and longer and sleeker than their working sisters. And they have a curved sting, shaped like a scimitar, while the others have a straight one.

A common bee will sting any one or anybody, but a royalty stings royalties only. A common bee will sting and kill another common bee, for cause, but when it is necessary to kill the queen other ways are employed. When a queen has grown old and slack and does not lay eggs enough one of her royal daughters is allowed to come to attack her, the rest of the bees looking on at the duel and seeing fair play. It is a duel with the curved stings. If one of the fighters gets hard pressed and gives it up and runs, she is brought back and must try again—once, maybe twice; then, if she runs yet once more for her life, judicial death is her portion; her children pack themselves into a ball around her person and hold her in that compact grip two or three days, until she starves to death or is suffocated. Meantime the victor bee is receiving royal honors and performing the one royal function —laying eggs.

As regards the ethics of the judicial assassination of the queen, that is a matter of politics, and will be discussed later, in its proper place.

During substantially the whole of her short life of five or six years the queen lives in the Egyptian darkness and stately seclusion of the royal apartments, with none about her but plebeian servants, who give her empty lip-affection in place of the love which her heart hungers for; who spy upon her in the interest of her waiting heirs, and report and exaggerate her defects and deficiencies to them; who fawn upon her and flatter her to her face and slander her behind her back; who grovel before her in the day of her power and forsake her in her age and weakness. There she sits, friendless, upon her throne through the long night of her life, cut off from the consoling sympathies and sweet companionship and loving endearments which she craves, by the gilded barriers of her awful rank; a forlorn exile in her own house and home, weary object of formal ceremonies and machine-made worship, winged child of the sun, native to the free air and the blue skies and the flowery fields, doomed by the splendid accident of her birth to trade this priceless heritage for a black captivity, a tinsel grandeur, and a loveless life, with shame and insult at the end and a cruel death—and condemned by the human instinct in her to hold the bargain valuable!

Huber, Lubbock, Maeterlinck—in fact, all the great authorities—are agreed in denying that the bee is a member of the human family. I do not know why they have done this, but I think it is from dishonest motives. Why, the innumerable facts brought to light by their own painstaking and exhaustive experiments prove that if there is a master fool in the world, it is the bee. That seems to settle it.

But that is the way of the scientist. He will spend thirty years in building up a mountain range of facts with the intent to prove a certain theory; then he is so happy in his achievement that as a rule he overlooks the main chief fact of all—that his accumulation proves an entirely different thing. When you point out this miscarriage to him he does not answer your letters; when you call to convince him, the servant prevaricates and you do not get in. Scientists have odious manners, except when you prop up their theory; then you can borrow money of them.

To be strictly fair, I will concede that now and then one of them will answer your letter, but when they do they avoid the issue—you cannot pin them down. When I discovered that the bee was human I wrote about it to all those scientists whom I have just mentioned. For evasions, I have seen nothing to equal the answers I got.

After the queen, the personage next in importance in the hive is the virgin. The virgins are fifty thousand or one hundred thousand in number, and they are the workers, the laborers. No work is done, in the hive or out of it, save by them. The males do not work, the queen does no work, unless laying eggs is work, but it does not seem so to me. There are only two million of them, anyway, and all of five months to finish the contract in. The distribution of work in a hive is as cleverly and elaborately specialized as it is in a vast American machine-shop or factory. A bee that has been trained to one of the many and various industries of the concern doesn't know how to exercise any other, and would be offended if asked to take a hand in anything outside of her profession. She is as human as a cook; and if you should ask the cook to wait on the table, you know what would happen. Cooks will play the piano if you like, but they draw the line there. In my time I have asked a cook to chop wood, and I know about these things. Even the hired girl has her frontiers; true, they are vague, they are ill-defined, even flexible, but they are there. This is not conjecture; it is founded on the absolute. And then the butler. You ask the butler to wash the dog. It is just as I say; there is much to be learned in these ways, without going to books. Books are very well, but books do not cover the whole domain of esthetic human culture. Pride of profession is one of the boniest bones of existence, if not the boniest. Without doubt it is so in the hive.

A Majestic Literary Fossil

If I were required to guess offhand, and without collusion with higher minds, what is the bottom cause of the amazing material and intellectual advancement of the last fifty years, I should guess that it was the modern-born and previously non-existent disposition on the part of men to believe that a new idea can have value. With the long roll of the mighty names of history present in our minds, we are not privileged to doubt that for the past twenty or thirty centuries every conspicuous civilization in the world has produced intellects able to invent and create the things which make our day a wonder; perhaps we may be justified in inferring, then, that the reason they did not do it was that the public reverence for old ideas and hostility to new ones always stood in their way, and was a wall they could not break down or climb over. The prevailing tone of old books regarding new ideas is one of suspicion and uneasiness at times, and at other times contempt. By contrast, our day is indifferent to old ideas, and even considers that their age makes their value questionable, but jumps at a new idea with enthusiasm and high hope—a hope which is high because it has not been accustomed to being disappointed. I make no guess as to just when this disposition was born to us, but it certainly is ours, was not possessed by any century before us, is our peculiar mark and badge, and is doubtless the bottom reason why we are a race of lightning-shod Mercuries, and proud of it—instead of being, like our ancestors, a race of plodding crabs, and proud of that.

So recent is this change from a three or four thousand year twilight to the flash and glare of open day that I have walked in both, and yet am not old. Nothing is to-day as it was when I was an urchin; but when I was an urchin, nothing was much different from what it had always been in this world. Take a single detail, for example—medicine. Galen could have come into my sick-room at any time during my first seven years—I mean any day when it wasn't fishing weather, and there wasn't any choice but school or sickness—and he could have sat down there and stood my doctor's watch without asking a question. He would have smelt around among the wilderness of cups and bottles and vials on the table and the shelves, and missed not a stench that used to glad him two thousand years before, nor discovered one that was of a later date. He would have examined me, and run across only one disappointment—I was already salivated; I would have him there; for I was always salivated, calomel was so cheap. He would get out his lancet then; but I would have him again; our family doctor didn't allow blood to accumulate in the system. However, he could take dipper and ladle, and freight me up with old familiar doses that had come down from Adam to his time and mine; and he could go out with a wheelbarrow and gather weeds and offal, and build some more, while those others were getting in their work. And if our reverend doctor came and found him there, he would be dumb with awe, and would get down and worship him. Whereas if Galen should appear among us to-day, he could not stand anybody's watch; he would inspire no awe; he would be told he was a back number, and it would surprise him to see that that fact counted against him, instead of in his favor. He wouldn't know our medicines; he wouldn't know our practice; and the first time he tried to introduce his own we would hang him.

This introduction brings me to my literary relic. It is a *Dictionary of Medicine,* by Dr. James, of London, assisted by Mr. Boswell's Doctor Samuel Johnson, and is a hundred and fifty years old, it having been published at the time of the rebellion of '45. If it had been sent against the Pretender's troops there probably wouldn't have been a survivor. In 1861 this deadly book was still working the cemeteries—down in Virginia. For three generations and a half it had been going quietly along, enriching the earth with its slain. Up to its last free day it was trusted and believed in, and its devastating advice taken, as was shown by notes inserted between its leaves. But our troops captured it and brought it home, and it has been out of business since. These remarks from its preface are in the true spirit of the olden time, sodden with worship of the old, disdain of the new:

> If we inquire into the Improvements which have been made by the Moderns, we shall be forced to confess that we have so little Reason to value ourselves beyond the Antients, or to be tempted to condemn them, that we cannot give stronger or more convincing Proofs of our own Ignorance, as well as our Pride.
>
> Among all the systematical Writers, I think there are very few who refuse the Preference to *Hieron, Fabricius ab Aquapendente,* as a Person of unquestion'd Learning and Judgment; and yet is he not asham'd to let his Readers know that *Celsus* among the Latins, *Paulus Ægineta* among the Greeks, and *Albucasis* among the Arabians, whom I am unwilling to place among the Moderns, tho' he liv'd but six hundred Years since, are the Triumvirate to whom he principally stands indebted, for the Assistance he had receiv'd from them in composing his excellent Book.
>
> [In a previous paragraph are puffs of Galen, Hippocrates, and other debris of the Old Silurian Period of Medicine.] How many Operations are there now in Use which were unknown to the Antients?

That is true. The surest way for a nation's scientific men to prove that they were proud and ignorant was to claim to have found out something fresh in the course of a thousand years or so. Evidently the peoples of this book's day regarded themselves as children, and their remote ancestors as the only grown-up people that had existed. Consider the contrast: without offense, without over-egotism, our own scientific men may and do regard themselves as grown people and their grandfathers as children. The change here presented is probably the most sweeping that has ever come over mankind in the history of the race. It is the utter reversal, in a couple of generations, of an attitude which had been maintained without challenge or interruption from the earliest antiquity. It amounts to creating man over again on a new plan; he was a canal-boat before, he is an ocean greyhound to-day. The change from reptile to bird was not more tremendous, and it took longer.

It is curious. If you read between the lines what this author says about Brer Albucasis, you detect that in venturing to compliment him he has to whistle a little to keep his courage up, because Albucasis "liv'd but six hundred Years since," and therefore came so uncomfortably near being a "modern" that one couldn't respect him without risk.

Phlebotomy, Venesection—terms to signify bleeding—are not often heard in our day, because we have ceased to believe that the best way to make a bank or a body healthy is to squander its capital; but in our author's time the physician went around with a hatful of lancets on his person all the time, and took a hack at every patient whom he found still alive. He robbed his man of pounds and pounds of blood at a single operation. The details of this sort in this book make terrific reading. Apparently even the healthy did not escape, but were bled twelve times a year, on a particular day of the month, and exhaustively purged besides. Here is a specimen of the vigorous old-time practice; it occurs in our author's adoring biography of a Doctor Aretæus, a licensed assassin of Homer's time, or thereabouts:

> In a Quinsey he used Venesection, and allow'd the Blood to flow till the Patient was ready to faint away.

There is no harm in trying to cure a headache—in our day. You can't do it, but you get more or less entertainment out of trying, and that is something; besides, you live to tell about it, and that is more. A century or so ago you could have had the first of these features in rich variety, but you might fail of the other once—and once would do. I quote:

> As Dissections of Persons who have died of severe Head-achs, which have been related by Authors, are too numerous to be inserted in this Place, we shall here abridge some of the most curious and important Observations relating to this Subject, collected by the celebrated *Bonetus.*

The celebrated Bonetus's "Observation No. 1" seems to me a sufficient sample, all by itself, of what people used to have to stand any time between the creation of the world and the birth of your father and mine when they had the disastrous luck to get a "Head-ach":

> A certain Merchant, about forty Years of Age, of a Melancholic Habit, and deeply involved in the Cares of the World, was, during the Dog-days, seiz'd with a violent pain of his Head, which some time after oblig'd him to keep his Bed.

I, being call'd, order'd Venesection in the Arms, the Application of Leeches to the Vessels of his Nostrils, Forehead, and Temples, as also to those behind his Ears; I likewise prescrib'd the Application of Cupping-glasses, with Scarification, to his Back: But notwithstanding these Precautions, he dy'd. If any Surgeon, skill'd in Arteriotomy, had been present, I should have also order'd that Operation.

I looked for "Arteriotomy" in this same Dictionary, and found this definition: "The opening of an Artery with a View of taking away Blood." Here was a person who was being bled in the arms, forehead, nostrils, back, temples, and behind the ears, yet the celebrated Bonetus was not satisfied, but wanted to open an artery "with a View" to insert a pump, probably. "Notwithstanding these Precautions"—he dy'd. No art of speech could more quaintly convey this butcher's innocent surprise. Now that we know what the celebrated Bonetus did when he wanted to relieve a Head-ach, it is no trouble to infer that if he wanted to comfort a man that had a Stomach-ach he disemboweled him.

I have given one "Observation"—a single Head-ach case; but the celebrated Bonetus follows it with eleven more. Without enlarging upon the matter, I merely note this coincidence—they all "dy'd." Not one of these people got well; yet this obtuse hyena sets down every little gory detail of the several assassinations as complacently as if he imagined he was doing a useful and meritorious work in perpetuating the methods of his crimes. "Observations," indeed! They are confessions.

According to this book, "the Ashes of an Ass's hoof mix'd with Woman's milk cures chilblains." Length of time required not stated. Another item: "The constant Use of Milk is bad for the Teeth, and causes them to rot, and loosens the Gums." Yet in our day babies use it constantly without hurtful results. This author thinks you ought to wash out your mouth with wine before venturing to drink milk. Presently, when we come to notice what fiendish decoctions those people introduced into their stomachs by way of medicine, we shall wonder that they could have been afraid of milk.

It appears that they had false teeth in those days. They were made of ivory sometimes, sometimes of bone, and were thrust into the natural sockets, and lashed to each other and to the neighboring teeth with wires or with silk threads. They were not to eat with, nor to laugh with, because they dropped out when not in repose. You could smile with them, but you had to practise first, or you would overdo it. They were not for business, but just decoration. They filled the bill according to their lights.

This author says "the Flesh of Swine nourishes above all other eatables." In another place he mentions a number of things, and says "these are very easy to be digested; so is Pork." This is probably a lie. But he is pretty handy in that line; and when he hasn't anything of the sort in stock himself he gives some other expert an opening. For instance, under the head of "Attractives" he introduces Paracelsus, who tells of a nameless "Specific"—quantity of it not set down—which is able to draw a hundred pounds of flesh to itself—distance not stated—and then proceeds, "It happen'd in our own Days that an Attractive of this Kind drew a certain Man's Lungs up into his Mouth, by which he had the Misfortune to be suffocated." This is more than doubtful. In the first place, his Mouth couldn't accommodate his Lungs—in fact, his Hat couldn't; secondly, his Heart being more eligibly Situated, it would have got the Start of his Lungs, and, being a lighter Body, it would have Sail'd in ahead and Occupied the Premises; thirdly, you will Take Notice a Man with his Heart in his Mouth hasn't any Room left for his Lungs—he has got all he can Attend to; and finally, the Man must have had the Attractive in his Hat, and when he saw what was going to Happen he would have Remov'd it and Sat Down on it. Indeed, he would; and then how could it Choke him to Death? I don't believe the thing ever happened at all.

Paracelsus adds this effort: "I myself saw a Plaister which attracted as much Water as was sufficient to fill a Cistern; and by these very Attractives Branches may be torn from Trees; and, which is still more surprising, a Cow may be carried up into the Air." Paracelsus is dead now; he was always straining himself that way.

They liked a touch of mystery along with their medicine in the olden time; and the medicine-man of that day, like the medicine-man of our Indian tribes, did what he could to meet the requirement:

> *Arcanum.* A Kind of Remedy whose Manner of Preparation, or singular Efficacy, is industriously concealed, in order to enhance its Value. By the Chymists it is generally defined a thing secret, incorporeal, and immortal, which cannot be Known by Man, unless by Experience; for it is the Virtue of every thing, which operates a thousand times more than the thing itself.

To me the butt end of this explanation is not altogether clear. A little of what they knew about natural history in the early times is exposed here and there in the Dictionary.

> *The Spider.* It is more common than welcome in Houses. Both the Spider and its Web are used in Medicine: The Spider is said to avert the Paroxysms of Fevers, if it be apply'd to the Pulse of the Wrist, or the Temples; but it is peculiarly recommended against a Quartan, being enclosed in the Shell of a Hazlenut.
>
> Among approved Remedies, I find that the distill'd Water of Black Spiders is an excellent Cure for Wounds, and that this was one of the choice Secrets of Sir Walter Raleigh.
>
> The Spider which some call the Catcher, or Wolf, being beaten into a Plaister, then sew'd up in Linen, and apply'd to the Forehead or Temples, prevents the Returns of a Tertian.
>
> There is another Kind of Spider, which spins a white, fine, and thick Web. One of this Sort, wrapp'd in Leather, and hung about the Arm, will avert the Fit of a Quartan. Boil'd in Oil of Roses, and instilled into the Ears, it eases Pains in those Parts. *Dioscorides, Lib. 2, Cap. 68.*
>
> Thus we find that Spiders have in all Ages been celebrated for their febrifuge Virtues; and it is worthy of Remark, that a Spider is usually given to Monkeys, and is esteem'd a sovereign Remedy for the Disorders those Animals are principally subject to.

Then follows a long account of how a dying woman, who had suffered nine hours a day with an ague during eight weeks, and who had been bled dry some dozens of times meantime without apparent benefit, was at last forced to swallow several wads of "Spiders-web," whereupon she straightway mended, and promptly got well. So the sage is full of enthusiasm over the spider-webs, and mentions only in the most casual way the discontinuance of the daily bleedings, plainly never suspecting that this had anything to do with the cure.

> As concerning the venomous Nature of Spiders, *Scaliger* takes notice of a certain Species of them (which he had forgotten) whose Poison was of so great Force as to affect one *Vincentinus* thro' the Sole of his Shoe, by only treading on it.

The sage takes that in without a strain, but the following case was a trifle too bulky for him, as his comment reveals:

In Gascony, observes *Scaliger,* there is a very small Spider, which, running over a Looking-glass, will crack the same by the Force of her Poison. *(A mere Fable.)*

But he finds no fault with the following facts:

Remarkable is the Enmity recorded between this Creature and the Serpent, as also the Toad: Of the former it is reported, That, lying (as he thinks securely) under the Shadow of some Tree, the Spider lets herself down by her Thread, and, striking her Proboscis or Sting into the Head, with that Force and Efficacy, injecting likewise her venomous Juice, that, wringing himself about, he immediately grows giddy, and quickly after dies.

When the Toad is bit or stung in Fight with this Creature, the Lizard, Adder, or other that is poisonous, she finds relief from Plantain, to which she resorts. In her Combat with the Toad, the Spider useth the same Stratagem as with the Serpent, hanging by her own Thread from the Bough of some Tree, and striking her Sting into her enemy's Head, upon which the other, enraged, swells up, and sometimes bursts.

To this Effect is the Relation of *Erasmus,* which he saith he had from one of the Spectators, of a Person lying along upon the Floor of his Chamber, in the Summer-time, to sleep in a supine Posture, when a Toad, creeping out of some green Rushes, brought just before in, to adorn the Chimney, gets upon his Face, and with his Feet sits across his Lips. To force off the Toad, says the Historian, would have been accounted sudden Death to the Sleeper; and to leave her there, very cruel and dangerous; so that upon Consultation it was concluded to find out a Spider, which, together with her Web, and the Window she was fasten'd to, was brought carefully, and so contrived as to be held perpendicularly to the Man's Face; which was no sooner done, but the Spider, discovering his Enemy, let himself down, and struck in his Dart, afterwards betaking himself up again to his Web; the Toad swell'd, but as yet kept his station: The second Wound is given quickly after by the Spider, upon which he swells yet more, but remain'd alive still.—The Spider, coming down again by his Thread, gives the third Blow; and the Toad, taking off his Feet from over the Man's Mouth, fell off dead.

To which the sage appends this grave remark, "And so much for the historical Part." Then he passes on to a consideration of "the Effects and Cure of the Poison."

One of the most interesting things about this tragedy is the double sex of the Toad, and also of the Spider.

Now the sage quotes from one Turner:

I remember, when a very young Practitioner, being sent for to a certain Woman, whose Custom was usually, when she went to the Cellar by Candle-light, to go also a Spider-hunting, setting Fire to their Webs, and burning them with the Flame of the Candle still as she pursued them. It happen'd at length, after this Whimsy had been follow'd a long time, one of them sold his Life much dearer than those Hundreds she had destroy'd; for, lighting upon the melting Tallow of her Candle, near the Flame, and his legs being entangled therein, so that he could not extricate himself, the Flame or Heat coming on, he was made a Sacrifice to his cruel Persecutor, who delighting her Eyes with the Spectacle, still waiting for the Flame to take hold of him, he presently burst with a great Crack, and threw his Liquor, some into her Eyes, but mostly upon her Lips; by means of which, flinging away her Candle, she cry'd out for Help, as fansying herself kill'd already with the Poison. However in the Night her Lips swell'd up excessively, and one of her Eyes was much inflam'd; also her Tongue and Gums were somewhat affected; and, whether from the Nausea excited by the Thoughts of the Liquor getting into her Mouth, or from the poisonous Impressions communicated by the nervous *Fibrillæ* of those Parts to those of the Ventricle, a continual Vomiting attended: To take off which, when I was call'd, I order'd a Glass of mull'd Sack, with a Scruple of Salt of Wormwood, and some hours after a Theriacal Bolus, which she flung up again. I embrocated the Lips with the Oil of Scorpions mix'd with the Oil of Roses; and, in Consideration of the Ophthalmy, tho' I was not certain but the Heat of the Liquor, rais'd by the Flame of the Candle before the Body of the Creature burst, might, as well as the Venom, excite the Disturbance, (altho' Mr. *Boyle's* Case of a Person blinded by this Liquor dropping from the living Spider, makes the latter sufficient;) yet observing the great Tumefaction of the Lips, together with the other Symptoms not likely to arise from simple Heat, I was inclin'd to believe a real Poison in the Case; and therefore not daring to let her Blood in the Arm [If a man's throat were cut in those old days, the doctor would come and bleed the other end of him], I did, however, with good Success, set Leeches to her Temples, which took off much of the Inflammation; and her Pain was likewise abated, by instilling into her Eyes a thin Mucilage of the Seeds of Quinces and white Poppies extracted with Rose-water; yet the Swelling on the Lips increased; upon which, in the Night, she wore a Cataplasm prepared by boiling the Leaves of Scordium, Rue, and Elder-flowers, and afterwards thicken'd with the Meal of Vetches. In the mean time, her Vomiting having left her, she had given her, between whiles, a little Draught of Distill'd Water of Carduus Benedictus and Scordium, with some of the Theriaca dissolved; and upon going off of the Symptoms, an old Woman came luckily in, who, with Assurance suitable to those People, (whose Ignorance and Poverty is their Safety and Protection,) took off the Dressings, promising to cure her in two Days' time, altho' she made it as many Weeks, yet had the Reputation of the Cure; applying only Plantain Leaves bruis'd and mixed with Cobwebs, dropping the Juice into her Eye, and giving some Spoonfuls of the same inwardly, two or three times a day.

So ends the wonderful affair. Whereupon the sage gives Mr. Turner the following shot—strengthening it with italics—and passes calmly on:

I must remark upon this History, that the Plantain, as a Cooler, was much more likely to cure this Disorder than warmer Applications and Medicines.

How strange that narrative sounds to-day, and how grotesque, when one reflects that it was a grave contribution to medical "science" by an old and reputable physician! Here was all this to-do—two weeks of it—over a woman who had scorched her eye and her lips with candle grease. The poor wench is as elaborately dosed, bled, embrocated, and otherwise harried and bedeviled as if there had been really something the matter with her; and when a sensible old woman comes along at last, and treats the trivial case in a sensible way, the educated ignoramus rails at her ignorance, serenely unconscious of his own. It is pretty suggestive of the former snail-pace of medical progress that the spider retained his terrors during three thousand years, and only lost them within the last thirty or forty.

Observe what imagination can do. "This same young Woman" used to be so affected by the strong (imaginary) smell which emanated from the burning spiders that "the Objects about her seem'd to turn round; she grew faint also with cold Sweats, and sometimes a light Vomiting." There could have been Beer in that cellar as well as Spiders.

Here are some more of the effects of imagination: "*Sennertus* takes Notice of the Signs of the Bite or Sting of this Insect to be a Stupor or Numbness upon the Part, with a sense of Cold, Horror, or Swelling of the Abdomen, Paleness of the Face, involuntary Tears, Trembling, Contractions, a (. . .), Convulsions, cold Sweats; but these latter chiefly when the Poison has been received inwardly," whereas the modern physician holds that a few spiders taken inwardly, by a bird or a man, will do neither party any harm.

The above "Signs" are not restricted to spider bites—often they merely indicate fright. I have seen a person with a hornet in his pantaloons exhibit them all.

> As to the Cure, not slighting the usual Alexipharmics taken internally, the Place bitten must be immediately washed with Salt Water, or a Sponge dipped in hot Vinegar, or fomented with a Decoction of Mallows, Origanum, and Mother of Thyme; after which a Cataplasm must be laid on of the Leaves of Bay, Rue, Leeks, and the Meal of Barley, boiled with Vinegar, or of Garlick and Onions, contused with Goat's Dung and fat Figs. Meantime the Patient should eat Garlick and drink Wine freely.

As for me, I should prefer the spider bite. Let us close this review with a sample or two of the earthquakes which the old-time doctor used to introduce into his patient when he could find room. Under this head we have "Alexander's Golden Antidote," which is good for—well, pretty much everything. It is probably the old original first patent-medicine. It is built as follows:

> Take of Afarabocca, Henbane, Carpobalsamum, each two Drams and a half; of Cloves, Opium, Myrrh, Cyperus, each two Drams; of Opobalsamum, Indian Leaf, Cinnamon, Zedoary, Ginger, Coftus, Coral, Cassia, Euphorbium, Gum Tragacanth, Frankincense, Styrax Calamita, Celtic, Nard, Spignel, Hartwort, Mustard, Saxifrage, Dill, Anise, each one Dram; of Xylaloes, Rheum, Ponticum, Alipta Moschata, Castor, Spikenard, Galangals, Opoponax, Anacardium, Mastich, Brimstone, Peony, Eringo, Pulp of Dates, red and white Hermodactyls, Roses, Thyme, Acorns, Penyroyal, Gentian, the Bark of the Root of Mandrake, Germander, Valerian, Bishops Weed, Bay-berries, long and white Pepper, Xylobalsamum, Carnabadium, Macodonian, Parsley-seeds, Lovage, the Seeds of Rue, and Sinon, of each a Dram and a half; of pure Gold, pure Silver, Pearls not perforated, the Blatta Byzantina, the Bone of the Stag's Heart, of each the Quantity of fourteen Grains of Wheat; of Sapphire, Emerald, and Jasper Stones, each one Dram; of Haslenut, two Drams; of Pellitory of Spain, Shavings of Ivory, Calamus Odoratus, each the Quantity of twenty-nine Grains of Wheat; of Honey or Sugar a sufficient Quantity.

Serve with a shovel. No; one might expect such an injunction after such formidable preparation; but it is not so. The dose recommended is "the Quantity of an Haslenut." Only that; it is because there is so much jewelry in it, no doubt.

> *Aqua Limacum.* Take a great Peck of Garden-snails, and wash them in a great deal of Beer, and make your Chimney very clean, and set a Bushel of Charcoal on Fire; and when they are thoroughly kindled, make a Hole in the Middle of the Fire, and put the Snails in, and scatter more Fire amongst them, and let them roast till they make a Noise; then take them out, and, with a Knife and coarse Cloth, pick and wipe away all the green froth: Then break them, Shells and all, in a Stone Mortar. Take also a Quart of Earth-worms, and scour them with Salt, divers times over. Then take two Handfuls of Angelica and lay them in the Bottom of the Still; next lay two Handfuls of Celandine; next a Quart of Rosemary-flowers; then two Handfuls of Bears-foot and Agrimony; then Fenugreek; then Turmerick; of each one Ounce: Red Dock-root, Bark of Barberry-trees, Wood-sorrel, Betony, of each two Handfuls.—Then lay the Snails and Worms on the top of the Herbs; and then two Handfuls of Goose Dung, and two Handfuls of Sheep Dung. Then put in three Gallons of Strong Ale, and place the pot where you mean to set Fire under it: Let it stand all Night, or longer; in the Morning put in three Ounces of Cloves well beaten, and a small Quantity of Saffron, dry'd to Powder; then six Ounces of Shavings of Hartshorn, which must be uppermost. Fix on the Head and Refrigeratory, and distil according to Art.

There. The book does not say whether this is all one dose, or whether you have a right to split it and take a second chance at it, in case you live. Also, the book does not seem to specify what ailment it was for; but it is of no consequence, for of course that would come out on the inquest.

Upon looking further, I find that this formidable nostrum is "good for raising Flatulencies in the Stomach"—meaning *from* the stomach, no doubt. So it would appear that when our progenitors chanced to swallow a sigh, they emptied a sewer down their throats to expel it. It is like dislodging skippers from cheese with artillery.

When you reflect that your own father had to take such medicines as the above, and that you would be taking them to-day yourself but for the introduction of homeopathy, which forced the old-school doctor to stir around and learn something of a rational nature about his business, you may honestly feel grateful that homeopathy survived the attempts of the allopathists to destroy it, even though you may never employ any physician but an allopathist while you live.

At the Appetite Cure

This establishment's name is Hochberghaus. It is in Bohemia, a short day's journey from Vienna, and being in the Austrian Empire is, of course, a health resort. The empire is made up of health resorts; it distributes health to the whole world. Its waters are all medicinal. They are bottled and sent throughout the earth; the natives themselves drink beer. This is self-sacrifice, apparently—but outlanders who have drunk Vienna beer have another idea about it. Particularly the Pilsener which one gets in a small cellar up an obscure back lane in the First Bezirk—the name has escaped me, but the place is easily found: You inquire for the Greek church; and when you get to it, go right along by—the next house is that little beer-mill. It is remote from all traffic and all noise; it is always Sunday there. There are two small rooms, with low ceilings supported by massive arches; the arches and ceilings are whitewashed, otherwise the rooms would pass for cells in the dungeons of a bastille. The furniture is plain and cheap, there is no ornamentation anywhere; yet it is a heaven for the self-sacrificers, for the beer there is incomparable; there is nothing like it elsewhere in the world. In the first room you will find twelve or fifteen ladies and gentlemen of civilian quality; in the other one a dozen generals and ambassadors. One may live in Vienna many months and not hear of this place; but having once heard of it and sampled it the sampler will afterward infest it.

However, this is all incidental—a mere passing note of gratitude for blessings received—it has nothing to do with my subject. My subject is health resorts. All unhealthy people ought to domicile themselves in Vienna, and use that as a base, making flights from time to time to the outlying resorts, according to need. A flight to Marienbad to get rid of fat; a flight to Carlsbad to get rid of rheumatism; a flight to Kaltenleutgeben to take the water cure and get rid of the rest of the diseases. It is all so handy. You can stand in Vienna and toss a biscuit into Kaltenleutgeben, with a twelve-inch gun. You can run out thither at any time of the day; you go by the phenomenally slow trains, and yet inside of an hour you have exchanged the glare and swelter of the city for wooded hills, and shady forest paths, and soft, cool airs, and the music of birds, and the repose and peace of paradise.

And there are plenty of other health resorts at your service and convenient to get at from Vienna; charming places, all of them; Vienna sits in the center of a beautiful world of mountains with now and then a lake and forests; in fact, no other city is so fortunately situated.

There are abundance of health resorts, as I have said. Among them this place—Hochberghaus. It stands solitary on the top of a densely wooded mountain, and is a building of great size. It is called the Appetite Anstalt, and people who have lost their appetites come here to get them restored. When I arrived I was taken by Professor Haimberger to his consulting-room and questioned:

"It is six o'clock. When did you eat last?"

"At noon."

"What did you eat?"

"Next to nothing."

"What was on the table?"

"The usual things."

"Chops, chickens, vegetables, and so on?"

"Yes; but don't mention them—I can't bear it."

"Are you tired of them?"

"Oh, utterly. I wish I might never hear of them again."

"The mere sight of food offends you, does it?"

"More, it revolts me."

The doctor considered awhile, then got out a long menu and ran his eye slowly down it.

"I think," said he, "that what you need to eat is—but here, choose for yourself."

I glanced at the list, and my stomach threw a handspring. Of all the barbarous layouts that were ever contrived, this was the most atrocious. At the top stood "tough, underdone, overdue tripe, garnished with garlic"; half-way down the bill stood "young cat; old cat; scrambled cat"; at the bottom stood "sailor-boots, softened with tallow—served raw." The wide intervals of the bill were packed with dishes calculated to insult a cannibal. I said:

"Doctor, it is not fair to joke over so serious a case as mine. I came here to get an appetite, not to throw away the remnant that's left."

He said, gravely, "I am not joking; why should I joke?"

"But I can't eat these horrors."

"Why not?"

He said it with a naïveté that was admirable, whether it was real or assumed.

"Why not? Because—why, doctor, for months I have seldom been able to endure anything more substantial than omelettes and custards. These unspeakable dishes of yours—"

"Oh, you will come to like them. They are very good. And you *must* eat them. It is the rule of the place, and is strict. I cannot permit any departure from it."

I said, smiling: "Well, then, doctor, you will have to permit the departure of the patient. I am going."

He looked hurt, and said in a way which changed the aspect of things:

"I am sure you would not do me that injustice. I accepted you in good faith—you will not shame that confidence. This appetite cure is my whole living. If you should go forth from it with the sort of appetite which you now have, it could become known, and you can see, yourself, that people would say my cure failed in your case and hence can fail in other cases. You will not go; you will not do me this hurt."

I apologized and said I would stay.

"That is right. I was sure you would not go; it would take the food from my family's mouths."

"Would they mind that? Do they eat these fiendish things?"

"They? My family?" His eyes were full of gentle wonder. "Of course not."

"Oh, they don't! Do you?"

"Certainly not."

"I see. It's another case of a physician who doesn't take his own medicine."

"I don't need it. It is six hours since you lunched. Will you have supper now—or later?"

"I am not hungry, but now is as good a time as any, and I would like to be done with it and have it off my mind. It is about my usual time, and regularity is commanded by all the authorities. Yes, I will try to nibble a little now—I wish a light horse-whipping would answer instead."

The professor handed me that odious menu.

"Choose—or will you have it later?"

"Oh, dear me, show me to my room; I forgot your hard rule."

"Wait just a moment before you finally decide. There is another rule. If you choose now, the order will be filled at once; but if you wait, you will have to await my pleasure. You cannot get a dish from that entire bill until I consent."

"All right. Show me to my room, and send the cook to bed; there is not going to be any hurry."

The professor took me up one flight of stairs and showed me into a most inviting and comfortable apartment consisting of parlor, bedchamber, and bath-room.

The front windows looked out over a far-reaching spread of green glades and valleys, and tumbled hills clothed with forests—a noble solitude unvexed by the fussy world. In the parlor were many shelves filled with books. The professor said he would now leave me to myself; and added:

"Smoke and read as much as you please, drink all the water you like. When you get hungry, ring and give your order, and I will decide whether it shall be filled or not. Yours is a stubborn, bad case, and I think the first fourteen dishes in the bill are each and all too delicate for its needs. I ask you as a favor to restrain yourself and not call for them."

"Restrain myself, is it? Give yourself no uneasiness. You are going to save money by me. The idea of coaxing a sick man's appetite back with this buzzard fare is clear insanity."

I said it with bitterness, for I felt outraged by this calm, cold talk over these heartless new engines of assassination. The doctor looked grieved, but not offended. He laid the bill of fare on the commode at my bed's head, "so that it would be handy," and said:

"Yours is not the worst case I have encountered, by any means; still it is a bad one and requires robust treatment; therefore I shall be gratified if you will restrain yourself and skip down to No. 15 and begin with that."

Then he left me and I began to undress, for I was dog-tired and very sleepy. I slept fifteen hours and woke up finely refreshed at ten the next morning. Vienna coffee! It was the first thing I thought of—that unapproachable luxury—that sumptuous coffee-house coffee, compared with which all other European coffee and all American hotel coffee is mere fluid poverty. I rang, and ordered it; also Vienna bread, that delicious invention. The servant spoke through the wicket in the door and said—but you know what he said. He referred me to the bill of fare. I allowed him to go—I had no further use for him.

After the bath I dressed and started for a walk, and got as far as the door. It was locked on the outside. I rang and the servant came and explained that it was another rule. The seclusion of the patient was required until after the first meal. I had not been particularly anxious to get out before; but it was different now. Being locked in makes a person wishful to get out. I soon began to find it difficult to put in the time. At two o'clock I had been twenty-six hours without food. I had been growing hungry for some time; I recognized that I was not only hungry now, but hungry with a strong adjective in front of it. Yet I was not hungry enough to face the bill of fare.

I must put in the time somehow. I would read and smoke. I did it; hour by hour. The books were all of one breed—shipwrecks; people lost in deserts; people shut up in caved-in mines; people starving in besieged cities. I read about all the revolting dishes that ever famishing men had stayed their hunger with. During the first hours these things nauseated me; hours followed in which they did not so affect me; still other hours followed in which I found myself smacking my lips over some tolerably infernal messes. When I had been without food forty-five hours I ran eagerly to the bell and ordered the second dish in the bill, which was a sort of dumplings containing a compost made of caviar and tar.

It was refused me. During the next fifteen hours I visited the bell every now and then and ordered a dish that was further down the list. Always a refusal. But I was conquering prejudice after prejudice, right along; I was making sure progress; I was creeping up on No. 15 with deadly certainty, and my heart beat faster and faster, my hopes rose higher and higher.

At last when food had not passed my lips for sixty hours, victory was mine, and I ordered No. 15:

"Soft-boiled spring chicken—in the egg; six dozen, hot and fragrant!"

In fifteen minutes it was there; and the doctor along with it, rubbing his hands with joy. He said with great excitement:

"It's a cure, it's a cure! I knew I could do it. Dear sir, my grand system never fails—never. You've got your appetite back—you know you have; say it and make me happy."

"Bring on your carrion—I can eat anything in the bill!"

"Oh, this is noble, this is splendid—but I knew I could do it, the system never fails. How are the birds?"

"Never was anything so delicious in the world; and yet as a rule I don't care for game. But don't interrupt me, don't— I can't spare my mouth, I really can't."

Then the doctor said:

"The cure is perfect. There is no more doubt nor danger. Let the poultry alone; I can trust you with a beefsteak now."

The beefsteak came—as much as a basketful of it—with potatoes, and Vienna bread and coffee; and I ate a meal then that was worth all the costly preparation I had made for it. And dripped tears of gratitude into the gravy all the time—gratitude to the doctor for putting a little plain common sense into me when I had been empty of it so many, many years.

II

Thirty years ago Haimberger went off on a long voyage in a sailing-ship. There were fifteen passengers on board. The table-fare was of the regulation pattern of the day: At seven in the morning, a cup of bad coffee in bed; at nine, breakfast: bad coffee, with condensed milk; soggy rolls, crackers, salt fish; at 1 P.M., luncheon: cold tongue, cold ham, cold corned beef, soggy cold rolls, crackers; 5 P.M., dinner: thick pea-soup, salt fish, hot corned beef and sauerkraut, boiled pork and beans, pudding; 9 till 11 P.M., supper: tea, with condensed milk, cold tongue, cold ham, pickles, sea-biscuit, pickled oysters, pickled pig's feet, grilled bones, golden buck.

At the end of the first week eating had ceased, nibbling had taken its place. The passengers came to the table, but it was partly to put in the time, and partly because the wisdom of the ages commanded them to be regular in their meals. They were tired of the coarse and monotonous fare, and took no interest in it, had no appetite for it. All day and every day they roamed the ship half hungry, plagued by their gnawing stomachs, moody, untalkative, miserable. Among them were three confirmed dyspeptics. These became shadows in the course of three weeks. There was also a bedridden invalid; he lived on boiled rice; he could not look at the regular dishes.

Now came shipwreck and life in open boats, with the usual paucity of food. Provisions ran lower and lower. The appetites improved, then. When nothing was left but raw ham and the ration of that was down to two ounces a day per person, the appetites were perfect. At the end of fifteen days the dyspeptics, the invalid and the most delicate ladies in the party were chewing sailor-boots in ecstasy, and only complaining because the supply of them was limited. Yet these were the same people who couldn't endure the ship's tedious corned beef and sauerkraut and other crudities. They were rescued by an English vessel. Within ten days the whole fifteen were in as good condition as they had been when the shipwreck occurred.

"They had suffered no damage by their adventure," said the professor. "Do you note that?"

"Yes."

"Do you note it well?"

"Yes—I think I do."

"But you don't. You hesitate. You don't rise to the importance of it. I will say it again—with emphasis—*not one of them suffered any damage.*"

"Now I begin to see. Yes, it was indeed remarkable."

"Nothing of the kind. It was perfectly natural. There was no reason why they should suffer damage. They were undergoing Nature's Appetite Cure, the best and wisest in the world."

"Is that where you got your idea?"

"That is where I got it."

"It taught those people a valuable lesson."

"What makes you think that?"

"Why shouldn't I? You seem to think it taught you one."

"That is nothing to the point. I am not a fool."

"I see. Were they fools?"

"They were human beings."

"Is it the same thing?"

"Why do you ask? You know it yourself. As regards his health—and the rest of the things—the average man is what his environment and his superstitions have made him; and their function is to make him an ass. He can't add up three or four new circumstances together and perceive what they mean; it is beyond him. He is not capable of observing for himself. He has to get everything at second hand. If what are miscalled the lower animals were as silly as man is, they would all perish from the earth in a year."

"Those passengers learned no lesson, then?"

"Not a sign of it. They went to their regular meals in the English ship, and pretty soon they were nibbling again—nibbling, appetiteless, disgusted with the food, moody, miserable, half hungry, their outraged stomachs cursing and swearing and whining and supplicating all day long. And in vain, for they were the stomachs of fools."

"Then, as I understand it, your scheme is—"

"Quite simple. Don't eat till you are hungry. If the food fails to taste good, fails to satisfy you, rejoice you, comfort you, don't eat again until you are *very* hungry. Then it will rejoice you—and do you good, too."

"And I observe no regularity, as to hours?"

"When you are conquering a bad appetite—no. After it is conquered, regularity is no harm, so long as the appetite remains good. As soon as the appetite wavers, apply the corrective again—which is starvation, long or short according to the needs of the case."

"The best diet, I suppose—I mean the wholesomest—"

"All diets are wholesome. Some are wholesomer than others, but all the ordinary diets are wholesome enough for the people who use them. Whether the food be fine or coarse, it will taste good and it will nourish if a watch be kept upon the appetite and a little starvation introduced every time it weakens. Nansen was used to fine fare, but when his meals were restricted to bear-meat months at a time he suffered no damage and no discomfort, because his appetite was kept at par through the difficulty of getting his bear-meat regularly."

"But doctors arrange carefully considered and delicate diets for invalids."

"They can't help it. The invalid is full of inherited superstitions and won't starve himself. He believes it would certainly kill him."

"It would weaken him, wouldn't it?"

"Nothing to hurt. Look at the invalids in our shipwreck. They lived fifteen days on pinches of raw ham, a suck at sailor-boots, and general starvation. It weakened them, but it didn't hurt them. It put them in fine shape to eat heartily of hearty food and build themselves up to a condition of robust health. But they did not perceive that; they lost their opportunity; they remained invalids; it served them right. Do you know the tricks that the health-resort doctors play?"

"What is it?"

"My system disguised—covert starvation. Grape-cure, bath-cure, mud-cure—it is all the same. The grape and the bath and the mud make a show and do a trifle of the work—the real work is done by the surreptitious starvation. The patient accustomed to four meals and late hours—at both ends of the day—now consider what he has to do at a health resort. He gets up at six in the morning. Eats one egg. Tramps up and down a promenade two hours with the other fools. Eats a butterfly. Slowly drinks a glass of filtered sewage that smells like a buzzard's breath. Promenades another two hours, but alone; if you speak to him he says anxiously, 'My water!—I am walking off my water!—please don't interrupt,' and goes stumping along again. Eats a candied rose-leaf. Lies at rest in the silence and solitude of his room for hours; mustn't speak, mustn't read, mustn't smoke. The doctor comes and feels of his heart, now, and his pulse, and thumps his breast and his back and his stomach, and listens for results through a penny flageolet; then orders the man's bath—half a degree, Réaumur, cooler than yesterday. After the bath, another egg. A glass of sewage at three or four in the afternoon, and promenade solemnly with the other freaks. Dinner at six—half a doughnut and a cup of tea. Walk again. Half past eight, supper—more butterfly; at nine, to bed. Six weeks of this régime—think of it. It starves a man out and puts him in splendid condition. It would have the same effect in London, New York, Jericho—anywhere."

"How long does it take to put a person in condition here?"

"It ought to take but a day or two; but in fact it takes from one to six weeks, according to the character and mentality of the patient."

"How is that?"

"Do you see that crowd of women playing football, and boxing, and jumping fences yonder? They have been here six or seven weeks. They were spectral poor weaklings when they came. They were accustomed to nibbling at dainties and delicacies at set hours four times a day, and they had no appetite for anything. I questioned them, and then locked them into their rooms, the frailest ones to starve nine or ten hours, the others twelve or fifteen. Before long they began to beg; and indeed they suffered a good deal. They complained of nausea, headache, and so on. It was good to see them eat when the time was up. They could not remember when the devouring of a meal had afforded them such rapture—that was their word. Now, then, that ought to have ended their cure, but it didn't. They were free to go to any meals in the house, and they chose their accustomed four. Within a day or two I had to interfere. Their appetites were weakening. I made them knock out a meal. That set them up again. Then they resumed the four. I begged them to learn to knock out a meal themselves, without waiting for me. Up to a fortnight ago they couldn't; they really hadn't manhood enough; but they were gaining it, and now I think they are safe. They drop out a meal every now and then of their own accord. They are in fine condition now, and they might safely go home, I think, but their confidence is not quite perfect yet, so they are waiting awhile."

"Other cases are different?"

"Oh, yes. Sometimes a man learns the whole trick in a week. Learns to regulate his appetite and keep it in perfect order. Learns to drop out a meal with frequency and not mind it."

"But why drop the entire meal out? Why not a part of it?"

"It's a poor device, and inadequate. If the stomach doesn't call vigorously—with a shout, as you may say—it is better not to pester it, but just give it a real rest. Some people can eat more meals than others, and still thrive. There are all sorts of people, and all sorts of appetites. I will show you a man presently who was accustomed to nibble at eight meals a day. It was beyond the proper gait of his appetite by two. I have got him down to six a day, now, and he is all right, and enjoys life. How many meals do you effect per day?"

"Formerly—for twenty-two years—a meal and a half; during the past two years, two and a half: coffee and a roll at nine, luncheon at one, dinner at seven-thirty or eight."

"Formerly a meal and a half—that is, coffee and a roll at nine, dinner in the evening, nothing between—is that it?"

"Yes."

"Why did you add a meal?"

"It was the family's idea. They were uneasy. They thought I was killing myself."

"You found a meal and a half per day enough, all through the twenty-two years?"

"Plenty."

"Your present poor condition is due to the extra meal. Drop it out. You are trying to eat oftener than your stomach demands. You don't gain, you lose. You eat less food now, in a day, on two and a half meals, than you formerly ate on one and a half."

"True—a good deal less; for in those old days my dinner was a very sizable thing."

"Put yourself on a single meal a day, now—dinner—for a few days, till you secure a good, sound, regular, trustworthy appetite, then take to your one and a half permanently, and don't listen to the family any more. When you have any ordinary ailment, particularly of a feverish sort, eat nothing at all during twenty-four hours. That will cure it. It will cure the stubbornest cold in the head, too. No cold in the head can survive twenty-four hours on modified starvation."

"I know it. I have proved it many a time."

TWAIN *and* HUMAN NATURE

My Watch

An Instructive Little Tale

My beautiful new watch had run eighteen months without losing or gaining, and without breaking any part of its machinery or stopping. I had come to believe it infallible in its judgments about the time of day, and to consider its constitution and its anatomy imperishable. But at last, one night, I let it run down. I grieved about it as if it were a recognized messenger and forerunner of calamity. But by and by I cheered up, set the watch by guess, and commanded my bodings and superstitions to depart. Next day I stepped into the chief jeweler's to set it by the exact time, and the head of the establishment took it out of my hand and proceeded to set it for me. Then he said, "She is four minutes slow—regulator wants pushing up." I tried to stop him—tried to make him understand that the watch kept perfect time. But no; all this human cabbage could see was that the watch was four minutes slow, and the regulator *must* be pushed up a little; and so, while I danced around him in anguish, and implored him to let the watch alone, he calmly and cruelly did the shameful deed. My watch began to gain. It gained faster and faster day by day. Within the week it sickened to a raging fever, and its pulse went up to a hundred and fifty in the shade. At the end of two months it had left all the timepieces of the town far in the rear, and was a fraction over thirteen days ahead of the almanac. It was away into November enjoying the snow, while the October leaves were still turning. It hurried up house rent, bills payable, and such things, in such a ruinous way that I could not abide it. I took it to the watchmaker to be regulated. He asked me if I had ever had it repaired. I said no, it had never needed any repairing. He looked a look of vicious happiness and eagerly pried the watch open, and then put a small dice-box into his eye and peered into its machinery. He said it wanted cleaning and oiling, besides regulating—come in a week. After being cleaned and oiled, and regulated, my watch slowed down to that degree that it ticked like a tolling bell. I began to be left by trains, I failed all appointments, I got to missing my dinner; my watch strung out three days' grace to four and let me go to protest; I gradually drifted back into yesterday, then day before, then into last week, and by and by the comprehension came upon me that all solitary and alone I was lingering along in week before last, and the world was out of sight. I seemed to detect in myself a sort of sneaking fellow-feeling for the mummy in the museum, and a desire to swap news with him. I went to a watchmaker again. He took the watch all to pieces while I waited, and then said the barrel was "swelled." He said he could reduce it in three days. After this the watch *averaged* well, but nothing more. For half a day it would go like the very mischief, and keep up such a barking and wheezing and whooping and sneezing and snorting, that I could not hear myself think for the disturbance; and as long as it held out there was not a watch in the land that stood any chance against it. But the rest of the day it would keep on slowing down and fooling along until all the clocks it had left behind caught up again. So at last, at the end of twenty-four hours, it would trot up to the judges' stand all right and just in time. It would show a fair and square average, and no man could say it had done more or less than its duty. But a correct average is only a mild virtue in a watch, and I took this instrument to another watchmaker. He said the king-bolt was broken. I said I was glad it was nothing more serious. To tell the plain truth, I had no idea what the king-bolt was, but I did not choose to appear ignorant to a stranger. He repaired the king-bolt, but what the watch gained in one way it lost in another. It would run awhile and then stop awhile, and then run awhile again, and so on, using its own discretion about the intervals. And every time it went off it kicked back like a musket. I padded my breast for a few days, but finally took the watch to another watchmaker. He picked it all to pieces, and turned the ruin over and over under his glass; and then he said there appeared to be something the matter with the hair-trigger. He fixed it, and gave it a fresh start. It did well now, except that always at ten minutes to ten the hands would shut together like a pair of scissors, and from that time forth they would travel together. The oldest man in the world could not make head or tail of the time of day by such a watch, and so I went again to have the thing repaired. This person said that the crystal had got bent, and that the mainspring was not straight. He also remarked that part of the works needed half-soling. He made these things all right, and then my timepiece performed unexceptionably, save that now and then, after working along quietly for nearly eight hours, everything inside would let go all of a sudden and begin to buzz like a bee, and the hands would straightway begin to spin round and round so fast that their individuality was lost completely, and they simply seemed a delicate spider's web over the face of the watch. She would reel off the next twenty-four hours in six or seven minutes, and then stop with a bang. I went with a heavy heart to one more watchmaker, and looked on while he took her to pieces. Then I prepared to cross-question him rigidly, for this thing was getting serious. The watch had cost two hundred dollars originally, and I seemed to have paid out two or three thousand for repairs. While I waited and looked on I presently recognized in this watchmaker an old acquaintance—a steamboat engineer of other days, and not a good engineer, either. He examined all the parts carefully, just as the other watchmakers had done, and then delivered his verdict with the same confidence of manner.

He said:

"She makes too much steam—you want to hang the monkey-wrench on the safety-valve!"

I brained him on the spot, and had him buried at my own expense.

My uncle William (now deceased, alas!) used to say that a good horse was a good horse until it had run away once, and that a good watch was a good watch until the repairers got a chance at it. And he used to wonder what became of all the unsuccessful tinkers, and gunsmiths, and shoemakers, and engineers, and blacksmiths; but nobody could ever tell him.

Mental Telegraphy

A Manuscript with a History

NOTE TO THE EDITOR.—By glancing over the inclosed bundle of rusty old manuscript, you will perceive that I once made a great discovery: the discovery that certain sorts of thing which, from the beginning of the world, had always been regarded as merely "curious coincidences"—that is to say, accidents—were no more accidental than is the sending and receiving of a telegram an accident. I made this discovery sixteen or seventeen years ago, and gave it a name—"Mental Telegraphy." It is the same thing around the outer edges of which the Psychical Society of England began to group (and play with) four or five years ago, and which they named "Telepathy." Within the last two or three years they have penetrated toward the heart of the matter, however, and have found out that mind can act upon mind in a quite detailed and elaborate way over vast stretches of land and water. And they have succeeded in doing, by their great credit and influence, what I could never have done—they have convinced the world that mental telegraphy is not a jest, but a fact, and that it is a thing not rare, but exceedingly common. They have done our age a service—and a very great service, I think.

In this old manuscript you will find mention of an extraordinary experience of mine in the mental telegraphic line, of date about the year 1874 or 1875—the one concerning the Great Bonanza book. It was this experience that called my attention to the matter under consideration. I began to keep a record, after that, of such experiences of mine as seemed explicable by the theory that minds telegraph thoughts to each other. In 1878 I went to Germany and began to write the book called *A Tramp Abroad.* The bulk of this old batch of manuscript was written at that time and for that book. But I removed it when I came to revise the volume for the press; for I feared that the public would treat the thing as a joke and throw it aside, whereas I was in earnest.

At home, eight or ten years ago, I tried to creep in under shelter of an authority grave enough to protect the article from ridicule—*The North American Review.* But Mr. Metcalf was too wary for me. He said that to treat these mere "coincidences" seriously was a thing which the *Review* couldn't dare to do; that I must put either my name or my *nom de plume* to the article, and thus save the *Review* from harm. But I couldn't consent to that; it would be the surest possible way to defeat my desire that the public should receive the thing seriously, and be willing to stop and give it some fair degree of attention. So I pigeonholed the MS., because I could not get it published anonymously.

Now see how the world has moved since then. These small experiences of mine, which were too formidable at that time for admission to a grave magazine—if the magazine must allow them to appear as something above and beyond "accidents" and "coincidences"—are trifling and commonplace now, since the flood of light recently cast upon mental telegraphy by the intelligent labors of the Psychical Society. But I think they are worth publishing, just to show what harmless and ordinary matters were considered dangerous and incredible eight or ten years ago.

As I have said, the bulk of this old manuscript was written in 1878; a later part was written from time to time two, three, and four years afterward. The "Postscript" I add to-day.—M.T.

May, '78.—Another of those apparently trifling things has happened to me which puzzle and perplex all men every now and then, keep them thinking an hour or two, and leave their minds barren of explanation or solution at last. Here it is—and it looks inconsequential enough, I am obliged to say. A few days ago I said: "It must be that Frank Millet doesn't know we are in Germany, or he would have written long before this. I have been on the point of dropping him a line at least a dozen times during the past six weeks, but I always decided to wait a day or two longer, and see if we shouldn't hear from him. But now I *will* write." And so I did. I directed the letter to Paris, and thought, "*Now* we shall hear from him before this letter is fifty miles from Heidelberg—it always happens so."

True enough; but *why* should it? That is the puzzling part of it. We are always talking about letters "crossing" each other, for that is one of the very commonest accidents of this life. We call it "accident," but perhaps we misname it. We have the instinct a dozen times a year that the letter we are writing is going to "cross" the other person's letter; and if the reader will rack his memory a little he will recall the fact that this presentiment had strength enough to it to make him cut his letter down to a decided briefness, because it would be a waste of time to write a letter which was going to "cross," and hence be a useless letter. I think that in my experience this instinct has generally come to me in cases where I had put off my letter a good while in the hope that the other person would write.

Yes, as I was saying, I had waited five or six weeks; then I wrote but three lines, because I felt and seemed to know that a letter from Millet would cross mine. And so it did. He wrote the same day that I wrote. The letters crossed each other. His letter went to Berlin, care of the American minister, who sent it to me. In this letter Millet said he had been trying for six weeks to stumble upon somebody who knew my German address, and at last the idea had occurred to him that a letter sent to the care of the embassy at Berlin might possibly find me. Maybe it was an "accident" that he finally determined to write me at the same moment that I finally determined to write him, but I think not.

With me the most irritating thing has been to wait a tedious time in a purely business matter, hoping that the other party will do the writing, and then sit down and do it myself, perfectly satisfied that that other man is sitting down at the same moment to write a letter which will "cross" mine. And yet one must go on writing, just the same; because if you get up from your table and postpone, that other man will do the same thing, exactly as if you two were harnessed together like the Siamese twins, and must duplicate each other's movements.

Several months before I left home a New York firm did some work about the house for me, and did not make a success of it, as it seemed to me. When the bill came, I wrote and said I wanted the work perfected before I paid. They replied that they were very busy, but that as soon as they could spare the proper man the thing should be done. I waited more than two months, enduring as patiently as possible the companionship of bells which would fire away of their own accord sometimes when nobody was touching them, and at other times wouldn't ring though you struck the button with a sledgehammer. Many a time I got ready to write and then postponed it; but at last I sat down one evening and poured out my grief to the extent of a page or so, and then cut my letter suddenly short, because a strong instinct told me that the firm had begun to move in the matter. When I came down to breakfast next morning the postman had not yet taken my letter away, but the electrical man had been there, done his work, and was gone again! He had received his orders the previous evening from his employers, and had come up by the night train.

If that was an "accident," it took about three months to get it up in good shape.

One evening last summer I arrived in Washington, registered at the Arlington Hotel, and went to my room. I read and smoked until ten o'clock; then, finding I was not yet sleepy, I thought I would take a breath of fresh air. So I went forth in the rain, and tramped through one street after another in an aimless and enjoyable way. I knew that Mr. O——, a friend of mine, was in town, and I wished I might run across him; but I did not propose to hunt for him at midnight, especially as I did not know where he was stopping. Toward twelve o'clock the streets had become so deserted that I felt lonesome; so I stepped into a cigar shop far up the avenue, and remained there fifteen minutes, listening to some bummers discussing national politics. Suddenly the spirit of prophecy came upon me, and I said to myself, "Now I will go out at this door, turn to the left, walk ten steps, and meet Mr. O—— face to face." I did it, too! I could not see his face, because he had an umbrella before it, and it was pretty dark anyhow, but he interrupted the man he was walking and talking with, and I recognized his voice and stopped him.

That I should step out there and stumble upon Mr. O—— was nothing, but that I should know beforehand that I was going to do it was a good deal. It is a very curious thing when you come to look at it. I stood far within the cigar shop when I delivered my prophecy; I walked about five steps to the door, opened it, closed it after me, walked down a flight of three steps to the sidewalk, then turned to the left and walked four or five more, and found my man. I repeat that in itself the thing was nothing; but to know it would happen so *beforehand,* wasn't that really curious?

I have criticized absent people so often, and then discovered, to my humiliation, that I was talking with their relatives, that I have grown superstitious about that sort of thing and dropped it. How like an idiot one feels after a blunder like that!

We are always mentioning people, and in that very instant they appear before us. We laugh, and say, "Speak of the devil," and so forth, and there we drop it, considering it an "accident." It is a cheap and convenient way of disposing of a grave and very puzzling mystery. The fact is, it does seem to happen too often to be an accident.

Now I come to the oddest thing that ever happened to me. Two or three years ago I was lying in bed, idly musing, one morning—it was the

2d of March—when suddenly a red-hot new idea came whistling down into my camp, and exploded with such comprehensive effectiveness as to sweep the vicinity clean of rubbishy reflections and fill the air with their dust and flying fragments. This idea, stated in simple phrase, was that the time was ripe and the market ready for a certain book; a book which ought to be written at once; a book which must command attention and be of peculiar interest—to wit, a book about the Nevada silver-mines. The "Great Bonanza" was a new wonder then, and everybody was talking about it. It seemed to me that the person best qualified to write this book was Mr. William H. Wright, a journalist of Virginia, Nevada, by whose side I had scribbled many months when I was a reporter there ten or twelve years before. He might be alive still; he might be dead; I could not tell; but I would write him, anyway. I began by merely and modestly suggesting that he make such a book; but my interest grew as I went on, and I ventured to map out what I thought ought to be the plan of the work, he being an old friend, and not given to taking good intentions for ill. I even dealt with details, and suggested the order and sequence which they should follow. I was about to put the manuscript in an envelope, when the thought occurred to me that if this book should be written at my suggestion, and then no publisher happened to want it, I should feel uncomfortable; so I concluded to keep my letter back until I should have secured a publisher. I pigeonholed my document, and dropped a note to my own publisher, asking him to name a day for a business consultation. He was out of town on a far journey.

My note remained unanswered, and at the end of three or four days the whole matter had passed out of my mind. On the 9th of March the postman brought three or four letters, and among them a thick one whose superscription was in a hand which seemed dimly familiar to me. I could not "place" it at first, but presently I succeeded. Then I said to a visiting relative who was present:

"Now I will do a miracle. I will tell you everything this letter contains—date, signature, and all—without breaking the seal. It is from a Mr. Wright, of Virginia, Nevada, and is dated the 2d of March—seven days ago. Mr. Wright proposes to make a book about the silver-mines and the Great Bonanza, and asks what I, as a friend, think of the idea. He says his subjects are to be so and so, their order and sequence so and so, and he will close with a history of the chief feature of the book, the Great Bonanza."

I opened the letter, and showed that I had stated the date and the contents correctly. Mr. Wright's letter simply contained what my own letter, written on the same date, contained, and mine still lay in its pigeon-hole, where it had been lying during the seven days since it was written.

There was no clairvoyance about this, if I rightly comprehend what clairvoyance is. I think the clairvoyant professes to actually *see* concealed writing, and read it off word for word. This was not my case. I only seemed to know, and to know absolutely, the contents of the letter in detail and due order, but I had to *word* them myself. I translated them, so to speak, out of Wright's language into my own.

Wright's letter and the one which I had written to him but never sent were in substance the same.

Necessarily this could not come by accident; such elaborate accidents cannot happen. Chance might have duplicated one or two of the details, but she would have broken down on the rest. I could not doubt—there was no tenable reason for doubting—that Mr. Wright's mind and mine had been in close and crystal-clear communication with each other across three thousand miles of mountain and desert on the morning of the 2d of March. I did not consider that both minds *originated* that succession of ideas, but that one mind originated it, and simply telegraphed it to the other. I was curious to know which brain was the telegrapher and which the receiver, so I wrote and asked for particulars. Mr. Wright's reply showed that his mind had done the originating and telegraphing, and mine the receiving. Mark that significant thing now; consider for a moment how many a splendid "original" idea has been unconsciously stolen from a man three thousand miles away! If one should question that this is so, let him look into the cyclopedia and con once more that curious thing in the history of inventions which has puzzled every one so much—that is, the frequency with which the same machine or other contrivance has been invented at the same time by several persons in different quarters of the globe. The world was without an electric telegraph for several thousand years; then Professor Henry, the American, Wheatstone in England, Morse on the sea, and a German in Munich, all invented it at the same time. The discovery of certain ways of applying steam was made in two or three countries in the same year. Is it not possible that inventors are constantly and unwittingly stealing each other's ideas whilst they stand thousands of miles asunder?

Last spring a literary friend of mine,[1] who lived a hundred miles away, paid me a visit, and in the course of our talk he said he had made a

1. W. D. Howells.—M.T.

discovery—conceived an entirely new idea—one which certainly had never been used in literature. He told me what it was. I handed him a manuscript, and said he would find substantially the same idea in that—a manuscript which I had written a week before. The idea had been in my mind since the previous November; it had only entered his while I was putting it on paper, a week gone by. He had not yet written his; so he left it unwritten, and gracefully made over all his right and title in the idea to me.

The following statement, which I have clipped from a newspaper, is true. I had the facts from Mr. Howells's lips when the episode was new:

> A remarkable story of a literary coincidence is told of Mr. Howells's *Atlantic Monthly* serial, "Dr. Breen's Practice." A lady of Rochester, New York, contributed to the magazine after "Dr. Breen's Practice" was in type, a short story which so much resembled Mr. Howells's that he felt it necessary to call upon her and explain the situation of affairs in order that no charge of plagiarism might be preferred against him. He showed her the proof-sheets of his story, and satisfied her that the similarity between her work and his was one of those strange coincidences which have from time to time occurred in the literary world.

I had read portions of Mr. Howells's story, both in MS. and in proof, before the lady offered her contribution to the magazine.

Here is another case. I clip it from a newspaper:

> The republication of Miss Alcott's novel *Moods* recalls to a writer in the Boston *Post* a singular coincidence which was brought to light before the book was first published: "Miss Anna M. Crane, of Baltimore, published *Emily Chester,* a novel which was pronounced a very striking and strong story. A comparison of this book with *Moods* showed that the two writers, though entire strangers to each other, and living hundreds of miles apart, had both chosen the same subject for their novels, had followed almost the same line of treatment up to a certain point, where the parallel ceased, and the dénouements were entirely opposite. And even more curious, the leading characters in both books had identically the same names, so that the names in Miss Alcott's novel had to be changed. Then the book was published by Loring."

Four or five times within my recollection there has been a lively newspaper war in this country over poems whose authorship was claimed by two or three different people at the same time. There was a war of this kind over "Nothing to Wear," "Beautiful Snow," "Rock me to Sleep, Mother," and also over one of Mr. Will Carleton's early ballads, I think. These were all blameless cases of unintentional and unwitting mental telegraphy, I judge.

A word more as to Mr. Wright. He had had his book in mind some time; consequently he, and not I, had originated the idea of it. The subject was entirely foreign to my thoughts; I was wholly absorbed in other things. Yet this friend, whom I had not seen and had hardly thought of for eleven years, was able to shoot his thoughts at me across three thousand miles of country, and fill my head with them, to the exclusion of every other interest, in a single moment. He had begun his letter after finishing his work on the morning paper—a little after three o'clock, he said. When it was three in the morning in Nevada it was about six in Hartford, where I lay awake thinking about nothing in particular; and just about that time his ideas came pouring into my head from across the continent, and I got up and put them on paper, under the impression that they were my own original thoughts.

I have never seen any mesmeric or clairvoyant performances or spiritual manifestations which were in the least degree convincing—a fact which is not of consequence, since my opportunities have been meager; but I am forced to believe that one human mind (still inhabiting the flesh) can communicate with another, over any sort of a distance, and without any *artificial* preparation of "sympathetic conditions" to act as a transmitting agent. I suppose that when the sympathetic conditions happen to exist the two minds communicate with each other, and that otherwise they don't; and I suppose that if the sympathetic conditions could be kept up right along, the two minds would continue to correspond without limit as to time.

Now there is that curious thing which happens to everybody: suddenly a succession of thoughts or sensations flocks in upon you, which startles you with the weird idea that you have ages ago experienced just this succession of thoughts or sensations in a previous existence. The previous existence is possible, no doubt, but I am persuaded that the solution of this hoary mystery lies not there, but in the fact that some far-off stranger has been telegraphing his thoughts and sensations into your consciousness, and that he stopped because some counter-current or other obstruction intruded and broke the line of communication. Perhaps they seem repetitions to you because they *are* repetitions, got at second hand from the other man. Possibly Mr. Brown, the "mind-reader," reads other people's minds, possibly he does not; but I know of a surety that I have read another man's mind, and therefore I do not see why Mr. Brown shouldn't do the like also.

I wrote the foregoing about three years ago, in Heidelberg, and laid the manuscript aside, purposing to add to it instances of mind-telegraphing from time to time as they should fall under my experience. Meantime the "crossing" of letters has been so frequent as to become monotonous. However, I have managed to get something useful out of this hint; for now, when I get tired of waiting upon a man whom I very much wish to hear from, I sit down and *compel* him to write, whether he wants to or not; that is to say, I sit down and write him, and then tear my letter up, satisfied that my act has forced him to write me at the same moment. I do not need to mail my letter—the writing it is the only essential thing.

Of course I have grown superstitious about this letter-crossing business—this was natural. We stayed awhile in Venice after leaving Heidelberg. One day I was going down the Grand Canal in a gondola, when I heard a shout behind me, and looked around to see what the matter was; a gondola was rapidly following, and the gondolier was making signs to me to stop. I did so, and the pursuing boat ranged up alongside. There was an American lady in it—a resident of Venice. She was in a good deal of distress. She said:

"There's a New York gentleman and his wife at the Hotel Britannia who arrived a week ago, expecting to find news of their son, whom they have heard nothing about during eight months. There was no news. The lady is down sick with despair; the gentleman can't sleep or eat. Their son arrived at San Francisco eight months ago, and announced the fact in a letter to his parents the same day. That is the last trace of him. The parents have been in Europe ever since; but their trip has been spoiled, for they have occupied their time simply in drifting restlessly from place to place, and writing letters everywhere and to everybody, begging for news of their son; but the mystery remains as dense as ever. Now the gentleman wants to stop writing and go calling. He wants to cable San Francisco. He has never done it before, because he is afraid of—of he doesn't know what—death of his son, no doubt. But he wants somebody to *advise* him to cable; wants me to do it. Now I simply can't; for if no news came, that mother yonder would die. So I have chased you up in order to get you to support me in urging him to be patient, and put the thing off a week or two longer; it may be the saving of this lady. Come along; let's not lose any time."

So I went along, but I had a program of my own. When I was introduced to the gentleman I said: "I have some superstitions, but they are worthy of respect. If you will cable San Francisco immediately, you will hear news of your son inside of twenty-four hours. I don't know that you will get the news from San Francisco, but you will get it from somewhere. The only necessary thing is to *cable*—that is all. The news will come within twenty-four hours. Cable Peking, if you prefer; there is no choice in this matter. This delay is all occasioned by your not cabling long ago, when you were first moved to do it."

It seems absurd that this gentleman should have been cheered up by this nonsense, but he was; he brightened up at once, and sent his cablegram; and next day, at noon, when a long letter arrived from his lost son, the man was as grateful to me as if I had really had something to do with the hurrying up of that letter. The son had shipped from San Francisco in a sailing-vessel, and his letter was written from the first port he touched at, months afterward.

This incident argues nothing, and is valueless. I insert it only to show how strong is the superstition which "letter-crossing" has bred in me. I was so sure that a cablegram sent to any place, no matter where, would defeat itself by "crossing" the incoming news, that my confidence was able to raise up a hopeless man and make him cheery and hopeful.

But here are two or three incidents which come strictly under the head of mind-telegraphing. One Monday morning, about a year ago, the mail came in, and I picked up one of the letters and said to a friend: "Without opening this letter I will tell you what it says. It is from Mrs. ——, and she says she was in New York last Saturday, and was purposing to run up here in the afternoon train and surprise us, but at the last moment changed her mind and returned westward to her home."

I was right; my details were exactly correct. Yet we had had no suspicion that Mrs. —— was coming to New York, or that she had even a remote intention of visiting us.

I smoke a good deal—that is to say, all the time—so, during seven years, I have tried to keep a box of matches handy, behind a picture on the mantelpiece; but I have had to take it out in trying, because George (colored), who makes the fires and lights the gas, always uses my matches and never replaces them. Commands and persuasions have gone for nothing with him all these seven years. One day last summer, when our family had been away from home several months, I said to a member of the household:

"Now, with all this long holiday, and nothing in the way to interrupt—"

"I can finish the sentence for you," said the member of the household.

"Do it, then," said I.

"George ought to be able, by practising, to learn to let those matches alone."

It was correctly done. That was what I was going to say. Yet until that moment George and the matches had not been in my mind for three months, and it is plain that the part of the sentence which I uttered offers not the least cue or suggestion of what I was purposing to follow it with.

My mother[1] is descended from the younger of two English brothers named Lambton, who settled in this country a few generations ago. The tradition goes that the elder of the two eventually fell heir to a certain estate in England (now an earldom), and died right away. This has always been the way with our family. They always die when they could make anything by not doing it. The two Lambtons left plenty of Lambtons behind them; and when at last, about fifty years ago, the English baronetcy was exalted to an earldom, the great tribe of American Lambtons began to bestir themselves—that is, those descended from the elder branch. Ever since that day one or another of these has been fretting his life uselessly away with schemes to get at his "rights." The present "rightful earl"—I mean the American one—used to write me occasionally, and try to interest me in his projected raids upon the title and estates by offering me a share in the latter portion of the spoil; but I have always managed to resist his temptations.

Well, one day last summer I was lying under a tree, thinking about nothing in particular, when an absurd idea flashed into my head, and I said to a member of the household, "Suppose I should live to be ninety-two, and dumb and blind and toothless, and just as I was gasping out what was left of me on my death-bed—"

"Wait, I will finish the sentence," said a member of the household.

"Go on," said I.

"Somebody should rush in with a document, and say, 'All the other heirs are dead, and you are the Earl of Durham!' "

That is truly what I was going to say. Yet until that moment the subject had not entered my mind or been referred to in my hearing for months before. A few years ago this thing would have astounded me, but the like could not much surprise me now, though it happened every week; for I

1. She was still living when this was written.—M.T.

think I *know* now that mind can communicate accurately with mind without the aid of the slow and clumsy vehicle of speech.

This age does seem to have exhausted invention nearly; still, it has one important contract on its hands yet—the invention of the *phrenophone;* that is to say, a method whereby the communicating of mind with mind may be brought under command and reduced to certainty and system. The telegraph and the telephone are going to become too slow and wordy for our needs. We must have the *thought* itself shot into our minds from a distance; then, if we need to put it into words, we can do that tedious work at our leisure. Doubtless the something which conveys our thoughts through the air from brain to brain is a finer and subtler form of electricity, and all we need do is to find out how to capture it and how to force it to do its work, as we have had to do in the case of the electric currents. Before the day of telegraphs neither one of these marvels would have seemed any easier to achieve than the other.

While I am writing this, doubtless somebody on the other side of the globe is writing it, too. The question is, am I inspiring him or is he inspiring me? I cannot answer that; but that these thoughts have been passing through somebody else's mind all the time I have been setting them down I have no sort of doubt.

I will close this paper with a remark which I found some time ago in Boswell's *Johnson:*

> Voltaire's *Candide* is wonderfully similar in its plan and conduct to Johnson's *Rasselas;* insomuch that I have heard Johnson say that if they had not been published so closely one after the other that there was not time for imitation, *it would have been in vain to deny that the scheme of that which came latest was taken from the other.*

The two men were widely separated from each other at the time, and the sea lay between them.

Postscript

In the *Atlantic* for June, 1882, Mr. John Fiske refers to the often-quoted Darwin-and-Wallace "coincidence":

> I alluded, just now, to the "unforeseen circumstance" which led Mr. Darwin in 1859 to break his long silence, and to write and publish the *Origin*

of Species. This circumstance served, no less than the extraordinary success of his book, to show how ripe the minds of men had become for entertaining such views as those which Mr. Darwin propounded. In 1858 Mr. Wallace, who was then engaged in studying the natural history of the Malay Archipelago, sent to Mr. Darwin (as the man most likely to understand him) a paper in which he sketched the outlines of a theory identical with that upon which Mr. Darwin had so long been at work. The same sequence of observed facts and inferences that had led Mr. Darwin to the discovery of natural selection and its consequences had led Mr. Wallace to the very threshold of the same discovery; but in Mr. Wallace's mind the theory had by no means been wrought out to the same degree of completeness to which it had been wrought in the mind of Mr. Darwin. In the preface to his charming book on Natural Selection, Mr. Wallace, with rare modesty and candor, acknowledges that whatever value his speculations may have had, they have been utterly surpassed in richness and cogency of proof by those of Mr. Darwin. This is no doubt true, and Mr. Wallace has done such good work in further illustration of the theory that he can well afford to rest content with the second place in the first announcement of it.

The coincidence, however, between Mr. Wallace's conclusions and those of Mr. Darwin was very remarkable. But, after all, coincidences of this sort have not been uncommon in the history of scientific inquiry. Nor is it at all surprising that they should occur now and then, when we remember that a great and pregnant discovery must always be concerned with some question which many of the foremost minds in the world are busy thinking about. It was so with the discovery of the differential calculus, and again with the discovery of the planet Neptune. It was so with the interpretation of the Egyptian hieroglyphics, and with the establishment of the undulatory theory of light. It was so, to a considerable extent, with the introduction of the new chemistry, with the discovery of the mechanical equivalent of heat, and the whole doctrine of the correlation of forces. It was so with the invention of the electric telegraph and with the discovery of spectrum analysis. And it is not at all strange that it should have been so with the doctrine of the origin of species through natural selection.

He thinks these "coincidences" were apt to happen because the matters from which they sprang were matters which many of the foremost minds in the world were busy thinking about. But perhaps *one* man in each case did the telegraphing to the others. The aberrations which gave Leverrier the idea that there must be a planet of such and such mass and such and such orbit hidden from sight out yonder in the remote abysses of space were not new; they had been noticed by astronomers for generations. Then why should it happen to occur to three people, widely separated—Leverrier,

Mrs. Somerville, and Adams—to suddenly go to worrying about those aberrations all at the same time, and set themselves to work to find out what caused them, and to measure and weigh an invisible planet, and calculate its orbit, and hunt it down and catch it?—a strange project which nobody but they had ever thought of before. If one astronomer had invented that odd and happy project fifty years before, don't you think he would have telegraphed it to several others without knowing it?

But now I come to a puzzler. How is it that *inanimate* objects are able to affect the mind? They seem to do that. However, I wish to throw in a parenthesis first—just a reference to a thing everybody is familiar with—the experience of receiving a clear and particular *answer* to your telegram before your telegram has reached the sender of the answer. That is a case where your telegram has gone straight from your brain to the man it was meant for, far outstripping the wire's slow electricity, and it is an exercise of mental telegraphy which is as common as dining. To return to the influence of inanimate things. In the cases of non-professional clairvoyance examined by the Psychical Society the clairvoyant has usually been blindfolded, then some object which has been touched or worn by a person is placed in his hand; the clairvoyant immediately describes that person, and goes on and gives a history of some event with which the text object has been connected. If the inanimate object is able to affect and inform the clairvoyant's mind, maybe it can do the same when it is working in the interest of mental telegraphy. Once a lady in the West wrote me that her son was coming to New York to remain three weeks, and would pay me a visit if invited, and she gave me his address. I mislaid the letter, and forgot all about the matter till the three weeks were about up. Then a sudden and fiery irruption of remorse burst up in my brain that illuminated all the region round about, and I sat down at once and wrote to the lady and asked for that lost address. But, upon reflection, I judged that the stirring up of my recollection had not been an accident, so I added a postscript to say, never mind, I should get a letter from her son before night. And I did get it; for the letter was already in the town, although not delivered yet. It had influenced me somehow. I have had so many experiences of this sort—a dozen of them at least—that I am nearly persuaded that inanimate objects do not confine their activities to helping the clairvoyant, but do every now and then give the mental telegraphist a lift.

The case of mental telegraphy which I am coming to now comes under I don't exactly know what head. I clipped it from one of our local papers six or eight years ago. I know the details to be right and true, for the story was told to me in the same form by one of the two persons concerned (a clergyman of Hartford) at the time that the curious thing happened:

A REMARKABLE COINCIDENCE

Strange coincidences make the most interesting of stories and most curious of studies. Nobody can quite say how they come about, but everybody appreciates the fact when they do come, and it is seldom that any more complete and curious coincidence is recorded of minor importance than the following, which is absolutely true and occurred in this city.

At the time of the building of one of the finest residences of Hartford, which is still a very new house, a local firm supplied the wall-paper for certain rooms, contracting both to furnish and to put on the paper. It happened that they did not calculate the size of one room exactly right, and the paper of the design selected for it fell short just half a roll. They asked for delay enough to send on to the manufacturers for what was needed, and were told that there was no especial hurry. It happened that the manufacturers had none on hand, and had destroyed the blocks from which it was printed. They wrote that they had a full list of the dealers to whom they had sold that paper, and that they would write to each of these and get from some of them a roll. It might involve a delay of a couple of weeks, but they would surely get it.

In the course of time came a letter saying that, to their great surprise, they could not find a single roll. Such a thing was very unusual, but in this case it had so happened. Accordingly the local firm asked for further time, saying they would write to their own customers who had bought of that pattern, and would get the piece from them. But to their surprise, this effort also failed. A long time had now elapsed, and there was no use of delaying any longer. They had contracted to paper the room, and their only course was to take off that which was insufficient and put on some other of which there was enough to go around. Accordingly at length a man was sent out to remove the paper. He got his apparatus ready, and was about to begin to work, under the direction of the owner of the building, when the latter was for the moment called away. The house was large and very interesting, and so many people had rambled about it that finally admission had been refused by a sign at the door. On the occasion, however, when a gentleman had knocked and asked for leave to look about, the owner, being on the premises, had been sent for to reply to the request in person. That was the call that for the moment delayed the final preparations. The gentleman went to the door and admitted the stranger, saying he would show him about the house, but first must return for a moment to that room to finish his directions there, and he told the curious story about the paper as they went on. They entered the room together, and the first thing the stranger, who lived fifty miles away, said on looking about was, "Why, I have that very paper on a room in my house, and I have an extra roll of it laid away, which is at your service." In a few days the wall was papered according to the original contract. Had not the owner been at the house, the stranger would not have been admitted; had he called a day later, it would have been too late; had not the facts been almost accidentally told to him, he would probably have said nothing of the paper, and so on. The exact fitting of all the circumstances is something very remarkable, and makes one of those stories that seem hardly accidental in their nature.

Something that happened the other day brought my hoary MS. to mind, and that is how I came to dig it out from its dusty pigeonhole grave for publication. The thing that happened was a question. A lady asked: "Have you ever had a vision—when awake?" I was about to answer promptly, when the last two words of the question began to grow and spread and swell, and presently they attained to vast dimensions. She did not know that they were important; and I did not at first, but I soon saw that they were putting me on the track of the solution of a mystery which had perplexed me a good deal. You will see what I mean when I get down to it. Ever since the English Society for Psychical Research began its investigations of ghost stories, haunted houses, and apparitions of the living and the dead, I have read their pamphlets with avidity as fast as they arrived. Now one of their commonest inquiries of a dreamer or a vision-seer is, "Are you sure you were awake at the time?" If the man can't say he is sure he was awake, a doubt falls upon his tale right there. But if he is positive he was awake, and offers reasonable evidence to substantiate it, the fact counts largely for the credibility of his story. It does with the society, and it did with me until that lady asked me the above question the other day.

The question set me to considering, and brought me to the conclusion that you can be asleep—at least, wholly unconscious—for a time, and not suspect that it has happened, and not have any way to prove that it *has* happened. A memorable case was in my mind. About a year ago I was standing on the porch one day, when I saw a man coming up the walk. He was a stranger, and I hoped he would ring and carry his business into the house without stopping to argue with me; he would have to pass the front door to get to me, and I hoped he wouldn't take the trouble; to help, I tried to look like a stranger myself—it often works. I was looking straight at that man; he had got to within ten feet of the door and within twenty-five feet of me—and suddenly he disappeared. It was as astounding as if a church should vanish from before your face and leave nothing behind it but a vacant lot. I was unspeakably delighted. I had seen an apparition at last, with my own eyes, in broad daylight. I made up my mind to write an account of it to the society. I ran to where the specter had been, to make sure he was playing fair, then I ran to the other end of the porch, scanning the open grounds as I went. No, everything was perfect; he couldn't have escaped without my seeing him; he was an apparition, without the slightest doubt, and I would write him up before he was cold. I ran, hot with excitement, and let myself in with a latch-key. When I stepped into the hall my lungs collapsed and my heart stood still. For there sat that same apparition in a chair all alone, and as quiet and reposeful as if he had come to stay a year! The shock kept me dumb for a moment or two; then I said, "Did you come in at that door?"

"Yes."

"Did *you* open it, or did you ring?"

"I rang, and the colored man opened it."

I said to myself: "This is astonishing. It takes George all of two minutes to answer the door-bell when he is in a hurry, and I have never seen him in a hurry. How *did* this man stand two minutes at that door, within five steps of me, and I did not see him?"

I should have gone to my grave puzzling over that riddle but for that lady's chance question last week: "Have you ever had a vision—when awake?" It stands explained now. During at least sixty seconds that day I was asleep, or at least totally unconscious, without suspecting it. In that interval the man came to my immediate vicinity, rang, stood there and waited, then entered and closed the door, and I did not see him and did not hear the door slam.

If he had slipped around the house in that interval and gone into the cellar—he had time enough—I should have written him up for the society, and magnified him, and gloated over him, and hurrahed about him, and thirty yoke of oxen could not have pulled the belief out of me that I was of the favored ones of the earth, and had seen a vision—while wide awake.

Now how are you to tell when you are awake? What are you to go by? People bite their fingers to find out. Why, you can do that in a dream.

Mental Telegraphy Again

I have three or four curious incidents to tell about. They seem to come under the head of what I named "Mental Telegraphy" in a paper written seventeen years ago, and published long afterward.

Several years ago I made a campaign on the platform with Mr. George W. Cable. In Montreal we were honored with a reception. It began at two in the afternoon in a long drawing-room in the Windsor Hotel. Mr. Cable and I stood at one end of this room, and the ladies and gentlemen entered it at the other end, crossed it at that end, then came up the long left-hand side, shook hands with us, said a word or two, and passed on, in the usual way. My sight is of the telescopic sort, and I presently recognized a familiar face among the throng of strangers drifting in at the distant door, and I said to myself, with surprise and high gratification, "That is Mrs. R——; I had forgotten that she was a Canadian." She had been a great friend of mine in Carson City, Nevada, in the early days. I had not seen her or heard of her for twenty years; I had not been thinking about her; there was nothing to suggest her to me, nothing to bring her to my mind; in fact, to me she had long ago ceased to exist, and had disappeared from my consciousness. But I knew her instantly; and I saw her so clearly that I was able to note some of the particulars of her dress, and did note them, and they remained in my mind. I was impatient for her to come. In the midst of the hand-shakings I snatched glimpses of her and noted her progress with the slow-moving file across the end of the room; then I saw her start up the side, and this gave me a full front view of her face. I saw her last when she was within twenty-five feet of me. For an hour I kept thinking she must still be in the room somewhere and would come at last, but I was disappointed.

When I arrived in the lecture-hall that evening some one said: "Come into the waiting-room; there's a friend of yours there who wants to see you. You'll not be introduced—you are to do the recognizing without help if you can."

I said to myself: "It is Mrs. R——; I sha'n't have any trouble."

There were perhaps ten ladies present, all seated. In the midst of them was Mrs. R——, as I had expected. She was dressed exactly as she was when I had seen her in the afternoon. I went forward and shook hands with her and called her by name, and said:

"I knew you the moment you appeared at the reception this afternoon."

She looked surprised, and said: "But I was not at the reception. I have just arrived from Quebec, and have not been in town an hour."

It was my turn to be surprised now. I said: "I can't help it. I give you my word of honor that it is as I say. I saw you at the reception, and you were dressed precisely as you are now. When they told me a moment ago that I should find a friend in this room, your image rose before me, dress and all, just as I had seen you at the reception."

Those are the facts. She was not at the reception at all, or anywhere near it; but I saw her there nevertheless, and most clearly and unmistakably. To that I could make oath. How is one to explain this? I was not thinking of her at the time; had not thought of her for years. But she had been thinking of me, no doubt; did her thoughts flit through leagues of air to me, and bring with it that clear and pleasant vision of herself? I think so. That was and remains my sole experience in the matter of apparitions—I mean apparitions that come when one is (ostensibly) awake. I could have been asleep for a moment; the apparition could have been the creature of a dream. Still, that is nothing to the point; the feature of interest is the happening of the thing just at that time, instead of at an earlier or later time, which is argument that its origin lay in thought-transference.

My next incident will be set aside by most persons as being merely a "coincidence," I suppose. Years ago I used to think sometimes of making a lecturing trip through the antipodes and the borders of the Orient, but always gave up the idea, partly because of the great length of the journey and partly because my wife could not well manage to go with me. Toward the end of last January that idea, after an interval of years, came suddenly into my head again—forcefully, too, and without any apparent reason. Whence came it? What suggested it? I will touch upon that presently.

I was at that time where I am now—in Paris. I wrote at once to Henry M. Stanley (London), and asked him some questions about his Australian lecture tour, and inquired who had conducted him and what were the terms. After a day or two his answer came. It began:

> The lecture agent for Australia and New Zealand is *par excellence* Mr. R. S. Smythe, of Melbourne.

He added his itinerary, terms, sea expenses, and some other matters, and advised me to write Mr. Smythe, which I did—February 3d. I began my letter by saying in substance that, while he did not know me personally, we had a mutual friend in Stanley, and that would answer for an introduction. Then I proposed my trip, and asked if he would give me the same terms which he had given Stanley.

I mailed my letter to Mr. Smythe February 6th, and three days later I got a letter from the selfsame Smythe, dated Melbourne, December 17th. I would as soon have expected to get a letter from the late George Washington. The letter began somewhat as mine to him had begun—with a self-introduction:

> DEAR MR. CLEMENS.—It is so long since Archibald Forbes and I spent that pleasant afternoon in your comfortable house at Hartford that you have probably quite forgotten the occasion.

In the course of his letter this occurs:

> I am willing to give you [here he named the terms which he had given Stanley] for an antipodean tour to last, say, three months.

Here was the single essential detail of my letter answered three days after I had mailed my inquiry. I might have saved myself the trouble and the postage—and a few years ago I would have done that very thing, for I would have argued that my sudden and strong impulse to write and ask some questions of a stranger on the under side of the globe meant that the impulse came from that stranger, and that he would answer my questions of his own motion if I would let him alone.

Mr. Smythe's letter probably passed under my nose on its way to lose three weeks traveling to America and back, and gave me a whiff of its contents as it went along. Letters often act like that. Instead of the *thought* coming to you in an instant from Australia, the (apparently) unsentient letter imparts it to you as it glides invisibly past your elbow in the mail-bag.

Next incident. In the following month—March—I was in America. I spent a Sunday at Irvington-on-the-Hudson with Mr. John Brisben Walker, of the *Cosmopolitan* magazine. We came into New York next morning, and went to the Century Club for luncheon. He said some praiseful things about the character of the club and the orderly serenity and pleasantness of its quarters, and asked if I had never tried to acquire membership in it. I said I had not, and that New York clubs were a continuous expense to the country members without being of frequent use or benefit to them.

"And now I've got an idea!" said I. "There's the Lotos—the first New York club I was ever a member of—my very earliest love in that line. I have been a member of it for considerably more than twenty years, yet have seldom had a chance to look in and see the boys. They turn gray and grow old while I am not watching. And *my dues go on.* I am going to Hartford this afternoon for a day or two, but as soon as I get back I will go to John Elderkin very privately and say: 'Remember the veteran and confer distinction upon him, for the sake of old times. Make me an honorary member and abolish the tax. If you haven't any such thing as honorary membership, all the better—create it for my honor and glory.' That would be a great thing; I will go to John Elderkin as soon as I get back from Hartford."

I took the last express that afternoon, first telegraphing Mr. F. G. Whitmore to come and see me next day. When he came he asked:

"Did you get a letter from Mr. John Elderkin, secretary of the Lotos Club, before you left New York?"

"No."

"Then it just missed you. If I had known you were coming I would have kept it. It is beautiful, and will make you proud. The Board of Directors, by unanimous vote, have made your a life member, and *squelched those dues;* and you are to be on hand and receive your distinction on the night of the 30th, which is the twenty-fifth anniversary of the founding of the club, and it will not surprise me if they have some great times there."

What put the honorary membership in my head that day in the Century Club? for I had never thought of it before. I don't know what brought the thought to me at *that* particular time instead of earlier, but I am well satisfied that it originated with the Board of Directors, and had been on its way to my brain through the air ever since the moment that saw their vote recorded.

Another incident. I was in Hartford two or three days as a guest of the Rev. Joseph H. Twichell. I have held the rank of Honorary Uncle to his children for a quarter of a century, and I went out with him in the trolley-car to visit one of my nieces, who is at Miss Porter's famous school in Farmington. The distance is eight or nine miles. On the way, talking, I illustrated something with an anecdote. This is the anecdote:

Two years and a half ago I and the family arrived at Milan on our way to Rome, and stopped at the Continental. After dinner I went below and took a seat in the stone-paved court, where the customary lemon trees stand in the customary tubs, and said to myself, "Now *this* is comfort, comfort and repose, and nobody to disturb it; I do not know anybody in Milan."

Then a young gentleman stepped up and shook hands, which damaged my theory. He said, in substance:

"You won't remember me, Mr. Clemens, but I remember you very well. I was a cadet at West Point when you and Rev. Joseph H. Twichell came there some years ago and talked to us on a Hundredth Night. I am a lieutenant in the regular army now, and my name is H——. I am in Europe, all alone, for a modest little tour; my regiment is in Arizona."

We became friendly and sociable, and in the course of the talk he told me of an adventure which had befallen him—about to this effect:

"I was at Bellagio, stopping at the big hotel there, and ten days ago I lost my letter of credit. I did not know what in the world to do. I was a stranger; I knew no one in Europe; I hadn't a penny in my pocket; I couldn't even send a telegram to London to get my lost letter replaced; my hotel bill was a week old, and the presentation of it imminent—so imminent that it could happen at any moment now. I was so frightened that my wits seemed to leave me. I tramped and tramped, back and forth, like a crazy person. If anybody approached me I hurried away, for no matter what a person looked like, I took him for the head waiter with the bill.

"I was at last in such a desperate state that I was ready to do any wild thing that promised even the shadow of help, and so this is the insane thing that I did. I saw a family lunching at a small table on the veranda, and recognized their nationality—Americans—father, mother, and several young daughters—young, tastefully dressed, and pretty—the rule with our people. I went straight there in my civilian costume, named my name, said I was a lieutenant in the army, and told my story and asked for help.

"What do you suppose the gentleman did? But you would not guess in twenty years. He took out a handful of gold coin and told me to help myself—freely. That is what he did."

The next morning the lieutenant told me his new letter of credit had arrived in the night, so we strolled to Cook's to draw money to pay back the benefactor with. We got it, and then went strolling through the great arcade. Presently he said, "Yonder they are; come and be introduced." I was introduced to the parents and the young ladies; then we separated, and I never saw him or them any m—

"Here we are at Farmington," said Twichell, interrupting.

We left the trolley-car and tramped through the mud a hundred yards or so to the school, talking about the time we and Warner walked out there years ago, and the pleasant time we had.

We had a visit with my niece in the parlor, then started for the trolley again. Outside the house we encountered a double rank of twenty or thirty of Miss Porter's young ladies arriving from a walk, and we stood aside, ostensibly to let them have room to file past, but really to look at them. Presently one of them stepped out of the rank and said:

"You don't know me, Mr. Twichell, but I know your daughter and that gives me the privilege of shaking hands with you."

Then she put out her hand to me, and said:

"And I wish to shake hands with you too, Mr. Clemens. You don't remember me, but you were introduced to me in the arcade in Milan two years and a half ago by Lieutenant H——."

What had put that story into my head after all that stretch of time? Was it just the proximity of that young girl, or was it merely an odd accident?

Concerning Tobacco

As concerns tobacco, there are many superstitions. And the chiefest is this—that there is a *standard* governing the matter, whereas there is nothing of the kind. Each man's own preference is the only standard for him, the only one which he can accept, the only one which can command him. A congress of all the tobacco-lovers in the world could not elect a standard which would be binding upon you or me, or would even much influence us.

The next superstition is that a man has a standard of his own. He hasn't. He thinks he has, but he hasn't. He thinks he can tell what he regards as a good cigar from what he regards as a bad one—but he can't. He goes by the brand, yet imagines he goes by the flavor. One may palm off the worst counterfeit upon him; if it bears his brand he will smoke it contentedly and never suspect.

Children of twenty-five, who have seven years of experience, try to tell me what is a good cigar and what isn't. Me, who never learned to smoke, but always smoked; me, who came into the world asking for a light.

No one can tell me what is a good cigar—for me. I am the only judge. People who claim to know say that I smoke the worst cigars in the world. They bring their own cigars when they come to my house. They betray an unmanly terror when I offer them a cigar; they tell lies and hurry away to meet engagements which they have not made when they are threatened with the hospitalities of my box. Now then, observe what superstition, assisted by a man's reputation, can do. I was to have twelve personal friends to supper one night. One of them was as notorious for costly and elegant cigars as I was for cheap and devilish ones. I called at his house and when no one was looking borrowed a double handful of his very choicest; cigars which cost him forty cents apiece and bore red-and-gold labels in sign of their nobility. I removed the labels and put the cigars into a box with my favorite brand on it—a brand which those people all knew, and which cowed them as men are cowed by an epidemic. They took these cigars when offered at the end of the supper, and lit them and sternly struggled with them—in dreary silence, for hilarity died when the fell brand came into view and started around—but their fortitude held for a short time only; then they made excuses and filed out, treading on one another's heels with indecent eagerness; and in the morning when I went out to observe results the cigars lay all between the front door and the gate. All except one—that one lay in the plate of the man from whom I had cabbaged the lot. One or two whiffs was all he could stand. He told me afterward that some day I would get shot for giving people that kind of cigars to smoke.

Am I certain of my own standard? Perfectly; yes, absolutely—unless somebody fools me by putting my brand on some other kind of cigar; for no doubt I am like the rest, and know my cigar by the brand instead of by the flavor. However, my standard is a pretty wide one and covers a good deal of territory. To me, almost any cigar is good that nobody else will smoke, and to me almost all cigars are bad that other people consider good. Nearly any cigar will do me, except a Havana. People think they hurt my feelings when they come to my house with their life-preservers on —I mean, with their own cigars in their pockets. It is an error; I take care of myself in a similar way. When I go into danger—that is, into rich people's houses, where, in the nature of things, they will have high-tariff cigars, red-and-gilt girdled and nested in a rosewood box along with a damp sponge, cigars which develop a dismal black ash and burn down the side and smell, and will grow hot to the fingers, and will go on growing hotter and hotter, and go on smelling more and more infamously and unendurably the deeper the fire tunnels down inside below the thimbleful of honest tobacco that is in the front end, the furnisher of it praising it all the time and telling you how much the deadly thing cost—yes, when I go into that sort of peril I carry my own defense along; I carry my own brand —twenty-seven cents a barrel—and I live to see my family again. I may seem to light his red-gartered cigar, but that is only for courtesy's sake; I smuggle it into my pocket for the poor, of whom I know many, and light one of my own; and while he praises it I join in, but when he says it cost forty-five cents I say nothing, for I know better.

However, to say true, my tastes are so catholic that I have never seen any cigars that I really could not smoke, except those that cost a dollar apiece. I have examined those and know that they are made of dog-hair, and not good dog-hair at that.

I have a thoroughly satisfactory time in Europe, for all over the Continent one finds cigars which not even the most hardened newsboys in New York would smoke. I brought cigars with me, the last time; I will not do that any more. In Italy, as in France, the Government is the only cigar-peddler. Italy has three or four domestic brands: the Minghetti, the Trabuco, the Virginia, and a very coarse one which is a modification of the Virginia. The Minghettis are large and comely, and cost three dollars and sixty cents a hundred; I can smoke a hundred in seven days and enjoy every one of them. The Trabucos suit me, too; I don't remember the price. But one has to learn to like the Virginia, nobody is born friendly to it. It looks like a rat-tail file, but smokes better, some think. It has a straw through it; you pull this out, and it leaves a flue, otherwise there would be no draught, not even as much as there is to a nail. Some prefer a nail at first. However, I like all the French, Swiss, German, and Italian domestic cigars, and have never cared to inquire what they are made of; and nobody would know, anyhow, perhaps. There is even a brand of European smoking-tobacco that I like. It is a brand used by the Italian peasants. It is loose and dry and black, and looks like tea-grounds. When the fire is applied it expands, and climbs up and towers above the pipe, and presently tumbles off inside of one's vest. The tobacco itself is cheap, but it raises the insurance. It is as I remarked in the beginning—the taste for tobacco is a matter of superstition. There are no standards—no real standards. Each man's preference is the only standard for him, the only one which he can accept, the only one which can command him.

Does the Race of Man Love a Lord?

Often a quite assified remark becomes sanctified by use and petrified by custom; it is then a permanency, its term of activity a geologic period.

The day after the arrival of Prince Henry I met an English friend, and he rubbed his hands and broke out with a remark that was charged to the brim with joy—joy that was evidently a pleasant salve to an old sore place:

"Many a time I've had to listen without retort to an old saying that is irritatingly true, and until now seemed to offer no chance for a return jibe: 'An Englishman does dearly love a lord'; but after this I shall talk back, and say 'How about the Americans?' "

It is a curious thing, the currency that an idiotic saying can get. The man that first says it thinks he has made a discovery. The man he says it to, thinks the same. It departs on its travels, is received everywhere with admiring acceptance, and not only as a piece of rare and acute observation, but as being exhaustively true and profoundly wise; and so it presently takes its place in the world's list of recognized and established wisdoms, and after that no one thinks of examining it to see whether it is really entitled to its high honors or not. I call to mind instances of this in two well-established proverbs, whose dullness is not surpassed by the one about the Englishman and his love for a lord: one of them records the American's Adoration of the Almighty Dollar, the other the American millionaire-girl's ambition to trade cash for a title, with a husband thrown in.

It isn't merely the American that adores the Almighty Dollar, it is the human race. The human race has always adored the hatful of shells, or the bale of calico, or the half-bushel of brass rings, or the handful of steel fish-hooks, or the houseful of black wives, or the zareba full of cattle, or the two-score camels and asses, or the factory, or the farm, or the block of buildings, or the railroad bonds, or the bank stock, or the hoarded cash, or —anything that stands for wealth and consideration and independence, and can secure to the possessor that most precious of all things, another man's envy. It was a dull person that invented the idea that the American's devotion to the dollar is more strenuous than another's.

Rich American girls do buy titles, but they did not invent that idea; it had been worn threadbare several hundred centuries before America was discovered. European girls still exploit it as briskly as ever; and, when a title is not to be had for the money in hand, they buy the husband without it. They must put up the "dot," or there is no trade. The commercialization of brides is substantially universal, except in America. It exists with us, to some little extent, but in no degree approaching a custom.

"The Englishman dearly loves a lord."

What is the soul and source of his love? I think the thing could be more correctly worded:

"The human race dearly envies a lord."

That is to say, it envies the lord's place. Why? On two accounts, I think: its Power and its Conspicuousness.

Where Conspicuousness carries with it a Power which, by the light of our own observation and experience, we are able to measure and comprehend, I think our envy of the possessor is as deep and as passionate as is that of any other nation. No one can care less for a lord than the backwoodsman, who has had no personal contact with lords and has seldom heard them spoken of; but I will not allow that any Englishman has a profounder envy of a lord than has the average American who has lived long years in a European capital and fully learned how immense is the position the lord occupies.

Of any ten thousand Americans who eagerly gather, at vast inconvenience, to get a glimpse of Prince Henry, all but a couple of hundred will be there out of an immense curiosity; they are burning up with desire to see a personage who is so much talked about. They envy him; but it is Conspicuousness they envy mainly, not the Power that is lodged in his royal quality and position, for they have but a vague and spectral knowledge and appreciation of that; through their environment and associations they have been accustomed to regard such things lightly, and as not being very real; consequently, they are not able to value them enough to consumingly envy them.

But, whenever an American (or other human being) is in the presence, for the first time, of a combination of great Power and Conspicuousness which he thoroughly understands and appreciates, his eager curiosity and pleasure will be well-sodden with that other passion—envy—whether he suspect it or not. At any time, on any day, in any part of America, you can confer a happiness upon any passing stranger by calling his attention to any other passing stranger and saying:

"Do you see that gentleman going along there? It is Mr. Rockfeller."

Watch his eye. It is a combination of power and conspicuousness which the man understands.

When we understand rank, we always like to rub against it. When a man is conspicuous, we always want to see him. Also, if he will pay us an attention we will manage to remember it. Also, we will mention it now and then, casually; sometimes to a friend, or if a friend is not handy, we will make out with a stranger.

Well, then, what is rank, and what is conspicuousness? At once we think of kings and aristocracies, and of world-wide celebrities in soldierships, the arts, letters, etc., and we stop there. But that is a mistake. Rank holds its court and receives its homage on every round of the ladder, from the emperor down to the rat-catcher; and distinction, also, exists on every round of the ladder, and commands its due of deference and envy.

To worship rank and distinction is the dear and valued privilege of all the human race, and it is freely and joyfully exercised in democracies as well as in monarchies—and even, to some extent, among those creatures whom we impertinently call the Lower Animals. For even they have some poor little vanities and foibles, though in this matter they are paupers as compared to us.

A Chinese Emperor has the worship of his four hundred million of subjects, but the rest of the world is indifferent to him. A Christian Emperor has the worship of his subjects and of a large part of the Christian world outside of his dominions; but he is a matter of indifference to all China. A king, class A, has an extensive worship; a king, class B, has a less extensive worship; class C, class D, class E get a steadily diminishing share of worship; class L (Sultan of Zanzibar), class P (Sultan of Sulu), and class W (half-king of Samoa), get no worship at all outside their own little patch of sovereignty.

Take the distinguished people along down. Each has his group of homage-payers. In the navy, there are many groups; they start with the Secretary and the Admiral, and go down to the quartermaster—and below; for there will be groups among the sailors, and each of these groups will have a tar who is distinguished for his battles, or his strength, or his daring, or his profanity, and is admired and envied by his group. The same with the army; the same with the literary and journalistic craft, the publishing craft; the cod-fishery craft; Standard Oil; U. S. Steel; the class A hotel—and the rest of the alphabet in that line; the class A prize-fighter—and the rest of the alphabet in his line—clear down to the lowest and obscurest six-boy gang of little gamins, with its one boy that can thrash the rest, and to whom he is king of Samoa, bottom of the royal race, but looked up to with a most ardent admiration and envy.

There is something pathetic, and funny, and pretty, about this human race's fondness for contact with power and distinction, and for the reflected glory it gets out of it. The king, class A, is happy in the state banquet and the military show which the emperor provides for him, and he goes home and gathers the queen and the princelings around him in the privacy of the spare room, and tells them all about it, and says:

"His Imperial Majesty put his hand on my shoulder in the most friendly way—just as friendly and familiar, oh, you can't imagine it!—and everybody *seeing* him do it; charming, perfectly charming!"

The king, class G, is happy in the cold collation and the police parade provided for him by the king, class B, and goes home and tells the family all about it, and says:

"And His Majesty took me into his own private cabinet for a smoke and a chat, and there we sat just as sociable, and talking away and laughing and chatting, just the same as if we had been born in the same bunk; and all the servants in the anteroom could see us doing it! Oh, it was too lovely for anything!"

The king, class Q, is happy in the modest entertainment furnished him by the king, class M, and goes home and tells the household about it, and is as grateful and joyful over it as were his predecessors in the gaudier attentions that had fallen to their larger lot.

Emperors, kings, artisans, peasants, big people, little people—at bottom we are all alike and all the same; all just alike on the inside, and when our clothes are off, nobody can tell which of us is which. We are unanimous in the pride we take in good and genuine compliments paid us, in distinctions conferred upon us, in attentions shown us. There is not one of us, from the emperor down, but is made like that. Do I mean attentions shown us by the great? No, I mean simply flattering attentions, let them come whence they may. We despise no source that can pay us a pleasing attention—there is no source that is humble enough for that. You have heard a dear little girl say to a frowzy and disreputable dog: "He came right to me and let me pat him on the head, and he wouldn't let the others touch him!" and you have seen her eyes dance with pride in that high distinction. You have often seen that. If the child were a princess, would that random dog be able to confer the like glory upon her with his pretty compliment? Yes; and even in her mature life and seated upon a throne, she would still remember it, still recall it, still speak of it with frank satisfaction. That charming and lovable German princess and poet, Carmen Sylva, Queen of Roumania, remembers yet that the flowers of the woods and fields "talked to her" when she was a girl, and she sets it down in her latest book; and that the squirrels conferred upon her and her father the valued compliment of not being afraid of them; and "once one of them, holding a nut between its sharp little teeth, ran right up against my father"—it has the very note of "He came right to me and let me pat him on the head"—"and when it saw itself reflected in his boot it was very much surprised, and stopped for a long time to contemplate itself in the polished leather"—then it went its way. And the birds! she still remembers with pride that "they came boldly into my room," when she had neglected her "duty" and put no food on the window-sill for them; she knew all the wild birds, and forgets the royal crown on her head to remember with pride that they knew her; also that the wasp and the bee were personal friends of hers, and never forgot that gracious relationship to her injury: "never have I been stung by a wasp or a bee." And here is that proud note again that sings in that little child's elation in being singled out, among all the company of children, for the random dog's honor-conferring attentions. "Even in the very worst summer for wasps, when, in lunching out of doors, our table was covered with them and every one else was stung, they never hurt me."

When a queen whose qualities of mind and heart and character are able to add distinction to so distinguished a place as a throne, remembers with grateful exultation, after thirty years, honors and distinctions conferred upon her by the humble, wild creatures of the forest, we are helped to realize that complimentary attentions, homage, distinctions, are of no caste, but are above all caste—that they are a nobility-conferring power apart.

We all like these things. When the gate-guard at the railway-station passes me through unchallenged and examines other people's tickets, I feel as the king, class A, felt when the emperor put the imperial hand on his shoulder, "everybody seeing him do it"; and as the child felt when the random dog allowed her to pat his head and ostracized the others; and as the princess felt when the wasps spared her and stung the rest; and I felt just so, four years ago in Vienna (and remember it yet), when the helmeted police shut me off, with fifty others, from a street which the Emperor was to pass through, and the captain of the squad turned and saw the situation and said indignantly to that guard:

"Can't you see it is the Herr Mark Twain? Let him through!"

It was four years ago; but it will be four hundred before I forget the wind of self-complacency that rose in me, and strained my buttons when I marked the deference for me evoked in the faces of my fellow-rabble, and noted, mingled with it, a puzzled and resentful expression which said, as plainly as speech could have worded it: "And who in the nation is the Herr Mark Twain *um Gotteswillen?*"

How many times in your life have you heard this boastful remark:

"I stood as close to him as I am to you; I could have put out my hand and touched him."

We have all heard it many and many a time. It was a proud distinction to be able to say those words. It brought envy to the speaker, a kind of glory; and he basked in it and was happy through all his veins. And who was it he stood so close to? The answer would cover all the grades. Sometimes it was a king; sometimes it was a renowned highwayman; sometimes it was an unknown man killed in an extraordinary way and made suddenly famous by it; always it was a person who was for the moment the subject of public interest—the public interest of a nation, maybe only the public interest of a village.

"I was there, and I saw it myself." That is a common and envy-compelling remark. It can refer to a battle; to a hanging; to a coronation; to the killing of Jumbo by the railway-train; to the arrival of Jenny Lind at the Battery; to the meeting of the President and Prince Henry; to the chase of a murderous maniac; to the disaster in the tunnel; to the explosion in the subway; to a remarkable dog-fight; to a village church struck by lightning. It will be said, more or less casually, by everybody in America who has seen Prince Henry do anything, or try to. The man who was absent and didn't see him do anything, will scoff. It is his privilege; and he can make capital out of it, too; he will seem, even to himself, to be different from other Americans, and better. As his opinion of his superior Americanism grows, and swells, and concentrates and coagulates, he will go further and try to belittle the distinction of those that saw the Prince do things, and will spoil their pleasure in it if he can. My life has been embittered by that kind of persons. If you are able to tell of a special distinction that has fallen to your lot, it gravels them; they cannot bear it; and they try to make believe that the thing you took for a special distinction was nothing of the kind and was meant in quite another way. Once I was received in private audience by an emperor. Last week I was telling a jealous person about it, and I could see him wince under it, see it bite, see him suffer. I revealed the whole episode to him with considerable elaboration and nice attention to detail. When I was through, he asked me what had impressed me most. I said:

"His Majesty's delicacy. They told me to be sure and back out from the presence, and find the door-knob as best I could; it was not allowable to face around. Now the Emperor knew it would be a difficult ordeal for me, because of lack of practice; and so, when it was time to part, he turned, with exceeding delicacy, and pretended to fumble with things on his desk, so that I could get out in my own way, without his seeing me."

It went home! It was vitriol! I saw the envy and disgruntlement rise in the man's face; he couldn't keep it down. I saw him trying to fix up something in his mind to take the bloom off that distinction. I enjoyed that, for I judged that he had his work cut out for him. He struggled along inwardly for quite a while; then he said, with the manner of a person who has to say something and hasn't anything relevant to say:

"You said he had a handful of special-brand cigars lying on the table?"

"Yes; *I* never saw anything to match them."

I had him again. He had to fumble around in his mind as much as another minute before he could play; then he said in as mean a way as I ever heard a person say anything:

"He could have been counting the cigars, you know."

I cannot endure a man like that. It is nothing to him how unkind he is, so long as he takes the bloom off. It is all he cares for.

"An Englishman (or other human being) does dearly love a lord (or other conspicuous person)." It includes us all. We love to be noticed by the conspicuous person; we love to be associated with such, or with a conspicuous event, even in a seventh-rate fashion, even in a forty-seventh, if we cannot do better. This accounts for some of our curious tastes in mementos. It accounts for the large private trade in the Prince of Wales's hair, which chambermaids were able to drive in that article of commerce when the Prince made the tour of the world in the long ago—hair which probably did not always come from his brush, since enough of it was marketed to refurnish a bald comet; it accounts for the fact that the rope which lynches a negro in the presence of ten thousand Christian spectators is salable five minutes later at two dollars an inch; it accounts for the mournful fact that a royal personage does not venture to wear buttons on his coat in public.

We do love a lord—and by that term I mean any person whose situation is higher than our own. The lord of a group, for instance: a group of peers, a group of millionaires, a group of hoodlums, a group of sailors, a group of newsboys, a group of saloon politicians, a group of college girls. No royal person has ever been the object of a more delirious loyalty and slavish adoration than is paid by the vast Tammany herd to its squalid idol of Wantage. There is not a bifurcated animal in that menagerie that would not be proud to appear in a newspaper picture in his company. At the same time, there are some in that organization who would scoff at the people who have been daily pictured in company with Prince Henry, and would say vigorously that *they* would not consent to be photographed with him—a statement which would not be true in any instance. There are hundreds of people in America who would frankly say to you that they would not be proud to be photographed in a group with the Prince, if invited; and some of these unthinking people would believe it when they said it; yet in no instance would it be true. We have a large population, but we have not a large enough one, by several millions, to furnish that man. He has not yet been begotten, and in fact he is not begettable.

You may take any of the printed groups, and there isn't a person in it who isn't visibly glad to be there; there isn't a person in the dim background who isn't visibly trying to be vivid; if it is a crowd of ten thousand —ten thousand proud, untamed democrats, horny-handed sons of toil and of politics, and fliers of the eagle—there isn't one who isn't conscious of the camera, there isn't one who is trying to keep out of range, there isn't one who isn't plainly meditating a purchase of the paper in the morning, with the intention of hunting himself out in the picture and of framing and keeping it if he shall find so much of his person in it as his starboard ear.

We all love to get some of the drippings of Conspicuousness, and we will put up with a single, humble drip, if we can't get any more. We may pretend otherwise, in conversation; but we can't pretend it to ourselves privately—and we don't. We do confess in public that we are the noblest work of God, being moved to it by long habit, and teaching, and superstition; but deep down in the secret places of our souls we recognize that, if we *are* the noblest work, the less said about it the better.

We of the North poke fun at the South for its fondness for titles—a fondness for titles pure and simple, regardless of whether they are genuine or pinchbeck. We forget that whatever a Southerner likes the rest of the human race likes, and that there is no law of predilection lodged in one people that is absent from another people. There is no variety in the human race. We are all children, all children of the one Adam, and we love toys. We can soon acquire that Southern disease if some one will give it a start. It already has a start, in fact. I have been personally acquainted with over eighty-four thousand persons who, at one time or another in their lives, have served for a year or two on the staffs of our multitudinous governors, and through that fatality have been generals temporarily, and colonels temporarily, and judge-advocates temporarily; but I have known only nine among them who could be hired to let the title go when it ceased to be legitimate. I know thousands and thousands of governors who ceased to be governors away back in the last century; but I am acquainted with only three who would answer your letter if you failed to call them "Governor" in it. I know acres and acres of men who have done time in a legislature in prehistoric days, but among them is not half an acre whose resentment you would not raise if you addressed them as "Mr." instead of "Hon." The first thing a legislature does is to convene in an impressive legislative attitude, and get itself photographed. Each member frames his copy and takes it to the woods and hangs it up in the most aggressively conspicuous place in his house; and if you visit the house and fail to inquire what that accumulation is, the conversation will be brought around to it by that aforetime legislator, and he will show you a figure in it which in the course of years he has almost obliterated with the smut of his finger-marks, and say with a solemn joy, "It's me!"

Have you ever seen a country Congressman enter the hotel breakfast-room in Washington with his letters?—and sit at his table and let on to read them?—and wrinkle his brows and frown statesman-like?—keeping a furtive watch-out over his glasses all the while to see if he is being observed and admired?—those same old letters which he fetches in every morning? Have you seen it? Have you seen him show off? It is *the* sight of the national capital. Except one; a pathetic one. That is the ex-Congressman:

the poor fellow whose life has been ruined by a two-year taste of glory and of fictitious consequence: who has been superseded, and ought to take his heartbreak home and hide it, but cannot tear himself away from the scene of his lost little grandeur; and so he lingers, and still lingers, year after year, unconsidered, sometimes snubbed, ashamed of his fallen estate, and valiantly trying to look otherwise; dreary and depressed, but counterfeiting breeziness and gaiety, hailing with chummy familiarity, which is not always welcomed, the more-fortunates who are still in place and were once his mates. Have you seen him? He clings piteously to the one little shred that is left of his departed distinction—the "privilege of the floor"; and works it hard and gets what he can out of it. That is the saddest figure I know of.

Yes, we do so love our little distinctions! And then we loftily scoff at a Prince for enjoying his larger ones; forgetting that if we only had his chance—ah! "Senator" is not a legitimate title. A Senator has no more right to be addressed by it than have you or I; but, in the several state capitals and in Washington, there are five thousand Senators who take very kindly to that fiction, and who purr gratefully when you call them by it—which you may do quite unrebuked. Then those same Senators smile at the self-constructed majors and generals and judges of the South!

Indeed, we do love our distinctions, get them how we may. And we work them for all they are worth. In prayer we call ourselves "worms of the dust," but it is only on a sort of tacit understanding that the remark shall not be taken at par. *We*—worms of the dust! Oh, no, we are not that. Except in fact; and we do not deal much in fact when we are contemplating ourselves.

As a race, we do certainly love a lord—let him be Croker, or a duke, or a prize-fighter, or whatever other personage shall chance to be the head of our group. Many years ago, I saw a greasy youth in overalls standing by the *Herald* office, with an expectant look in his face. Soon a large man passed out, and gave him a pat on the shoulder. That was what the boy was waiting for—the large man's notice. The pat made him proud and happy, and the exultation inside of him shone out through his eyes; and his mates were there to see the pat and envy it and wish they could have that glory. The boy belonged down cellar in the press-room, the large man was king of the upper floors, foreman of the composing-room. The light in the boy's face was worship, the foreman was his lord, head of his group. The pat was an accolade. It was as precious to the boy as it would have been if he had been an aristocrat's son and the accolade had been delivered by his sovereign with a sword. The quintessence of the honor was all there; there was no difference in values; in truth there was no difference present except an artificial one—clothes.

All the human race loves a lord—that is, it loves to look upon or be noticed by the possessor of Power or Conspicuousness; and sometimes animals, born to better things and higher ideals, descend to man's level in this matter. In the Jardin des Plantes I have seen a cat that was so vain of being the personal friend of an elephant that I was ashamed of her.

A Telephonic Conversation

Consider that a conversation by telephone—when you are simply sitting by and not taking any part in that conversation—is one of the solemnest curiosities of this modern life. Yesterday I was writing a deep article on a sublime philosophical subject while such a conversation was going on in the room. I notice that one can always write best when somebody is talking through a telephone close by. Well, the thing began in this way. A member of our household came in and asked me to have our house put into communication with Mr. Bagley's, downtown. I have observed, in many cities, that the sex always shrink from calling up the central office themselves. I don't know why, but they do. So I touched the bell, and this talk ensued:

Central Office. (Gruffly.) Hello!

I. Is it the Central Office?

C. O. Of course it is. What do you want?

I. Will you switch me on to the Bagleys, please?

C. O. All right. Just keep your ear to the telephone.

Then I heard, *k-look, k-look, k'look—klook-klook-klook-look-look!* then a horrible "gritting" of teeth, and finally a piping female voice: Y-e-s? *(Rising inflection.)* Did you wish to speak to me?

Without answering, I handed the telephone to the applicant, and sat down. Then followed that queerest of all the queer things in this world—a conversation with only one end to it. You hear questions asked; you don't hear the answer. You hear invitations given; you hear no thanks in return. You have listening pauses of dead silence, followed by apparently irrelevant and unjustifiable exclamations of glad surprise or sorrow or dismay. You can't make head or tail of the talk, because you never hear anything that the person at the other end of the wire says. Well, I heard the following remarkable series of observations, all from the one tongue, and all shouted—for you can't ever persuade the sex to speak gently into a telephone:

Yes? Why, how did *that* happen?

Pause.

What did you say?

Pause.

Oh no, I don't think it was

Pause.

No! Oh no, I didn't mean *that.* I meant, put it in while it is still boiling—or just before it *comes* to a boil.

Pause.

WHAT?

Pause.

I turned it over with a backstitch on the selvage edge.

Pause.

Yes, I like that way, too; but I think it's better to baste it on with Valenciennes or bombazine, or something of that sort. It gives it such an air—and attracts so much notice.

Pause.

It's forty-ninth Deuteronomy, sixty-fourth to ninety-seventh inclusive. I think we ought all to read it often.

Pause.

Perhaps so; I generally use a hair-pin.

Pause.

What did you say? *(Aside.)* Children, do be quiet!

Pause.

Oh! B *flat!* Dear me, I thought you said it was the cat!

Pause.

Since *when?*

Pause.

Why, *I* never heard of it.

Pause.

You astound me! It seems utterly impossible!

Pause.

Who did?

Pause.

Good-ness gracious!

Pause.

Well, what *is* this world coming to? Was it right in *church?*

Pause.

And was her *mother* there?

Pause.

Why, Mrs. Bagley, I should have died of humiliation! What did they *do?*

Long pause.

I can't be perfectly sure, because I haven't the notes by me; but I think it goes something like this: te-rolly-loll-loll, loll lolly-loll-loll, O tolly-loll-loll-*lee-ly-li-i*-do! And then *repeat,* you know.

Pause.

Yes, I think it *is* very sweet—and very solemn and impressive, if you get the andantino and the pianissimo right.

Pause.

Oh, gum-drops, gum-drops! But I never allow them to eat striped candy. And of course they *can't,* till they get their teeth, anyway.

Pause.

What?

Pause.

Oh, not in the least—go right on. He's here writing—it doesn't bother *him.*

Pause.

Very well, I'll come if I can. *(Aside.)* Dear me, how it does tire a person's arm to hold this thing up so long! I wish she'd—

Pause.

Oh no, not at all; I *like* to talk—but I'm afraid I'm keeping you from your affairs.

Pause.

Visitors?

Pause.

No, we never use butter on them.

Pause.

Yes, that is a very good way; but all the cookbooks say they are very unhealthy when they are out of season. And *he* doesn't like them, anyway —especially canned.

Pause.

Oh, I think that is too high for them; we have never paid over fifty cents a bunch.

Pause.

Must you go? Well, *good*-by.

Pause.

Yes, I think so. *Good*-by.

Pause.

Four o'clock, then—I'll be ready. *Good*-by.

Pause.

Thank you ever so much. *Good*-by.

Pause.

Oh, not at all!—just as fresh— *Which?* Oh, I'm glad to hear you say that. *Good*-by.

(Hangs up the telephone and says, "Oh, it *does* tire a person's arm so!")

A man delivers a single brutal "Good-by," and that is the end of it. Not so with the gentle sex—I say it in their praise; they cannot abide abruptness.

Wit Inspirations of the "Two-Year-Olds"

All infants appear to have an impertinent and disagreeable fashion nowadays of saying "smart" things on most occasions that offer, and especially on occasions when they ought not to be saying anything at all. Judging by the average published specimens of smart sayings, the rising generation of children are little better than idiots. And the parents must surely be but little better than the children, for in most cases they are the publishers of the sunbursts of infantile imbecility which dazzle us from the pages of our periodicals. I may seem to speak with some heat, not to say a suspicion of personal spite; and I do admit that it nettles me to hear about so many gifted infants in these days, and remember that I seldom said anything smart when I was a child. I tried it once or twice, but it was not popular. The family were not expecting brilliant remarks from me, and so they snubbed me sometimes and spanked me the rest. But it makes my flesh creep and my blood run cold to think what might have happened to me if I had dared to utter some of the smart things of this generation's "four-year-olds" where my father could hear me. To have simply skinned me alive and considered his duty at an end would have seemed to him criminal leniency toward one so sinning. He was a stern, unsmiling man, and hated all forms of precocity. If I had said some of the things I have referred to, and said them in his hearing, he would have destroyed me. He would, indeed. He would, provided the opportunity remained with him. But it would not, for I would have had judgment enough to take some strychnine first and say my smart thing afterward. The fair record of my life has been tarnished by just one pun. My father overheard that, and he hunted me over four or five townships seeking to take my life. If I had been full-grown, of course he would have been right; but, child as I was, I could not know how wicked a thing I had done.

I made one of those remarks ordinarily called "smart things" before that, but it was not a pun. Still, it came near causing a serious rupture between my father and myself. My father and mother, my uncle Ephraim and his wife, and one or two others were present, and the conversation turned on a name for me. I was lying there trying some India-rubber rings of various patterns, and endeavoring to make a selection, for I was tired of trying to cut my teeth on people's fingers, and wanted to get hold of something that would enable me to hurry the thing through and get something else. Did you ever notice what a nuisance it was cutting your teeth on your nurse's finger, or how back-breaking and tiresome it was trying to cut them on your big toe? And did you never get out of patience and wish your teeth were in Jericho long before you got them half cut? To me it seems as if these things happened yesterday. And they did, to some children. But I digress. I was lying there trying the India-rubber rings. I remember looking at the clock and noticing that in an hour and twenty-five minutes I would be two weeks old, and thinking how little I had done to merit the blessings that were so unsparingly lavished upon me. My father said:

"Abraham is a good name. My grandfather was named Abraham."

My mother said:

"Abraham is a good name. Very well. Let us have Abraham for one of his names."

I said:

"Abraham suits the subscriber."

My father frowned, my mother looked pleased; my aunt said:

"What a little darling it is!"

My father said:

"Isaac is a good name, and Jacob is a good name."

My mother assented, and said:

"No names are better. Let us add Isaac and Jacob to his names."

I said:

"All right. Isaac and Jacob are good enough for yours truly. Pass me that rattle, if you please. I can't chew India-rubber rings all day."

Not a soul made a memorandum of these sayings of mine, for publication. I saw that, and did it myself, else they would have been utterly lost. So far from meeting with a generous encouragement like other children when developing intellectually, I was now furiously scowled upon by my father; my mother looked grieved and anxious, and even my aunt had about her an expression of seeming to think that maybe I had gone too far. I took a vicious bite out of an India-rubber ring, and covertly broke the rattle over the kitten's head, but said nothing. Presently my father said:

"Samuel is a very excellent name."

I saw that trouble was coming. Nothing could prevent it. I laid down my rattle; over the side of the cradle I dropped my uncle's silver watch, the clothes-brush, the toy dog, my tin soldier, the nutmeg-grater, and other matters which I was accustomed to examine, and meditate upon and make pleasant noises with, and bang and batter and break when I needed wholesome entertainment. Then I put on my little frock and my little bonnet, and took my pygmy shoes in one hand and my licorice in the other, and climbed out on the floor. I said to myself, Now, if the worst comes to worst, I am ready. Then I said aloud, in a firm voice:

"Father, I cannot, cannot wear the name of Samuel."

"My son!"

"Father, I mean it. I cannot."

"Why?"

"Father, I have an invincible antipathy to that name."

"My son, this is unreasonable. Many great and good men have been named Samuel."

"Sir, I have yet to hear of the first instance."

"What! There was Samuel the prophet. Was not he great and good?"

"No so very."

"My son! With His own voice the Lord called him."

"Yes, sir, and had to call him a couple of times before he would come!"

And then I sallied forth, and that stern old man sallied forth after me. He overtook me at noon the following day, and when the interview was over I had acquired the name of Samuel, and a thrashing, and other useful information; and by means of this compromise my father's wrath was appeased and a misunderstanding bridged over which might have become a permanent rupture if I had chosen to be unreasonable. But just judging by this episode, what would my father have done to me if I had ever uttered in his hearing one of the flat, sickly things these "two-year-olds" say in print nowadays? In my opinion there would have been a case of infanticide in our family.

Concerning the Jews

Some months ago I published a magazine article descriptive of a remarkable scene in the Imperial Parliament in Vienna. Since then I have received from Jews in America several letters of inquiry. They were difficult letters to answer, for they were not very definite. But at last I received a definite one. It is from a lawyer, and he really asks the questions which the other writers probably believed they were asking. By help of this text I will do the best I can to publicly answer this correspondent, and also the others—at the same time apologizing for having failed to reply privately. The lawyer's letter reads as follows:

> I have read "Stirring Times in Austria." One point in particular is of vital import to not a few thousand people, including myself, being a point about which I have often wanted to address a question to some disinterested person. The show of military force in the Austrian Parliament, which precipitated the riots, was not introduced by any Jew. No Jew was a member of that body. No Jewish question was involved in the *Ausgleich* or in the language proposition. No Jew was insulting anybody. In short, no Jew was doing any mischief toward anybody whatsoever. In fact, the Jews were the only ones of the nineteen different races in Austria which did not have a party—they are

absolutely non-participants. Yet in your article you say that in the rioting which followed, all classes of people were unanimous only on one thing—*viz.,* in being against the Jews. Now will you kindly tell me why, in your judgment, the Jews have thus ever been, and are even now, in these days of supposed intelligence, the butt of baseless, vicious animosities? I dare say that for centuries there has been no more quiet, undisturbing, and well-behaving citizens, as a class, than that same Jew. It seems to me that ignorance and fanaticism cannot alone account for these horrible and unjust persecutions.

Tell me, therefore, from your vantage-point of cold view, what in your mind is the cause. Can American Jews do anything to correct it either in America or abroad? Will it ever come to an end? Will a Jew be permitted to live honestly, decently, and peaceably like the rest of mankind? What has become of the golden rule?

I will begin by saying that if I thought myself prejudiced against the Jew, I should hold it fairest to leave this subject to a person not crippled in that way. But I think I have no such prejudice. A few years ago a Jew observed to me that there was no uncourteous reference to his people in my books, and asked how it happened. It happened because the disposition was lacking. I am quite sure that (bar one) I have no race prejudices, and I think I have no color prejudices nor caste prejudices nor creed prejudices. Indeed, I know it. I can stand any society. All that I care to know is that a man is a human being—that is enough for me; he can't be any worse. I have no special regard for Satan; but I can at least claim that I have no prejudice against him. It may even be that I lean a little his way, on account of his not having a fair show. All religions issue bibles against him, and say the most injurious things about him, but we never hear *his* side. We have none but the evidence for the prosecution, and yet we have rendered the verdict. To my mind, this is irregular. It is un-English; it is un-American; it is French. Without this precedent Dreyfus could not have been condemned. Of course Satan has some kind of a case, it goes without saying. It may be a poor one, but that is nothing; that can be said about any of us. As soon as I can get at the facts I will undertake his rehabilitation myself, if I can find an unpolitic publisher. It is a thing which we ought to be willing to do for any one who is under a cloud. We may not pay him reverence, for that would be indiscreet, but we can at least respect his talents. A person who has for untold centuries maintained the imposing position of spiritual head of four-fifths of the human race, and political head of the whole of it, must be granted the possession of executive abilities of the loftiest order. In his large presence the other popes and politicians shrink to midges for the microscope. I would like to see him. I would rather see him and shake him by the tail than any other member of the European Concert. In the present paper I shall allow myself to use the word Jew as if it stood for both religion and race. It is handy; and, besides, that is what the term means to the general world.

In the above letter one notes these points:

1. The Jew is a well-behaved citizen.
2. Can ignorance and fanaticism *alone* account for his unjust treatment?
3. Can Jews do anything to improve the situation?
4. The Jews have no party; they are non-participants.
5. Will the persecution ever come to an end?
6. What has become of the golden rule?

Point No. 1.—We must grant proposition No. 1, for several sufficient reasons. The Jew is not a disturber of the peace of any country. Even his enemies will concede that. He is not a loafer, he is not a sot, he is not noisy, he is not a brawler nor a rioter, he is not quarrelsome. In the statistics of crime his presence is conspicuously rare—in all countries. With murder and other crimes of violence he has but little to do: he is a stranger to the hangman. In the police court's daily long roll of "assaults" and "drunk and disorderlies" his name seldom appears. That the Jewish home is a home in the truest sense is a fact which no one will dispute. The family is knitted together by the strongest affections; its members show each other every due respect; and reverence for the elders is an inviolate law of the house. The Jew is not a burden on the charities of the state nor of the city; these could cease from their functions without affecting him. When he is well enough, he works; when he is incapacitated, his own people take care of him. And not in a poor and stingy way, but with a fine and large benevolence. His race is entitled to be called the most benevolent of all the races of men. A Jewish beggar is not impossible, perhaps; such a thing may exist, but there are few men that can say they have seen that spectacle. The Jew has been staged in many uncomplimentary forms, but, so far as I know, no dramatist has done him the injustice to stage him as a beggar. Whenever a Jew has real need to beg, his people save him from the necessity of doing it. The charitable institutions of the Jews are supported by Jewish money, and amply. The Jews make no noise about it; it is done quietly; they do not nag and pester and harass us for contributions; they give us peace, and set us an example—an example which we have not found ourselves able to follow; for by nature we are not free givers, and have to be patiently and persistently hunted down in the interest of the unfortunate.

These facts are all on the credit side of the proposition that the Jew is a good and orderly citizen. Summed up, they certify that he is quiet, peaceable, industrious, unaddicted to high crimes and brutal dispositions; that his family life is commendable; that he is not a burden upon public charities; that he is not a beggar; that in benevolence he is above the reach of competition. These are the very quintessentials of good citizenship. If you can add that he is as honest as the average of his neighbors— But I think that question is affirmatively answered by the fact that he is a successful business man. The basis of successful business is honesty; a business cannot thrive where the parties to it cannot trust each other. In the matter of numbers the Jew counts for little in the overwhelming population of New York; but that his honesty counts for much is guaranteed by the fact that the immense wholesale business of Broadway, from the Battery to Union Square, is substantially in his hands.

I suppose that the most picturesque example in history of a trader's trust in his fellow-trader was one where it was not Christian trusting Christian, but Christian trusting Jew. That Hessian Duke who used to sell his subjects to George III. to fight George Washington with got rich at it; and by and by, when the wars engendered by the French Revolution made his throne too warm for him, he was obliged to fly the country. He was in a hurry, and had to leave his earnings behind—nine million dollars. He had to risk the money with some one without security. He did not select a Christian, but a Jew—a Jew of only modest means, but of high character; a character so high that it left him lonesome—Rothschild of Frankfort. Thirty years later, when Europe had become quiet and safe again, the Duke came back from overseas, and the Jew returned the loan, with interest added.[1]

1. Here is another piece of picturesque history; and it reminds us that shabbiness and dishonesty are not the monopoly of any race or creed, but are merely human:

"Congress passed a bill to pay $379.56 to Moses Pendergrass, of Libertyville, Missouri. The story of the reason of this liberality is pathetically interesting, and shows the sort of pickle that an honest man may get into who undertakes to do an honest job of work for Uncle Sam. In 1886 Moses Pendergrass put in a bid for the contract to carry the mail on the route from Knob Lick to Libertyville and Coffman, thirty miles a day, from July 1, 1887, for one year. He got the postmaster at Knob Lick to write the letter for him, and while Moses intended that his bid should be $400, his scribe carelessly made it $4. Moses got the contract, and did not find out about the mistake until the end

The Jew has his other side. He has some discreditable ways, though he has not a monopoly of them, because he cannot get entirely rid of vexatious Christian competition. We have seen that he seldom transgresses the laws against crimes of violence. Indeed, his dealings with courts are almost restricted to matters connected with commerce. He has a reputation for various small forms of cheating, and for practising oppressive usury, and for burning himself out to get the insurance, and arranging for cunning contracts which leave him an exit but lock the other man in, and for smart evasions which find him safe and comfortable just within the strict letter of the law, when court and jury know very well that he has violated the spirit of it. He is a frequent and faithful and capable officer in the civil service, but he is charged with an unpatriotic disinclination to stand by the flag as a soldier—like the Christian Quaker.

Now if you offset these discreditable features by the creditable ones summarized in a preceding paragraph beginning with the words, "These facts are all on the credit side," and strike a balance, what must the verdict be? This, I think: that, the merits and demerits being fairly weighed and measured on both sides, the Christian can claim no superiority over the Jew in the matter of good citizenship.

of the first quarter, when he got his first pay. When he found at what rate he was working he was sorely cast down, and opened communication with the Post Office Department. The department informed him that he must either carry out his contract or throw it up, and that if he threw it up his bondsmen would have to pay the government $1,459.85 damages. So Moses carried out his contract, walked thirty miles every weekday for a year, and carried the mail, and received for his labor $4—or, to be accurate, $6.84; for, the route being extended after his bid was accepted, the pay was proportionately increased. Now, after ten years, a bill was finally passed to pay to Moses the difference between what he earned in that unlucky year and what he received."

The *Sun,* which tells the above story, says that bills were introduced in three or four Congresses for Moses' relief, and that committees repeatedly investigated his claim.

It took six Congresses, containing in their persons the compressed virtues of 70,000,000 of people, and cautiously and carefully giving expression to those virtues in the fear of God and the next election, eleven years to find out some way to cheat a fellow-Christian out of about $13 on his honestly executed contract, and out of nearly $300 due him on its enlarged terms. And they succeeded. During the same time they paid out $1,000,000,000 in pensions—a third of it unearned and undeserved. This indicates a splendid all-around competency in theft, for it starts with farthings, and works its industries all the way up to ship-loads. It may be possible that the Jews can beat this, but the man that bets on it is taking chances.—M.T.

Yet, in all countries, from the dawn of history, the Jew has been persistently and implacably hated, and with frequency persecuted.

Point No. 2.—"Can fanaticism *alone* account for this?"

Years ago I used to think that it was responsible for nearly all of it, but latterly I have come to think that this was an error. Indeed, it is now my conviction that it is responsible for hardly any of it. In this connection I call to mind Genesis, chapter xlvii.

We have all thoughtfully—or unthoughtfully—read the pathetic story of the years of plenty and the years of famine in Egypt, and how Joseph, with that opportunity, made a corner in broken hearts, and the crusts of the poor, and human liberty—a corner whereby he took a nation's money all away, to the last penny; took a nation's land away, to the last acre; then took the nation itself, buying it for bread, man by man, woman by woman, child by child, till all were slaves; a corner which took everything, left nothing; a corner so stupendous that, by comparison with it, the most gigantic corners in subsequent history are but baby things, for it dealt in hundreds of millions of bushels, and its profits were reckonable by hundreds of millions of dollars, and it was a disaster so crushing that its effects have not wholly disappeared from Egypt today, more than three thousand years after the event.

Is it presumable that the eye of Egypt was upon Joseph, the foreign Jew, all this time? I think it likely. Was it friendly? We must doubt it. Was Joseph establishing a character for his race which would survive long in Egypt? And in time would his name come to be familiarly used to express that character—like Shylock's? It is hardly to be doubted. Let us remember that this was *centuries before the crucifixion.*

I wish to come down eighteen hundred years later and refer to a remark made by one of the Latin historians. I read it in a translation many years ago, and it comes back to me now with force. It was alluding to a time when people were still living who could have seen the Saviour in the flesh. Christianity was so new that the people of Rome had hardly heard of it, and had but confused notions of what it was. The substance of the remark was this: Some Christians were persecuted in Rome through error, they being *"mistaken for Jews."*

The meaning seems plain. These pagans had nothing against Christians, but they were quite ready to persecute Jews. For some reason or other they hated a Jew before they even knew what a Christian was. May I not assume, then, that the persecution of Jews is a thing which *antedates*

Christianity and was not born of Christianity? I think so. What was the origin of the feeling?

When I was a boy, in the back settlements of the Mississippi Valley, where a gracious and beautiful Sunday-school simplicity and unpracticality prevailed, the "Yankee" (citizen of the New England states) was hated with a splendid energy. But religion had nothing to do with it. In a trade, the Yankee was held to be about five times the match of the Westerner. His shrewdness, his insight, his judgment, his knowledge, his enterprise, and his formidable cleverness in applying these forces were frankly confessed, and most competently cursed.

In the cotton states, after the war, the simple and ignorant negroes made the crops for the white planter on shares. The Jew came down in force, set up shop on the plantation, supplied all the negro's wants on credit, and at the end of the season was proprietor of the negro's share of the present crop and of part of his share of the next one. Before long, the whites detested the Jew, and it is doubtful if the negro loved him.

The Jew is being legislated out of Russia. The reason is not concealed. The movement was instituted because the Christian peasant and villager stood no chance against his commercial abilities. He was always ready to lend money on a crop, and sell vodka and other necessaries of life on credit while the crop was growing. When settlement day came he owned the crop; and next year or year after he owned the farm, like Joseph.

In the dull and ignorant England of John's time everybody got into debt to the Jew. He gathered all lucrative enterprises into his hands; he was the king of commerce; he was ready to be helpful in all profitable ways; he even financed crusades for the rescue of the Sepulcher. To wipe out his account with the nation and restore business to its natural and incompetent channels he had to be banished the realm.

For the like reasons Spain had to banish him four hundred years ago, and Austria about a couple of centuries later.

In all the ages Christian Europe has been obliged to curtail his activities. If he entered upon a mechanical trade, the Christian had to retire from it. If he set up as a doctor, he was the best one, and he took the business. If he exploited agriculture, the other farmers had to get at something else. Since there was no way to successfully compete with him in any vocation, the law had to step in and save the Christian from the poorhouse. Trade after trade was taken away from the Jew by statute till practically none was left. He was forbidden to engage in agriculture; he was forbidden to practise law; he was forbidden to practise medicine, except among Jews; he was forbidden the handicrafts. Even the seats of learning and the schools of science had to be closed against this tremendous antagonist. Still, almost bereft of employments, he found ways to make money, even ways to get rich. Also ways to invest his takings well, for usury was not denied him. In the hard conditions suggested, the Jew without brains could not survive, and the Jew with brains had to keep them in good training and well sharpened up, or starve. Ages of restriction to the one tool which the law was not able to take from him—his brain—have made that tool singularly competent; ages of compulsory disuse of his hands have atrophied them, and he never uses them now. This history has a very, very commercial look, a most sordid and practical commercial look, the business aspect of a Chinese cheap-labor crusade. Religious prejudices may account for one part of it, but not for the other nine.

Protestants have persecuted Catholics, but they did not take their livelihoods away from them. The Catholics have persecuted the Protestants with bloody and awful bitterness, but they never closed agriculture and the handicrafts against them. Why was that? That has the candid look of genuine religious persecution, not a trade-union boycott in a religious disguise.

The Jews are harried and obstructed in Austria and Germany, and lately in France; but England and America give them an open field and yet survive. Scotland offers them an unembarrassed field too, but there are not many takers. There are a few Jews in Glasgow, and one in Aberdeen; but that is because they can't earn enough to get away. The Scotch pay themselves that compliment, but it is authentic.

I feel convinced that the Crucifixion has not much to do with the world's attitude toward the Jew; that the reasons for it are older than that event, as suggested by Egypt's experience and by Rome's regret for having persecuted an unknown quantity called a Christian, under the mistaken impression that she was merely persecuting a Jew. *Merely* a Jew—a skinned eel who was used to it, presumably. I am persuaded that in Russia, Austria, and Germany nine-tenths of the hostility to the Jew comes from the average Christian's inability to compete successfully with the average Jew in business—in either straight business or the questionable sort.

In Berlin, a few years ago, I read a speech which frankly urged the expulsion of the Jews from Germany; and the agitator's *reason* was as frank as his proposition. It was this: *that eighty-five per cent.* of the successful lawyers of Berlin were Jews, and that about the same percentage of the great and lucrative businesses of all sorts in Germany were in the hands of the Jewish race! Isn't it an amazing confession? It was but another way of saying that in a population of 48,000,000, of whom only 500,000 were registered as Jews, eighty-five per cent. of the brains and honesty of the whole was lodged in the Jews. I must insist upon the honesty—it is an essential of successful business, taken by and large. Of course it does not rule out rascals entirely, even among Christians, but it is a good working rule, nevertheless. The speaker's figures may have been inexact, but *the motive of persecution* stands out as clear as day.

The man claimed that in Berlin the banks, the newspapers, the theaters, the great mercantile, shipping, mining, and manufacturing interests, the big army and city contracts, the tramways, and pretty much all other properties of high value, and *also* the small businesses—were in the hands of the Jews. He said the Jew was pushing the Christian to the wall all along the line; that it was all a Christian could do to scrape together a living; and that the Jew *must* be banished, and soon—there was no other way of saving the Christian. Here in Vienna, last autumn, an agitator said that all these disastrous details were true of Austria-Hungary also; and in fierce language he demanded the expulsion of the Jews. When politicians come out without a blush and read the baby act in this frank way, *unrebuked,* it is a very good indication that they have a market back of them, and know where to fish for votes.

You note the crucial point of the mentioned agitation; the argument is that the Christian cannot *compete* with the Jew, and that hence his very bread is in peril. To human beings this is a much more hate-inspiring thing than is any detail connected with religion. With most people, of a necessity, bread and meat take first rank, religion second. I am convinced that the persecution of the Jew is not due in any large degree to religious prejudice.

No, the Jew is a money-getter; and in getting his money he is a very serious obstruction to less capable neighbors who are on the same quest. I think that that is the trouble. In estimating worldly values the Jew is not shallow, but deep. With precocious wisdom he found out in the morning of time that some men worship rank, some worship heroes, some worship power, some worship God, and that over these ideals they dispute and cannot unite—but that they all worship money; so he made it the end and aim of his life to get it. He was at it in Egypt thirty-six centuries ago; he was at it in Rome when that Christian got persecuted by mistake for him; he has been at it ever since. The cost to him has been heavy; his success has made the whole human race his enemy—but it has paid, for it has brought him envy, and that is the only thing which men will sell both soul and body to get. He long ago observed that a millionaire commands respect, a two-millionaire homage, a multi-millionaire the deepest deeps of adoration. We all know that feeling; we have seen it express itself. We have noticed that when the average man mentions the name of a multi-millionaire he does it with that mixture in his voice of awe and reverence and lust which burns in a Frenchman's eye when it falls on another man's centime.

Point No. 4.—"The Jews have no party; they are non-participants."

Perhaps you have let the secret out and given yourself away. It seems hardly a credit to the race that it is able to say that; or to you, sir, that you can say it without remorse; more, that you should offer it as a plea against maltreatment, injustice, and oppression. Who gives the Jew the right, who gives any race the right, to sit still, in a free country, and let somebody else look after its safety? The oppressed Jew was entitled to all pity in the former times under brutal autocracies, for he was weak and friendless, and had no way to help his case. But he has ways now, and he has had them for a century, but I do not see that he has tried to make serious use of them. When the Revolution set him free in France it was an act of grace—the grace of other people; he does not appear in it as a helper. I do not know that he helped when England set him free. Among the Twelve Sane Men of France who have stepped forward with great Zola at their head to fight (and win, I hope and believe[1]) the battle for the most infamously misused Jew of modern times, do you find a great or rich or illustrious Jew helping? In the United States he was created free in the beginning—he did not need to help, of course. In Austria, and Germany, and France he has a vote, but of what considerable use is it to him? He doesn't seem to know how to apply it to the best effect. With all his splendid capacities and all his fat wealth he is to-day not politically important in any country. In America, as early as 1854, the ignorant Irish hod-carrier, who had a spirit of his own and a way of exposing it to the weather, made it apparent to all that he must be politically reckoned with; yet fifteen years before that we

1. This article was written in the summer of 1898. The "misused Jew" was Capt. Alfred Dreyfus (1859–1935), falsely accused and convicted of conveying French army secrets to the Germans. Through the efforts of writer Emile Zola (1840–1902) and others, Dreyfus was later released from imprisonment on Devil's Island, and his conviction eventually overturned.—EDITOR.

hardly knew what an Irishman looked like. As an intelligent force, and numerically, he has always been away down, but he has governed the country just the same. It was because he was *organized.* It made his vote valuable—in fact, essential.

You will say the Jew is everywhere numerically feeble. That is nothing to the point—with the Irishman's history for an object-lesson. But I am coming to your numerical feebleness presently. In all parliamentary countries you could no doubt elect Jews to the legislatures—and even *one* member in such a body is sometimes a force which counts. How deeply have you concerned yourselves about this in Austria, France, and Germany? Or even in America for that matter? You remark that the Jews were not to blame for the riots in this Reichsrath here, and you add with satisfaction that there wasn't one in that body. That is not strictly correct; if it were, would it not be in order for you to explain it and apologize for it, not try to make a merit of it? But I think that the Jew was by no means in as large force there as he ought to have been, with his chances. Austria opens the suffrage to him on fairly liberal terms, and it must surely be his own fault that he is so much in the background politically.

As to your numerical weakness. I mentioned some figures awhile ago—500,000—as the Jewish population of Germany. I will add some more—6,000,000 in Russia, 5,000,000 in Austria, 250,000 in the United States. I take them from memory; I read them in the *Encyclopædia Britannica* about ten years ago. Still, I am entirely sure of them. If those statistics are correct, my argument is not as strong as it ought to be as concerns America, but it still has strength. It is plenty strong enough as concerns Austria, for ten years ago 5,000,000 was nine per cent. of the empire's population. The Irish would govern the Kingdom of Heaven if they had a strength there like that.

I have some suspicions; I got them at second hand, but they have remained with me these ten or twelve years. When I read in the *E. B.* that the Jewish population of the United States was 250,000, I wrote the editor, and explained to him that I was personally acquainted with more Jews than that in my country, and that his figures were without doubt a misprint for 25,000,000. I also added that I was personally acquainted with *that* many there; but that was only to raise his confidence in me, for it was not true. His answer miscarried, and I never got it; but I went around talking about the matter, and people told me they had reason to suspect that for business reasons many Jews whose dealings were mainly with the Christians did not report themselves as Jews in the census. It looked plausible; it looks plausible yet. Look at the city of New York; and look at Boston, and Philadelphia, and New Orleans, and Chicago, and Cincinnati, and San Francisco—how your race swarms in those places!—and everywhere else in America, down to the least little village. Read the signs on the marts of commerce and on the shops: Goldstein (gold stone), Edelstein (precious stone), Blumenthal (flower-vale), Rosenthal (rose-vale), Veilchenduft (violet odor), Singvogel (song-bird), Rosenzweig (rose branch), and all the amazing list of beautiful and enviable names which Prussia and Austria glorified you with so long ago. It is another instance of Europe's coarse and cruel persecution of your race; not that it was coarse and cruel to outfit it with pretty and poetical names like those, but that it was coarse and cruel to make it *pay* for them or else take such hideous and often indecent names that to-day their owners never use them; or, if they do, only on official papers. And it was the many, not the few, who got the odious names, they being too poor to bribe the officials to grant them better ones.

Now why was the race renamed? I have been told that in Prussia it was given to using fictitious names, and often changing them, so as to beat the tax-gatherer, escape military service, and so on; and that finally the idea was hit upon of furnishing all the inmates of a house with *one and the same surname,* and then holding the house responsible right along for those inmates, and accountable for any disappearances that might occur; it made the Jews keep track of *each other,* for self-interest's sake, and saved the government the trouble.[1]

If that explanation of how the Jews of Prussia came to be renamed is correct, if it is true that they fictitiously registered themselves to gain certain advantages, it may possibly be true that in America they refrain from registering themselves as Jews to fend off the damaging prejudices of the Christian customer. I have no way of knowing whether this notion is well founded or not. There may be other and better ways of explaining why only that poor little 250,000 of our Jews got into the *Encyclopædia.* I

1. In Austria the renaming was merely done because the Jews in some newly acquired regions had no surnames, but were mostly named Abraham and Moses, and therefore the tax-gatherer could not tell t'other from which, and was likely to lose his reason over the matter. The renaming was put into the hands of the War Department, and a charming mess the graceless young lieutenants made of it. To them a Jew was of no sort of consequence, and they labeled the race in a way to make the angels weep. As an example take these two! *Abraham Bellyache* and *Schmul Godbedamned.—Culled from "Namens Studien," by Karl Emil Franzos.*—M.T.

may, of course, be mistaken, but I am strongly of the opinion that we have an immense Jewish population in America.

Point No. 3.—"Can Jews do anything to improve the situation?"

I think so. If I may make a suggestion without seeming to be trying to teach my grandmother how to suck eggs, I will offer it. In our days we have learned the value of combination. We apply it everywhere—in railway systems, in trusts, in trade-unions, in Salvation Armies, in minor politics, in major politics, in European Concerts. Whatever our strength may be, big or little, we *organize* it. We have found out that that is the only way to get the most out of it that is in it. We know the weakness of individual sticks, and the strength of the concentrated fagot. Suppose you try a scheme like this, for instance. In England and America put every Jew on the census-book *as* a Jew (in case you have not been doing that). Get up volunteer regiments composed of Jews solely, and, when the drum beats, fall in and go to the front, so as to remove the reproach that you have few Massénas among you, and that you feed on a country but don't like to fight for it. Next, in politics, organize your strength, band together, and deliver the casting vote where you can, and, where you can't, compel as good terms as possible. You huddle to yourselves already in all countries, but you huddle to no sufficient purpose, politically speaking. You do not seem to be organized, except for your charities. There you are omnipotent; there you compel your due of recognition—you do not have to beg for it. It shows what you can do when you band together for a definite purpose.

And then from America and England you can encourage your race in Austria, France, and Germany, and materially help it. It was a pathetic tale that was told by a poor Jew in Galicia a fortnight ago during the riots, after he had been raided by the Christian peasantry and despoiled of everything he had. He said his vote was of no value to him, and he wished he could be excused from casting it, for indeed casting it was a sure *damage* to him, since no matter which party he voted for, the other party would come straight and take its revenge out of him. Nine per cent. of the population of the empire, these Jews, and apparently they cannot put a plank into any candidate's platform! If you will send our Irish lads over here I think they will organize your race and change the aspect of the Reichsrath.

You seem to think that the Jews take no hand in politics here, that they are "absolutely non-participants." I am assured by men competent to speak that this is a very large error, that the Jews are exceedingly active in politics all over the empire, but that they scatter their work and their votes among the numerous parties, and thus lose the advantages to be had by concentration. I think that in America they scatter too, but you know more about that than I do.

Speaking of concentration, Dr. Herzl has a clear insight into the value of that. Have you heard of his plan? He wishes to gather the Jews of the world together in Palestine, with a government of their own—under the suzerainty of the Sultan, I suppose. At the convention of Berne, last year, there were delegates from everywhere, and the proposal was received with decided favor. I am not the Sultan, and I am not objecting; but if that concentration of the cunningest brains in the world was going to be made in a free country (bar Scotland), I think it would be politic to stop it. It will not be well to let that race find out its strength. If the horses knew theirs, we should not ride any more.

Point No. 5.—"Will the persecution of the Jews ever come to an end?"

On the score of religion, I think it has already come to an end. On the score of race prejudice and trade, I have the idea that it will continue. That is, here and there in spots about the world, where a barbarous ignorance and a sort of mere animal civilization prevail; but I do not think that elsewhere the Jew need now stand in any fear of being robbed and raided. Among the high civilizations he seems to be very comfortably situated indeed, and to have more than his proportionate share of the prosperities going. It has that look in Vienna. I suppose the race prejudice cannot be removed; but he can stand that; it is no particular matter. By his make and ways he is substantially a foreigner wherever he may be, and even the angels dislike a foreigner. I am using this word foreigner in the German sense—*stranger*. Nearly all of us have an antipathy to a stranger, even of our own nationality. We pile gripsacks in a vacant seat to keep him from getting it; and a dog goes further, and does as a savage would—challenges him on the spot. The German dictionary seems to make no distinction between a stranger and a foreigner; in its view a stranger *is* a foreigner—a sound position, I think. You will always be by ways and habits and predilections substantially strangers—foreigners—wherever you are, and that will probably keep the race prejudice against you alive.

But you were the favorites of Heaven originally, and your manifold and unfair prosperities convince me that you have crowded back into that snug place again. Here is an incident that is significant. Last week in Vienna a hail-storm struck the prodigious Central Cemetery and made wasteful destruction there. In the Christian part of it, according to the official figures,

621 window-panes were broken; more than 900 singing-birds were killed; five great trees and many small ones were torn to shreds and the shreds scattered far and wide by the wind; the ornamental plants and other decorations of the graves were ruined, and more than a hundred tomb-lanterns shattered; and it took the cemetery's whole force of 300 laborers more than three days to clear away the storm's wreckage. In the report occurs this remark—and in its italics you can hear it grit its Christian teeth: ". . . lediglich die *israelitische* Abtheilung des Friedhofes vom Hagelwetter *ganzlich verschont* worden war." Not a hailstone hit the Jewish reservation! Such nepotism makes me tired.

Point No. 6.—"What has become of the golden rule?"

It exists, it continues to sparkle, and is well taken care of. It is Exhibit A in the Church's assets, and we pull it out every Sunday and give it an airing. But you are not permitted to try to smuggle it into this discussion, where it is irrelevant and would not feel at home. It is strictly religious furniture, like an acolyte, or a contribution-plate, or any of those things. It has never been intruded into business; and Jewish persecution is not a religious passion, it is a business passion.

To conclude.—If the statistics are right, the Jews constitute but *one per cent.* of the human race. It suggests a nebulous dim puff of star dust lost in the blaze of the Milky Way. Properly the Jew ought hardly to be heard of; but he is heard of, has always been heard of. He is as prominent on the planet as any other people, and his commercial importance is extravagantly out of proportion to the smallness of his bulk. His contributions to the world's list of great names in literature, science, art, music, finance, medicine, and abstruse learning are also away out of proportion to the weakness of his numbers. He has made a marvelous fight in this world, in all the ages; and has done it with his hands tied behind him. He could be vain of himself, and be excused for it. The Egyptian, the Babylonian, and the Persian rose, filled the planet with sound and splendor, then faded to dream-stuff and passed away; the Greek and the Roman followed, and made a vast noise, and they are gone; other peoples have sprung up and held their torch high for a time, but it burned out, and they sit in twilight now, or have vanished. The Jew saw them all, beat them all, and is now what he always was, exhibiting no decadence, no infirmities of age, no weakening of his parts, no slowing of his energies, no dulling of his alert and aggressive mind. All things are mortal but the Jew; all other forces pass, but he remains. What is the secret of his immortality?

Postscript—The Jew as Soldier

When I published the above article in Harper's Monthly, I was ignorant—like the rest of the Christian world—of the fact that the Jew had a record as a soldier. I have since seen the official statistics, and I find that he furnished soldiers and high officers to the Revolution, the War of 1812, and the Mexican War. In the Civil War he was represented in the armies and navies of both the North and the South by 10 per cent. of his numerical strength—the same percentage that was furnished by the Christian populations of the two sections. This large fact means more than it seems to mean; for it means that the Jew's patriotism was not merely level with the Christian's, but overpassed it. When the Christian volunteer arrived in camp he got a welcome and applause, but as a rule the Jew got a snub. His company was not desired, and he was made to feel it. That he nevertheless conquered his wounded pride and sacrificed both that and his blood for his flag raises the average and quality of his patriotism above the Christian's. His record for capacity, for fidelity, and for gallant soldiership in the field is as good as any one's. This is true of the Jewish private soldiers and the Jewish generals alike. Major-General O. O. Howard speaks of one of his Jewish staff-officers as being "of the bravest and best"; of another—killed at Chancellorsville—as being "a true friend and a brave officer"; he highly praises two of his Jewish brigadier-generals; finally, he uses these strong words: "Intrinsically there are no more patriotic men to be found in the country than those who claim to be of Hebrew descent, and who served with me in parallel commands or more directly under my instructions."

Fourteen Jewish Confederate and Union families contributed, between them, fifty-one soldiers to the war. Among these, a father and three sons; and another, a father and four sons.

In the above article I was not able to endorse the common reproach that the Jew is willing to feed upon a country but not to fight for it, because I did not know whether it was true or false. I supposed it to be true, but it is not allowable to endorse wandering maxims upon supposition—except when one is trying to make out a case. That slur upon the Jew cannot hold up its head in presence of the figures of the War Department. It has done its work, and done it long and faithfully, and with high approval: it ought to be pensioned off now, and retired from active service.—M.T.

Extracts from Adam's Diary

Monday.—This new creature with the long hair is a good deal in the way. It is always hanging around and following me about. I don't like this; I am not used to company. I wish it would stay with the other animals. . . . Cloudy to-day, wind in the east; think we shall have rain. . . . *We?* Where did I get that word?—I remember now—the new creature uses it.

Tuesday.—Been examining the great waterfall. It is the finest thing on the estate, I think. The new creature calls it Niagara Falls—why, I am sure I do not know. Says it *looks* like Niagara Falls. That is not a reason, it is mere waywardness and imbecility. I get no chance to name anything myself. The new creature names everything that comes along, before I can get in a protest. And always that same pretext is offered—it *looks* like the thing. There is the dodo, for instance. Says the moment one looks at it one sees at a glance that it "looks like a dodo." It will have to keep that name, no doubt. It wearies me to fret about it, and it does no good, anyway. Dodo! It looks no more like a dodo than I do.

Wednesday.—Built me a shelter against the rain, but could not have it to myself in peace. The new creature intruded. When I tried to put it out it shed water out of the holes it looks with, and wiped it away with the back of its paws, and made a noise such as some of the other animals make when they are in distress. I wish it would not talk; it is always talking. That sounds like a cheap fling at the poor creature, a slur; but I do not mean it so. I have never heard the human voice before, and any new and strange sound intruding itself here upon the solemn hush of these dreaming solitudes offends my ear and seems a false note. And this new sound is so close to me; it is right at my shoulder, right at my ear, first on one side and then on the other, and I am used only to sounds that are more or less distant from me.

Friday.—The naming goes recklessly on, in spite of anything I can do. I had a very good name for the estate, and it was musical and pretty—GARDEN OF EDEN. Privately, I continue to call it that, but not any longer publicly. The new creature says it is all woods and rocks and scenery, and therefore has no resemblance to a garden. Says it *looks* like a park, and does not look like anything *but* a park. Consequently, without consulting me, it has been new-named—NIAGARA FALLS PARK. This is sufficiently high-handed, it seems to me. And already there is a sign up:

KEEP OFF
THE GRASS

My life is not as happy as it was.

Saturday.—The new creature eats too much fruit. We are going to run short, most likely. "We" again—that is *its* word; mine, too, now, from hearing it so much. Good deal of fog this morning. I do not go out in the fog myself. The new creature does. It goes out in all weathers, and stumps right in with its muddy feet. And talks. It used to be so pleasant and quiet here.

Sunday.—Pulled through. This day is getting to be more and more trying. It was selected and set apart last November as a day of rest. I had already six of them per week before. This morning found the new creature trying to clod apples out of that forbidden tree.

Monday.—The new creature says its name is Eve. That is all right, I have no objections. Says it is to call it by, when I want it to come. I said it was superfluous, then. The word evidently raised me in its respect; and indeed it is a large, good word and will bear repetition. It says it is not an It, it is a She. This is probably doubtful; yet it is all one to me; what she is were nothing to me if she would but go by herself and not talk.

Tuesday.—She has littered the whole estate with execrable names and offensive signs:

THIS WAY TO THE WHIRLPOOL
THIS WAY TO GOAT ISLAND
CAVE OF THE WINDS THIS WAY

She says this park would make a tidy summer resort if there was any custom for it. Summer resort—another invention of hers—just words, without any meaning. What is a summer resort? But it is best not to ask her, she has such a rage for explaining.

Friday.—She has taken to beseeching me to stop going over the Falls. What harm does it do? Says it makes her shudder. I wonder why; I have always done it—always liked the plunge, and coolness. I supposed it was what the Falls were for. They have no other use that I can see, and they must have been made for something. She says they were only made for scenery—like the rhinoceros and the mastodon.

I went over the Falls in a barrel—not satisfactory to her. Went over in a tub—still not satisfactory. Swam the Whirlpool and the Rapids in a fig-leaf suit. It got much damaged. Hence, tedious complaints about my extravagance. I am too much hampered here. What I need is change of scene.

Saturday.—I escaped last Tuesday night, and traveled two days, and built me another shelter in a secluded place, and obliterated my tracks as well as I could, but she hunted me out by means of a beast which she has tamed and calls a wolf, and came making that pitiful noise again, and shedding that water out of the places she looks with. I was obliged to return with her, but will presently emigrate again when occasion offers. She engages herself in many foolish things; among others, to study out why the animals called lions and tigers live on grass and flowers, when, as she says, the sort of teeth they wear would indicate that they were intended to eat each other. This is foolish, because to do that would be to kill each other, and that would introduce what, as I understand it, is called "death"; and death, as I have been told, has not yet entered the Park. Which is a pity, on some accounts.

Sunday.—Pulled through.

Monday.—I believe I see what the week is for: it is to give time to rest up from the weariness of Sunday. It seems a good idea. . . . She has been climbing that tree again. Clodded her out of it. She said nobody was looking. Seems to consider that a sufficient justification for chancing any dangerous thing. Told her that. The word justification moved her admiration—and envy, too, I thought. It is a good word.

Tuesday.—She told me she was made out of a rib taken from my body. This is at least doubtful, if not more than that. I have not missed any rib. . . . She is in much trouble about the buzzard; says grass does not agree with it; is afraid she can't raise it; thinks it was intended to live on decayed flesh. The buzzard must get along the best it can with what it is provided. We cannot overturn the whole scheme to accommodate the buzzard.

Saturday.—She fell in the pond yesterday when she was looking at herself in it, which she is always doing. She nearly strangled, and said it was most uncomfortable. This made her sorry for the creatures which live in there, which she calls fish, for she continues to fasten names on to things that don't need them and don't come when they are called by them, which is a matter of no consequence to her, she is such a numskull, anyway; so she got a lot of them out and brought them in last night and put them in my bed to keep warm, but I have noticed them now and then all day and I don't see that they are any happier there than they were before, only quieter. When night comes I shall throw them outdoors. I will not sleep with them again, for I find them clammy and unpleasant to lie among when a person hasn't anything on.

Sunday.—Pulled through.

Tuesday.—She has taken up with a snake now. The other animals are glad, for she was always experimenting with them and bothering them; and I am glad because the snake talks, and this enables me to get a rest.

Friday.—She says the snake advises her to try the fruit of that tree, and says the result will be a great and fine and noble education. I told her there would be another result, too—it would introduce death into the world. That was a mistake—it had been better to keep the remark to myself; it only gave her an idea—she could save the sick buzzard, and furnish fresh meat to the despondent lions and tigers. I advised her to keep away from the tree. She said she wouldn't. I foresee trouble. Will emigrate.

Wednesday.—I have had a variegated time. I escaped last night, and rode a horse all night as fast as he could go, hoping to get clear out of the Park and hide in some other country before the trouble should begin; but it was not to be. About an hour after sun-up, as I was riding through a flowery plain where thousands of animals were grazing, slumbering, or playing with each other, according to their wont, all of a sudden they broke into a tempest of frightful noises, and in one moment the plain was a frantic commotion and every beast was destroying its neighbor. I knew what it meant—Eve had eaten that fruit, and death was come into the world. . . . The tigers ate my horse, paying no attention when I ordered them to desist, and they would have eaten me if I had stayed—which I didn't, but went away in much haste. . . . I found this place, outside the Park, and was fairly comfortable for a few days, but she has found me out. Found me out, and has named the place Tonawanda—says it *looks* like that. In fact I was not sorry she came, for there are but meager pickings here, and she brought some of those apples. I was obliged to eat them, I was so hungry. It was against my principles, but I find that principles have no real force except when one is well fed. . . . She came curtained in boughs and bunches of leaves, and when I asked her what she meant by such nonsense, and snatched them away and threw them down, she tittered and blushed. I had never seen a person titter and blush before, and to me it seemed unbecoming and idiotic. She said I would soon know how it was myself. This was correct. Hungry as I was, I laid down the apple half-eaten—certainly the best one I ever saw, considering the lateness of the season—and arrayed myself in the discarded boughs and branches, and then spoke to her with some severity and ordered her to go and get some more and not make such a spectacle of herself. She did it, and after this we crept down to where the wild-beast battle had been, and collected some skins, and I made her patch together a couple of suits proper for public occasions. They are uncomfortable, it is true, but stylish, and that is the main point about clothes. . . . I find she is a good deal of a companion. I see I should be lonesome and depressed without her, now that I have lost my property. Another thing, she says it is ordered that we work for our living hereafter. She will be useful. I will superintend.

Ten Days Later.—She accuses *me* of being the cause of our disaster! She says, with apparent sincerity and truth, that the Serpent assured her that the forbidden fruit was not apples, it was chestnuts. I said I was innocent, then, for I had not eaten any chestnuts. She said the Serpent informed her that "chestnut" was a figurative term meaning an aged and moldy joke. I turned pale at that, for I have made many jokes to pass the weary time, and some of them could have been of that sort, though I had honestly supposed that they were new when I made them. She asked me if I had made one just at the time of the catastrophe. I was obliged to admit that I had made one to myself, though not aloud. It was this. I was thinking about the Falls, and I said to myself, "How wonderful it is to see that vast body of water tumble down there!" Then in an instant a bright thought flashed into my head, and I let it fly, saying, "It would be a deal more wonderful to see it tumble *up* there!"—and I was just about to kill myself with laughing at it when all nature broke loose in war and death and I had to flee for my life. "There," she said, with triumph, "that is just it; the Serpent mentioned that very jest, and called it the First Chestnut, and said it was coeval with the creation." Alas, I am indeed to blame. Would that I were not witty; oh, that I had never had that radiant thought!

Next Year.—We have named it Cain. She caught it while I was up country trapping on the North Shore of the Erie; caught it in the timber a couple of miles from our dug-out—or it might have been four, she isn't certain which. It resembles us in some ways, and may be a relation. That is what she thinks, but this is an error, in my judgment. The difference in size warrants the conclusion that it is a different and new kind of animal—a fish, perhaps, though when I put it in the water to see, it sank, and she plunged in and snatched it out before there was opportunity for the experiment to determine the matter. I still think it is a fish, but she is indifferent about what it is, and will not let me have it to try. I do not understand this. The coming of the creature seems to have changed her whole nature and made her unreasonable about experiments. She thinks more of it than she does of any of the other animals, but is not able to explain why. Her mind is disordered—everything shows it. Sometimes she carries the fish in her arms half the night when it complains and wants to get to the water. At such times the water comes out of the places in her face that she looks out of, and she pats the fish on the back and makes soft sounds with her mouth to soothe it, and betrays sorrow and solicitude in a hundred ways. I have never seen her do like this with any other fish, and it troubles me greatly. She used to carry the young tigers around so, and play with them, before we lost our property, but it was only play; she never took on about them like this when their dinner disagreed with them.

Sunday.—She doesn't work, Sundays, but lies around all tired out, and likes to have the fish wallow over her; and she makes fool noises to amuse it, and pretends to chew its paws, and that makes it laugh. I have not seen a fish before that could laugh. This makes me doubt. . . . I have come to like Sunday myself. Superintending all the week tires a body so. There ought to be more Sundays. In the old days they were tough, but now they come handy.

Wednesday.—It isn't a fish. I cannot quite make out what it is. It makes curious devilish noises when not satisfied, and says "goo-goo" when it is. It is not one of us, for it doesn't walk; it is not a bird, for it doesn't fly; it is not a frog, for it doesn't hop; it is not a snake, for it doesn't crawl; I feel sure it is not a fish, though I cannot get a chance to find out whether it can swim or not. It merely lies around, and mostly on its back, with its feet up. I have not seen any other animal do that before. I said I believed it was an enigma; but she only admired the word without understanding it. In my judgment it is either an enigma or some kind of a bug. If it dies, I will take it apart and see what its arrangements are. I never had a thing perplex me so.

Three Months Later.—The perplexity augments instead of diminishing. I sleep but little. It has ceased from lying around, and goes about on its four legs now. Yet it differs from the other four-legged animals, in that its front legs are unusually short, consequently this causes the main part of its person to stick up uncomfortably high in the air, and this is not attractive. It is built much as we are, but its method of traveling shows that it is not of our breed. The short front legs and long hind ones indicate that it is of the kangaroo family, but it is a marked variation of the species, since the true kangaroo hops, whereas this one never does. Still it is a curious and interesting variety, and has not been catalogued before. As I discovered it, I have felt justified in securing the credit of the discovery by attaching my name to it, and hence have called it *Kangaroorum Adamiensis*. . . . It must have been a young one when it came, for it has grown exceedingly since. It must be five times as big, now, as it was then, and when discontented it is able to make from twenty-two to thirty-eight times the noise it made at first. Coercion does not modify this, but has the contrary effect. For this reason I discontinued the system. She reconciles it by persuasion, and by giving it things which she had previously told me she wouldn't give it. As already observed, I was not at home when it first came, and she told me she found it in the woods. It seems odd that it should be the only one, yet it must be so, for I have worn myself out these many weeks trying to find another one to add to my collection, and for this one to play with; for surely then it would be quieter and we could tame it more easily. But I find none, nor any vestige of any; and strangest of all, no tracks. It has to live on the ground, it cannot help itself; therefore, how does it get about without leaving a track? I have set a dozen traps, but they do no good. I catch all small animals except that one; animals that merely go into the trap out of curiosity, I think, to see what the milk is there for. They never drink it.

Three Months Later.—The Kangaroo still continues to grow, which is very strange and perplexing. I never knew one to be so long getting its growth. It has fur on its head now; not like kangaroo fur, but exactly like our hair except that it is much finer and softer, and instead of being black is red. I am like to lose my mind over the capricious and harassing developments of this unclassifiable zoological freak. If I could catch another one —but that is hopeless; it is a new variety, and the only sample; this is plain. But I caught a true kangaroo and brought it in, thinking that this one, being lonesome, would rather have that for company than have no kin at all, or any animal it could feel a nearness to or get sympathy from in its forlorn condition here among strangers who do not know its ways or habits, or what to do to make it feel that it is among friends; but it was a mistake—it went into such fits at the sight of the kangaroo that I was convinced it had never seen one before. I pity the poor noisy little animal, but there is nothing I can do to make it happy. If I could tame it—but that is out of the question; the more I try the worse I seem to make it. It grieves me to the heart to see it in its little storms of sorrow and passion. I wanted to let it go, but she wouldn't hear of it. That seemed cruel and not like her; and yet she may be right. It might be lonelier than ever; for since I cannot find another one, how could *it?*

Five Months Later.—It is not a kangaroo. No, for it supports itself by holding to her finger, and thus goes a few steps on its hind legs, and then falls down. It is probably some kind of a bear; and yet it has no tail—as yet —and no fur, except on its head. It still keeps on growing—that is a curious circumstance, for bears get their growth earlier than this. Bears are dangerous—since our catastrophe—and I shall not be satisfied to have this one prowling about the place much longer without a muzzle on. I have offered to get her a kangaroo if she would let this one go, but it did no good—she is determined to run us into all sorts of foolish risks, I think. She was not like this before she lost her mind.

A Fortnight Later.—I examined its mouth. There is no danger yet: it has only one tooth. It has no tail yet. It makes more noise now than it ever did before—and mainly at night. I have moved out. But I shall go over, mornings, to breakfast, and see if it has more teeth. If it gets a mouthful of teeth it will be time for it to go, tail or no tail, for a bear does not need a tail in order to be dangerous.

Four Months Later.—I have been off hunting and fishing a month, up in the region that she calls Buffalo; I don't know why, unless it is because there are not any buffaloes there. Meantime the bear has learned to paddle around all by itself on its hind legs, and says "poppa" and "momma." It is certainly a new species. This resemblance to words may be purely accidental, of course, and may have no purpose or meaning; but even in that case it is still extraordinary, and is a thing which no other bear can do. This imitation of speech, taken together with general absence of fur and entire absence of tail, sufficiently indicates that this is a new kind of bear. The further study of it will be exceedingly interesting. Meantime I will go off on a far expedition among the forests of the north and make an exhaustive search. There must certainly be another one somewhere, and this one will be less dangerous when it has company of its own species. I will go straightway; but I will muzzle this one first.

Three Months Later.—It has been a weary, weary hunt, yet I have had no success. In the mean time, without stirring from the home estate, she has caught another one! I never saw such luck. I might have hunted these woods a hundred years, I never would have run across that thing.

Next Day.—I have been comparing the new one with the old one, and it is perfectly plain that they are the same breed. I was going to stuff one of them for my collection, but she is prejudiced against it for some reason or other; so I have relinquished the idea, though I think it is a mistake. It would be an irreparable loss to science if they should get away. The old one is tamer than it was and can laugh and talk like the parrot, having learned this, no doubt, from being with the parrot so much, and having the imitative faculty in a highly developed degree. I shall be astonished if it turns out to be a new kind of parrot; and yet I ought not to be astonished, for it has already been everything else it could think of since those first days when it was a fish. The new one is as ugly now as the old one was at first; has the same sulphur-and-raw-meat complexion and the same singular head without any fur on it. She calls it Abel.

Ten Years Later.—They are *boys;* we found it out long ago. It was their coming in that small, immature shape that puzzled us; we were not used to it. There are some girls now. Abel is a good boy, but if Cain had stayed a bear it would have improved him. After all these years, I see that I was mistaken about Eve in the beginning; it is better to live outside the Garden with her than inside it without her. At first I thought she talked too much; but now I should be sorry to have that voice fall silent and pass out of my life. Blessed be the chestnut that brought us near together and taught me to know the goodness of her heart and the sweetness of her spirit!

Eve's Diary

TRANSLATED FROM THE ORIGINAL

Saturday.—I am almost a whole day old, now. I arrived yesterday. That is as it seems to me. And it must be so, for if there was a day-before-yesterday I was not there when it happened, or I should remember it. It could be, of course, that it did happen, and that I was not noticing. Very well; I will be very watchful now, and if any day-before-yesterdays happen I will make a note of it. It will be best to start right and not let the record get confused, for some instinct tells me that these details are going to be important to the historian some day. For I feel like an experiment, I feel exactly like an experiment; it would be impossible for a person to feel more like an experiment than I do, and so I am coming to feel convinced that that is what I *am*—an experiment; just an experiment, and nothing more.

Then if I am an experiment, am I the whole of it? No, I think not; I think the rest of it is part of it. I am the main part of it, but I think the rest of it has its share in the matter. Is my position assured, or do I have to watch it and take care of it? The latter, perhaps. Some instinct tells me that eternal vigilance is the price of supremacy. [That is a good phrase, I think, for one so young.]

Everything looks better to-day than it did yesterday. In the rush of finishing up yesterday, the mountains were left in a ragged condition, and some of the plains were so cluttered with rubbish and remnants that the aspects were quite distressing. Noble and beautiful works of art should not be subjected to haste; and this majestic new world is indeed a most noble and beautiful work. And certainly marvelously near to being perfect, notwithstanding the shortness of the time. There are too many stars in some places and not enough in others, but that can be remedied presently, no doubt. The moon got loose last night, and slid down and fell out of the scheme—a very great loss; it breaks my heart to think of it. There isn't another thing among the ornaments and decorations that is comparable to it for beauty and finish. It should have been fastened better. If we can only get it back again—

But of course there is no telling where it went to. And besides, whoever gets it will hide it; I know it because I would do it myself. I believe I can be honest in all other matters, but I already begin to realize that the core and center of my nature is love of the beautiful, a passion for the beautiful, and that it would not be safe to trust me with a moon that belonged to another person and that person didn't know I had it. I could give up a moon that I found in the daytime, because I should be afraid some one was looking; but if I found it in the dark, I am sure I should find some kind of an excuse for not saying anything about it. For I do love moons, they are so pretty and so romantic. I wish we had five or six; I would never go to bed; I should never get tired lying on the moss-bank and looking up at them.

Stars are good, too. I wish I could get some to put in my hair. But I suppose I never can. You would be surprised to find how far off they are, for they do not look it. When they first showed, last night, I tried to knock some down with a pole, but it didn't reach, which astonished me; then I tried clods till I was all tired out, but I never got one. It was because I am left-handed and cannot throw good. Even when I aimed at the one I wasn't after I couldn't hit the other one, though I did make some close shots, for I saw the black blot of the clod sail right into the midst of the golden clusters forty or fifty times, just barely missing them, and if I could have held out a little longer maybe I could have got one.

So I cried a little, which was natural, I suppose, for one of my age, and after I was rested I got a basket and started for a place on the extreme rim of the circle, where the stars were close to the ground and I could get them with my hands, which would be better, anyway, because I could gather them tenderly then, and not break them. But it was farther than I thought, and at last I had to give it up; I was so tired I couldn't drag my feet another step; and besides, they were sore and hurt me very much.

I couldn't get back home; it was too far and turning cold; but I found some tigers and nestled in among them and was most adorably comfortable, and their breath was sweet and pleasant, because they live on strawberries. I had never seen a tiger before, but I knew them in a minute by the stripes. If I could have one of those skins, it would make a lovely gown.

To-day I am getting better ideas about distances. I was so eager to get hold of every pretty thing that I giddily grabbed for it, sometimes when it was too far off, and sometimes when it was but six inches away but seemed a foot—alas, with thorns between! I learned a lesson; also I made an axiom, all out of my own head—my very first one: *The scratched Experiment shuns the thorn.* I think it is a very good one for one so young.

I followed the other Experiment around, yesterday afternoon, at a distance, to see what it might be for, if I could. But I was not able to make out. I think it is a man. I had never seen a man, but it looked like one, and I feel sure that that is what it is. I realize that I feel more curiosity about it than about any of the other reptiles. If it is a reptile, and I suppose it is; for it has frowsy hair and blue eyes, and looks like a reptile. It has no hips; it tapers like a carrot; when it stands, it spreads itself apart like a derrick; so I think it is a reptile, though it may be architecture.

I was afraid of it at first, and started to run every time it turned around, for I thought it was going to chase me; but by and by I found it was only trying to get away, so after that I was not timid any more, but tracked it along, several hours, about twenty yards behind, which made it nervous and unhappy. At last it was a good deal worried, and climbed a tree. I waited a good while, then gave it up and went home.

To-day the same thing over. I've got it up the tree again.

Sunday.—It is up there yet. Resting, apparently. But that is a subterfuge: Sunday isn't the day of rest; Saturday is appointed for that. It looks to me like a creature that is more interested in resting than in anything else. It would tire me to rest so much. It tires me just to sit around and watch the tree. I do wonder what it is for; I never see it do anything.

They returned the moon last night, and I was *so* happy! I think it is very honest of them. It slid down and fell off again, but I was not distressed; there is no need to worry when one has that kind of neighbors; they will fetch it back. I wish I could do something to show my appreciation. I would like to send them some stars, for we have more than we can use. I mean I, not we, for I can see that the reptile cares nothing for such things.

It has low tastes, and is not kind. When I went there yesterday evening in the gloaming it had crept down and was trying to catch the little speckled fishes that play in the pool, and I had to clod it to make it go up the tree again and let them alone. I wonder if *that* is what it is for? Hasn't it any heart? Hasn't it any compassion for those little creatures? Can it be that it was designed and manufactured for such ungentle work? It has the look of it. One of the clods took it back of the ear, and it used language. It gave me a thrill, for it was the first time I had ever heard speech, except my own. I did not understand the words, but they seemed expressive.

When I found it could talk I felt a new interest in it, for I love to talk; I talk, all day, and in my sleep, too, and I am very interesting, but if I had another to talk to I could be twice as interesting, and would never stop, if desired.

If this reptile is a man, it isn't an *it,* is it? That wouldn't be grammatical, would it? I think it would be *he.* I think so. In that case one would parse it thus: nominative, *he;* dative, *him;* possessive, *his'n.* Well, I will consider it a man and call it he until it turns out to be something else. This will be handier than having so many uncertainties.

Next week Sunday.—All the week I tagged around after him and tried to get acquainted. I had to do the talking, because he was shy, but I didn't mind it. He seemed pleased to have me around, and I used the sociable "we" a good deal, because it seemed to flatter him to be included.

Wednesday.—We are getting along very well indeed, now, and getting better and better acquainted. He does not try to avoid me any more, which is a good sign, and shows that he likes to have me with him. That pleases me, and I study to be useful to him in every way I can, so as to increase his regard. During the last day or two I have taken all the work of naming things off his hands, and this has been a great relief to him, for he has not gift in that line, and is evidently very grateful. He can't think of a rational name to save him, but I do not let him see that I am aware of his defect. Whenever a new creature comes along I name it before he has time to expose himself by an awkward silence. In this way I have saved him many embarrassments. I have no defect like his. The minute I set eyes on an animal I know what it is. I don't have to reflect a moment; the right name comes out instantly, just as if it were an inspiration, as no doubt it is, for I am sure it wasn't in me half a minute before. I seem to know just by the shape of the creature and the way it acts what animal it is.

When the dodo came along he thought it was a wildcat—I saw it in his eye. But I saved him. And I was careful not to do it in a way that could hurt his pride. I just spoke up in a quite natural way of pleased surprise, and not as if I was dreaming of conveying information, and said, "Well, I do declare, if there isn't the dodo!" I explained—without seeming to be explaining—how I knew it for a dodo, and although I thought maybe he was a little piqued that I knew the creature when he didn't, it was quite evident that he admired me. That was very agreeable, and I thought of it more than once with gratification before I slept. How little a thing can make us happy when we feel that we have earned it!

Thursday.—My first sorrow. Yesterday he avoided me and seemed to wish I would not talk to him. I could not believe it, and thought there was some mistake, for I loved to be with him, and loved to hear him talk, and so how could it be that he could feel unkind toward me when I had not done anything? But at last it seemed true, so I went away and sat lonely in the place where I first saw him the morning that we were made and I did not know what he was and was indifferent about him; but now it was a mournful place, and every little thing spoke of him, and my heart was very sore. I did not know why very clearly, for it was a new feeling; I had not experienced it before, and it was all a mystery, and I could not make it out.

But when night came I could not bear the lonesomeness, and went to the new shelter which he has built, to ask him what I had done that was wrong and how I could mend it and get back his kindness again; but he put me out in the rain, and it was my first sorrow.

Sunday.—It is pleasant again, now, and I am happy; but those were heavy days; I do not think of them when I can help it.

I tried to get him some of those apples, but I cannot learn to throw straight. I failed, but I think the good intention pleased him. They are forbidden, and he says I shall come to harm; but so I come to harm through pleasing him, why shall I care for that harm?

Monday.—This morning I told him my name, hoping it would interest him. But he did not care for it. It is strange. If he should tell me his name, I would care. I think it would be pleasanter in my ears than any other sound.

He talks very little. Perhaps it is because he is not bright, and is sensitive about it and wishes to conceal it. It is such a pity that he should feel so, for brightness is nothing; it is in the heart that the values lie. I wish I could make him understand that a loving good heart is riches, and riches enough, and that without it intellect is poverty.

Although he talks so little, he has quite a considerable vocabulary. This morning he used a surprisingly good word. He evidently recognized, himself, that it was a good one, for he worked it in twice afterward, casually. It was not good casual art, still it showed that he possesses a certain quality of perception. Without a doubt that seed can be made to grow, if cultivated.

Where did he get that word? I do not think I have ever used it.

No, he took no interest in my name. I tried to hide my disappointment, but I suppose I did not succeed. I went away and sat on the moss-bank with my feet in the water. It is where I go when I hunger for companionship, some one to look at, some one to talk to. It is not enough—that lovely white body painted there in the pool—but it is something, and something is better than utter loneliness. It talks when I talk; it is sad when I am sad; it comforts me with its sympathy; it says, "Do not be downhearted, you poor friendless girl; I will be your friend." It *is* a good friend to me, and my only one; it is my sister.

That first time that she forsook me! ah, I shall never forget that—never, never. My heart was lead in my body! I said, "She was all I had, and now she is gone!" In my despair I said, "Break, my heart; I cannot bear my life any more!" and hid my face in my hands, and there was no solace for me. And when I took them away, after a little, there she was again, white and shining and beautiful, and I sprang into her arms!

That was perfect happiness; I had known happiness before, but it was not like this, which was ecstasy. I never doubted her afterward. Sometimes she stayed away—maybe an hour, maybe almost the whole day, but I waited and did not doubt; I said, "She is busy, or she is gone a journey, but she will come." And it was so: she always did. At night she would not come if it was dark, for she was a timid little thing; but if there was a moon she would come. I am not afraid of the dark, but she is younger than I am; she was born after I was. Many and many are the visits I have paid her; she is my comfort and my refuge when my life is hard—and it is mainly that.

Tuesday.—All the morning I was at work improving the estate; and I purposely kept away from him in the hope that he would get lonely and come. But he did not.

At noon I stopped for the day and took my recreation by flitting all about with the bees and the butterflies and reveling in the flowers, those beautiful creatures that catch the smile of God out of the sky and preserve it! I gathered them, and made them into wreaths and garlands and clothed myself in them while I ate my luncheon—apples, of course; then I sat in the shade and wished and waited. But he did not come.

But no matter. Nothing would have come of it, for he does not care for flowers. He calls them rubbish, and cannot tell one from another, and thinks it is superior to feel like that. He does not care for me, he does not care for flowers, he does not care for the painted sky at eventide—is there anything he does care for, except building shacks to coop himself up in from the good clean rain, and thumping the melons, and sampling the grapes, and fingering the fruit on the trees, to see how those properties are coming along?

I laid a dry stick on the ground and tried to bore a hole in it with another one, in order to carry out a scheme that I had, and soon I got an awful fright. A thin, transparent bluish film rose out of the hole, and I dropped everything and ran! I thought it was a spirit, and I *was* so frightened! But I looked back, and it was not coming; so I leaned against a rock and rested and panted, and let my limbs go on trembling until they got steady again; then I crept warily back, alert, watching, and ready to fly if there was occasion; and when I was come near, I parted the branches of a rose-bush and peeped through—wishing the man was about, I was looking so cunning and pretty—but the sprite was gone. I went there, and there was a pinch of delicate pink dust in the hole. I put my finger in, to feel it, and said *ouch!* and took it out again. It was a cruel pain. I put my finger in my mouth; and by standing first on one foot and then the other, and grunting, I presently eased my misery; then I was full of interest, and began to examine.

I was curious to know what the pink dust was. Suddenly the name of it occurred to me, though I had never heard of it before. It was *fire!* I was as certain of it as a person could be of anything in the world. So without hesitation I named it that—fire.

I had created something that didn't exist before; I had added a new thing to the world's uncountable properties; I realized this, and was proud of my achievement, and was going to run and find him and tell him about it, thinking to raise myself in his esteem—but I reflected, and did not do it. No—he would not care for it. He would ask what it was good for, and what could I answer? for if it was not *good* for something, but only beautiful, merely beautiful—

So I sighed, and did not go. For it wasn't good for anything; it could not build a shack, it could not improve melons, it could not hurry a fruit crop; it was useless, it was a foolishness and a vanity; he would despise it and say cutting words. But to me it was not despicable; I said, "Oh, you fire, I love you, you dainty pink creature, for you are *beautiful*—and that is enough!" and was going to gather it to my breast. But refrained. Then I made another maxim out of my own head, though it was so nearly like the first one that I was afraid it was only a plagiarism: *"The burnt Experiment shuns the fire."*

I wrought again; and when I had made a good deal of fire-dust I emptied it into a handful of dry brown grass, intending to carry it home and keep it always and play with it; but the wind struck it and it sprayed up and spat out at me fiercely, and I dropped it and ran. When I looked back the blue spirit was towering up and stretching and rolling away like a cloud, and instantly I thought of the name of it—*smoke!*—though, upon my word, I had never heard of smoke before.

Soon, brilliant yellow and red flares shot up through the smoke, and I named them in an instant—*flames*—and I was right, too, though these were the very first flames that had ever been in the world. They climbed the trees, they flashed splendidly in and out of the vast and increasing volume of tumbling smoke, and I had to clap my hands and laugh and dance in my rapture, it was so new and strange and so wonderful and so beautiful!

He came running, and stopped and gazed, and said not a word for many minutes. Then he asked what it was. Ah, it was too bad that he should ask such a direct question. I had to answer it, of course, and I did. I said it was fire. If it annoyed him that I should know and he must ask, that was not my fault; I had no desire to annoy him. After a pause he asked:

"How did it come?"

Another direct question, and it also had to have a direct answer.

"I made it."

The fire was traveling farther and farther off. He went to the edge of the burned place and stood looking down, and said:

"What are these?"

"Fire-coals."

He picked up one to examine it, but changed his mind and put it down again. Then he went away. *Nothing* interests him.

But I was interested. There were ashes, gray and soft and delicate and pretty—I knew what they were at once. And the embers; I knew the embers, too. I found my apples, and raked them out, and was glad; for I am very young and my appetite is active. But I was disappointed; they were all burst open and spoiled. Spoiled apparently; but it was not so; they were better than raw ones. Fire is beautiful; some day it will be useful, I think.

Friday.—I saw him again, for a moment, last Monday at nightfall, but only for a moment. I was hoping he would praise me for trying to improve the estate, for I had meant well and had worked hard. But he was not pleased, and turned away and left me. He was also displeased on another account: I tried once more to persuade him to stop going over the Falls. That was because the fire had revealed to me a new passion—quite new, and distinctly different from love, grief, and those others which I had already discovered—*fear.* And it is horrible!—I wish I had never discovered it; it gives me dark moments, it spoils my happiness, it makes me shiver and tremble and shudder. But I could not persuade him, for he has not discovered fear yet, and so he could not understand me.

Extract from Adam's Diary

Perhaps I ought to remember that she is very young, a mere girl, and make allowances. She is all interest, eagerness, vivacity; the world is to her a charm, a wonder, a mystery, a joy; she can't speak for delight when she finds a new flower, she must pet it and caress it and smell it and talk to it, and pour out endearing names upon it. And she is color-mad: brown rocks, yellow sand, gray moss, green foliage, blue sky; the pearl of the dawn, the purple shadows on the mountains, the golden islands floating in crimson seas at sunset, the pallid moon sailing through the shredded cloud-rack, the star-jewels glittering in the wastes of space—none of them is of any practical value, so far as I can see, but because they have color and majesty, that is enough for her, and she loses her mind over them. If she could quiet down and keep still a couple of minutes at a time, it would be a reposeful spectacle. In that case I think I could enjoy looking at her; indeed I am sure I could, for I am coming to realize that she is a quite remarkably comely creature—lithe, slender, trim, rounded, shapely, nimble, graceful; and once when she was standing marble-white and sun-drenched on a boulder, with her young head tilted back and her hand shading her eyes, watching the flight of a bird in the sky, I recognized that she was beautiful.

Monday noon.—*If there is anything on the planet that she is not interested in it is not in my list. There are animals that I am indifferent to, but it is not so with her. She has no discrimination, she takes to all of them, she thinks they are all treasures, every new one is welcome.*

When the mighty brontosaurus came striding into camp, she regarded it as an acquisition, I considered it a calamity; that is a good sample of the lack of harmony that prevails in our views of things. She wanted to domesticate it, I wanted to make it a present of the homestead and move out. She believed it could be tamed by kind treatment and would be a good pet; I said a pet twenty-one feet high and eighty-four feet long would be no proper thing to have about the place, because, even with the best intentions and without meaning any harm, it could sit down on the house and mash it, for any one could see by the look of its eye that it was absent-minded.

Still, her heart was set upon having that monster, and she couldn't give it up. She thought we could start a dairy with it, and wanted me to help her milk it; but I wouldn't; it was too risky. The sex wasn't right, and we hadn't any ladder anyway. Then she wanted to ride it, and look at the scenery. Thirty or forty feet of its tail was lying on the ground, like a fallen tree, and she thought she could climb it, but she was mistaken; when she got to the steep place it was too slick and down she came, and would have hurt herself but for me.

Was she satisfied now? No. Nothing ever satisfies her but demonstration; untested theories are not in her line, and she won't have them. It is the right spirit, I concede it; it attracts me; I feel the influence of it; if I were with her more I think I should take it up myself. Well, she had one theory remaining about this colossus: she thought that if we could tame him and make him friendly we could stand him in the river and use him for a bridge. It turned out that he was already plenty tame enough—at least as far as she was concerned—so she tried her theory, but it failed: every time she got him properly placed in the river and went ashore to cross over on him, he came out and followed her around like a pet mountain. Like the other animals. They all do that.

Friday.—Tuesday—Wednesday—Thursday—and to-day: all without seeing him. It is a long time to be alone; still, it is better to be alone than unwelcome.

I *had* to have company—I was made for it, I think—so I made friends with the animals. They are just charming, and they have the kindest disposition and the politest ways; they never look sour, they never let you feel that you are intruding, they smile at you and wag their tail, if they've got one, and they are always ready for a romp or an excursion or anything you want to propose. I think they are perfect gentlemen. All these days we have had such good times, and it hasn't been lonesome for me, ever. Lonesome!

No, I should say not. Why, there's always a swarm of them around—sometimes as much as four or five acres—you can't count them; and when you stand on a rock in the midst and look out over the furry expanse it is so mottled and splashed and gay with color and frisking sheen and sun-flash, and so rippled with stripes, that you might think it was a lake, only you know it isn't; and there's storms of sociable birds, and hurricanes of whirring wings; and when the sun strikes all that feathery commotion, you have a blazing up of all the colors you can think of, enough to put your eyes out.

We have made long excursions, and I have seen a great deal of the world; almost all of it, I think; and so I am the first traveler, and the only one. When we are on the march, it is an imposing sight—there's nothing like it anywhere. For comfort I ride a tiger or a leopard, because it is soft and has a round back that fits me, and because they are such pretty animals; but for long distance or for scenery I ride the elephant. He hoists me up with his trunk, but I can get off myself; when we are ready to camp, he sits and I slide down the back way.

The birds and animals are all friendly to each other, and there are no disputes about anything. They all talk, and they all talk to me, but it must be a foreign language, for I cannot make out a word they say; yet they often understand me when I talk back, particularly the dog and the elephant. It makes me ashamed. It shows that they are brighter than I am, and are therefore my superiors. It annoys me, for I want to be the principal Experiment myself—and I intend to be, too.

I have learned a number of things, and am educated, now, but I wasn't at first. I was ignorant at first. At first it used to vex me because, with all my watching, I was never smart enough to be around when the water was running uphill; but now I do not mind it. I have experimented and experimented until now I know it never does run uphill, except in the dark. I know it does in the dark, because the pool never goes dry, which it would, of course, if the water didn't come back in the night. It is best to prove things by actual experiment; then you *know;* whereas if you depend on guessing and supposing and conjecturing, you will never get educated.

Some things you *can't* find out; but you will never know you can't by guessing and supposing: no, you have to be patient and go on experimenting until you find out that you can't find out. And it is delightful to have it that way, it makes the world so interesting. If there wasn't anything to find out, it would be dull. Even trying to find out and not finding out is just as interesting as trying to find out and finding out, and I don't know but more so. The secret of the water was a treasure until I *got* it; then the excitement all went away, and I recognized a sense of loss.

By experiment I know that wood swims, and dry leaves, and feathers, and plenty of other things; therefore by all that cumulative evidence you know that a rock will swim; but you have to put up with simply knowing it, for there isn't any way to prove it—up to now. But I shall find a way—then *that* excitement will go. Such things make me sad; because by and by when I have found out everything there won't be any more excitements, and I do love excitements so! The other night I couldn't sleep for thinking about it.

At first I couldn't make out what I was made for, but now I think it was to search out the secrets of this wonderful world and be happy and thank the Giver of it all for devising it. I think there are many things to learn yet —I hope so; and by economizing and not hurrying too fast I think they will last weeks and weeks. I hope so. When you cast up a feather it sails away on the air and goes out of sight; then you throw up a clod and it doesn't. It comes down, every time. I have tried it and tried it, and it is always so. I wonder why it is? Of course it *doesn't* come down, but why should it *seem* to? I suppose it is an optical illusion. I mean, one of them is. I don't know which one. I may be the feather, it may be the clod; I can't prove which it is, I can only demonstrate that one or the other is a fake, and let a person take his choice.

By watching, I know that the stars are not going to last. I have seen some of the best ones melt and run down the sky. Since one can melt, they can all melt; since they can all melt, they can all melt the same night. That sorrow will come—I know it. I mean to sit up every night and look at them as long as I can keep awake; and I will impress those sparkling fields on my memory, so that by and by when they are taken away I can by my fancy restore those lovely myriads to the black sky and make them sparkle again, and double them by the blur of my tears.

After the Fall

When I look back, the Garden is a dream to me. It was beautiful, surpassingly beautiful, enchantingly beautiful; and now it is lost, and I shall not see it any more.

The Garden is lost, but I have found *him,* and am content. He loves me as well as he can; I love him with all the strength of my passionate nature, and this, I think, is proper to my youth and sex. If I ask myself why I love him, I find I do not know, and do not really much care to know; so I suppose that this kind of love is not a product of reasoning and statistics, like one's love for other reptiles and animals. I think that this must be so. I love certain birds because of their song; but I do not love Adam on account of his singing—no, it is not that; the more he sings the more I do not get reconciled to it. Yet I ask him to sing, because I wish to learn to like everything he is interested in. I am sure I can learn, because at first I could not stand it, but now I can. It sours the milk, but it doesn't matter; I can get used to that kind of milk.

It is not on account of his brightness that I love him—no, it is not that. He is not to blame for his brightness, such as it is, for he did not make it himself; he is as God made him, and that is sufficient. There was a wise purpose in it, *that* I know. In time it will develop, though I think it will not be sudden; and besides, there is no hurry; he is well enough just as he is.

It is not on account of his gracious and considerate ways and his delicacy that I love him. No, he has lacks in these regards, but he is well enough just so, and is improving.

It is not on account of his industry that I love him—no, it is not that. I think he has it in him, and I do not know why he conceals it from me. It is my only pain. Otherwise he is frank and open with me, now. I am sure he keeps nothing from me but this. It grieves me that he should have a secret from me, and sometimes it spoils my sleep, thinking of it, but I will put it out of my mind; it shall not trouble my happiness, which is otherwise full to overflowing.

It is not on account of his education that I love him—no, it is not that. He is self-educated, and does really know a multitude of things, but they are not so.

It is not on account of his chivalry that I love him—no, it is not that. He told on me, but I do not blame him; it is a peculiarity of sex, I think, and he did not make his sex. Of course I would not have told on him, I would have perished first; but that is a peculiarity of sex, too, and I do not take credit for it, for I did not make my sex.

Then why is it that I love him? *Merely because he is masculine,* I think.

At bottom he is good, and I love him for that, but I could love him without it. If he should beat me and abuse me, I should go on loving him. I know it. It is a matter of sex, I think.

He is strong and handsome, and I love him for that, and I admire him and am proud of him, but I could love him without those qualities. If he were plain, I should love him; if he were a wreck, I should love him; and I would work for him, and slave over him, and pray for him, and watch by his bedside until I died.

Yes, I think I love him merely because he is *mine* and is *masculine.* There is no other reason, I suppose. And so I think it is as I first said: that this kind of love is not a product of reasoning and statistics. It just *comes*—none knows whence—and cannot explain itself. And doesn't need to.

It is what I think. But I am only a girl, and the first that has examined this matter, and it may turn out that in my ignorance and inexperience I have not got it right.

Forty Years Later

It is my prayer, it is my longing, that we may pass from this life together—a longing which shall never perish from the earth, but shall have place in the heart of every wife that loves, until the end of time; and it shall be called by my name.

But if one of us must go first, it is my prayer that it shall be I; for he is strong, I am weak, I am not so necessary to him as he is to me—life without him would not be life; how could I endure it? This prayer is also immortal, and will not cease from being offered up while my race continues. I am the first wife; and in the last wife I shall be repeated.

At Eve's Grave

ADAM: Wheresoever she was, *there* was Eden.

TWAIN *and the* LEARNING PROCESS

Taming the Bicycle

In the early 1880s, when he was nearly fifty, Mark Twain learned to ride one of the old high-wheel bicycles of that time.—Editor.

I

I thought the matter over, and concluded I could do it. So I went down and bought a barrel of Pond's Extract and a bicycle. The Expert came home with me to instruct me. We chose the back yard, for the sake of privacy, and went to work.

Mine was not a full-grown bicycle, but only a colt—a fifty-inch, with the pedals shortened up to forty-eight—and skittish, like any other colt. The Expert explained the thing's points briefly, then he got on its back and rode around a little, to show me how easy it was to do. He said that the dismounting was perhaps the hardest thing to learn, and so we would leave that to the last. But he was in error there. He found, to his surprise and joy, that all that he needed to do was to get me on to the machine and stand out of the way; I could get off, myself. Although I was wholly inexperienced, I dismounted in the best time on record. He was on that side, shoving up the machine; we all came down with a crash, he at the bottom, I next, and the machine on top.

We examined the machine, but it was not in the least injured. This was hardly believable. Yet the Expert assured me that it was true; in fact, the examination proved it. I was partly to realize, then, how admirably these things are constructed. We applied some Pond's Extract, and resumed. The Expert got on the *other* side to shove up this time, but I dismounted on that side; so the result was as before.

The machine was not hurt. We oiled ourselves up again, and resumed. This time the Expert took up a sheltered position behind, but somehow or other we landed on him again.

He was full of surprised admiration; said it was abnormal. She was all right, not a scratch on her, not a timber started anywhere. I said it was wonderful, while we were greasing up, but he said that when I came to know these steel spider-webs I would realize that nothing but dynamite could cripple them. Then he limped out to position, and we resumed once more. This time the Expert took up the position of short-stop, and got a man to shove up behind. We got up a handsome speed, and presently traversed a brick, and I went out over the top of the tiller and landed, head down, on the instructor's back, and saw the machine fluttering in the air between me and the sun. It was well it came down on us, for that broke the fall, and it was not injured.

Five days later I got out and was carried down to the hospital, and found the Expert doing pretty fairly. In a few more days I was quite sound. I attribute this to my prudence in always dismounting on something soft. Some recommend a feather bed, but I think an Expert is better.

The Expert got out at last, brought four assistants with him. It was a good idea. These four held the graceful cobweb upright while I climbed into the saddle; then they formed in column and marched on either side of me while the Expert pushed behind; all hands assisted at the dismount.

The bicycle had what is called the "wabbles," and had them very badly. In order to keep my position, a good many things were required of me, and in every instance the thing required was against nature. Against nature, but not against the *laws* of nature. That is to say, that whatever the needed thing might be, my nature, habit, and breeding moved me to attempt it in one way, while some immutable and unsuspected law of physics required that it be done in just the other way. I perceived by this how radically and grotesquely wrong had been the life-long education of my body and members. They were steeped in ignorance; they knew nothing—nothing which it could profit them to know. For instance, if I found myself falling to the right, I put the tiller hard down the other way, by a quite natural impulse, and so violated a law, and kept on going down. The law required the opposite thing—the big wheel must be turned in the direction in which you are falling. It is hard to believe this, when you are told it. And not merely hard to believe it, but impossible; it is opposed to all your notions. And it is just as hard to do it, after you do come to believe it. Believing it, and knowing by the most convincing proof that it is true, does not help it: you can't any more *do* it than you could before; you can neither force nor persuade yourself to do it at first. The intellect has to come to the front, now. It has to teach the limbs to discard their old education and adopt the new.

The steps of one's progress are distinctly marked. At the end of each lesson he knows he has acquired something, and he also knows what that something is, and likewise that it will stay with him. It is not like studying German, where you mull along, in a groping, uncertain way, for thirty years; and at last, just as you think you've got it, they spring the subjunctive on you, and there you are. No—and I see now, plainly enough, that the great pity about the German language is, that you can't fall off it and hurt yourself. There is nothing like that feature to make you attend strictly to business. But I also see, by what I have learned of bicycling, that the right and only sure way to learn German is by the bicycling method. That is to say, take a grip on one villainy of it at a time, and learn it—not ease up and shirk to the next, leaving that one half learned.

When you have reached the point in bicycling where you can balance the machine tolerably fairly and propel it and steer it, then comes your next task—how to mount it. You do it in this way: you hop along behind it on your right foot, resting the other on the mounting-peg, and grasping the tiller with your hands. At the word, you rise on the peg, stiffen your left leg, hang your other one around in the air in a general and indefinite way, lean your stomach against the rear of the saddle, and then fall off, maybe on one side, maybe on the other; but you fall off. You get up and do it again; and once more; and then several times.

By this time you have learned to keep your balance; and also to steer without wrenching the tiller out by the roots (I say tiller because it *is* a tiller; "handle-bar" is a lamely descriptive phrase). So you steer along, straight ahead, a little while, then you rise forward, with a steady strain, bringing your right leg, and then your body, into the saddle, catch your breath, fetch a violent hitch this way and then that, and down you go again.

But you have ceased to mind the going down by this time; you are getting to light on one foot or the other with considerable certainty. Six more attempts and six more falls make you perfect. You land in the saddle comfortably, next time, and stay there—that is, if you can be content to let your legs dangle, and leave the pedals alone awhile; but if you grab at once for the pedals, you are gone again. You soon learn to wait a little and perfect your balance before reaching for the pedals; then the mounting-art is acquired, is complete, and a little practice will make it simple and easy to you, though spectators ought to keep off a rod or two to one side, along at first, if you have nothing against them.

And now you come to the voluntary dismount; you learned the other kind first of all. It is quite easy to tell one how to do the voluntary dismount; the words are few, the requirement simple, and apparently undifficult; let your left pedal go down till your left leg is nearly straight, turn your wheel to the left, and get off as you would from a horse. It certainly does sound exceedingly easy; but it isn't. I don't know why it isn't, but it isn't. Try as you may, you don't get down as you would from a horse, you get down as you would from a house afire. You make a spectacle of yourself every time.

II

During eight days I took a daily lesson of an hour and a half. At the end of this twelve working-hours' apprenticeship I was graduated—in the rough. I was pronounced competent to paddle my own bicycle without outside help. It seems incredible, this celerity of acquirement. It takes considerably longer than that to learn horseback-riding in the rough.

Now it is true that I could have learned without a teacher, but it would have been risky for me, because of my natural clumsiness. The self-taught man seldom knows anything accurately, and he does not know a tenth as much as he could have known if he had worked under teachers; and, besides, he brags, and is the means of fooling other thoughtless people into going and doing as he himself has done. There are those who imagine that the unlucky accidents of life—life's "experiences"—are in some way useful to us. I wish I could find out how. I never knew one of them to happen twice. They always change off and swap around and catch you on your inexperienced side. If personal experience can be worth anything as an education, it wouldn't seem likely that you could trip Methuselah; and yet if that old person could come back here it is more than likely that one of the first things he would do would be to take hold of one of these electric wires and tie himself all up in a knot. Now the surer thing and the wiser thing would be for him to ask somebody whether it was a good thing to take hold of. But that would not suit him; he would be one of the self-taught kind that go by experience; he would want to examine for himself. And he would find, for his instruction, that the coiled patriarch shuns the electric wire; and it would be useful to him, too, and would leave his education in quite a complete and rounded-out condition, till he should come again, some day, and go to bouncing a dynamite-can around to find out what was in it.

But we wander from the point. However, get a teacher; it saves much time and Pond's Extract.

Before taking final leave of me, my instructor inquired concerning my physical strength, and I was able to inform him that I hadn't any. He said that that was a defect which would make up-hill wheeling pretty difficult for me at first; but he also said the bicycle would soon remove it. The contrast between his muscles and mine was quite marked. He wanted to test mine, so I offered my biceps—which was my best. It almost made him smile. He said, "It is pulpy, and soft, and yielding, and rounded; it evades pressure, and glides from under the fingers; in the dark a body might think it was an oyster in a rag." Perhaps this made me look grieved, for he added, briskly: "Oh, that's all right; you needn't worry about that; in a little while you can't tell it from a petrified kidney. Just go right along with your practice; you're all right."

Then he left me, and I started out alone to seek adventures. You don't really have to seek them—that is nothing but a phrase—they come to you.

I chose a reposeful Sabbath-day sort of a back street which was about thirty yards wide between the curbstones. I knew it was not wide enough; still, I thought that by keeping strict watch and wasting no space unnecessarily I could crowd through.

Of course I had trouble mounting the machine, entirely on my own responsibility, with no encouraging moral support from the outside, no sympathetic instructor to say, "Good! now you're doing well—good again—don't hurry—there, now, you're all right—brace up, go ahead." In place of this I had some other support. This was a boy, who was perched on a gate-post munching a hunk of maple sugar.

He was full of interest and comment. The first time I failed and went down he said that if he was me he would dress up in pillows, that's what he would do. The next time I went down he advised me to go and learn to ride a tricycle first. The third time I collapsed he said he didn't believe I could stay on a horse-car. But next time I succeeded, and got clumsily under way in a weaving, tottering, uncertain fashion, and occupying pretty much all of the street. My slow and lumbering gait filled the boy to the chin with scorn, and he sung out, "My, but don't he rip along!" Then he got down from his post and loafed along the sidewalk, still observing and occasionally commenting. Presently he dropped into my wake and followed along behind. A little girl passed by, balancing a wash-board on her head, and giggled, and seemed about to make a remark, but the boy said, rebukingly, "Let him alone, he's going to a funeral."

I had been familiar with that street for years, and had always supposed it was a dead level; but it was not, as the bicycle now informed me, to my surprise. The bicycle, in the hands of a novice, is as alert and acute as a spirit-level in the detecting of delicate and vanishing shades of difference in these matters. It notices a rise where your untrained eye would not observe that one existed; it notices any decline which water will run down. I was toiling up a slight rise, but was not aware of it. It made me tug and pant and perspire; and still, labor as I might, the machine came almost to a standstill every little while. At such times the boy would say: "That's it! take a rest—there ain't no hurry. They can't hold the funeral without *you.*"

Stones were a bother to me. Even the smallest ones gave me a panic when I went over them. I could hit any kind of a stone, no matter how small, if I tried to miss it; and of course at first I couldn't help trying to do that. It is but natural. It is part of the ass that is put in us all, for some inscrutable reason.

I was at the end of my course, at last, and it was necessary for me to round to. This is not a pleasant thing, when you undertake it for the first time on your own responsibility, and neither is it likely to succeed. Your confidence oozes away, you fill steadily up with nameless apprehensions, every fiber of you is tense with a watchful strain, you start a cautious and gradual curve, but your squirmy nerves are all full of electric anxieties, so the curve is quickly demoralized into a jerky and perilous zigzag; then suddenly the nickel-clad horse takes the bit in its mouth and goes slanting for the curbstone, defying all prayers and all your powers to change its mind—your heart stands still, your breath hangs fire, your legs forget to work, straight on you go, and there are but a couple of feet between you and the curb now. And now is the desperate moment, the last chance to save yourself; of course all your instructions fly out of your head, and you whirl your wheel *away* from the curb instead of *toward* it, and so you go sprawling on that granite-bound inhospitable shore. That was my luck;

that was my experience. I dragged myself out from under the indestructible bicycle and sat down on the curb to examine.

I started on the return trip. It was now that I saw a farmer's wagon poking along down toward me, loaded with cabbages. If I needed anything to perfect the precariousness of my steering, it was just that. The farmer was occupying the middle of the road with his wagon, leaving barely fourteen or fifteen yards of space on either side. I couldn't shout at him—a beginner can't shout; if he opens his mouth he is gone; he must keep all his attention on his business. But in this grisly emergency, the boy came to the rescue, and for once I had to be grateful to him. He kept a sharp lookout on the swiftly varying impulses and inspirations of my bicycle, and shouted to the man accordingly:

"To the left. Turn to the left, or this jackass'll run over you!" The man started to do it. "No, to the right, to the right! Hold on! *that* won't do!—to the left!—to the right!—to the *left!*—right! left—ri— Stay where you *are,* or you're a goner!"

And just then I caught the off horse in the starboard and went down in a pile. I said, "Hang it! Couldn't you *see* I was coming?"

"Yes, I see you was coming, but I couldn't tell which *way* you was coming. Nobody could—now, *could* they? You couldn't yourself—now, *could* you? So what could *I* do?"

There was something in that, and so I had the magnanimity to say so. I said I was no doubt as much to blame as he was.

Within the next five days I achieved so much progress that the boy couldn't keep up with me. He had to go back to his gate-post, and content himself with watching me fall at long range.

There was a row of low stepping-stones across one end of the street, a measured yard apart. Even after I got so I could steer pretty fairly I was so afraid of those stones that I always hit them. They gave me the worst falls I ever got in that street, except those which I got from dogs. I have seen it stated that no expert is quick enough to run over a dog; that a dog is always able to skip out of his way. I think that that may be true: but I think that the reason he couldn't run over the dog was because he was trying to. I did not try to run over any dog. But I ran over every dog that came along. I think it makes a great deal of difference. If you try to run over the dog he knows how to calculate, but if you are trying to miss him he does not know how to calculate, and is liable to jump the wrong way every time. It was always so in my experience. Even when I could not hit a wagon I could hit a dog that came to see me practise. They all liked to see me practise, and they all came, for there was very little going on in our neighborhood to entertain a dog. It took time to learn to miss a dog, but I achieved even that.

I can steer as well as I want to, now, and I will catch that boy out one of these days and run over *him* if he doesn't reform.

Get a bicycle. You will not regret it, if you live.

How to Make History Dates Stick

These chapters are for children, and I shall try to make the words large enough to command respect. In the hope that you are listening, and that you have confidence in me, I will proceed. Dates are difficult things to acquire; and after they are acquired it is difficult to keep them in the head. But they are very valuable. They are like the cattle-pens of a ranch—they shut in the several brands of historical cattle, each within its own fence, and keep them from getting mixed together. Dates are hard to remember because they consist of figures; figures are monotonously unstriking in appearance, and they don't take hold, they form no pictures, and so they give the eye no chance to help. Pictures are the thing. Pictures can make dates stick. They can make nearly anything stick—particularly *if you make the pictures yourself.* Indeed, that is the great point—make the pictures *yourself.* I know about this from experience. Thirty years ago I was delivering a memorized lecture every night, and every night I had to help myself with a page of notes to keep from getting myself mixed. The notes consisted of beginnings of sentences, and were eleven in number, and they ran something like this:

"In that region the weather—"

"At that time it was a custom—"

"But in California one never heard—"

Eleven of them. They initialed the brief divisions of the lecture and protected me against skipping. But they all looked about alike on the page; they formed no picture; I had them by heart, but I could never with certainty remember the order of their succession; therefore I always had to keep those notes by me and look at them every little while. Once I mislaid them; you will not be able to imagine the terrors of that evening. I now saw that I must invent some other protection. So I got ten of the initial letters by heart in their proper order—I, A, B, and so on—and I went on the platform the next night with these marked in ink on my ten finger-nails. But it didn't answer. I kept track of the fingers for a while; then I lost it, and after that I was never quite sure which finger I had used last. I couldn't lick off a letter after using it, for while that would have made success certain it would also have provoked too much curiosity. There was curiosity enough without that. To the audience I seemed more interested in my fingernails than I was in my subject; one or two persons asked me afterward what was the matter with my hands.

It was now that the idea of pictures occurred to me; then my troubles passed away. In two minutes I made six pictures with a pen, and they did the work of the eleven catch-sentences, and did it perfectly. I threw the pictures away as soon as they were made, for I was sure I could shut my eyes and see them any time. That was a quarter of a century ago; the lecture vanished out of my head more than twenty years ago, but I could rewrite it from the pictures—for they remain. Here are three of them: (Fig. 1).

FIG. 1

The first one is a haystack—below it a rattlesnake—and it told me where to begin to talk ranch-life in Carson Valley. The second one told me where to begin to talk about a strange and violent wind that used to burst upon Carson City from the Sierra Nevadas every afternoon at two o'clock and try to blow the town away. The third picture, as you easily perceive, is lightning; its duty was to remind me when it was time to begin to talk about San Francisco weather, where there *is* no lightning—nor thunder, either—and it never failed me.

I will give you a valuable hint. When a man is making a speech and you are to follow him don't jot down notes to speak from, jot down *pictures.* It is awkward and embarrassing to have to keep referring to notes; and besides it breaks up your speech and makes it ragged and non-coherent; but you can tear up your pictures as soon as you have made them—they will stay fresh and strong in your memory in the order and sequence in which you scratched them down. And many will admire to see what a good memory you are furnished with, when perhaps your memory is not any better than mine.

Sixteen years ago when my children were little creatures the governess was trying to hammer some primer histories into their heads. Part of this fun—if you like to call it that—consisted in the memorizing of the accession dates of the thirty-seven personages who had ruled over England from the Conqueror down. These little people found it a bitter, hard contract. It was all dates, they all looked alike, and they wouldn't stick. Day after day of the summer vacation dribbled by, and still the kings held the fort; the children couldn't conquer any six of them.

With my lecture experience in mind I was aware that I could invent some way out of the trouble with pictures, but I hoped a way could be found which would let them romp in the open air while they learned the kings. I found it, and then they mastered all the monarchs in a day or two.

The idea was to make them *see* the reigns with their eyes; that would be a large help. We were at the farm then. From the house-porch the grounds sloped gradually down to the lower fence and rose on the right to the high ground where my small work-den stood. A carriage-road wound through the grounds and up the hill. I staked it out with the English monarchs, beginning with the Conqueror, and you could stand on the porch and clearly see every reign and its length, from the Conquest down to Victoria, then in the forty-sixth year of her reign—*eight hundred and seventeen years* of English history under your eye at once!

English history was an unusually live topic in America just then. The world had suddenly realized that while it was not noticing the Queen had passed Henry VIII., passed Henry VI. and Elizabeth, and gaining in length every day. Her reign had entered the list of the long ones; everybody was interested now—it was watching a race. Would she pass the long Edward? There was a possibility of it. Would she pass the long Henry? Doubtful, most people said. The long George? Impossible! Everybody said it. But we have lived to see her leave him two years behind.

I measured off 817 feet of the roadway, a foot representing a year, and at the beginning and end of each reign I drove a three-foot white-pine stake in the turf by the roadside and wrote the name and dates on it. Abreast the middle of the porch-front stood a great granite flower-vase overflowing with a cataract of bright-yellow flowers—I can't think of their name. The vase was William the Conqueror. We put his name on it and his accession date, 1066. We started from that and measured off twenty-one feet of the road, and drove William Rufus's stake; then thirteen feet and drove the first Henry's stake; then thirty-five feet and drove Stephen's; then nineteen feet, which brought us just past the summer-house on the left; then we staked out thirty-five, ten, and seventeen for the second Henry and Richard and John; turned the curve and entered upon just what was needed for Henry III.—a level, straight stretch of fifty-six feet of road without a crinkle in it. And it lay exactly in front of the house, in the middle of the grounds. There couldn't have been a better place for that long reign; you could stand on the porch and see those two wide-apart stakes almost with your eyes shut. (Fig. 2.)

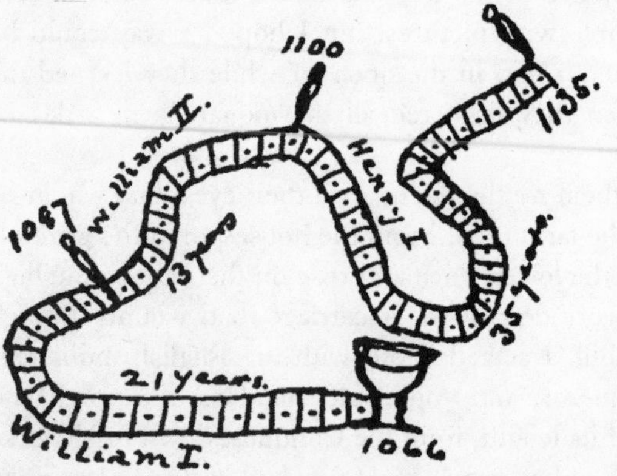

FIG. 2

That isn't the shape of the road—I have bunched it up like that to save room. The road had some great curves in it, but their gradual sweep was such that they were no mar to history. No, in our road one could tell at a glance who was who by the size of the vacancy between stakes—with *locality* to help, of course.

Although I am away off here in a Swedish village and those stakes did not stand till the snow came, I can see them to-day as plainly as ever; and whenever I think of an English monarch his stakes rise before me of their own accord and I notice the large or small space which he takes up on our road. Are your kings spaced off in your mind? When you think of Richard III. and of James II. do the durations of their reigns seem about alike to you? It isn't so to me; I always notice that there's a foot's difference. When you think of Henry III. do you see a great long stretch of straight road? I do; and just at the end where it joins on to Edward I. I always see a small pear-bush with its green fruit hanging down. When I think of the Commonwealth I see a shady little group of these small saplings which we called the oak parlor; when I think of George III. I see him stretching up the hill, part of him occupied by a flight of stone steps; and I can locate Stephen to an inch when he comes into my mind, for he just filled the stretch which went by the summer-house. Victoria's reign reached almost to my study door on the first little summit; there's sixteen feet to be added now; I believe that that would carry it to a big pine-tree that was shattered by some lightning one summer when it was trying to hit me.

We got a good deal of fun out of the history road; and exercise, too. We trotted the course from the Conqueror to the study, the children calling out the names, dates, and length of reigns as we passed the stakes, going a good gait along the long reigns, but slowing down when we came upon people like Mary and Edward VI., and the short Stuart and Plantagenet, to give time to get in the statistics. I offered prizes, too—apples. I threw one as far as I could send it, and the child that first shouted the reign it fell in got the apple.

The children were encouraged to stop locating things as being "over by the arbor," or "in the oak parlor," or "up at the stone steps," and say instead that the things were in Stephen, or in the Commonwealth, or in George III. They got the habit without trouble. To have the long road mapped out with such exactness was a great boon for me, for I had the habit of leaving books and other articles lying around everywhere, and had not previously been able to definitely name the place, and so had often been obliged to go to fetch them myself, to save time and failure; but now I could name the reign I left them in, and send the children.

Next I thought I would measure off the French reigns, and peg them alongside the English ones, so that we could always have contemporaneous French history under our eyes as we went our English rounds. We pegged them down to the Hundred Years' War, then threw the idea aside, I do not now remember why. After that we made the English pegs fence in European and American history as well as English, and that answered very well. English and alien poets, statesmen, artists, heroes, battles, plagues, cataclysms, revolutions—we shoveled them all into the English fences according to their dates. Do you understand? We gave Washington's birth to

George II.'s pegs and his death to George III.'s; George II. got the Lisbon earthquake and George III. the Declaration of Independence. Goethe, Shakespeare, Napoleon, Savonarola, Joan of Arc, the French Revolution, the Edict of Nantes, Clive, Wellington, Waterloo, Plassey, Patay, Cowpens, Saratoga, the Battle of the Boyne, the invention of the logarithms, the microscope, the steam-engine, the telegraph—anything and everything all over the world—we dumped it all in among the English pegs according to its date and regardless of its nationality.

If the road-pegging scheme had not succeeded I should have lodged the kings in the children's heads by means of pictures—that is, I should have tried. It might have failed, for the pictures could only be effective *when made by the pupil,* not the master, for it is the work put upon the drawing that makes the drawing stay in the memory, and my children were too little to make drawings at that time. And, besides, they had no talent for art, which is strange, for in other ways they are like me.

But I will develop the picture plan now, hoping that you will be able to use it. It will come good for indoors when the weather is bad and one cannot go outside and peg a road. Let us imagine that the kings are a procession, and that they have come out of the Ark and down Ararat for exercise and are now starting back again up the zigzag road. This will bring several of them into view at once, and each zigzag will represent the length of a king's reign.

And so on. You will have plenty of space, for by my project you will use the parlor wall. You do not mark on the wall; that would cause trouble. You only attach bits of paper to it with pins or thumb-tacks. These will leave no mark.

Take your pen now, and twenty-one pieces of white paper, each two inches square, and we will do the twenty-one years of the Conqueror's reign. On each square draw a picture of a whale and write the dates and term of service. We choose the whale for several reasons: its name and William's begin with the same letter; it is the biggest fish that swims, and William is the most conspicuous figure in English history in the way of a landmark; finally, a whale is about the easiest thing to draw. By the time you have drawn twenty-one whales and written "William I.—1066—1087—twenty-one years" twenty-one times, those details will be your property; you cannot dislodge them from your memory with anything but dynamite. I will make a sample for you to copy: (Fig. 3).

I have got his chin up too high, but that is no matter; he is looking for Harold. It may be that a whale hasn't that fin up there on his back, but I do not remember; and so, since there is a doubt, it is best to err on the safe side. He looks better, anyway, than he would without it.

Be very careful and *attentive* while you are drawing your first whale from my sample and writing the word and figures under it, so that you will not need to copy the sample any more. Compare your copy with the sample; examine closely; if you find you have got everything right and can shut your eyes and see the picture and call the words and figures, then turn the sample and the copy upside down and make the next copy from memory; and also the next and next, and so on, always drawing and writing from memory until you have finished the whole twenty-one. This will take you twenty minutes, or thirty, and by that time you will find that you can make a whale in less time than an unpractised person can make a sardine; also, up to the time you die you will always be able to furnish William's dates to any ignorant person that inquires after them.

FIG. 3

You will now take thirteen pieces of *blue* paper, each two inches square, and do William II. (Fig. 4.)

Make him spout his water forward instead of backward; also make him small, and stick a harpoon in him and give him that sick look in the eye. Otherwise you might seem to be continuing the other William, and that would be confusing and a damage. It is quite right to make him small; he was only about a No. 11 whale, or along there somewhere; there wasn't room in him for his father's great spirit. The barb of that harpoon ought not to show like that, because it is down inside the whale and ought to be out of sight, but it

FIG. 4

FIG. 5

cannot be helped; if the barb were removed people would think some one had stuck a whip-stock into the whale. It is best to leave the barb the way it is, then every one will know it is a harpoon and attending to business. Remember—draw from the copy only once; make your other twelve and the inscription from memory.

Now the truth is that whenever you have copied a picture and its inscription once from my sample and two or three times from memory the details will stay with you and be hard to forget. After that, if you like, you may make merely the whale's *head and water-spout* for the Conqueror till you end his reign, each time *saying* the inscription in place of writing it; and in the case of William II. make the *harpoon* alone, and say over the inscription each time you do it. You see, it will take nearly twice as long to do the first set as it will to do the second, and that will give you a marked sense of the difference in length of the two reigns.

FIG. 6

Next do Henry I. on thirty-five squares of *red* paper. (Fig. 5.)

That is a hen, and suggests Henry by furnishing the first syllable. When you have repeated the hen and the inscription until you are perfectly sure of them, draw merely the hen's head the rest of the thirty-five times, saying over the inscription each time. Thus: (Fig. 6).

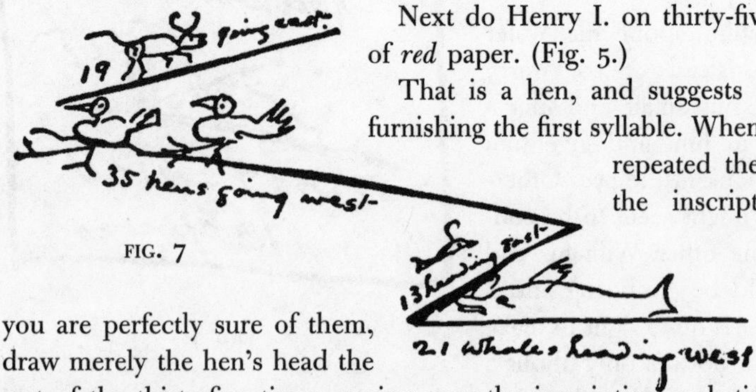

FIG. 7

You begin to understand now how this procession is going to look when it is on the wall. First, there will be the Conqueror's twenty-one whales and water-spouts, the twenty-one white squares joined to one another and making a white stripe three and one-half feet long; the thirteen blue squares of William II. will be joined to that—a blue stripe two feet, two inches long, followed by Henry's red stripe five feet, ten inches long, and so on. The colored divisions will smartly show to the eye the difference in the length of the reigns and impress the proportions on the memory and the understanding. (Fig. 7.)

Stephen of Blois comes next. He requires nineteen two-inch squares of *yellow* paper. (Fig. 8.)

FIG. 8

That is a steer. The sound suggests the beginning of Stephen's name. I choose it for that reason. I can make a better steer than that when I am not excited. But this one will do. It is a good-enough steer for history. The tail is defective, but it only wants straightening out.

Next comes Henry II. Give him thirty-five squares of *red* paper. These hens must face west, like the former ones. (Fig. 9.)

FIG. 9

This hen differs from the other one. He is on his way to inquire what has been happening at Canterbury.

Now we arrive at Richard I., called Richard of the Lion-heart because he was a brave fighter and was never so contented as when he was leading crusades in Palestine and neglecting his affairs at home. Give him ten squares of *white* paper. (Fig. 10.)

That is a lion. His office is to remind you of the lion-hearted Richard. There is something the matter with his legs, but I do not quite know what it is, they do not seem right. I think the hind ones are the most unsatisfactory; the front ones are well enough, though it would be better if they were rights and lefts.

FIG. 10

Next comes King John, and he was a poor circumstance. He was called Lackland. He gave his realm to the Pope. Let him have seventeen squares of *yellow* paper. (Fig. 11.)

FIG. 11

That creature is a jamboree. It looks like a trademark, but that is only an accident and not intentional. It is prehistoric and extinct. It used to roam the earth in the Old Silurian times, and lay eggs and catch fish and climb trees and live on fossils; for it was of a mixed breed, which was the fashion then. It was very fierce, and the Old Silurians were afraid of it, but this is a tame one. Physically it has no representative now, but its mind has been transmitted. First I drew it sitting down, but have turned it the other way now because I think it looks more attractive and spirited when one end of it is galloping. I love to think that in this attitude it gives us a pleasant idea of John coming all in a happy excitement to see what the barons have been arranging for him at Runnymede, while the other one gives us an idea of him sitting down to wring his hands and grieve over it.

FIG. 12

We now come to Henry III.; *red* squares again, of course—fifty-six of them. We must make all the Henrys the same color; it will make their long reigns show up handsomely on the wall. Among all the eight Henrys there were but two short ones. A lucky name, as far as longevity goes. The reigns of six of the Henrys cover 227 years. It might have been well to name all the royal princes Henry, but this was overlooked until it was too late. (Fig. 12.)

That is the best one yet. He is on his way (1265) to have a look at the first House of Commons in English history. It was a monumental event, the situation of the House, and was the second great liberty landmark which the century had set up. I have made Henry looking glad, but this was not intentional.

Edward I. comes next; *light-brown* paper, thirty-five squares. (Fig. 13.)

FIG. 13

That is an editor. He is trying to think of a word. He props his feet on the chair, which is the editor's way; then he can think better. I do not care much for this one; his ears are not alike; still, editor suggests the sound of Edward, and he will do. I could make him better if I had a model, but I made this one from memory. But it is no particular matter; they all look alike, anyway. They are conceited and troublesome, and don't pay enough. Edward was the first really English king that had yet occupied the throne. The editor in the picture probably looks just as Edward looked when it was first borne in upon him that this was so. His whole attitude expressed gratification and pride mixed with stupefaction and astonishment.

Edward II. now; twenty *blue* squares. (Fig. 14.)

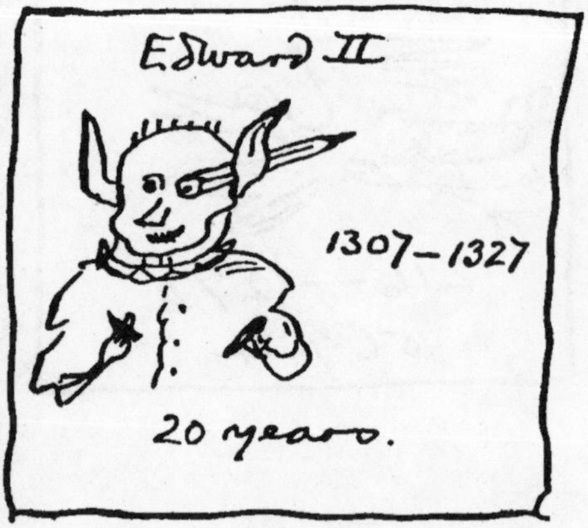

FIG. 14

Another editor. That thing behind his ear is his pencil. Whenever he finds a bright thing in your manuscript he strikes it out with that. That does him good, and makes him smile and show his teeth, the way he is doing in the picture. This one has just been striking out a smart thing, and now he is sitting there with his thumbs in his vest-holes, gloating. They are full of envy and malice, editors are. This picture will serve to remind you that Edward II. was the first English king who was *deposed.* Upon demand, he signed his deposition himself. He had found kingship a most aggravating and disagreeable occupation, and you can see by the look of him that he is glad he resigned. He has put his blue pencil up for good now. He had struck out many a good thing with it in his time.

Edward III. next; fifty *red* squares. (Fig. 15.)

FIG. 15

This editor is a critic. He has pulled out his carving-knife and his tomahawk and is starting after a book which he is going to have for breakfast. This one's arms are put on wrong. I did not notice it at first, but I see it now. Somehow he has got his right arm on his left shoulder, and his left arm on the right shoulder, and this shows us the back of his hands in both instances. It makes him left-handed all around, which is a thing which has never happened before, except perhaps in a museum. That is the way with art, when it is not acquired but born to you: you start in to make some simple little thing, not suspecting that your genius is beginning to work and swell and strain in secret, and all of a sudden there is a convulsion and you fetch out something astonishing. This is called inspiration. It is an accident; you never know when it is coming. I might have tried as much as a year to think of such a strange thing as an all-around left-handed man and I could not have done it, for the more you try to think of an unthinkable thing the more it eludes you; but it can't elude inspiration; you have only to bait with inspiration and you will get it every time. Look at Botticelli's "Spring." Those snaky women were unthinkable, but inspiration secured them for us, thanks to goodness. It is too late to reorganize this editor-critic now; we will leave him as he is. He will serve to remind us.

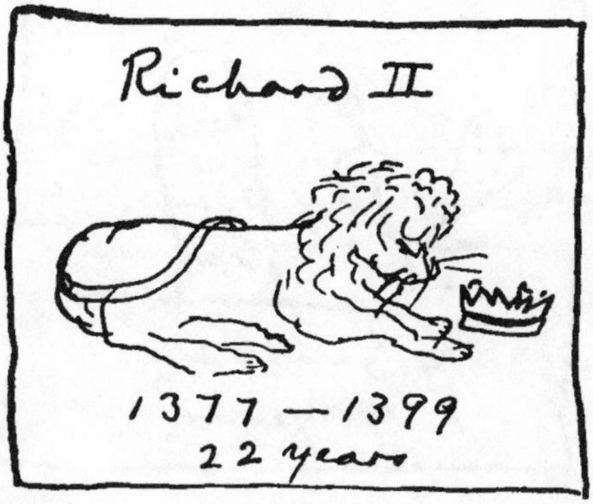

FIG. 16

Richard II. next; twenty-two *white* squares. (Fig. 16.)

We use the lion again because this is another Richard. Like Edward II., he was *deposed.* He is taking a last sad look at his crown before they take it away. There was not room enough and I have made it too small; but it never fitted him, anyway.

Now we turn the corner of the century with a new line of monarchs—the Lancastrian kings.

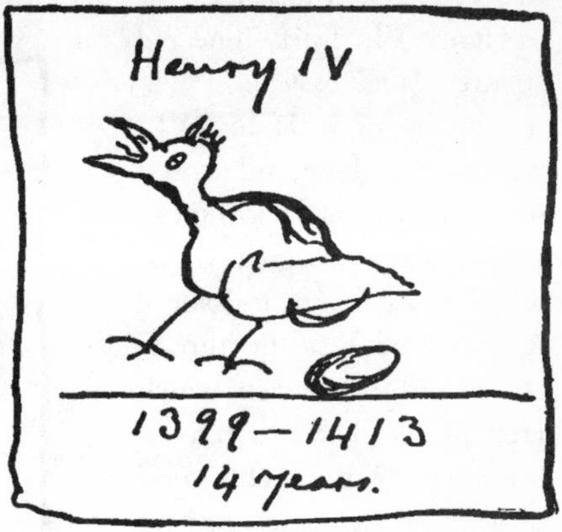

FIG. 17

Henry IV.; fourteen squares of *yellow* paper. (Fig. 17.)

This hen has laid the egg of a new dynasty and realizes the imposing magnitude of the event. She is giving notice in the usual way. You notice that I am improving in the construction of hens. At first I made them too much like other animals, but this one is orthodox. I mention this to encourage you. You will find that the more you practise the more accurate you will become. I could always draw animals, but before I was educated I could not tell what kind they were when I got them done, but now I can. Keep up your courage; it will be the same with you, although you may not think it. This Henry died the year after Joan of Arc was born.

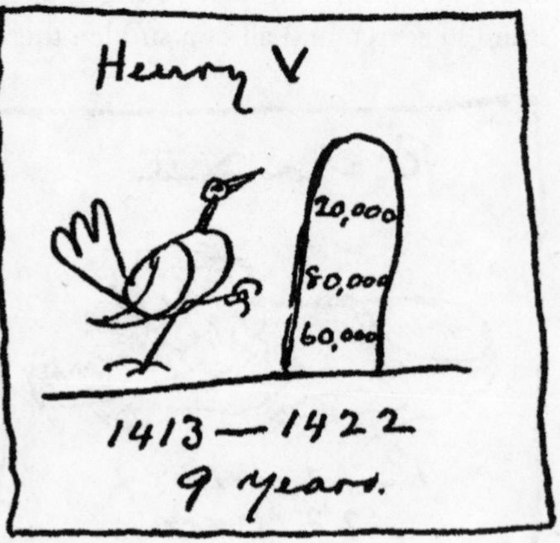

FIG. 18

Henry V.; nine *blue* squares. (Fig. 18.)

There you see him lost in meditation over the monument which records the amazing figures of the battle of Agincourt. French history says 20,000 Englishmen routed 80,000 Frenchmen there; and English historians say that the French loss, in killed and wounded, was 60,000.

Henry VI.; thirty-nine *red* squares. (Fig. 19.)

This is poor Henry VI., who reigned long and scored many misfortunes and humiliations. Also two great disasters: he lost France to Joan of Arc and he lost the throne and ended the dynasty which Henry IV. had started in business with such good prospects. In the picture we see him sad and weary and downcast, with the scepter falling from his nerve-

FIG. 19

less grasp. It is a pathetic quenching of a sun which had risen in such splendor.

Edward IV.; twenty-two *light-brown* squares. (Fig. 20.)

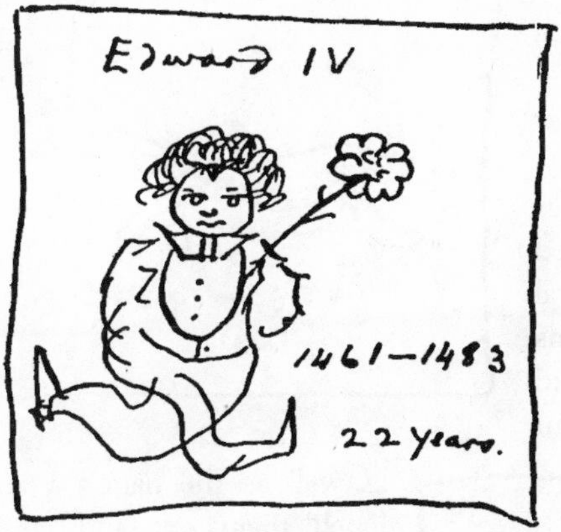

FIG. 20

That is a society editor, sitting there elegantly dressed, with his legs crossed in that indolent way, observing the clothes the ladies wear, so that he can describe them for his paper and make them out finer than they are and get bribes for it and become wealthy. That flower which he is wearing in his buttonhole is a rose—a white rose, a York rose—and will serve to remind us of the Wars of the Roses, and that the white one was the winning color when Edward got the throne and dispossessed the Lancastrian dynasty.

Edward V.; one-third of a *black* square. (Fig. 21.)

FIG. 21

His uncle Richard had him murdered in the tower. When you get the reigns displayed upon the wall this one will be conspicuous and easily remembered. It is the shortest one in English history except Lady Jane Grey's, which was only nine days. She is never officially recognized as a monarch of England, but if you or I should ever occupy a throne we should like to have proper notice taken of it; and it would be only fair and right, too, particularly if we gained nothing by it and lost our lives besides.

Richard III.; two *white* squares. (Fig. 22.)

That is not a very good lion, but Richard was not a very good king. You would think that this lion has two heads, but that is not so; one is only a shadow. There would be shadows for the rest of him, but there was not light enough to go round, it being a dull day, with only fleeting sun-glimpses now and then. Richard had a humped back and a hard heart, and fell at the battle of Bosworth. I do not know the name of that flower in the pot, but we will use it as Richard's trade-mark, for it is said that it grows in only one place in the world—Bosworth Field—and tradition says it never grew there until Richard's royal blood warmed its hidden seed to life and made it grow.

FIG. 22

Henry VII.; twenty-four *blue* squares. (Fig. 23.)

Henry VII. had no liking for wars and turbulence; he preferred peace and quiet and the general prosperity which such conditions create. He liked to sit on that kind of eggs on his own private account as well as the nation's, and hatch them out and count up the result. When he died he left his heir £2,000,000, which was a most unusual fortune for a king to possess in those days. Columbus's great achievement gave him the discovery-fever, and he sent Sebastian Cabot to the New World to search out some foreign territory for England. That is Cabot's ship up there in the corner. This was the first time that England went far abroad to enlarge her estate—but not the last.

FIG. 23

Henry VIII.; thirty-eight *red* squares. (Fig. 24.)

That is Henry VIII. suppressing a monastery in his arrogant fashion.

FIG. 24

Edward VI.; six squares of *yellow* paper. (Fig. 25.)

He is the last Edward to date. It is

indicated by that thing over his head, which is a *last*—shoemaker's last.

Mary; five squares of *black* paper. (Fig. 26.)

The picture represents a burning martyr. He is in back of the smoke.

FIG. 25

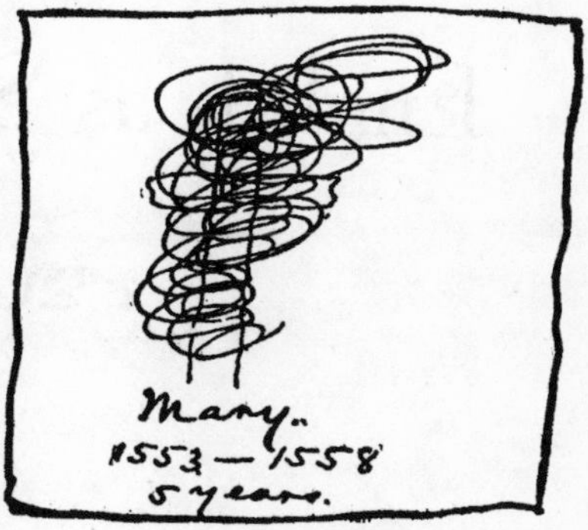

FIG. 26

The first three letters of Mary's name and the first three of the word martyr are the same. Martyrdom was going out in her day and martyrs were becoming scarcer, but she made several. For this reason she is sometimes called Bloody Mary.

This brings us to the reign of Elizabeth, after passing through a period of nearly five hundred years of England's history—492 to be exact. I think you may now be trusted to go the rest of the way without further lessons in art or inspirations in the matter of ideas. You have the scheme now, and something in the ruler's name or career will suggest the pictorial symbol. The effort of inventing such things will not only help your memory, but will develop originality in art. See what it has done for me. If you do not find the parlor wall big enough for all of England's history, continue it into the dining-room and into other rooms. This will make the walls interesting and instructive and really worth something instead of being just flat things to hold the house together.

English as She Is Taught

In the appendix to Croker's Boswell's Johnson one finds this anecdote:

Cato's Soliloquy.—One day Mrs. Gastrel set a little girl to repeat to him [Dr. Samuel Johnson] Cato's Soliloquy, which she went through very correctly. The Doctor, after a pause, asked the child:

"What was to bring Cato to an end?"

She said it was a knife.

"No, my dear, it was not so."

"My aunt Polly said it was a knife."

"Why, Aunt Polly's knife *may do,* but it was a *dagger,* my dear."

He then asked her the meaning of "bane and antidote," which she was unable to give. Mrs. Gastrel said:

"You cannot expect so young a child to know the meaning of such words."

He then said:

"My dear, how many pence are there in *sixpence?*"

"I cannot tell, sir," was the half-terrified reply.

On this, addressing himself to Mrs. Gastrel, he said:

"Now, my dear lady, can anything be more ridiculous than to teach a child Cato's Soliloquy, who does not know how many pence there are in sixpence?"

In a lecture before the Royal Geographical Society Professor Ravenstein quoted the following list of frantic questions, and said that they had been asked in an examination:

Mention all the names of places in the world derived from Julius Cæsar or Augustus Cæsar.

Where are the following rivers: Pisuerga, Sakaria, Guadalete, Jalon, Mulde?

All you know of the following: Machacha, Pilmo, Schebulos, Crivoscia, Basecs, Mancikert, Taxhem, Citeaux, Meloria, Zutphen.

The highest peaks of the Karakorum range.

The number of universities in Prussia.

Why are the tops of mountains continually covered with snow [*sic*]?

Name the length and breadth of the streams of lava which issued from the Skaptar Jokul in the eruption of 1783.

That list would oversize nearly anybody's geographical knowledge. Isn't it reasonably possible that in our schools many of the questions in all studies are several miles ahead of where the pupil is?—that he is set to struggle with things that are ludicrously beyond his present reach, hopelessly beyond his present strength? This remark in passing, and by way of text; now I come to what I was going to say.

I have just now fallen upon a darling literary curiosity. It is a little book, a manuscript compilation, and the compiler sent it to me with the request that I say whether I think it ought to be published or not. I said, Yes; but as I slowly grow wise I briskly grow cautious; and so, now that the publication is imminent, it has seemed to me that I should feel more comfortable if I could divide up this responsibility with the public by adding them to the court. Therefore I will print some extracts from the book, in the hope that they may make converts to my judgment that the volume has merit which entitles it to publication.

As to its character. Every one has sampled "English as She Is Spoke" and "English as She Is Wrote"; this little volume furnishes us an instructive array of examples of "English as She Is Taught"—in the public schools of—well, this country. The collection is made by a teacher in those schools, and all the examples in it are genuine; none of them have been tampered with, or doctored in any way. From time to time, during several years, whenever a pupil has delivered himself of anything peculiarly quaint or toothsome in the course of his recitations, this teacher and her associates have privately set that thing down in a memorandum-book; strictly following the original, as to grammar, construction, spelling, and all; and the result is this literary curiosity.

The contents of the book consist mainly of answers given by the boys and girls to questions, said answers being given sometimes verbally, sometimes in writing. The subjects touched upon are fifteen in number: I. Etymology; II. Grammar; III. Mathematics; IV. Geography; V. "Original"; VI. Analysis; VII. History; VIII. "Intellectual"; IX. Philosophy; X. Physiology; XI. Astronomy; XII. Politics; XIII. Music; XIV. Oratory; XV. Metaphysics.

You perceive that the poor little young idea has taken a shot at a good many kinds of game in the course of the book. Now as to results. Here are some quaint definitions of words. It will be noticed that in all of these instances the sound of the word, or the look of it on paper, has misled the child:

Aborigines, a system of mountains.
Alias, a good man in the Bible.
Amenable, anything that is mean.
Ammonia, the food of the gods.
Assiduity, state of being an acid.
Auriferous, pertaining to an orifice.
Capillary, a little caterpillar.
Corniferous, rocks in which fossil corn is found.
Emolument, a headstone to a grave.
Equestrian, one who asks questions.
Eucharist, one who plays euchre.
Franchise, anything belonging to the French.
Idolater, a very idol person.
Ipecac, a man who likes a good dinner.
Irrigate, to make fun of.
Mendacious, what can be mended.
Mercenary, one who feels for another.
Parasite, a kind of umbrella.
Parasite, the murder of an infant.
Publican, a man who does his prayers in public.
Tenacious, ten acres of land.

Here is one where the phrase "publicans and sinners" has got mixed up in the child's mind with politics, and the result is a definition which takes one in a sudden and unexpected way:

Republican, a sinner mentioned in the Bible.

Also in Democratic newspapers now and then. Here are two where the mistake has resulted from sound assisted by remote fact:

Plagiarist, a writer of plays.
Demagogue, a vessel containing beer and other liquids.

I cannot quite make out what it was that misled the pupil in the following instances; it would not seem to have been the sound of the word, nor the look of it in print:

Asphyxia, a grumbling, fussy temper.
Quarternions, a bird with a flat beak and no bill, living in New Zealand.
Quarternions, the name given to a style of art practiced by the Phœnicians.
Quarternions, a religious convention held every hundred years.
Sibilant, the state of being idiotic.
Crosier, a staff carried by the Deity.

In the following sentences the pupil's ear has been deceiving him again:

The marriage was illegible.
He was totally dismasted with the whole performance.
He enjoys riding on a philosopher.
She was very quick at repertoire.
He prayed for the waters to subsidize.
The leopard is watching his sheep.
They had a strawberry vestibule.

Here is one which—well, now, how often we do slam right into the truth without ever suspecting it:

The men employed by the Gas Company go around and speculate the meter.

Indeed they do, dear; and when you grow up, many and many's the time you will notice it in the gas bill. In the following sentences the little people have some information to convey, every time; but in my case they fail to connect: the light always went out on the keystone word:

> The coercion of some things is remarkable; as bread and molasses.
> Her hat is contiguous because she wears it on one side.
> He preached to an egregious congregation.
> The captain eliminated a bullet through the man's heart.
> You should take caution and be precarious.
> The supercilious girl acted with vicissitude when the perennial time came.

That last is a curiously plausible sentence; one seems to know what it means, and yet he knows all the time that he doesn't. Here is an odd (but entirely proper) use of a word, and a most sudden descent from a lofty philosophical altitude to a very practical and homely illustration:

> We should endeavor to avoid extremes—like those of wasps and bees.

And here—with "zoological" and "geological" in his mind, but not ready to his tongue—the small scholar has innocently gone and let out a couple of secrets which ought never to have been divulged in any circumstances:

> There are a good many donkeys in theological gardens.
> Some of the best fossils are found in theological cabinets.

Under the head of "Grammar" the little scholars furnish the following information:

> Gender is the distinguishing nouns without regard to sex.
> A verb is something to eat.
> Adverbs should always be used as adjectives and adjectives as adverbs.
> Every sentence and name of God must begin with a caterpillar.

"Caterpillar" is well enough, but capital letter would have been stricter. The following is a brave attempt at a solution, but it failed to liquify:

When they are going to say some prose or poetry before they say the poetry or prose they must put a semicolon just after the introduction of the prose or poetry.

The chapter on "Mathematics" is full of fruit. From it I take a few samples—mainly in an unripe state.

A straight line is any distance between two places.
Parallel lines are lines that can never meet until they run together.
A circle is a round straight line with a hole in the middle.
Things which are equal to each other are equal to anything else.
To find the number of square feet in a room you multiply the room by the number of the feet. The product is the result.

Right you are. In the matter of geography this little book is unspeakably rich. The questions do not appear to have applied the microscope to the subject, as did those quoted by Professor Ravenstein; still, they proved plenty difficult enough without that. These pupils did not hunt with a microscope, they hunted with a shot-gun; this is shown by the crippled condition of the game they brought in:

America is divided into the Passiffic slope and the Mississippi valey.
North America is separated by Spain.
America consists from north to south about five hundred miles.
The United States is quite a small country compared with some other countrys, but is about as industrious.
The capital of the United States is Long Island.
The five seaports of the U. S. are Newfunlan and Sanfrancisco.
The principal products of the U. S. is earthquakes and volcanoes.
The Alaginnies are mountains in Philadelphia.
The Rocky Mountains are on the western side of Philadelphia.
Cape Hateras is a vast body of water surrounded by land and flowing into the Gulf of Mexico.
Mason and Dixon's line is the Equater.
One of the leading industries of the United States is mollasses, book-covers, numbers, gas, teaching, lumber, manufacturers, paper-making, publishers, coal.
In Austria the principal occupation is gathering Austrich feathers.
Gibraltar is an island built on a rock.
Russia is very cold and tyrannical.
Sicily is one of the Sandwich Islands.

Hindoostan flows through the Ganges and empties into the Mediterranean Sea.

Ireland is called the Emigrant Isle because it is so beautiful and green.

The width of the different zones Europe lies in depend upon the surrounding country.

The imports of a country are the things that are paid for, the exports are the things that are not.

Climate lasts all the time and weather only a few days.

The two most famous volcanoes of Europe are Sodom and Gomorrah.

The chapter headed "Analysis" shows us that the pupils in our public schools are not merely loaded up with those showy facts about geography, mathematics, and so on, and left in that incomplete state; no, there's machinery for clarifying and expanding their minds. They are required to take poems and analyze them, dig out their common sense, reduce them to statistics, and reproduce them in a luminous prose translation which shall tell you at a glance what the poet was trying to get at. One sample will do. Here is a stanza from "The Lady of the Lake," followed by the pupil's impressive explanation of it:

Alone, but with unbated zeal,
The horseman plied with scourge and steel;
For jaded now and spent with toil,
Embossed with foam and dark with soil,
While every gasp with sobs he drew,
The laboring stag strained full in view.

The man who rode on the horse performed the whip and an instrument made of steel alone with strong ardor not diminishing, for, being tired from the time passed with hard labor overworked with anger and ignorant with weariness, while every breath for labor he drew with cries full of sorrow, the young deer made imperfect who worked hard filtered in sight.

I see, now, that I never understood that poem before. I have had glimpses of its meaning, in moments when I was not as ignorant with weariness as usual, but this is the first time the whole spacious idea of it ever filtered in sight. If I were a public-school pupil I would put those other studies aside and stick to analysis; for, after all, it is the thing to spread your mind.

We come now to historical matters, historical remains, one might say.

As one turns the pages he is impressed with the depth to which one date has been driven into the American child's head—1492. The date is there, and it is there to stay. And it is always at hand, always deliverable at a moment's notice. But the Fact that belongs with it? That is quite another matter. Only the date itself is familiar and sure: its vast Fact has failed of lodgment. It would appear that whenever you ask a public-school pupil when a thing—anything, no matter what—happened, and he is in doubt, he always rips out his 1492. He applies it to everything, from the landing of the ark to the introduction of the horse-car. Well, after all, it is our first date, and so it is right enough to honor it, and pay the public schools to teach our children to honor it:

George Washington was born in 1492.

Washington wrote the Declareation of Independence in 1492.

St. Bartholemew was massacred in 1492.

The Brittains were the Saxons who entered England in 1492 under Julius Cæsar.

The earth is 1492 miles in circumference.

To proceed with "History"

Christopher Columbus was called the Father of his Country.

Queen Isabella of Spain sold her watch and chain and other millinery so that Columbus could discover America.

The Indian wars were very desecrating to the country.

The Indians pursued their warfare by hiding in the bushes and then scalping them.

Captain John Smith has been styled the father of his country. His life was saved by his daughter Pochahantas.

The Puritans found an insane asylum in the wilds of America.

The Stamp Act was to make everybody stamp all materials so they should be null and void.

Washington died in Spain almost broken-hearted. His remains were taken to the cathedral in Havana.

Gorilla warfare was where men rode on gorillas.

John Brown was a very good insane man who tried to get fugitives slaves into Virginia. He captured all the inhabitants, but was finally conquered and condemned to his death. The Confederasy was formed by the fugitive slaves.

Alfred the Great reigned 872 years. He was distinguished for letting some buckwheat cakes burn, and the lady scolded him.

Henry Eight was famous for being a great widower haveing lost several wives.

Lady Jane Grey studied Greek and Latin and was beheaded after a few days.

John Bright is noted for an incurable disease.

Lord James Gordon Bennett instigated the Gordon Riots.

The Middle Ages come in between antiquity and posterity.

Luther introduced Christianity into England a good many thousand years ago. His birthday was November 1883. He was once a Pope. He lived at the time of the Rebellion of Worms.

Julius Cæsar is noted for his famous telegram dispatch I came I saw I conquered.

Julius Cæsar was really a very great man. He was a very great soldier and wrote a book for beginners in the Latin.

Cleopatra was caused by the death of an asp which she dissolved in a wine cup.

The only form of government in Greece was a limited monkey.

The Persian war lasted about 500 years.

Greece had only 7 wise men.

Socrates . . . destroyed some statues and had to drink Shamrock.

Here is a fact correctly stated; and yet it is phrased with such ingenious infelicity that it can be depended upon to convey misinformation every time it is uncarefully read:

By the Salic law no woman or descendant of a woman could occupy the throne.

To show how far a child can travel in history with judicious and diligent boosting in the public school, we select the following mosaic:

Abraham Lincoln was born in Wales in 1599.

In the chapter headed "Intellectual" I find a great number of most interesting statements. A sample or two may be found not amiss:

Bracebridge Hall was written by Henry Irving.

Snow Bound was written by Peter Cooper.

The House of the Seven Gables was written by Lord Bryant.

Edgar A. Poe was a very curdling writer.

Cotton Mather was a writer who invented the cotten gin and wrote histories.

Beowulf wrote the Scriptures.

Ben Johnson survived Shakspeare in some respects.

In the Canterbury Tale it gives account of King Alfred on his way to the shrine of Thomas Bucket.

Chaucer was the father of English pottery.

Chaucer was a bland verse writer of the third century.

Chaucer was succeeded by H. Wads. Longfellow an American Writer. His writings were chiefly prose and nearly one hundred years elapsed.

Shakspere translated the Scriptures and it was called St. James because he did it.

In the middle of the chapter I find many pages of information concerning Shakespeare's plays, Milton's works, and those of Bacon, Addison, Samuel Johnson, Fielding, Richardson, Sterne, Smollett, De Foe, Locke, Pope, Swift, Goldsmith, Burns, Cowper, Wordsworth, Gibbon, Byron, Coleridge, Hood, Scott, Macaulay, George Eliot, Dickens, Bulwer, Thackeray, Browning, Mrs. Browning, Tennyson, and Disraeli—a fact which shows that into the restricted stomach of the public-school pupil is shoveled every year the blood, bone, and viscera of a gigantic literature, and the same is there digested and disposed of in a most successful and characteristic and gratifying public-school way. I have space for but a trifling few of the results:

Lord Byron was the son of an heiress and a drunken man.

Wm. Wordsworth wrote the Barefoot Boy and Imitations on Immortality.

Gibbon wrote a history of his travels in Italy. This was original.

George Eliot left a wife and children who mourned greatly for his genius.

George Eliot Miss Mary Evans Mrs. Cross Mrs. Lewis was the greatest female poet unless George Sands is made an exception of.

Bulwell is considered a good writer.

Sir Walter Scott Charles Bronte Alfred the Great and Johnson were the first great novelists.

Thomas Babinton Makorlay graduated at Harvard and then studied law, he was raised to the peerage as baron in 1557 and died in 1776.

Here are two or three miscellaneous facts that may be of value, if taken in moderation:

Homer's writings are Homer's Essays Virgil the Aneid and Paradise lost some people say that these poems were not written by Homer but by another man of the same name.

A sort of sadness kind of shone in Bryant's poems.

Holmes is a very profligate and amusing writer.

When the public-school pupil wrestles with the political features of the Great Republic, they throw him sometimes:

A bill becomes a law when the President vetoes it.

The three departments of the government is the President rules the world, the governor rules the State, the mayor rules the city.

The first conscientious Congress met in Philadelphia.

The Constitution of the United States was established to ensure domestic hostility.

Truth crushed to earth will rise again. As follows:

The Constitution of the United States is that part of the book at the end which nobody reads.

And here she rises once more and untimely. There should be a limit to public-school instruction; it cannot be wise or well to let the young find out everything:

Congress is divided into civilized half civilized and savage.

Here are some results of study in music and oratory:

An interval in music is the distance on the keyboard from one piano to the next.

A rest means you are not to sing it.

Emphasis is putting more distress on one word than another.

The chapter on "Physiology" contains much that ought not to be lost to science:

Physillogigy is to study about your bones stummick and vertebry.

Occupations which are injurious to health are cabolic acid gas which is impure blood.

We have an upper and a lower skin. The lower skin moves all the time and the upper skin moves when we do.

The body is mostly composed of water and about one half is avaricious tissue.

The stomach is a small pear-shaped bone situated in the body.

The gastric juice keeps the bones from creaking.

The Chyle flows up the middle of the backbone and reaches the heart where it meets the oxygen and is purified.

The salivary glands are used to salivate the body.

In the stomach starch is changed to cane sugar and cane sugar to sugar cane.

The olfactory nerve enters the cavity of the orbit and is developed into the special sense of hearing.

The growth of a tooth begins in the back of the mouth and extends to the stomach.

If we were on a railroad track and a train was coming the train would deafen our ears so that we couldn't see to get off the track.

If, up to this point, none of my quotations have added flavor to the Johnsonian anecdote at the head of this article, let us make another attempt:

The theory that intuitive truths are discovered by the light of nature originated from St. John's interpretation of a passage in the Gospel of Plato.

The weight of the earth is found by comparing a mass of known lead with that of a mass of unknown lead.

To find the weight of the earth take the length of a degree on a meridian and multiply by $62\frac{1}{2}$ pounds.

The spheres are to each other as the squares of their homologous sides.

A body will go just as far in the first second as the body will go plus the force of gravity and that's equal to twice what the body will go.

Specific gravity is the weight to be compared weight of an equal volume of or that is the weight of a body compared with the weight of an equal volume.

The law of fluid pressure divide the different forms of organized bodies by the form of attraction and the number increased will be the form.

Inertia is that property of bodies by virtue of which it cannot change its own condition of rest or motion. In other words it is the negative quality of passiveness either in recoverable latency or insipient latescence.

If a laugh is fair here, not the struggling child, nor the unintelligent teacher—or rather the unintelligent Boards, Committees, and Trustees—

are the proper target for it. All through this little book one detects the signs of a certain probable fact—that a large part of the pupil's "instruction" consists in cramming him with obscure and wordy "rules" which he does not understand and has no time to understand. It would be as useful to cram him with brickbats; they would at least stay. In a town in the interior of New York, a few years ago, a gentleman set forth a mathematical problem and proposed to give a prize to every public-school pupil who should furnish the correct solution of it. Twenty-two of the brightest boys in the public schools entered the contest. The problem was not a very difficult one for pupils of their mathematical rank and standing, yet they all failed—by a hair—through one trifling mistake or another. Some searching questions were asked, when it turned out that these lads were as glib as parrots with the "rules," but could not reason out a single rule or explain the principle underlying it. Their memories had been stocked, but not their understandings. It was a case of brickbat culture, pure and simple.

There are several curious "compositions" in the little book, and we must make room for one. It is full of naïveté, brutal truth, and unembarrassed directness, and is the funniest (genuine) boy's composition I think I have ever seen:

ON GIRLS

Girls are very stuck up and dignefied in their maner and be have your. They think more of dress than anything and like to play with dowls and rags. They cry if they see a cow in a far distance and are afraid of guns. They stay at home all the time and go to church on Sunday. They are al-ways sick. They are al-ways funy and making fun of boy's hands and they say how dirty. They cant play marbels. I pity them poor things. They make fun of boys and then turn round and love them. I dont beleave they ever kiled a cat or anything. They look out every nite and say oh ant the moon lovely. Thir is one thing I have not told and that is they al-ways now their lessons bettern boys.

From Mr. Edward Channing's recent article in *Science:*

The marked difference between the books now being produced by French, English, and American travelers, on the one hand, and German explorers, on the other, is too great to escape attention. That difference is due entirely to the fact that in school and university the German is taught, in the first place to see, and in the second place to understand what he does see.

Italian without a Master

It is almost a fortnight now that I am domiciled in a medieval villa in the country, a mile or two from Florence. I cannot speak the language; I am now too old to learn how, also too busy when I am busy, and too indolent when I am not; wherefore some will imagine that I am having a dull time of it. But it is not so. The "help" are all natives; they talk Italian to me, I answer in English; I do not understand them, they do not understand me, consequently no harm is done, and everybody is satisfied. In order to be just and fair, I throw in an Italian word when I have one, and this has a good influence. I get the word out of the morning paper. I have to use it while it is fresh, for I find that Italian words do not keep in this climate. They fade toward night, and next morning they are gone. But it is no matter; I get a new one out of the paper before breakfast, and thrill the domestics with it while it lasts. I have no dictionary, and I do not want one; I can select my words by the sound, or by orthographic aspect. Many of them have a French or German or English look, and these are the ones I enslave for the day's service. That is, as a rule. Not always. If I find a learnable phrase that has an imposing look and warbles musically along I do not care to know the meaning of it; I pay it out to the first applicant, knowing that if I pronounce it carefully *he* will understand it, and that's enough.

Yesterday's word was *avanti.* It sounds Shakespearian, and probably means Avaunt and quit my sight. To-day I have a whole phrase: *sono dispiacentissimo.* I do not know what it means, but it seems to fit in everywhere and give satisfaction. Although as a rule my words and phrases are good for one day and train only, I have several that stay by me all the time, for some unknown reason, and these come very handy when I get into a long conversation and need things to fire up with in monotonous stretches. One of the best ones is *Dov' è il gatto.* It nearly always produces a pleasant surprise, therefore I save it up for places where I want to express applause or admiration. The fourth word has a French sound, and I think the phrase means "that takes the cake."

During my first week in the deep and dreamy stillness of this woodsy and flowery place I was without news of the outside world, and was well content without it. It had been four weeks since I had seen a newspaper, and this lack seemed to give life a new charm and grace, and to saturate it with a feeling verging upon actual delight. Then came a change that was to be expected: the appetite for news began to rise again, after this invigorating rest. I had to feed it, but I was not willing to let it make me its helpless slave again; I determined to put it on a diet, and a strict and limited one. So I examined an Italian paper, with the idea of feeding it on that, and on that exclusively. On that exclusively, and without help of a dictionary. In this way I should surely be well protected against overloading and indigestion.

A glance at the telegraphic page filled me with encouragement. There were no scare-heads. That was good—supremely good. But there were headings—one-liners and two-liners—and that was good too; for without these, one must do as one does with a German paper—pay our precious time in finding out what an article is about, only to discover, in many cases, that there is nothing in it of interest to you. The head-line is a valuable thing.

Necessarily we are all fond of murders, scandals, swindles, robberies, explosions, collisions, and all such things, when we know the people, and when they are neighbors and friends, but when they are strangers we do not get any great pleasure out of them, as a rule. Now the trouble with an American paper is that it has no discrimination; it rakes the whole earth for blood and garbage, and the result is that you are daily overfed and suffer a surfeit. By habit you stow this muck every day, but you come by and by to take no vital interest in it—indeed, you almost get tired of it. As a rule, forty-nine-fiftieths of it concerns strangers only—people away off yonder, a thousand miles, two thousand miles, ten thousand miles from where you are. Why, when you come to think of it, who cares what becomes of those people? I would not give the assassination of one personal friend for a whole massacre of those others. And, to my mind, one relative or neighbor mixed up in a scandal is more interesting than a whole Sodom and Gomorrah of outlanders gone rotten. Give me the home product every time.

Very well. I saw at a glance that the Florentine paper would suit me: five out of six of its scandals and tragedies were local; they were adventures of one's very neighbors, one might almost say one's friends. In the matter of world news there was not too much, but just about enough. I subscribed. I have had no occasion to regret it. Every morning I get all the news I need for the day; sometimes from the head-lines, sometimes from the text. I have never had to call for a dictionary yet. I read the paper with ease. Often I do not quite understand, often some of the details escape me, but no matter, I get the idea. I will cut out a passage or two, then you will see how limpid the language is:

ILL RITORNO, DEI REALI D'ITALIA

ELARGIZIONE DEL RE ALL' OSPEDALE ITALIANO

The first line means that the Italian sovereigns are coming back—they have been to England. The second line seems to mean that they enlarged the King at the Italian hospital. With a banquet, I suppose. An English banquet has that effect. Further:

ILL RITORNO DEI SOVRANI

A ROMA

ROMA, 24, ore 22,50. - I Sovrani e le Principessine Reali si attendono a Roma domani alle ore 15,51.

Return of the sovereigns to Rome, you see. Date of the telegram, Rome, November 24, ten minutes before twenty-three o'clock. The telegram seems to say, "The Sovereigns and the Royal Children expect themselves at Rome to-morrow at fifty-one minutes after fifteen o'clock."

I do not know about Italian time, but I judge it begins at midnight and runs through the twenty-four hours without breaking bulk. In the following ad. the theaters open at half-past twenty. If these are not matinées, 20.30 must mean 8.30 P.M., by my reckoning.

SPETTACOLL DEL DI 25

TEATRO DELLA PERGOLA—(Ore 20,30)—Opera: *Bohème.*

TEATRO ALFIERI.—Compagnia drammatica Drago—(Ore 20,30) — *La Legge.*

ALHAMBRA—(Ore 20,30)—Spettacolo variato.

SALA EDISON—Grandioso spettacolo Cinematografico: *Quo-Vadis?*—Inaugurazione della Chiesa Russa—In coda al Direttissimo—Vedute di Firenze con gran movimento—America: Trasporto tronchi giganteschi—I ladri in casa del Diavolo—Scene comiche.

CINEMATOGRAFO—Via Brunelleschi n. 4.—Programma straordinaro, *Don Chisciotte* — Prezzi popolari.

The whole of that is intelligible to me—and sane and rational, too—except the remark about the Inauguration of a Russian Cheese. That one oversizes my hand. Gimme five cards.

This is a four-page paper; and as it is set in long primer leaded and has a page of advertisements, there is no room for the crimes, disasters, and general sweepings of the outside world—thanks be! To-day I find only a single importation of the off-color sort:

UNA PRINCIPESSA

CHE FUGGE CON UN COCCHIERE

PARIGI, 24.—Il *Matin* ha da Berlino che la principessa Schovenbsre-Waldenbura scomparve il 9 novembre. Sarebbe partita col suo cocchiere.

La Principessa ha 27 anni.

Twenty-seven years old, and scomparve—scampered—on the 9th November. You see by the added detail that she departed with her coachman. I hope Sarebbe has not made a mistake, but I am afraid the chances are that she has. *Sono dispiacentissimo.*

There are several fires: also a couple of accidents. This is one of them:

GRAVE DISGRAZIA SUL PONTE VECCHIO

Stamattina, circa le 7,30, mentre Giuseppe Sciatti, di anni 55, di Casellina e Torri, passava dal-Ponte Vecchio, stando seduto sopra un barroccio carico di verdura, perse l' equilibrio e cadde al suolo, rimanendo con la gamba destra sotto una ruota del veicolo.

Lo Sciatti fu subito raccolto da alcuni cittadini, che, per mezzo della pubblica vettura n. 365, lo trasportarono a San Giovanni di Dio.

Ivi il medico di guardia gli riscontrò la frattura della gamba destra e alcune lievi escoriazioni giudicandolo guaribile in 50 giorni salvo complicazioni.

What it seems to say is this: "Serious Disgrace on the Old Old Bridge. This morning about 7.30, Mr. Joseph Sciatti, aged 55, of Casellina and Torri, while standing up in a sitting posture on top of a carico barrow of verdure (foliage? hay? vegetables?), lost his equilibrium and fell on himself, arriving with his left leg under one of the wheels of the vehicle.

"Said Sciatti was suddenly harvested (gathered in?) by several citizens, who by means of public cab No. 365 transported him to St. John of God."

Paragraph No. 3 is a little obscure, but I think it says that the medico set the broken left leg—right enough, since there was nothing the matter with the other one—and that several are encouraged to hope that fifty days will fetch him around in quite giudicandolo-guaribile way, if no complications intervene.

I am sure I hope so myself.

There is a great and peculiar charm about reading news-scraps in a language which you are not acquainted with—the charm that always goes with the mysterious and the uncertain. You can never be absolutely sure of the meaning of anything you read in such circumstances; you are chasing an alert and gamy riddle all the time, and the baffling turns and dodges of the prey make the life of the hunt. A dictionary would spoil it. Sometimes a single word of doubtful purport will cast a veil of dreamy and golden uncertainty over a whole paragraph of cold and practical certainties, and leave steeped in a haunting and adorable mystery an incident which had been vulgar and commonplace but for that benefaction. Would you be wise to draw a dictionary on that gracious word? would you be properly grateful?

After a couple of days' rest I now come back to my subject and seek a case in point. I find it without trouble, in the morning paper; a cablegram from Chicago and Indiana by way of Paris. All the words save one are guessable by a person ignorant of Italian:

REVOLVERATE IN TEATRO

PARIGI, 27.—La *Patrie* ha da Chicago:

Il guardiano del teatro dell'opera di Wallace (Indiana), avendo voluto espellere uno spettatore che continuava a fumare malgrado il divieto, questo spalleggiato dai suoi amici tiro diversi colpi di rivoltella. Il guardiano rispose. Nacque una scarica generale. Grande panico tra-gli spettatori. Nessun ferito.

Translation.—"REVOLVERATION IN THEATER. *Paris,* 27th. *La Patrie* has from Chicago: The cop of the theater of the opera of Wallace, Indiana, had willed to expel a spectator which continued to smoke in spite of the prohibition, who, spalleggiato by his friends, tirò (Fr. *tiré,* Anglice *pulled*) manifold revolver-shots. The cop responded. Result, a general scare; great panic among the spectators. Nobody hurt."

It is bettable that that harmless cataclysm in the theater of the opera of Wallace, Indiana, excited not a person in Europe but me, and so came near to not being worth cabling to Florence by way of France. But it does excite me. It excites me because I cannot make out, for sure, what it was that moved that spectator to resist the officer. I was gliding along smoothly and without obstruction or accident, until I came to that word "spalleggiato," then the bottom fell out. You notice what a rich gloom, what a somber and pervading mystery, that word sheds all over the whole Wallachian tragedy. That is the charm of the thing, that is the delight of it. This is where you begin, this is where you revel. You can guess and guess, and have all the fun you like; you need not be afraid there will be an end to it; none is possible, for no amount of guessing will ever furnish you a meaning for that word that you can be sure is the right one. All the other words give you hints, by their form, their sound, or their spelling—this one doesn't, this one throws out no hints, this one keeps its secret. If there is even the slightest slight shadow of a hint anywhere, it lies in the very meagerly suggestive fact that "spalleggiato" carries our word "egg" in its stomach. Well, make the most out of it, and then where are you at? You conjecture that the spectator which was smoking in spite of the prohibition and become reprohibited by the guardians, was "egged on" by his friends, and that it was owing to that evil influence that he initiated the revolveration in theater that has galloped under the sea and come crashing through the European press without exciting anybody but me. But are you sure, are you dead sure, that that was the way of it? No. Then the uncertainty remains, the mystery abides, and with it the charm. Guess again.

If I had a phrase-book of a really satisfactory sort I would study it, and not give all my free time to undictionarial readings, but there is no such work on the market. The existing phrase-books are inadequate. They are well enough as far as they go, but when you fall down and skin your leg they don't tell you what to say.

Italian with Grammar

I found that a person of large intelligence could read this beautiful language with considerable facility without a dictionary, but I presently found that to such a person a grammar could be of use at times. It is because, if he does not know the *Were's* and the *Was's* and the *May-be's* and the *Has-been's* apart, confusions and uncertainties can arise. He can get the idea that a thing is going to happen next week when the truth is that it has already happened week before last. Even more previously, sometimes. Examination and inquiry showed me that the adjectives and such things were frank and fair-minded and straightforward, and did not shuffle; it was the Verb that mixed the hands, it was the Verb that lacked stability, it was the Verb that had no permanent opinion about anything, it was the Verb that was always dodging the issue and putting out the light and making all the trouble.

Further examination, further inquiry, further reflection, confirmed this judgment, and established beyond peradventure the fact that the Verb was the storm-center. This discovery made plain the right and wise course to pursue in order to acquire certainty and exactness in understanding the statements which the newspaper was daily endeavoring to convey to me: I must catch a Verb and tame it. I must find out its ways, I must spot its eccentricities, I must penetrate its disguises, I must intelligently foresee and forecast at least the commoner of the dodges it was likely to try upon a stranger in given circumstances, I must get in on its main shifts and head them off, I must learn its game and play the limit.

I had noticed, in other foreign languages, that verbs are bred in families, and that the members of each family have certain features or resemblances that are common to that family and distinguish it from the other families—the other kin, the cousins and what not. I had noticed that this family-mark is not usually the nose or the hair, so to speak, but the tail—the Termination—and that these tails are quite definitely differentiated; insomuch that an expert can tell a Pluperfect from a Subjunctive by its tail as easily and as certainly as a cowboy can tell a cow from a horse by the like process, the result of observation and culture. I should explain that I am speaking of legitimate verbs, those verbs which in the slang of the grammar are called Regular. There are others—I am not meaning to conceal this; others called Irregulars, born out of wedlock, of unknown and uninteresting parentage, and naturally destitute of family resemblances, as regards all features, tails included. But of these pathetic outcasts I have nothing to say. I do not approve of them, I do not encourage them; I am prudishly delicate and sensitive, and I do not allow them to be used in my presence.

But, as I have said, I decided to catch one of the others and break it to harness. One is enough. Once familiar with its assortment of tails, you are immune; after that, no regular verb can conceal its specialty from you and make you think it is working the past or the future or the conditional or the unconditional when it is engaged in some other line of business—its tail will give it away. I found out all these things by myself, without a teacher.

I selected the verb *Amare, to love.* Not for any personal reason, for I am indifferent about verbs; I care no more for one verb than for another, and have little or no respect for any of them; but in foreign languages you always begin with that one. Why, I do not know. It is merely habit, I suppose; the first teacher chose it, Adam was satisfied, and there hasn't been a successor since with originality enough to start a fresh one. For they *are* a pretty limited lot, you will admit that? Originality is not in their line; they can't think up anything new, anything to freshen up the old moss-grown dullness of the language lesson and put life and "go" into it, and charm and grace and picturesqueness.

I knew I must look after those details myself; therefore I thought them out and wrote them down, and sent for the *facchino* and explained them to him, and said he must arrange a proper plant, and get together a good stock company among the *contadini,* and design the costumes, and distribute the parts; and drill the troupe, and be ready in three days to begin on this Verb in a shipshape and workman-like manner. I told him to put each grand division of it under a foreman, and each subdivision under a subordinate of the rank of sergeant or corporal or something like that, and to have a different uniform for each squad, so that I could tell a Pluperfect from a Compound Future without looking at the book; the whole battery to be under his own special and particular command, with the rank of Brigadier, and I to pay the freight.

I then inquired into the character and possibilities of the selected verb, and was much disturbed to find that it was over my size, it being chambered for fifty-seven rounds—fifty-seven ways of saying *I love* without reloading; and yet none of them likely to convince a girl that was laying for a title, or a title that was laying for rocks.

It seemed to me that with my inexperience it would be foolish to go into action with this mitrailleuse, so I ordered it to the rear and told the facchino to provide something a little more primitive to start with, something less elaborate, some gentle old-fashioned flint-lock, smooth-bore, double-barreled thing, calculated to cripple at two hundred yards and kill at forty—an arrangement suitable for a beginner who could be satisfied with moderate results on the offstart and did not wish to take the whole territory in the first campaign.

But in vain. He was not able to mend the matter, all the verbs being of the same build, all Gatlings, all of the same caliber and delivery, fifty-seven to the volley, and fatal at a mile and a half. But he said the auxiliary verb AVERE, *to have,* was a tidy thing, and easy to handle in a seaway, and less likely to miss stays in going about than some of the others; so, upon his recommendation I chose that one, and told him to take it along and scrape its bottom and break out its spinnaker and get it ready for business.

I will explain that a facchino is a general-utility domestic. Mine was a horse-doctor in his better days, and a very good one.

At the end of three days the facchino-doctor-brigadier was ready. I was also ready, with a stenographer. We were in the room called the Rope-Walk. This is a formidably long room, as is indicated by its facetious name, and is a good place for reviews. At 9:30 the F.-D.-B. took his place near me and gave the word of command; the drums began to rumble and thunder, the head of the forces appeared at an upper door, and the "march-past" was on. Down they filed, a blaze of variegated color, each squad gaudy in a uniform of its own and bearing a banner inscribed with its verbal rank and quality: first the Present Tense in Mediterranean blue and old gold, then the Past Definite in scarlet and black, then the Imperfect in green and yellow, then the Indicative Future in the stars and stripes, then the Old Red Sandstone Subjunctive in purple and silver—and so on and so on, fifty-seven privates and twenty commissioned and non-commissioned officers; certainly one of the most fiery and dazzling and eloquent sights I have ever beheld. I could not keep back the tears. Presently:

"Halt!" commanded the Brigadier.

"Front—face!"

"Right dress!"

"Stand at ease!"

"One—two—three. In unison—*recite!*"

It was fine. In one noble volume of sound all the fifty-seven Haves in the Italian language burst forth in an exalting and splendid confusion. Then came commands:

"About—face! Eyes—front! Helm alee—hard aport! Forward—march!" and the drums let go again.

When the last Termination had disappeared, the commander said the instruction drill would now begin, and asked for suggestions. I said:

"They say *I have, thou hast, he has,* and so on, but they don't say *what.* It will be better, and more definite, if they have something to have; just an object, you know, a something—anything will do; anything that will give the listener a sort of personal as well as grammatical interest in their joys and complaints, you see."

He said:

"It is a good point. Would a dog do?"

I said I did not know, but we could try a dog and see. So he sent out an aide-de-camp to give the order to add the dog.

The six privates of the Present Tense now filed in, in charge of Sergeant Avere *(to have),* and displaying their banner. They formed in line of battle, and recited, one at a time, thus:

"Io ho un cane, I have a dog."

"Tu hai un cane, thou hast a dog."

"Egli ha un cane, he has a dog."

"Noi abbiamo un cane, we have a dog."

"Voi avete un cane, you have a dog."

"Eglino hanno un cane, they have a dog."

No comment followed. They returned to camp, and I reflected awhile. The commander said:

"I fear you are disappointed."

"Yes," I said; "they are too monotonous, too singsong, too dead-and-alive; they have no expression, no elocution. It isn't natural; it could never happen in real life. A person who had just acquired a dog is either blame' glad or blame' sorry. He is not on the fence. I never saw a case. What the nation do you suppose is the matter with these people?"

He thought maybe the trouble was with the dog. He said:

"These are *contadini,* you know, and they have a prejudice against dogs—that is, against marimane. Marimana dogs stand guard over people's vines and olives, you know, and are very savage, and thereby a grief and an inconvenience to persons who want other people's things at night. In my judgment they have taken this dog for a marimana, and have soured on him."

I saw that the dog was a mistake, and not functionable: we must try something else; something, if possible, that could evoke sentiment, interest, feeling.

"What is cat, in Italian?" I asked.

"Gatto."

"Is it a gentleman cat, or a lady?"

"Gentleman cat."

"How are these people as regards that animal?"

"We-ll, they—they—"

"You hesitate: that is enough. How are they about chickens?"

He tilted his eyes toward heaven in mute ecstasy. I understood.

"What is chicken, in Italian?" I asked.

"Pollo, *podere."* (Podere is Italian for master. It is a title of courtesy, and conveys reverence and admiration.) "Pollo is one chicken by itself; when there are enough present to constitute a plural, it is *polli."*

"Very well, polli will do. Which squad is detailed for duty next?"

"The Past Definite."

"Send out and order it to the front—with chickens. And let them understand that we don't want any more of this cold indifference."

He gave the order to an aide, adding, with a haunting tenderness in his tone and a watering mouth in his aspect:

"Convey to them the conception that these are unprotected chickens."

He turned to me, saluting with his hand to his temple, and explained, "It will inflame their interest in the poultry, sire."

A few minutes elapsed. Then the squad marched in and formed up, their faces glowing with enthusiasm, and the file-leader shouted:

"Ebbi polli, I had chickens!"

"Good!" I said. "Go on, the next."

"Avesti polli, thou hadst chickens!"

"Fine! Next!"

"Ebbe polli, he had chickens!"

"Moltimoltissimo! Go on, the next!"

"Avemmo polli, we had chickens!"

"Basta-basta aspettatto avanti—last man—*charge!"*

"Ebbero polli, they had chickens!"

Then they formed in echelon, by columns of fours, refusing the left, and retired in great style on the double-quick. I was enchanted, and said:

"Now, doctor, that is something *like!* Chickens are the ticket, there is no doubt about it. What is the next squad?"

"The Imperfect."

"How does it go?"

"Io aveva, I had, *tu avevi,* thou hadst, *egli aveva,* he had, *noi av—"*

"Wait—we've just *had* the hads. What are you giving me?"

"But this is another breed."

"What do we want of another breed? Isn't one breed enough? *Had* is HAD, and your tricking it out in a fresh way of spelling isn't going to make it any hadder than it was before; now you know that yourself."

"But there is a distinction—they are not just the same Hads."

"How do you make it out?"

"Well, you use that first Had when you are referring to something that happened at a named and sharp and perfectly definite moment; you use the other when the thing happened at a vaguely defined time and in a more prolonged and indefinitely continuous way."

"Why, doctor, it is pure nonsense; you know it yourself. Look here: If I have had a had, or have wanted to have had a had, or was in a position right then and there to have had a had that hadn't had any chance to go out hadding on account of this foolish discrimination which lets one Had go hadding in any kind of indefinite grammatical weather but restricts the other one to definite and datable meteoric convulsions, and keeps it pining around and watching the barometer all the time, and liable to get sick through confinement and lack of exercise, and all that sort of thing, why—why, the inhumanity of it is enough, let alone the wanton superfluity and uselessness of any such a loafing consumptive hospital-bird of a Had taking up room and cumbering the place for nothing. These finical refinements revolt me; it is not right, it is not honorable; it is constructive nepotism to keep in office a Had that is so delicate it can't come out when the wind's in the nor'west—I won't have this dude on the pay-roll. Cancel his exequatur; and look here—"

"But you miss the point. It is like this. You see—"

"Never mind explaining, I don't care anything about it. Six Hads is enough for me; anybody that needs twelve, let him subscribe; I don't want any stock in a Had Trust. Knock out the Prolonged and Indefinitely Continuous; four-fifths of it is water, anyway."

"But I beg you, podere! It is often quite indispensable in cases where—"

"Pipe the next squad to the assault!"

But it was not to be; for at that moment the dull boom of the noon gun floated up out of far-off Florence, followed by the usual softened jangle of church-bells, Florentine and suburban, that bursts out in murmurous response; by labor-union law the *colazione* [1] must stop; stop promptly, stop instantly, stop definitely, like the chosen and best of the breed of Hads.

1. Colazione is Italian for a collection, a meeting, a séance, a sitting.—M.T.

The Awful German Language

A little learning makes the whole world kin.
—PROVERBS XXXII, 7.

I went often to look at the collection of curiosities in Heidelberg Castle, and one day I surprised the keeper of it with my German. I spoke entirely in that language. He was greatly interested; and after I had talked awhile he said my German was very rare, possibly a "unique"; and wanted to add it to his museum.

If he had known what it had cost me to acquire my art, he would also have known that it would break any collector to buy it. Harris and I had been hard at work on our German during several weeks at that time, and although we had made good progress, it had been accomplished under great difficulty and annoyance, for three of our teachers had died in the meantime. A person who has not studied German can form no idea of what a perplexing language it is.

Surely there is not another language that is so slipshod and systemless, and so slippery and elusive to the grasp. One is washed about in it, hither and hither, in the most helpless way; and when at last he thinks he has captured a rule which offers firm ground to take a rest on amid the general rage and turmoil of the ten parts of speech, he turns over the page and reads, "Let the pupil make careful note of the following *exceptions.*" He runs his eye down and finds that there are more exceptions to the rule than instances of it. So overboard he goes again, to hunt for another Ararat and find another quicksand. Such has been, and continues to be, my experience. Every time I think I have got one of these four confusing "cases" where I am master of it, a seemingly insignificant preposition intrudes itself into my sentence, clothed with an awful and unsuspected power, and crumbles the ground from under me. For instance, my book inquires after a certain bird—(it is always inquiring after things which are of no sort of consequence to anybody): "Where is the bird?" Now the answer to this question, according to the book, is that the bird is waiting in the blacksmith shop on account of the rain. Of course no bird would do that, but then you must stick to the book. Very well, I begin to cipher out the German for that answer. I begin at the wrong end, necessarily, for that is the German idea. I say to myself, "*Regen* (rain) is masculine—or maybe it is feminine—or possibly neuter—it is too much trouble to look now. Therefore, it is either *der* (the) Regen, or *die* (the) Regen, or *das* (the) Regen, according to which gender it may turn out to be when I look. In the interest of science, I will cipher it out on the hypothesis that it is masculine. Very well—then *the* rain is *der* Regen, if it is simply in the quiescent state of being *mentioned,* without enlargement or discussion—Nominative case; but if this rain is lying around, in a kind of a general way on the ground, it is then definitely located, it is *doing something*—that is, *resting* (which is one of the German grammar's ideas of doing something), and this throws the rain into the Dative case, and makes it *dem* Regen. However, this rain is not resting, but is doing something *actively;* it is falling—to interfere with the bird, likely—and this indicates *movement,* which has the effect of sliding it into the Accusative case and changing *dem* Regen into *den* Regen." Having completed the grammatical horoscope of this matter, I answer up confidently and state in German that the bird is staying in the blacksmith shop "wegen (on account of) *den* Regen." Then the teacher lets me softly down with the remark that whenever the word "wegen" drops into a sentence, it *always* throws that subject into the *Genitive* case, regardless of consequences—and that therefore this bird staid in the blacksmith shop "wegen *des* Regens."

N.B.—I was informed, later, by a higher authority, that there was an "exception" which permits one to say "wegen *den* Regen" in certain peculiar and complex circumstances, but that this exception is not extended to anything *but* rain.

There are ten parts of speech, and they are all troublesome. An average sentence, in a German newspaper, is a sublime and impressive curiosity; it occupies a quarter of a column; it contains all the ten parts of speech—not in regular order, but mixed; it is built mainly of compound words constructed by the writer on the spot, and not to be found in any dictionary—six or seven words compacted into one, without joint or seam—that is, without hyphens; it treats of fourteen or fifteen different subjects, each enclosed in a parenthesis of its own, with here and there extra parentheses which re-enclose three or four of the minor parentheses, making pens within pens: finally, all the parentheses and reparentheses are massed together between a couple of king-parentheses, one of which is placed in the first line of the majestic sentence and the other in the middle of the last line of it—*after which comes the* VERB, and you find out for the first time what the man has been talking about; and after the verb—merely by way of ornament, as far as I can make out—the writer shovels in *"haven sind gewesen gehabt haben geworden sein,"* or words to that effect, and the monument is finished. I suppose that this closing hurrah is in the nature of the flourish to a man's signature—not necessary, but pretty. German books are easy enough to read when you hold them before the looking-glass or stand on your head—so as to reverse the construction—but I think that to learn to read and understand a German newspaper is a thing which must always remain an impossibility to a foreigner.

Yet even the German books are not entirely free from attacks of the Parenthesis distemper—though they are usually so mild as to cover only a few lines, and therefore when you at last get down to the verb it carries some meaning to your mind because you are able to remember a good deal of what has gone before.

Now here is a sentence from a popular and excellent German novel—with a slight parenthesis in it. I will make a perfectly literal translation, and throw in the parenthesis-marks and some hyphens for the assistance of the reader, though in the original there are no parenthesis-marks or hyphens, and the reader is left to flounder through to the remote verb the best way he can:

"But when he, upon the street, the (in-satin-and-silk-covered-now-very-unconstrainedly-after-the-newest-fashion-dressed) government counsellor's wife *met,"* etc., etc.*

That is from "The Old Mamselle's Secret," by Mrs. Marlitt. And that

* "Wenn er aber auf der Strasse der in Sammt und Seide gehüllten jetz sehr ungenirt nach der neusten mode gekleideten Regierungsrathin begegnet."

sentence is constructed upon the most approved German model. You observe how far that verb is from the reader's base of operations; well, in a German newspaper they put their verb away over on the next page; and I have heard that sometimes after stringing along on exciting preliminaries and parentheses for a column or two, they get in a hurry and have to go to press without getting to the verb at all. Of course, then, the reader is left in a very exhausted and ignorant state.

We have the Parenthesis disease in our literature, too; and one may see cases of it every day in our books and newspapers: but with us it is the mark and sign of an unpractised writer or a cloudy intellect, whereas with the Germans it is doubtless the mark and sign of a practised pen and of the presence of that sort of luminous intellectual fog which stands for clearness among these people. For surely it is *not* clearness—it necessarily can't be clearness. Even a jury would have penetration enough to discover that. A writer's ideas must be a good deal confused, a good deal out of line and sequence, when he starts out to say that a man met a counsellor's wife in the street, and then right in the midst of this so simple undertaking halts these approaching people and makes them stand still until he jots down an inventory of the woman's dress. That is manifestly absurd. It reminds a person of those dentists who secure your instant and breathless interest in a tooth by taking a grip on it with the forceps, and then stand there and drawl through a tedious anecdote before they give the dreaded jerk. Parentheses in literature and dentistry are in bad taste.

The Germans have another kind of parenthesis, which they make by splitting a verb in two and putting half of it at the beginning of an exciting chapter and the *other half* at the end of it. Can any one conceive of anything more confusing than that? These things are called "separable verbs." The German grammar is blistered all over with separable verbs; and the wider the two portions of one of them are spread apart, the better the author of the crime is pleased with his performance. A favorite one is *reiste ab,* which means *departed.* Here is an example which I culled from a novel and reduced to English:

"The trunks being now ready, he DE-after kissing his mother and sisters, and once more pressing to his bosom his adored Gretchen, who, dressed in simple white muslin, with a single tuberose in the ample folds of her rich brown hair, had tottered feebly down the stairs, still pale from the terror and excitement of the past evening, but longing to lay her poor aching head yet once again upon the breast of him whom she loved more dearly than life itself, PARTED."

However, it is not well to dwell too much on the separable verbs. One is sure to lose his temper early; and if he sticks to the subject, and will not be warned, it will at last either soften his brain or petrify it. Personal pronouns and adjectives are a fruitful nuisance in this language, and should have been left out. For instance, the same sound, *sie,* means *you,* and it means *she* and it means *her,* and it means *it,* and it means *they,* and it means *them.* Think of the ragged poverty of a language which has to make one word do the work of six—and a poor little weak thing of only three letters at that. But mainly, think of the exasperation of never knowing which of these meanings the speaker is trying to convey. This explains why, whenever a person says *sie* to me, I generally try to kill him, if a stranger.

Now observe the Adjective. Here was a case where simplicity would have been an advantage; therefore, for no other reason, the inventor of this language complicated it all he could. When we wish to speak of our "good friend or friends," in our enlightened tongue, we stick to the one form and have no trouble or hard feeling about it; but with the German tongue it is different. When a German gets his hands on an adjective, he declines it, and keeps on declining it until the common sense is all declined out of it. It is as bad as Latin. He says, for instance:

SINGULAR.

Nominative—Mein gut*er* Freund, my good friend.
Genitive—Mein*es* gut*en* Freund*es,* of my good friend.
Dative—Mein*em* gut*en* Freund, to my good friend.
Accusative—Mein*en* gut*en* Freund, my good friend.

PLURAL.

N.—Mein*e* gut*en* Freund*e,* my good friends.
G.—Mein*er* gut*en* Freund*e,* of my good friends.
D.—Mein*en* gut*en* Freund*en,* to my good friends.
A.—Mein*e* gut*en* Freund*e,* my good friends.

Now let the candidate for the asylum try to memorize those variations, and see how soon he will be elected. One might better go without friends in Germany than take all this trouble about them. I have shown what a bother it is to decline a good (male) friend; well this is only a third of the work, for there is a variety of new distortions of the adjective to be learned when the object is feminine, and still another when the object is neuter. Now there are more adjectives in this language than there are black cats in Switzerland, and they must all be as elaborately declined as the examples above suggested. Difficult?—troublesome?—these words cannot describe it. I heard a Californian student in Heidelberg say, in one of his calmest moods, that he would rather decline two drinks than one German adjective.

The inventor of the language seems to have taken pleasure in complicating it in every way he could think of. For instance, if one is casually referring to a house, *Haus,* or a horse, *Pferd,* or a dog, *Hund,* he spells these words as I have indicated; but if he is referring to them in the Dative case, he sticks on a foolish and unnecessary *e* and spells them Hause, Pferde, Hunde. So, as an added *e* often signifies the plural, as the *s* does with us, the new student is likely to go on for a month making twins out of a Dative dog before he discovers his mistake; and on the other hand, many a new student who could ill afford loss, has bought and paid for two dogs and only got one of them, because he ignorantly bought that dog in the Dative singular when he really supposed he was talking plural—which left the law on the seller's side, of course, by the strict rules of grammar, and therefore a suit for recovery could not lie.

In German, all the Nouns begin with a capital letter. Now that is a good idea; and a good idea, in this language, is necessarily conspicuous from its lonesomeness. I consider this capitalizing of nouns a good idea, because by reason of it you are almost always able to tell a noun the minute you see it. You fall into error occasionally, because you mistake the name of a person for the name of a thing, and waste a good deal of time trying to dig a meaning out of it. German names almost always do mean something, and this helps to deceive the student. I translated a passage one day, which said that "the infuriated tigress broke loose and utterly ate up the unfortunate fir-forest" *(Tannenwald).* When I was girding up my loins to doubt this, I found out that Tannenwald, in this instance, was a man's name.

Every noun has a gender, and there is no sense or system in the distribution; so the gender of each must be learned separately and by heart. There is no other way. To do this one has to have a memory like a memorandum book. In German, a young lady has no sex, while a turnip has. Think what overwrought reverence that shows for the turnip, and what callous disrespect for the girl. See how it looks in print—I translate this from a conversation in one of the best of the German Sunday-school books:

"*Gretchen.* Wilhelm, where is the turnip?

"*Wilhelm.* She has gone to the kitchen.

"*Gretchen.* Where is the accomplished and beautiful English maiden?

"*Wilhelm.* It has gone to the opera."

To continue with the German genders: a tree is male, its buds are female, its leaves are neuter; horses are sexless, dogs are male, cats are female—Tom-cats included, of course; a person's mouth, neck, bosom, elbows, fingers, nails, feet, and body, are of the male sex, and his head is male or neuter according to the word selected to signify it, and *not* according to the sex of the individual who wears it, for in Germany all the women wear either male heads or sexless ones; a person's nose, lips, shoulders, breast, hands, hips, and toes are of the female sex; and his hair, ears, eyes, chin, legs, knees, heart, and conscience, haven't any sex at all. The inventor of the language probably got what he knew about a conscience from hearsay.

Now, by the above dissection, the reader will see that in Germany a man may *think* he is a man, but when he comes to look into the matter closely, he is bound to have his doubts; he finds that in sober truth he is a most ridiculous mixture; and if he ends by trying to comfort himself with the thought that he can at least depend on a third of this mess as being manly and masculine, the humiliating second thought will quickly remind him that in this respect he is no better off than any woman or cow in the land.

In the German it is true that by some oversight of the inventor of the language, a Woman is a female; but a Wife *(Weib)* is not—which is unfortunate. A Wife, here, has no sex; she is neuter; so, according to the grammar, a fish is *he,* his scales are *she,* but a fishwife is neither. To describe a wife as sexless may be called under-description; that is bad enough, but over-description is surely worse. A German speaks of an Englishman as the *Engländer;* to change the sex, he adds *inn,* and that stands for Englishwoman—*Engländerinn.* That seems descriptive enough, but still it is not exact enough for a German; so he precedes the word with that article which indicates that the creature to follow is feminine, and writes it down thus: "*die* Engländer*inn,*" which means "the *she-Englishwoman.*" I consider that that person is over-described.

Well, after the student has learned the sex of a great number of nouns, he is still in a difficulty, because he finds it impossible to persuade his tongue to refer to things as "*he*" and "*she,*" and "*him*" and "*her,*" which it has been always accustomed to refer to as "*it.*" When he even frames a German sentence in his mind, with the hims and hers in the right places, and then works up his courage to the utterance-point, it is no use; the moment he begins to speak his tongue flies the track and all those labored males and females come out as *"its."* And even when he is reading German to himself, he always calls those things *"it,"* whereas he ought to read in this way:

TALE OF THE FISHWIFE AND ITS SAD FATE[1]

It is a bleak Day. Hear the Rain, how he pours, and the Hail, how he rattles; and see the Snow, how he drifts along, and oh the Mud, how deep he is! Ah the poor Fishwife, it is stuck fast in the Mire; it has dropped its Basket of Fishes; and its Hands have been cut by the Scales as it seized some of the falling Creatures; and one Scale has even got into its Eye, and it cannot get her out. It opens its Mouth to cry for Help; but if any Sound comes out of him, alas he is drowned by the raging of the Storm. And now a Tomcat has got one of the Fishes and she will surely escape with him. No, she bites off a Fin, she holds her in her Mouth—will she swallow her? No, the Fishwife's brave Mother-dog deserts his Puppies and rescues the Fin—which he eats, himself, as his Reward. O, horror, the Lightning has struck the Fishbasket; he sets him on Fire; see the Flame, how she licks the doomed Utensil with her red and angry Tongue; now she attacks the helpless Fishwife's Foot; she burns him up, all but the big Toe, and even *she* is partly consumed; and still she spreads, still she waves her fiery Tongues; she attacks the Fishwife's Leg and destroys *it;* she attacks its Hand and destroys *her;* she attacks its poor worn Garment and destroys *her* also; she attacks its Body and consumes *him;* she wreathes herself about its Heart and *it* is consumed; next about its Breast, and in a Moment *she* is a Cinder; now she reaches its Neck—*he* goes; now its Chin—*it* goes; now its Nose—*she* goes. In another Moment, except Help come, the Fishwife will be no more. Time presses; is there none to succor and save? Yes! Joy, joy, with flying Feet the she-Englishwoman comes! But alas, the generous she-Female is too late: where now is the fated Fishwife? It has ceased from its Sufferings, it has gone to a better Land; all that is left of it for its loved Ones to lament over, is this poor smouldering Ash-heap. Ah, woful, woful Ash-heap! Let us take him up tenderly, reverently, upon the lowly Shovel, and bear him to his long Rest, with the Prayer that when he rises again it will be in a Realm where he will have one good square responsible Sex, and have it all to himself, instead of having a mangy lot of assorted Sexes scattered all over him in Spots.

There, now, the reader can see for himself that this pronoun business is a very awkward thing for the unaccustomed tongue.

1. I capitalize the nouns, in the German (and ancient English) fashion.—M.T.

I suppose that in all languages the similarities of look and sound between words which have no similarity in meaning are a fruitful source of perplexity to the foreigner. It is so in our tongue, and it is notably the case in the German. Now there is that troublesome word *vermählt:* to me it has so close a resemblance—either real or fancied—to three or four other words, that I never know whether it means despised, painted, suspected, or married; until I look in the dictionary, and then I find it means the latter. There are lots of such words and they are a great torment. To increase the difficulty there are words which *seem* to resemble each other, and yet do not; but they make just as much trouble as if they did. For instance, there is the word *vermiethen* (to let, to lease, to hire); and the word *verheirathen* (another way of saying to *marry).* I heard of an Englishman who knocked at a man's door in Heidelberg and proposed, in the best German he could command, to "verheirathen" that house. Then there are some words which mean one thing when you emphasize the first syllable, but mean something very different if you throw the emphasis on the last syllable. For instance, there is a word which means a runaway, or the act of glancing through a book, according to the placing of the emphasis; and another word which signifies to *associate* with a man, or to *avoid* him, according to where you put the emphasis—and you can generally depend on putting it in the wrong place and getting into trouble.

There are some exceedingly useful words in this language. *Schlag,* for example; and *Zug.* There are three-quarters of a column of Schlags in the dictionary, and a column and a half of Zugs. The word Schlag means Blow, Stroke, Dash, Hit, Shock, Clap, Slap, Time, Bar, Coin, Stamp, Kind, Sort, Manner, Way, Apoplexy, Wood-Cutting, Enclosure, Field, Forest-Clearing. This is its simple and *exact* meaning, that is to say, its restricted, its fettered meaning; but there are ways by which you can set it free, so that it can soar away, as on the wings of the morning, and never be at rest. You can hang any word you please to its tail, and make it mean anything you want to. You can begin with *Schlag-ader,* which means artery, and you can hang on the whole dictionary, word by word, clear through the alphabet to *Schlag-wasser,* which means bilge-water, and including *Schlag-mutter,* which means mother-in-law.

Just the same with *Zug.* Strictly speaking, Zug means Pull, Tug, Draught, Procession, March, Progress, Flight, Direction, Expedition, Train, Caravan, Passage, Stroke, Touch, Line, Flourish, Trait of Character, Feature, Lineament, Chess-move, Organ-stop, Team, Whiff, Bias, Drawer, Propensity, Inhalation, Disposition: but that thing which it does *not* mean, when all its legitimate pendants have been hung on, has not been discovered yet.

One cannot over-estimate the usefulness of Schlag and Zug. Armed just with these two, and the word *Also,* what cannot the foreigner on German soil accomplish? The German word *Also* is the equivalent of the English phrase "You know," and does not mean anything at all—in *talk,* though it sometimes does in print. Every time a German opens his mouth an *Also* falls out; and every time he shuts it he bites one in two that was trying to *get* out.

Now, the foreigner, equipped with these three noble words, is master of the situation. Let him talk right along, fearlessly; let him pour his indifferent German forth, and when he lacks for a word, let him heave a *Schlag* into the vacuum; all the chances are that it fits it like a plug, but if it doesn't let him promptly heave a *Zug* after it; the two together can hardly fail to bung the hole; but if, by a miracle, they *should* fail, let him simply say *Also!* and this will give him a moment's chance to think of the needful word. In Germany, when you load your conversational gun it is always best to throw in a *Schlag* or two and a *Zug* or two, because it doesn't make any difference how much the rest of the charge may scatter, you are bound to bag something with *them.* Then you blandly say *Also,* and load up again. Nothing gives such an air of grace and elegance and unconstraint to a German or an English conversation as to scatter it full of "Also's" or "You-knows."

In my note-book I find this entry:

> *July* 1.—In the hospital yesterday, a word of thirteen syllables was successfully removed from a patient, a North-German from near Hamburg; but as most unfortunately the surgeons had opened him in the wrong place, under the impression that he contained a panorama, he died. The sad event has cast a gloom over the whole community.

That paragraph furnishes a text for a few remarks about one of the most curious and notable features of my subject: the length of German words. Some German words are so long that they have a perspective. Observe these examples:

Freundschaftsbezeigungen.

Dilettantenaufdringlichkeiten.

Stadtverordnetenversammlungen.

These things are not words, they are alphabetical processions. And they are not rare; one can open a German newspaper any time and see them marching majestically across the page—and if he has any imagination he can see the banners and hear the music, too. They impart a martial thrill to the meekest subject. I take a great interest in these curiosities. Whenever I come across a good one, I stuff it and put it in my museum. In this way I have made quite a valuable collection. When I get duplicates, I exchange with other collectors, and thus increase the variety of my stock. Here are some specimens which I lately bought at an auction sale of the effects of a bankrupt bric-a-brac hunter:

GENERALSTAATSVERORDNETENVERSAMMLUNGEN.

ALTERTHUMSWISSENSCHAFTEN.

KINDERBEWAHRUNGSANSTALTEN.

UNABHAENGIGKEITSERKLAERUNGEN.

WIEDERERSTELLUNGSBESTREBUNGEN.

WAFFENSTILLSTANDSUNTERHANDLUNGEN.

Of course when one of these grand mountain ranges goes stretching across the printed page, it adorns and ennobles that literary landscape—but at the same time it is a great distress to the new student, for it blocks up his way; he cannot crawl under it, or climb over it, or tunnel through it. So he resorts to the dictionary for help, but there is no help there. The dictionary must draw the line somewhere, so it leaves this sort of words out. And it is right, because these long things are hardly legitimate words, but are rather combinations of words, and the inventor of them ought to have been killed. They are compound words with the hyphens left out. The various words used in building them are in the dictionary, but in a very scattered condition; so you can hunt the materials out, one by one, and get at the meaning at last, but it is a tedious and harassing business. I have tried this process upon some of the above examples. "Freundschaftsbezeigungen" seems to be "Friendshipdemonstrations," which is only a foolish and clumsy way of saying "demonstrations of friendship." "Unabhaengigkeitserklaerungen" seems to be "Independencedeclarations," which is no improvement upon "Declarations of Independence," so far as I can see. "Generalstaatsverordnetenversammlungen" seems to be "Generalstatesrepresentativesmeetings," as nearly as I can get at it—a mere rhythmical, gushy euphuism for "meetings of the legislature," I judge. We used to have a good deal of this sort of crime in our literature, but it has gone out now. We used to speak of a thing as a "never-to-be-forgotten" circumstance, instead of cramping it into the simple and sufficient word "memorable" and then going calmly about our business as if nothing had happened. In those days we were not content to embalm the thing and bury it decently, we wanted to build a monument over it.

But in our newspapers the compounding-disease lingers a little to the present day, but with the hyphens left out, in the German fashion. This is the shape it takes: instead of saying "Mr. Simmons, clerk of the county and district courts, was in town yesterday," the new form puts it thus: "Clerk of the County and District Court Simmons was in town yesterday." This saves neither time nor ink, and has an awkward sound besides. One often sees a remark like this in our papers: "*Mrs.* Assistant District Attorney Johnson returned to her city residence yesterday for the season." That is a case of really unjustifiable compounding; because it not only saves no time or trouble, but confers a title on Mrs. Johnson which she has no right to. But these little instances are trifles indeed, contrasted with the ponderous and dismal German system of piling jumbled compounds together. I wish to submit the following local item, from a Mannheim journal, by way of illustration:

"In the daybeforeyesterdayshortlyaftereleveno'clock Night, the inthistownstandingtavern called 'The Wagoner' was downburnt. When the fire to the onthedownburninghouseresting Stork's Nest reached, flew the parent Storks away. But when the bytheraging, firesurrounded Nest *itself* caught Fire, straightway plunged the quickreturning Mother Stork into the Flames and died, her Wings over her young ones outspread."

Even the cumbersome German construction is not able to take the pathos out of that picture—indeed, it somehow seems to strengthen it. This item is dated away back yonder months ago. I could have used it sooner, but I was waiting to hear from the Father-Stork. I am still waiting.

"*Also!*" If I have not shown that the German is a difficult language, I have at least intended to do it. I have heard of an American student who was asked how he was getting along with his German, and who answered promptly: "I am not getting along at all. I have worked at it hard for three level months, and all I have got to show for it is one solitary German phrase: '*Zwei glas*' (two glasses of beer)." He paused a moment, reflectively; then added with feeling: "But I've got that *solid!*"

And if I have not also shown that German is a harassing and infuriating study, my execution has been at fault, and not my intent. I heard lately of a worn and sorely-tried American student who used to fly to a certain German word for relief when he could bear up under his aggravations no longer—the only word in the whole language whose sound was sweet and precious to his ear and healing to his lacerated spirit. This was the word *Damit.* It was only the *sound* that helped him, not the meaning; [1] and so, at last, when he learned that the emphasis was not on the first syllable, his only stay and support was gone, and he faded away and died.

I think that a description of any loud, stirring, tumultuous episode must be tamer in German than in English. Our descriptive words of this character have such a deep, strong, resonant sound, while their German equivalents do seem so thin and mild and energyless. Boom, burst, crash, roar, storm, bellow, blow, thunder, explosion; howl, cry, shout, yell, groan; battle, hell. These are magnificent words; they have a force and magnitude of sound befitting the things which they describe. But their German equivalents would be ever so nice to sing the children to sleep with, or else my awe-inspiring ears were made for display and not for superior usefulness in analyzing sounds. Would any man want to die in a battle which was called by so tame a term as a *Schlacht?* Or would not a consumptive feel too much bundled up, who was about to go out, in a shirt collar and a seal ring, into a storm which the bird-song word *Gewitter* was employed to describe? And observe the strongest of the several German equivalents for explosion: *Ausbruch.* Our word Toothbrush is more powerful than that. It seems to me that the Germans could do worse than import it into their language to describe particularly tremendous explosions with. The German word for hell—*Hölle*—sounds more like *helly* than anything else; therefore, how necessarily chipper, frivolous, and unimpressive it is. If a man were told in German to go there, could he really rise to the dignity of feeling insulted?

Having now pointed out, in detail, the several vices of this language, I now come to the brief and pleasant task of pointing out its virtues. The capitalizing of the nouns I have already mentioned. But far before this virtue stands another—that of spelling a word according to the sound of it. After one short lesson in the alphabet, the student can tell how any German word is pronounced without having to ask; whereas in our language if a student should inquire of us, "What does B, O, W, spell?" we should be obliged to reply, "Nobody can tell what it spells when you set it off by itself; you can only tell by referring to the context and finding out what it signifies—whether it is a thing to shoot arrows with, or a nod of one's head, or the forward end of a boat."

There are some German words which are singularly and powerfully

1. It merely means, in its general sense, "herewith."—M.T.

effective. For instance, those which describe lowly, peaceful, and affectionate home life; those which deal with love, in any and all forms, from mere kindly feeling and honest good will toward the passing stranger, clear up to courtship; those which deal with outdoor Nature, in its softest and loveliest aspects—with meadows and forests, and birds and flowers, the fragrance and sunshine of summer, and the moonlight of peaceful winter nights; in a word, those which deal with any and all forms of rest, repose, and peace; those also which deal with the creatures and marvels of fairyland; and lastly and chiefly, in those words which express pathos, is the language surpassingly rich and effective. There are German songs which can make a stranger to the language cry. That shows that the *sound* of the words is correct—it interprets the meanings with truth and with exactness; and so the ear is informed, and through the ear, the heart.

The Germans do not seem to be afraid to repeat a word when it is the right one. They repeat it several times, if they choose. That is wise. But in English, when we have used a word a couple of times in a paragraph, we imagine we are growing tautological, and so we are weak enough to exchange it for some other word which only approximates exactness, to escape what we wrongly fancy is a greater blemish. Repetition may be bad, but surely inexactness is worse.

There are people in the world who will take a great deal of trouble to point out the faults in a religion or a language, and then go blandly about their business without suggesting any remedy. I am not that kind of a person. I have shown that the German language needs reforming. Very well, I am ready to reform it. At least I am ready to make the proper suggestions. Such a course as this might be immodest in another; but I have devoted upwards of nine full weeks, first and last, to a careful and critical study of this tongue, and thus have acquired a confidence in my ability to reform it which no mere superficial culture could have conferred upon me.

In the first place, I would leave out the Dative Case. It confuses the plurals; and, besides, nobody ever knows when he is in the Dative Case, except he discover it by accident—and then he does not know when or where it was that he got into it, or how long he has been in it, or how he is ever going to get out of it again. The Dative Case is but an ornamental folly—it is better to discard it.

In the next place, I would move the Verb further up to the front. You may load up with ever so good a Verb, but I notice that you never really bring down a subject with it at the present German range; you only cripple it. So I insist that this important part of speech should be brought forward to a position where it may be easily seen with the naked eye.

Thirdly, I would import some strong words from the English tongue—to swear with, and also to use in describing all sorts of vigorous things in a vigorous way.[1]

Fourthly, I would reorganize the sexes, and distribute them according to the will of the Creator. This as a tribute of respect, if nothing else.

Fifthly, I would do away with those great long compounded words; or require the speaker to deliver them in sections, with intermissions for refreshments. To wholly do away with them would be best, for ideas are more easily received and digested when they come one at a time than when they come in bulk. Intellectual food is like any other; it is pleasanter and more beneficial to take it with a spoon than with a shovel.

Sixthly, I would require a speaker to stop when he is done, and not hang a string of those useless "haben sind gewesen gehabt haben geworden seins" to the end of his oration. This sort of gew-gaws undignify a speech, instead of adding a grace. They are, therefore, an offense, and should be discarded.

Seventhly, I would discard the Parenthesis. Also the re-parenthesis, the re-re-parenthesis, and the re-re-re-re-re-re-parentheses, and likewise the final wide-reaching all-enclosing King-parenthesis. I would require every individual, be he high or low, to unfold a plain straightforward tale, or else coil it and sit on it and hold his peace. Infractions of this law should be punishable with death.

And eighthly and last, I would retain *Zug* and *Schlag,* with their pendants, and discard the rest of the vocabulary. This would simplify the language.

I have now named what I regard as the most necessary and important

1. "Verdammt," and its variations and enlargements, are words which have plenty of meaning, but the *sounds* are so mild and ineffectual that German ladies can use them without sin. German ladies who could not be induced to commit a sin by any persuasion or compulsion, promptly rip out one of these harmless little words when they tear their dresses or don't like the soup. It sounds about as wicked as our "My gracious." German ladies are constantly saying, "Ach! Gott!" "Mein Gott!" "Gott in Himmel!" "Herr Gott!" "Der Herr Jesus!" etc. They think our ladies have the same custom, perhaps; for I once heard a gentle and lovely old German lady say to a sweet young American girl: "The two languages are so alike—how pleasant that is; we say 'Ach! Gott!' you say '*Goddam.*' "—M.T.

changes. These are perhaps all I could be expected to name for nothing; but there are other suggestions which I can and will make in case my proposed application shall result in my being formally employed by the government in the work of reforming the language.

My philological studies have satisfied me that a gifted person ought to learn English (barring spelling and pronouncing) in thirty hours, French in thirty days, and German in thirty years. It seems manifest, then, that the latter tongue ought to be trimmed down and repaired. If it is to remain as it is, it ought to be gently and reverently set aside among the dead languages, for only the dead have time to learn it.

A FOURTH OF JULY ORATION IN THE GERMAN TONGUE, DELIVERED AT A BANQUET OF THE ANGLO-AMERICAN CLUB OF STUDENTS BY THE AUTHOR OF THIS BOOK.

GENTLEMEN: Since I arrived, a month ago, in this old wonderland, this vast garden of Germany, my English tongue has so often proved a useless piece of baggage to me, and so troublesome to carry around, in a country where they haven't the checking system for luggage, that I finally set to work, last week, and learned the German language. Also! Es freut mich dass dies so ist, denn es muss, in ein hauptsächlich degree, höflich sein, dass man auf ein occasion like this, sein Rede in die Sprache des Landes worin he boards, aussprechen soll. Dafür habe ich, aus reinische Verlegenheit—no, Vergangenheit—no, I mean Höflichkeit—aus reinische Höflichkeit habe ich resolved to tackle this business in the German language, um Gottes willen! Also! Sie müssen so freundlich sein, und verzeih mich die interlarding von ein oder zwei Englischer Worte, hie und da, denn ich finde dass die deutsche is not a very copious language, and so when you've really got anything to say, you've got to draw on a language that can stand the strain.

Wenn aber man kann nicht meinem Rede verstehen, so werde ich ihm später dasselbe übersetz, wenn er solche Dienst verlangen wollen haben werden sollen sein hätte. (I don't know what wollen haben werden sollen sein hätte means, but I notice they always put it at the end of a German sentence—merely for general literary gorgeousness, I suppose.)

This is a great and justly honored day—a day which is worthy of the veneration in which it is held by the true patriots of all climes and nationalities, a day which offers a fruitful theme for thought and speech; und meinem Freunde—no, mein*en* Freund*en*—mein*es* Freun*des*—well, take your choice, they're all the same price; I don't know which one is right—also! ich habe gehabt haben worden gewesen sein, as Goethe says in his Paradise Lost—ich—ich—that is to say—ich—but let us change cars.

Also! Die Anblick so viele Grossbrittanischer und Amerikanischer hier zusammengetroffen in Bruderliche concord, ist zwar a welcome and inspiriting spectacle. And what has moved you to it? Can the terse German tongue rise to the expression of this impulse? Is it Freundschaftsbezeigungenstadtverordnetenversammlungenfamilieneigenthümlichkeiten? Nein, o nein! This is a crisp and noble word, but it fails to pierce the marrow of the impulse which has gathered this friendly meeting and produced diese Anblick—eine Anblick welche ist gut zu sehen—gut für die Augen in a foreign land and a far country—eine Anblick solche als in die gewöhnliche Heidelberger phrase nennt man ein "schönes Aussicht!" Ja, freilich natürlich wahrscheinlich ebensowohl! Also! Die Aussicht auf dem Königsstuhl mehr grösserer ist, aber geistlische sprechend nicht so schön, lob' Gott! Because sie sind hier zusammengetroffen, in Bruderlichem concord, ein grossen Tag zu feiern, whose high benefits were not for one land and one locality only, but have conferred a measure of good upon all lands that know liberty to-day, and love it. Hundert Jahre vorüber, waren die Engländer und die Amerikaner Feinde; aber heute sind sie herzlichen Freunde, Gott sei Dank! May this good fellowship endure; may these banners here blended in amity so remain; may they never any more wave over opposing hosts, or be stained with blood which was kindred, is kindred, and always will be kindred, until a line drawn upon a map shall be able to say: "*This* bars the ancestral blood from flowing in the veins of the descendant!"

TWAIN *and* LITERATURE

Fenimore Cooper's Literary Offenses

The Pathfinder and *The Deerslayer* stand at the head of Cooper's novels as artistic creations. There are others of his works which contain parts as perfect as are to be found in these, and scenes even more thrilling. Not one can be compared with either of them as a finished whole.

The defects in both of these tales are comparatively slight. They were pure works of art. —PROF. LOUNSBURY.

The five tales reveal an extraordinary fullness of invention.

. . . One of the very greatest characters in fiction, Natty Bumppo. . . .

The craft of the woodsman, the tricks of the trapper, all the delicate art of the forest, were familiar to Cooper from his youth up.

—PROF. BRANDER MATTHEWS.

Cooper is the greatest artist in the domain of romantic fiction yet produced by America. —WILKIE COLLINS.

It seems to me that it was far from right for the Professor of English Literature in Yale, the Professor of English Literature in Columbia, and Wilkie Collins to deliver opinions on Cooper's literature without having read some of it. It would have been much more decorous to keep silent and let persons talk who have read Cooper.

Cooper's art has some defects. In one place in *Deerslayer,* and in the restricted space of two-thirds of a page, Cooper has scored 114 offenses against literary art out of a possible 115. It breaks the record.

There are nineteen rules governing literary art in the domain of romantic fiction—some say twenty-two. In *Deerslayer* Cooper violated eighteen of them. These eighteen require:

1. That a tale shall accomplish something and arrive somewhere. But the *Deerslayer* tale accomplishes nothing and arrives in the air.

2. They require that the episodes of a tale shall be necessary parts of the tale, and shall help to develop it. But as the *Deerslayer* tale is not a tale, and accomplishes nothing and arrives nowhere, the episodes have no rightful place in the work, since there was nothing for them to develop.

3. They require that the personages in a tale shall be alive, except in the case of corpses, and that always the reader shall be able to tell the corpses from the others. But this detail has often been overlooked in the *Deerslayer* tale.

4. They require that the personages in a tale, both dead and alive, shall exhibit a sufficient excuse for being there. But this detail also has been overlooked in the *Deerslayer* tale.

5. They require that when the personages of a tale deal in conversation, the talk shall sound like human talk, and be talk such as human beings would be likely to talk in the given circumstances, and have a discoverable meaning, also a discoverable purpose, and a show of relevancy, and remain in the neighborhood of the subject in hand, and be interesting to the reader, and help out the tale, and stop when the people cannot think of anything more to say. But this requirement has been ignored from the beginning of the *Deerslayer* tale to the end of it.

6. They require that when the author describes the character of a personage in his tale, the conduct and conversation of that personage shall justify said description. But this law gets little or no attention in the *Deerslayer* tale, as Natty Bumppo's case will amply prove.

7. They require that when a personage talks like an illustrated, gilt-edged, tree-calf, hand-tooled, seven-dollar Friendship's Offering in the beginning of a paragraph, he shall not talk like a negro minstrel in the end of it. But this rule is flung down and danced upon in the *Deerslayer* tale.

8. They require that crass stupidities shall not be played upon the reader as "the craft of the woodsman, the delicate art of the forest," by either the author or the people in the tale. But this rule is persistently violated in the *Deerslayer* tale.

9. They require that the personages of a tale shall confine themselves to possibilities and let miracles alone; or, if they venture a miracle, the author must so plausibly set it forth as to make it look possible and reasonable. But these rules are not respected in the *Deerslayer* tale.

10. They require that the author shall make the reader feel a deep interest in the personages of his tale and in their fate; and that he shall make the reader love the good people in the tale and hate the bad ones. But the reader of the *Deerslayer* tale dislikes the good people in it, is indifferent to the others, and wishes they would all get drowned together.

11. They require that the characters in a tale shall be so clearly defined that the reader can tell beforehand what each will do in a given emergency. But in the *Deerslayer* tale this rule is vacated.

In addition to these large rules there are some little ones. These require that the author shall

12. *Say* what he is proposing to say, not merely come near it.
13. Use the right word, not its second cousin.
14. Eschew surplusage.
15. Not omit necessary details.
16. Avoid slovenliness of form.
17. Use good grammar.
18. Employ a simple and straightforward style.

Even these seven are coldly and persistently violated in the *Deerslayer* tale.

Cooper's gift in the way of invention was not a rich endowment; but such as it was he liked to work it, he was pleased with the effects, and indeed he did some quite sweet things with it. In his little box of stage-properties he kept six or eight cunning devices, tricks, artifices for his savages and woodsmen to deceive and circumvent each other with, and he was never so happy as when he was working these innocent things and seeing them go. A favorite one was to make a moccasined person tread in the tracks of the moccasined enemy, and thus hide his own trail. Cooper wore out barrels and barrels of moccasins in working that trick. Another stage-property that he pulled out of his box pretty frequently was his broken twig. He prized his broken twig above all the rest of his effects, and worked it the hardest. It is a restful chapter in any book of his when somebody doesn't step on a dry twig and alarm all the reds and whites for two hundred yards around. Every time a Cooper person is in peril, and absolute silence is worth four dollars a minute, he is sure to step on a dry twig. There may be a hundred handier things to step on, but that wouldn't satisfy Cooper. Cooper requires him to turn out and find a dry twig; and if he can't do it, go and borrow one. In fact, the Leatherstocking Series ought to have been called the Broken Twig Series.

I am sorry there is not room to put in a few dozen instances of the delicate art of the forest, as practised by Natty Bumppo and some of the other Cooperian experts. Perhaps we may venture two or three samples. Cooper was a sailor—a naval officer; yet he gravely tells us how a vessel, driving toward a lee shore in a gale, is steered for a particular spot by her skipper because he knows of an *undertow* there which will hold her back against the gale and save her. For just pure woodcraft, or sailorcraft, or whatever it is, isn't that neat? For several years Cooper was daily in the society of artillery, and he ought to have noticed that when a cannon-ball strikes the ground it either buries itself or skips a hundred feet or so; skips again a hundred feet or so—and so on, till finally it gets tired and rolls. Now in one place he loses some "females"—as he always calls women—in the edge of a wood near a plain at night in a fog, on purpose to give Bumppo a chance to show off the delicate art of the forest before the reader. These mislaid people are hunting for a fort. They hear a cannon-blast, and a cannon-ball presently comes rolling into the wood and stops at their feet. To the females this suggests nothing. The case is very different with the admirable Bumppo. I wish I may never know peace again if he doesn't strike out promptly and *follow the track* of that cannon-ball across the plain through the dense fog and find the fort. Isn't it a daisy? If Cooper had any real knowledge of Nature's ways of doing things, he had a most delicate art in concealing the fact. For instance: one of his acute Indian experts, Chingachgook (pronounced Chicago, I think), has lost the trail of a person he is tracking through the forest. Apparently that trail is hopelessly lost. Neither you nor I could ever have guessed out the way to find it. It was very different with Chicago. Chicago was not stumped for long. He turned a running stream out of its course, and there, in the slush in its old bed, were that person's moccasin tracks. The current did not wash them away, as it would have done in all other like cases—no, even the eternal laws of Nature have to vacate when Cooper wants to put up a delicate job of woodcraft on the reader.

We must be a little wary when Brander Matthews tell us that Cooper's books "reveal an extraordinary fullness of invention." As a rule, I am quite willing to accept Brander Matthews's literary judgments and applaud his lucid and graceful phrasing of them; but that particular statement needs to be taken with a few tons of salt. Bless your heart, Cooper hadn't any more invention than a horse; and I don't mean a high-class horse, either; I mean a clothes-horse. It would be very difficult to find a really clever "situation" in Cooper's books, and still more difficult to find one of any kind which he has failed to render absurd by his handling of it. Look at the episodes of "the caves"; and at the celebrated scuffle between Maqua and those others on the table-land a few days later; and at Hurry Harry's queer water-transit from the castle to the ark; and at Deerslayer's half-hour with his first corpse; and at the quarrel between Hurry Harry and Deerslayer later; and at—but choose for yourself; you can't go amiss.

If Cooper had been an observer his inventive faculty would have worked better; not more interestingly, but more rationally, more plausibly. Cooper's proudest creations in the way of "situations" suffer noticeably from the absence of the observer's protecting gift. Cooper's eye was splendidly inaccurate. Cooper seldom saw anything correctly. He saw nearly all things as through a glass eye, darkly. Of course a man who cannot see the commonest little every-day matters accurately is working at a disadvantage when he is constructing a "situation." In the *Deerslayer* tale Cooper has a stream which is fifty feet wide where it flows out of a lake; it presently narrows to twenty as it meanders along for no given reason, and yet when a stream acts like that it ought to be required to explain itself. Fourteen pages later the width of the brook's outlet from the lake has suddenly shrunk thirty feet, and become "the narrowest part of the stream." This shrinkage is not accounted for. The stream has bends in it, a sure indication that it has alluvial banks and cuts them; yet these bends are only thirty and fifty feet long. If Cooper had been a nice and punctilious observer he would have noticed that the bends were oftener nine hundred feet long than short of it.

Cooper made the exit of that stream fifty feet wide, in the first place, for no particular reason; in the second place, he narrowed it to less than twenty to accommodate some Indians. He bends a "sapling" to the form of an arch over this narrow passage, and conceals six Indians in its foliage. They are "laying" for a settler's scow or ark which is coming up the stream on its way to the lake; it is being hauled against the stiff current by a rope whose stationary end is anchored in the lake; its rate of progress cannot be more than a mile an hour. Cooper describes the ark, but pretty obscurely. In the matter of dimensions "it was little more than a modern canal-boat." Let us guess, then, that it was about one hundred and forty feet long. It was of "greater breadth than common." Let us guess, then, that it was about sixteen feet wide. This leviathan had been prowling down bends which were but a third as long as itself, and scraping between banks where it had only two feet of space to spare on each side. We cannot too much admire this miracle. A low-roofed log dwelling occupies "two-thirds of the ark's length"—a dwelling ninety feet long and sixteen feet wide, let us say—a kind of vestibule train. The dwelling has two rooms—each forty-five feet long and sixteen feet wide, let us guess. One of them is the bedroom of the Hutter girls, Judith and Hetty; the other is the parlor in the daytime, at night it is papa's bedchamber. The ark is arriving at the stream's exit now, whose width has been reduced to less than twenty feet to accommodate the Indians—say to eighteen. There is a foot to spare on each side of the boat. Did the Indians notice that there was going to be a tight squeeze there? Did they notice that they could make money by climbing down out of that arched sapling and just stepping aboard when the ark scraped by? No, other Indians would have noticed these things, but Cooper's Indians never notice anything. Cooper thinks they are marvelous creatures for noticing, but he was almost always in error about his Indians. There was seldom a sane one among them.

The ark is one hundred and forty-feet long; the dwelling is ninety feet long. The idea of the Indians is to drop softly and secretly from the arched sapling to the dwelling as the ark creeps along under it at the rate of a mile an hour, and butcher the family. It will take the ark a minute and a half to pass under. It will take the ninety-foot dwelling a minute to pass under. Now, then, what did the six Indians do? It would take you thirty years to guess, and even then you would have to give it up, I believe. Therefore, I will tell you what the Indians did. Their chief, a person of quite extraordinary intellect for a Cooper Indian, warily watched the canal-boat as it squeezed along under him, and when he had got his calculations fined down to exactly the right shade, as he judged, he let go and dropped. And *missed the house!* That is actually what he did. He missed the house, and landed in the stern of the scow. It was not much of a fall, yet it knocked him silly. He lay there unconscious. If the house had been ninety-seven feet long he would have made the trip. The fault was Cooper's, not his. The error lay in the construction of the house. Cooper was no architect.

There still remained in the roost five Indians. The boat has passed under and is now out of their reach. Let me explain what the five did—you would not be able to reason it out for yourself. No. 1 jumped for the boat, but fell in the water astern of it. Then No. 2 jumped for the boat, but fell in the water still farther astern of it. Then No. 3 jumped for the boat, and fell a good way astern of it. Then No. 4 jumped for the boat, and fell in the water *away* astern. Then even No. 5 made a jump for the boat—for he was a Cooper Indian. In the matter of intellect, the difference between a Cooper Indian and the Indian that stands in front of the cigar-shop is not spacious. The scow episode is really a sublime burst of invention; but it does not thrill, because the inaccuracy of the details throws a sort of air of fictitiousness and general improbability over it. This comes of Cooper's inadequacy as an observer.

The reader will find some examples of Cooper's high talent for inaccurate observation in the account of the shooting-match in *The Pathfinder*.

> A common wrought nail was driven lightly into the target, its head having been first touched with paint.

The color of the paint is not stated—an important omission, but Cooper deals freely in important omissions. No, after all, it was not an important omission; for this nail-head is *a hundred yards from* the marksmen, and could not be seen by them at that distance, no matter what its color might be. How far can the best eyes see a common house-fly? A hundred yards? It is quite impossible. Very well; eyes that cannot see a house-fly that is a hundred yards away cannot see an ordinary nail-head at that distance, for the size of the two objects is the same. It takes a keen eye to see a fly or a nail-head at fifty yards—one hundred and fifty feet. Can the reader do it?

The nail was lightly driven, its head painted, and game called. Then the Cooper miracles began. The bullet of the first marksman chipped an edge of the nail-head; the next man's bullet drove the nail a little way into the target—and removed all the paint. Haven't the miracles gone far enough now? Not to suit Cooper; for the purpose of this whole scheme is to show off his prodigy, Deerslayer-Hawkeye-Long-Rifle-Leatherstocking-Pathfinder-Bumppo before the ladies.

> "Be all ready to clench it, boys!" cried out Pathfinder, stepping into his friend's tracks the instant they were vacant. "Never mind a new nail; I can see that, though the paint is gone, and what I can see I can hit at a hundred yards, though it were only a mosquito's eye. Be ready to clench!"
>
> The rifle cracked, the bullet sped its way, and the head of the nail was buried in the wood, covered by the piece of flattened lead.

There, you see, is a man who could hunt flies with a rifle, and command a ducal salary in a Wild West show to-day if we had him back with us.

The recorded feat is certainly surprising just as it stands; but it is not surprising enough for Cooper. Cooper adds a touch. He has made Pathfinder do this miracle with another man's rifle; and not only that, but Pathfinder did not have even the advantage of loading it himself. He had everything against him, and yet he made that impossible shot; and not only made it, but did it with absolute confidence, saying, "Be ready to clench." Now a person like that would have undertaken that same feat with a brickbat, and with Cooper to help he would have achieved it, too.

Pathfinder showed off handsomely that day before the ladies. His very first feat was a thing which no Wild West show can touch. He was standing with the group of marksmen, observing—a hundred yards from the target, mind; one Jasper raised his rifle and drove the center of the bull's-eye. Then the Quartermaster fired. The target exhibited no result this time. There was a laugh. "It's a dead miss," said Major Lundie. Pathfinder waited an impressive moment or two; then said, in that calm, indifferent, know-it-all way of his, "No, Major, he has covered Jasper's bullet, as will be seen if any one will take the trouble to examine the target."

Wasn't it remarkable! How *could* he see that little pellet fly through the air and enter that distant bullet-hole? Yet that is what he did; for nothing is impossible to a Cooper person. Did any of those people have any deep-seated doubts about this thing? No; for that would imply sanity, and these were all Cooper people.

> The respect for Pathfinder's skill and for his *quickness and accuracy of sight* [the italics are mine] was so profound and general, that the instant he made this declaration the spectators began to distrust their own opinions, and a dozen rushed to the target in order to ascertain the fact. There, sure enough, it was found that the Quartermaster's bullet had gone through the hole made by Jasper's, and that, too, so accurately as to require a minute examination to be certain of the circumstance, which, however, was soon clearly established by discovering one bullet over the other in the stump against which the target was placed.

They made a "minute" examination; but never mind, how could they know that there were two bullets in that hole without digging the latest one out? for neither probe nor eyesight could prove the presence of any more than one bullet. Did they dig? No; as we shall see. It is the Pathfinder's turn now; he steps out before the ladies, takes aim, and fires.

But, alas! here is a disappointment; an incredible, an unimaginable disappointment—for the target's aspect is unchanged; there is nothing there but that same old bullet-hole!

> "If one dared to hint at such a thing," cried Major Duncan, "I should say that the Pathfinder has also missed the target!"

As nobody had missed it yet, the "also" was not necessary; but never mind about that, for the Pathfinder is going to speak.

> "No, no, Major," said he, confidently, "that *would* be a risky declaration. I didn't load the piece, and can't say what was in it; but if it was lead, you will find the bullet driving down those of the Quartermaster and Jasper, else is not my name Pathfinder."
>
> A shout from the target announced the truth of this assertion.

Is the miracle sufficient as it stands? Not for Cooper. The Pathfinder speaks again, as he "now slowly advances toward the stage occupied by the females":

> "That's not all, boys, that's not all; if you find the target touched at all, I'll own to a miss. The Quartermaster cut the wood, but you'll find no wood cut by that last messenger."

The miracle is at last complete. He knew—doubtless *saw*—at the distance of a hundred yards—that his bullet had passed into the hole *without fraying the edges.* There were now three bullets in that one hole—three bullets embedded processionally in the body of the stump back of the target. Everybody knew this—somehow or other—and yet nobody had dug any of them out to make sure. cooper is not a close observer, but he is interesting. He is certainly always that, no matter what happens. And he is more interesting when he is not noticing what he is about than when he is. This is a considerable merit.

The conversations in the Cooper books have a curious sound in our modern ears. To believe that such talk really ever came out of people's mouths would be to believe that there was a time when time was of no value to a person who thought he had something to say; when it was the custom to spread a two-minute remark out to ten; when a man's mouth was a rolling-mill, and busied itself all day long in turning four-foot pigs of thought into thirty-foot bars of conversational railroad iron by attenuation;

when subjects were seldom faithfully stuck to, but the talk wandered all around and arrived nowhere; when conversations consisted mainly of irrelevancies, with here and there a relevancy, a relevancy with an embarrassed look, as not being able to explain how it got there.

Cooper was certainly not a master in the construction of dialogue. Inaccurate observation defeated him here as it defeated him in so many other enterprises of his. He even failed to notice that the man who talks corrupt English six days in the week must and will talk it on the seventh, and can't help himself. In the *Deerslayer* story he lets Deerslayer talk the showiest kind of book-talk sometimes, and at other times the basest of base dialects. For instance, when some one asks him if he has a sweetheart, and if so, where she abides, this is his majestic answer:

> "She's in the forest—hanging from the boughs of the trees, in a soft rain—in the dew on the open grass—the clouds that float about in the blue heavens—the birds that sing in the woods—the sweet springs where I slake my thirst—and in all the other glorious gifts that come from God's Providence!"

And he preceded that, a little before, with this:

> "It consarns me as all things that touches a fri'nd consarns a fri'nd."

And this is another of his remarks:

> "If I was Injin born, now, I might tell of this, or carry in the scalp and boast of the expl'ite afore the whole tribe; or if my inimy had only been a bear"—[and so on].

We cannot imagine such a thing as a veteran Scotch Commander-in-Chief comporting himself in the field like a windy melodramatic actor, but Cooper could. On one occasion Alice and Cora were being chased by the French through a fog in the neighborhood of their father's fort:

> *"Point de quartier aux coquins!"* cried an eager pursuer, who seemed to direct the operations of the enemy.
>
> "Stand firm and be ready, my gallant 60ths!" suddenly exclaimed a voice above them; "wait to see the enemy; fire low, and sweep the glacis."
>
> "Father! father" exclaimed a piercing cry from out the mist; "it is I! Alice! thy own Elsie! spare, O! save your daughters!"
>
> "Hold!" shouted the former speaker, in the awful tones of parental agony,

the sound reaching even to the woods, and rolling back in solemn echo. " 'Tis she! God has restored me my children! Throw open the sally-port; to the field, 60ths, to the field! pull not a trigger, lest ye kill my lambs! Drive off these dogs of France with your steel!"

Cooper's word-sense was singularly dull. When a person has a poor ear for music he will flat and sharp right along without knowing it. He keeps near the tune, but it is *not* the tune. When a person has a poor ear for words, the result is a literary flatting and sharping; you perceive what he is intending to say, but you also perceive that he doesn't *say* it. This is Cooper. He was not a word-musician. His ear was satisfied with the *approximate* word. I will furnish some circumstantial evidence in support of this charge. My instances are gathered from half a dozen pages of the tale called *Deerslayer.* He uses "verbal" for "oral"; "precision" for "facility"; "phenomena" for "marvels"; "necessary" for "predetermined"; "unsophisticated" for "primitive"; "preparation" for "expectancy"; "rebuked" for "subdued"; "dependent on" for "resulting from"; "fact" for "condition"; "fact" for "conjecture"; "precaution" for "caution"; "explain" for "determine"; "mortified" for "disappointed"; "meretricious" for "factitious"; "materially" for "considerably"; "decreasing" for "deepening"; "increasing" for "disappearing"; "embedded" for "inclosed"; "treacherous" for "hostile"; "stood" for "stooped"; "softened" for "replaced"; "rejoined" for "remarked"; "situation" for "condition"; "different" for "differing"; "insensible" for "unsentient"; "brevity" for "celerity"; "distrusted" for "suspicious"; "mental imbecility" for "imbecility"; "eyes" for "sight"; "counteracting" for "opposing"; "funeral obsequies" for "obsequies."

There have been daring people in the world who claimed that Cooper could write English, but they are all dead now—all dead but Lounsbury. I don't remember that Lounsbury makes the claim in so many words, still he makes it, for he says that *Deerslayer* is a "pure work of art." Pure, in that connection, means faultless—faultless in all details—and language is a detail. If Mr. Lounsbury had only compared Cooper's English with the English which he writes himself—but it is plain that he didn't; and so it is likely that he imagines until this day that Cooper's is as clean and compact as his own. Now I feel sure, deep down in my heart, that Cooper wrote about the poorest English that exists in our language, and that the English of *Deerslayer* is the very worst that even Cooper ever wrote.

I may be mistaken, but it does seem to me that *Deerslayer* is not a work of art in any sense; it does seem to me that it is destitute of every detail that goes to the making of a work of art; in truth, it seems to me that *Deerslayer* is just simply a literary *delirium tremens.*

A work of art? It has no invention; it has no order, system, sequence, or result; it has no lifelikeness, no thrill, no stir, no seeming of reality; its characters are confusedly drawn, and by their acts and words they prove that they are not the sort of people the author claims that they are; its humor is pathetic; its pathos is funny; its conversations are—oh! indescribable; its love-scenes odious; its English a crime against the language.

Counting these out, what is left is Art. I think we must all admit that.

William Dean Howells

Is it true that the sun of a man's mentality touches noon at forty and then begins to wane toward setting? Doctor Osler is charged with saying so. Maybe he said it, maybe he didn't; I don't know which it is. But if he said it, I can point him to a case which proves his rule. Proves it by being an exception to it. To this place I nominate Mr. Howells.

I read his *Venetian Days* about forty years ago. I compare it with his paper on Machiavelli in a late number of *Harper,* and I cannot find that his English has suffered any impairment. For forty years his English has been to me a continual delight and astonishment. In the sustained exhibition of certain great qualities—clearness, compression, verbal exactness, and unforced and seemingly unconscious felicity of phrasing—he is, in my belief, without his peer in the English-writing world. *Sustained.* I intrench myself behind that protecting word. There are others who exhibit those great qualities as greatly as does he, but only by intervaled distributions of rich moonlight, with stretches of veiled and dimmer landscape between; whereas Howells's moon sails cloudless skies all night and all the nights.

In the matter of verbal exactness Mr. Howells has no superior, I suppose. He seems to be almost always able to find that elusive and shifty grain of gold, the *right word.* Others have to put up with approximations, more or less frequently; he has better luck. To me, the others are miners working with the gold-pan—of necessity some of the gold washes over and escapes; whereas, in my fancy, he is quicksilver raiding down a riffle—no grain of the metal stands much chance of eluding him. A powerful agent is the right word: it lights the reader's way and makes it plain; a close approximation to it will answer, and much traveling is done in a well-enough fashion by its help, but we do not welcome it and applaud it and rejoice in it as we do when *the* right one blazes out on us. Whenever we come upon one of those intensely right words in a book or a newspaper the resulting effect is physical as well as spiritual, and electrically prompt: it tingles exquisitely around through the walls of the mouth and tastes as tart and crisp and good as the autumn-butter that creams the sumac-berry. One has no time to examine the word and vote upon its rank and standing, the automatic recognition of its supremacy is so immediate. There is a plenty of acceptable literature which deals largely in approximations, but it may be likened to a fine landscape seen through the rain; the right word would dismiss the rain, then you would see it better. It doesn't rain when Howells is at work.

And where does he get the easy and effortless flow of his speech? and its cadenced and undulating rhythm? and its architectural felicities of construction, its graces of expression, its pemmican quality of compression, and all that? Born to him, no doubt. All in shining good order in the beginning, all extraordinary; and all just as shining, just as extraordinary to-day, after forty years of diligent wear and tear and use. He passed his fortieth year long and long ago; but I think his English of to-day—his perfect English, I wish to say—can throw down the glove before his English of that antique time and not be afraid.

I will go back to the paper on Machiavelli now, and ask the reader to examine this passage from it which I append. I do not mean examine it in a bird's-eye way; I mean search it, study it. And, of course, read it aloud. I may be wrong, still it is my conviction that one cannot get out of finely wrought literature all that is in it by reading it mutely:

> Mr. Dyer is rather of the opinion, first luminously suggested by Macaulay, that Machiavelli was in earnest, but must not be judged as a political moralist of our time and race would be judged. He thinks that Machiavelli was in earnest, as none but an idealist can be, and he is the first to imagine him an idealist immersed in realities, who involuntarily transmutes the events under his eye into something like the visionary issues of reverie. The Machiavelli

whom he depicts does not cease to be politically a republican and socially a just man because he holds up an atrocious despot like Cæsar Borgia as a mirror for rulers. What Machiavelli beheld round him in Italy was a civic disorder in which there was oppression without statecraft, and revolt without patriotism. When a miscreant like Borgia appeared upon the scene and reduced both tyrants and rebels to an apparent quiescence, he might very well seem to such a dreamer the savior of society whom a certain sort of dreamers are always looking for. Machiavelli was no less honest when he honored the diabolical force of Cæsar Borgia than Carlyle was when at different times he extolled the strong man who destroys liberty in creating order. But Carlyle has only just ceased to be mistaken for a reformer, while it is still Machiavelli's hard fate to be so trammeled in his material that his name stands for whatever is most malevolent and perfidious in human nature.

You see how easy and flowing it is; how unvexed by ruggednesses, clumsinesses, broken meters; how simple and—so far as you or I can make out—unstudied; how clear, how limpid, how understandable, how unconfused by cross-currents, eddies, undertows; how seemingly unadorned, yet is all adornment, like the lily-of-the-valley; and how compressed, how compact, without a complacency-signal hung out anywhere to call attention to it.

There are twenty lines in the quoted passage. After reading it several times aloud, one perceives that a good deal of matter is crowded into that small space. I think it is a model of compactness. When I take its materials apart and work them over and put them together in my way, I find I cannot crowd the result back into the same hole, there not being room enough. I find it a case of a woman packing a man's trunk: he can get the things out, but he can't ever get them back again.

The proffered paragraph is a just and fair sample; the rest of the article is as compact as it is; there are no waste words. The sample is just in other ways: limpid, fluent, graceful, and rhythmical as it is, it holds no superiority in these respects over the rest of the essay. Also, the choice phrasing noticeable in the sample is not lonely; there is a plenty of its kin distributed through the other paragraphs. This is claiming much when that kin must face the challenge of a phrase like the one in the middle sentence: "an idealist immersed in realities who involuntarily transmutes the events under his eye into something like the visionary issues of reverie." With a hundred words to do it with, the literary artisan could catch that airy thought and tie it down and reduce it to a concrete condition, visible, substantial, understandable and all right, like a cabbage; but the artist does it with twenty, and the result is a flower.

The quoted phrase, like a thousand others that have come from the same source, has the quality of certain scraps of verse which take hold of us and stay in our memories, we do not understand why, at first: all the words being the right words, none of them is conspicuous, and so they all seem inconspicuous, therefore we wonder what it is about them that makes their message take hold.

> The mossy marbles rest
> On the lips that he has prest
>   In their bloom,
> And the names he loved to hear
> Have been carved for many a year
>   On the tomb.

It is like a dreamy strain of moving music, with no sharp notes in it. The words are all "right" words, and all the same size. We do not notice it at first. We get the effect, it goes straight home to us, but we do not know why. It is when the right words are conspicuous that they thunder:

> The glory that was Greece and the grandeur that was Rome!

When I go back from Howells old to Howells young I find him arranging and clustering English words well, but not any better than now. He is not more felicitous in concreting abstractions now than he was in translating, then, the visions of the eyes of flesh into words that reproduced their forms and colors:

> In Venetian streets they give the fallen snow no rest. It is at once shoveled into the canals by hundreds of half-naked *facchini;* and now in St. Mark's Place the music of innumerable shovels smote upon my ear; and I saw the shivering legion of poverty as it engaged the elements in a struggle for the possession of the Piazza. But the snow continued to fall, and through the twilight of the descending flakes all this toil and encounter looked like that weary kind of effort in dreams, when the most determined industry seems only to renew the task. The lofty crest of the bell-tower was hidden in the folds of falling snow, and I could no longer see the golden angel upon its

summit. But looked at across the Piazza, the beautiful outline of St. Mark's Church was perfectly penciled in the air, and the shifting threads of the snowfall were woven into a spell of novel enchantment around the structure that always seemed to me too exquisite in its fantastic loveliness to be anything but the creation of magic. The tender snow had compassionated the beautiful edifice for all the wrongs of time, and so hid the stains and ugliness of decay that it looked as if just from the hand of the builder—or, better said, just from the brain of the architect. There was marvelous freshness in the colors of the mosaics in the great arches of the façade, and all that gracious harmony into which the temple rises, of marble scrolls and leafy exuberance airily supporting the statues of the saints, was a hundred times etherealized by the purity and whiteness of the drifting flakes. The snow lay lightly on the golden globes that tremble like peacock-crests above the vast domes, and plumed them with softest white; it robed the saints in ermine; and it danced over all its work, as if exulting in its beauty—beauty which filled me with subtle, selfish yearning to keep such evanescent loveliness for the little-while-longer of my whole life, and with despair to think that even the poor lifeless shadow of it could never be fairly reflected in picture or poem.

Through the wavering snowfall, the Saint Theodore upon one of the granite pillars of the Piazzetta did not show so grim as his wont is, and the winged lion on the other might have been a winged lamb, so gentle and mild he looked by the tender light of the storm. The towers of the island churches loomed faint and far away in the dimness; the sailors in the rigging of the ships that lay in the Basin wrought like phantoms among the shrouds; the gondolas stole in and out of the opaque distance more noiselessly and dreamily than ever; and a silence, almost palpable, lay upon the mutest city in the world.

The spirit of Venice is there: of a city where Age and Decay, fagged with distributing damage and repulsiveness among the other cities of the planet in accordance with the policy and business of their profession, come for rest and play between seasons, and treat themselves to the luxury and relaxation of sinking the shop and inventing and squandering charms all about, instead of abolishing such as they find, as is their habit when not on vacation.

In the working season they do business in Boston sometimes, and a character in *The Undiscovered Country* takes accurate note of pathetic effects wrought by them upon the aspects of a street of once dignified and elegant homes whose occupants have moved away and left them a prey to neglect and gradual ruin and progressive degradation; a descent which reaches bottom at last, when the street becomes a roost for humble professionals of the faith-cure and fortune-telling sort.

> What a queer, melancholy house, what a queer, melancholy street! I don't think I was ever in a street before where quite so many professional ladies, with English surnames, preferred Madam to Mrs. on their door-plates. And the poor old place has such a desperately conscious air of going to the deuce. Every house seems to wince as you go by, and button itself up to the chin for fear you should find out it had no shirt on—so to speak. I don't know what's the reason, but these material tokens of a social decay afflict me terribly: a tipsy woman isn't dreadfuler than a haggard old house, that's once been a home, in a street like this.

Mr. Howells's pictures are not mere stiff, hard, accurate photographs; they are photographs with feeling in them, and sentiment, photographs taken in a dream, one might say.

As concerns his humor, I will not try to say anything, yet I would try, if I had the words that might approximately reach up to its high place. I do not think any one else can play with humorous fancies so gracefully and delicately and deliciously as he does, nor has so many to play with, nor can come so near making them look as if they were doing the playing themselves and he was not aware that they were at it. For they are unobtrusive, and quiet in their ways, and well conducted. His is a humor which flows softly all around about and over and through the mesh of the page, pervasive, refreshing, health-giving, and makes no more show and no more noise than does the circulation of the blood.

There is another thing which is contentingly noticeable in Mr. Howells's books. That is his "stage directions"—those artifices which authors employ to throw a kind of human naturalness around a scene and a conversation, and help the reader to see the one and get at meanings in the other which might not be perceived if intrusted unexplained to the bare words of the talk. Some authors overdo the stage directions, they elaborate them quite beyond necessity; they spend so much time and take up so much room in telling us how a person said a thing and how he looked and acted when he said it that we get tired and vexed and wish he hadn't said it at all. Other authors' directions are brief enough, but it is seldom that the brevity contains either wit or information. Writers of this school go in rags, in the matter of stage directions; the majority of them have nothing in stock but a cigar, a laugh, a blush, and a bursting into tears. In their poverty they work these sorry things to the bone. They say:

". . . replied Alfred, flipping the ash from his cigar." (This explains nothing; it only wastes space.)

". . . responded Richard, with a laugh." (There was nothing to laugh about; there never is. The writer puts it in from habit—automatically; he is paying no attention to his work, or he would see that there is nothing to laugh at; often, when a remark is unusually and poignantly flat and silly, he tries to deceive the reader by enlarging the stage direction and making Richard break into "frenzies of uncontrollable laughter." This makes the reader sad.)

". . . murmured Gladys, blushing." (This poor old shop-worn blush is a tiresome thing. We get so we would rather Gladys would fall out of the book and break her neck than do it again. She is always doing it, and usually irrelevantly. Whenever it is her turn to murmur she hangs out her blush; it is the only thing she's got. In a little while we hate her, just as we do Richard.)

". . . repeated Evelyn, bursting into tears." (This kind keep a book damp all the time. They can't say a thing without crying. They cry so much about nothing that by and by when they have something to cry *about* they have gone dry; they sob, and fetch nothing; we are not moved. We are only glad.)

They gravel me, these stale and overworked stage directions, these carbon films that got burnt out long ago and cannot now carry any faintest thread of light. It would be well if they could be relieved from duty and flung out in the literary back yard to rot and disappear along with the discarded and forgotten "steeds" and "halidomes" and similar stage-properties once so dear to our grandfathers. But I am friendly to Mr. Howells's stage directions; more friendly to them than to any one else's, I think. They are done with a competent and discriminating art, and are faithful to the requirements of a stage direction's proper and lawful office, which is to inform. Sometimes they convey a scene and its conditions so well that I believe I could see the scene and get the spirit and meaning of the accompanying dialogue if some one would read merely the stage directions to me and leave out the talk. For instance, a scene like this, from *The Undiscovered Country:*

". . . and she laid her arms with a beseeching gesture on her father's shoulder."

". . . she answered, following his gesture with a glance."

". . . she said, laughing nervously."

". . . she asked, turning swiftly upon him that strange, searching glance."

". . . she answered, vaguely."

". . . she reluctantly admitted."

". . . but her voice died wearily away, and she stood looking into his face with puzzled entreaty."

Mr. Howells does not repeat his forms, and does not need to; he can invent fresh ones without limit. It is mainly the repetition over and over again, by the third-rates, of worn and commonplace and juiceless forms that makes their novels such a weariness and vexation to us, I think. We do not mind one or two deliveries of their wares, but as we turn the pages over and keep on meeting them we presently get tired of them and wish they would do other things for a change:

". . . replied Alfred, flipping the ash from his cigar."

". . . responded Richard, with a laugh."

". . . murmured Gladys, blushing."

". . . repeated Evelyn, bursting into tears."

". . . replied the Earl, flipping the ash from his cigar."

". . . responded the undertaker, with a laugh."

". . . murmured the chambermaid, blushing."

". . . repeated the burglar, bursting into tears."

". . . replied the conductor, flipping the ash from his cigar."

". . . responded Arkwright, with a laugh."

". . . murmured the chief of police, blushing."

". . . repeated the house-cat, bursting into tears."

And so on and so on; till at last it ceases to excite. I always notice stage directions, because they fret me and keep me trying to get out of their way, just as the automobiles do. At first; then by and by they become monotonous and I get run over.

Mr. Howells has done much work, and the spirit of it is as beautiful as the make of it. I have held him in admiration and affection so many years that I know by the number of those years that he is old now; but his heart isn't, nor his pen, and years do not count. Let him have plenty of them: there is profit in them for us.

Is Shakespeare Dead?

(FROM MY AUTOBIOGRAPHY)

I

Scattered here and there through the stacks of unpublished manuscript which constitute this formidable Autobiography and Diary of mine, certain chapters will in some distant future be found which deal with "Claimants"—claimants historically notorious: Satan, Claimant; the Golden Calf, Claimant; the Veiled Prophet of Khorassan, Claimant; Louis XVII., Claimant; William Shakespeare, Claimant; Arthur Orton, Claimant; Mary Baker G. Eddy, Claimant—and the rest of them. Eminent Claimants, successful Claimants, defeated Claimants, royal Claimants, pleb Claimants, showy Claimants, shabby Claimants, revered Claimants, despised Claimants, twinkle star-like here and there and yonder through the mists of history and legend and tradition—and, oh, all the darling tribe are clothed in mystery and romance, and we read about them with deep interest and discuss them with loving sympathy or with rancorous resentment, according to which side we hitch ourselves to. It has always been so with the human race. There was never a Claimant that couldn't get a hearing, nor one that couldn't accumulate a rapturous following, no matter how flimsy and apparently unauthentic his claim might be. Arthur Orton's claim that he was the lost Tichborne baronet come to life again was as flimsy as Mrs. Eddy's that she wrote *Science and Health* from the direct dictation of the Deity; yet in England near forty years ago Orton had a huge army of devotees and incorrigible adherents, many of whom remained stubbornly unconvinced after their fat god had been proven an imposter and jailed as a perjurer, and to-day Mrs. Eddy's following is not only immense, but is daily augmenting in numbers and enthusiasm. Orton had many fine and educated minds among his adherents, Mrs. Eddy has had the like among hers from the beginning. Her Church is as well equipped in those particulars as is any other Church. Claimants can always count upon a following, it doesn't matter who they are, nor what they claim, nor whether they come with documents or without. It was always so. Down out of the long-vanished past, across the abyss of the ages, if you listen, you can still hear the believing multitudes shouting for Perkin Warbeck and Lambert Simnel.

A friend has sent me a new book, from England—*The Shakespeare Problem Restated*—well restated and closely reasoned; and my fifty years' interest in that matter—asleep for the last three years—is excited once more. It is an interest which was born of Delia Bacon's book—away back in that ancient day—1857, or maybe 1856. About a year later my pilot-master, Bixby, transferred me from his own steamboat to the *Pennsylvania,* and placed me under the orders and instructions of George Ealer—dead now, these many, many years. I steered for him a good many months—as was the humble duty of the pilot-apprentice: stood a daylight watch and spun the wheel under the severe superintendence and correction of the master. He was a prime chess-player and an idolater of Shakespeare. He would play chess with anybody; even with me, and it cost his official dignity something to do that. Also—quite uninvited—he would read Shakespeare to me; not just casually, but by the hour, when it was his watch and I was steering. He read well, but not profitably for me, because he constantly injected commands into the text. That broke it all up, mixed it all up, tangled it all up—to that degree, in fact, that if we were in a risky and difficult piece of river an ignorant person couldn't have told, sometimes, which observations were Shakespeare's and which were Ealer's. For instance:

> What man dare, I dare!
> Approach thou *what* are you laying in the leads for? what a hell of an idea!

like the rugged ease her off a little, ease her off! rugged Russian bear, the armed rhinoceros or the *there* she goes! meet her, meet her! didn't you *know* she'd smell the reef if you crowded it like that? Hyrcan tiger; take any shape but that and my firm nerves she'll be in the *woods* the first you know! stop the starboard! come ahead strong on the larboard! back the starboard! . . . *Now* then, you're all right; come ahead on the starboard; straighten up and go 'long, never tremble: or be alive again, and dare me to the desert *damnation* can't you keep away from that greasy water? pull her down! snatch her! snatch her baldheaded! with thy sword; if trembling I inhabit then, lay in the leads!—no, only the starboard one, leave the other alone, protest me the baby of a girl. Hence horrible shadow! eight bells—that watchman's asleep again, I reckon, go down and call Brown yourself, unreal mockery, hence!

He certainly was a good reader, and splendidly thrilling and stormy and tragic, but it was a damage to me, because I have never since been able to read Shakespeare in a calm and sane way. I cannot rid it of his explosive interlardings, they break in everywhere with their irrelevant, "What in hell are you up to *now!* pull her down! more! *more!*—there now, steady as you go," and the other disorganizing interruptions that were always leaping from his mouth. When I read Shakespeare now I can hear them as plainly as I did in that long-departed time—fifty-one years ago. I never regarded Ealer's readings as educational. Indeed, they were a detriment to me.

His contributions to the text seldom improved it, but barring that detail he was a good reader; I can say that much for him. He did not use the book, and did not need to; he knew his Shakespeare as well as Euclid ever knew his multiplication table.

Did he have something to say—this Shakespeare-adoring Mississippi pilot—anent Delia Bacon's book?

Yes. And he said it; said it all the time, for months—in the morning watch, the middle watch, and dog watch; and probably kept it going in his sleep. He bought the literature of the dispute as fast as it appeared, and we discussed it all through thirteen hundred miles of river four times traversed in every thirty-five days—the time required by that swift boat to achieve two round trips. We discussed, and discussed, and discussed, and disputed and disputed and disputed; at any rate, *he* did, and I got in a word now and then when he slipped a cog and there was a vacancy. He did his arguing with heat, with energy, with violence; and I did mine with the reserve and moderation of a subordinate who does not like to be flung out of a pilot-house that is perched forty feet above the water. He was fiercely loyal to Shakespeare and cordially scornful of Bacon and of all the pretensions of the Baconians. So was I—at first. And at first he was glad that that was my attitude. There were even indications that he admired it; indications dimmed, it is true, by the distance that lay between the lofty boss-pilotical altitude and my lowly one, yet perceptible to me; perceptible, and translatable into a compliment—compliment coming down from above the snow-line and not well thawed in the transit, and not likely to set anything afire, not even a cub-pilot's self-conceit; still a detectable compliment, and precious.

Naturally it flattered me into being more loyal to Shakespeare—if possible—than I was before, and more prejudiced against Bacon—if possible—than I was before. And so we discussed and discussed, both on the same side, and were happy. For a while. Only for a while. Only for a very little while, a very, very, very little while. Then the atmosphere began to change; began to cool off.

A brighter person would have seen what the trouble was, earlier than I did, perhaps, but I saw it early enough for all practical purposes. You see, he was of an argumentative disposition. Therefore it took him but a little time to get tired of arguing with a person who agreed with everything he said and consequently never furnished him a provocative to flare up and show what he could do when it came to clear, cold, hard, rose-cut, hundred-faceted, diamond-flashing *reasoning.* That was his name for it. It has been applied since, with complacency, as many as several times, in the Bacon-Shakespeare scuffle. On the Shakespeare side.

Then the thing happened which has happened to more persons than to me when principle and personal interest found themselves in opposition to each other and a choice had to be made: I let principle go, and went over to the other side. Not the entire way, but far enough to answer the requirements of the case. That is to say, I took this attitude—to wit, I only *believed* Bacon wrote Shakespeare, whereas I *knew* Shakespeare didn't. Ealer was satisfied with that, and the war broke loose. Study, practice, experience in handling my end of the matter presently enabled me to take my new position almost seriously; a little bit later, utterly seriously; a little later still, lovingly, gratefully, devotedly; finally: fiercely, rabidly, uncompromisingly. After that I was welded to my faith, I was theoretically ready to die for it, and I looked down with compassion not unmixed with scorn upon everybody else's faith that didn't tally with mine. That faith, imposed upon me by self-interest in that ancient day, remains my faith to-day, and in it I find comfort, solace, peace, and never-failing joy. You see how curiously theological it is. The "rice Christian" of the Orient goes through the very same steps, when he is after rice and the missionary is after *him;* he goes for rice, and remains to worship.

Ealer did a lot of our "reasoning"—not to say substantially all of it. The slaves of his cult have a passion for calling it by that large name. We others do not call our inductions and deductions and reductions by any name at all. They show for themselves what they are, and we can with tranquil confidence leave the world to ennoble them with a title of its own choosing.

Now and then when Ealer had to stop to cough, I pulled my induction-talents together and hove the controversial lead myself: always getting eight feet, eight and a half, often nine, sometimes even quarter-less-twain—as *I* believed; but always "no bottom," as *he* said.

I got the best of him only once. I prepared myself. I wrote out a passage from Shakespeare—it may have been the very one I quoted awhile ago, I don't remember—and riddled it with his wild steamboatful interlardings. When an unrisky opportunity offered, one lovely summer day, when we had sounded and buoyed a tangled patch of crossings known as Hell's Half Acre, and were aboard again and he had sneaked the *Pennsylvania* triumphantly through it without once scraping sand, and the *A. T. Lacey* had followed in our wake and got stuck, and he was feeling good, I showed it to him. It amused him. I asked him to fire it off—*read* it; read it, I diplomatically added, as only *he* could read dramatic poetry. The compliment touched him where he lived. He did read it; read it with surpassing fire and spirit; read it as it will never be read again; for *he* knew how to put the right music into those thunderous interlardings and make them seem a part of the text, make them sound as if they were bursting from Shakespeare's own soul, each one of them a golden inspiration and not to be left out without damage to the massed and magnificent whole.

I waited a week, to let the incident fade; waited longer; waited until he brought up for reasonings and vituperation my pet position, my pet argument, the one which I was fondest of, the one which I prized far above all others in my ammunition-wagon—to wit, that Shakespeare couldn't have written Shakespeare's works, for the reason that the man who wrote them was limitlessly familiar with the laws, and the law-courts, and law-proceedings, and lawyer-talk, and lawyer-ways—and if Shakespeare was possessed of the infinitely divided star-dust that constituted this vast wealth, *how* did he get it, and *where,* and *when?*

"From books."

From books! That was always the idea. I answered as my readings of the champions of my side of the great controversy had taught me to answer: that a man can't handle glibly and easily and comfortably and successfully the argot of a trade at which he has not personally served. He will make mistakes; he will not, and cannot, get the trade-phrasings precisely and exactly right; and the moment he departs, by even a shade, from a common trade-form, the reader who has served that trade will know the writer *hasn't.* Ealer would not be convinced; he said a man could learn how to correctly handle the subtleties and mysteries and free-masonries of *any* trade by careful reading and studying. But when I got him to read again the passage from Shakespeare with the interlardings, he perceived, himself, that books couldn't teach a student a bewildering multitude of pilot-phrases so thoroughly and perfectly that he could talk them off in book and play or conversation and make no mistake that a pilot would not immediately discover. It was a triumph for me. He was silent awhile, and I knew what was happening—he was losing his temper. And I knew he would presently close the session with the same old argument that was always his stay and his support in time of need; the same old argument, the one I couldn't answer, because I dasn't—the argument that I was an ass, and better shut up. He delivered it, and I obeyed.

Oh dear, how long ago it was—how pathetically long ago! And here am I, old, forsaken, forlorn, and alone, arranging to get that argument out of somebody again.

When a man has a passion for Shakespeare, it goes without saying that he keeps company with other standard authors. Ealer always had several high-class books in the pilot-house, and he read the same ones over and over again, and did not care to change to newer and fresher ones. He played well on the flute, and greatly enjoyed hearing himself play. So did I. He had a notion that a flute would keep its health better if you took it apart when it was not standing a watch; and so, when it was not on duty it took its rest, disjointed, on the compass-shelf under the breastboard. When the *Pennsylvania* blew up and became a drifting rack-heap freighted with wounded and dying poor souls (my young brother Henry among them), pilot Brown had the watch below, and was probably asleep and never knew what killed him; but Ealer escaped unhurt. He and his pilot-house were shot up into the air; then they fell, and Ealer sank through the ragged cavern where the hurricane-deck and the boiler-deck had been, and landed in a nest of ruins on the main deck, on top of one of the unexploded boilers, where he lay prone in a fog of scald and deadly steam. But not for long. He did not lose his head—long familiarity with danger had taught him to keep it, in any and all emergencies. He held his coat-lapels to his nose with one hand, to keep out the steam, and scrabbled around with the other till he found the joints of his flute, then he took measures to save himself alive, and was successful. I was not on board. I had been put ashore in New Orleans by Captain Klinefelter. The reason—however, I have told all about it in the book called *Old Times on the Mississippi*, and it isn't important, anyway, it is so long ago.

II

When I was a Sunday-school scholar, something more than sixty years ago, I became interested in Satan, and wanted to find out all I could about him. I began to ask questions, but my class-teacher, Mr. Barclay, the stone-mason, was reluctant about answering them, it seemed to me. I was anxious to be praised for turning my thoughts to serious subjects when there wasn't another boy in the village who could be hired to do such a thing. I was greatly interested in the incident of Eve and the serpent, and thought Eve's calmness was perfectly noble. I asked Mr. Barclay if he had ever heard of another woman who, being approached by a serpent, would not excuse herself and break for the nearest timber. He did not answer my question, but rebuked me for inquiring into matters above my age and comprehension. I will say for Mr. Barclay that he was willing to tell me the facts of Satan's history, but he stopped there: he wouldn't allow any discussion of them.

In the course of time we exhausted the facts. There were only five or six of them; you could set them all down on a visiting-card. I was disappointed. I had been meditating a biography, and was grieved to find that there were no materials. I said as much, with the tears running down. Mr. Barclay's sympathy and compassion were aroused, for he was a most kind and gentle-spirited man, and he patted me on the head and cheered me up by saying there was a whole vast ocean of materials! I can still feel the happy thrill which these blessed words shot through me.

Then he began to bail out that ocean's riches for my encouragement and joy. Like this: it was "conjectured"—though not established—that Satan was originally an angel in heaven; that he fell; that he rebelled, and brought on a war; that he was defeated, and banished to perdition. Also, "we have reason to believe" that later he did so and so; that "we are warranted in supposing" that at a subsequent time he traveled extensively, seeking whom he might devour; that a couple of centuries afterward, "as tradition instructs us," he took up the cruel trade of tempting people to their ruin, with vast and fearful results; that by and by, "as the probabilities seem to indicate," he may have done certain things, he might have done certain other things, he must have done still other things.

And so on and so on. We set down the five known facts by themselves, on a piece of paper, and numbered it "page 1"; then on fifteen hundred other pieces of paper we set down the "conjectures," and "suppositions," and "maybes," and "perhapses," and "doubtlesses," and "rumors," and "guesses," and "probabilities," and "likelihoods," and "we are permitted to thinks," and "we are warranted in believings," and "might have beens," and "could have beens," and "must have beens," and "unquestionablys," and "without a shadow of doubts"—and behold!

Materials? Why, we had enough to build a biography of Shakespeare!

Yet he made me put away my pen; he would not let me write the history of Satan. Why? Because, as he said, he had suspicions—suspicions that my attitude in this matter was not reverent, and that a person must be reverent when writing about the sacred characters. He said any one who spoke flippantly of Satan would be frowned upon by the religious world and also be brought to account.

I assured him, in earnest and sincere words, that he had wholly misconceived my attitude; that I had the highest respect for Satan, and that my reverence for him equaled, and possibly even exceeded, that of any member of any church. I said it wounded me deeply to perceive by his words that he thought I would make fun of Satan, and deride him, laugh at him, scoff at him; whereas in truth I had never thought of such a thing, but had only a warm desire to make fun of those others and laugh at *them.* "What others?" "Why, the Supposers, the Perhapsers, the Might-Have-Beeners, the Could-Have-Beeners, the Must-Have-Beeners, the Without-a-Shadow-of-Doubters, the We-Are-Warranted-In-Believingers, and all that funny crop of solemn architects who have taken a good solid foundation of five indisputable and unimportant facts and built upon it a Conjectural Satan thirty miles high."

What did Mr. Barclay do then? Was he disarmed? Was he silenced? No. He was shocked. He was so shocked that he visibly shuddered. He said the Satanic Traditioners and Perhapsers and Conjecturers were *themselves* sacred! As sacred as their work. So sacred that whoso ventured to mock them or make fun of their work, could not afterward enter any respectable house, even by the back door.

How true were his words, and how wise! How fortunate it would have been for me if I had heeded them. But I was young, I was but seven years of age, and vain, foolish, and anxious to attract attention. I wrote the biography, and have never been in a respectable house since.

III

How curious and interesting is the parallel—as far as poverty of biographical details is concerned—between Satan and Shakespeare. It is wonderful, it is unique, it stands quite alone, there is nothing resembling it in history, nothing resembling it in romance, nothing approaching it even in tradition. How sublime is their position, and how overtopping, how sky-reaching, how supreme—the two Great Unknowns, the two Illustrious Conjecturabilities! They are the best-known unknown persons that have ever drawn breath upon the planet.

For the instruction of the ignorant I will make a list, now, of those details of Shakespeare's history which are *facts*—verified facts, established facts, undisputed facts.

Facts

He was born on the 23d of April, 1564.

Of good farmer-class parents who could not read, could not write, could not sign their names.

At Stratford, a small back settlement which in that day was shabby and unclean, and densely illiterate. Of the nineteen important men charged with the government of the town, thirteen had to "make their mark" in attesting important documents, because they could not write their names.

Of the first eighteen years of his life *nothing* is known. They are a blank.

On the 27th of November (1582) William Shakespeare took out a license to marry Anne Whateley.

Next day William Shakespeare took out a license to marry Anne Hathaway. She was eight years his senior.

William Shakespeare married Anne Hathaway. In a hurry. By grace of a reluctantly granted dispensation there was but one publication of the banns.

Within six months the first child was born.

About two (blank) years followed, during which period *nothing at all happened to Shakespeare,* so far as anybody knows.

Then came twins—1585. February.

Two blank years follow.

Then—1587—he makes a ten-year visit to London, leaving the family behind.

Five blank years follow. During this period *nothing happened to him,* as far as anybody actually knows.

Then—1592—there is mention of him as an actor.

Next year—1593—his name appears in the official list of players.

Next year—1594—he played before the queen. A detail of no consequence: other obscurities did it every year of the forty-five of her reign. And remained obscure.

Three pretty full years follow. Full of play-acting. Then

In 1597 he bought New Place, Stratford.

Thirteen or fourteen busy years follow; years in which he accumulated money, and also reputation as actor and manager.

Meantime his name, liberally and variously spelt, had become associated with a number of great plays and poems, as (ostensibly) author of the same.

Some of these, in these years and later, were pirated, but he made no protest.

Then—1610-11—he returned to Stratford and settled down for good and all, and busied himself in lending money, trading in tithes, trading in land and houses; shirking a debt of forty-one shillings, borrowed by his wife during his long desertion of his family; suing debtors for shillings and coppers; being sued himself for shillings and coppers; and acting as confederate to a neighbor who tried to rob the town of its rights in a certain common, and did not succeed.

He lived five or six years—till 1616—in the joy of these elevated pursuits. Then he made a will, and signed each of its three pages with his name.

A thoroughgoing business man's will. It named in minute detail every item of property he owned in the world—houses, lands, sword, silver-gilt bowl, and so on—all the way down to his "second-best bed" and its furniture.

It carefully and calculatingly distributed his riches among the members of his family, overlooking no individual of it. Not even his wife: the wife he had been enabled to marry in a hurry by urgent grace of a special dispensation before he was nineteen; the wife whom he had left husbandless so many years; the wife who had had to borrow forty-one shillings in her need, and which the lender was never able to collect of the prosperous husband, but died at last with the money still lacking. No, even this wife was remembered in Shakespeare's will.

He left her that "second-best bed."

And *not another thing;* not even a penny to bless her lucky widowhood with.

It was eminently and conspicuously a business man's will, not a poet's.

It mentioned *not a single book.*

Books were much more precious than swords and silver-gilt bowls and second-best beds in those days, and when a departing person owned one he gave it a high place in his will.

The will mentioned *not a play, not a poem, not an unfinished literary work, not a scrap of manuscript of any kind.*

Many poets have died poor, but this is the only one in history that has died *this* poor; the others all left literary remains behind. Also a book. Maybe two.

If Shakespeare had owned a dog—but we need not go into that: we know he would have mentioned it in his will. If a good dog, Susanna would have got it; if an inferior one his wife would have got a dower interest in it. I wish he had had a dog, just so we could see how painstakingly he would have divided that dog among the family, in his careful business way.

He signed the will in three places.

In earlier years he signed two other official documents.

These five signatures still exist.

There are *no other specimens of his penmanship in existence.* Not a line.

Was he prejudiced against the art? His granddaughter, whom he loved, was eight years old when he died, yet she had had no teaching, he left no provision for her education, although he was rich, and in her mature womanhood she couldn't write and couldn't tell her husband's manuscript from anybody else's—she thought it was Shakespeare's.

When Shakespeare died in Stratford *it was not an event.* It made no more stir in England than the death of any other forgotten theater-actor would have made. Nobody came down from London; there were no lamenting poems, no eulogies, no national tears—there was merely silence, and nothing more. A striking contrast with what happened when Ben Jonson, and Francis Bacon, and Spenser, and Raleigh, and the other distinguished literary folk of Shakespeare's time passed from life! No praiseful voice was lifted for the lost Bard of Avon; even Ben Jonson waited seven years before he lifted his.

So far as anybody actually knows and can prove, Shakespeare of Stratford-on-Avon never wrote a play in his life.

So far as anybody knows and can prove, he never wrote a letter to anybody in his life.

So far as any one knows, he received only one letter during his life.

So far as any one *knows and can prove,* Shakespeare of Stratford wrote only one poem during his life. This one is authentic. He did write that one —a fact which stands undisputed; he wrote the whole of it; he wrote the whole of it out of his own head. He commanded that this work of art be engraved upon his tomb, and he was obeyed. There it abides to this day. This is it:

> Good friend for Iesus sake forbeare
> To digg the dust encloased heare:
> Blest be ye man yt spares thes stones
> And curst be he yt moves my bones.

In the list as above set down will be found *every positively known* fact of Shakespeare's life, lean and meager as the invoice is. Beyond these details we know *not a thing* about him. All the rest of his vast history, as furnished by the biographers, is built up, course upon course, of guesses, inferences, theories, conjectures—an Eiffel Tower of artificialities rising sky-high from a very flat and very thin foundation of inconsequential facts.

IV

Conjectures

The historians "suppose" that Shakespeare attended the Free School in Stratford from the time he was seven years old till he was thirteen. There is *no evidence* in existence that he ever went to school at all.

The historians "infer" that he got his Latin in that school—the school which they "suppose" he attended.

They "suppose" his father's declining fortunes made it necessary for him to leave the school they supposed he attended, and get to work and help support his parents and their ten children. But there is no evidence that he ever entered or returned from the school they suppose he attended.

They "suppose" he assisted his father in the butchering business; and that, being only a boy, he didn't have to do full-grown butchering, but only slaughtered calves. Also, that whenever he killed a calf he made a high-flown speech over it. This supposition rests upon the testimony of a man who wasn't there at the time; a man who got it from a man who could have been there, but did not say whether he was or not; and neither of them thought to mention it for decades, and decades, and decades, and two more decades after Shakespeare's death (until old age and mental decay had refreshed and vivified their memories). They hadn't two facts in stock about the long-dead distinguished citizen, but only just the one: he slaughtered calves and broke into oratory while he was at it. Curious. They had only one fact, yet the distinguished citizen had spent twenty-six years in that little town—just half his lifetime. However, rightly viewed, it was the most important fact, indeed almost the only important fact, of Shakespeare's life in Stratford. Rightly viewed. For experience is an author's most valuable asset; experience is the thing that puts the muscle and the breath and the warm blood into the book he writes. Rightly viewed, calf-butchering accounts for "Titus Andronicus," the only play—ain't it?—that the Stratford Shakespeare ever wrote; and yet it is the only one everybody tries to chouse him out of, the Baconians included.

The historians find themselves "justified in believing" that the young Shakespeare poached upon Sir Thomas Lucy's deer preserves and got haled before that magistrate for it. But there is no shred of respectworthy evidence that anything of the kind happened.

The historians, having argued the thing that *might* have happened into the thing that *did* happen, found no trouble in turning Sir Thomas Lucy into Mr. Justice Shallow. They have long ago convinced the world—on surmise and without trustworthy evidence—that Shallow *is* Sir Thomas.

The next addition to the young Shakespeare's Stratford history comes easy. The historian builds it out of the surmised deer-stealing, and the surmised trial before the magistrate, and the surmised vengeance-prompted satire upon the magistrate in the play: result, the young Shakespeare was a wild, wild, wild, oh, *such* a wild young scamp, and that gratuitous slander is established for all time! It is the very way Professor Osborn and I built the colossal skeleton brontosaur that stands fifty-seven feet long and sixteen feet high in the Natural History Museum, the awe and admiration of all the world, the stateliest skeleton that exists on the planet. We had nine bones, and we built the rest of him out of plaster of Paris. We ran short of plaster of Paris, or we'd have built a brontosaur that could sit down beside the Stratford Shakespeare and none but an expert could tell which was biggest or contained the most plaster.

Shakespeare pronounced "Venus and Adonis" "the first heir of his invention," apparently implying that it was his first effort at literary composition. He should not have said it. It has been an embarrassment to his historians these many, many years. They have to make him write that graceful and polished and flawless and beautiful poem before he escaped from Stratford and his family—1586 or '87—age, twenty-two, or along there; because within the next five years he wrote five great plays, and could not have found time to write another line.

It is sorely embarrassing. If he began to slaughter calves, and poach deer, and rollick around, and learn English, at the earliest likely moment—say at thirteen, when he was supposably wrenched from that school where he was supposably storing up Latin for future literary use—he had his youthful hands full, and much more than full. He must have had to put aside his Warwickshire dialect, which wouldn't be understood in London, and study English very hard. Very hard indeed; incredibly hard, almost, if the result of that labor was to be the smooth and rounded and flexible and letter-perfect English of the "Venus and Adonis" in the space of ten years; and at the same time learn great and fine and unsurpassable literary *form.*

However, it is "conjectured" that he accomplished all this and more, much more: learned law and its intricacies; and the complex procedure of the law-courts; and all about soldiering, and sailoring, and the manners and customs and ways of royal courts and aristocratic society; and likewise accumulated in his one head every kind of knowledge the learned then possessed, and every kind of humble knowledge possessed by the lowly and the ignorant; and added thereto a wider and more intimate knowledge of the world's great literatures, ancient and modern, than was possessed by any other man of his time—for he was going to make brilliant and easy and admiration-compelling use of these splendid treasures the moment he got to London. And according to the surmisers, that is what he did. Yes, although there was no one in Stratford able to teach him these things, and no library in the little village to dig them out of. His father could not read, and even the surmisers surmise that he did not keep a library.

It is surmised by the biographers that the young Shakespeare got his vast knowledge of the law and his familiar and accurate acquaintance with the manners and customs and shop-talk of lawyers through being for a time the *clerk of a Stratford court;* just as a bright lad like me, reared in a village on the banks of the Mississippi, might become perfect in knowledge of the Bering Strait whale-fishery and the shop-talk of the veteran exercises of that adventure-bristling trade through catching catfish with a "trot-line" Sundays. But the surmise is damaged by the fact that there is no evidence —and not even tradition—that the young Shakespeare was ever clerk of a law-court.

It is further surmised that the young Shakespeare accumulated his law-treasures in the first years of his sojourn in London, through "amusing himself" by learning book-law in his garret and by picking up lawyer-talk and the rest of it through loitering about the law-courts and listening. But it is only surmise; there is no *evidence* that he ever did either of those things. They are merely a couple of chunks of plaster of Paris.

There is a legend that he got his bread and butter by holding horses in front of the London theaters, mornings and afternoons. Maybe he did. If he did, it seriously shortened his law-study hours and his recreation-time in the courts. In those very days he was writing great plays, and needed all the time he could get. The horse-holding legend ought to be strangled; it too formidably increases the historian's difficulty in accounting for the young Shakespeare's erudition—an erudition which he was acquiring, hunk by hunk and chunk by chunk, every day in those strenuous times, and emptying each day's catch into next day's imperishable drama.

He had to acquire a knowledge of war at the same time; and a knowledge of soldier-people and sailor-people and their ways and talk; also a knowledge of some foreign lands and their languages: for he was daily emptying fluent streams of these various knowledges, too, into his dramas. How did he acquire these rich assets?

In the usual way: by surmise. It is *surmised* that he traveled in Italy and Germany and around, and qualified himself to put their scenic and social aspects upon paper; that he perfected himself in French, Italian, and Spanish on the road; that he went in Leicester's expedition to the Low Countries, as soldier or sutler or something, for several months or years—or whatever length of time a surmiser needs in his business—and thus became familiar with soldiership and soldier-ways and soldier-talk and generalship and general-ways and general-talk, and seamanship and sailor-ways and sailor-talk.

Maybe he did all these things, but I would like to know who held the horses in the mean time; and who studied the books in the garret; and who frollicked in the law-courts for recreation. Also, who did the call-boying and the play-acting.

For he became a call-boy; and as early as '93 he became a "vagabond"—

the law's ungentle term for an unlisted actor; and in '94 a "regular" and properly and officially listed member of that (in those days) lightly valued and not much respected profession.

Right soon thereafter he became a stockholder in two theaters, and manager of them. Thenceforward he was a busy and flourishing business man, and was raking in money with both hands for twenty years. Then in a noble frenzy of poetic inspiration he wrote his one poem—his only poem, his darling—and laid him down and died:

> Good friend for Iesus sake forbeare
> To digg the dust encloased heare:
> Blest be ye man yt spares thes stones
> And curst be he yt moves my bones.

He was probably dead when he wrote it. Still, this is only conjecture. We have only circumstantial evidence. Internal evidence.

Shall I set down the rest of the Conjectures which constitute the giant Biography of William Shakespeare? It would strain the Unabridged Dictionary to hold them. He is a brontosaur: nine bones and six hundred barrels of plaster of Paris.

V

"We May Assume"

In the Assuming trade three separate and independent cults are transacting business. Two of these cults are known as the Shakespearites and the Baconians, and I am the other one—the Brontosaurian.

The Shakespearite knows that Shakespeare wrote Shakespeare's Works; the Baconian knows that Francis Bacon wrote them; the Brontosaurian doesn't really know which of them did it, but is quite composedly and contentedly sure that Shakespeare *didn't,* and strongly suspects that Bacon *did.* We all have to do a good deal of assuming, but I am fairly certain that in every case I can call to mind the Baconian assumers have come out ahead of the Shakespearites. Both parties handle the same materials, but the Baconians seem to me to get much more reasonable and rational and persuasive results out of them than is the case with the Shakespearites. The Shakespearite conducts his assuming upon a definite principle, an unchanging and immutable law: which is: 2 and 8 and 7 and 14, added together, make 165. I believe this to be an error. No matter, you cannot get a habit-sodden Shakespearite to cipher-up his materials upon any other basis. With the Baconian it is different. If you place before him the above figures and set him to adding them up, he will never in any case get more than 45 out of them, and in nine cases out of ten he will get just the proper 31.

Let me try to illustrate the two systems in a simple and homely way calculated to bring the idea within the grasp of the ignorant and unintelligent. We will suppose a case: take a lap-bred, house-fed, uneducated, inexperienced kitten; take a rugged old Tom that's scarred from stem to rudder-post with the memorials of strenuous experience, and is so cultured, so educated, so limitlessly erudite that one may say of him "all cat-knowledge is his province"; also, take a mouse. Lock the three up in a holeless, crackless, exitless prison-cell. Wait half an hour, then open the cell, introduce a Shakespearite and a Baconian, and let them cipher and assume. The mouse is missing: the question to be decided is, where is it? You can guess both verdicts beforehand. One verdict will say the kitten contains the mouse; the other will as certainly say the mouse is in the tom-cat.

The Shakespearite will Reason like this—(that is not my word, it is his). He will say the kitten *may have been* attending school when nobody was noticing; therefore *we are warranted in assuming* that it did so; also, it *could have been* training in a court-clerk's office when no one was noticing; since that could have happened, *we are justified in assuming* that it did happen; it *could have studied catology in a garret* when no one was noticing—therefore it *did;* it *could have* attended cat-assizes on the shed-roof nights, for recreation, when no one was noticing, and have harvested a knowledge of cat court-forms and cat lawyer-talk in that way: it *could* have done it, therefore without a doubt it *did;* it *could have* gone soldiering with a war-tribe when no one was noticing, and learned soldier-wiles and soldier-ways, and what to do with a mouse when opportunity offers; the plain inference, therefore, is that that is what it *did.* Since all these manifold things *could* have occurred, we have *every right to believe* they did occur. These patiently and painstakingly accumulated vast acquirements and competences needed but one thing more—opportunity—to convert themselves into triumphant action. The opportunity came, we have the result; *beyond shadow of question* the mouse is in the kitten.

It is proper to remark that when we of the three cults plant a *"We think we may assume,"* we expect it, under careful watering and fertilizing and tending, to grow up into a strong and hardy and weather-defying *"there isn't a shadow of a doubt"* at last—and it usually happens.

We know what the Baconian's verdict would be: *"There is not a rag of evidence that the kitten has had any training, any education, any experience qualifying it for the present occasion, or is indeed equipped for any achievement above lifting such unclaimed milk as comes its way; but there is abundant evidence—unassailable proof, in fact—that the other animal is equipped, to the last detail, with every qualification necessary for the event. Without shadow of doubt the tom-cat contains the mouse."*

VI

When Shakespeare died, in 1616, great literary productions attributed to him as author had been before the London world and in high favor for twenty-four years. Yet his death was not an event. It made no stir, it attracted no attention. Apparently his eminent literary contemporaries did not realize that a celebrated poet had passed from their midst. Perhaps they knew a play-actor of minor rank had disappeared, but did not regard him as the author of his Works. "We are justified in assuming" this.

His death was not even an event in the little town of Stratford. Does this mean that in Stratford he was not regarded as a celebrity of *any* kind?

"We are privileged to assume"—no, we are indeed *obliged* to assume—that such was the case. He had spent the first twenty-two or twenty-three years of his life there, and of course knew everybody and was known by everybody of that day in the town, including the dogs and the cats and the horses. He had spent the last five or six years of his life there, diligently trading in every big and little thing that had money in it; so we are compelled to assume that many of the folk there in those said latter days knew him personally, and the rest by sight and hearsay. But not as a *celebrity?* Apparently not. For everybody soon forgot to remember any contact with him or any incident connected with him. The dozens of townspeople, still alive, who had known of him or known about him in the first twenty-three years of his life were in the same unremembering condition: if they knew of any incident connected with that period of his life they didn't tell about it. Would they if they had been asked? It is most likely. Were they asked? It is pretty apparent that they were not. Why weren't they? It is a very plausible guess that nobody there or elsewhere was interested to know.

For seven years after Shakespeare's death nobody seems to have been interested in him. Then the quarto was published, and Ben Jonson awoke out of his long indifference and sang a song of praise and put it in the front of the book. Then silence fell *again.*

For sixty years. Then inquiries into Shakespeare's Stratford life began to be made, of Stratfordians. Of Stratfordians who had known Shakespeare or had seen him? No. Then of Stratfordians who had seen people who had known or seen people who had seen Shakespeare? No. Apparently the inquiries were only made of Stratfordians who were not Stratfordians of Shakespeare's day, but later comers; and what they had learned had come to them from persons who had not seen Shakespeare; and what they had learned was not claimed as *fact,* but only as legend—dim and fading and indefinite legend; legend of the calf-slaughtering rank, and not worth remembering either as history or fiction.

Has it ever happened before—or since—that a celebrated person who had spent exactly half of a fairly long life in the village where he was born and reared, was able to slip out of this world and leave that village voiceless and gossipless behind him—utterly voiceless, utterly gossipless? And permanently so? I don't believe it has happened in any case except Shakespeare's. And couldn't and wouldn't have happened in his case if he had been regarded as a celebrity at the time of his death.

When I examine my own case—but let us do that, and see if it will not be recognizable as exhibiting a condition of things quite likely to result, most likely to result, indeed substantially *sure* to result in the case of a celebrated person, a benefactor of the human race. Like me.

My parents brought me to the village of Hannibal, Missouri, on the banks of the Mississippi, when I was two and a half years old. I entered school at five years of age, and drifted from one school to another in the village during nine and a half years. Then my father died, leaving his family in exceedingly straitened circumstances; wherefore my book-education came to a standstill forever, and I became a printer's apprentice, on board and clothes, and when the clothes failed I got a hymn-book in place of them. This for summer wear, probably. I lived in Hannibal fifteen and a half years, altogether, then ran away, according to the custom of persons who are intending to become celebrated. I never lived there afterward. Four years later I became a "cub" on a Mississippi steamboat in the St. Louis and New Orleans trade, and after a year and a half of hard study and hard work the U.S. inspectors rigorously examined me through a couple of long sittings and decided that I knew every inch of the Mississippi—thirteen hundred miles—in the dark and in the day—as well as a baby knows the way to its mother's paps day or night. So they licensed me as a pilot—knighted me, so to speak—and I rose up clothed with authority, a responsible servant of the United States Government.

Now then. Shakespeare died young—he was only fifty-two. He had lived in his native village twenty-six years, or about that. He died celebrated (if you believe everything you read in the books). Yet when he died nobody there or elsewhere took any notice of it; and for sixty years afterward no townsman remembered to say anything about him or about his life in Stratford. When the inquirer came at last he got but one fact—no, *legend*—and got that one at second hand, from a person who had only heard it as a rumor and didn't claim copyright in it as a production of his own. He couldn't, very well, for its date antedated his own birth-date. But necessarily a number of persons were still alive in Stratford who, in the days of their youth, had seen Shakespeare nearly every day in the last five years of his life, and they would have been able to tell that inquirer some first-hand things about him if he had in those last days been a celebrity and therefore a person of interest to the villagers. Why did not the inquirer hunt them up and interview them? Wasn't it worth while? Wasn't the matter of sufficient consequence? Had the inquirer an engagement to see a dog-fight and couldn't spare the time?

It all seems to mean that he never had any literary celebrity, there or elsewhere, and no considerable repute as actor and manager.

Now then, I am away along in life—my seventy-third year being already well behind me—yet *sixteen* of my Hannibal schoolmates are still alive to-day, and can tell—and do tell—inquirers dozens and dozens of incidents of their young lives and mine together; things that happened to us in the morning of life, in the blossom of our youth, in the good days, the dear days, "the days when we went gipsying, a long time ago." Most of them creditable to me, too. One child to whom I paid court when she was five years old and I eight still lives in Hannibal, and she visited me last summer, traversing the necessary ten or twelve hundred miles of railroad without damage to her patience or to her old-young vigor. Another little lassie to whom I paid attention in Hannibal when she was nine years old and I the same, is still alive—in London—and hale and hearty, just as I am. And on the few surviving steamboats—those lingering ghosts and remembrancers of great fleets that plied the big river in the beginning of my water-career—which is exactly as long ago as the whole invoice of the life-years of Shakespeare numbers—there are still findable two or three river-pilots who saw me do creditable things in those ancient days; and several white-headed engineers; and several roustabouts and mates; and several deck-hands who used to heave the lead for me and send up on the still night air the "Six—feet—*scant!*" that made me shudder, and the "M-a-r-k—*twain!*" that took the shudder away, and presently the darling "By the d-e-e-p—*four!*" that lifted me to heaven for joy.[1] They know about me, and can tell. And so do printers, from St. Louis to New York; and so do newspaper reporters, from Nevada to San Francisco. And so do the police. If Shakespeare had really been celebrated, like me, Stratford could have told things about him; and if my experience goes for anything, they'd have done it.

VII

If I had under my superintendence a controversy appointed to decide whether Shakespeare wrote Shakespeare or not, I believe I would place before the debaters only the one question, *Was Shakespeare ever a practising lawyer?* and leave everything else out.

It is maintained that the man who wrote the plays was not merely myriad-minded, but also myriad-accomplished: that he not only knew some thousands of things about human life in all its shades and grades, and about the hundred arts and trades and crafts and professions which men busy themselves in, but that he could *talk* about the men and their grades and trades accurately, making no mistakes. Maybe it is so, but have the experts spoken, or is it only Tom, Dick, and Harry? Does the exhibit stand upon wide, and loose, and eloquent generalizing—which is not evidence, and not proof—or upon details, particulars, statistics, illustrations, demonstrations?

Experts of unchallengeable authority have testified definitely as to only one of Shakespeare's multifarious craft-equipments, so far as my recollections of Shakespeare-Bacon talk abide with me—his law-equipment. I do not remember that Wellington or Napoleon ever examined Shakespeare's battles and sieges and strategies, and then decided and established for good and all that they were militarily flawless; I do not remember that any Nelson, or Drake, or Cook ever examined his seamanship and said it

1. Four fathoms—twenty-four feet.—M.T.

showed profound and accurate familiarity with that art; I don't remember that any king or prince or duke has ever testified that Shakespeare was letter-perfect in his handling of royal court-manners and the talk and manners of aristocracies; I don't remember that any illustrious Latinist or Grecian or Frenchman or Spaniard or Italian has proclaimed him a past-master in those languages; I don't remember—well, I don't remember that there is *testimony*—great testimony—imposing testimony—unanswerable and unattackable testimony as to any of Shakespeare's hundred specialties, except one—the law.

Other things change, with time, and the student cannot trace back with certainty the changes that various trades and their processes and technicalities have undergone in the long stretch of a century or two and find out what their processes and technicalities were in those early days, but with the law it is different: it is mile-stoned and documented all the way back, and the master of that wonderful trade, that complex and intricate trade, that awe-compelling trade, has competent ways of knowing whether Shakespeare-law is good law or not; and whether his law-court procedure is correct or not, and whether his legal shop-talk is the shop-talk of a veteran practitioner or only a machine-made counterfeit of it gathered from books and from occasional loiterings in Westminster.

Richard H. Dana served two years before the mast, and had every experience that falls to the lot of the sailor before the mast of our day. His sailor-talk flows from his pen with the sure touch and the ease and confidence of a person who has *lived* what he is talking about, not gathered it from books and random listenings. Hear him:

> Having hove short, cast off the gaskets, and made the bunt of each sail fast by the jigger, with a man on each yard, at the word the whole canvas of the ship was loosed, and with the greatest rapidity possible everything was sheeted home and hoisted up, the anchor tripped and cat-headed, and the ship under headway.

Again:

> The royal yards were all crossed at once, and royals and sky-sails set, and, as we had the wind free, the booms were run out, and all were aloft, active as cats, laying out on the yards and booms, reeving the studding-sail gear; and sail after sail the captain piled upon her, until she was covered with canvas, her sails looking like a great white cloud resting upon a black speck.

Once more. A race in the Pacific:

> Our antagonist was in her best trim. Being clear of the point, the breeze became stiff, and the royal-masts bent under our sails, but we would not take them in until we saw three boys spring into the rigging of the *California;* then they were all furled at once, but with orders to our boys to stay aloft at the top-gallant mast-heads and loose them again at the word. It was my duty to furl the fore-royal; and while standing by to loose it again, I had a fine view of the scene. From where I stood, the two vessels seemed nothing but spars and sails, while their narrow decks, far below, slanting over by the force of the wind aloft, appeared hardly capable of supporting the great fabrics raised upon them. The *California* was to windward of us, and had every advantage; yet, while the breeze was stiff we held our own. As soon as it began to slacken she ranged a little ahead, and the order was given to loose the royals. In an instant the gaskets were off and the bunt dropped. "Sheet home the fore-royal!"—"Weather sheet's home!"—"Lee sheet's home!"—"Hoist away, sir!" is bawled from aloft. "Overhaul your clew-lines!" shouts the mate. "Aye-aye, sir, all clear!"—"Taut leech! belay! Well the lee brace; haul taut to windward!" and the royals are set.

What would the captain of any sailing-vessel of our time say to that? He would say, "The man that wrote that didn't learn his trade out of a book, he has *been* there!" But would this same captain be competent to sit in judgment upon Shakespeare's seamanship—considering the changes in ships and ship-talk that have necessarily taken place, unrecorded, unremembered, and lost to history in the last three hundred years? It is my conviction that Shakespeare's sailor-talk would be Choctaw to him. For instance—from "The Tempest":

> *Master.* Boatswain!
>
> *Boatswain.* Here, master; what cheer?
>
> *Master.* Good, speak to the mariners: fall to 't, yarely, or we run ourselves to ground; bestir, bestir!
>
> *(Enter mariners.)*
>
> *Boatswain.* Heigh, my hearts! cheerly, cheerly, my hearts! yare, yare! Take in the topsail. Tend to the master's whistle. . . . Down with the topmast! yare! lower, lower! Bring her to try wi' the main course. . . . Lay her a-hold, a-hold! Set her two courses. Off to sea again; lay her off.

That will do, for the present; let us yare a little, now, for a change. If a man should write a book and in it make one of his characters say,

"Here, devil, empty the quoins into the standing galley and the imposing-stone into the hell-box; assemble the comps around the frisket and let them jeff for takes and be quick about it," I should recognize a mistake or two in the phrasing, and would know that the writer was only a printer theoretically, not practically.

I have been a quartz miner in the silver regions—a pretty hard life; I know all the palaver of that business: I know all about discovery claims and the subordinate claims; I know all about lodes, ledges, outcroppings, dips, spurs, angles, shafts, drifts, inclines, levels, tunnels, air-shafts, "horses," clay casings, granite casings; quartz mills and their batteries; arastras, and how to charge them with quicksilver and sulphate of copper; and how to clean them up, and how to reduce the resulting amalgam in the retorts, and how to cast the bullion into pigs; and finally I know how to screen tailings, and also how to hunt for something less robust to do, and find it. I know the argot of the quartz-mining and milling industry familiarly; and so whenever Bret Harte introduces that industry into a story, the first time one of his miners opens his mouth I recognize from his phrasing that Harte got the phrasing by listening—like Shakespeare—I mean the Stratford one—not by experience. No one can talk the quartz dialect correctly without learning it with pick and shovel and drill and fuse.

I have been a surface miner—gold—and I know all its mysteries, and the dialect that belongs with them; and whenever Harte introduces that industry into a story I know by the phrasing of his characters that neither he nor they have ever served that trade.

I have been a "pocket" miner—a sort of gold mining not findable in any but one little spot in the world, so far as I know. I know how, with horn and water, to find the trail of a pocket and trace it step by step and stage by stage up the mountain to its source, and find the compact little nest of yellow metal reposing in its secret home under the ground. I know the language of that trade, that capricious trade, that fascinating buried-treasure trade, and can catch any writer who tries to use it without having learned it by the sweat of his brow and the labor of his hands.

I know several other trades and the argot that goes with them; and whenever a person tries to talk the talk peculiar to any of them without having learned it at its source I can trap him always before he gets far on his road.

And so, as I have already remarked, if I were required to superintend a Bacon-Shakespeare controversy, I would narrow the matter down to a single question—the only one, so far as the previous controversies have informed me, concerning which illustrious experts of unimpeachable competency have testified: *Was the author of Shakespeare's Works a lawyer?*—a lawyer deeply read and of limitless experience? I would put aside the guesses and surmises, and perhapses, and might-have-beens, and could-have-beens, and must-have-beens, and we-are-justified-in-presumings, and the rest of those vague specters and shadows and indefinitenesses, and stand or fall, win or lose, by the verdict rendered by the jury upon that single question. If the verdict was Yes, I should feel quite convinced that the Stratford Shakespeare, the actor, manager, and trader who died so obscure, so forgotten, so destitute of even village consequence, that sixty years afterward no fellow-citizen and friend of his later days remembered to tell anything about him, did not write the Works.

Chapter XIII of *The Shakespeare Problem Restated* bears the heading "Shakespeare as a Lawyer," and comprises some fifty pages of expert testimony, with comments thereon, and I will copy the first nine, as being sufficient all by themselves, as it seems to me, to settle the question which I have conceived to be the master-key to the Shakespeare-Bacon puzzle.

VIII

Shakespeare as a Lawyer[1]

The Plays and Poems of Shakespeare supply ample evidence that their author not only had a very extensive and accurate knowledge of law, but that he was well acquainted with the manners and customs of members of the Inns of Court and with legal life generally.

"While novelists and dramatists are constantly making mistakes as to the laws of marriage, of wills, and inheritance, to Shakespeare's law, lavishly as he expounds it, there can neither be demurrer, nor bill of exceptions, nor writ of error." Such was the testimony borne by one of the most distinguished lawyers of the nineteenth century who was raised to the high office of Lord Chief Justice in 1850, and subsequently became Lord Chancellor. Its weight will, doubtless, be more appreciated by lawyers than by laymen, for only lawyers know how impossible it is for those who have not served an apprenticeship to the law to avoid displaying their ignorance if they venture to employ legal terms and to discuss legal doctrines. "There is nothing so dangerous," wrote Lord Campbell, "as for one not of the craft to tamper

1. From Chapter XIII of *The Shakespeare Problem Restated.* By George G. Greenwood, M.P. John Lane Company, publishers.—M.T.

with our freemasonry." A layman is certain to betray himself by using some expression which a lawyer would never employ. Mr. Sidney Lee himself supplies us with an example of this. He writes (p. 164): "On February 15, 1609, Shakespeare . . . obtained judgment from a jury against Addenbroke for the payment of No. 6, and No. 1, 5s. od. costs." Now a lawyer would never have spoken of obtaining "judgment from a jury," for it is the function of a jury not to deliver judgment (which is the prerogative of the court), but to find a verdict on the facts. The error is, indeed, a venial one, but it is just one of those little things which at once enable a lawyer to know if the writer is a layman or "one of the craft."

But when a layman ventures to plunge deeply into legal subjects, he is naturally apt to make an exhibition of his incompetence. "Let a non-professional man, however acute," writes Lord Campbell again, "presume to talk law, or to draw illustrations from legal science in discussing other subjects, and he will speedily fall into laughable absurdity."

And what does the same high authority say about Shakespeare? He had "a deep technical knowledge of the law," and an easy familiarity with "some of the most abstruse proceedings in English jurisprudence." And again: "Whenever he indulges this propensity he uniformly lays down good law." Of "Henry IV.," Part 2, he says: "If Lord Eldon could be supposed to have written the play, I do not see how he could be chargeable with having forgotten any of his law while writing it." Charles and Mary Cowden Clarke speak of "the marvelous intimacy which he displays with legal terms, his frequent adoption of them in illustration, and his curiously technical knowledge of their form and force." Malone, himself a lawyer, wrote: "His knowledge of legal terms is not merely such as might be acquired by the casual observation of even his all-comprehending mind; it has the appearance of technical skill." Another lawyer and well-known Shakespearian, Richard Grant White, says: "No dramatist of the time, not even Beaumont, who was the younger son of a judge of the Common Pleas, and who after studying in the Inns of Court abandoned law for the drama, used legal phrases with Shakespeare's readiness and exactness. And the significance of this fact is heightened by another, that it is only to the language of the law that he exhibits this inclination. The phrases peculiar to other occupations serve him on rare occasions by way of description, comparison, or illustration, generally when something in the scene suggests them, but legal phrases flow from his pen as part of his vocabulary and parcel of his thought. Take the word 'purchase' for instance, which, in ordinary use, means to acquire by giving value, but applies in law to all legal modes of obtaining property except by inheritance or descent, and in this peculiar sense the word occurs five times in Shakespeare's thirty-four plays, and only in one single instance in the fifty-four plays of Beaumont and Fletcher. It has been suggested that it was in attendance upon the courts in London that he picked up his legal vocabulary. But this supposition not only fails to account for Shakespeare's peculiar freedom and exactness in the use of that phraseology, it does not even place him in the way of learning those terms his use of which is most remarkable, which are not such as he would have heard at ordinary proceedings at *nisi prius,* but such as refer to the tenure or transfer of real property, 'fine and recovery,' 'statutes merchant,' 'purchase,' 'indenture,' 'tenure,' 'double voucher,' 'fee simple,' 'fee farm,' 'remainder,' 'reversion,' 'forfeiture,' etc. This conveyancer's jargon could not have been picked up by hanging round the courts of law in London two hundred and fifty years ago, when suits as to the title of real property were comparatively rare. And besides, Shakespeare uses his law just as freely in his first plays, written in his first London years, as in those produced at a later period. Just as exactly, too; for the correctness and propriety with which these terms are introduced have compelled the admiration of a Chief Justice and a Lord Chancellor."

Senator Davis wrote: "We seem to have something more than a sciolist's temerity of indulgence in the terms of an unfamiliar art. No legal solecisms will be found. The abstrusest elements of the common law are impressed into a disciplined service. Over and over again, where such knowledge is unexampled in writers unlearned in the law, Shakespeare appears in perfect possession of it. In the law of real property, its rules of tenure and descents, its entails, its fines and recoveries, their vouchers and double vouchers, in the procedure of the Courts, the method of bringing writs and arrests, the nature of actions, the rules of pleading, the law of escapes and of contempt of court, in the principles of evidence, both technical and philosophical, in the distinction between the temporal and spiritual tribunals, in the law of attainder and forfeiture, in the requisites of a valid marriage, in the presumption of legitimacy, in the learning of the law of prerogative, in the inalienable character of the Crown, this mastership appears with surprising authority."

To all this testimony (and there is much more which I have not cited) may now be added that of a great lawyer of our own times, *viz.:* Sir James Plaisted Wilde, Q.C. 1855, created a Baron of the Exchequer in 1860, promoted to the post of Judge-Ordinary and Judge of the Courts of Probate and Divorce in 1863, and better known to the world as Lord Penzance, to which dignity he was raised in 1869. Lord Penzance, as all lawyers know, and as the late Mr. Inderwick, K.C., has testified, was one of the first legal authorities of his day, famous for his "remarkable grasp of legal principles," and "endowed by nature with a remarkable facility for marshaling facts, and for a clear expression of his views."

Lord Penzance speaks of Shakespeare's "perfect familiarity with not only the principles, axioms, and maxims, but the technicalities of English law, a knowledge so perfect and intimate that he was never incorrect and never at fault. . . . The mode in which this knowledge was pressed into service on all occasions to express his meaning and illustrate his thoughts was quite unexampled. He seems to have had a special pleasure in his complete and ready mastership of it in all its branches. As manifested in the plays, this legal knowledge and learning had therefore a special character which places it on a wholly different footing from the rest of the multifarious knowledge which is exhibited in page after page of the plays. At every turn and point at which the author required a metaphor, simile, or illustration, his mind ever turned *first* to the law. He seems almost to have *thought* in legal phrases, the commonest of legal expressions were ever at the end of his pen in description or illustration. That he should have descanted in lawyer language when he had a forensic subject in hand, such as Shylock's bond, was to be expected, but the knowledge of law in 'Shakespeare' was exhibited in a far different manner: it protruded itself on all occasions, appropriate or inappropriate, and mingled itself with strains of thought widely divergent from forensic subjects." Again: "To acquire a perfect familiarity with legal principles, and an accurate and ready use of the technical terms and phrases not only of the conveyancer's office, but of the pleader's chambers and the Courts at Westminster, nothing short of employment in some career involving constant contact with legal questions and general legal work would be requisite. But a continuous employment involves the element of time, and time was just what the manager of two theaters had not at his disposal. In what portion of Shakespeare's *(i.e.,* Shakspere's) career would it be possible to point out that time could be found for the interposition of a legal employment in the chambers or offices of practising lawyers?"

Stratfordians, as is well known, casting about for some possible explanation of Shakespeare's extraordinary knowledge of law, have made the suggestion that Shakespeare might, conceivably, have been a clerk in an attorney's office before he came to London. Mr. Collier wrote to Lord Campbell to ask his opinion as to the probability of this being true. His answer was as follows: "You require us to believe implicitly a fact, of which, if true, positive and irrefragable evidence in his own handwriting might have been forthcoming to establish it. Not having been actually enrolled as an attorney, neither the records of the local court at Stratford nor of the superior Courts at Westminster would present his name as being concerned in any suit as an attorney, but it might reasonably have been expected that there would be deeds or wills witnessed by him still extant, and after a very diligent search none such can be discovered."

Upon this Lord Penzance comments: "It cannot be doubted that Lord Campbell was right in this. No young man could have been at work in an attorney's office without being called upon continually to act as a witness, and in many other ways leaving traces of his work and name." There is not a single fact or incident in all that is known of Shakespeare, even by rumor or tradition, which supports this notion of a clerkship. And after much argument and surmise which has been indulged in on this subject, we may, I think, safely put the notion on one side, for no less an authority than Mr. Grant White says finally that the idea of his having been clerk to an attorney has been "blown to pieces."

It is altogether characteristic of Mr. Churton Collins that he, nevertheless, adopts this exploded myth. "That Shakespeare was in early life employed as a clerk in an attorney's office may be correct. At Stratford there was by royal charter a Court of Record sitting every fortnight, with six attorneys, besides the town clerk, belonging to it, and it is certainly not straining probability to suppose that the young Shakespeare may have had employment in one of them. There is, it is true, no tradition to this effect, but such traditions as we have about Shakespeare's occupation between the time of leaving school and going to London are so loose and baseless that no confidence can be placed in them. It is, to say the least, more probable that he was in an attorney's office than that he was a butcher killing calves 'in a high style,' and making speeches over them."

This is a charming specimen of Stratfordian argument. There is, as we have seen, a very old tradition that Shakespeare was a butcher's apprentice. John Dowdall, who made a tour in Warwickshire in 1693, testifies to it as coming from the old clerk who showed him over the church, and it is unhesitatingly accepted as true by Mr. Halliwell-Phillipps. (Vol. I, p. 11, and Vol. II, pp. 71, 72.) Mr. Sidney Lee sees nothing improbable in it, and it is supported by Aubrey, who must have written his account some time before 1680, when his manuscript was completed. Of the attorney's clerk hypothesis, on the other hand, there is not the faintest vestige of a tradition. It has been evolved out of the fertile imaginations of embarrassed Stratfordians, seeking for some explanation of the Stratford rustic's marvelous acquaintance with law and legal terms and legal life. But Mr. Churton Collins has not the least hesitation in throwing over the tradition which has the warrant of antiquity and setting up in its stead this ridiculous invention, for which not only is there no shred of positive evidence, but which, as Lord Campbell and Lord Penzance point out, is really put out of court by the negative evidence, since "no young man could have been at work in an attorney's office without being called upon continually to act as a witness, and in many other ways leaving traces of his work and name." And as Mr. Edwards further points out, since the day when Lord Campbell's book was published (between forty and fifty years ago), "every old deed or will, to say nothing of other legal papers, dated during the period of William Shakespeare's youth, has been scrutinized over half a dozen shires, and not one signature of the young man has been found."

Moreover, if Shakespeare had served as clerk in an attorney's office it is clear that he must have so served for a considerable period in order to have gained (if, indeed, it is credible that he could have so gained) his remarkable knowledge of law. Can we then for a moment believe that, if this had been so, tradition would have been absolutely silent on the matter? That Dowdall's old clerk, over eighty years of age, should have never heard of it (though he was sure enough about the butcher's apprentice), and that all the other ancient witnesses should be in similar ignorance!

But such are the methods of Stratfordian controversy. Tradition is to be scouted when it is found inconvenient, but cited as irrefragable truth when it suits the case. Shakespeare of Stratford was the author of the Plays and Poems, but the author of the Plays and Poems could not have been a butcher's apprentice. Away, therefore, with tradition. But the author of the Plays and Poems *must* have had a very large and a very accurate knowledge of the law. Therefore, Shakespeare of Stratford must have been an attorney's clerk! The method is simplicity itself. By similar reasoning Shakespeare has been made a country schoolmaster, a soldier, a physician, a printer, and a good many other things besides, according to the inclination and the exigencies of the commentator. It would not be in the least surprising to find that he was studying Latin as a schoolmaster and law in an attorney's office at the same time.

However, we must do Mr. Collins the justice of saying that he has fully recognized, what is indeed tolerably obvious, that Shakespeare must have had a sound legal training. "It may, of course, be urged," he writes, "that Shakespeare's knowledge of medicine, and particularly that branch of it which related to morbid psychology, is equally remarkable, and that no one has ever contended that he was a physician. (Here Mr. Collins is wrong; that contention also has been put forward.) It may be urged that his acquaintance with the technicalities of other crafts and callings, notably of marine and military affairs, was also extraordinary, and yet no one has suspected him of being a sailor or a soldier. (Wrong again. Why, even Messrs. Garnett and Gosse "suspect" that he was a soldier!) This may be conceded, but the concession hardly furnishes an analogy. To these and all other subjects he recurs occasionally, and in season, but with reminiscences of the law his memory, as is abundantly clear, was simply saturated. In season and out of season now in manifest, now in recondite application, he presses it into the service of expression and illustration. At least a third of his myriad metaphors are derived from it. It would indeed be difficult to find a single act in any of his dramas, nay, in some of them, a single scene, the diction and imagery of which are not colored by it. Much of his law may have been acquired from three books easily accessible to him—namely, Tottell's *Precedents* (1572), Pulton's *Statutes* (1578), and Fraunce's *Lawier's Logike* (1588), works with which he certainly seems to have been familiar; but much of it could only have come from one who had an intimate acquaintance with legal proceedings. We quite agree with Mr. Castle that Shakespeare's legal knowledge is not what could have been picked up in an attorney's office, but could only have been learned by an actual attendance at the Courts, at a Pleader's Chambers, and on circuit, or by associating intimately with members of the Bench and Bar."

This is excellent. But what is Mr. Collins's explanation? "Perhaps the simplest solution of the problem is to accept the hypothesis that in early life he was in an attorney's office (!), that he there contracted a love for the law which never left him, that as a young man in London he continued to study or dabble in it for his amusement, to stroll in leisure hours into the Courts, and to frequent the society of lawyers. On no other supposition is it possible to explain the attraction which the law evidently had for him, and his minute and undeviating accuracy in a subject where no layman who has indulged in such copious and ostentatious display of legal technicalities has ever yet succeeded in keeping himself from tripping."

A lame conclusion. "No other supposition" indeed! Yes, there is another, and a very obvious supposition—namely, that Shakespeare was himself a lawyer, well versed in his trade, versed in all the ways of the courts, and living in close intimacy with judges and members of the Inns of Court.

One is, of course, thankful that Mr. Collins has appreciated the fact that Shakespeare must have had a sound legal training, but I may be forgiven if I do not attach quite so much importance to his pronouncements on this branch of the subject as to those of Malone, Lord Campbell, Judge Holmes, Mr. Castle, K.C., Lord Penzance, Mr. Grant White, and other lawyers, who have expressed their opinion on the matter of Shakespeare's legal acquirements. . . .

Here it may, perhaps, be worth while to quote again from Lord Penzance's book as to the suggestion that Shakespeare had somehow or other managed "to acquire a perfect familiarity with legal principles, and an accurate and ready use of the technical terms and phrases, not only of the conveyancer's office, but of the pleader's chambers and the Courts at Westminster." This, as Lord Penzance points out, "would require nothing short of employment in some career involving *constant contact* with legal questions and general legal work." But "in what portion of Shakespeare's career would it be possible to point out that time could be found for the interposition of a legal employment in the chambers or offices of practising lawyers? . . . It is beyond doubt that at an early period he was called upon to abandon his attendance at school and assist his father, and was soon after, at the age of sixteen, bound apprentice to a trade. While under the obligation of this bond he could not have pursued any other employment. Then he leaves Stratford and comes to London. He has to provide himself with the means of a livelihood, and this he did in some capacity at the theater. No one doubts that. The holding of horses is scouted by many, and perhaps with justice, as being unlikely and certainly unproved; but whatever the nature of his employment was at the theater, there is hardly room for the belief that it could have been other than continuous, for his progress there was so rapid. Ere long he had been taken into the company as an actor, and was soon spoken of as a 'Johannes Factotum.' His rapid accumulation of wealth speaks volumes for the constancy and activity of his services. One fails to see when there could be a break in the current of his life at this period of it, giving room or opportunity for legal or indeed any other employment. 'In 1589,' says Knight, 'we have undeniable evidence that he had not only a casual engagement, was not only a salaried servant, as many players were, but was a shareholder in the company of the Queen's players with other shareholders below him on the list.' This (1589) would be within two years after his arrival in London, which is placed by White and Halliwell-Phillipps about the year 1587. The difficulty in supposing that, starting with a state of ignorance in 1587, when he is supposed to have come to London, he was induced to enter upon a course of most extended study and mental culture, is almost insuperable. Still it was physically possible, provided always that he could have had access to the needful books. But this legal training seems to me to stand on a different footing. It is not only unaccountable and incredible, but it is actually negatived by the known facts of his career." Lord Penzance then refers to the fact that "by 1592 (according to the best authority, Mr. Grant White) several of the plays had been written. 'The Comedy of Errors' in 1589, 'Love's Labour's Lost' in 1589, 'Two Gentlemen of Verona' in 1589 or 1590," and so forth, and then asks, "with this catalogue of dramatic work on hand . . . was it possible that he could have taken a leading part in the management and conduct of two theaters, and if Mr. Phillipps is to be relied upon, taken his share in the performances of the provincial tours of his company—and at the same time devoted himself to the study of the law in all its branches so efficiently as to make himself complete master of its principles and practice, and saturate his mind with all its most technical terms?"

I have cited this passage from Lord Penzance's book, because it lay before me, and I had already quoted from it on the matter of Shakespeare's legal knowledge; but other writers have still better set forth the insuperable difficulties, as they seem to me, which beset the idea that Shakespeare might have found time in some unknown period of early life, amid multifarious other occupations, for the study of classics, literature, and law, to say nothing of languages and a few other matters. Lord Penzance further asks his readers: "Did you ever meet with or hear of an instance in which a young man in this country gave himself up to legal studies and engaged in legal employments, which is the only way of becoming familiar with the technicalities of practice, unless with the view of practising in that profession? I do not believe that it would be easy, or indeed possible, to produce an instance in which the law has been seriously studied in all its branches, except as a qualification for practice in the legal profession."

This testimony is so strong, so direct, so authoritative; and so uncheapened, unwatered by guesses, and surmises, and maybe-so's, and might-have-beens, and could-have-beens, and must-have-beens, and the rest of that ton of plaster of Paris out of which the biographers have built the colossal brontosaur which goes by the Stratford actor's name, that it quite convinces me that the man who wrote Shakespeare's Works knew all about law and lawyers. Also, that that man could not have been the Stratford Shakespeare—and *wasn't.*

Who did write these Works, then?

I wish I knew.

IX

Did Francis Bacon write Shakespeare's Works?

Nobody knows.

We cannot say we *know* a thing when that thing has not been proved. *Know* is too strong a word to use when the evidence is not final and absolutely conclusive. We can infer, if we want to, like those slaves. . . . No, I will not write that word, it is not kind, it is not courteous. The upholders of the Stratford-Shakespeare superstition call *us* the hardest names they can think of, and they keep doing it all the time; very well, if they like to descend to that level, let them do it, but I will not so undignify myself as to follow them. I cannot call them harsh names; the most I can do is to indicate them by terms reflecting my disapproval; and this without malice, without venom.

To resume. What I was about to say was, those thugs have built their entire superstition upon *inferences,* not upon known and established facts. It is a weak method, and poor, and I am glad to be able to say our side never resorts to it while there is anything else to resort to.

But when we must, we must; and we have now arrived at a place of that sort. . . . Since the Stratford Shakespeare couldn't have written the Works, we infer that somebody did. Who was it, then? This requires some more inferring.

Ordinarily when an unsigned poem sweeps across the continent like a tidal wave whose roar and boom and thunder are made up of admiration, delight, and applause, a dozen obscure people rise up and claim the authorship. Why a dozen, instead of only one or two? One reason is, because there are a dozen that are recognizably competent to do that poem. Do you remember "Beautiful Snow"? Do you remember "Rock Me to Sleep, Mother, Rock Me to Sleep"? Do you remember "Backward, turn backward, O Time, in thy flight! Make me a child again just for to-night"? I remember them very well. Their authorship was claimed by most of the grown-up people who were alive at the time, and every claimant had one plausible argument in his favor, at least—to wit, he could have done the authoring; he was competent.

Have the Works been claimed by a dozen? They haven't. There was good reason. The world knows there was but one man on the planet at the time who was competent—not a dozen, and not two. A long time ago the dwellers in a far country used now and then to find a procession of prodigious footprints stretching across the plain—footprints that were three miles apart, each footprint a third of a mile long and a furlong deep, and with forests and villages mashed to mush in it. Was there any doubt as to who made that mighty trail? Were there a dozen claimants? Were there two? No—the people knew who it was that had been along there: there was only one Hercules.

There has been only one Shakespeare. There couldn't be two; certainly there couldn't be two at the same time. It takes ages to bring forth a Shakespeare, and some more ages to match him. This one was not matched before his time; nor during his time; and hasn't been matched since. The prospect of matching him in our time is not bright.

The Baconians claim that the Stratford Shakespeare was not qualified to write the Works, and that Francis Bacon was. They claim that Bacon possessed the stupendous equipment—both natural and acquired—for the miracle; and that no other Englishman of his day possessed the like; or, indeed, anything closely approaching it.

Macaulay, in his Essay, has much to say about the splendor and horizonless magnitude of that equipment. Also, he has synopsized Bacon's history—a thing which cannot be done for the Stratford Shakespeare, for he hasn't any history to synopsize. Bacon's history is open to the world, from his boyhood to his death in old age—a history consisting of known facts, displayed in minute and multitudinous detail; *facts,* not guesses and conjectures and might-have-beens.

Whereby it appears that he was born of a race of statesmen, and had a Lord Chancellor for his father, and a mother who was "distinguished both as a linguist and a theologian: she corresponded in Greek with Bishop Jewell, and translated his *Apologia* from the Latin so correctly that neither he nor Archbishop Parker could suggest a single alteration." It is the atmosphere we are reared in that determines how our inclinations and aspirations shall tend. The atmosphere furnished by the parents to the son in this present case was an atmosphere saturated with learning; with thinkings and ponderings upon deep subjects; and with polite culture. It had its natural effect. Shakespeare of Stratford was reared in a house which had no use for books, since its owners, his parents, were without education. This may have had an effect upon the son, but we do not know, because we have no history of him of an informing sort. There were but few books anywhere, in that day, and only the well-to-do and highly educated possessed them, they being almost confined to the dead languages. "All the valuable books then extant in all the vernacular dialects of Europe would hardly have filled a single shelf"—imagine it! The few existing books were in the Latin tongue mainly. "A person who was ignorant of it was shut out from all acquaintance—not merely with Cicero and Virgil, but with the most interesting memoirs, state papers, and pamphlets of his own time"—a literature necessary to the Stratford lad, for his fictitious reputation's sake, since the writer of his Works would begin to use it wholesale and in a most masterly way before the lad was hardly more than out of his teens and into his twenties.

At fifteen Bacon was sent to the university, and he spent three years there. Thence he went to Paris in the train of the English Ambassador, and there he mingled daily with the wise, the cultured, the great, and the aristocracy of fashion, during another three years. A total of six years spent at the sources of knowledge; knowledge both of books and of men. The three spent at the university were coeval with the second and last three spent by the little Stratford lad at Stratford school supposedly, and perhapsedly, and maybe, and by inference—with nothing to infer from. The second three of the Baconian six were "presumably" spent by the Stratford lad as apprentice to a butcher. That is, the thugs presume it—on no evidence of any kind. Which is their way, when they want a historical fact. Fact and presumption are, for business purposes, all the same to them. They know the difference, but they also know how to blink it. They know, too, that while in history-building a fact is better than a presumption, it doesn't take a presumption long to bloom into a fact when *they* have the handling of it. They know by old experience that when they get hold of a presumption-tadpole he is not going to *stay* tadpole in their history-tank; no, they know how to develop him into the giant four-legged bullfrog of *fact,* and make him sit up on his hams, and puff out his chin, and look important and insolent and come-to-stay; and assert his genuine simon-pure authenticity with a thundering bellow that will convince everybody because it is so loud. The thug is aware that loudness convinces sixty persons where reasoning convinces but one. I wouldn't be a thug, not even if—but never mind about that, it has nothing to do with the argument, and it is not noble in spirit besides. If I am better than a thug, is the merit mine? No, it is His. Then to Him be the praise. That is the right spirit.

They "presume" the lad severed his "presumed" connection with the Stratford school to become apprentice to a butcher. They also "presume" that the butcher was his father. They don't know. There is no written record of it, nor any other actual evidence. If it would have helped their case any, they would have apprenticed him to thirty butchers, to fifty butchers, to a wilderness of butchers—all by their patented method "presumption." If it will help their case they will do it yet; and if it will further help it, they will "presume" that all those butchers were his father. And the week after, they will *say* it. Why, it is just like being the past tense of the compound reflexive adverbial incandescent hypodermic irregular accusative Noun of Multitude; which is father to the expression which the grammarians call Verb. It is like a whole ancestry, with only one posterity.

To resume. Next, the young Bacon took up the study of law, and mastered that abstruse science. From that day to the end of his life he was daily in close contact with lawyers and judges; not as a casual onlooker in intervals between holding horses in front of a theater, but as a practising lawyer—a great and successful one, a renowned one, a Launcelot of the bar, the most formidable lance in the high brotherhood of the legal Table Round; he lived in the law's atmosphere thenceforth, all his years, and by sheer ability forced his way up its difficult steeps to its supremest summit, the Lord-Chancellorship, leaving behind him no fellow-craftsman qualified to challenge his divine right to that majestic place.

When we read the praises bestowed by Lord Penzance and the other illustrious experts upon the legal condition and legal aptnesses, brilliances, profundities, and felicities so prodigally displayed in the Plays, and try to fit them to the historyless Stratford stage-manager, they sound wild, strange, incredible, ludicrous; but when we put them in the mouth of Bacon they do not sound strange, they seem in their natural and rightful place, they seem at home there. Please turn back and read them again. Attributed to Shakespeare of Stratford they are meaningless, they are inebriate extravagancies—intemperate admirations of the dark side of the moon, so to speak; attributed to Bacon, they are admirations of the golden glories of the moon's front side, the moon at the full—and not intemperate, not overwrought, but sane and right, and justified. "At every turn and point at which the author required a metaphor, simile, or illustration, his mind ever turned *first* to the law; he seems almost to have *thought* in legal phrases; the commonest legal phrases, the commonest of legal expressions, were ever at the end of his pen." That could happen to no one but a person whose *trade* was the law; it could not happen to a dabbler in it. Veteran mariners fill their conversation with sailor-phrases and draw all their similes from the ship and the sea and the storm, but no mere *passenger* ever does it, be he of Stratford or elsewhere; or could do it with anything resembling accuracy, if he were hardy enough to try. Please read again what Lord Campbell and the other great authorities have said about Bacon when they thought they were saying it about Shakespeare of Stratford.

X

The Rest of the Equipment

The author of the Plays was equipped, beyond every other man of his time, with wisdom, erudition, imagination, capaciousness of mind, grace, and majesty of expression. Every one has said it, no one doubts it. Also, he had humor, humor in rich abundance, and always wanting to break out. We have no evidence of any kind that Shakespeare of Stratford possessed any of these gifts or any of these acquirements. The only lines he ever wrote, so far as we know, are substantially barren of them—barren of all of them.

Good friend for Iesus sake forbeare
To digg the dust encloased heare:
Blest be ye man yt spares thes stones
And curst be he yt moves my bones.

Ben Jonson says of Bacon, as orator:

His language, *where he could spare and pass by a jest,* was nobly censorious. No man ever spoke more neatly, more pressly, more weightily, or suffered less emptiness, less idleness, in what he uttered. No member of his speech but consisted of his (its) own graces. . . . The fear of every man that heard him was lest he should make an end.

From Macaulay:

He continued to distinguish himself in Parliament, particularly by his exertions in favor of one excellent measure on which the King's heart was set —the union of England and Scotland. It was not difficult for such an intellect to discover many irresistible arguments in favor of such a scheme. He conducted the great case of the *Post Nati* in the Exchequer Chamber; and the decision of the judges—a decision the legality of which may be questioned, but the beneficial effect of which must be acknowledged—was in a great measure attributed to his dexterous management.

Again:

While actively engaged in the House of Commons and in the courts of law, he still found leisure for letters and philosophy. The noble treatise on the *Advancement of Learning,* which at a later period was expanded into the *De Augmentis,* appeared in 1605.

The *Wisdom of the Ancients,* a work which, if it had proceeded from any other writer, would have been considered as a masterpiece of wit and learning, was printed in 1609.

In the mean time the *Novum Organum* was slowly proceeding. Several distinguished men of learning had been permitted to see portions of that extraordinary book, and they spoke with the greatest admiration of his genius.

Even Sir Thomas Bodley, after perusing the *Cogitata et Visa,* one of the most precious of those scattered leaves out of which the great oracular volume was afterward made up, acknowledged that "in all proposals and plots in that book, Bacon showed himself a master workman"; and that "it could not be gainsaid but all the treatise over did abound with choice conceits of the present state of learning, and with worthy contemplations of the means to procure it."

In 1612 a new edition of the *Essays* appeared, with additions surpassing the original collection both in bulk and quality.

Nor did these pursuits distract Bacon's attention from a work the most arduous, the most glorious, and the most useful that even his mighty powers could have achieved, "the reducing and recompiling," to use his own phrase, "of the laws of England."

To serve the exacting and laborious offices of Attorney-General and Solicitor-General would have satisfied the appetite of any other man for hard work, but Bacon had to add the vast literary industries just described, to satisfy his. He was a born worker.

> The service which he rendered to letters during the last five years of his life, amid ten thousand distractions and vexations, increase the regret with which we think on the many years which he had wasted, to use the words of Sir Thomas Bodley, "on such study as was not worthy such a student."
>
> He commenced a digest of the laws of England, a History of England under the Princes of the House of Tudor, a body of National History, a Philosophical Romance. He made extensive and valuable additions to his Essays. He published the inestimable *Treatise De Augmentis Scientiarum.*

Did these labors of Hercules fill up his time to his contentment, and quiet his appetite for work? Not entirely:

> The trifles with which he amused himself in hours of pain and languor bore the mark of his mind. *The best jest-book in the world* is that which he dictated from memory, without referring to any book, on a day on which illness had rendered him incapable of serious study.

Here are some scattered remarks (from Macaulay) which throw light upon Bacon, and seem to indicate—and maybe demonstrate—that he was competent to write the Plays and Poems:

> With great minuteness of observation he had an amplitude of comprehension such as has never yet been vouchsafed to any other human being.

> The *Essays* contain abundant proofs that no nice feature of character, no peculiarity in the ordering of a house, a garden, or a court-masque, could escape the notice of one whose mind was capable of taking in the whole world of knowledge.

> His understanding resembled the tent which the fairy Paribanou gave to Prince Ahmed: fold it, and it seemed a toy for the hand of a lady; spread it, and the armies of powerful Sultans might repose beneath its shade.

The knowledge in which Bacon excelled all men was a knowledge of the mutual relations of all departments of knowledge.

In a letter written when he was only thirty-one, to his uncle, Lord Burleigh, he said, "I have taken all knowledge to be my province."

Though Bacon did not arm his philosophy with the weapons of logic, he adorned her profusely with all the richest decorations of rhetoric.

The practical faculty was powerful in Bacon; but not, like his wit, so powerful as occasionally to usurp the place of his reason and to tyrannize over the whole man.

There are too many places in the Plays where this happens. Poor old dying John of Gaunt volleying second-rate puns at his own name, is a pathetic instance of it. "We may assume" that it is Bacon's fault, but the Stratford Shakespeare has to bear the blame.

No imagination was ever at once so strong and so thoroughly subjugated. It stopped at the first check from good sense.

In truth, much of Bacon's life was passed in a visionary world—amid things as strange as any that are described in the *Arabian Tales* . . . amid buildings more sumptuous than the palace of Aladdin, fountains more wonderful than the golden water of Parizade, conveyances more rapid than the hippogryph of Ruggiero, arms more formidable than the lance of Astolfo, remedies more efficacious than the balsam of Fierabras. Yet in his magnificent day-dreams there was nothing wild—nothing but what sober reason sanctioned.

Bacon's greatest performance is the first book of the *Novum Organum*. . . . Every part of it blazes with wit, but with wit which is employed only to illustrate and decorate truth. No book ever made so great a revolution in the mode of thinking, overthrew so many prejudices, introduced so many new opinions.

But what we most admire is the vast capacity of that intellect which, without effort, takes in at once all the domains of science—all the past, the present and the future, all the errors of two thousand years, all the encouraging signs of the passing times, all the bright hopes of the coming age.

He had a wonderful talent for packing thought close and rendering it portable.

His eloquence would alone have entitled him to a high rank in literature.

It is evident that he had each and every one of the mental gifts and each and every one of the acquirements that are so prodigally displayed in the Plays and Poems, and in much higher and richer degree than any other man of his time or of any previous time. He was a genius without a mate, a prodigy not matable. There was only one of him; the planet could not produce two of him at one birth, nor in one age. He could have written anything that is in the Plays and Poems. He could have written this:

The cloud-cap'd towers, the gorgeous palaces,
The solemn temples, the great globe itself,
Yea, all which it inherit, shall dissolve,
And, like an insubstantial pageant faded,
Leave not a rack behind. We are such stuff
As dreams are made on, and our little life
Is rounded with a sleep.

Also, he could have written this, but he refrained:

Good friend for Iesus sake forbeare
To digg the dust encloased heare:
Blest be ye man yt spares thes stones
And curst be he yt moves my bones.

When a person reads the noble verses about the cloud-cap'd towers, he ought not to follow it immediately with Good friend for Iesus sake forbeare, because he will find the transition from great poetry to poor prose too violent for comfort. It will give him a shock. You never notice how commonplace and unpoetic gravel is until you bite into a layer of it in a pie.

XI

Am I trying to convince anybody that Shakespeare did not write Shakespeare's Works? Ah, now, what do you take me for? Would I be so soft as that, after having known the human race familiarly for nearly seventy-four years? It would grieve me to know that any one could think so injuriously of me, so uncomplimentarily, so unadmiringly of me. No, no, I am aware that when even the brightest mind in our world has been trained up from childhood in a superstition of any kind, it will never be possible for that mind, in its maturity, to examine sincerely, dispassionately, and conscientiously any evidence or any circumstance which shall seem to cast a doubt upon the validity of that superstition. I doubt if I could do it myself. We always get at second hand our notions about systems of government; and high tariff and low tariff; and prohibition and anti-prohibition; and the holiness of peace and the glories of war; and codes of honor and codes of morals; and approval of the duel and disapproval of it; and our beliefs concerning the nature of cats; and our ideas as to whether the murder of helpless wild animals is base or is heroic; and our preferences in the matter of religious and political parties; and our acceptance or rejection of the Shakespeares and the Arthur Ortons and the Mrs. Eddys. We get them all at second hand, we reason none of them out for ourselves. It is the way we are made. It is the way we are all made, and we can't help it, we can't change it. And whenever we have been furnished a fetish, and have been taught to believe in it, and love it and worship it, and refrain from examining it, there is no evidence, howsoever clear and strong, that can persuade us to withdraw from it our loyalty and our devotion. In morals, conduct, and beliefs we take the color of our environment and associations, and it is a color that can safely be warranted to wash. Whenever we have been furnished with a tar baby ostensibly stuffed with jewels, and warned that it will be dishonorable and irreverent to disembowel it and test the jewels, we keep our sacrilegious hands off it. We submit, not reluctantly, but rather gladly, for we are privately afraid we should find, upon examination, that the jewels are of the sort that are manufactured at North Adams, Mass.

I haven't any idea that Shakespeare will have to vacate his pedestal this side of the year 2209. Disbelief in him cannot come swiftly, disbelief in a healthy and deeply-loved tar baby has never been known to disintegrate swiftly; it is a very slow process. It took several thousand years to convince our fine race—including every splendid intellect in it—that there is no such thing as a witch; it has taken several thousand years to convince that same fine race—including every splendid intellect in it—that there is no such person as Satan; it has taken several centuries to remove perdition from the Protestant Church's program of post-mortem entertainments; it has taken a weary long time to persuade American Presbyterians to give up infant damnation and try to bear it the best they can; and it looks as if their Scotch brethren will still be burning babies in the everlasting fires when Shakespeare comes down from his perch.

We are The Reasoning Race. We can't prove it by the above examples, and we can't prove it by the miraculous "histories" built by those Stratfordolaters out of a hatful of rags and a barrel of sawdust, but there is a plenty of other things we can prove it by, if I could think of them. We are The Reasoning Race, and when we find a vague file of chipmunk-tracks stringing through the dust of Stratford village, we know by our reasoning powers that Hercules has been along there. I feel that our fetish is safe for three centuries yet. The bust, too—there in the Stratford Church. The precious bust, the priceless bust, the calm bust, the serene bust, the emotionless bust, with the dandy mustache, and the putty face, unseamed of care—that face which has looked passionlessly down upon the awed pilgrim for a hundred and fifty years and will still look down upon the awed pilgrim three hundred more, with the deep, deep, deep, subtle, subtle, subtle, expression of a bladder.

XII

Irreverence

One of the most trying defects which I find in these—these—what shall I call them? for I will not apply injurious epithets to them, the way they do to us, such violations of courtesy being repugnant to my nature and my dignity. The farthest I can go in that direction is to call them by names of limited reverence—names merely descriptive, never unkind, never offensive, never tainted by harsh feeling. If *they* would do like this, they would feel better in their hearts. Very well, then—to proceed. One of the most trying defects which I find in these Stratfordolaters, these Shakesperiods, these thugs, these bangalores, these troglodytes, these herumfrodites, these blatherskites, these buccaneers, these bandoleers, is their spirit of irreverence. It is detectable in every utterance of theirs when they are talking about us. I am thankful that in me there is nothing of that spirit. When a thing is sacred to me it is impossible for me to be irreverent toward it. I cannot call to mind a single instance where I have ever been irreverent, except toward the things which were sacred to other people. Am I in the right? I think so. But I ask no one to take my unsupported word; no, look at the dictionary; let the dictionary decide. Here is the definition:

> *Irreverence.* The quality or condition of irreverence toward God and sacred things.

What does the Hindu say? He says it is correct. He says irreverence is lack of respect for Vishnu, and Brahma, and Chrishna, and his other gods, and for his sacred cattle, and for his temples and the things within them. He indorses the definition, you see; and there are 300,000,000 Hindus or their equivalents back of him.

The dictionary had the acute idea that by using the capital G it could restrict irreverence to lack of reverence for *our* Deity and our sacred things, but that ingenious and rather sly idea miscarried: for by the simple process of spelling *his* deities with capitals the Hindu confiscates the definition and restricts it to his own sects, thus making it clearly compulsory upon us to revere *his* gods and *his* sacred things, and nobody's else. We can't say a word, for he has our own dictionary at his back, and its decision is final.

This law, reduced to its simplest terms, is this: 1. Whatever is sacred to the Christian must be held in reverence by everybody else; 2. whatever is sacred to the Hindu must be held in reverence by everybody else; 3. therefore, by consequence, logically, and indisputably, whatever is sacred to *me* must be held in reverence by everybody else.

Now then, what aggravates me is that these troglodytes and muscovites and bandoleers and buccaneers are *also* trying to crowd in and share the benefit of the law, and compel everybody to revere their Shakespeare and hold him sacred. We can't have that: there's enough of us already. If you go on widening and spreading and inflating the privilege, it will presently come to be conceded that each man's sacred things are the *only* ones, and the rest of the human race will have to be humbly reverent toward them or suffer for it. That can surely happen, and when it happens, the word Irreverence will be regarded as the most meaningless, and foolish, and self-conceited, and insolent, and impudent, and dictatorial word in the language. And people will say, "Whose business is it what gods I worship and what things hold sacred? Who has the right to dictate to my conscience, and where did he get that right?"

We cannot afford to let that calamity come upon us. We must save the word from this destruction. There is but one way to do it, and that is to stop the spread of the privilege and strictly confine it to its present limits—that is, to all the Christian sects, to all the Hindu sects, and me. We do not need any more, the stock is watered enough, just as it is.

It would be better if the privilege were limited to me alone. I think so because I am the only sect that knows how to employ it gently, kindly, charitably, dispassionately. The other sects lack the quality of self-restraint. The Catholic Church says the most irreverent things about matters which are sacred to the Protestants, and the Protestant Church retorts in kind about the confessional and other matters which Catholics hold sacred; then both of these irreverencers turn upon Thomas Paine and charge *him* with irreverence. This is all unfortunate, because it makes it difficult for students equipped with only a low grade of mentality to find out what Irreverence really *is*.

It will surely be much better all around if the privilege of regulating the irreverent and keeping them in order shall eventually be withdrawn from all the sects but me. Then there will be no more quarreling, no more bandying of disrespectful epithets, no more heartburnings.

There will then be nothing sacred involved in this Bacon-Shakespeare controversy except what is sacred to me. That will simplify the whole matter, and trouble will cease. There will be irreverence no longer, because I will not allow it. The first time those criminals charge me with irreverence for calling their Stratford myth an Arthur-Orton-Mary-Baker-Thompson-Eddy-Louis-the-Seventeenth-Veiled-Prophet-of-Khorassan will be the last. Taught by the methods found effective in extinguishing earlier offenders by the Inquisition, of holy memory, I shall know how to quiet them.

XIII

Isn't it odd, when you think of it, that you may list all the celebrated Englishmen, Irishmen, and Scotchmen of modern times, clear back to the first Tudors—a list containing five hundred names, shall we say?—and you can go to the histories, biographies, and cyclopedias and learn the particulars of the lives of every one of them. Every one of them except one—the most famous, the most renowned—by far the most illustrious of them all—Shakespeare! You can get the details of the lives of all the celebrated ecclesiastics in the list; all the celebrated tragedians, comedians, singers, dancers, orators, judges, lawyers, poets, dramatists, historians, biographers, editors, inventors, reformers, statesmen, generals, admirals, discoverers, prize-fighters, murderers, pirates, conspirators, horse-jockeys, bunco-steerers, misers, swindlers, explorers, adventurers by land and sea, bankers, financiers, astronomers, naturalists, claimants, impostors, chemists, biologists, geologists, philologists, college presidents and professors, architects, engineers, painters, sculptors, politicians, agitators, rebels, revolutionists, patriots, demagogues, clowns, cooks, freaks, philosophers, burglars, highwaymen, journalists, physicians, surgeons—you can get the life-histories of all of them but *one.* Just *one*—the most extraordinary and the most celebrated of them all—Shakespeare!

You may add to the list the thousand celebrated persons furnished by the rest of Christendom in the past four centuries, and you can find out the life-histories of all those people, too. You will then have listed fifteen hundred celebrities, and you can trace the authentic life-histories of the whole of them. Save one—far and away the most colossal prodigy of the entire accumulation—Shakespeare! About him you can find out *nothing.* Nothing of even the slightest importance. Nothing worth the trouble of stowing away in your memory. Nothing that even remotely indicates that he was ever anything more than a distinctly commonplace person—a manager, an actor of inferior grade, a small trader in a small village that did not regard him as a person of any consequence, and had forgotten all about him before he was fairly cold in his grave. We can go to the records and find out the life-history of every renowned *race-horse* of modern times—but not Shakespeare's! There are many reasons why, and they have been furnished in cart-loads (of guess and conjecture) by those troglodytes; but there is one that is worth all the rest of the reasons put together, and is abundantly sufficient all by itself—*he hadn't any history to record.* There is no way of getting around that deadly fact. And no sane way has yet been discovered of getting around its formidable significance.

Its quite plain significance—to any but those thugs (I do not use the term unkindly) is, that Shakespeare had no prominence while he lived, and none until he had been dead two or three generations. The Plays enjoyed high fame from the beginning; and if he wrote them it seems a pity the world did not find it out. He ought to have explained that he was the author, and not merely a *nom de plume* for another man to hide behind. If he had been less intemperately solicitous about his bones, and more solicitous about his Works, it would have been better for his good name, and a kindness to us. The bones were not important. They will moulder away, they will turn to dust, but the Works will endure until the last sun goes down.

MARK TWAIN.

P.S.—March 25. About two months ago I was illuminating this Autobiography with some notions of mine concerning the Bacon-Shakespeare controversy, and I then took occasion to air the opinion that the Stratford Shakespeare was a person of no public consequence or celebrity during his lifetime, but was utterly obscure and unimportant. And not only in great London, but also in the little village where he was born, where he lived a quarter of a century, and where he died and was buried. I argued that if he had been a person of any note at all, aged villagers would have had much to tell about him many and many a year after his death, instead of being unable to furnish inquirers a single fact connected with him. I believed, and I still believe, that if he had been famous, his notoriety would have lasted as long as mine has lasted in my native village out in Missouri. It is a good argument, a prodigiously strong one, and a most formidable one for even the most gifted and ingenious and plausible Stratfordolater to get around or explain away. To-day a Hannibal *Courier-Post* of recent date has reached me, with an article in it which reinforces my contention that a really celebrated person cannot be forgotten in his village in the short space of sixty years. I will make an extract from it:

> Hannibal, as a city, may have many sins to answer for, but ingratitude is not one of them, or reverence for the great men she has produced, and as the years go by her greatest son, Mark Twain, or S. L. Clemens as a few of the unlettered call him, grows in the estimation and regard of the residents of the town he made famous and the town that made him famous. His name is associated with every old building that is torn down to make way for the modern structures demanded by a rapidly growing city, and with every hill or cave over or through which he might by any possibility have roamed, while the many points of interest which he wove into his stories, such as Holiday Hill, Jackson's Island, or Mark Twain Cave, are now monuments to his genius. Hannibal is glad of any opportunity to do him honor as he has honored her.
>
> So it has happened that the "old timers" who went to school with Mark or were with him on some of his usual escapades have been honored with large audiences whenever they were in a reminiscent mood and condescended to tell of their intimacy with the ordinary boy who came to be a very extraordinary humorist and whose every boyish act is now seen to have been indica-

tive of what was to come. Like Aunt Becky and Mrs. Clemens, they can now see that Mark was hardly appreciated when he lived here and that the things he did as a boy and was whipped for doing were not all bad, after all. So they have been in no hesitancy about drawing out the bad things he did as well as the good in their efforts to get a "Mark Twain" story, all incidents being viewed in the light of his present fame, until the volume of "Twainiana" is already considerable and growing in proportion as the "old timers" drop away and the stories are retold second and third hand by their descendants. With some seventy-three years young and living in a villa instead of a house, he is a fair target, and let him incorporate, copyright, or patent himself as he will, there are some of his "works" that will go swooping up Hannibal chimneys as long as graybeards gather about the fires and begin with, "I've heard father tell," or possibly, "Once when I."

The Mrs. Clemens referred to is my mother—*was* my mother.

And here is another extract from a Hannibal paper, of date twenty days ago:

> Miss Becca Blankenship died at the home of William Dickason, 408 Rock Street, at 2.30 o'clock yesterday afternoon, aged 72 years. The deceased was a sister of "Huckleberry Finn," one of the famous characters in Mark Twain's *Tom Sawyer.* She had been a member of the Dickason family—the housekeeper—for nearly forty-five years, and was a highly respected lady. For the past eight years she had been an invalid, but was as well cared for by Mr. Dickason and his family as if she had been a near relative. She was a member of the Park Methodist Church and a Christian woman.

I remember her well. I have a picture of her in my mind which was graven there, clear and sharp and vivid, sixty-three years ago. She was at that time nine years old, and I was about eleven. I remember where she stood, and how she looked; and I can still see her bare feet, her bare head, her brown face, and her short tow-linen frock. She was crying. What it was about I have long ago forgotten. But it was the tears that preserved the picture for me, no doubt. She was a good child, I can say that for her. She knew me nearly seventy years ago. Did she forget me, in the course of time? I think not. If she had lived in Stratford in Shakespeare's time, would she have forgotten him? Yes. For he was never famous during his lifetime, he was utterly obscure in Stratford, and there wouldn't be any occasion to remember him after he had been dead a week.

"Injun Joe," "Jimmy Finn," and "General Gaines" were prominent and very intemperate ne'er-do-wells in Hannibal two generations ago. Plenty of grayheads there remember them to this day, and can tell you about them. Isn't it curious that two "town drunkards" and one half-breed loafer should leave behind them, in a remote Missourian village, a fame a hundred times greater and several hundred times more particularized in the matter of definite facts than Shakespeare left behind him in the village where he had lived the half of his lifetime?

A Helpless Situation

Once or twice a year I get a letter of a certain pattern, a pattern that never materially changes, in form and substance, yet I cannot get used to that letter—it always astonishes me. It affects me as the locomotive always affects me: I say to myself, "I have seen you a thousand times, you always look the same way, yet you are always a wonder, and you are always impossible; to contrive you is clearly beyond human genius—you can't exist, you don't exist, yet here you are!"

I have a letter of that kind by me, a very old one. I yearn to print it, and where is the harm? The writer of it is dead years ago, no doubt, and if I conceal her name and address—her this-world address—I am sure her shade will not mind. And with it I wish to print the answer which I wrote at the time but probably did not send. If it went—which is not likely—it went in the form of a copy, for I find the original still here, pigeonholed with the said letter. To that kind of letters we all write answers which we do not send, fearing to hurt where we have no desire to hurt; I have done it many a time, and this is doubtless a case of the sort.

The Letter

X——., CALIFORNIA, *June 3, 1879*.

MR. S. L. CLEMENS, *Hartford, Conn.*

DEAR SIR,—You will doubtless be surprised to know who has presumed to write and ask a favor of you. Let your memory go back to your days in the Humboldt mines—'62–'63. You will remember, you and Clagett and Oliver and the old blacksmith Tillou lived in a lean-to which was half-way up the gulch, and there were six log cabins in the camp—strung pretty well separated up the gulch from its mouth at the desert to where the last claim was, at the divide. The lean-to you lived in was the one with a canvas roof that the cow fell down through one night, as told about by you in *Roughing It*—my uncle Simmons remembers it very well. He lived in the principal cabin, half-way up the divide, along with Dixon and Parker and Smith. It had two rooms, one for kitchen and the other for bunks, and was the only one that had. You and your party were there on the great night, the time they had dried-apple-pie, Uncle Simmons often speaks of it. It seems curious that dried-apple-pie should have seemed such a great thing, but it was, and it shows how far Humboldt was out of the world and difficult to get to, and how slim the regular bill of fare was. Sixteen years ago—it is a long time. I was a little girl then, only fourteen. I never saw you, I lived in Washoe. But Uncle Simmons ran across you every now and then, all during those weeks that you and party were there working your claim which was like the rest. The camp played out long and long ago, there wasn't silver enough in it to make a button. You never saw my husband, but he was there after you left, *and lived in that very lean-to,* a bachelor then but married to me now. He often wishes there had been a photographer there in those days, he would have taken the lean-to. He got hurt in the old Hal Clayton claim that was abandoned like the others, putting in a blast and not climbing out quick enough, though he scrambled the best he could. It landed him clear down on the trail and hit a Piute. For weeks they thought he would not get over it but he did, and is all right, now. Has been ever since. This is a long introduction but it is the only way I can make myself known. The favor I ask I feel assured your generous heart will grant: Give me some advice about a book I have written. I do not claim anything for it only it is mostly true and as interesting as most of the books of the times. I am unknown in the literary world and you know what that means unless one has some one of influence (like yourself) to help you by speaking a good word for you. I would like to place the book on royalty basis plan with any one you would suggest.

This is a secret from my husband and family. I intend it as a surprise in case I get it published.

Feeling you will take an interest in this and if possible write me a letter to some publisher, or, better still, if you could see them for me and then let me hear.

I appeal to you to grant me this favor. With deepest gratitude I thank you for your attention.

One knows, without inquiring, that the twin of that embarrassing letter is forever and ever flying in this and that and the other direction across the continent in the mails, daily, nightly, hourly, unceasingly, unrestingly. It goes to every well-known merchant, and railway official, and manufacturer, and capitalist, and Mayor, and Congressman, and Governor, and editor, and publisher, and author, and broker, and banker—in a word, to every person who is supposed to have "influence." It always follows the one pattern: "You do not know me, *but you once knew a relative of mine,*" etc., etc. We should all like to help the applicants, we should all be glad to do it, we should all like to return the sort of answer that is desired, but—Well, there is not a thing we can do that would be a help, for not in any instance does that letter ever come from anyone who *can* be helped. The struggler whom you *could* help does his own helping; it would not occur to him to apply to you, a stranger. He has talent and knows it, and he goes into his fight eagerly and with energy and determination—all alone, preferring to be alone. That pathetic letter which comes to you from the incapable, the unhelpable—how do you who are familiar with it answer it? What do you find to say? You do not want to inflict a wound; you hunt ways to avoid that. What do you find? How do you get out of your hard place with a contented conscience? Do you try to explain? The old reply of mine to such a letter shows that I tried that once. Was I satisfied with the result? Possibly; and possibly not; probably not; almost certainly not. I have long ago forgotten all about it. But, anyway, I append my effort:

The Reply

I know Mr. H., and I will go to him, dear madam, if upon reflection you find you still desire it. There will be a conversation. I know the form it will take. It will be like this:

Mr. H. How do her books strike you?
Mr. Clemens. I am not acquainted with them.
H. Who has been her publisher?
C. I don't know.
H. She *has* one, I suppose?
C. I—I think not.
H. Ah. You think this is her first book?
C. Yes—I suppose so. I think so.
H. What is it about? What is the character of it?
C. I believe I do not know.
H. Have you seen it?
C. Well—no, I haven't.
H. Ah-h. How long have you known her?
C. I don't know her.
H. Don't know her?
C. No.
H. Ah-h. How did you come to be interested in her book, then?
C. Well, she—she wrote and asked me to find a publisher for her, and mentioned you.
H. Why should she apply to you instead of to me?
C. She wished me to use my influence.
H. Dear me, what has *influence* to do with such a matter?
C. Well, I think she thought you would be more likely to examine her book if you were influenced.
H. Why, what we are here *for* is to examine books—anybody's book that comes along. It's our *business.* Why should we turn away a book unexamined because it's a stranger's? It would be foolish. No publisher does it. On what ground did she request your influence, since you do not know her? She must have thought you knew her literature and could speak for it. Is that it?
C. No; she knew I didn't.

H. Well, what then? She had a reason of *some* sort for believing you competent to recommend her literature, and also under obligations to do it?

C. Yes, I—I knew her uncle.

H. Knew her *uncle?*

C. Yes.

H. Upon my word! So, you knew her uncle; her uncle knows her literature; he indorses it to you; the chain is complete, nothing further needed; you are satisfied, and therefore—

C. No, that isn't all, there are other ties. I know the cabin her uncle lived in, in the mines; I knew his partners, too; also I came near knowing her husband before she married him, and I *did* know the abandoned shaft where a premature blast went off and he went flying through the air and clear down to the trail and hit an Indian in the back with almost fatal consequences.

H. To *him,* or to the Indian?

C. She didn't say which it was.

H. *(With a sigh).* It certainly beats the band! You don't know *her,* you don't know her literature, you don't know who got hurt when the blast went off, you don't know a single thing for us to build an estimate of her book upon, so far as I—

C. I knew her uncle. You are forgetting her uncle.

H. Oh, what use is *he?* Did you know him long? How long was it?

C. Well, I don't know that I really knew him, but I must have met him, anyway. I think it was that way; you can't tell about these things, you know, except when they are recent.

H. Recent? When was all this?

C. Sixteen years ago.

H. What a basis to judge a book upon! At first you said you knew him, and now you don't know whether you did or not.

C. Oh yes, I knew him; anyway, I think I thought I did; I'm perfectly certain of it.

H. What makes you think you thought you knew him?

C. Why, she says I did, herself.

H. *She* says so!

C. Yes, she does, and I *did* know him, too, though I don't remember it now.

H. Come—how can you know it when you don't remember it?

C. I don't know. That is, I don't know the process, but I *do* know lots of things that I don't remember, and remember lots of things that I don't know. It's so with every educated person.

H. (After a pause.) Is your time valuable?

C. No—well, not very.

H. Mine is.

So I came away then, because he was looking tired. Overwork, I reckon; I never do that; I have seen the evil effects of it. My mother was always afraid I would overwork myself, but I never did.

Dear madam, you see how it would happen if I went there. He would ask me those questions, and I would try to answer them to suit him, and he would hunt me here and there and yonder and get me embarrassed more and more all the time, and at last he would look tired on account of overwork, and there it would end and nothing done. I wish I could be useful to you, but, you see, they do not care for uncles or any of those things; it doesn't move them, it doesn't have the least effect, they don't care for anything but the literature itself, and they as good as despise influence. But they do care for books, and are eager to get them and examine them, no matter whence they come, nor from whose pen. If you will send yours to a publisher—any publisher—he will certainly examine it, I can assure you of that.

The First Writing-Machines

(FROM MY UNPUBLISHED AUTOBIOGRAPHY)

Some days ago a correspondent sent in an old typewritten sheet, faded by age, containing the following letter over the signature of Mark Twain

"HARTFORD, *March 19, 1875.*

"Please do not use my name in any way. Please do not even divulge the fact that I own a machine. I have entirely stopped using the typewriter, for the reason that I never could write a letter with it to anybody without receiving a request by return mail that I would not only describe the machine, but state what progress I had made in the use of it, etc., etc. I don't like to write letters, and so I don't want people to know I own this curiosity-breeding little joker."

A note was sent to Mr. Clemens asking him if the letter was genuine and whether he really had a typewriter as long ago as that. Mr. Clemens replied that his best answer is in the following chapter from his unpublished autobiography:

1904. VILLA QUARTO, FLORENCE, *January.*

Dictating autobiography to a typewriter is a new experience for me, but it goes very well, and is going to save time and "language"—the kind of language that soothes vexation.

I have dictated to a typewriter before—but not autobiography. Between that experience and the present one there lies a mighty gap—more than thirty years! It is a sort of lifetime. In that wide interval much has happened—to the type-machine as well as to the rest of us. At the beginning of that interval a type-machine was a curiosity. The person who owned one was a curiosity, too. But now it is the other way about: the person who *doesn't* own one is a curiosity. I saw a type-machine for the first time in—what year? I suppose it was 1873—because Nasby was with me at the time, and it was in Boston. We must have been lecturing, or we could not have been in Boston, I take it. I quitted the platform that season.

But never mind about that, it is no matter. Nasby and I saw the machine through a window, and went in to look at it. The salesman explained it to us, showed us samples of its work, and said it could do fifty-seven words a minute—a statement which we frankly confessed that we did not believe. So he put his type-girl to work, and we timed her by the watch. She actually did the fifty-seven in sixty seconds. We were partly convinced, but said it probably couldn't happen again. But it did. We timed the girl over and over again—with the same result always: she won out. She did her work on narrow slips of paper, and we pocketed them as fast as she turned them out, to show as curiosities. The price of the machine was one hundred and twenty-five dollars. I bought one, and we went away very much excited.

At the hotel we got out our slips and were a little disappointed to find that they all contained the same words. The girl had economized time and labor by using a formula which she knew by heart. However, we argued—safely enough—that the *first* type-girl must naturally take rank with the first billiard-player: neither of them could be expected to get out of the game any more than a third or a half of what was in it. If the machine survived—*if* it survived—experts would come to the front, by and by, who would double this girl's output without a doubt. They would do one hundred words a minute—my talking speed on the platform. That score has long ago been beaten.

At home I played with the toy, repeating and repeating and repeating "The Boy stood on the Burning Deck," until I could turn that boy's adventure out at the rate of twelve words a minute; then I resumed the pen, for business, and only worked the machine to astonish inquiring visitors. They carried off many reams of the boy and his burning deck.

By and by I hired a young woman, and did my first dictating (letters, merely), and my last until now. The machine did not do both capitals and lower case (as now), but only capitals. Gothic capitals they were, and sufficiently ugly. I remember the first letter I dictated. It was to Edward Bok, who was a boy then. I was not acquainted with him at that time. His present enterprising spirit is not new—he had it in that early day. He was accumulating autographs, and was not content with mere signatures, he wanted a whole autograph *letter.* I furnished it—in type-machine capitals, *signature and all.* It was long; it was a sermon; it contained advice; also reproaches. I said writing was my *trade,* my bread-and-butter; I said it was not fair to ask a man to give away samples of his trade; would he ask the blacksmith for a horseshoe? would he ask the doctor for a corpse?

Now I come to an important matter—as I regard it. In the year '74 the young woman copied a considerable part of a book of mine *on the machine.* In a previous chapter of this Autobiography I have claimed that I was the first person in the world that ever had a telephone in his house for practical purposes; I will now claim—until dispossessed—that I was the first person in the world to *apply the type-machine to literature.* That book must have been *The Adventures of Tom Sawyer.* I wrote the first half of it in '72, the rest of it in '74. My machinist type-copied a book for me in '74, so I concluded it was that one.

That early machine was full of caprices, full of defects—devilish ones. It had as many immoralities as the machine of to-day has virtues. After a year or two I found that it was degrading my character, so I thought I would give it to Howells. He was reluctant, for he was suspicious of novelties and unfriendly toward them, and he remains so to this day. But I persuaded him. He had great confidence in me, and I got him to believe things about the machine that I did not believe myself. He took it home to Boston, and my morals began to improve, but his have never recovered.

He kept it six months, and then returned it to me. I gave it away twice after that, but it wouldn't stay; it came back. Then I gave it to our coachman, Patrick McAleer, who was very grateful, because he did not know the animal, and thought I was trying to make him wiser and better. As soon as he got wiser and better he traded it to a heretic for a side-saddle which he could not use, and there my knowledge of its history ends.

A Cure for the Blues

By courtesy of Mr. Cable I came into possession of a singular book eight or ten years ago. It is likely that mine is now the only copy in existence. Its title-page, unabbreviated, reads as follows:

"The Enemy Conquered; or, Love Triumphant. By G. Ragsdale McClintock,[1] author of 'An Address,' etc., delivered at Sunflower Hill, South Carolina, and member of the Yale Law School. New Haven: published by T. H. Pease, 83 Chapel Street, 1845."

No one can take up this book and lay it down again unread. Whoever reads one line of it is caught, is chained; he has become the contented slave of its fascinations; and he will read and read, devour and devour, and will not let it go out of his hand till it is finished to the last line, though the house be on fire over his head. And after a first reading he will not throw it aside, but will keep it by him, with his Shakespeare and his Homer, and will take it up many and many a time, when the world is dark and his spirits are low, and be straightway cheered and refreshed. Yet this work has been allowed to lie wholly neglected, unmentioned, and apparently unregretted, for nearly half a century.

1. The name here given is a substitute for the one actually attached to the pamphlet.—M.T.

The reader must not imagine that he is to find in it wisdom, brilliancy, fertility of invention, ingenuity of construction, excellence of form, purity of style, perfection of imagery, truth to nature, clearness of statement, humanly possible situations, humanly possible people, fluent narrative, connected sequence of events—or philosophy, or logic, or sense. No; the rich, deep, beguiling charm of the book lies in the total and miraculous *absence* from it of all these qualities—a charm which is completed and perfected by the evident fact that the author, whose naïve innocence easily and surely wins our regard, and almost our worship, does not know that they are absent, does not even suspect that they are absent. When read by the light of these helps to an understanding of the situation, the book is delicious—profoundly and satisfyingly delicious.

I call it a book because the author calls it a book, I call it a work because he calls it a work; but, in truth, it is merely a duodecimo pamphlet of thirty-one pages. It was written for fame and money, as the author very frankly—yes, and very hopefully, too, poor fellow—says in his preface. The money never came—no penny of it ever came; and how long, how pathetically long, the fame has been deferred—forty-seven years! He was young then, it would have been so much to him then; but will he care for it now?

As time is measured in America, McClintock's epoch is antiquity. In his long-vanished day the Southern author had a passion for "eloquence"; it was his pet, his darling. He would be eloquent, or perish. And he recognized only one kind of eloquence—the lurid, the tempestuous, the volcanic. He liked words—big words, fine words, grand words, rumbling, thundering, reverberating words; with sense attaching if it could be got in without marring the sound, but not otherwise. He loved to stand up before a dazed world, and pour forth flame and smoke and lava and pumice-stone into the skies, and work his sub-terranean thunders, and shake himself with earthquakes, and stench himself with sulphur fumes. If he consumed his own fields and vineyards, that was a pity, yes; but he would have his eruption at any cost. Mr. McClintock's eloquence—and he is always eloquent, his crater is always spouting—is of the pattern common to his day, but he departs from the custom of the time in one respect: his brethren allowed sense to intrude when it did not mar the sound, but he does not allow it to intrude at all. For example, consider this figure, which he uses in the village "Address" referred to with such candid complacency in the title-page above quoted—"like the topmost topaz of an ancient tower." Please read it again; contemplate it; measure it; walk around it; climb up it; try to get at an approximate realization of the size of it. Is the fellow to that to be found in literature, ancient or modern, foreign or domestic, living or dead, drunk or sober? One notices how fine and grand it sounds. We know that if it was loftily uttered, it got a noble burst of applause from the villagers; yet there isn't a ray of sense in it, or meaning to it.

McClintock finished his education at Yale in 1843, and came to Hartford on a visit that same year. I have talked with men who at that time talked with him, and felt of him, and knew he was real. One needs to remember that fact and to keep fast hold of it; it is the only way to keep McClintock's book from undermining one's faith in McClintock's actuality.

As to the book. The first four pages are devoted to an inflamed eulogy of Woman—simply Woman in general, or perhaps as an Institution—wherein, among other compliments to her details, he pays a unique one to her voice. He says it "fills the breast with fond alarms, echoed by every rill." It sounds well enough, but it is not true. After the eulogy he takes up his real work and the novel begins. It begins in the woods, near the village of Sunflower Hill.

> Brightening clouds seemed to rise from the mist of the fair Chattahoochee, to spread their beauty over the thick forest, to guide the hero whose bosom beats with aspirations to conquer the enemy that would tarnish his name, and to win back the admiration of his long-tried friend.

It seems a general remark, but it is not general; the hero mentioned is the to-be hero of the book; and in this abrupt fashion, and without name or description, he is shoveled into the tale. "With aspirations to conquer the enemy that would tarnish his name" is merely a phrase flung in for the sake of the sound—let it not mislead the reader. No one is trying to tarnish this person; no one has thought of it. The rest of the sentence is also merely a phrase; the man has no friend as yet, and of course has had no chance to try him, or win back his admiration, or disturb him in any other way.

The hero climbs up over "Sawney's Mountain," and down the other side, making for an old Indian "castle"—which becomes "the red man's hut" in the next sentence; and when he gets there at last, he "surveys with wonder and astonishment" the invisible structure, "which time had buried in the dust, and thought to himself his happiness was not yet complete." One doesn't know why it wasn't, nor how near it came to being complete, nor what was still wanting to round it up and make it so. Maybe it was the Indian; but the book does not say. At this point we have an episode:

Beside the shore of the brook sat a young man, about eighteen or twenty, who seemed to be reading some favorite book, and who had a remarkably noble countenance—eyes which betrayed more than a common mind. This of course made the youth a welcome guest, and gained him friends in whatever condition of life he might be placed. The traveler observed that he was a well-built figure which showed strength and grace in every movement. He accordingly addressed him in quite a gentlemanly manner, and inquired of him the way to the village. After he had received the desired information, and was about taking his leave, the youth said, "Are you not Major Elfonzo, the great musician[1]—the champion of a noble cause—the modern Achilles, who gained so many victories in the Florida War?" "I bear that name," said the Major, "and those titles, trusting at the same time that the ministers of grace will carry me triumphantly through all my laudable undertakings, and if," continued the Major, "you, sir, are the patronizer of noble deeds, I should like to make you my confidant and learn your address." The youth looked somewhat amazed, bowed low, mused for a moment, and began: "My name is Roswell. I have been recently admitted to the bar, and can only give a faint outline of my future success in that honorable profession; but I trust, sir, like the Eagle, I shall look down from lofty rocks upon the dwellings of man, and shall ever be ready to give you any assistance in my official capacity, and whatever this muscular arm of mine can do, whenever it shall be called from its buried *greatness.*" The Major grasped him by the hand, and exclaimed: "O! thou exalted spirit of inspiration—thou flame of burning prosperity, may the Heaven-directed blaze be the glare of thy soul, and battle down every rampart that seems to impede your progress!"

There is a strange sort of originality about McClintock; he imitates other people's styles, but nobody can imitate his, not even an idiot. Other people can be windy, but McClintock blows a gale; other people can blubber sentiment, but McClintock spews it; other people can mishandle metaphors, but only McClintock knows how to make a business of it. McClintock is always McClintock, he is always consistent, his style is always his own style. He does not make the mistake of being relevant on one page and irrelevant on another; he is irrelevant on all of them. He does not make the mistake of being lucid in one place and obscure in another; he is obscure all the time. He does not make the mistake of slipping in a name here and there that is out of character with his work; he always uses names that exactly and fantastically fit his lunatics. In the matter of undeviating

1. Further on it will be seen that he is a country expert on the fiddle, and has a three-township fame.—M.T.

consistency he stands alone in authorship. It is this that makes his style unique, and entitles it to a name of its own—McClintockian. It is this that protects it from being mistaken for anybody else's. Uncredited quotations from other writers often leave a reader in doubt as to their authorship, but McClintock is safe from that accident; an uncredited quotation from him would always be recognizable. When a boy nineteen years old, who had just been admitted to the bar, says, "I trust, sir, like the Eagle, I shall look down from lofty rocks upon the dwellings of man," we know who is speaking through that boy; we should recognize that note anywhere. There be myriads of instruments in this world's literary orchestra, and a multitudinous confusion of sounds that they make, wherein fiddles are drowned, and guitars smothered, and one sort of drum mistaken for another sort; but whensoever the brazen note of the McClintockian trombone breaks through that fog of music, that note is recognizable, and about it there can be no blur of doubt.

The novel now arrives at the point where the Major goes home to see his father. When McClintock wrote this interview he probably believed it was pathetic.

> The road which led to the town presented many attractions Elfonzo had bid farewell to the youth of deep feeling, and was now wending his way to the dreaming spot of his fondness. The south winds whistled through the woods, as the waters dashed against the banks, as rapid fire in the pent furnace roars. This brought him to remember while alone, that he quietly left behind the hospitality of a father's house, and gladly entered the world, with higher hopes than are often realized. But as he journeyed onward, he was mindful of the advice of his father, who had often looked sadly on the ground, when tears of cruelly deceived hope moistened his eyes. Elfonzo had been somewhat of a dutiful son; yet fond of the amusements of life—had been in distant lands—had enjoyed the pleasure of the world, and had frequently returned to the scenes of his boyhood, almost destitute of many of the comforts of life. In this condition, he would frequently say to his father, "Have I offended you, that you look upon me as a stranger, and frown upon me with stinging looks? Will you not favor me with the sound of your voice? If I have trampled upon your veneration, or have spread a humid veil of darkness around your expectations, send me back into the world, where no heart beats for me—where the foot of man has never yet trod; but give me at least one kind word—allow me to come into the presence sometimes of thy winter-worn locks." "Forbid it, Heaven, that I should be angry with thee," answered the father, "my son, and yet I send thee back to the children of the world—to the cold charity of the combat, and to a land of victory. I read

another destiny in thy countenance—I learn thy inclinations from the flame that has already kindled in my soul a strange sensation. It will seek thee, my dear *Elfonzo,* it will find thee—thou canst not escape that lighted torch, which shall blot out from the remembrance of men a long train of prophecies which they have foretold against thee. I once thought not so. Once, I was blind; but now the path of life is plain before me, and my sight is clear; yet, Elfonzo, return to thy worldly occupation—take again in thy hand that chord of sweet sounds—struggle with the civilized world and with your own heart; fly swiftly to the enchanted ground—let the night-*Owl* send forth its screams from the stubborn oak—let the sea sport upon the beach, and the stars sing together; but learn of these, Elfonzo, thy doom, and thy hiding-place. Our most innocent as well as our most lawful *desires* must often be denied us, that we may learn to sacrifice them to a Higher will."

Remembering such admonitions with gratitude, Elfonzo was immediately urged by the recollection of his father's family to keep moving.

McClintock has a fine gift in the matter of surprises; but as a rule they are not pleasant ones, they jar upon the feelings. His closing sentence in the last quotation is of that sort. It brings one down out of the tinted clouds in too sudden and collapsed a fashion. It incenses one against the author for a moment. It makes the reader want to take him by his winter-worn locks, and trample on his veneration, and deliver him over to the cold charity of combat, and blot him out with his own lighted torch. But the feeling does not last. The master takes again in his hand that concord of sweet sounds of his, and one is reconciled, pacified.

His steps became quicker and quicker—he hastened through the *piny* woods, dark as the forest was, and with joy he very soon reached the little village of repose, in whose bosom rested the boldest chivalry. His close attention to every important object—his modest questions about whatever was new to him—his reverence for wise old age, and his ardent desire to learn many of the fine arts, soon brought him into respectable notice.

One mild winter day, as he walked along the streets toward the Academy, which stood upon a small eminence, surrounded by native growth—some venerable in its appearance, others young and prosperous—all seemed inviting, and seemed to be the very place for learning as well as for genius to spend its research beneath its spreading shades. He entered its classic walls in the usual mode of southern manners.

The artfulness of this man! None knows so well as he how to pique the curiosity of the reader—and how to disappoint it. He raises the hope, here, that he is going to tell all about how one enters a classic wall in the usual mode of Southern manners; but does he? No; he smiles in his sleeve, and turns aside to other matters.

> The principal of the Institution begged him to be seated and listen to the recitations that were going on. He accordingly obeyed the request, and seemed to be much pleased. After the school was dismissed, and the young hearts regained their freedom, with the songs of the evening, laughing at the anticipated pleasures of a happy home, while others tittered at the actions of the past day, he addressed the teacher in a tone that indicated a resolution—with an undaunted mind. He said he had determined to become a student, if he could meet with his approbation. "Sir," said he, "I have spent much time in the world. I have traveled among the uncivilized inhabitants of America. I have met with friends, and combated with foes; but none of these gratify my ambition, or decide what is to be my destiny. I see the learned world have an influence with the voice of the people themselves. The despoilers of the remotest kingdoms of the earth refer their differences to this class of persons. This the illiterate and inexperienced little dream of; and now if you will receive me as I am, with these deficiencies—with all my misguided opinions, I will give you my honor, sir, that I will never disgrace the Institution, or those who have placed you in this honorable station." The instructor, who had met with many disappointments, knew how to feel for a stranger who had been thus turned upon the charities of an unfeeling community. He looked at him earnestly, and said: "Be of good cheer—look forward, sir, to the high destination you may attain. Remember, the more elevated the mark at which you aim, the more sure, the more glorious, the more magnificent the prize." From wonder to wonder, his encouragement led the impatient listener. A strange nature bloomed before him—giant streams promised him success—gardens of hidden treasures opened to his view. All this, so vividly described, seemed to gain a new witchery from his glowing fancy.

It seems to me that this situation is new in romance. I feel sure it has not been attempted before. Military celebrities have been disguised and set at lowly occupations for dramatic effect, but I think McClintock is the first to send one of them to school. Thus, in this book, you pass from wonder to wonder, through gardens of hidden treasure, where giant streams bloom before you, and behind you, and all around, and you feel as happy, and groggy, and satisfied with your quart of mixed metaphor aboard as you would if it had been mixed in a sample-room and delivered from a jug.

Now we come upon some more McClintockian surprises—a sweetheart who is sprung upon us without any preparation, along with a name for her which is even a little more of a surprise than she herself is.

> In 1842 he entered the class, and made rapid progress in the English and Latin departments. Indeed, he continued advancing with such rapidity that he was like to become the first in his class, and made such unexpected progress, and was so studious, that he had almost forgotten the pictured saint of his affections. The fresh wreaths of the pine and cypress had waited anxiously to drop once more the dews of Heaven upon the heads of those who had so often poured forth the tender emotions of their souls under its boughs. He was aware of the pleasure that he had seen there. So one evening, as he was returning from his reading, he concluded he would pay a visit to this enchanting spot. Little did he think of witnessing a shadow of his former happiness, though no doubt he wished it might be so. He continued sauntering by the roadside, meditating on the past. The nearer he approached the spot, the more anxious he became. At that moment a tall female figure flitted across his path, with a bunch of roses in her hand; her countenance showed uncommon vivacity, with a resolute spirit; her ivory teeth already appeared as she smiled beautifully, promenading—while her ringlets of hair dangled unconsciously around her snowy neck. Nothing was wanting to complete her beauty. The tinge of the rose was in full bloom upon her cheek; the charms of sensibility and tenderness were always her associates. In Ambulinia's bosom dwelt a noble soul—one that never faded—one that never was conquered.

Ambulinia! It can hardly be matched in fiction. The full name is Ambulinia Valeer. Marriage will presently round it out and perfect it. Then it will be Mrs. Ambulinia Valeer Elfonzo. It takes the chromo.

> Her heart yielded to no feeling but the love of Elfonzo, on whom she gazed with intense delight, and to whom she felt herself more closely bound, because he sought the hand of no other. Elfonzo was roused from his apparent reverie. His books no longer were his inseparable companions—his thoughts arrayed themselves to encourage him to the field of victory. He endeavored to speak to his supposed Ambulinia, but his speech appeared not in words. No, his effort was a stream of fire, that kindled his soul into a flame of admiration, and carried his senses away captive. Ambulinia had disappeared, to make him more mindful of his duty. As she walked speedily away through the piny woods, she calmly echoed: "O! Elfonzo, thou wilt now look from thy sunbeams. Thou shalt now walk in a new path—perhaps thy way leads through darkness; but fear not, the stars foretell happiness."

To McClintock that jingling jumble of fine words meant something, no doubt, or seemed to mean something; but it is useless for us to try to divine what it was. Ambulinia comes—we don't know whence nor why; she mysteriously intimates—we don't know what; and then she goes echoing away—we don't know whither; and down comes the curtain. McClintock's art is subtle; McClintock's art is deep.

> Not many days afterward, as surrounded by fragrant flowers she sat one evening at twilight, to enjoy the cool breeze that whispered notes of melody along the distant groves, the little birds perched on every side, as if to watch the movements of their new visitor. The bells were tolling, when Elfonzo silently stole along by the wild wood flowers, holding in his hand his favorite instrument of music—his eye continually searching for Ambulinia, who hardly seemed to perceive him, as she played carelessly with the songsters that hopped from branch to branch. Nothing could be more striking than the difference between the two. Nature seemed to have given the more tender soul to Elfonzo, and the stronger and more courageous to Ambulinia. A deep feeling spoke from the eyes of Elfonzo—such a feeling as can only be expressed by those who are blessed as admirers, and by those who are able to return the same with sincerity of heart. He was a few years older than Ambulinia: she had turned a little into her seventeenth. He had almost grown up in the Cherokee country, with the same equal proportions as one of the natives. But little intimacy had existed between them until the year forty-one—because the youth felt that the character of such a lovely girl was too exalted to inspire any other feeling than that of quiet reverence. But as lovers will not always be insulted, at all times and under all circumstances, by the frowns and cold looks of crabbed old age, which should continually reflect dignity upon those around, and treat the unfortunate as well as the fortunate with a graceful mien, he continued to use diligence and perseverance. All this lighted a spark in his heart that changed his whole character, and like the unyielding Deity that follows the storm to check its rage in the forest, he resolves for the first time to shake off his embarrassment and return where he had before only worshiped.

At last we begin to get the Major's measure. We are able to put this and that casual fact together, and build the man up before our eyes, and look at him. And after we have got him built, we find him worth the trouble. By the above comparison between his age and Ambulinia's, we guess the war-worn veteran to be twenty-two; and the other facts stand thus: he had grown up in the Cherokee country with the same equal proportions as one of the natives—how flowing and graceful the language, and yet how tantalizing as to meaning!—he had been turned adrift by his father, to whom he had been "somewhat of a dutiful son"; he wandered in distant lands; came back frequently "to the scenes of his boyhood, almost destitute of many of the comforts of life," in order to get into the presence of his father's winter-worn locks, and spread a humid veil of darkness around his expectations; but he was always promptly sent back to the cold charity of the combat again; he learned to play the fiddle, and made a name for himself in that line; he had dwelt among the wild tribes; he had philosophized about the despoilers of the kingdoms of the earth, and found out—the cunning creature—that they refer their differences to the learned for settlement; he had achieved a vast fame as a military chieftain, the Achilles of the Florida campaigns, and then had got him a spelling-book and started to school; he had fallen in love with Ambulinia Valeer while she was teething, but had kept it to himself awhile, out of the reverential awe which he felt for the child; but now at last, like the unyielding Deity who follows the storm to check its rage in the forest, he resolves to shake off his embarrassment, and to return where before he had only worshiped. The Major, indeed, has made up his mind to rise up and shake his faculties together, and to see if *he* can't do that thing himself. This is not clear. But no matter about that: there stands the hero, compact and visible; and he is no mean structure, considering that his creator had never created anything before, and hadn't anything but rags and wind to build with this time. It seems to me that no one can contemplate this odd creature, this quaint and curious blatherskite, without admiring McClintock, or, at any rate, loving him and feeling grateful to him; for McClintock made him, he gave him to us; without McClintock we could not have had him, and would now be poor.

But we must come to the feast again. Here is a courtship scene, down there in the romantic glades among the raccoons, alligators, and things, that has merit, peculiar literary merit. See how Achilles woos. Dwell upon the second sentence (particularly the close of it) and the beginning of the third. Never mind the new personage, Leos, who is intruded upon us unheralded and unexplained. That is McClintock's way; it is his habit; it is a part of his genius; he cannot help it; he never interrupts the rush of his narrative to make introductions.

> It could not escape Ambulinia's penetrating eye that he sought an interview with her, which she as anxiously avoided, and assumed a more distant calmness than before, seemingly to destroy all hope. After many efforts and struggles with his own person, with timid steps the Major approached the

damsel, with the same caution as he would have done in a field of battle. "Lady Ambulinia," said he, trembling, "I have long desired a moment like this. I dare not let it escape. I fear the consequences; yet I hope your indulgence will at least hear my petition. Can you not anticipate what I would say, and what I am about to express? Will not you, like Minerva, who sprung from the brain of Jupiter, release me from thy winding chains or cure me—" "Say no more, Elfonzo," answered Ambulinia, with a serious look, raising her hand as if she intended to swear eternal hatred against the whole world; "another lady in my place would have perhaps answered your question in bitter coldness. I know not the little arts of my sex. I care but little for the vanity of those who would chide me, and am unwilling as well as ashamed to be guilty of anything that would lead you to think 'all is not gold that glitters'; so be not rash in your resolution. It is better to repent now, than to do it in a more solemn hour. Yes, I know what you would say. I know you have a costly gift for me—the noblest that man can make—*your heart!* You should not offer it to one so unworthy. Heaven, you know, has allowed my father's house to be made a house of solitude, a home of silent obedience, which my parents say is more to be admired than big names and high-sounding titles. Notwithstanding all this, let me speak the emotions of an honest heart—allow me to say in the fullness of my hopes that I anticipate better days. The bird may stretch its wings toward the sun, which it can never reach; and flowers of the field appear to ascend in the same direction, because they cannot do otherwise; but man confides his complaints to the saints in whom he believes; for in their abodes of light they know no more sorrow. From your confession and indicative looks, I must be that person; if so deceive not yourself."

Elfonzo replied, "Pardon me, my dear madam, for my frankness. I have loved you from my earliest days—everything grand and beautiful hath borne the image of Ambulinia; while precipices on every hand surrounded me, your *guardian angel* stood and beckoned me away from the deep abyss. In every trial, in every misfortune, I have met with your helping hand; yet I never dreamed or dared to cherish thy love, till a voice impaired with age encouraged the cause, and declared they who acquired thy favor should win a victory. I saw how Leos worshiped thee. I felt my own unworthiness. I began to *know jealousy,* a strong guest—indeed, in my bosom,—yet I could see if I gained your admiration Leos was to be my rival. I was aware that he had the influence of your parents, and the wealth of a deceased relative, which is too often mistaken for permanent and regular tranquillity; yet I have determined by your permission to beg an interest in your prayers—to ask you to animate my drooping spirits by your smiles and your winning looks; for if you but speak I shall be conqueror, my enemies shall stagger like Olympus shakes. And though earth and sea may tremble, and the charioteer of the sun may forget his dashing steed, yet I am assured that it is only to arm me with divine weapons which will enable me to complete my long-tried intention."

"Return to yourself, Elfonzo," said Ambulinia, pleasantly: "a dream of vision has disturbed your intellect; you are above the atmosphere, dwelling in the celestial regions; nothing is there that urges or hinders, nothing that brings discord into our present litigation. I entreat you to condescend a little, and be a man, and forget it all. When Homer describes the battle of the gods and noble men fighting with giants and dragons, they represent under this image our struggles with the delusions of our passions. You have exalted me, an unhappy girl, to the skies; you have called me a saint, and portrayed in your imagination an angel in human form. Let her remain such to you, let her continue to be as you have supposed, and be assured that she will consider a share in your esteem as her highest treasure. Think not that I would allure you from the path in which your conscience leads you; for you know I respect the conscience of others, as I would die for my own. Elfonzo, if I am worthy of thy love, let such conversation never again pass between us. Go, seek a nobler theme! we will seek it in the stream of time, as the sun set in the Tigris." As she spake these words she grasped the hand of Elfonzo, saying at the same time—"Peace and prosperity attend you, my hero; be up and doing!" Closing her remarks with this expression, she walked slowly away, leaving Elfonzo astonished and amazed. He ventured not to follow or detain her. Here he stood alone, gazing at the stars; confounded as he was, here he stood.

Yes; there he stood. There seems to be no doubt about that. Nearly half of this delirious story has now been delivered to the reader. It seems a pity to reduce the other half to a cold synopsis. Pity! it is more than a pity, it is a crime; for to synopsize McClintock is to reduce a sky-flushing conflagration to dull embers, it is to reduce barbaric splendor to ragged poverty. McClintock never wrote a line that was not precious; he never wrote one that could be spared; he never framed one from which a word could be removed without damage. Every sentence that this master has produced may be likened to a perfect set of teeth, white, uniform, beautiful. If you pull one, the charm is gone.

Still, it is now necessary to begin to pull, and to keep it up; for lack of space requires us to synopsize.

We left Elfonzo standing there amazed. At what, we do not know. Not at the girl's speech. No; we ourselves should have been amazed at it, of course, for none of us has ever heard anything resembling it; but Elfonzo was used to speeches made up of noise and vacancy, and could listen to them with undaunted mind like the "topmost topaz of an ancient tower"; he was used to making them himself; he—but let it go, it cannot be guessed out; we shall never know what it was that astonished him. He stood there awhile; then he said, "Alas! am I now Grief's disappointed son at last?" He did not stop to examine his mind, and to try to find out what he probably meant by that, because, for one reason, "a mixture of ambition and greatness of soul moved upon his young heart," and started him for the village. He resumed his bench in school, "and reasonably progressed in his education." His heart was heavy, but he went into society, and sought surcease of sorrow in its light distractions. He made himself popular with his violin, "which seemed to have a thousand chords—more symphonious than the Muses of Apollo, and more enchanting than the ghost of the Hills." This is obscure, but let it go.

During this interval Leos did some unencouraged courting, but at last, "choked by his undertaking," he desisted.

Presently "Elfonzo again wends his way to the stately walls and new-built village." He goes to the house of his beloved; she opens the door herself. To my surprise—for Ambulinia's heart had still seemed free at the time of their last interview—love beamed from the girl's eyes. One sees that Elfonzo was surprised, too; for when he caught that light, "a halloo of smothered shouts ran through every vein." A neat figure—a very neat figure, indeed! Then he kissed her. "The scene was overwhelming." They went into the parlor. The girl said it was safe, for her parents were abed, and would never know. Then we have this fine picture—flung upon the canvas with hardly an effort, as you will notice.

> Advancing toward him, she gave a bright display of her rosy neck, and from her head the ambrosial locks breathed divine fragrance; her robe hung waving to his view, while she stood like a goddess confessed before him.

There is nothing of interest in the couple's interview. Now at this point the girl invites Elfonzo to a village show, where jealousy is the motive of the play, for she wants to teach him a wholesome lesson, if he is a jealous person. But this is a sham, and pretty shallow. McClintock merely wants a pretext to drag in a plagiarism of his upon a scene or two in "Othello."

The lovers went to the play. Elfonzo was one of the fiddlers. He and Ambulinia must not be seen together, lest trouble follow with the girl's malignant father; we are made to understand that clearly. So the two sit together in the orchestra, in the midst of the musicians. This does not seem to be good art. In the first place, the girl would be in the way, for orchestras are always packed closely together, and there is no room to spare for people's girls; in the next place, one cannot conceal a girl in an orchestra without everybody taking notice of it. There can be no doubt, it seems to me, that this is bad art.

Leos is present. Of course, one of the first things that catches his eye is the maddening spectacle of Ambulinia "leaning upon Elfonzo's chair." This poor girl does not seem to understand even the rudiments of concealment. But she is "in her seventeenth," as the author phrases it, and that is her justification.

Leos meditates, constructs a plan—with personal violence as a basis, of course. It was their way down there. It is a good plain plan, without any imagination in it. He will go out and stand at the front door, and when these two come out he will "arrest Ambulinia from the hands of the insolent Elfonzo," and thus make for himself a "more prosperous field of immortality than ever was decreed by Omnipotence, or ever pencil drew or artist imagined." But, dear me, while he is waiting there the couple climb out at the back window and scurry home! This is romantic enough, but there is a lack of dignity in the situation.

At this point McClintock puts in the whole of his curious play—which we skip.

Some correspondence follows now. The bitter father and the distressed lovers write the letters. Elopements are attempted. They are idiotically planned, and they fail. Then we have several pages of romantic powwow and confusion signifying nothing. Another elopement is planned; it is to take place on Sunday, when everybody is at church. But the "hero" cannot keep the secret; he tells everybody. Another author would have found another instrument when he decided to defeat this elopement; but that is not McClintock's way. He uses the person that is nearest at hand.

The evasion failed, of course. Ambulinia, in her flight, takes refuge in a neighbor's house. Her father drags her home. The villagers gather, attracted by the racket.

> Elfonzo was moved at this sight. The people followed on to see what was going to become of Ambulinia, while he, with downcast looks, kept at a distance, until he saw them enter the abode of the father, thrusting her, that was the sigh of his soul, out of his presence into a solitary apartment, when she exclaimed, "Elfonzo! Elfonzo! oh, Elfonzo! where art thou, with all thy heroes? haste, oh! haste, come thou to my relief. Ride on the wings of the

> wind! Turn thy force loose like a tempest, and roll on thy army like a whirlwind, over this mountain of trouble and confusion. Oh, friends! if any pity me, let your last efforts throng upon the green hills, and come to the relief of Ambulinia, who is guilty of nothing but innocent love." Elfonzo called out with a loud voice, "My God, can I stand this! arouse up, I beseech you, and put an end to this tyranny. Come, my brave boys," said he, "are you ready to go forth to your duty?" They stood around him. "Who," said he, "will call us to arms? Where are my thunderbolts of war? Speak ye, the first who will meet the foe! Who will go forward with me in this ocean of grievous temptation? If there is one who desires to go, let him come and shake hands upon the altar of devotion, and swear that he will be a hero; yes, a Hector in a cause like this, which calls aloud for a speedy remedy." "Mine be the deed," said a young lawyer, "and mine alone; Venus alone shall quit her station before I will forsake one jot or tittle of my promise to you; what is death to me? what is all this warlike army, if it is not to win a victory? I love the sleep of the lover and the mighty; nor would I give it over till the blood of my enemies should wreak with that of my own. But God forbid that our fame should soar on the blood of the slumberer." Mr. Valeer stands at his door with the frown of a demon upon his brow, with his dangerous weapon[1] ready to strike the first man who should enter his door. "Who will arise and go forward through blood and carnage to the rescue of my Ambulinia?" said Elfonzo. "All," exclaimed the multitude; and onward they went, with their implements of battle. Others, of a more timid nature, stood among the distant hills to see the result of the contest.

It will hardly be believed that after all this thunder and lightning not a drop of rain fell; but such is the fact. Elfonzo and his gang stood up and blackguarded Mr. Valeer with vigor all night, getting their outlay back with interest; then in the early morning the army and its general retired from the field, leaving the victory with their solitary adversary and his crowbar. This is the first time this has happened in romantic literature. The invention is original. Everything in this book is original; there is nothing hackneyed about it anywhere. Always, in other romances, when you find the author leading up to a climax, you know what is going to happen. But in this book it is different; the thing which seems inevitable and unavoidable never happens; it is circumvented by the art of the author every time.

Another elopement was attempted. It failed.

We have now arrived at the end. But it is not exciting. McClintock thinks it is; but it isn't. One day Elfonzo sent Ambulinia another note—a

1. It is a crowbar.—M.T.

note proposing elopement No. 16. This time the plan is admirable; admirable, sagacious, ingenious, imaginative, deep—oh, everything, and perfectly easy. One wonders why it was never thought of before. This is the scheme. Ambulinia is to leave the breakfast-table, ostensibly to "attend to the placing of those flowers, which should have been done a week ago"—artificial ones, of course; the others wouldn't keep so long—and then, instead of fixing the flowers, she is to walk out to the grove, and go off with Elfonzo. The invention of this plan overstrained the author, that is plain, for he straightway shows failing powers. The details of the plan are not many or elaborate. The author shall state them himself—this good soul, whose intentions are always better than his English:

> "You walk carelessly toward the academy grove, where you will find me with a lightning steed, elegantly equipped to bear you off where we shall be joined in wedlock with the first connubial rights."

Last scene of all, which the author, now much enfeebled, tries to smarten up and make acceptable to his spectacular heart by introducing some new properties—silver bow, golden harp, olive branch—things that can all come good in an elopement, no doubt, yet are not to be compared to an umbrella for real handiness and reliability in an excursion of that kind.

> And away she ran to the sacred grove, surrounded with glittering pearls, that indicated her coming. Elfonzo hails her with his silver bow and his golden harp. They meet—Ambulinia's countenance brightens—Elfonzo leads up the winged steed. "Mount," said he, "ye true-hearted, ye fearless soul—the day is ours." She sprang upon the back of the young thunderbolt, a brilliant star sparkles upon her head, with one hand she grasps the reins, and with the other she holds an olive branch. "Lend thy aid, ye strong winds," they exclaimed, "ye moon, ye sun, and all ye fair host of heaven, witness the enemy conquered." "Hold," said Elfonzo, "thy dashing steed." "Ride on," said Ambulinia, "the voice of thunder is behind us." And onward they went, with such rapidity that they very soon arrived at Rural Retreat, where they dismounted, and were united with all the solemnities that usually attend such divine operations.

There is but one Homer, there is but one Shakespeare, there is but one McClintock—and his immortal book is before you. Homer could not have written this book, Shakespeare could not have written it, I could not have done it myself. There is nothing just like it in the literature of any country or of any epoch. It stands alone; it is monumental. It adds G. Ragsdale McClintock's to the sum of the republic's imperishable names.

A Petition to the Queen of England

HARTFORD, *Nov. 6, 1887.*

MADAM: You will remember that last May Mr. Edward Bright, the clerk of the Inland Revenue Office, wrote me about a tax which he said was due from me to the government on books of mine published in London—that is to say, an income tax on the royalties. I do not know Mr. Bright, and it is embarrassing to me to correspond with strangers; for I was raised in the country and have always lived there, the early part in Marion County, Missouri, before the war, and this part in Hartford County, Connecticut, near Bloomfield and about eight miles this side of Farmington, though some call it nine, which it is impossible to be, for I have walked it many and many a time in considerably under three hours, and General Hawley says he has done it in two and a quarter, which is not likely; so it has seemed best that I write your Majesty. It is true that I do not know your Majesty personally, but I have met the Lord Mayor, and if the rest of the family are like him, it is but just that it should be named royal; and likewise plain that in a family matter like this, I cannot better forward my case than to frankly carry it to the head of the family itself. I have also met the Prince of Wales once in the fall of 1873, but it was not in any familiar way, but in a quite informal way, being casual, and was, of course, a surprise to us both. It was in Oxford Street, just where you come out of Oxford into Regent Circus, and just as he turned up one side of the circle at the head of a procession, I went down the other side on the top of an omnibus. He will remember me on account of a gray coat with flap pockets that I wore, as I was the only person on the omnibus that had on that kind of a coat; I remember him of course as easy as I would a comet. He looked quite proud and satisfied, but that is not to be wondered at, he has a good situation. And once I called on your Majesty, but you were out.

But that is no matter, it happens with everybody. However, I have wandered a little away from what I started about. It was this way. Young Bright wrote my London publishers, Chatto and Windus—their place is the one on the left as you come down Piccadilly, about a block and a half above where the minstrel show is—he wrote them that he wanted them to pay income tax on the royalties of some foreign authors, namely, "Miss De La Ramé (Ouida), Dr. Oliver Wendell Holmes, Mr. Francis Bret Harte, and Mr. Mark Twain." Well, Mr. Chatto diverted him from the others, and tried to divert him from me, but in this case he failed. So then young Bright wrote me. And not only that, but he sent me a printed document the size of a newspaper, for me to sign all over in different places. Well, it was that kind of a document that the more you study it the more it undermines you and makes everything seem uncertain to you; and so, while in that condition, and really not responsible for my acts, I wrote Mr. Chatto to pay the tax and charge to me. Of course my idea was that it was for only one year, and that the tax would be only about one per cent. or along there somewhere, but last night I met Professor Sloane of Princeton —you may not know him, but you have probably seen him every now and then, for he goes to England a good deal, a large man and very handsome and absorbed in thought, and if you have noticed such a man on platforms after the train is gone, that is the one, he generally gets left, like all those specialists and other scholars who know everything but how to apply it—and he said it was a back tax for *three* years, and not one per cent., but two and a half!

That gave what had seemed a little matter a new aspect. I then began to study the printed document again, to see if I could find anything in it that might modify my case, and I had what seems to be a quite promising success. For instance, it opens thus—polite and courteous, the way those English government documents always are—I do not say that to hear myself talk, it is just the fact, and it is a credit:

"To Mr. Mark Twain: IN PURSUANCE of the Acts of Parliament for granting to Her Majesty Duties and Profits," etc.

I had not noticed that before. My idea had been that it was for the government, and so I wrote *to* the government; but now I saw that it was a private matter, a family matter, and that the proceeds went to yourself, not the government. I would always rather treat with principals, and I am glad I noticed that clause. With a principal, one can always get at a fair and right understanding, whether it is about potatoes, or continents, or any of those things, or something entirely different; for the size or nature of the thing does not affect the fact; whereas, as a rule, a subordinate is more or less troublesome to satisfy. And yet this is not against them, but the other way. They have their duties to do, and must be harnessed to rules, and not allowed any discretion. Why, if your Majesty should equip young Bright with discretion—I mean his own discretion—it is an even guess that he would discretion you out of house and home in two or three years. He would not *mean* to get the family into straits, but that would be the upshot, just the same. Now then, with Bright out of the way, this is not going to be any Irish question; it is going to be settled pleasantly and satisfactorily for all of us, and when it is finished your Majesty is going to stand with the American people just as you have stood for fifty years, and surely no monarch can require better than that of an alien nation. They do not all pay a British income tax, but the most of them will in time, for we have shoals of new authors coming along every year; and of the population of your Canada, upward of four-fifths are wealthy Americans, and more going there all the time.

Well, another thing which I noticed in the Document was an item about "Deductions." I will come to that presently, your Majesty. And another thing was this: that Authors are not mentioned in the Document at all. No, we have "Quarries, Mines, Iron-works, Salt-springs, Alum-mines, Water-works, Canals, Docks, Drains, Levels, Fishings, Fairs, Tolls, Bridges, Ferries," and so forth and so forth and so on—well, as much as a yard or a yard and a half of them, I should think—anyway a very large quantity or number. I read along—down, and down, and down the list, further, and further, and further, and as I approached the bottom my hopes began to rise higher and higher, because I saw that everything in England *that* far was taxed by name and in detail, except perhaps the family, and maybe Parliament, and yet still no mention of Authors. Apparently they were going to be overlooked. And sure enough, they were! My heart gave a great bound. But I was too soon. There was a footnote, in Mr. Bright's hand, which said: "You are taxed under Schedule D, section 14." I turned to that place, and found these three things: "Trades, Offices, Gas-works."

Of course, after a moment's reflection, hope came up again, and then certainty: Mr. Bright was in error, and clear off the track; for Authorship is not a Trade, it is an inspiration; Authorship does not keep an Office, its habitation is all out under the sky, and everywhere where the winds are blowing and the sun is shining and the creatures of God are free. Now then, since I have no Trade and keep no Office, I am not taxable under Schedule D, section 14. Your Majesty sees that; so I will go on to that other thing that I spoke of, the "deductions"—deductions from my tax which I may get allowed, under conditions. Mr. Bright says all deductions to be claimed by me must be restricted to the provisions made in Paragraph No. 8, entitled "Wear and Tear of Machinery, or Plant." This is curious, and shows how far he has gotten away on his wrong course after once he has got started wrong: for Offices and Trades do not have Plant, they do not have Machinery, such a thing was never heard of; and, moreover, they do not wear and tear. You see that, your Majesty, and that it is true. Here is the Paragraph No. 8:

> Amount claimed as a deduction for diminished value by reason of Wear and Tear, where the Machinery or Plant belongs to the Person or Company carrying on the Concern, or is let to such Person or Company so that the Lessee is bound to maintain and deliver over the same in good condition:
>
> *Amout* £________

There it is—the very words.

I could answer Mr. Bright thus:

It is my pride to say that my Brain is my Plant; and I do not claim any deduction for diminished value by reason of Wear and Tear, for the reason that it does not wear and tear, but stays sound and whole all the time. Yes, I could say to him, my Brain is my Plant, my Skull is my Workshop, my Hand is my Machinery, and I am the Person carrying on the Concern; it is not leased to anybody, and so there is no Lessee bound to maintain and deliver over the same in good condition. There. I do not wish to any way overrate this argument and answer, dashed off just so, and not a word of it altered from the way I first wrote it, your Majesty, but indeed it does seem to pulverize that young fellow, you can see that yourself. But that is all I say; I stop there; I never pursue a person after I have got him down.

Having thus shown your Majesty that I am not taxable, but am the victim of the error of a clerk who mistakes the nature of my commerce, it only remains for me to beg that you will of your justice annul my letter that I spoke of, so that my publisher can keep back that tax-money which, in the confusion and aberration caused by the Document, I ordered him to pay. You will not miss the sum, but this is a hard year for authors; and as for lectures, I do not suppose your Majesty ever saw such a dull season.

With always great and ever-increasing respect, I beg to sign myself your Majesty's servant to command,

MARK TWAIN.

HER MAJESTY THE QUEEN, LONDON.

TWAIN *the* TRAVELER

Concerning Chambermaids

Against all chambermaids, of whatsoever age or nationality, I launch the curse of bachelordom! Because:

They always put the pillows at the opposite end of the bed from the gas-burner, so that while you read and smoke before sleeping (as is the ancient and honored custom of bachelors), you have to hold your book aloft, in an uncomfortable position, to keep the light from dazzling your eyes.

When they find the pillows removed to the other end of the bed in the morning, they receive not the suggestion in a friendly spirit; but, glorying in their absolute sovereignty, and unpitying your helplessness, they make the bed just as it was originally, and gloat in secret over the pang their tyranny will cause you.

Always after that, when they find you have transposed the pillows, they undo your work, and thus defy and seek to embitter the life that God has given you.

If they cannot get the light in an inconvenient position any other way, they move the bed.

If you pull your trunk out six inches from the wall, so that the lid will stay up when you open it, they always shove that trunk back again. They do it on purpose.

If you want the spittoon in a certain spot, where it will be handy, they don't, and so they move it.

They always put your other boots into inaccessible places. They chiefly enjoy depositing them as far under the bed as the wall will permit. It is because this compels you to get down in an undignified attitude and make wild sweeps for them in the dark with the bootjack, and swear.

They always put the matchbox in some other place. They hunt up a new place for it every day, and put up a bottle, or other perishable glass thing, where the box stood before. This is to cause you to break that glass thing, groping in the dark, and get yourself into trouble.

They are for ever and ever moving the furniture. When you come in in the night you can calculate on finding the bureau where the wardrobe was in the morning. And when you go out in the morning, if you leave the slop-bucket by the door and rocking-chair by the window, when you come in at midnight or thereabout, you will fall over that rocking-chair, and you will proceed toward the window and sit down in that slop-tub. This will disgust you. They like that.

No matter where you put anything, they are not going to let it stay there. They will take it and move it the first chance they get. It is their nature. And, besides, it gives them pleasure to be mean and contrary this way. They would die if they couldn't be villains.

They always save up all the old scraps of printed rubbish you throw on the floor, and stack them up carefully on the table, and start the fire with your valuable manuscripts. If there is any one particular old scrap that you are more down on than any other, and which you are gradually wearing your life out trying to get rid of, you may take all the pains you possibly can in that direction, but it won't be of any use, because they will always fetch that old scrap back and put it in the same old place again every time. It does them good.

And they use up more hair-oil than any six men. If charged with purloining the same, they lie about it. What do they care about a hereafter? Absolutely nothing.

If you leave the key in the door for convenience' sake, they will carry it down to the office and give it to the clerk. They do this under the vile pretense of trying to protect your property from thieves; but actually they do it because they want to make you tramp back down-stairs after it when you come home tired, or put you to the trouble of sending a waiter for it, which waiter will expect you to pay him something. In which case I suppose the degraded creatures divide.

They keep always trying to make your bed before you get up, thus destroying your rest and inflicting agony upon you; but after you get up, they don't come any more till next day.

They do all the mean things they can think of, and they do them just out of pure cussedness, and nothing else.

Chambermaids are dead to every human instinct.

If I can get a bill through the legislature abolishing chambermaids, I mean to do it.

The Portier

Omar Khayám, the poet-prophet of Persia, writing more than eight hundred years ago, has said:

> In the four parts of the earth are many that are able to write learned books, many that are able to lead armies, and many also that are able to govern kingdoms and empires; but few there be that can keep a hotel.

A word about the European hotel *portier.* He is a most admirable invention, a most valuable convenience. He always wears a conspicuous uniform; he can always be found when he is wanted, for he sticks closely to his post at the front door; he is as polite as a duke; he speaks from four to ten languages; he is your surest help and refuge in time of trouble or perplexity. He is not the clerk, he is not the landlord; he ranks above the clerk, and represents the landlord, who is seldom seen. Instead of going to the clerk for information, as we do at home, you go to the portier. It is the pride of our average hotel clerk to know nothing whatever; it is the pride of the portier to know everything. You ask the portier at what hours the trains leave—he tells you instantly; or you ask him who is the best physician in town; or what is the hack tariff; or how many children the mayor has; or what days the galleries are open, and whether a permit is required, and where you are to get it, and what you must pay for it; or when the theaters open and close, what the plays are to be, and the price of seats; or what is the newest thing in hats; or how the bills of mortality average; or "who struck Billy Patterson." It does not matter what you ask him: in nine cases out of ten he knows, and in the tenth case he will find out for you before you can turn around three times. There is nothing he will not put his hand to. Suppose you tell him you wish to go from Hamburg to Peking by the way of Jericho, and are ignorant of routes and prices—the next morning he will hand you a piece of paper with the whole thing worked out on it to the last detail. Before you have been long on European soil, you find yourself still *saying* you are relying on Providence, but when you come to look closer you will see that in reality you are relying on the portier. He discovers what is puzzling you, or what is troubling you, or what your need is, before you can get the half of it out, and he promptly says, "Leave that to me." Consequently, you easily drift into the habit of leaving everything to him. There is a certain embarrassment about applying to the average American hotel clerk, a certain hesitancy, a sense of insecurity against rebuff; but you feel no embarrassment in your intercourse with the portier; he receives your propositions with an enthusiasm which cheers, and plunges into their accomplishment with an alacrity which almost inebriates. The more requirements you can pile upon him, the better he likes it. Of course the result is that you cease from doing anything for yourself. He calls a hack when you want one; puts you into it; tells the driver whither to take you; receives you like a long lost child when you return; sends you about your business, does all the quarreling with the hackman himself, and pays him his money out of his own pocket. He sends for your theater tickets, and pays for them; he sends for any possible article you can require, be it a doctor, an elephant, or a postage stamp; and when you leave, at last, you will find a subordinate seated with the cab driver who will put you in your railway compartment, buy your tickets, have your baggage weighed, bring you the printed tags, and tell you everything is in your bill and paid for. At home you get such elaborate, excellent, and willing service as this only in the best hotels of our large cities; but in Europe you get it in the mere back country towns just as well.

What is the secret of the portier's devotion? It is very simple: he gets *fees, and no salary*. His fee is pretty closely regulated, too. If you stay a week in the house, you give him five marks—a dollar and a quarter, or about eighteen cents a day. If you stay a month, you reduce this average somewhat. If you stay two or three months or longer, you cut it down half, or even more than half. If you stay only one day, you give the portier a mark.

The head waiter's fee is a shade less than the portier's; the Boots, who not only blacks your boots and brushes your clothes, but is usually the porter and handles your baggage, gets a somewhat smaller fee than the head waiter; the chambermaid's fee ranks below that of the Boots. You fee only these four, and no one else. A German gentleman told me that when he remained a week in a hotel, he gave the portier five marks, the head waiter four, the Boots three, and the chambermaid two; and if he staid three months he divided ninety marks among them, in about the above proportions. Ninety marks make $22.50.

None of these fees are ever paid until you leave the hotel, though it be a year—except one of these four servants should go away in the meantime; in that case he will be sure to come and bid you good-bye and give you the opportunity to pay him what is fairly coming to him. It is considered very bad policy to fee a servant while you are still to remain longer in the hotel, because if you gave him too little he might neglect you afterward, and if you gave him too much he might neglect somebody else to attend to you. It is considered best to keep his expectations "on a string" until your stay is concluded.

I do not know whether hotel servants in New York get any wages or not, but I do know that in some of the hotels there the feeing system in vogue is a heavy burden. The waiter expects a quarter at breakfast—and gets it. You have a different waiter at luncheon, and so he gets a quarter. Your waiter at dinner is another stranger; consequently he gets a quarter. The boy who carries your satchel to your room and lights your gas fumbles around and hangs around significantly, and you fee him to get rid of him. Now you may ring for ice water; and ten minutes later for a lemonade; and ten minutes afterward, for a cigar; and by and by for a newspaper—and what is the result? Why, a new boy has appeared every time and fooled and fumbled around until you have paid him something. Suppose you boldly put your foot down, and say it is the hotel's business to pay its servants?—and suppose you stand your ground and stop feeing? You will have to ring your bell ten or fifteen times before you get a servant there; and when he goes off to fill your order you will grow old and infirm before you see him again. You may struggle nobly for twenty-four hours, maybe, if you are an adamantine sort of person, but in the meantime you will have been so wretchedly served, and so insolently, that you will haul down your colors, and go to impoverishing yourself with fees.

It seems to me that it would be a happy idea to import the European feeing system into America. I believe it would result in getting even the bells of the Philadelphia hotels answered, and cheerful service rendered.

The greatest American hotels keep a number of clerks and a cashier, and pay them salaries which mount up to a considerable total in the course of a year. The great continental hotels keep a cashier on a trifling salary, and a portier *who pays the hotel a salary.* By the latter system both the hotel and the public save money and are better served than by our system. One of our consuls told me that the portier of a great Berlin hotel paid $5,000 a year for his position, and yet cleared $6,000 for himself. The position of portier in the chief hotels of Saratoga, Long Branch, New York, and similar centers of resort, would be one which the holder could afford to pay even more than $5,000 for, perhaps.

When we borrowed the feeing fashion from Europe a dozen years ago, the salary system ought to have been discontinued, of course. We might make this correction now, I should think. And we might add the portier, too. Since I first began to study the portier, I have had opportunities to observe him in the chief cities of Germany, Switzerland, and Italy; and the more I have seen of him the more I have wished that he might be adopted in America, and become there, as he is in Europe, the stranger's guardian angel.

Yes, what was true eight hundred years ago, is just as true to-day: "Few there be that can keep hotel." Perhaps it is because the landlords and their subordinates have in too many cases taken up their trade without first learning it. In Europe the trade of hotel-keeper is taught. The apprentice begins at the bottom of the ladder and masters the several grades one after the other. Just as in our country printing-offices the apprentice first learns how to sweep out and bring water; then learns to "roll"; then to sort "pi"; then to set type; and finally rounds and completes his education with job-work and presswork; so the landlord-apprentice serves as call-boy; then as underwaiter; then as a parlor waiter; then as head-waiter, in which position he often has to make out all the bills; then as clerk or cashier; then as portier. His trade is learned now, and by and by he will assume the style and dignity of landlord, and be found conducting a hotel of his own.

Now in Europe, the same as in America, when a man has kept a hotel so thoroughly well during a number of years as to give it a great reputation, he has his reward. He can live prosperously on that reputation. He can let his hotel run down to the last degree of shabbiness and yet have it full of people all the time. For instance, there is the Hôtel de Ville, in Milan. It swarms with mice and fleas, and if the rest of the world were destroyed it could furnish dirt enough to start another one with. The food would create an insurrection in a poorhouse; and yet if you go outside to get your meals that hotel makes up its loss by over-charging you on all sorts of trifles—and without making any denials or excuses about it, either. But the Hôtel de Ville's old excellent reputation still keeps its dreary rooms crowded with travelers who would be elsewhere if they had only had some wise friend to warn them.

Heidelberg Castle

Heidelberg Castle must have been very beautiful before the French battered and bruised and scorched it two hundred years ago. The stone is brown, with a pinkish tint, and does not seem to stain easily. The dainty and elaborate ornamentation upon its two chief fronts is as delicately carved as if it had been intended for the interior of a drawing-room rather than for the outside of a house. Many fruit and flower-clusters, human heads and grim projecting lion's heads are still as perfect in every detail as if they were new. But the statues which are ranked between the windows have suffered. These are life-size statues of old-time emperors, electors, and similar grandees, clad in mail and bearing ponderous swords. Some have lost an arm, some a head, and one poor fellow is chopped off at the middle. There is a saying that if a stranger will pass over the drawbridge and walk across the court to the castle front without saying anything, he can make a wish and it will be fulfilled. But they say that the truth of this thing has never had a chance to be proved, for the reason that before any stranger can walk from the drawbridge to the appointed place, the beauty of the palace front will extort an exclamation of delight from him.

A ruin must be rightly situated, to be effective. This one could not have been better placed. It stands upon a commanding elevation, it is buried in green woods, there is no level ground about it, but, on the contrary, there are wooded terraces upon terraces, and one looks down through shining leaves into profound chasms and abysses where twilight reigns and the sun cannot intrude. Nature knows how to garnish a ruin to get the best effect. One of these old towers is split down the middle, and one half has tumbled aside. It tumbled in such a way as to establish itself in a picturesque attitude. Then all it lacked was a fitting drapery, and Nature has furnished that; she has robed the rugged mass in flowers and verdure, and made it a charm to the eye. The standing half exposes its arched and cavernous rooms to you, like open, toothless mouths; there, too, the vines and flowers have done their work of grace. The rear portion of the tower has not been neglected, either, but is clothed with a clinging garment of polished ivy which hides the wounds and stains of time. Even the top is not left bare, but is crowned with a flourishing group of trees and shrubs. Misfortune has done for this old tower what it has done for the human character sometimes—improved it.

A gentleman remarked, one day, that it might have been fine to live in the castle in the day of its prime, but that we had one advantage which its vanished inhabitants lacked—the advantage of having a charming ruin to visit and muse over. But that was a hasty idea. Those people had the advantage of *us.* They had the fine castle to live in, and they could cross the Rhine valley and muse over the stately ruin of Trifels besides. The Trifels people, in their day, five hundred years ago, could go and muse over majestic ruins which have vanished, now, to the last stone. There have always been ruins, no doubt; and there have always been pensive people to sigh over them, and asses to scratch upon them their names and the important date of their visit. Within a hundred years after Adam left Eden, the guide probably gave the usual general flourish with his hand and said: "Place where the animals were named, ladies and gentlemen; place where the tree of the forbidden fruit stood; exact spot where Adam and Eve first met; and here, ladies and gentlemen, adorned and hallowed by the names and addresses of three generations of tourists, we have the crumbling remains of Cain's altar—fine old ruin!" Then, no doubt, he taxed them a shekel apiece and let them go.

An illumination of Heidelberg Castle is one of the sights of Europe. The Castle's picturesque shape; its commanding situation, midway up the steep and wooded mountain side; its vast size—these features combine to make an illumination a most effective spectacle. It is necessarily an expensive show, and consequently rather infrequent. Therefore whenever one of these exhibitions is to take place, the news goes about in the papers and Heidelberg is sure to be full of people on that night. I and my agent had one of these opportunities, and improved it.

About half past seven on the appointed evening, we crossed the lower bridge, with some American students, in a pouring rain, and started up the road which borders the Neunheim side of the river. This roadway was densely packed with carriages and foot passengers; the former of all ages, and the latter of all ages and both sexes. This black and solid mass was struggling painfully onward, through the slop, the darkness, and the deluge. We waded along for three-quarters of a mile, and finally took up a position in an unsheltered beer garden directly opposite the Castle. We could not *see* the Castle—or anything else, for that matter—but we could dimly discern the outlines of the mountain over the way, through the pervading blackness, and knew whereabouts the Castle was located. We stood on one of the hundred benches in the garden, under our umbrellas; the other ninety-nine were occupied by standing men and women, and they also had umbrellas. All the region round about, and up and down the river-road, was a dense wilderness of humanity hidden under an unbroken pavement of carriage tops and umbrellas. Thus we stood during two drenching hours. No rain fell on my head, but the converging whalebone points of a dozen neighboring umbrellas poured little cooling streams of water down my neck, and sometimes into my ears, and thus kept me from getting hot and impatient. I had the rheumatism, too, and had heard that this was good for it. Afterward, however, I was led to believe that the water treatment is *not* good for rheumatism. There were even little girls in that dreadful place. A man held one in his arms, just in front of me, for as much as an hour, with umbrella-drippings soaking into her clothing all the time.

In the circumstances, two hours was a good while for us to have to wait, but when the illumination did at last come, we felt repaid. It came unexpectedly, of course—things always do, that have been long looked and longed for. With a perfectly breath-taking suddenness several vast sheaves of varicolored rockets were vomited skyward out of the black throats of the castle towers, accompanied by a thundering crash of sound, and instantly every detail of the prodigious ruin stood revealed against the mountain side and glowing with an almost intolerable splendor of fire and color. For some little time the whole building was a blinding crimson mass, the towers continued to spout thick columns of rockets aloft, and overhead the sky was radiant with arrowy bolts which clove their way to the zenith, paused, curved gracefully downward, then burst into brilliant fountain sprays of richly-colored sparks. The red fires died slowly down, within the castle, and presently the shell grew nearly black outside; the angry glare that shone out through the broken arches and innumerable sashless windows, now, reproduced the aspect which the Castle must have borne in the old time when the French spoilers saw the monster bonfire which they had made there fading and smouldering toward extinction.

While we still gazed and enjoyed, the ruin was suddenly enveloped in rolling and tumbling volumes of vaporous green fire; then in dazzling purple ones; then a mixture of many colors followed, and drowned the great fabric in its blended splendors. Meantime the nearest bridge had been illuminated, and from several rafts anchored in the river, meteor showers of rockets, Roman candles, bombs, serpents, and Catharine wheels were being discharged in wasteful profusion into the sky—a marvelous sight indeed to a person as little used to such spectacles as I was. For a while the whole region about us seemed as bright as day, and yet the rain was falling in torrents all the time. The evening's entertainment presently closed, and we joined the innumerable caravan of half-drowned spectators, and waded home again.

The Castle grounds are very ample and very beautiful; and as they joined the Hotel grounds, with no fences to climb, but only some nobly shaded stone stairways to descend, we spent a part of nearly every day in idling through their smooth walks and leafy groves. There was an attractive spot among the trees where were a great many wooden tables and benches; and there one could sit in the shade and pretend to sip at his foamy beaker of beer while he inspected the crowd. I say pretend, because I only pretended to sip, without really sipping. That is the polite way; but when you are ready to go, you empty the beaker at a draught. There was a brass band, and it furnished excellent music every afternoon. Sometimes so many people came that every seat was occupied, every table filled. And never a rough in the assemblage—all nicely dressed fathers and mothers, young gentlemen and ladies and children; and plenty of university students and glittering officers; with here and there a gray professor, or a peaceful old lady with her knitting; and always a sprinkling of gawky foreigners. Everybody had his glass of beer before him, or his cup of coffee, or his bottle of wine, or his hot cutlet and potatoes; young ladies chatted, or fanned themselves, or wrought at their crotcheting or embroidering; the students fed sugar to their dogs, or discussed duels, or illustrated new fencing-tricks with their little canes; and everywhere was comfort and enjoyment, and everywhere peace and good-will to men. The trees were jubilant with birds, and the paths with rollicking children. One could have a seat in that place and plenty of music, any afternoon, for about eight cents, or a family ticket for the season for two dollars.

For a change, when you wanted one, you could stroll to the castle, and burrow among its dungeons, or climb about its ruined towers, or visit its interior shows—the great Heidelberg Tun, for instance. Everybody has heard of the great Heidelberg Tun, and most people have seen it, no doubt. It is a wine cask as big as a cottage, and some traditions say it holds eighteen hundred thousand bottles, and other traditions say it holds eighteen hundred million barrels. I think it likely that one of these statements is a mistake, and the other one a lie. However, the mere matter of capacity is a thing of no sort of consequence, since the cask is empty, and indeed has always been empty, history says. An empty cask the size of a cathedral could excite but little emotion in me. I do not see any wisdom in building a monster cask to hoard up emptiness in, when you can get a better quality, outside, any day, free of expense. What could this cask have been built for? The more one studies over that, the more uncertain and unhappy he becomes. Some historians say that thirty couples, some say thirty thousand couples, can dance on the head of this cask at the same time. Even this does not seem to me to account for the building of it. It does not even throw light on it. A profound and scholarly Englishman—a specialist—who had made the great Heidelberg Tun his sole study for fifteen years, told me he had at last satisfied himself that the ancients built it to make German cream in. He said that the average German cow yielded from one to two and a half teaspoonfuls of milk, when she was not worked in the plow or the hay wagon more than eighteen or nineteen hours a day. This milk was very sweet and good, and of a beautiful transparent bluish tint; but in order to get cream from it in the most economical way, a peculiar process was necessary. Now he believed that the habit of the ancients was to collect several milkings in a teacup, pour it into the Great Tun, fill up with water, and then skim off the cream from time to time as the needs of the German Empire demanded.

This began to look reasonable. It certainly began to account for the German cream which I had encountered and marveled over in so many hotels and restaurants. But a thought struck me:

"Why did not each ancient dairyman take his own teacup of milk and his own cask of water, and mix them, without making a government matter of it?"

"Where could he get a cask large enough to contain the right proportion of water?"

Very true. It was plain that the Englishman had studied the matter from all sides. Still I thought I might catch him on one point; so I asked him why the modern empire did not make the nation's cream in the Heidelberg Tun, instead of leaving it to rot away unused. But he answered as one prepared:

"A patient and diligent examination of the modern German cream has satisfied me that they do not use the Great Tun now, because they have got a *bigger* one hid away somewhere. Either that is the case or they empty the spring milkings into the mountain torrents and then skim the Rhine all summer."

There is a museum of antiquities in the castle, and among its most treasured relics are ancient manuscripts connected with German history. There are hundreds of these, and their dates stretch back through many centuries. One of them is a decree signed and sealed by the hand of a successor of Charlemagne, in the year 896. A signature made by a hand which vanished out of this life near a thousand years ago, is a more impressive thing than even a ruined castle. Luther's wedding ring was shown me; also a fork belonging to a time anterior to our era, and an early bootjack. And there was a plaster cast of the head of a man who was assassinated about sixty years ago. The stab-wounds in the face were duplicated with unpleasant fidelity. One or two real hairs still remained sticking in the eyebrows of the cast. That trifle seemed to almost change the counterfeit into a corpse.

There are many aged portraits—some valuable, some worthless; some of great interest, some of none at all. I bought a couple—one a gorgeous duke of the olden time, and the other a comely blue-eyed damsel, a princess, maybe. I bought them to start a portrait gallery of my ancestors with. I paid a dollar and a half for the duke and two and a half for the princess. One can lay in ancestors at even cheaper rates than these, in Europe, if he will mouse among old picture shops and look out for chances.

The College Prison

It seems that the student may break a good many of the public laws without having to answer to the public authorities. His case must come before the University for trial and punishment. If a policeman catches him in an unlawful act and proceeds to arrest him, the offender proclaims that he is a student, and perhaps shows his matriculation card, whereupon the officer asks for his address, then goes his way, and reports the matter at headquarters. If the offense is one over which the city has no jurisdiction, the authorities report the case officially to the University, and give themselves no further concern about it. The University court send for the student, listen to the evidence, and pronounce judgment. The punishment usually inflicted is imprisonment in the University prison. As I understand it, a student's case is often tried without his being present at all. Then something like this happens: A constable in the service of the University visits the lodgings of the said student, knocks, is invited to come in, does so, and says politely:

"If you please, I am here to conduct you to prison."

"Ah," says the student, "I was not expecting it. What have I been doing?"

"Two weeks ago the public peace had the honor to be disturbed by you."

"It is true; I had forgotten it. Very well: I have been complained of, tried, and found guilty—is that it?"

"Exactly. You are sentenced to two days' solitary confinement in the College prison, and I am sent to fetch you."

Student. "O, I can't go to-day!"

Officer. "If you please, why?"

Student. "Because I've got an engagement."

Officer. "To-morrow, then, perhaps?"

Student. "No, I am going to the opera, to-morrow."

Officer. "Could you come Friday?"

Student. (Reflectively.) "Let me see—Friday—Friday. I don't seem to have anything on hand Friday."

Officer. "Then, if you please, I will expect you on Friday."

Student. "All right, I'll come around Friday."

Officer. "Thank you. Good day, sir."

Student. "Good day."

So on Friday the student goes to the prison of his own accord, and is admitted.

It is questionable if the world's criminal history can show a custom more odd than this. Nobody knows, now, how it originated. There have always been many noblemen among the students, and it is presumed that all students are gentlemen; in the old times it was usual to mar the convenience of such folk as little as possible; perhaps this indulgent custom owes its origin to this.

One day I was listening to some conversation upon this subject when an American student said that for some time he had been under sentence for a slight breach of the peace and had promised the constable that he would presently find an unoccupied day and betake himself to prison. I asked the young gentleman to do me the kindness to go to jail as soon as he conveniently could, so that I might try to get in there and visit him, and see what college captivity was like. He said he would appoint the very first day he could spare.

His confinement was to endure twenty-four hours. He shortly chose his day, and sent me word. I started immediately. When I reached the University Place, I saw two gentlemen talking together, and, as they had portfolios under their arms, I judged they were tutors or elderly students; so I asked them in English to show me the college jail. I had learned to take it for granted that anybody in Germany who knows anything, knows English, so I had stopped afflicting people with my German. These gentlemen seemed a trifle amused—and a trifle confused, too—but one of them said he would walk around the corner with me and show me the place. He asked me why I wanted to get in there, and I said to see a friend—and for curiosity. He doubted if I would be admitted, but volunteered to put in a word or two for me with the custodian.

He rang the bell, a door opened, and we stepped into a paved way and then into a small living-room, where we were received by a hearty and good-natured German woman of fifty. She threw up her hands with a surprised "Ach Gott, Herr Professor!" and exhibited a mighty deference for my new acquaintance. By the sparkle in her eye I judged she was a good deal amused, too. The "Herr Professor" talked to her in German, and I understood enough of it to know that he was bringing very plausible reasons to bear for admitting me. They were successful. So the Herr Professor received my earnest thanks and departed. The old dame got her keys, took me up two or three flights of stairs, unlocked a door, and we stood in the presence of the criminal. Then she went into a jolly and eager description of all that had occurred downstairs, and what the Herr Professor had said, and so forth and so on. Plainly, she regarded it as quite a superior joke that I had waylaid a Professor and employed him in so odd a service. But I wouldn't have done it if I had known he was a Professor; therefore my conscience was not disturbed.

Now the dame left us to ourselves. The cell was not a roomy one; still it was a little larger than an ordinary prison cell. It had a window of good size, iron-grated; a small stove; two wooden chairs: two oaken tables, very old and most elaborately carved with names, mottoes, faces, armorial bearings, etc.—the work of several generations of imprisoned students; and a narrow wooden bedstead with a villainous old straw mattress, but no sheets, pillows, blankets, or coverlets, for these the student must furnish at his own cost if he wants them. There was no carpet, of course.

The ceiling was completely covered with names, dates, and monograms, done with candle smoke. The walls were thickly covered with pictures and portraits (in profile), some done with ink, some with soot, some with a pencil, and some with red, blue, and green chalks; and wherever an inch or two of space had remained between the pictures, the captives had written plaintive verses, or names and dates. I do not think I was ever in a more elaborately frescoed apartment.

Against the wall hung a placard containing the prison laws. I made a note of one or two of these. For instance: The prisoner must pay, for the "privilege" of entering, a sum equivalent to 20 cents of our money; for the privilege of leaving, when his term has expired, 20 cents; for every day spent in the prison, 12 cents; for fire and light, 12 cents a day. The jailer furnishes coffee, mornings, for a small sum; dinners and suppers may be ordered from outside if the prisoner chooses—and he is allowed to pay for them, too.

Here and there, on the walls, appeared the names of American students, and in one place the American arms and motto were displayed in colored chalks.

With the help of my friend I translated many of the inscriptions. Some of them were cheerful, others the reverse. I will give the reader a few specimens:

"In my tenth semester (my best one), I am cast here through the complaints of others. Let those who follow me take warning."

"III Tage ohne Grund angeblich aus Neugierde." Which is to say, he had a curiosity to know what prison life was like; so he made a breach in some law and got three days for it. It is more than likely that he never had the same curiosity again.

(Translation.) "E. Glinicke, four days for being too eager a spectator of a row."

"F. Graf Bismarck—27–29, II, '74." Which means that Count Bismarck, son of the great statesman, was a prisoner two days in 1874.

(Translation.) "R. Diergandt—for Love—4 days." Many people in this world have caught it heavier than that for the same indiscretion.

This one is terse. I translate:

"Four weeks for *misinterpreted gallantry*."

I wish the sufferer had explained a little more fully. A four-weeks term is a rather serious matter.

There were many uncomplimentary references, on the walls, to a certain unpopular college dignitary. One sufferer had got three days for not saluting him. Another had "here two days slept and three nights lain awake," on account of this same "Dr. K—." In one place was a picture of Dr. K— hanging on a gallows.

Here and there, lonesome prisoners had eased the heavy time by altering the records left by predecessors. Leaving the name standing, and the date and length of the captivity, they had erased the description of the misdemeanor, and written in its place, in staring capitals, "FOR THEFT!" or "FOR MURDER!" or some other gaudy crime. In one place, all by itself, stood this blood-curdling word:

"Rache!"[1]

There was no name signed, and no date. It was an inscription well calculated to pique curiosity. One would greatly like to know the nature of the wrong that had been done, and what sort of vengeance was wanted, and whether the prisoner ever achieved it or not. But there was no way of finding out these things.

Occasionally, a name was followed simply by the remark, "II days, for disturbing the peace," and without comment upon the justice or injustice of the sentence.

In one place was a hilarious picture of a student of the green-cap corps with a bottle of champagne in each hand; and below was the legend: "These make an evil fate endurable."

There were two prison cells, and neither had space left on walls or ceiling for another name or portrait or picture. The inside surfaces of the two doors were completely covered with cartes de visite of former prisoners, ingeniously let into the wood and protected from dirt and injury by glass.

I very much wanted one of the sorry old tables which the prisoners had spent so many years in ornamenting with their pocket-knives, but red tape was in the way. The custodian could not sell one without an order from a superior; and that superior would have to get it from *his* superior; and this one would have to get it from a higher one—and so on up and up until the faculty should sit on the matter and deliver final judgment. The system was right, and nobody could find fault with it; but it did not seem justifiable to bother so many people, so I proceeded no further. It might have cost me more than I could afford, anyway; for one of those prison tables, which was at that time in a private museum in Heidelberg, was afterward sold at auction for two hundred and fifty dollars. It was not worth more than a dollar, or possibly a dollar and a half, before the captive students began their work on it. Persons who saw it at the auction said it was so curiously and wonderfully carved that it was worth the money that was paid for it.

Among the many who have tasted the college prison's dreary hospitality was a lively young fellow from one of the Southern States of America, whose first year's experience of German university life was rather peculiar. The day he arrived in Heidelberg he enrolled his name on the college books, and was so elated with the fact that his dearest hope had found

1. "Revenge!"—M.T.

fruition and he was actually a student of the old and renowned university, that he set to work that very night to celebrate the event by a grand lark in company with some other students. In the course of his lark he managed to make a wide breach in one of the university's most stringent laws. Sequel: before noon, next day, he was in the college prison—booked for three months. The twelve long weeks dragged slowly by, and the day of deliverance came at last. A great crowd of sympathizing fellow-students received him with a rousing demonstration as he came forth, and of course there was another grand lark, in the course of which he managed to make a wide breach in one of the *city's* most stringent laws. Sequel: before noon, next day, he was safe in the city lockup—booked for three months. This second tedious captivity drew to an end in the course of time, and again a great crowd of sympathizing fellow-students gave him a rousing reception as he came forth; but his delight in his freedom was so boundless that he could not proceed soberly and calmly, but must go hopping and skipping and jumping down the sleety street from sheer excess of joy. Sequel: he slipped and broke his leg, and actually lay in the hospital during the next three months!

When he at last became a free man again, he said he believed he would hunt up a brisker seat of learning; the Heidelberg lectures might be good, but the opportunities of attending them were too rare, the educational process too slow; he said he had come to Europe with the idea that the acquirement of an education was only a matter of time, but if he had averaged the Heidelburg system correctly, it was rather a matter of eternity.

The German Chicago

I feel lost in Berlin. It has no resemblance to the city I had supposed it was. There was once a Berlin which I would have known, from descriptions in books—the Berlin of the last century and the beginning of the present one: a dingy city in a marsh, with rough streets, muddy and lantern-lighted, dividing straight rows of ugly houses all alike, compacted into blocks as square and plain and uniform and monotonous and serious as so many dry-goods boxes. But that Berlin has disappeared. It seems to have disappeared totally, and left no sign. The bulk of the Berlin of to-day has about it no suggestion of a former period. The site it stands on has traditions and a history, but the city itself has no traditions and no history. It is a new city; the newest I have ever seen. Chicago would seem venerable beside it; for there are many old-looking districts in Chicago, but not many in Berlin. The main mass of the city looks as if it had been built last week, the rest of it has a just perceptibly graver tone, and looks as if it might be six or even eight months old.

The next feature that strikes one is the spaciousness, the roominess of the city. There is no other city, in any country, whose streets are so generally wide. Berlin is not merely *a* city of wide streets, it is *the* city of wide streets. As a wide-street city it has never had its equal, in any age of the world. "Unter den Linden" is three streets in one; the Potsdamerstrasse is bordered on both sides by sidewalks which are themselves wider than some of the historic thoroughfares of the old European capitals; there seem to be no lanes or alleys; there are no short cuts; here and there, where several important streets empty into a common center, that center's circumference is of a magnitude calculated to bring that word spaciousness into your mind again. The park in the middle of the city is so huge that it calls up that expression once more.

The next feature that strikes one is the straightness of the streets. The short ones haven't so much as a waver in them; the long ones stretch out to prodigious distances and then tilt a little to the right or left, then stretch out on another immense reach as straight as a ray of light. A result of this arrangement is, that at night Berlin is an inspiring sight to see. Gas and the electric light are employed with a wasteful liberality, and so, wherever one goes, he has always double ranks of brilliant lights stretching far down into the night on every hand, with here and there a wide and splendid constellation of them spread out over an intervening "Platz"; and between the interminable double procession of street lamps one has the swarming and darting cab lamps, a lively and pretty addition to the fine spectacle, for they counterfeit the rush and confusion and sparkle of an invasion of fireflies.

There is one other noticeable feature—the absolutely level surface of the site of Berlin. Berlin—to recapitulate—is newer to the eye than is any other city, and also blonder of complexion and tidier; no other city has such an air of roominess, freedom from crowding; no other city has so many straight streets; and with Chicago it contests the chromo for flatness of surface and for phenomenal swiftness of growth. Berlin is the European Chicago. The two cities have about the same population—say a million and a half. I cannot speak in exact terms, because I only know what Chicago's population was week before last; but at that time it was about a million and a half. Fifteen years ago Berlin and Chicago were large cities, of course, but neither of them was the giant it now is.

But now the parallels fail. Only parts of Chicago are stately and beautiful, whereas all of Berlin is stately and substantial, and it is not merely in parts but uniformly beautiful. There are buildings in Chicago that are architecturally finer than any in Berlin, I think, but what I have just said above is still true. These two flat cities would lead the world for phenomenal good health if London were out of the way. As it is, London leads by a point or two. Berlin's death rate is only nineteen in the thousand. Fourteen years ago the rate was a third higher.

Berlin is a surprise in a great many ways—in a multitude of ways, to speak strongly and be exact. It seems to be the most governed city in the world, but one must admit that it also seems to be the best governed. Method and system are observable on every hand—in great things, in little things, in all details, of whatsoever size. And it is not method and system on paper, and there an end—it is method and system in practice. It has a rule for everything, and puts the rule in force; puts it in force against the poor and powerful alike, without favor or prejudice. It deals with great matters and minute particulars with equal faithfulness, and with a plodding and painstaking diligence and persistency which compel admiration—and sometimes regret. There are several taxes, and they are collected quarterly. Collected is the word; they are not merely levied, they are collected—every time. This makes light taxes. It is in cities and countries where a considerable part of the community shirk payment that taxes have to be lifted to a burdensome rate. Here the police keep coming, calmly and patiently, until you pay your tax. They charge you five or ten cents per visit after the first call. By experiment you will find that they will presently collect that money.

In one respect the million and a half of Berlin's population are like a family: the head of this large family knows the names of its several members, and where the said members are located, and when and where they were born, and what they do for a living, and what their religious brand is. Whoever comes to Berlin must furnish these particulars to the police immediately; moreover, if he knows how long he is going to stay, he must say so. If he take a house he will be taxed on the rent and taxed also on his income. He will not be asked what his income is, and so he may save some lies for home consumption. The police will estimate his income from the house rent he pays, and tax him on that basis.

Duties on imported articles are collected with inflexible fidelity, be the sum large or little; but the methods are gentle, prompt, and full of the spirit of accommodation. The postman attends to the whole matter for you, in cases where the article comes by mail, and you have no trouble and suffer no inconvenience. The other day a friend of mine was informed that there was a package in the post-office for him, containing a lady's silk belt with gold clasp, and a gold chain to hang a bunch of keys on. In his first agitation he was going to try to bribe the postman to chalk it through, but acted upon his sober second thought and allowed the matter to take its proper and regular course. In a little while the postman brought the package and made these several collections: duty on the silk belt, 7½ cents; duty on the gold chain, 10 cents; charge for fetching the package, 5 cents. These devastating imposts are exacted for the protection of German home industries.

The calm, quiet, courteous, cussed persistence of the police is the most admirable thing I have encountered on this side. They undertook to persuade me to send and get a passport for a Swiss maid whom we had brought with us, and at the end of six weeks of patient, tranquil, angelic daily effort they succeeded. I was not intending to give them trouble, but I was lazy and I thought they would get tired. Meanwhile they probably thought I would be the one. It turned out just so.

One is not allowed to build unstable, unsafe, or unsightly houses in Berlin; the result is this comely and conspicuously stately city, with its security from conflagrations and breakdowns. It is built of architectural Gibraltars. The building commissioners inspect while the building is going up. It has been found that this is better than to wait till it falls down. These people are full of whims.

One is not allowed to cram poor folk into cramped and dirty tenement houses. Each individual must have just so many cubic feet of room-space, and sanitary inspections are systematic and frequent.

Everything is orderly. The fire brigade march in rank, curiously uniformed, and so grave is their demeanor that they look like a Salvation Army under conviction of sin. People tell me that when a fire alarm is sounded, the firemen assemble calmly, answer to their names when the roll is called, then proceed to the fire. There they are ranked up, military fashion, and told off in detachments by the chief, who parcels out to the detachments the several parts of the work which they are to undertake in putting out that fire. This is all done with low-voiced propriety, and strangers think these people are working a funeral. As a rule, the fire is confined to a single floor in these great masses of bricks and masonry, and consequently there is little or no interest attaching to a fire here for the rest of the occupants of the house.

There is abundance of newspapers in Berlin, and there was also a newsboy, but he died. At intervals of half a mile on the thoroughfares there are booths, and it is at these that you buy your papers. There are plenty of theaters, but they do not advertise in a loud way. There are no big posters of any kind, and the display of vast type and of pictures of actors and performance framed on a big scale and done in rainbow colors is a thing unknown. If the big show-bills existed there would be no place to exhibit them; for there are no poster-fences, and one would not be allowed to disfigure dead walls with them. Unsightly things are forbidden here; Berlin is a rest to the eye.

And yet the saunterer can easily find out what is going on at the theaters. All over the city, at short distances apart, there are neat round pillars eighteen feet high and about as thick as a hogshead, and on these the little black and white theater bills and other notices are posted. One generally finds a group around each pillar reading these things. There are plenty of things in Berlin worth importing to America. It is these that I have particularly wished to make a note of. When Buffalo Bill was here his biggest poster was probably not larger than the top of an ordinary trunk.

There is a multiplicity of clean and comfortable horse-cars, but whenever you think you know where a car is going to you would better stop ashore, because that car is not going to that place at all. The car routes are marvelously intricate, and often the drivers get lost and are not heard of for years. The signs on the cars furnish no details as to the course of the journey; they name the end of it, and then experiment around to see how much territory they can cover before they get there. The conductor will collect your fare over again every few miles, and give you a ticket which he hasn't apparently kept any record of, and you keep it till an inspector comes aboard by and by and tears a corner off it (which he does not keep), then you throw the ticket away and get ready to buy another. Brains are of no value when you are trying to navigate Berlin in a horse-car. When the ablest of Brooklyn's editors was here on a visit he took a horse-car in the early morning, and wore it out trying to go to a point in the center of the city. He was on board all day and spent many dollars in fares, and then did not arrive at the place which he had started to go to. This is the most thorough way to see Berlin, but it is also the most expensive.

But there are excellent features about the car system, nevertheless. The car will not stop for you to get on or off, except at certain places a block or two apart where there is a sign to indicate that that is a halting-station. This system saves many bones. There are twenty places inside the car; when these seats are filled, no more can enter. Four or five persons may stand on each platform—the law decrees the number—and when these standing-places are all occupied the next applicant is refused. As there is no crowding, and as no rowdyism is allowed, women stand on the platforms as well as the men; they often stand there when there are vacant seats inside, for these places are comfortable, there being little or no jolting. A native tells me that when the first car was put on, thirty or forty years ago, the public had such a terror of it that they didn't feel safe inside of it, or outside either. They made the company keep a man at every crossing with a red flag in his hand. Nobody would travel in the car except convicts on the way to the gallows. This made business in only one direction, and the car had to go back light. To save the company, the city government transferred the convict cemetery to the other end of the line. This made traffic in both directions and kept the company from going under. This sounds like some of the information which traveling foreigners are furnished with in America. To my mind it has a doubtful ring about it.

The first-class cab is neat and trim, and has leather-cushion seats and a swift horse. The second-class cab is an ugly and lubberly vehicle, and is always old. It seems a strange thing that they have never built any new ones. Still, if such a thing were done everybody that had time to flock would flock to see it, and that would make a crowd, and the police do not like crowds and disorder here. If there were an earthquake in Berlin the police would take charge of it and conduct it in that sort of orderly way that would make you think it was a prayer-meeting. That is what an earthquake generally ends in, but this one would be different from those others; it would be kind of soft and self-contained, like a republican praying for a mugwump.

For a course (a quarter of an hour or less), one pays twenty-five cents in a first-class cab, and fifteen cents in a second-class. The first-class will take you along faster, for the second-class horse is old—always old—as old as his cab, some authorities say—and ill-fed and weak. He has been a first-class once, but has been degraded to second class for long and faithful service.

Still, he must take you as *far* for fifteen cents as the other horse takes you for twenty-five. If he can't do his fifteen-minute distance in fifteen minutes, he must still do the distance for the fifteen cents. Any stranger can check the distance off—by means of the most curious map I am acquainted with. It is issued by the city government and can be bought in any shop for a trifle. In it every street is sectioned off like a string of long beads of different colors. Each long bead represents a minute's travel, and when you have covered fifteen of the beads you have got your money's worth. This map of Berlin is a gay-colored maze, and looks like pictures of the circulation of the blood.

The streets are very clean. They are kept so—not by prayer and talk and the other New York methods, but by daily and hourly work with scrapers and brooms; and when an asphalted street has been tidily scraped after a rain or a light snowfall, they scatter clean sand over it. This saves some of the horses from falling down. In fact, this is a city government which seems to stop at no expense where the public convenience, comfort, and health are concerned—except in one detail. That is the naming of the streets and the numbering of the houses. Sometimes the name of a street will change in the middle of a block. You will not find it out till you get to the next corner and discover the new name on the wall, and of course you don't know just when the change happened.

The names are plainly marked on the corners—on all the corners—there are no exceptions. But the numbering of the houses—there has never been anything like it since original chaos. It is not possible that it was done by this wise city government. At first one thinks it was done by an idiot; but there is too much variety about it for that; an idiot could not think of so many different ways of making confusion and propagating blasphemy. The numbers run up one side the street and down the other. That is endurable, but the rest isn't. They often use one number for three or four houses—and sometimes they put the number on only one of the houses and let you guess at the others. Sometimes they put a number on a house—4, for instance—then put *4a, 4b, 4c,* on the succeeding houses, and one becomes old and decrepit before he finally arrives at 5. A result of this systemless system is that when you are at No. 1 in a street you haven't any idea how far it may be to No. 150; it may be only six or eight blocks, it may be a couple of miles. Frederick Street is long, and is one of the great thoroughfares. The other day a man put up his money behind the assertion that there were more refreshment places in that street than numbers on the houses—and he won. There were 254 numbers and 257 refreshment places. Yet as I have said, it is a long street.

But the worst feature of all this complex business is that in Berlin the numbers do not travel in any one direction; no, they travel along until they get to 50 or 60, perhaps, then suddenly you find yourself up in the hundreds—140, maybe; the next will be 139—then you perceive by that sign that the numbers are now traveling toward you from the opposite direction. They will keep that sort of insanity up as long as you travel that street; every now and then the numbers will turn and run the other way. As a rule, there is an arrow under the number, to show by the direction of its flight which way the numbers are proceeding. There are a good many suicides in Berlin; I have seen six reported in a single day. There is always a deal of learned and laborious arguing and ciphering going on as to the cause of this state of things. If they will set to work and number their houses in a rational way perhaps they will find out what was the matter.

More than a month ago Berlin began to prepare to celebrate Professor Virchow's seventieth birthday. When the birthday arrived, the middle of October, it seemed to me that all the world of science arrived with it; deputation after deputation came, bringing the homage and reverence of far cities and centers of learning, and during the whole of a long day the hero of it sat and received such witness of his greatness as has seldom been vouchsafed to any man in any walk of life in any time, ancient or modern. These demonstrations were continued in one form or another day after day, and were presently merged in similar demonstrations to his twin in science and achievement, Professor Helmholtz, whose seventieth birthday is separated from Virchow's by only about three weeks; so nearly as this did these two extraordinary men come to being born together. Two such births have seldom signalized a single year in human history.

But perhaps the final and closing demonstration was peculiarly grateful to them. This was a Commers given in their honor the other night by 1,000 students. It was held in a huge hall, very long and very lofty, which had five galleries, far above everybody's head, which were crowded with ladies—four or five hundred, I judged.

It was beautifully decorated with clustered flags and various ornamental devices, and was brilliantly lighted. On the spacious floor of this place were ranged, in files, innumerable tables, seating twenty-four persons each, extending from one end of the great hall clear to the other, and with narrow aisles between the files. In the center on one side was a high and tastefully decorated platform twenty or thirty feet long, with a long table on it behind which sat the half-dozen chiefs of the givers of the Commers in the rich medieval costumes of as many different college corps. Behind these youths a band of musicians was concealed. On the floor directly in front of this platform were half a dozen tables which were distinguished from the outlying continent of tables by being covered instead of left naked. Of these the central table was reserved for the two heroes of the occasion and twenty particularly eminent professors of the Berlin University, and the other covered tables were for the occupancy of a hundred less distinguished professors.

I was glad to be honored with a place at the table of the two heroes of the occasion, although I was not really learned enough to deserve it.

Indeed, there was a pleasant strangeness in being in such company; to be thus associated with twenty-three men who forget more every day than I ever knew. Yet there was nothing embarrassing about it, because loaded men and empty ones look about alike, and I knew that to that multitude there I was a professor. It required but little art to catch the ways and attitude of those men and imitate them, and I had no difficulty in looking as much like a professor as anybody there.

We arrived early; so early that only Professors Virchow and Helmholtz and a dozen guests of the special tables were ahead of us, and three hundred or four hundred students. But people were arriving in floods now, and within fifteen minutes all but the special tables were occupied, and the great house was crammed, the aisles included. It was said that there were four thousand men present. It was a most animated scene, there is no doubt about that; it was a stupendous beehive. At each end of each table stood a corps student in the uniform of his corps. These quaint costumes are of brilliant colored silks and velvets, with sometimes a high plumed hat, sometimes a broad Scotch cap, with a great plume wound about it, sometimes—oftenest—a little shallow silk cap on the tip of the crown, like an inverted saucer; sometimes the pantaloons are snow-white, sometimes of other colors; the boots in all cases come up well above the knee; and in all cases also white gauntlets are worn; the sword is a rapier with a bowl-shaped guard for the hand, painted in several colors. Each corps has a uniform of its own, and all are of rich material, brilliant in color, and exceedingly picturesque; for they are survivals of the vanished costumes of the Middle Ages, and they reproduce for us the time when men were beautiful to look at. The student who stood guard at our end of the table was of grave countenance and great frame and grace of form, and he was doubtless an accurate reproduction, clothes and all, of some ancestor of his of two or three centuries ago—a reproduction as far as the outside, the animal man, goes, I mean.

As I say, the place was now crowded. The nearest aisle was packed with students standing up, and they made a fence which shut off the rest of the house from view. As far down this fence as you could see all these wholesome young faces were turned in one direction, all these intent and worshiping eyes were centered upon one spot—the place where Virchow and Helmholtz sat. The boys seemed lost to everything, unconscious of their own existence; they devoured these two intellectual giants with their eyes, they feasted upon them, and the worship that was in their hearts shone in their faces. It seemed to me that I would rather be flooded with a glory like that, instinct with sincerity, innocent of self-seeking, than win a hundred battles and break a million hearts.

There was a big mug of beer in front of each of us, and more to come when wanted. There was also a quarto pamphlet containing the words of the songs to be sung. After the names of the officers of the feast were these words in large type:

Während des Kommerses herrscht allgemeiner Burgfriede.

I was not able to translate this to my satisfaction, but a professor helped me out. This was his explanation: The students in uniform belong to different college corps; not all students belong to corps; none join the corps except those who enjoy fighting. The corps students fight duels with swords every week, one corps challenging another corps to furnish a certain number of duelists for the occasion, and it is only on this battle-field that students of different corps exchange courtesies. In common life they do not drink with each other or speak. The above line now translates itself: there is truce during the Commers, war is laid aside and fellowship takes its place.

Now the performance began. The concealed band played a piece of martial music; then there was a pause. The students on the platform rose to their feet, the middle one gave a toast to the Emperor, then all the house rose, mugs in hand. At the call "One—two—three!" all glasses were drained and then brought down with a slam on the tables in unison. The result was as good an imitation of thunder as I have ever heard. From now on, during an hour, there was singing, in mighty chorus. During each interval between songs a number of the special guests—the professors—arrived. There seemed to be some signal whereby the students on the platform were made aware that a professor had arrived at the remote door of entrance; for you would see them suddenly rise to their feet, strike an erect military attitude, then draw their swords; the swords of all their brethren standing guard at the innumerable tables would flash from their scabbards and be held aloft—a handsome spectacle! Three clear bugle notes would ring out, then all these swords would come down with a crash, twice repeated, on the tables, and be uplifted and held aloft again; then in the distance you would see the gay uniforms and uplifted swords of a guard of honor clearing the way and conducting the guest down to his place. The songs were stirring, the immense outpour from young life and young lungs, the crash of swords and the thunder of the beer-mugs gradually worked a body up to what seemed the last possible summit of excitement. It surely seemed to me that I had reached that summit, that I had reached my limit, and that there was no higher lift desirable for me. When apparently the last eminent guest had long ago taken his place, again those three bugle blasts rang out and once more the swords leaped from their scabbards. Who might this late comer be? Nobody was interested to inquire. Still, indolent eyes were turned toward the distant entrance; we saw the silken gleam and the lifted swords of a guard of honor plowing through the remote crowds. Then we saw that end of the house rising to its feet; saw it rise abreast the advancing guard all along, like a wave. This supreme honor had been offered to no one before. Then there was an excited whisper at our table—"MOMMSEN!" and the whole house rose. Rose and shouted and stamped and clapped, and banged the beer-mugs. Just simply a storm! Then the little man with his long hair and Emersonian face edged his way past us and took his seat. I could have touched him with my hand—Mommsen!—think of it!

This was one of those immense surprises that can happen only a few times in one's life. I was not dreaming of him, he was to me only a giant myth, a world-shadowing specter, not a reality. The surprise of it all can be only comparable to a man's suddenly coming upon Mont Blanc, with its awful form towering into the sky, when he didn't suspect he was in its neighborhood. I would have walked a great many miles to get a sight of him, and here he was, without trouble or tramp or cost of any kind. Here he was, clothed in a Titanic deceptive modesty which made him look like other men. Here he was, carrying the Roman world and all the Cæsars in his hospitable skull, and doing it as easily as that other luminous vault, the skull of the universe, carries the Milky Way and the constellations.

One of the professors said that once upon a time an American young lady was introduced to Mommsen, and found herself badly scared and speechless. She dreaded to see his mouth unclose, for she was expecting him to choose a subject several miles above her comprehension, and didn't suppose he *could* get down to the world that other people lived in; but when his remark came, her terrors disappeared: "Well, how do you do? Have you read Howells's last book? *I* think it's his best."

The active ceremonies of the evening closed with the speeches of welcome delivered by two students and the replies made by Professors Virchow and Helmholtz.

Virchow has long been a member of the city government of Berlin. He works as hard for the city as does any other Berlin alderman, and gets the same pay—nothing. I don't know that we in America could venture to ask our most illustrious citizen to serve in a board of aldermen, and if we might venture it I am not positively sure that we could elect him. But here the municipal system is such that the best men in the city consider it an honor to serve gratis as aldermen, and the people have the good sense to prefer these men and to elect them year after year. As a result Berlin is a thoroughly well-governed city. It is a free city; its affairs are not meddled with by the state; they are managed by its own citizens, and after methods of their own devising.

At the Shrine of St. Wagner

BAYREUTH, *Aug. 2d, 1891.*

It was at Nuremberg that we struck the inundation of music-mad strangers that was rolling down upon Bayreuth. It had been long since we had seen such multitudes of excited and struggling people. It took a good half-hour to pack them and pair them into the train—and it was the longest train we have yet seen in Europe. Nuremberg had been witnessing this sort of experience a couple of times a day for about two weeks. It gives one an impressive sense of the magnitude of this biennial pilgrimage. For a pilgrimage is what it is. The devotees come from the very ends of the earth to worship their prophet in his own Kaaba in his own Mecca.

If you are living in New York or San Francisco or Chicago or anywhere else in America, and you conclude, by the middle of May, that you would like to attend the Bayreuth opera two months and a half later, you must use the cable and get about it immediately or you will get no seats, and you must cable for lodgings, too. Then if you are lucky you will get seats in the last row and lodgings in the fringe of the town. If you stop to write you will get nothing. There were plenty of people in Nuremberg when we passed through who had come on pilgrimage without first securing seats and lodgings. They had found neither in Bayreuth; they had walked Bayreuth streets awhile in sorrow, then had gone to Nuremberg and found neither beds nor standing room, and had walked those quaint streets all night, waiting for the hotels to open and empty their guests into the trains, and so make room for these, their defeated brethren and sisters in the faith. They had endured from thirty to forty hours' railroading on the continent of Europe—with all which that implies of worry, fatigue, and financial impoverishment—and all they had got and all they were to get for it was handiness and accuracy in kicking themselves, acquired by practice in the back streets of the two towns when other people were in bed; for back they must go over that unspeakable journey with their pious mission unfulfilled. These humiliated outcasts had the frowsy and unbrushed and apologetic look of wet cats, and their eyes were glazed with drowsiness, their bodies were adroop from crown to sole, and all kind-hearted people refrained from asking them if they had been to Bayreuth and failed to connect, as knowing they would lie.

We reached here (Bayreuth) about mid-afternoon of a rainy Saturday. We were of the wise, and had secured lodgings and opera seats months in advance.

I am not a musical critic, and did not come here to write essays about the operas and deliver judgment upon their merits. The little children of Bayreuth could do that with a finer sympathy and a broader intelligence than I. I only care to bring four or five pilgrims to the operas, pilgrims able to appreciate them and enjoy them. What I write about the performance to put in my odd time would be offered to the public as merely a cat's view of a king, and not of didactic value.

Next day, which was Sunday, we left for the opera-house—that is to say, the Wagner temple—a little after the middle of the afternoon. The great building stands all by itself, grand and lonely, on a high ground outside the town. We were warned that if we arrived after four o'clock we should be obliged to pay two dollars and a half apiece extra by way of fine. We saved that; and it may be remarked here that this is the only opportunity that Europe offers of saving money. There was a big crowd in the grounds about the building, and the ladies' dresses took the sun with fine effect. I do not mean to intimate that the ladies were in full dress, for that was not so. The dresses were pretty, but neither sex was in evening dress.

The interior of the building is simple—severely so; but there is no occasion for color and decoration, since the people sit in the dark. The auditorium has the shape of a keystone, with the stage at the narrow end. There is an aisle on each side, but no aisle in the body of the house. Each row of seats extends in an unbroken curve from one side of the house to the other. There are seven entrance doors on each side of the theater and four at the butt, eighteen doors to admit and emit 1,650 persons. The number of the particular door by which you are to enter the house or leave it is printed on your ticket, and you can use no door but that one. Thus, crowding and confusion are impossible. Not so many as a hundred people use any one door. This is better than having the usual (and useless) elaborate fireproof arrangements. It is the model theater of the world. It can be emptied while the second hand of a watch makes its circuit. It would be entirely safe, even if it were built of lucifer matches.

If your seat is near the center of a row and you enter late you must work your way along a rank of about twenty-five ladies and gentlemen to get to it. Yet this causes no trouble, for everybody stands up until all the seats are full, and the filling is accomplished in a very few minutes. Then all sit down, and you have a solid mass of fifteen hundred heads, making a steep cellar-door slant from the rear of the house down to the stage.

All the lights were turned low, so low that the congregation sat in a deep and solemn gloom. The funereal rustling of dresses and the low buzz of conversation began to die swiftly down, and presently not the ghost of a sound was left. This profound and increasingly impressive stillness endured for some time—the best preparation for music, spectacle, or speech conceivable. I should think our show people would have invented or imported that simple and impressive device for securing and solidifying the attention of an audience long ago; instead of which they continue to this day to open a performance against a deadly competition in the form of noise, confusion, and a scattered interest.

Finally, out of darkness and distance and mystery soft rich notes rose upon the stillness, and from his grave the dead magician began to weave his spells about his disciples and steep their souls in his enchantments. There was something strangely impressive in the fancy which kept intruding itself that the composer was conscious in his grave of what was going on here, and that these divine sounds were the clothing of thoughts which were at this moment passing through his brain, and not recognized and familiar ones which had issued from it at some former time.

The entire overture, long as it was, was played to a dark house with the curtain down. It was exquisite; it was delicious. But straightway thereafter, of course, came the singing, and it does seem to me that nothing can make a Wagner opera absolutely perfect and satisfactory to the untutored but to leave out the vocal parts. I wish I could see a Wagner opera done in pantomime once. Then one would have the lovely orchestration unvexed to listen to and bathe his spirit in, and the bewildering beautiful scenery to intoxicate his eyes with, and the dumb acting couldn't mar these pleasures, because there isn't often anything in the Wagner opera that one would call by such a violent name as acting; as a rule all you would see would be a couple of silent people, one of them standing still, the other catching flies. Of course I do not really mean that he would be catching flies; I only mean that the usual operatic gestures which consist in reaching first one hand out into the air and then the other might suggest the sport I speak of if the operator attended strictly to business and uttered no sound.

This present opera was "Parsifal." Madame Wagner does not permit its representation anywhere but in Bayreuth. The first act of the three occupied two hours, and I enjoyed that in spite of the singing.

I trust that I know as well as anybody that singing is one of the most entrancing and bewitching and moving and eloquent of all the vehicles invented by man for the conveying of feeling; but it seems to me that the chief virtue in song is melody, air, tune, rhythm, or what you please to call it, and that when this feature is absent what remains is a picture with the color left out. I was not able to detect in the vocal parts of "Parsifal" anything that might with confidence be called rhythm or tune or melody; one person performed at a time—and a long time, too—often in a noble, and always in a high-toned, voice; but he only pulled out long notes, then some short ones, then another long one, then a sharp, quick, peremptory bark or two—and so on and so on; and when he was done you saw that the information which he had conveyed had not compensated for the disturbance. Not always, but pretty often. If two of them would but put in a duet occasionally and blend the voices; but no, they don't do that. The great master, who knew so well how to make a hundred instruments rejoice in unison and pour out their souls in mingled and melodious tides of delicious sound, deals only in barren solos when he puts in the vocal parts. It may be that he was deep, and only added the singing to his operas for the sake of the contrast it would make with the music. Singing! It does seem the wrong name to apply to it. Strictly described, it is a practising of difficult and unpleasant intervals, mainly. An ignorant person gets tired of listening to gymnastic intervals in the long run, no matter how pleasant they may be. In "Parsifal" there is a hermit named Gurnemanz who stands on the stage in one spot and practises by the hour, while first one and then another character of the cast endures what he can of it and then retires to die.

During the evening there was an intermission of three-quarters of an hour after the first act and one an hour long after the second. In both instances the theater was totally emptied. People who had previously engaged tables in the one sole eating-house were able to put in their time very satisfactorily; the other thousand went hungry. The opera was concluded at ten in the evening or a little later. When we reached home we had been gone more than seven hours. Seven hours at five dollars a ticket is almost too much for the money.

While browsing about the front yard among the crowd between the acts I encountered twelve or fifteen friends from different parts of America, and those of them who were most familiar with Wagner said that "Parsifal" seldom pleased at first, but that after one had heard it several times it was almost sure to become a favorite. It seemed impossible, but it was true, for the statement came from people whose word was not to be doubted.

And I gathered some further information. On the ground I found part of a German musical magazine, and in it a letter written by Uhlic thirty-three years ago, in which he defends the scorned and abused Wagner against people like me, who found fault with the comprehensive absence of what our kind regards as singing. Uhlic says Wagner despised *"Jene plapperude musik,"* and therefore "runs, trills, and *schnorkel* are discarded by him." I don't know what a *schnorkel* is, but now that I know it has been left out of these operas I never have missed so much in my life. And Uhlic further says that Wagner's song is true: that it is "simply emphasized intoned speech." That certainly describes it—in "Parsifal" and some of the other operas; and if I understand Uhlic's elaborate German he apologizes for the beautiful airs in "Tannhäuser." Very well; now that Wagner and I understand each other, perhaps we shall get along better, and I shall stop calling him Waggner, on the American plan, and thereafter call him Wagner as per German custom, for I feel entirely friendly now. The minute we get reconciled to a person, how willing we are to throw aside little needless punctilios and pronounce his name right!

Of course I came home wondering why people should come from all corners of America to hear these operas, when we have lately had a season or two of them in New York with these same singers in the several parts, and possibly this same orchestra. I resolved to think that out at all hazards.

Tuesday.—Yesterday they played the only operatic favorite I have ever had—an opera which has always driven me mad with ignorant delight whenever I have heard it—"Tannhäuser." I heard it first when I was a youth; I heard it last in the last German season in New York. I was busy yesterday and I did not intend to go, knowing I should have another "Tannhäuser" opportunity in a few days; but after five o'clock I found myself free and walked out to the opera-house and arrived about the beginning of the second act. My opera ticket admitted me to the grounds in front, past the policeman and the chain, and I thought I would take a rest on a bench for an hour or two and wait for the third act.

In a moment or so the first bugles blew, and the multitude began to crumble apart and melt into the theater. I will explain that this bugle-call is one of the pretty features here. You see, the theater is empty, and hundreds of the audience are a good way off in the feeding-house; the first bugle-call is blown about a quarter of an hour before time for the curtain to rise. This company of buglers, in uniform, march out with military step and send out over the landscape a few bars of the theme of the approaching act, piercing the distances with the gracious notes; then they march to the other entrance and repeat. Presently they do this over again. Yesterday only about two hundred people were still left in front of the house when the second call was blown; in another half-minute they would have been in the house, but then a thing happened which delayed them—the one solitary thing in this world which could be relied on with certainty to accomplish it, I suppose—an imperial princess appeared in the balcony above them. They stopped dead in their tracks and began to gaze in a stupor of gratitude and satisfaction. The lady presently saw that she must disappear or the doors would be closed upon these worshipers, so she returned to her box. This daughter-in-law of an emperor was pretty; she had a kind face; she was without airs; she is known to be full of common human sympathies. There are many kinds of princesses, but this kind is the most harmful of all, for wherever they go they reconcile people to monarchy and set back the clock of progress. The valuable princes, the desirable princes, are the czars and their sort. By their mere dumb presence in the world they cover with derision every argument that can be invented in favor of royalty by the most ingenious casuist. In his time the husband of this princess was valuable. He led a degraded life, he ended it with his own hand in circumstances and surroundings of a hideous sort, and was buried like a god.

In the opera-house there is a long loft back of the audience, a kind of open gallery, in which princes are displayed. It is sacred to them; it is the holy of holies. As soon as the filling of the house is about complete the standing multitude turn and fix their eyes upon the princely layout and gaze mutely and longingly and adoringly and regretfully like sinners looking into heaven. They become rapt, unconscious, steeped in worship.

There is no spectacle anywhere that is more pathetic than this. It is worth crossing many oceans to see. It is somehow not the same gaze that people rivet upon a Victor Hugo, or Niagara, or the bones of the mastodon, or the guillotine of the Revolution, or the great pyramid, or distant Vesuvius smoking in the sky, or any man long celebrated to you by his genius and achievements, or thing long celebrated to you by the praises of books and pictures—no, that gaze is only the gaze of intense curiosity, interest, wonder, engaged in drinking delicious deep draughts that taste good all the way down and appease and satisfy the thirst of a lifetime. Satisfy it—that is the word. Hugo and the mastodon will still have a degree of intense interest thereafter when encountered, but never anything approaching the ecstasy of that first view. The interest of a prince is different. It may be envy, it may be worship, doubtless it is a mixture of both—and it does not satisfy its thirst with one view, or even noticeably diminish it. Perhaps the essence of the thing is the value which men attach to a valuable something which has come by luck and not been earned. A dollar picked up in the road is more satisfaction to you than the ninety-and-nine which you had to work for, and money won at faro or in stocks snuggles into your heart in the same way. A prince picks up grandeur, power, and a permanent holiday and gratis support by a pure accident, the accident of birth, and he stands always before the grieved eye of poverty and obscurity a monumental representative of luck. And then—supremest value of all—his is the only high fortune on the earth which is secure. The commercial millionaire may become a beggar; the illustrious statesman can make a vital mistake and be dropped and forgotten; the illustrious general can lose a decisive battle and with it the consideration of men; but once a prince always a prince—that is to say, an imitation god, and neither hard fortune nor an infamous character nor an addled brain nor the speech of an ass can undeify him. By common consent of all the nations and all the ages the most valuable thing in this world is the homage of men, whether deserved or undeserved. It follows without doubt or question, then, that the most desirable position possible is that of a prince. And I think it also follows that the so-called usurpations with which history is littered are the most excusable misdemeanors which men have committed. To usurp a usurpation—that is all it amounts to, isn't it?

A prince is not to us what he is to a European, of course. We have not been taught to regard him as a god, and so one good look at him is likely to so nearly appease our curiosity as to make him an object of no greater interest the next time. We want a fresh one. But it is not so with the

European. I am quite sure of it. The same old one will answer; he never stales. Eighteen years ago I was in London and I called at an Englishman's house on a bleak and foggy and dismal December afternoon to visit his wife and married daughter by appointment. I waited half an hour and then they arrived, frozen. They explained that they had been delayed by an unlooked-for circumstance: while passing in the neighborhood of Marlborough House they saw a crowd gathering and were told that the Prince of Wales was about to drive out, so they stopped to get a sight of him. They had waited half an hour on the sidewalk, freezing with the crowd, but were disappointed at last—the Prince had changed his mind. I said, with a good deal of surprise, "Is it possible that you two have lived in London all your lives and have never seen the Prince of Wales?"

Apparently it was their turn to be surprised, for they exclaimed: "What an idea! Why, we have seen him hundreds of times."

They had seen him hundreds of times, yet they had waited half an hour in the gloom and the bitter cold, in the midst of a jam of patients from the same asylum, on the chance of seeing him again. It was a stupefying statement, but one is obliged to believe the English, even when they say a thing like that. I fumbled around for a remark, and got out this one:

"I can't understand it at all. If I had never seen General Grant I doubt if I would do that even to get a sight of him." With a slight emphasis on the last word.

Their blank faces showed that they wondered where the parallel came in. Then they said, blankly: "Of course not. He is only a President."

It is doubtless a fact that a prince is a permanent interest, an interest not subject to deterioration. The general who was never defeated, the general who never held a council of war, the only general who ever commanded a connected battle-front twelve hundred miles long, the smith who welded together the broken parts of a great republic and re-established it where it is quite likely to outlast all the monarchies present and to come, was really a person of no serious consequence to these people. To them, with their training, my General was only a man, after all, while their Prince was clearly much more than that—a being of a wholly unsimilar construction and constitution, and being of no more blood and kinship with men than are the serene eternal lights of the firmament with the poor dull tallow candles of commerce that sputter and die and leave nothing behind but a pinch of ashes and a stink.

I saw the last act of "Tannhäuser." I sat in the gloom and the deep stillness, waiting—one minute, two minutes, I do not know exactly how long—then the soft music of the hidden orchestra began to breathe its rich, long sighs out from under the distant stage, and by and by the drop-curtain parted in the middle and was drawn softly aside, disclosing the twilighted wood and a wayside shrine, with a white-robed girl praying and a man standing near. Presently that noble chorus of men's voices was heard approaching, and from that moment until the closing of the curtain it was music, just music—music to make one drunk with pleasure, music to make one take scrip and staff and beg his way round the globe to hear it.

To such as are intending to come here in the Wagner season next year I wish to say, bring your dinner-pail with you. If you do, you will never cease to be thankful. If you do not, you will find it a hard fight to save yourself from famishing in Bayreuth. Bayreuth is merely a large village, and has no very large hotels or eating-houses. The principal inns are the Golden Anchor and the Sun. At either of these places you can get an excellent meal—no, I mean you can go there and see other people get it. There is no charge for this. The town is littered with restaurants, but they are small and bad, and they are overdriven with custom. You must secure a table hours beforehand, and often when you arrive you will find somebody occupying it. We have had this experience. We have had a daily scramble for life; and when I say we, I include shoals of people. I have the impression that the only people who do not have to scramble are the veterans—the disciples who have been here before and know the ropes. I think they arrive about a week before the first opera, and engage all the tables for the season. My tribe have tried all kinds of places—some outside of the town, a mile or two—and have captured only nibblings and odds and ends, never in any instance a complete and satisfying meal. Digestible? No, the reverse. These odds and ends are going to serve as souvenirs of Bayreuth, and in that regard their value is not to be over-estimated. Photographs fade, bric-à-brac gets lost, busts of Wagner get broken, but once you absorb a Bayreuth-restaurant meal it is your possession and your property until the time comes to embalm the rest of you. Some of these pilgrims here become, in effect, cabinets; cabinets of souvenirs of Bayreuth. It is believed among scientists that you could examine the crop of a dead Bayreuth pilgrim anywhere in the earth and tell where he came from. But I like this ballast. I think a "Hermitage" scrape-up at eight in the evening, when all the famine-breeders have been there and laid in their mementoes and gone, is the quietest thing you can lay on your keelson except gravel.

Thursday.—They keep two teams of singers in stock for the chief rôles, and one of these is composed of the most renowned artists in the world, with Materna and Alvary in the lead. I suppose a double team is necessary; doubtless a single team would die of exhaustion in a week, for all the plays last from four in the afternoon till ten at night. Nearly all the labor falls upon the half-dozen head singers, and apparently they are required to furnish all the noise they can for the money. If they feel a soft, whispery, mysterious feeling they are required to open out and let the public know it. Operas are given only on Sundays, Mondays, Wednesdays, and Thursdays, with three days of ostensible rest per week, and two teams to do the four operas; but the ostensible rest is devoted largely to rehearsing. It is said that the off days are devoted to rehearsing from some time in the morning till ten at night. Are there two orchestras also? It is quite likely, since there are one hundred and ten names in the orchestra list.

Yesterday the opera was "Tristan and Isolde." I have seen all sorts of audiences—at theaters, operas, concerts, lectures, sermons, funerals—but none which was twin to the Wagner audience of Bayreuth for fixed and reverential attention. Absolute attention and petrified retention to the end of an act of the attitude assumed at the beginning of it. You detect no movement in the solid mass of heads and shoulders. You seem to sit with the dead in the gloom of a tomb. You know that they are being stirred to their profoundest depths; that there are times when they want to rise and wave handkerchiefs and shout their approbation, and times when tears are running down their faces, and it would be a relief to free their pent emotions in sobs or screams; yet you hear not one utterance till the curtain swings together and the closing strains have slowly faded out and died; then the dead rise with one impulse and shake the building with their applause. Every seat is full in the first act; there is not a vacant one in the last. If a man would be conspicuous, let him come here and retire from the house in the midst of an act. It would make him celebrated.

This audience reminds me of nothing I have ever seen and of nothing I have read about except the city in the Arabian tale where all the inhabitants have been turned to brass and the traveler finds them after centuries mute, motionless, and still retaining the attitudes which they last knew in life. Here the Wagner audience dress as they please, and sit in the dark and worship in silence: At the Metropolitan in New York they sit in a glare, and wear their showiest harness; they hum airs, they squeak fans, they titter, and they gabble all the time. In some of the boxes the conversation and laughter are so loud as to divide the attention of the house with the stage. In large measure the Metropolitan is a show-case for rich fashionables who are not trained in Wagnerian music and have no reverence for it, but who like to promote art and show their clothes.

Can that be an agreeable atmosphere to persons in whom this music produces a sort of divine ecstasy and to whom its creator is a very deity, his stage a temple, the works of his brain and hands consecrated things, and the partaking of them with eye and ear a sacred solemnity? Manifestly, no. Then, perhaps the temporary expatriation, the tedious traversing of seas and continents, the pilgrimage to Bayreuth stands explained. These devotees would worship in an atmosphere of devotion. It is only here that they can find it without fleck or blemish or any worldly pollution. In this remote village there are no sights to see, there is no newspaper to intrude the worries of the distant world, there is nothing going on, it is always Sunday. The pilgrim wends to his temple out of town, sits out his moving service, returns to his bed with his heart and soul and his body exhausted by long hours of tremendous emotion, and he is in no fit condition to do anything but to lie torpid and slowly gather back life and strength for the next service. This opera of "Tristan and Isolde" last night broke the hearts of all witnesses who were of the faith, and I know of some who have heard of many who could not sleep after it, but cried the night away. I feel strongly out of place here. Sometimes I feel like the sane person in a community of the mad; sometimes I feel like the one blind man where all others see; the one groping savage in the college of the learned, and always, during service, I feel like a heretic in heaven.

But by no means do I ever overlook or minify the fact that this is one of the most extraordinary experiences of my life. I have never seen anything like this before. I have never seen anything so great and fine and real as this devotion.

Friday.—Yesterday's opera was "Parsifal" again. The others went and they show marked advance in appreciation; but I went hunting for relics and reminders of the Margravine Wilhelmina, she of the imperishable "Memoirs." I am properly grateful to her for her (unconscious) satire upon monarchy and nobility, and therefore nothing which her hand touched or her eye looked upon is indifferent to me. I am her pilgrim; the rest of this multitude here are Wagner's.

Tuesday.—I have seen my last two operas; my season is ended, and we cross over into Bohemia this afternoon. I was supposing that my musical regeneration was accomplished and perfected, because I enjoyed both of these operas, singing and all, and, moreover, one of them was "Parsifal," but the experts have disenchanted me. They say:

"Singing! That wasn't singing; that was the wailing, screeching of third-rate obscurities, palmed off on us in the interest of economy."

Well, I ought to have recognized the sign—the old, sure sign that has never failed me in matters of art. Whenever I enjoy anything in art it means that it is mighty poor. The private knowledge of this fact has saved me from going to pieces with enthusiasm in front of many and many a chromo. However, my base instinct does bring me profit sometimes; I was the only man out of thirty-two hundred who got his money back on those two operas.

About All Kinds of Ships

THE MODERN STEAMER AND THE OBSOLETE STEAMER

We are victims of one common superstition—the superstition that we realize the changes that are daily taking place in the world because we read about them and know what they are. I should not have supposed that the modern ship could be a surprise to me, but it is. It seems to be as much of a surprise to me as it could have been if I had never read anything about it. I walk about this great vessel, the *Havel,* as she plows her way through the Atlantic, and every detail that comes under my eye brings up the miniature counterpart of it as it existed in the little ships I crossed the ocean in fourteen, seventeen, eighteen, and twenty years ago.

In the *Havel* one can be in several respects more comfortable than he can be in the best hotels on the continent of Europe. For instance, she has several bathrooms, and they are as convenient and as nicely equipped as the bathrooms in a fine private house in America; whereas in the hotels of the Continent one bathroom is considered sufficient, and it is generally shabby and located in some out-of-the-way corner of the house; moreover, you need to give notice so long beforehand that you get over wanting a bath by the time you get it. In the hotels there are a good many different kinds of noises, and they spoil sleep; in my room in the ship I hear no sounds. In the hotels they usually shut off the electric light at midnight; in the ship one may burn it in one's room all night.

In the steamer *Batavia,* twenty years ago, one candle, set in the bulkhead between two staterooms, was there to light both rooms, but did not light either of them. It was extinguished at eleven at night, and so were all the saloon lamps except one or two, which were left burning to help the passenger see how to break his neck trying to get around in the dark. The passengers sat at table on long benches made of the hardest kind of wood; in the *Havel* one sits on a swivel chair with a cushioned back to it. In those old times the dinner bill of fare was always the same: a pint of some simple, homely soup or other, boiled codfish and potatoes, slab of boiled beef, stewed prunes for dessert—on Sundays "dog in a blanket," on Thursdays "plum duff." In the modern ship the menu is choice and elaborate, and is changed daily. In the old times dinner was a sad occasion; in our day a concealed orchestra enlivens it with charming music. In the old days the decks were always wet; in our day they are usually dry, for the promenade-deck is roofed over, and a sea seldom comes aboard. In a moderately disturbed sea, in the old days, a landsman could hardly keep his legs, but in such a sea in our day the decks are as level as a table. In the old days the inside of a ship was the plainest and barrenest thing, and the most dismal and uncomfortable that ingenuity could devise; the modern ship is a marvel of rich and costly decoration and sumptuous appointment, and is equipped with every comfort and convenience that money can buy. The old ships had no place of assembly but the dining-room, the new ones have several spacious and beautiful drawing-rooms. The old ships offered the passenger no chance to smoke except in the place that was called the "fiddle." It was a repulsive den made of rough boards (full of cracks) and its office was to protect the main hatch. It was grimy and dirty; there were no seats; the only light was a lamp of the rancid oil-and-rag kind; the place was very cold, and never dry, for the seas broke in through the cracks every little while and drenched the cavern thoroughly. In the modern ship there are three or four large smoking-rooms, and they have card-tables and cushioned sofas, and are heated by steam and lighted by electricity. There are few European hotels with such smoking-rooms.

The former ships were built of wood, and had two or three water-tight compartments in the hold with doors in them which were often left open, particularly when the ship was going to hit a rock. The modern leviathan is built of steel, and the water-tight bulkheads have no doors in them; they divide the ship into nine or ten water-tight compartments and endow her with as many lives as a cat. Their complete efficiency was established by the happy results following the memorable accident to the *City of Paris* a year or two ago.

One curious thing which is at once noticeable in the great modern ship is the absence of hubbub, clatter, rush of feet, roaring of orders. That is all gone by. The elaborate manœuvers necessary in working the vessel into her dock are conducted without sounds; one sees nothing of the processes, hears no commands. A Sabbath stillness and solemnity reign, in place of the turmoil and racket of the earlier days. The modern ship has a spacious bridge fenced chin-high with sail-cloth and floored with wooden gratings; and this bridge, with its fenced fore-and-aft annexes, could accommodate a seated audience of a hundred and fifty men. There are three steering equipments, each competent if the others should break. From the bridge the ship is steered, and also handled. The handling is not done by shout or whistle, but by signaling with patent automatic gongs. There are three telltales, with plainly lettered dials—for steering, handling the engines, and for communicating orders to the invisible mates who are conducting the landing of the ship or casting off. The officer who is astern is out of sight and too far away to hear trumpet-calls; but the gongs near him tell him to haul in, pay out, make fast, let go, and so on; he hears, but the passengers do not, and so the ship seems to land herself without human help.

This great bridge is thirty or forty feet above the water, but the sea climbs up there sometimes; so there is another bridge twelve or fifteen feet higher still, for use in these emergencies. The force of water is a strange thing. It slips between one's fingers like air, but upon occasion it acts like a solid body and will bend a thin iron rod. In the *Havel* it has splintered a heavy oaken rail into broom-straws instead of merely breaking it in two, as would have been the seemingly natural thing for it to do. At the time of the awful Johnstown disaster, according to the testimony of several witnesses, rocks were carried some distance on the surface of the stupendous torrent; and at St. Helena, many years ago, a vast sea-wave carried a battery of cannon forty feet up a steep slope and deposited the guns there in a row. But the water has done a still stranger thing, and it is one which is credibly vouched for. A marlin-spike is an implement about a foot long which tapers from its butt to the other extremity and ends in a sharp point. It is made of iron and is heavy. A wave came aboard a ship in a storm and raged aft, breast high, carrying a marlin-spike point first with it, and with such lightning-like swiftness and force as to drive it three or four inches into a sailor's body and kill him.

In all ways the ocean greyhound of to-day is imposing and impressive to one who carries in his head no ship pictures of a recent date. In bulk she comes near to rivaling the Ark; yet this monstrous mass of steel is driven five hundred miles through the waves in twenty-four hours. I remember the brag run of a steamer which I traveled in once on the Pacific—it was two hundred and nine miles in twenty-four hours; a year or so later I was a passenger in the excursion tub *Quaker City*, and on one occasion in a level and glassy sea it was claimed that she reeled off two hundred and eleven miles between noon and noon, but it was probably a campaign lie. That little steamer had seventy passengers, and a crew of forty men, and seemed a good deal of a beehive. But in this present ship we are living in a sort of solitude, these soft summer days, with sometimes a hundred passengers scattered about the spacious distances, and sometimes nobody in sight at all; yet, hidden somewhere in the vessel's bulk, there are (including crew) near eleven hundred people.

The stateliest lines in the literature of the sea are these:

> Britannia needs no bulwarks, no towers along the steep—
> Her march is o'er the mountain waves, her home is on the deep!

There it is. In those old times the little ships climbed over the waves and wallowed down into the trough on the other side; the giant ship of our day does not climb over the waves, but crushes her way through them. Her formidable weight and mass and impetus give her mastery over any but extraordinary storm waves.

The ingenuity of man! I mean in this passing generation. To-day I found in the chart-room a frame of removable wooden slats on the wall, and on the slats was painted uninforming information like this:

Trim-Tank	Empty
Double-Bottom No. 1	Full
Double-Bottom No. 2	Full
Double-Bottom No. 3	Full
Double-Bottom No. 4	Full

While I was trying to think out what kind of a game this might be and how a stranger might best go to work to beat it, a sailor came in and pulled out the "Empty" end of the first slat and put it back with its reverse side to the front, marked "Full." He made some other change, I did not notice what. The slat-frame was soon explained. Its function was to indicate how the ballast in the ship was distributed. The striking thing was that the ballast was water. I did not know that a ship had ever been ballasted with water. I had merely read, some time or other, that such an experiment was to be tried. But that is the modern way; between the experimental trial of a new thing and its adoption, there is no wasted time, if the trial proves its value.

On the wall, near the slat-frame, there was an outline drawing of the ship, and this betrayed the fact that this vessel has twenty-two considerable lakes of water in her. These lakes are in her bottom; they are imprisoned between her real bottom and a false bottom. They are separated from each other, thwartships, by water-tight bulkheads, and separated down the middle by a bulkhead running from the bow four-fifths of the way to the stern. It is a chain of lakes four hundred feet long and from five to seven feet deep. Fourteen of the lakes contain fresh-water brought from shore, and the aggregate weight of it is four hundred tons. The rest of the lakes contain salt-water—six hundred and eighteen tons. Upward of a thousand tons of water, altogether.

Think how handy this ballast is. The ship leaves port with the lakes all full. As she lightens forward through consumption of coal, she loses trim—her head rises, her stern sinks down. Then they spill one of the sternward lakes into the sea, and the trim is restored. This can be repeated right along as occasion may require. Also, a lake at one end of the ship can be moved to the other end by pipes and steam-pumps. When the sailor changed the slat-frame to-day, he was posting a transference of that kind. The seas had been increasing, and the vessel's head needed more weighting, to keep it from rising on the waves instead of plowing through them; therefore, twenty-five tons of water had been transferred to the bow from a lake situated well toward the stern.

A water compartment is kept either full or empty. The body of water must be compact, so that it cannot slosh around. A shifting ballast would not do, of course.

The modern ship is full of beautiful ingenuities, but it seems to me that this one is the king. I would rather be the originator of that idea than of any of the others. Perhaps the trim of a ship was never perfectly ordered and preserved until now. A vessel out of trim will not steer, her speed is maimed, she strains and labors in the seas. Poor creature, for six thousand years she has had no comfort until these latest days. For six thousand years she swam through the best and cheapest ballast in the world, the only perfect ballast, but she couldn't tell her master and he had not the wit to find it out for himself. It is odd to reflect that there is nearly as much water inside of this ship as there is outside, and yet there is no danger.

Noah's Ark

The progress made in the great art of ship-building since Noah's time is quite noticeable. Also, the looseness of the navigation laws in the time of Noah is in quite striking contrast with the strictness of the navigation laws of our time. It would not be possible for Noah to do in our day what he was permitted to do in his own. Experience has taught us the necessity of being more particular, more conservative, more careful of human life. Noah would not be allowed to sail from Bremen in our day. The inspectors would come and examine the Ark, and make all sorts of objections. A person who knows Germany can imagine the scene and the conversation without difficulty and without missing a detail. The inspector would be in a beautiful military uniform; he would be respectful, dignified, kindly, the perfect gentleman, but steady as the north star to the last requirement of his duty. He would make Noah tell him where he was born, and how old he was, and what religious sect he belonged to, and the amount of his income, and the grade and position he claimed socially, and the name and style of his occupation, and how many wives and children he had, and how many servants, and the name, sex, and age of the whole of them; and if he hadn't a passport he would be courteously required to get one right away. Then he would take up the matter of the Ark:

"What is her length?"

"Six hundred feet."

"Depth?"

"Sixty-five."

"Beam?"

"Fifty or sixty."

"Built of—"

"Wood."

"What kind?"

"Shittim and gopher."

"Interior and exterior decorations?"

"Pitched within and without."

"Passengers?"

"Eight."

"Sex?"

"Half male, the others female."

"Ages?"

"From a hundred years up."

"Up to where?"

"Six hundred."

"Ah—going to Chicago; good idea, too. Surgeon's name?"

"We have no surgeon."

"Must provide a surgeon. Also an undertaker—particularly the undertaker. These people must not be left without the necessities of life at their age. Crew?"

"The same eight."

"The same eight?"

"The same eight."

"And half of them women?"

"Yes, sir."

"Have they ever served as seamen?"

"No, sir."

"Have the men?"

"No, sir."

"Have any of you ever been to sea?"

"No, sir."

"Where were you reared?"

"On a farm—all of us."

"This vessel requires a crew of eight hundred men, she not being a steamer. You must provide them. She must have four mates and nine cooks. Who is captain?"

"I am, sir."

"You must get a captain. Also a chambermaid. Also sick-nurses for the old people. Who designed this vessel?"

"I did, sir."

"Is it your first attempt?"

"Yes, sir."

"I partly suspected it. Cargo?"

"Animals."

"Kind?"

"All kinds."

"Wild, or tame?"

"Mainly wild."

"Foreign or domestic?"

"Mainly foreign."

"Principal wild ones?"

"Megatherium, elephant, rhinoceros, lion, tiger, wolf, snakes—all the wild things of all climes—two of each."

"Securely caged?"

"No, not caged.

"They must have iron cages. Who feeds and waters the menagerie?"

"We do."

"The old people?"

"Yes, sir."

"It is dangerous—for both. The animals must be cared for by a competent force. How many animals are there?"

"Big ones, seven thousand; big and little together, ninety-eight thousand."

"You must provide twelve hundred keepers. How is the vessel lighted?"

"By two windows."

"Where are they?"

"Up under the eaves."

"Two windows for a tunnel six hundred feet long and sixty-five feet deep? You must put in the electric light—a few arc-lights and fifteen hundred incandescents. What do you do in case of leaks? How many pumps have you?"

"None, sir."

"You must provide pumps. How do you get water for the passengers and the animals?"

"We let down the buckets from the windows."

"It is inadequate. What is your motive power?"

"What is my which?"

"Motive power. What power do you use in driving the ship?"

"None."

"You must provide sails or steam. What is the nature of your steering apparatus?"

"We haven't any."

"Haven't you a rudder?"

"No, sir."

"How do you steer the vessel?"

"We don't."

"You must provide a rudder, and properly equip it. How many anchors have you?"

"None."

"You must provide six. One is not permitted to sail a vessel like this without that protection. How many life-boats have you?"

"None, sir."

"Provide twenty-five. How many life-preservers?"

"None."

"You will provide two thousand. How long are you expecting your voyage to last?"

"Eleven or twelve months."

"Eleven or twelve months. Pretty slow—but you will be in time for the Exposition. What is your ship sheathed with—copper?"

"Her hull is bare—not sheathed at all."

"Dear man, the wood-boring creatures of the sea would riddle her like a sieve and send her to the bottom in three months. She *cannot* be allowed to go away in this condition; she must be sheathed. Just a word more: Have you reflected that Chicago is an inland city and not reachable with a vessel like this?"

"Shecargo? What is Shecargo? I am not going to Shecargo."

"Indeed? Then may I ask what the animals are for?"

"Just to breed others from."

"Others? Is it possible that you haven't enough?"

"For the present needs of civilization, yes; but the rest are going to be drowned in a flood, and these are to renew the supply."

"A flood?"

"Yes, sir."

"Are you sure of that?"

"Perfectly sure. It is going to rain forty days and forty nights."

"Give yourself no concern about that, dear sir, it often does that here."

"Not this kind of rain. This is going to cover the mountain-tops, and the earth will pass from sight."

"Privately—but of course not officially—I am sorry you revealed this, for it compels me to withdraw the option I gave you as to sails or steam. I must require you to use steam. Your ship cannot carry the hundredth part of an eleven-months' water-supply for the animals. You will have to have condensed water."

"But I tell you I am going to dip water from outside with buckets."

"It will not answer. Before the flood reaches the mountain-tops the fresh waters will have joined the salt seas, and it will all be salt. You must put in steam and condense your water. I will now bid you good day, sir. Did I understand you to say that this was your very first attempt at ship-building?"

"My very first, sir, I give you the honest truth. I built this Ark without having ever had the slightest training or experience or instruction in marine architecture.

"It is a remarkable work, sir, a most remarkable work. I consider that it contains more features that are new—absolutely new and unhackneyed—than are to be found in any other vessel that swims the seas."

"This compliment does me infinite honor, dear sir, infinite; and I shall cherish the memory of it while life shall last. Sir, I offer my duty and most grateful thanks. Adieu."

No, the German inspector would be limitlessly courteous to Noah, and would make him feel that he was among friends, but he wouldn't let him go to sea with that Ark.

Columbus's Craft

Between Noah's time and the time of Columbus naval architecture underwent some changes, and from being unspeakably bad was improved to a point which may be described as less unspeakably bad. I have read somewhere, some time or other, that one of Columbus's ships was a ninety-ton vessel. By comparing that ship with the ocean greyhounds of our time one is able to get down to a comprehension of how small that Spanish bark was, and how little fitted she would be to run opposition in the Atlantic passenger trade to-day. It would take seventy-four of her to match the tonnage of the *Havel* and carry the *Havel*'s trip. If I remember rightly, it took her ten weeks to make the passage. With our ideas this would now be considered an objectionable gait. She probably had a captain, a mate, and a crew consisting of four seamen and a boy. The crew of a modern greyhound numbers two hundred and fifty persons.

Columbus's ship being small and very old, we know that we may draw from these two facts several absolute certainties in the way of minor details which history has left unrecorded. For instance: being small, we know that she rolled and pitched and tumbled in any ordinary sea, and stood on her head or her tail, or lay down with her ear in the water, when storm seas ran high; also, that she was used to having billows plunge aboard and wash her decks from stem to stern; also, that the storm racks were on the table all the way over, and that nevertheless a man's soup was oftener landed in his lap than in his stomach; also, that the dining-saloon was about ten feet by seven, dark, airless, and suffocating with oil-stench; also, that there was only about one state-room, the size of a grave, with a tier of two or three berths in it of the dimensions and comfortableness of coffins, and that when the light was out the darkness in there was so thick and real that you could bite into it and chew it like gum; also, that the only promenade was on the lofty poop-deck astern (for the ship was shaped like a high-quarter shoe)—a streak sixteen feet long by three feet wide, all the rest of the vessel being littered with ropes and flooded by the seas.

We know all these things to be true, from the mere fact that we know the vessel was small. As the vessel was old, certain other truths follow, as matters of course. For instance: she was full of rats; she was full of cockroaches; the heavy seas made her seams open and shut like your fingers, and she leaked like a basket; where leakage is, there also, of necessity, is bilge-water; and where bilge-water is, only the dead can enjoy life. This is on account of the smell. In the presence of bilge-water, Limburger cheese becomes odorless and ashamed.

From these absolutely sure data we can competently picture the daily life of the great discoverer. In the early morning he paid his devotions at the shrine of the Virgin. At eight bells he appeared on the poop-deck promenade. If the weather was chilly he came up clad from plumed helmet to spurred heel in magnificent plate armor inlaid with arabesques of gold, having previously warmed it at the galley fire. If the weather was warm he came up in the ordinary sailor toggery of the time—great slouch hat of blue velvet with a flowing brush of snowy ostrich plumes, fastened on with a flashing cluster of diamonds and emeralds; gold-embroidered doublet of green velvet with slashed sleeves exposing under-sleeves of crimson satin; deep collar and cuff ruffles of rich limp lace; trunk hose of pink velvet, with big knee-knots of brocaded yellow ribbon; pearl-tinted silk stockings, clocked and daintily embroidered; lemon-colored buskins of unborn kid, funnel-topped, and drooping low to expose the pretty stockings; deep gauntlets of finest white heretic skin, from the factory of the Holy Inquisition, formerly part of the person of a lady of rank; rapier with sheath crusted with jewels, and hanging from a broad baldric upholstered with rubies and sapphires.

He walked the promenade thoughtfully, he noted the aspects of the sky and the course of the wind; he kept an eye out for drifting vegetation and other signs of land; he jawed the man at the wheel for pastime; he got out an imitation egg and kept himself in practice on his old trick of making it stand on end; now and then he hove a life-line below and fished up a sailor who was drowning on the quarter-deck; the rest of his watch he gaped and yawned and stretched, and said he wouldn't make the trip again to discover six Americas. For that was the kind of natural human person Columbus was when not posing for posterity.

At noon he took the sun and ascertained that the good ship had made three hundred yards in twenty-four hours, and this enabled him to win the pool. Anybody can win the pool when nobody but himself has the privilege of straightening out the ship's run and getting it right.

The Admiral has breakfasted alone, in state: bacon, beans, and gin; at noon he dines alone, in state: bacon, beans, and gin; at six he sups alone, in state: bacon, beans, and gin; at eleven P.M. he takes a night relish alone, in state: bacon, beans, and gin. At none of these orgies is there any music; the ship orchestra is modern. After his final meal he returned thanks for his many blessings, a little overrating their value, perhaps, and then he laid off his silken splendors or his gilded hardware, and turned in, in his little coffin-bunk, and blew out his flickering stencher and began to refresh his lungs with inverted sighs freighted with the rich odors of rancid oil and bilge-water. The sighs returned as snores, and then the rats and the cockroaches swarmed out in brigades and divisions and army corps and had a circus all over him. Such was the daily life of the great discoverer in his marine basket during several historic weeks; and the difference between his ship and his comforts and ours is visible almost at a glance.

When he returned, the King of Spain, marveling, said—as history records:

"This ship seems to be leaky. Did she leak badly?"

"You shall judge for yourself, sire. I pumped the Atlantic Ocean through her sixteen times on the passage."

This is General Horace Porter's account. Other authorities say fifteen.

It can be shown that the differences between that ship and the one I am writing these historical contributions in are in several respects remarkable. Take the matter of decoration, for instance. I have been looking around again, yesterday and to-day, and have noted several details which I conceive to have been absent from Columbus's ship, or at least slurred over and not elaborated and perfected. I observe stateroom doors three inches thick, of solid oak and polished. I note companionway vestibules with walls, doors, and ceilings paneled in polished hard woods, some light, some dark, all dainty and delicate joiner-work, and yet every point compact and tight; with beautiful pictures inserted, composed of blue tiles—some of the pictures containing as many as sixty tiles—and the joinings of those tiles perfect. These are daring experiments. One would have said that the first time the ship went straining and laboring through a storm-tumbled sea those tiles would gape apart and drop out. That they have not done so is evidence that the joiner's art has advanced a good deal since the days when ships were so shackly that when a giant sea gave them a wrench the doors came unbolted. I find the walls of the dining-saloon upholstered with mellow pictures wrought in tapestry and the ceiling aglow with pictures done in oil. In other places of assembly I find great panels filled with embossed Spanish leather, the figures rich with gilding and bronze. Everywhere I find sumptuous masses of color—color, color, color—color all about, color of every shade and tint and variety; and, as a result, the ship is bright and cheery to the eye, and this cheeriness invades one's spirit and contents it. To fully appreciate the force and spiritual value of this radiant and opulent dream of color, one must stand outside at night in the pitch dark and the rain, and look in through a port, and observe it in the lavish splendor of the electric lights. The old-time ships were dull, plain, graceless, gloomy, and horribly depressing. They compelled the blues; one could not escape the blues in them. The modern idea is right: to surround the passenger with conveniences, luxuries, and abundance of inspiriting color. As a result, the ship is the pleasantest place one can be in, except, perhaps, one's home.

A Vanished Sentiment

One thing is gone, to return no more forever—the romance of the sea. Soft sentimentality about the sea has retired from the activities of this life, and is but a memory of the past, already remote and much faded. But within the recollection of men still living, it was in the breast of every individual; and the farther any individual lived from salt-water the more of it he kept in stock. It was as pervasive, as universal, as the atmosphere itself. The mere mention of the sea, the romantic sea, would make any company of people sentimental and mawkish at once. The great majority of the songs that were sung by the young people of the back settlements had the melancholy wanderer for subject and his mouthings about the sea for refrain. Picnic parties paddling down a creek in a canoe when the twilight shadows were gathering always sang:

> *Homeward bound, homeward bound,*
> *From a foreign shore;*

and this was also a favorite in the West with the passengers on stern-wheel steamboats. There was another:

> *My boat is by the shore*
> *And my bark is on the sea,*
> *But before I go, Tom Moore,*
> *Here's a double health to thee.*

And this one, also:

> *O pilot, 'tis a fearful night,*
> *There's danger on the deep.*

And this:

> *A life on the ocean wave*
> *And a home on the rolling deep,*
> *Where the scattered waters rave*
> *And the winds their revels keep!*

And this:

> *A wet sheet and a flowing sea,*
> *And a wind that follows fair.*

And this:

> *My foot is on my gallant deck,*
> *Once more the rover is free!*

And the "Larboard Watch"—the person referred to below is at the masthead, or somewhere up there:

Oh, who can tell what joy he feels,
As o'er the foam his vessel reels,
And his tired eyelids slumb'ring fall,
He rouses at the welcome call
Of "Larboard watch—ahoy!"

Yes, and there was forever and always some jackass-voiced person braying out:

Rocked in the cradle of the deep,
I lay me down in peace to sleep!

Other favorites had these suggestive titles: "The Storm at Sea"; "The Bird at Sea"; "The Sailor Boy's Dream"; "The Captive Pirate's Lament"; "We are far from Home on the Stormy Main"—and so on, and so on, the list is endless. Everybody on a farm lived chiefly amid the dangers of the deep in those days, in fancy.

But all that is gone now. Not a vestige of it is left. The iron-clad, with her unsentimental aspect and frigid attention to business, banished romance from the war marine, and the unsentimental steamer has banished it from the commercial marine. The dangers and uncertainties which made sea life romantic have disappeared and carried the poetic element along with them. In our day the passengers never sing sea-songs on board a ship, and the band never plays them. Pathetic songs about the wanderer in strange lands far from home, once so popular and contributing such fire and color to the imagination by reason of the rarity of that kind of wanderer, have lost their charm and fallen silent, because everybody is a wanderer in the far lands now, and the interest in that detail is dead. Nobody is worried about the wanderer; there are no perils of the sea for him, there are no uncertainties. He is safer in the ship than he would probably be at home, for there he is always liable to have to attend some friend's funeral and stand over the grave in the sleet, bareheaded—and that means pneumonia for him, if he gets his deserts; and the uncertainties of his voyage are reduced to whether he will arrive on the other side in the appointed afternoon, or have to wait till morning.

The first ship I was ever in was a sailing-vessel. She was twenty-eight days going from San Francisco to the Sandwich Islands. But the main reason for this particularly slow passage was that she got becalmed and lay in one spot fourteen days in the center of the Pacific two thousand miles from land. I hear no sea-songs in this present vessel, but I heard the entire lay-out in that one. There were a dozen young people—they are pretty old now, I reckon—and they used to group themselves on the stern, in the starlight or the moonlight, every evening, and sing sea-songs till after midnight, in that hot, silent, motionless calm. They had no sense of humor, and they always sang "Homeward Bound," without reflecting that that was practically ridiculous, since they were standing still and not proceeding in any direction at all; and they often followed that song with " 'Are we almost there, are we almost there?' said the dying girl as she drew near home."

It was a very pleasant company of young people, and I wonder where they are now. Gone, oh, none knows whither; and the bloom and grace and beauty of their youth, where is that? Among them was a liar; all tried to reform him, but none could do it. And so, gradually, he was left to himself; none of us would associate with him. Many a time since I have seen in fancy that forsaken figure, leaning forlorn against the taffrail, and have reflected that perhaps if we had tried harder, and been more patient, we might have won him from his fault and persuaded him to relinquish it. But it is hard to tell; with him the vice was extreme, and was probably incurable. I like to think—and, indeed, I do think—that I did the best that in me lay to lead him to higher and better ways.

There was a singular circumstance. The ship lay becalmed that entire fortnight in exactly the same spot. Then a handsome breeze came fanning over the sea, and we spread our white wings for flight. But the vessel did not budge. The sails bellied out, the gale strained at the ropes, but the vessel moved not a hair's-breadth from her place. The captain was surprised. It was some hours before we found out what the cause of the detention was. It was barnacles. They collect very fast in that part of the Pacific. They had fastened themselves to the ship's bottom; then others had fastened themselves to the first bunch, others to these, and so on, down and down and down, and the last bunch had glued the column hard and fast to the bottom of the sea, which is five miles deep at that point. So the ship was simply become the handle of a walking-cane five miles long—yes, no more moveable by wind and sail than a continent is. It was regarded by every one as remarkable.

Well, the next week—however, Sandy Hook is in sight.

The Danger of Lying in Bed

The man in the ticket-office said:

"Have an accident insurance ticket, also?"

"No," I said, after studying the matter over a little. "No, I believe not; I am going to be traveling by rail all day to-day. However, to-morrow I don't travel. Give me one for to-morrow."

The man looked puzzled. He said:

"But it is for accident insurance, and if you are going to travel by rail—"

"If I am going to travel by rail I sha'n't need it. Lying at home in bed is the thing *I* am afraid of."

I had been looking into this matter. Last year I traveled twenty thousand miles, almost entirely by rail; the year before, I traveled over twenty-five thousand miles, half by sea and half by rail; and the year before that I traveled in the neighborhood of ten thousand miles, exclusively by rail. I suppose if I put in all the little odd journeys here and there, I may say I have traveled sixty thousand miles during the three years I have mentioned. *And never an accident.*

For a good while I said to myself every morning: "Now I have escaped thus far, and so the chances are just that much increased that I shall catch it this time. I will be shrewd, and buy an accident ticket." And to a dead moral certainty I drew a blank, and went to bed that night without a joint started or a bone splintered. I got tired of that sort of daily bother, and fell to buying accident tickets that were good for a month. I said to myself, "A man *can't* buy thirty blanks in one bundle."

But I was mistaken. There was never a prize in the lot. I could read of railway accidents every day—the newspaper atmosphere was foggy with them; but somehow they never came my way. I found I had spent a good deal of money in the accident business, and had nothing to show for it. My suspicions were aroused, and I began to hunt around for somebody that had won in this lottery. I found plenty of people who had invested, but not an individual that had ever had an accident or made a cent. I stopped buying accident tickets and went to ciphering. The result was astounding. THE PERIL LAY NOT IN TRAVELING, BUT IN STAYING AT HOME.

I hunted up statistics, and was amazed to find that after all the glaring newspaper headings concerning railroad disasters, less than *three hundred* people had really lost their lives by those disasters in the preceding twelve months. The Erie road was set down as the most murderous in the list. It had killed forty-six—or twenty-six, I do not exactly remember which, but I know the number was double that of any other road. But the fact straightway suggested itself that the Erie was an immensely long road, and did more business than any other line in the country; so the double number of killed ceased to be matter for surprise.

By further figuring, it appeared that between New York and Rochester the Erie ran eight passenger-trains each way every day—16 altogether; and carried a daily average of 6,000 persons. That is about a million in six months—the population of New York City. Well, the Erie kills from 13 to 23 persons out of *its* million in six months; and in the same time 13,000 of New York's million die in their beds! My flesh crept, my hair stood on end. "This is appalling!" I said. "The danger isn't in traveling by rail, but in trusting to those deadly beds. I will never sleep in a bed again."

I had figured on considerably less than one-half the length of the Erie road. It was plain that the entire road must transport at least eleven or twelve thousand people every day. There are many short roads running out of Boston that do fully half as much; a great many such roads. There are many roads scattered about the Union that do a prodigious passenger business. Therefore it was fair to presume that an average of 2,500 passengers a day for each road in the country would be about correct. There are 846 railway lines in our country, and 846 times 2,500 are 2,115,000. So the railways of America move more than two millions of people every day; six hundred and fifty millions of people a year, without counting the Sundays.

They do that, too—there is no question about it; though where they get the raw material is clear beyond the jurisdiction of my arithmetic; for I have hunted the census through and through, and I find that there are not that many people in the United States, by a matter of six hundred and ten millions at the very least. They must use some of the same people over again, likely.

San Francisco is one-eighth as populous as New York; there are 60 deaths a week in the former and 500 a week in the latter—if they have luck. That is 3,120 deaths a year in San Francisco, and eight times as many in New York—say about 25,000 or 26,000. The health of the two places is the same. So we will let it stand as a fair presumption that this will hold good all over the country, and that consequently 25,000 out of every million of people we have must die every year. That amounts to one-fortieth of our total population. One million of us, then, die annually. Out of this million ten or twelve thousand are stabbed, shot, drowned, hanged, poisoned, or meet a similarly violent death in some other popular way, such as perishing by kerosene-lamp and hoop-skirt conflagrations, getting buried in coal-mines, falling off house-tops, breaking through church or lecture-room floors, taking patent medicines, or committing suicide in other forms. The Erie railroad kills from 23 to 46; the other 845 railroads kill an average of one-third of a man each; and the rest of that million, amounting in the aggregate to the appalling figure of 987,631 corpses, die naturally in their beds!

You will excuse me from taking any more chances on those beds. The railroads are good enough for me.

And my advice to all people is, Don't stay at home any more than you can help; but when you have *got* to stay at home a while, buy a package of those insurance tickets and sit up nights. You cannot be too cautious.

[One can see now why I answered that ticket-agent in the manner recorded at the top of this sketch.]

The moral of this composition is, that thoughtless people grumble more than is fair about railroad management in the United States. When we consider that every day and night of the year full fourteen thousand railway-trains of various kinds, freighted with life and armed with death, go thundering over the land, the marvel is, *not* that they kill three hundred human beings in a twelvemonth, but that they do not kill three hundred times three hundred!

TWAIN LOOKS BACK

My Boyhood Dreams

The dreams of my boyhood? No, they have not been realized. For all who are old, there is something infinitely pathetic about the subject which you have chosen, for in no gray-head's case can it suggest any but one thing—disappointment. Disappointment is its own reason for its pain: the quality or dignity of the hope that failed is a matter aside. The dreamer's valuation of a thing lost—not another man's—is the only standard to measure it by, and his grief for it makes it large and great and fine, and is worthy of our reverence in all cases. We should carefully remember that. There are sixteen hundred million people in the world. Of these there is but a trifling number—in fact, only thirty-eight million—who can understand why a person should have an ambition to belong to the French army; and why, belonging to it, he should be proud of that; and why, having got down that far, he should want to go on down, down, down till he struck bottom and got on the General Staff; and why, being stripped of his livery, or set free and reinvested with his self-respect by any other quick and thorough process, let it be what it might, he should wish to return to his strange serfage. But no matter: the estimate put upon these things by the fifteen hundred and sixty millions is no proper measure of their value: the proper measure, the just measure, is that which is put upon them by Dreyfus, and is cipherable merely upon the littleness or the vastness of the *disappointment* which their loss cost him.

There you have it: the measure of the magnitude of a dream-failure is the measure of the disappointment the failure cost the dreamer; the value, in others' eyes, of the thing lost, has nothing to do with the matter. With this straightening-out and classification of the dreamer's position to help us, perhaps we can put ourselves in his place and respect his dream—Dreyfus's, and the dreams our friends have cherished and reveal to us. Some that I call to mind, some that have been revealed to me, are curious enough; but we may not smile at them, for they were precious to the dreamers, and their failure has left scars which give them dignity and pathos. With this theme in my mind, dear heads that were brown when they and mine were young together rise old and white before me now, beseeching me to speak for them, and most lovingly will I do it.

Howells, Hay, Aldrich, Matthews, Stockton, Cable, Remus—how their young hopes and ambitions come flooding back to my memory now, out of the vague far past, the beautiful past, the lamented past! I remember it so well—that night we met together—it was in Boston, and Mr. Fields was there, and Mr. Osgood, and Ralph Keeler, and Boyle O'Reilly, lost to us now these many years—and under the seal of confidence revealed to each other what our boyhood dreams had been: dreams which had not as yet been blighted, but over which was stealing the gray of the night that was to come—a night which we prophetically *felt,* and this feeling oppressed us and made us sad. I remember that Howells's voice broke twice, and it was only with great difficulty that he was able to go on; in the end he wept. For he had hoped to be an auctioneer. He told of his early struggles to climb to his goal, and how at last he attained to within a single step of the coveted summit. But there misfortune after misfortune assailed him, and he went down, and down, and down, until now at last, weary and disheartened, he had for the present given up the struggle and become editor of the *Atlantic Monthly*. This was in 1830. Seventy years are gone since, and where now is his dream? It will never be fulfilled. And it is best so; he is no longer fitted for the position; no one would take him now; even if he got it, he would not be able to do himself credit in it, on account of his deliberateness of speech and lack of trained professional vivacity; he would be put on real estate, and would have the pain of seeing younger and abler men intrusted with the furniture and other such goods—goods which draw a mixed and intellectually low order of customers, who must be beguiled of their bids by a vulgar and specialized humor and sparkle, accompanied with antics.

But it is not the thing lost that counts, but only the *disappointment* the loss brings to the dreamer that had coveted that thing and had set his heart of hearts upon it; and when we remember this, a great wave of sorrow for Howells rises in our breasts, and we wish for his sake that his fate could have been different.

At that time Hay's boyhood dream was not yet past hope of realization, but it was fading, dimming, wasting away, and the wind of a growing apprehension was blowing cold over the perishing summer of his life. In the pride of his young ambition he had aspired to be a steamboat mate; and in fancy saw himself dominating a forecastle some day on the Mississippi and dictating terms to roustabouts in high and wounding tones. I look back now, from this far distance of seventy years, and note with sorrow the stages of that dream's destruction. Hay's history is but Howells's, with differences of detail. Hay climbed high toward his ideal; when success seemed almost sure, his foot upon the very gang-plank, his eye upon the capstan, misfortune came and his fall began. Down—down—down—ever down: Private Secretary to the President; Colonel in the field; Chargé d'Affaires in Paris; Chargé d'Affaires in Vienna; Poet; Editor of the *Tribune;* Biographer of Lincoln; Ambassador to England; and now at last there he lies—Secretary of State, Head of Foreign Affairs. And he has fallen like Lucifer, never to rise again. And his dream—where now is his dream? Gone down in blood and tears with the dream of the auctioneer.

And the young dream of Aldrich—where is that? I remember yet how he sat there that night fondling it, petting it; seeing it recede and ever recede; trying to be reconciled and give it up, but not able yet to bear the thought; for it had been his hope to be a horse-doctor. He also climbed high, but, like the others, fell; then fell again, and yet again, and again and again. And now at last he can fall no further. He is old now, he has ceased to struggle, and is only a poet. No one would risk a horse with him now. His dream is over.

Has *any* boyhood dream ever been fulfilled? I must doubt it. Look at Brander Matthews. He wanted to be a cowboy. What is he to-day? Nothing but a professor in a university. Will he ever be a cowboy? It is hardly conceivable.

Look at Stockton. What was Stockton's young dream? He hoped to be a barkeeper. See where *he* has landed.

Is it better with Cable? What was Cable's young dream? To be a ringmaster in the circus, and swell around and crack the whip. What is he today? Nothing but a theologian and novelist.

And Uncle Remus—what was his young dream? To be a buccaneer. Look at him now.

Ah, the dreams of our youth, how beautiful they are, and how perishable! The ruins of these might-have-beens, how pathetic! The heart-secrets that were revealed that night now so long vanished, how they touch me as I give them voice! Those sweet privacies, how they endeared us to each other! We were under oath never to tell any of these things, and I have always kept that oath inviolate when speaking with persons whom I thought not worthy to hear them.

Oh, our lost Youth—God keep its memory green in our hearts! for Age is upon us, with the indignity of its infirmities, and Death beckons!

TO THE ABOVE OLD PEOPLE

Sleep! for the Sun that scores another Day
Against the Tale allotted You to stay,
Reminding You, is Risen, and now
Serves Notice—ah, ignore it while You may!

The chill Wind blew, and those who stood before
The Tavern murmured, "Having drunk his Score,
Why tarries He with empty Cup? Behold,
The Wine of Youth once poured, is poured no more.

"Come leave the Cup, and on the Winter's Snow
Your Summer Garment of Enjoyment throw:
Your Tide of Life is ebbing fast, and it,
Exhausted once, for You no more shall flow."

While yet the Phantom of false Youth was mine,
I heard a Voice from out the Darkness whine,
"O Youth, O whither gone? Return,
And bathe my Age in thy reviving Wine."

In this subduing Draught of tender green
And kindly Absinthe, with its wimpling Sheen
Of dusky half-lights, let me drown
The haunting Pathos of the Might-Have-Been.

For every nickeled Joy, marred and brief,
We pay some day its Weight in golden Grief
Mined from our Hearts. Ah, murmur not—
From this one-sided Bargain dream of no Relief!

The Joy of Life, that streaming through their Veins
Tumultuous swept, falls slack—and wanes
The Glory in the Eye—and one by one
Life's Pleasures perish and make place for Pains.

Whether one hide in some secluded Nook—
Whether at Liverpool or Sandy Hook—
'Tis one. Old Age will search him out—and He—
He—He—when ready will know where to look.

From Cradle unto Grave I keep a House
Of Entertainment where may drowse
Bacilli and kindred Germs—or feed—or breed
Their festering Species in a deep Carouse.

Think—in this battered Caravanserai,
Whose Portals open stand all Night and Day,
How Microbe after Microbe with his Pomp
Arrives unasked, and comes to stay.

Our ivory Teeth, confessing to the Lust
Of masticating, once, now own Disgust
Of Clay-plug'd Cavities—full soon our Snags
Are emptied, and our Mouths are filled with Dust.

Our Gums forsake the Teeth and tender grow,
And fat, like over-ripened Figs—we know
The Sign—the Riggs Disease is ours, and we
Must list this Sorrow, add another Woe.

Our Lungs begin to fail and soon we Cough,
And chilly Streaks play up our Backs, and off
Our fever'd Foreheads drip an icy Sweat—
We scoffed before, but now we may not scoff.

Some for the Bunions that afflict us prate
Of Plasters unsurpassable, and hate
To cut a Corn—ah cut, and let the Plaster go,
Nor murmur if the Solace come too late.

Some for the Honors of Old Age, and some
Long for its Respite from the Hum
And Clash of sordid Strife—O Fools,
The Past should teach them what's to Come:

Lo, for the Honors, cold Neglect instead!
For Respite, disputatious Heirs a Bed
Of Thorns for them will furnish. Go,
Seek not Here for Peace—but Yonder—with the Dead.

For whether Zal and Rustam heed this Sign,
And even smitten thus, will not repine,
Let Zal and Rustam shuffle as they may,
The Fine once levied they must Cash the Fine.

O Voices of the Long Ago that were so dear!
Fall'n Silent, now, for many a Mold'ring Year,
O whither are ye flown? Come back,
And break my Heart, but bless my grieving ear.

Some happy Day my Voice will Silent fall,
And answer not when some that love it call:
Be glad for Me when this you note—and think
I've found the Voices lost, beyond the pall.

So let me grateful drain the Magic Bowl
That medicines hurt Minds and on the Soul
The Healing of its Peace doth lay—if then
Death claim me—Welcome be his Dole!

SANNA, SWEDEN, *September 15th.*

Private.—If you don't know what Riggs's Disease of the Teeth is, the dentist will tell you. I've had it—and it is more than interesting.—S.L.C.

EDITORIAL NOTE

Fearing that there might be some mistake, we submitted a proof of this article to the (American) gentlemen named in it, and asked them to correct any errors of detail that might have crept in among the facts. They reply with some asperity that errors cannot creep in among facts where there are no facts for them to creep in among; and that none are discoverable in this article, but only baseless aberrations of a disordered mind. They have no recollection of any such night in Boston, nor elsewhere; and in their opinion there was never any such night. They have *met* Mr. Twain, but have had the prudence not to intrust any privacies to him—particularly under oath; and they think they now see that this prudence was justified, since he has been untrustworthy enough to even betray privacies which had no existence. Further, they think it a strange thing that Mr. Twain, who was never invited to meddle with anybody's boyhood dreams but his own, has been so gratuitously anxious to see that other people's are placed before the world that he has quite lost his head in his zeal and forgotten to make any mention of his own at all. Provided we insert this explanation, they are willing to let his article pass; otherwise they must require its suppression in the interest of truth.

P.S.—These replies having left us in some perplexity, and also in some fear lest they might distress Mr. Twain if published without his privity, we judged it but fair to submit them to him and give him an opportunity to defend himself. But he does not seem to be troubled, or even aware that he is in a delicate situation. He merely says:

"Do not worry about those former young people. They can write good literature, but when it comes to speaking the truth, they have not had my training.—MARK TWAIN."

The last sentence seems obscure, and liable to an unfortunate construction. It plainly needs refashioning, but we cannot take the responsibility of doing it.—EDITOR.

A Burlesque Biography

Two or three persons having at different times intimated that if I would write an autobiography they would read it when they got leisure, I yield at last to this frenzied public demand and herewith tender my history.

Ours is a noble old house, and stretches a long way back into antiquity. The earliest ancestor the Twains have any record of was a friend of the family by the name of Higgins. This was in the eleventh century, when our people were living in Aberdeen, county of Cork, England. Why it is that our long line has ever since borne the maternal name (except when one of them now and then took a playful refuge in an alias to avert foolishness), instead of Higgins, is a mystery which none of us has ever felt much desire to stir. It is a kind of vague, pretty romance, and we leave it alone. All the old families do that way.

Arthour Twain was a man of considerable note—a solicitor on the highway in William Rufus's time. At about the age of thirty he went to one of those fine old English places of resort called Newgate, to see about something, and never returned again. While there he died suddenly.

Augustus Twain seems to have made something of a stir about the year 1160. He was as full of fun as he could be, and used to take his old saber and sharpen it up, and get in a convenient place on a dark night, and stick it through people as they went by, to see them jump. He was a born humorist. But he got to going too far with it; and the first time he was found stripping one of these parties, the authorities removed one end of him, and put it up on a nice high place on Temple Bar, where it could contemplate the people and have a good time. He never liked any situation so much or stuck to it so long.

Then for the next two hundred years the family tree shows a succession of soldiers—noble, high-spirited fellows, who always went into battle singing, right behind the army, and always went out a-whooping, right ahead of it.

This is a scathing rebuke to old dead Froissart's poor witticism that our family tree never had but one limb to it, and that that one stuck out at right angles, and bore fruit winter and summer.

Early in the fifteenth century we have Beau Twain, called "the Scholar." He wrote a beautiful, beautiful hand. And he could imitate anybody's hand so closely that it was enough to make a person laugh his head off to see it. He had infinite sport with his talent. But by and by he took a contract to break stone for a road, and the roughness of the work spoiled his hand. Still, he enjoyed life all the time he was in the stone business, which, with inconsiderable intervals, was some forty-two years. In fact, he died in harness. During all those long years he gave such satisfaction that he never was through with one contract a week till the government gave him another. He was a perfect pet. And he was always a favorite with his fellow-artists, and was a conspicuous member of their benevolent secret society, called the Chain Gang. He always wore his hair short, had a preference for striped clothes, and died lamented by the government. He was a sore loss to his country. For he was so regular.

Some years later we have the illustrious John Morgan Twain. He came over to this country with Columbus in 1492 as a passenger. He appears to have been of a crusty, uncomfortable disposition. He complained of the food all the way over, and was always threatening to go ashore unless there was a change. He wanted fresh shad. Hardly a day passed over his head that he did not go idling about the ship with his nose in the air, sneering about the commander, and saying he did not believe Columbus knew where he was going to or had ever been there before. The memorable cry of "Land ho!" thrilled every heart in the ship but his. He gazed awhile through a piece of smoked glass at the penciled line lying on the distant water, and then said: "Land be hanged—it's a raft!"

When this questionable passenger came on board the ship, he brought nothing with him but an old newspaper containing a handkerchief marked "B. G.," one cotton sock marked "L. W. C.," one woollen one marked "D. F.," and a night-shirt marked "O. M. R." And yet during the voyage he worried more about his "trunk," and gave himself more airs about it, than all the rest of the passengers put together. If the ship was "down by the head," and would not steer, he would go and move his "trunk" farther aft, and then watch the effect. If the ship was "by the stern," he would suggest to Columbus to detail some men to "shift that baggage." In storms he had to be gagged, because his wailings about his "trunk" made it impossible for the men to hear the orders. The man doės not appear to have been openly charged with any gravely unbecoming thing, but it is noted in the ship's log as a "curious circumstance" that albeit he brought his baggage on board the ship in a newspaper, he took it ashore in four trunks, a queensware crate, and a couple of champagne baskets. But when he came back insinuating, in an insolent, swaggering way, that some of his things were missing, and was going to search the other passengers' baggage, it was too much, and they threw him overboard. They watched long and wonderingly for him to come up, but not even a bubble rose on the quietly ebbing tide. But while every one was most absorbed in gazing over the side, and the interest was momentarily increasing, it was observed with consternation that the vessel was adrift and the anchor-cable hanging limp from the bow. Then in the ship's dimmed and ancient log we find this quaint note:

"In time it was discouvered yt ye troblesome passenger hadde gonne downe and got ye anchor, and toke ye same and solde it to ye dam sauvages from ye interior, saying yt he hadde founde it, ye sonne of a ghun!"

Yet this ancestor had good and noble instincts, and it is with pride that we call to mind the fact that he was the first white person who ever interested himself in the work of elevating and civilizing our Indians. He built a commodious jail and put up a gallows, and to his dying day he claimed with satisfaction that he had had a more restraining and elevating influence on the Indians than any other reformer that ever labored among them. At this point the chronicle becomes less frank and chatty, and closes abruptly by saying that the old voyager went to see his gallows perform on the first white man ever hanged in America, and while there received injuries which terminated in his death.

The great-grandson of the "Reformer" flourished in sixteen hundred and something, and was known in our annals as "the old Admiral," though in history he had other titles. He was long in command of fleets of swift vessels, well armed and manned, and did great service in hurrying up merchantmen. Vessels which he followed and kept his eagle eye on, always made good fair time across the ocean. But if a ship still loitered in spite of all he could do, his indignation would grow till he could contain himself no longer—and then he would take that ship home where he lived and keep it there carefully, expecting the owners to come for it, but they never did. And he would try to get the idleness and sloth out of the sailors of that ship by compelling them to take invigorating exercise and a bath. He called it "walking a plank." All the pupils liked it. At any rate, they never found any fault with it after trying it. When the owners were late coming for their ships, the Admiral always burned them, so that the insurance money should not be lost. At last this fine old tar was cut down in the fullness of his years and honors. And to her dying day, his poor heart-broken widow believed that if he had been cut down fifteen minutes sooner he might have been resuscitated.

Charles Henry Twain lived during the latter part of the seventeenth century, and was a zealous and distinguished missionary. He converted sixteen thousand South Sea islanders, and taught them that a dog-tooth necklace and a pair of spectacles was not enough clothing to come to divine service in. His poor flock loved him very, very dearly; and when his funeral was over, they got up in a body (and came out of the restaurant) with tears in their eyes, and saying, one to another, that he was a good tender missionary, and they wished they had some more of him.

Pah-go-to-wah-wah-pukketekeewis (Mighty-Hunter-with-a-Hog-Eye-Twain) adorned the middle of the eighteenth century, and aided General Braddock with all his heart to resist the oppressor Washington. It was this ancestor who fired seventeen times at our Washington from behind a tree. So far the beautiful romantic narrative in the moral story-books is correct; but when that narrative goes on to say that at the seventeenth round the awe-stricken savage said solemnly that that man was being reserved by the Great Spirit for some mighty mission, and he dared not lift his sacrilegious rifle against him again, the narrative seriously impairs the integrity of history. What he did say was:

"It ain't no (hic) no use. 'At man's so drunk he can't stan' still long enough for a man to hit him. I (hic) I can't 'ford to fool away any more am'nition on him."

That was why he stopped at the seventeenth round, and it was a good, plain, matter-of-fact reason, too, and one that easily commends itself to us by the eloquent, persuasive flavor of probability there is about it.

I always enjoyed the story-book narrative, but I felt a marring misgiving that every Indian at Braddock's Defeat who fired at a soldier a couple of times (two easily grows to seventeen in a century), and missed him, jumped to the conclusion that the Great Spirit was reserving that soldier for some grand mission; and so I somehow feared that the only reason why Washington's case is remembered and the others forgotten is, that in his the prophecy came true, and in that of the others it didn't. There are not books enough on earth to contain the record of the prophecies Indians and other unauthorized parties have made; but one may carry in his overcoat pockets the record of all the prophecies that have been fulfilled.

I will remark here, in passing, that certain ancestors of mine are so thoroughly well-known in history by their aliases, that I have not felt it to be worth while to dwell upon them, or even mention them in the order of their birth. Among these may be mentioned Richard Brinsley Twain, alias Guy Fawkes; John Wentworth Twain, alias Sixteen-String Jack; William Hogarth Twain, alias Jack Sheppard; Ananias Twain, alias Baron Munchausen; John George Twain, alias Captain Kydd; and then there are George Francis Train, Tom Pepper, Nebuchadnezzar, and Baalam's Ass—they all belong to our family, but to a branch of it somewhat distinctly removed from the honorable direct line—in fact, a collateral branch, whose members chifly differ from the ancient stock in that, in order to acquire the notoriety we have always yearned and hungered for, they have got into a low way of going to jail instead of getting hanged.

It is not well, when writing an autobiography, to follow your ancestry down too close to your own time—it is safest to speak only vaguely of your great-grandfather, and then skip from there to yourself, which I now do.

I was born without teeth—and there Richard III had the advantage of me; but I was born without a humpback, likewise, and there I had the advantage of him. My parents were neither very poor nor conspicuously honest.

But now a thought occurs to me. My own history would really seem so tame contrasted with that of my ancestors, that it is simply wisdom to leave it unwritten until I am hanged. If some other biographies I have read had stopped with the ancestry until a like event occurred, it would have been a felicitous thing for the reading public. How does it strike you?

The Death of Jean

The death of Jean Clemens occurred early in the morning of December 24, 1909. Mr. Clemens was in great stress of mind when I first saw him, but a few hours later I found him writing steadily.

"I am setting it down," he said, "everything. It is a relief to me to write it. It furnishes me an excuse for thinking." At intervals during that day and the next I looked in, and usually found him writing. Then on the evening of the 26th, when he knew that Jean had been laid to rest in Elmira, he came to my room with the manuscript in his hand.

"I have finished it," he said; "read it. I can form no opinion of it myself. If you think it worthy, some day—at the proper time—it can end my autobiography. It is the final chapter."

Four months later—almost to the day—(April 21st) he was with Jean.

—ALBERT BIGELOW PAINE.[1]

STORMFIELD, CHRISTMAS EVE, 11 A.M., *1909.*

Jean is dead!

Has any one ever tried to put upon paper all the little happenings connected with a dear one—happenings of the twenty-four hours preceding the sudden and unexpected death of that dear one? Would a book contain them? Would two books contain them? I think not. They

1. Twain's friend, literary executor, and biographer.—EDITOR.

pour into the mind in a flood. They are little things that have been always happening every day, and were always so unimportant and easily forgetable before—but now! Now, how different! how precious they are, how dear, how unforgetable, how pathetic, how sacred, how clothed with dignity!

Last night Jean, all flushed with splendid health, and I the same, from the wholesome effects of my Bermuda holiday, strolled hand in hand from the dinner-table and sat down in the library and chatted, and planned, and discussed, cheerily and happily (and how unsuspectingly!)—until nine—which is late for us—then went up-stairs, Jean's friendly German dog following. At my door Jean said, "I can't kiss you good night, father: I have a cold, and you could catch it." I bent and kissed her hand. She was moved—I saw it in her eyes—and she impulsively kissed my hand in return. Then with the usual gay "Sleep well, dear!" from both, we parted.

At half past seven this morning I woke, and heard voices outside my door. I said to myself, "Jean is starting on her usual horseback flight to the station for the mail." Then Katy[1] entered, stood quaking and gasping at my bedside a moment, then found her tongue:

"Miss Jean is dead!"

Possibly I know now what the soldier feels when a bullet crashes through his heart.

In her bathroom there she lay, the fair young creature, stretched upon the floor and covered with a sheet. And looking so placid, so natural, and as if asleep. We knew what had happened. She was an epileptic: she had been seized with a convulsion and heart failure in her bath. The doctor had to come several miles. His efforts, like our previous ones, failed to bring her back to life.

It is noon, now. How lovable she looks, how sweet and how tranquil! It is a noble face, and full of dignity; and that was a good heart that lies there so still.

In England, thirteen years ago, my wife and I were stabbed to the heart with a cablegram which said, "Susy was mercifully released to-day." I had to send a like shock to Clara, in Berlin, this morning. With the peremptory addition, "You must not come home." Clara and her husband sailed from here on the 11th of this month. How will Clara bear it? Jean, from her babyhood, was a worshiper of Clara.

1. Katy Leary, who had been in the service of the Clemens family for twenty-nine years. —EDITOR.

Four days ago I came back from a month's holiday in Bermuda in perfected health; but by some accident the reporters failed to perceive this. Day before yesterday, letters and telegrams began to arrive from friends and strangers which indicated that I was supposed to be dangerously ill. Yesterday Jean begged me to explain my case through the Associated Press. I said it was not important enough; but she was distressed and said I must think of Clara. Clara would see the report in the German papers, and as she had been nursing her husband day and night for four months[1] and was worn out and feeble, the shock might be disastrous. There was reason in that; so I sent a humorous paragraph by telephone to the Associated Press denying the "charge" that I was "dying," and saying "I would not do such a thing at my time of life."

Jean was a little troubled, and did not like to see me treat the matter so lightly; but I said it was best to treat it so, for there was nothing serious about it. This morning I sent the sorrowful facts of this day's irremediable disaster to the Associated Press. Will both appear in this evening's papers? —the one so blithe, the other so tragic.

I lost Susy thirteen years ago; I lost her mother—her incomparable mother!—five and a half years ago; Clara has gone away to live in Europe; and now I have lost Jean. How poor I am, who was once so rich! Seven months ago Mr. Rogers died—one of the best friends I ever had, and the nearest perfect, as man and gentleman, I have yet met among my race; within the last six weeks Gilder has passed away, and Laffan—old, old friends of mine. Jean lies yonder, I sit here; we are strangers under our own roof; we kissed hands good-by at this door last night—and it was forever, we never suspecting it. She lies there, and I sit here—writing, busying myself, to keep my heart from breaking. How dazzlingly the sunshine is flooding the hills around! It is like a mockery.

Seventy-four years old twenty-four days ago. Seventy-four years old yesterday. Who can estimate my age to-day?

I have looked upon her again. I wonder I can bear it. She looks just as her mother looked when she lay dead in that Florentine villa so long ago. The sweet placidity of death! it is more beautiful than sleep.

I saw her mother buried. I said I would never endure that horror again; that I would never again look into the grave of any one dear to me. I have kept to that. They will take Jean from this house to-morrow, and bear her

1. Mr. Gabrilowitsch had been operated on for appendicitis.—EDITOR.

to Elmira, New York, where lie those of us that have been released, but I shall not follow.

Jean was on the dock when the ship came in, only four days ago. She was at the door, beaming a welcome, when I reached this house the next evening. We played cards, and she tried to teach me a new game called "Mark Twain." We sat chatting cheerily in the library last night, and she wouldn't let me look into the loggia, where she was making Christmas preparations. She said she would finish them in the morning, and then her little French friend would arrive from New York—the surprise would follow; the surprise she had been working over for days. While she was out for a moment I disloyally stole a look. The loggia floor was clothed with rugs and furnished with chairs and sofas; and the uncompleted surprise was there; in the form of a Christmas tree that was drenched with silver film in a most wonderful way; and on a table was a prodigal profusion of bright things which she was going to hang upon it to-day. What desecrating hand will ever banish that eloquent unfinished surprise from that place? Not mine, surely. All these little matters have happened in the last four days. "Little." Yes—*then.* But not now. Nothing she said or thought or did is little now. And all the lavish humor!—what is become of it? It is pathos, now. Pathos, and the thought of it brings tears.

All these little things happened such a few hours ago—and now she lies yonder. Lies yonder, and cares for nothing any more. Strange—marvelous—incredible! I have had this experience before; but it would still be incredible if I had had it a thousand times.

"Miss Jean is dead!"

That is what Katy said. When I heard the door open behind the bed's head without a preliminary knock, I supposed it was Jean coming to kiss me good morning, she being the only person who was used to entering without formalities.

And so—

I have been to Jean's parlor. Such a turmoil of Christmas presents for servants and friends! They are everywhere; tables, chairs, sofas, the floor—everything is occupied, and over-occupied. It is many and many a year since I have seen the like. In that ancient day Mrs. Clemens and I used to slip softly into the nursery at midnight on Christmas Eve and look the array of presents over. The children were little then. And now here is Jean's parlor looking just as that nursery used to look. The presents are not labeled—the hands are forever idle that would have labeled them to-day. Jean's mother always worked herself down with her Christmas preparations. Jean did the same yesterday and the preceding days, and the fatigue has cost her her life. The fatigue caused the convulsion that attacked her this morning. She had had no attack for months.

Jean was so full of life and energy that she was constantly in danger of overtaxing her strength. Every morning she was in the saddle by half past seven, and off to the station for her mail. She examined the letters and I distributed them: some to her, some to Mr. Paine, the others to the stenographer and myself. She despatched her share and then mounted her horse again and went around superintending her farm and her poultry the rest of the day. Sometimes she played billiards with me after dinner, but she was usually too tired to play, and went early to bed.

Yesterday afternoon I told her about some plans I had been devising while absent in Bermuda, to lighten her burdens. We would get a housekeeper; also we would put her share of the secretary-work into Mr. Paine's hands.

No—she wasn't willing. She had been making plans herself. The matter ended in a compromise. I submitted. I always did. She wouldn't audit the bills and let Paine fill out the checks—she would continue to attend to that herself. Also, she would continue to be housekeeper, and let Katy assist. Also, she would continue to answer the letters of personal friends for me. Such was the compromise. Both of us called it by that name, though I was not able to see where any formidable change had been made.

However, Jean was pleased, and that was sufficient for me. She was proud of being my secretary, and I was never able to persuade her to give up any part of her share in that unlovely work.

In the talk last night I said I found everything going so smoothly that if she were willing I would go back to Bermuda in February and get blessedly out of the clash and turmoil again for another month. She was urgent that I should do it, and said that if I would put off the trip until March she would take Katy and go with me. We struck hands upon that, and said it was settled. I had a mind to write to Bermuda by to-morrow's ship and secure a furnished house and servants. I meant to write the letter this morning. But it will never be written, now.

For she lies yonder, and before her is another journey than that.

Night is closing down; the rim of the sun barely shows above the sky-line of the hills.

I have been looking at that face again that was growing dearer and dearer to me every day. I was getting acquainted with Jean in these last nine months. She had been long an exile from home when she came to us three-quarters of a year ago. She had been shut up in sanitariums, many miles from us. How eloquently glad and grateful she was to cross her father's threshold again!

Would I bring her back to life if I could do it? I would not. If a word would do it, I would beg for strength to withhold the word. And I would have the strength; I am sure of it. In her loss I am almost bankrupt, and my life is a bitterness, but I am content: for she has been enriched with the most precious of all gifts—that gift which makes all other gifts mean and poor—death. I have never wanted any released friend of mine restored to life since I reached manhood. I felt in this way when Susy passed away; and later my wife, and later Mr. Rogers. When Clara met me at the station in New York and told me Mr. Rogers had died suddenly that morning, my thought was, Oh, favorite of fortune—fortunate all his long and lovely life—fortunate to his latest moment! The reporters said there were tears of sorrow in my eyes. True—but they were for *me,* not for him. He had suffered no loss. All the fortunes he had ever made before were poverty compared with this one.

Why did I build this house, two years ago? To shelter this vast emptiness? How foolish I was! But I shall stay in it. The spirits of the dead hallow a house, for me. It was not so with other members of my family. Susy died in the house we built in Hartford. Mrs. Clemens would never enter it again. But it made the house dearer to me. I have entered it once since, when it was tenantless and silent and forlorn, but to me it was a holy place and beautiful. It seemed to me that the spirits of the dead were all about me, and would speak to me and welcome me if they could: Livy, and Susy, and George, and Henry Robinson, and Charles Dudley Warner. How good and kind they were, and how lovable their lives! In fancy I could see them all again, I could call the children back and hear them romp again with George—that peerless black ex-slave and children's idol who came one day—a flitting stranger—to wash windows, and stayed eighteen years. Until he died. Clara and Jean would never enter again the New York hotel which their mother had frequented in earlier days. They could not bear it. But I shall stay in this house. It is dearer to me to-night than ever it was before. Jean's spirit will make it beautiful for me always. Her lonely and tragic death—but I will not think of that now.

Jean's mother always devoted two or three weeks to Christmas shopping, and was always physically exhausted when Christmas Eve came. Jean was her very own child—she wore herself out present-hunting in New York these latter days. Paine has just found on her desk a long list of names—fifty, he thinks—people to whom she sent presents last night. Apparently she forgot no one. And Katy found there a roll of bank-notes, for the servants.

Her dog has been wandering about the grounds to-day, comradeless and forlorn. I have seen him from the windows. She got him from Germany. He has tall ears and looks exactly like a wolf. He was educated in Germany, and knows no language but the German. Jean gave him no orders save in that tongue. And so, when the burglar-alarm made a fierce clamor at midnight a fortnight ago, the butler, who is French and knows no German, tried in vain to interest the dog in the supposed burglar. Jean wrote me, to Bermuda, about the incident. It was the last letter I was ever to receive from her bright head and her competent hand. The dog will not be neglected.

There was never a kinder heart than Jean's. From her childhood up she always spent the most of her allowance on charities of one kind and another. After she became secretary and had her income doubled she spent her money upon these things with a free hand. Mine too, I am glad and grateful to say.

She was a loyal friend to all animals, and she loved them all, birds, beasts, and everything—even snakes—an inheritance from me. She knew all the birds: she was high up in that lore. She became a member of various humane societies when she was still a little girl—both here and abroad—and she remained an active member to the last. She founded two or three societies for the protection of animals, here and in Europe.

She was an embarrassing secretary, for she fished my correspondence out of the waste-basket and answered the letters. She thought all letters deserved the courtesy of an answer. Her mother brought her up in that kindly error.

She could write a good letter, and was swift with her pen. She had but an indifferent ear for music, but her tongue took to languages with an easy facility. She never allowed her Italian, French, and German to get rusty through neglect.

The telegrams of sympathy are flowing in, from far and wide, now, just as they did in Italy five years and a half ago, when this child's mother laid down her blameless life. They cannot heal the hurt, but they take away some of the pain. When Jean and I kissed hands and parted at my door last, how little did we imagine that in twenty-two hours the telegraph would be bringing words like these:

"From the bottom of our hearts we send our sympathy, dearest of friends."

For many and many a day to come, wherever I go in this house, remembrancers of Jean will mutely speak to me of her. Who can count the number of them?

She was in exile two years with the hope of healing her malady—epilepsy. There are no words to express how grateful I am that she did not meet her fate in the hands of strangers, but in the loving shelter of her own home.

"Miss Jean is dead!"

It is true. Jean is dead.

A month ago I was writing bubbling and hilarious articles for magazines yet to appear, and now I am writing—this.

Christmas Day. Noon.—Last night I went to Jean's room at intervals, and turned back the sheet and looked at the peaceful face, and kissed the cold brow, and remembered that heartbreaking night in Florence so long ago, in that cavernous and silent vast villa, when I crept down-stairs so many times, and turned back a sheet and looked at a face just like this one —Jean's mother's face—and kissed a brow that was just like this one. And last night I saw again what I had seen then—that strange and lovely miracle —the sweet, soft contours of early maidenhood restored by the gracious hand of death! When Jean's mother lay dead, all trace of care, and trouble, and suffering, and the corroding years had vanished out of the face, and I was looking again upon it as I had known and worshiped it in its young bloom and beauty a whole generation before.

About three in the morning, while wandering about the house in the deep silences, as one does in times like these, when there is a dumb sense that something has been lost that will never be found again, yet must be sought, if only for the employment the useless seeking gives, I came upon Jean's dog in the hall down-stairs, and noted that he did not spring to greet me, according to his hospitable habit, but came slow and sorrowfully; also I remembered that he had not visited Jean's apartment since the tragedy. Poor fellow, did he know? I think so. Always when Jean was abroad in the open he was with her; always when she was in the house he was with her, in the night as well as in the day. Her parlor was his bedroom. Whenever I happened upon him on the ground floor he always followed me about, and when I went up-stairs he went too—in a tumultuous gallop. But now it was different: after patting him a little I went to the library—he remained behind; when I went up-stairs he did not follow me, save with his wistful eyes. He has wonderful eyes—big, and kind, and eloquent. He can talk with them. He is a beautiful creature, and is of the breed of the New York police-dogs. I do not like dogs, because they bark when there is no occasion for it; but I have liked this one from the beginning, because he belonged to Jean, and because he never barks except when there is occasion—which is not oftener than twice a week.

In my wanderings I visited Jean's parlor. On a shelf I found a pile of my books, and I knew what it meant. She was waiting for me to come home from Bermuda and autograph them, then she would send them away. If I only knew whom she intended them for! But I shall never know. I will keep them. Her hand has touched them—it is an accolade—they are noble, now.

And in a closet she had hidden a surprise for me—a thing I have often wished I owned: a noble big globe. I couldn't see it for the tears. She will never know the pride I take in it, and the pleasure. Today the mails are full of loving remembrances for her: full of those old, old kind words she loved so well, "Merry Christmas to Jean!" If she could only have lived one day longer!

At last she ran out of money, and would not use mine. So she sent to one of those New York homes for poor girls all the clothes she could spare —and more, most likely.

Christmas Night.—This afternoon they took her away from her room. As soon as I might, I went down to the library, and there she lay, in her coffin, dressed in exactly the same clothes she wore when she stood at the other end of the same room on the 6th of October last, as Clara's chief bridesmaid. Her face was radiant with happy excitement then; it was the same face now, with the dignity of death and the peace of God upon it.

They told me the first mourner to come was the dog. He came uninvited, and stood up on his hind legs and rested his fore paws upon the trestle, and took a last long look at the face that was so dear to him, then went his way as silently as he had come. *He knows.*

At mid-afternoon it began to snow. The pity of it—that Jean could not see it! She so loved the snow.

The snow continued to fall. At six o'clock the hearse drew up to the door to bear away its pathetic burden. As they lifted the casket, Paine began playing on the orchestrelle Schubert's "Impromptu," which was Jean's favorite. Then he played the Intermezzo; that was for Susy; then he played the Largo; that was for their mother. He did this at my request. Elsewhere in my Autobiography I have told how the Intermezzo and the Largo came to be associated in my heart with Susy and Livy in their last hours in this life.

From my windows I saw the hearse and the carriages wind along the road and gradually grow vague and spectral in the falling snow, and presently disappear. Jean was gone out of my life, and would not come back any more. Jervis, the cousin she had played with when they were babies together—he and her beloved old Katy—were conducting her to her distant childhood home, where she will lie by her mother's side once more, in the company of Susy and Langdon.

December 26th. The dog came to see me at eight o'clock this morning. He was very affectionate, poor orphan! My room will be his quarters hereafter.

The storm raged all night. It has raged all the morning. The snow drives across the landscape in vast clouds, superb, sublime—and Jean not here to see.

2.30 P.M.—It is the time appointed. The funeral has begun. Four hundred miles away, but I can see it all, just as if I were there. The scene is the library in the Langdon homestead. Jean's coffin stands where her mother and I stood, forty years ago, and were married; and where Susy's coffin stood thirteen years ago; where her mother's stood five years and a half ago; and where mine will stand after a little time.

Five o'clock.—It is all over.

When Clara went away two weeks ago to live in Europe, it was hard, but I could bear it, for I had Jean left. I said *we* would be a family. We said we would be close comrades and happy—just we two. That fair dream was in my mind when Jean met me at the steamer last Monday; it was in my mind when she received me at the door last Tuesday evening. We were together; *we were a family!* the dream had come true—oh, precisely true, contentedly true, satisfyingly true! and remained true two whole days.

And now? Now Jean is in her grave!

In the grave—if I can believe it. God rest her sweet spirit!